THE HEART OF A SUNBURNED LAND

© Elizabeth Haran 2024

THE HEART OF A SUNBURNED LAND

FOREWARD

Riordan Magee entered the dank gloom of Chelms Wood, on the outskirts of Goold's Cross in County Tipperary, where he'd been told a band of gipsies were camped. Although he'd casually dismissed stories the 'wood ' was haunted by evil spirits, as he made his way between lofty, ancient trees, covered in lichen, an eerie chill swept over him, and he unconsciously reached for the cold reassurance of his pistol.

The 'wood' was part of Donaldbain Keefe's estate, a man the local children often referred to as the forest 'gargoyle'. He didn't take kindly to poachers or trespassers and introduced either to a round of shot from his antiquated blunderbuss. Since young Malachy Finn had disappeared under strange circumstances, no one from the village went near the 'wood'. The Inn keeper's wife claimed a search party had found strange markings on the ground, and concluded young Malachy was the victim of 'witchcraft'. She told Riordan about dogs howling when the moon was full, and the remains of mutilated animals found hanging in the trees.

Superstitious poppycock, Riordan thought as he glanced up at the moon, half covered by cloud. He'd bet the gipsies were to blame for the so-called 'strange happenings'. Gipsies always made God-fearing people uneasy.

Knowing it would be folly to light a lantern, Riordan felt his way over fallen logs and around thorny bracken, which tore at his breeches and scratched his legs. He crossed a trickling stream that looked like liquid silver in a beam of moonlight, then climbed a slippery, moss-covered incline. At the peak, gay music and coarse laughter drifted to him with wood smoke and the tantalizing aroma of poached game, but he could not see anything for the dark bulk of leafy trees around him.

The cry of a nightingale, directly overhead, startled, him, and he drew his pistol with lightning speed.

'Fer the love of God," he mumbled when the bird took flight. His heart was thumping so wildly, he thought he'd pass out, and leant on the tree for support, silently thanking the Lord he hadn't fired the gun, alerting the gipsies of his presence. He shuddered to think of the consequences.

"I must be raving mad," he told himself, as he proceeded on, knowing he could be killed if caught by the gipsies, notorious for guarding their women with their lives, a foolhardy risk he was more than willing to take.

A portrait of the beautiful Tara Killain had haunted him for months. In his mind, he could see the shadow of longing in the deep pools of her green eyes, set in a face that was a vision of beauty. He'd made a solemn promise that he'd find her but knew his reasons for risking his life were more personal than any vow.

Since Victoria had sent him the portrait of her niece, Tara had tormented his dreams and obsessed his every waking hour. She had become a ruling passion that dominated his life, - a fixation in his mind, that had obscured his judgment. His business had deteriorated, and with it his almost non-existent personal life, - and for what? A woman he didn't know personally, - although in his mind, he knew her intimately.

His friends questioned his sanity, as he followed any clue of her whereabouts. His health suffered, as he trudged the streets in snow and sleet, sometimes for days, searching any haunt the gipsies might frequent. He was driven by the horrors he imagined Tara faced at the hands of her barbaric captors, thoughts that almost drove him out of his mind.

Fortunately for Riordan the threatening rain had held off, and the moon was full. As he ventured on towards the sounds of revelry, the moving cloud allowed slivers of light to spear the trees and illuminate small, cleared pockets in the wood. His heart jumped again, as a hare scuttled for cover, and a field mouse crossed his path. Up ahead, through the shadowy trees, he could see the glow of a campfire, and hear the garish laughter of the women, guitar music, and the intoxicated slurs of men, and his heart began to thud with anticipation.

Colourful caravans formed a circle on the edge of a clearing, and a campfire blazed in the centre, casting shadows and a warm glow over the faces surrounding it. The eyes of the gipsies shone like black opals, contrasting with the flash of white teeth, and the deadly glint of a dagger. The warmth of the night, and the heat from the fire, made their skin glisten like bronze against vivid bandanas and multi-coloured skirts.

Riordan crouched between the gipsies horses, and the stallions, protective of the mares and foals, snorted in alarm. When the coast was clear, he dashed towards a caravan and slithered between the wheels. He soon discovered he had the company of sleeping pups, lousy with fleas. On the far side of the camp, some of the older children were also hiding beneath the caravans. He could see their shining eyes, greedily watching the festivities.

The stench under the caravan was a suffocating mixture of dog droppings, stale urine and rotting food, but Riordan was reluctant to move for fear of being discovered. If the gipsies caught him he could not rescue Tara from what he imagined to be an insufferable life of degradation. Overhead, he could hear tramping feet and an angry male voice, a baby crying, and a mother humming in soothing tones to quieten her child.

As Riordan's gaze wandered around the camp, the shadows on the faces of the men seemed distorted and sinister in the firelight. He could smell the sweat from their bodies, mingling with the acrid odour of the charred remains of the feast they had shared. Their shirts were tight fitting, and most wore black trousers, also taut, with wide studded leather belts. Nearly all wore their hair long, and some had tattoos on their forearms. As Riordan imagined them touching Tara, hatred filled his body, settling like a rock in the pit of his stomach. He envisaged her chained in a caravan, at their mercy. The thought made him want to vomit, so he pushed it from his mind. He realized he had no plan of action. He was blindly, - perhaps foolishly, following his heart.

The guitar music stopped abruptly, alerting Riordan to a change in mood. He waited in anxious anticipation for something to happen. A few moments later, the tattle of the tambourine broke the silence that had befallen the camp. He heard low cheers of encouragement from the men, as a woman made her way slowly and sensuously into the clearing around the fire, the tambourine held above her head, as she tantalizingly shook it. Riordan only caught glimpses of the woman, as the gathering crowd obscured his view. He moved until he had a clear view, and was shocked to see she had copper-coloured hair, flowing past her waist. Tara had hair the colour of burnished copper, but surely it could not possibly be her, dancing for her barbaric captors?

The woman continued to dance around the fire, her back to him. She wore a skirt that hung in tatters from her hips, like colourful strips of ribbon, revealing the full length of her golden legs. Her crimson peasant blouse was cut low over the sensuous curve of her breasts and shoulders, and her naked arms trailed by strands of hair, golden red with vibrancy in the firelight. From what Riordan could see, which included her profile, she was a beauty.

As the woman turned, and Riordan saw all of her face for the first time, he almost choked on the strangled gasp of shock rising in his throat. The very last thing he had been expecting to see was Tara, entertaining the people who held her prisoner. Yet it was her, of that he was sure. He'd been led to believe the gipsies had taken her from the sanctuary of her parent's home in the dead of night. Grasping for reasons for her behaviour, he thought it was likely they were forcing her to dance, perhaps threatening her. He became angrier, thinking of the humiliation that Tara must be suffering, being coerced to perform like an animal in a carnival.

As she whirled and twirled in a dance that was provocative and spellbinding, he watched through the smoke from the fire, mesmerized. She seemed in a trance, as if hypnotized.

He wondered if she had been drugged with one of their potions until he saw her lips part in gratification for her captured audience, as she rhythmically circled the fire.

As Riordan continued to watch, he had to painfully acknowledge she didn't look like she was being forced to perform, and he felt utterly betrayed. Although every fibre in him wanted to deny it, it was obvious her erotic conduct came as natural to her as breathing, and the power she held over her titillated subjects gave her as much pleasure as her dancing gave them. But where had she learned the dance of the gipsy, and who had taught her to use her body so provocatively? Certainly, no one in the strict confines of her family home would instruct her on such seductive behaviour. If her family could see her now….. They must never know, he vowed. Never!

As the tempo of the music quickened, Tara writhed and swayed to the beat. Her bare feet kicked up dust. She threw her head back, arching her curvaceous body, her lustrous hair flowing behind her. The men openly leered at her, as her movements became carnal and arousing. Riordan felt paralyzed with grief. His fantasies were crumbling into ruin; his life seemed to no longer have a purpose. In all his wildest dreams, he never expected to find Tara Killain 'enjoying' the company of the people accused of stealing her from a loving family and life of privilege and status. He'd thought of himself as her knight in shining armour, rescuing her from an abhorrent lifestyle. He could not have been more wrong, - and cursed himself for a fool.

Unable to turn away, he watched, his emotions lost to him. Like the rest of her audience, he was drawn like a moth to a flame, caught up in her spell, an unwilling slave to her beauty and the licentious movements of her shapely hips and breasts, even as his heart was breaking. He thought of the painting he'd looked at a million times, and could hardly believe it paled in comparison to the reality of the traitorous woman before him.

As the rhythm of the music quickened, so his heart raced to keep up, and beads of sweat formed on his face. Every sense was trained on her, blocking out the smells and sounds around him. In his wildest imagination, he could not have dreamt up anything so erotic. His body reacted, becoming more aroused than he had ever been in his life. He ached, throbbed, with unbearable pain. As the crowd closed in around her, spurring on the dance, they obstructed his vision yet again. He felt bereft, as cold as if he'd been doused with water. His body ached with torturous pain, as if addicted to an opiate, of which he was in frantic need.

In desperation not to miss a second of her frenzied, seductive performance, he carelessly left the safety of his hiding place. He pushed through the crowd, unnoticed in the shadows of night, and boldly ventured closer. Without realizing it, he found himself in the inner circle of those watching. Tara was so near, he could almost reach out and touch her glistening skin and silky hair. He imagined he felt the heat from her body, a body every fibre in him longed to caress, to possess. His mind was in turmoil, repulsed and disillusioned, yet too weak and aroused to turn away.

Their eyes met, and he was lost in the flames of desire reflected in hers, the colour of emeralds. It was as if they were the only two people in the woods. Hands clapped faster, and the guitar player strummed more forcefully, but it was as if the sounds were coming from miles away. All Riordan could hear was his own heart pumping wildly. He clapped to its rhythm, caught up in the music and the raw animal emotion it evoked, almost oblivious to the danger around him. Tara's feet stomped in the dust, her limbs writhed sensuously, as the dance reached fever pitch. It was almost agony waiting for the release that only the conclusion could bring. The desire for fulfilment, the crescendo.......

Suddenly Riordan was caught by the scruff of his neck and forced to the ground, surrounded by men. The music stopped abruptly. He reached for his pistol, but the gipsies were too quick for him. Black eyes, filled with hatred, bore into him. The last thing he remembered, after fists had slammed his face, and feet had pounded his body, was Tara's face, looking at him with terror in her eyes, before mercifully, blessed oblivion.

Birds happily chirping were the first conscious sounds to penetrate Riordan's fractured mind. The second was a painful prod in his shoulder, followed by some muffled, animal-like grunts. With great difficulty, he forced open one of his swollen eyes and squinted into the sunlight. A giant, bearded man was standing over him, pointing an ancient blunderbuss at his head. He tried to move his legs, and a wave of panic seized him, as he had no feeling below his waist. He quickly realized the lower half of his body was buried in dirt in a shallow grave. From the waist upward, every inch of his broken body seemed to be screaming in pain. His face was a bloody pulp.

    Riordan knew for certain that it was a miracle he was alive, but could feel no sense of relief, or joy. As the memory of what had happened just hours earlier, flooded his mind, he felt only a deep sense of sadness and utter betrayal.

    The gipsies were gone.

THE HEART OF A SUNBURNED LAND

CHAPTER ONE

SEVEN YEARS LATER

As 'Lady Morna Bowers' neared her destination, she nervously checked her appearance, making sure her veil concealed her face, and none of the delicate buttons on the front of her 'widow's weeds' had come loose again. The buttons unexpectedly reminded her of the last night she had spent with her family. It should have been a night of gaiety and fun, but the memory was devastating, and precisely the reason she was about to deceive good people, just so she could obtain the funds she needed to live.

Gripping her cumbersome parcel, not easily done in lacy gloves, 'Lady Bowers' glanced across Grafton Street, one of the busiest streets in Dublin, where she could see the Harcourt Gallery, her destination, in Darby Lane. Taking a deep, calming breath, she stepped from the curb.

"Look out," someone yelled.

Two carriage horses were startled by the horn of an automobile, and bolted, rattling past at speed. The carriage wheels sent up a spray of putrid water from a pothole in the road.

"You clumsy, scatter-brained, nincompoop," 'Lady Bowers' shouted after the automobile's driver. She was so startled, her parcel slipped through her fingers. "Damn these gloves," she mumbled irritably. "I can't hold a confounded thing. And to hell with this ridiculous veil. I can hardly see where I'm going."

Lifting the offending veil to inspect her parcel, she was relieved to see it wasn't damaged but noted the bottom of her gown was splashed with foul-smelling muck.

"Fer the love of Holy Moses," she muttered angrily. "Can anything else go wrong today?" The well-worn black gown, purchased from a charity auction for a bargain price, was found to have two buttons loose and gaped at the bust, which meant last-minute alterations. The only suitable shoes she could borrow were one size too large, so she'd had to stuff paper in the toes. Her horse had thrown a shoe, then she'd been caught in a downpour… She was suddenly conscious of a steadying arm around her tiny waist. "Are you hurt, madam?" a sympathetic male voice queried.

"Unhand me!" she snapped irritably, her attention taken with the stained hem of her gown. "That's all I bloody well need. To smell like a stable yard dung heap!"

Lady Bowers swung round, ready to give the cad with his hands on her, a tongue-lashing, but was effectively silenced by a pair of twinkling, grey-blue eyes. She quickly covered her face, but not before noticing the lively eyes watching her belonged to a very handsome gentleman, possibly just a few years her senior, who was dressed in a tailored overcoat made from the most luxurious cloth she had ever seen.

"Oh! Forgive me, sir?" Her hand came up to her mouth, as she thought that surely he must have been thinking the worst of her.

He removed his bowler hat, revealing a thick head of fair, wavy hair, which contrasted with his slightly ginger, well-trimmed moustache. Amidst the many unemployed men, trudging past in shabby attire, he looked quite out of place.

The gentleman brazenly looked her over. Her attire was somewhat 'old fashioned' for the times, so he'd been expecting a much older woman to be hiding beneath it. However, her silky voice, her actions, and certainly her colourful language, had all taken him by surprise. Luckily for him, he'd caught a glimpse of her face before she'd pulled down the ridiculous veil, and it was very pretty indeed.

"I think you'll agree, horse-drawn carriages and motor vehicles have no business being on the same road," he said and removed a snow-white, monogrammed handkerchief from his pocket. She watched in sheer disbelief, as he began wiping the hem of her gown.

"I most certainly do," Lady Bowers said passionately. "The drivers of motor vehicles have a devil-may-care attitude and absolutely no consideration for horses. I almost ended up in the ditch this morning…." She stopped abruptly, realizing he'd been advocating motor vehicles, and she was supposed to be playing the part of a 'lady', - one who had found herself left in an embarrassing financial situation, but a lady nevertheless. "That is, I've had to resort to my carriage. Like everything else, petrol is rather hard to obtain..."

He glanced up, as he continued to work on the hem of her gown, where he was only succeeding in smearing the muck. "There are ways to obtain almost anything if you have the right contacts."

Glancing at the top of his head, Lady Bowers softly snorted in annoyance. If his clothes were anything to go by, he could afford anything.

He straightened up and she forced herself to smile graciously.

"Are you sure you are unhurt?" he asked.

Despite her irritation, she found the timbre of his voice somewhat mesmerizing. "I'm quite sure," she replied and watched as he bent to retrieve her parcel. She was suddenly self-conscious of the brown paper wrapping and well-used string. "I should have looked before stepping onto the road. I wasn't thinking. I'm not usually so..." She batted her lashes coquettishly, trying to hide the fact that she was lost for an explanation for her unrefined behaviour.

"You were a victim of a clash between the past and progress," he suggested. "Allow me, if you will, to assist you across the road?"

For a fleeting moment, Lady Bowers enjoyed basking in the feeling of being treated so respectfully, but then she mentally reproached herself. She had to keep focused. "That won't be necessary." She hoped he would go about his business, which was precisely what she wanted to do before she lost her nerve completely.

"The traffic is heavy and your... painting is so cumbersome."

"I can manage."

"It would be my pleasure."

There was that devastating smile again. She felt her articulate plan unraveling before her eyes and again reminded herself of her goal. She was certain her life was about to take a dramatic turn for the worse, and she had to act quickly or find herself in a terrible position for a woman in her situation, - no longer in the first blush of womanhood, alone, and with no income.

"No, thank you. Now, if you will excuse me…"

"Is that your Phaeton carriage and driver?" He glanced at a shiny, black carriage at the curbside a few paces behind her, assuming it was hers. It was beautiful, but only in her wildest dreams could she afford such a carriage….. She felt hot colour creep into her cheeks and was yet again thankful she was wearing a veil.

"Yes, but I told my… footman I am quite capable of crossing the street, unaided." She attempted to retrieve her painting from him, but he held it firmly. She wasn't sure whether he possessed unshakable self-confidence, or was just annoyingly persistent. Whichever, he was trying her patience.

"Such spirited independence is an admirable quality, madam," he said, "especially under the circumstances in which you sadly find yourself, but I insist. Besides, I happen to have some influence at the gallery. I'd be honoured to personally escort you, and make sure you are treated with the utmost courtesy and consideration." He was certain something was not quite right, and was determined to discover what it was

Forgetting herself, she cast him a doubtful look. "Although you appear to have noble intentions, sir, I doubt even you could have that much influence over the prestigious Harcourt Gallery."

He looked startled and somewhat bemused.

Lady Bowers' mind was racing ahead, and she wasn't in the least repentant. "I have my own plan to ensure I receive fair treatment." She had contemplated the idea of putting a pillow under her gown, to make herself look expectant, but thought better of it.

"Really? I'm intrigued," he said.

His tone made her suddenly aware she wasn't sounding very much like a 'widow' in mourning.

"What I mean is, I'm hoping they'll be compassionate to my situation."

"Unfortunately madam, compassion and profits are usually worlds apart, even more so since the stock market crash. However, having someone on the inside such as a connection, can be a big help. May I ask if you are acquainted with anyone at the gallery?"

"Well... no."

He smiled to himself. "Allow me to introduce myself. Riordan Magee, at your service."

"Ta...." She cleared her throat, trying to cover her near blunder, but Riordan hadn't missed it.

"Lady Morna Bowers, sir." Remembering the hours of practiced mannerisms, she tentatively extended a gloved hand. He noted the golden brown skin between her gloves and the sleeve of her gown. A 'lady' didn't spend so much time outside.

"My pleasure, Lady Bowers." He bent over her extended hand. "I'm sure your 'plan' is well thought out, but I sincerely believe an escort would be to your advantage. Such establishments are a little stuffy about protocol, unfortunately even for someone in bereavement. I'd be honoured if you would allow me the privilege."

She studied him cautiously, realizing she needed every advantage. "Very well," she said, "as long as you don't interfere with my business. At the risk of sounding dramatic, so much depends upon the sale of this painting. I cannot afford to have anything go wrong." She noted Riordan looked curious, and she would rather lose a limb than admit she was on the verge of being homeless and alone, all because she had been unable to produce a child for her often absent husband. She reverted to her role as the grieving widow. "Since losing my... husband...." She sniffed into a handkerchief theatrically. "I must fend for myself. I hope you understand?"

"Of course, Lady Bowers. It's most unfortunate that your husband did not provide well for you."

'Morna's eyes widened, and she almost choked trying to push down hysterical laughter. It was hard to provide for a wife from the inside of a goal cell, where her husband often found himself.

"Although I was not personally acquainted with Lord Bowers," he added, "I had heard he was a very wealthy man."

Lady Bowers was taken off guard for a moment. She hadn't expected Riordan to know anything about her 'fictitious husband,' Lord Bowers. Her thoughts rushed ahead to her planned story. "That was some time ago, Mr. Magee. His passion for cards, particularly Black Jack, far exceeded his ability. We had to sell almost everything. I am very fond of this painting, but I have servants who depend upon me, and I do not have the heart to turn them onto the street....."

Riordan was quite convinced her 'story' was just that but was certainly enjoying watching her masquerade. He decided to disconcert her further. "I understand, and might I add, I'm so relieved the rumours about your husband aren't true."

She blinked in astonishment. "Rumours! What rumours?" "Well, I don't know if I should say...."

"Tell me, Mr. Magee. I have a right to know what people are saying about my... dearly departed Devlin."

He could barely stop himself grinning. "I'm sure there's not a ring of truth....."

"There isn't, of course, but nevertheless I should be informed about what's being said behind my back."

"Very well, Lady Bowers. It was rumoured Lord Bowers kept several mistresses." Although she should hardly have cared, her pride was miffed, and she was immediately indignant. "Of course, he didn't," she snapped.

"Please forgive my bluntness. Now that we've met, I could not believe it to be true. May I ask how Lord Bowers ... came to meet his untimely end? I have heard stories, but they can be so inaccurate, as I have shamelessly demonstrated."

"He... he er... was ill for some time, but alas his heart gave way eventually." She hoped being vague would cover almost any ailment the real Lord Bowers might have suffered.

Riordan's brows lifted. "Really? It's a relief to know he didn't die of syphilis. The rumour mill can be so unkind."

"Lady Bowers gasped in horror. How could she have picked such a cad for a bogus husband? She was about to give Riordan a piece of her mind for even suggesting... when she looked into his eyes and noted they were twinkling mischievously. Her suspicions, that he knew she was not really 'Lady Bowers', were practically confirmed, but she hoped he was enough of a gentleman not to openly make accusations. Anyway, he obviously didn't know Devlin Bowers personally, so she felt sure he could not prove she was lying, either way, without doing some investigation.

His eyes twinkled at her, and his lips twitched.

"I suspect, Mr. Magee," she said. 'under the very elegant facade of a gentleman, there beats the heart of a rogue. I must warn you, I am not easily taken for a fool."

Riordan pretended to take offence. "Please don't take this to heart, Lady Bowers, but I have the feeling it is 'I' who might learn something today from an expert in subterfuge." His words were softened by another wicked grin.

A brass bell jangled over the doorway, as Riordan Magee stepped aside for Lady Bowers to enter the Harcourt Gallery. Taking a deep breath to calm her sudden rush of nerves, she was immediately overawed by the prestige of the most famous art gallery in all of Ireland. Paintings in oils and watercolours, some framed elaborately, graced the walls, which had all the warmth of a mausoleum. Sculptures in bronze and stone were placed near ornate pillars and archways. Again, Lady Bowers suffered pangs of uncertainty. Under normal circumstances, she would never have dared to enter such an establishment.

Riordan Magee was detained in the doorway by a passing acquaintance, so she proceeded towards a smartly dressed gentleman at the back of the gallery without him. He watched her approach from his oversized chair, his features a mixture of mild curiosity and condescension. She swallowed the lump in her throat when she saw him glance at her brown paper-wrapped parcel, which Riordan had placed just inside the doorway, and the soiled hem of her gown. He stood up before she reached him, and 'Morna' noted his chair wasn't oversized, as it had first appeared, he was just exceptionally small in stature. Even so, she thought he looked quite unsympathetic and uncompromising, and his words soon confirmed her impression.

"If you are selling, madam, we do not do business with anyone who has not had a personal recommendation." His voice seemed to echo in the stillness of the gallery, enhancing the shame sweeping over her.

Her mind went blank. It took a few awkward moments to gather her thoughts. When she managed to find her voice, it was shamefully small. "Won't you please give me a few minutes of your time? I guarantee it will be worth your while." She sniffed into her handkerchief, but he appeared unmoved by her apparent distress.

"I'm sorry, madam. There are absolutely no exceptions." He didn't sound in the least penitent and dismissed her with a wave of his short-fingered hand.

Lady Bowers felt shocked and utterly humiliated. The hours of practicing her story flashed through her mind. She couldn't believe it had all been for nothing. Although being publicly humbled had become a way of life, she had never become used to it. To add to her misery, she was going to look a complete fool in front of Riordan Magee. Thankfully he had not witnessed her humiliating rebuff.

"I'm sorry to keep you waiting, Lady Bowers," he said from behind her, and she jumped.

She turned reluctantly, her mind racing to think of something to say that would conceal her shame. Nothing came to mind. To make matters worse, she felt on the verge of tears. "What a heartless man…" she stammered. The least she could hope for was sympathy. "He's apparently too busy to spare me a moment of his time after I travelled for hours to get here. My Devlin would turn in his grave…"

Riordan quickly summed up the situation. If he wasn't mistaken, Lady Bowers looked more embarrassed than disappointed. The manager of the gallery had obviously dealt with her swiftly and heartlessly.

"Lady Bowers," he said imploringly, "surely you aren't going to give up so easily. I was looking forward to seeing your plan executed."

She faltered, and heat swept through her.

Feeling tender-hearted towards her predicament, and genuinely disappointed that he wasn't going to witness her well-rehearsed performance, Riordan decided to help. Glancing at the man behind the desk, he whispered, "Perhaps he just needs to be reminded of 'who' you are?"

'Lady Bowers swept a sideways glance at the gentleman who had just dismissed her as if she was a 'nobody'. "You're right," she said, her determination re-surging. Lifting her chin and straightening her shoulders, she approached the desk again and stood looking down at the man behind it, who was concentrating on his paperwork.

"I am Lady Morna Bowers," she said with forceful flair. He looked up in surprise. "May I have your name and title, sir?"

For a second the man looked angry, and then Riordan stepped up behind her, and his expression changed to confusion.

"Have you suddenly lost your tongue?" she asked impatiently.

"No… madam I am Kelvin Kendrick, the manager of the gallery. I do apologize for my rudeness. I had no idea you were…" He cleared his throat nervously. "There is no excuse for my behaviour, but I often find myself confronted with all types claiming to be avant-garde artists, when in fact they are bohemian drop-outs, pushing their off-beat forms of art." His eyes darted from Riordan to her several times. "I'm not for a moment suggesting…" He felt himself go beet red. "Please forgive my inexcusable insolence." Lady Bowers' spirits surged. "If you will be so kind as to fetch the gallery owner, promptly, I will not mention your rudeness."

Kelvin Kendrick's pale face bore a blank expression. He glanced behind her again. "I er… I'm not sure the manager is … available."

"Well please see if you find out. I cannot stand here all day."

"If I may interrupt, Lady Bowers," Riordan said, "and suggest Mr. Kendrick show you to a private office, so that you may wait for the owner in comfort."

She turned to him. "Thank you, Riordan. As you can see, I have the situation well in hand." She lowered her voice. "The inane imbecile before me is at a loss for words. You may watch, and learn, but please remain silent."

Kelvin overheard what she said, and his face turned almost purple with humiliation. Lady Bowers turned back to him, while Riordan smothered a laugh. "If you have a private office, please lead the way," she said.

Kelvin was hesitant for only a moment. "Very well, madam. If you'll follow me, I'll see if I can … locate the owner."

"Please advise him I have connections in the European art world, and I won't be reticent in using them."

Kelvin's flush spread to his short neck, where the veins were bulging.

She turned to Riordan. "You can go now, Mr. Magee. I have everything under control."

"So I see," he said. "Goodbye, and good luck. I hope we meet again, soon."

She noted the twinkle of something akin to conciliatory mischief in his grey-blue eyes. "Thank you for escorting me here," she said. Picking up her painting, she followed Kelvin Kendrick down a hallway to a comfortable office. He showed her inside and left.

Lady Bowers noted the simple, elegant taste of the owner's private office. An antique desk and two comfortable leather chairs were the only pieces of furniture, apart from a small bookshelf and marble bust on a pedestal. Unlike the gallery, the office was tastefully carpeted, giving it a warmer appeal. As would be expected, the walls were adorned with beautiful artworks, mostly impressionist pieces, too off-beat for her liking.

In the corner behind the door, there were several more works of art, partially covered with a sheet. Curious, she removed the sheet and leafed through them casually. They were mostly landscapes and portraits. Suddenly she stopped and gasped. She was looking at a portrait of herself languishing beside a campfire, dressed in a provocative off-the-shoulder blouse, and a silk skirt, which revealed the full length of her shapely legs. The firelight caught the lustre in her burnished copper hair and deflected from her gold hoop earrings. Her skin, pale olive after a long, warm summer, glowed with vitality, and naked desire leapt in her eyes. It was a brief, happy time in her life, but it had all changed so quickly.

She wondered how the painting came to be in the gallery? It had been a gift to her aunt who swore she would never part with it. The last she knew of her, she'd moved overseas. That was several years ago. A noise behind her startled her.

"The owner is unavailable," Kelvin Kendrick said coldly. "Perhaps I can help you."

His offer sounded insincere, but she was only marginally disappointed. Even though she hadn't met the owner, she instinctively knew Kelvin Kendrick would be easier to manipulate, something she was not proud to do, as in her mind, the potential outcome justified the means.

Lady Bowers lifted the painting to the front of the pile. "Could you tell me where the gallery owner got this portrait?" she asked, trying to keep her voice unemotional.

Kelvin looked surprised. He had never particularly liked the painting. "I'm not sure. I believe he purchased it overseas, madam."

Something must have happened to her aunt. She vowed to come back to the gallery and speak to the owner.

"Mr...." Kelvin coughed, covering what he had been about to say. "Excuse me. I know it's not for sale, Lady Bowers," he said, again with a hint of condescension in his tone. "In my opinion, it's not technically good, but I believe there are personal reasons for the owner to have the painting in his possession. We do not usually keep this kind of work at the gallery."

She knew exactly what he meant. The painting of a gipsy woman was not considered worthy of a place on the Harcourt Gallery walls.

"For a reason unknown to me, the owner has been searching for the artist in the hope of purchasing more of his work," he said.

"Really!" She smiled in delight.

THE HEART OF A SUNBURNED LAND

CHAPTER TWO

Darkness was descending, the street lamps burning, when Lady Bowers and Mr. Kendrick concluded their business. He escorted her to the gallery door, just as a family of gipsies strolled past.

"Thieving scoundrels," Kelvin muttered. "Wait inside until they have passed, Lady Bowers, or you'll likely find yourself relieved of the handsome purse you carry."

'Morna' recognized the gipsies. Rosa and Jasper had five children to feed, and like many others suffering the Depression, were forced to do whatever they could to provide for them.

"The gipsies aren't as bad as people believe," she found herself saying in their defense, despite her own recent experiences. "They live by their own laws, which may be different to yours and mine, but I believe they are mostly honourable people."

Kelvin looked at her in astonishment. "Surely you don't know any personally, Lady Bowers? If you did, I'm certain your opinion would not be so generous."

"My father and my late uncle on my mother's side, used to allow the gipsies to camp on their land. My uncle had a moderate amount of talent as a painter, and I was told he used the gipsy women as models. As I was never allowed to see his work, I can only assume the paintings were on the risqué side."

Kelvin Kendrick's mouth dropped open, which made Lady Bowers feel smug.

"The gallery owner must like the one in his office," she added, "or he wouldn't have instructed you to purchase other work by the same artist."

Kelvin's look of distaste suggested the owner's fixation with the gipsy painting totally baffled him. Many times he had tried to get him to dispose of it, but he wouldn't consider the idea, even though he refused to hang it in his office, or anywhere else. It was as if he loathed it, but couldn't bear to part with it. The contradiction was perplexing for Kelvin.

"Good evening, Mr. Kendrick," she said when the danger had passed. "It was a pleasure doing business with you." This statement was an outright lie. Her gratification had nothing to do with the repugnant manager, but everything to do with successfully pulling off her ruse. That Kelvin Kendrick was willing to part with so much money for a painting he neither liked, nor believed had technical merit, confused her, but she decided not to question his motives or her luck. She'd put it down to long overdue good fortune.

Outside the gallery, Lady Bowers turned on her heel and hurried down the street. "Narrow-minded little twerp," she muttered angrily.

"Do I detect a note of dissatisfaction, Lady Bowers?"

Morna spun around, surprised to find Riordan Magee behind her. "Did your business not go well?" he asked, grinning wickedly.

"As a matter of fact, it went very well. Now if you will excuse me." She turned to go. Much about Lady Bowers intrigued Riordan, but at that moment he was especially curious about the painting she had sold the gallery. "I'm happy for you," he persisted, "but considering your good fortune, you seem rather piqued. Is something wrong?" Morna stopped and turned to face him. "I detest any form of bigotry," she snapped, then bit her tongue. What was she thinking, arousing his suspicions?

Riordan had been watching the gallery doorway, when the family of gipsies passed by, and saw Kelvin's expression of disgust as he held her inside.

"If you will excuse me, I really must be on my way." She turned away again but felt a hand on her arm.

"May I offer you a ride, Lady Bowers? Your carriage appears to have deserted you, and you never know who is lurking on the streets at this hour."

Lady Bowers was impatient to get away, but suddenly noticed a constable making his way towards them. Her eyes widened when she saw Jake, the leader of the band of gipsies camped on Liffey, closely shadowing him. She'd heard rumours her husband owed him money and knew he'd not rest until he got everything she owned. If he saw her talking to a gentleman of means or got wind of her sale...

"Perhaps you are right," she said. "Where is your carriage?"

Riordan Magee gestured to a black Model T Ford. It was gleaming under a streetlight at the curbside a few paces ahead of them. Morna's eyes widened when she saw it. She had never ridden in anything comparable to such modern luxury. Despite her impatience, she was suddenly filled with childish excitement. With no time to waste, she darted toward the door, instructing the driver through the open window. "Head for Merrion Square."

As Riordan followed her, he noted the constable coming towards them, and smiled to himself. Lady Bowers certainly was a beguiling woman. He suddenly realized it had been many years since he'd felt anything close to fascination for a woman.

As the car pulled away from the curb, Riordan said, "Now that there's just the two of us, you can tell me your real name?"

She hadn't expected him to be so blunt. "I beg your pardon," she said, hoping to stall for time. "I have no idea what you are talking about, and we're hardly alone." She glanced at his driver.

"Sykes is the most discreet of my staff. I can assure you, you may speak freely."

When she didn't reply, he went on. "You can drop the ruse, whatever your name is, for it's certainly not Morna Bowers. I'm acquainted with the real lady in question. Although Morna is a lovely person, she could only be described as minute in stature, and of substantial proportions."

Although embarrassed to be caught out, she almost smiled. Riordan was obviously too gentlemanly to describe Morna Bowers as 'short and rotund'.

"You hardly fit that description," he said. "I'd describe you as willowy, with a comely figure."

For a moment she was flattered, and almost taken off guard. Especially as his eyes seemed to be glinting with amusement, and not anger. She reminded herself to stay alert, at least until she found out what he wanted from her.

"Morna's husband, who was neither a card player nor a rake, died many years ago, under the most shocking circumstances. They were on their second honeymoon when he fell from a cruise ship off the coast of South Africa. I suppose his heart did give way." His lips twitched. "Mine would too, if I saw a shark swimming toward me. I believe he left Morna in a very comfortable position. Did you know she lives on the continent?"

She ignored his question, so he went on regardless. "Last I heard, she was very much in love with a wealthy count. I am hoping to be invited to the nuptials."

"I'm not interested in your perspective social life, Mr. Magee. Please get to the reason you have waylaid me, as I'm now more convinced than ever that my safety is the last thing on your mind." She gazed out of the window. Fog was rolling across the Liffey River, blanketing the streets. She could hardly make out where they were. As soon as they reached Merrion Square, she planned to take flight.

"Are you going to tell me why you are masquerading as Morna Bowers? You could be arrested for impersonation."

"I have committed no crime, but if you have any inclination to turn me into the police, I'll claim you were my co-conspirator. The manager of the gallery will be my witness."

He smiled. If only she knew the truth! "If you really believe yourself to be innocent, why were you avoiding the constable on the street outside the gallery."

It was her turn to look momentarily startled. "I can assure you I was not avoiding any constable. You offered me a ride, and I foolishly accepted, because you were quite correct when you referred to the unsavoury types that roam the streets. I am, of course, referring to the ruffian who was coming towards us outside the gallery."

Riordan did remember seeing an unpleasant type walking behind the constable. A gipsy! He realized the 'gipsy' might have given her away, as he probably knew her.

"You have my word as a gentleman, I have no intention of causing you trouble. I confess my curiosity is insatiable. I find a pretty lady and a mystery, an irresistible combination." Again his eyes gleamed and 'Morna' recognized a rogue in Mr. Magee. And yet, she instinctively felt she could trust him - to a degree.

"I believe you are a scoundrel, Magee. Tell me, how do you make your living?"

Riordan pretended to be indignant, his mind racing for an explanation that would not give him away. He was having too much fun to come clean. "I buy and sell.... valuable items," he said vaguely. "I don't believe that makes me a scoundrel. I prefer to think of myself as an 'opportunist'."

"Then being an 'opportunist' pays very well. Your coat is made of the finest cloth I have ever seen; even your handkerchiefs are monogrammed. And this motor vehicle must have cost a fortune. If I am not mistaken, there are very few Model T Ford's in Dublin, especially since the Depression began."

Her eye for detail astonished Riordan.

"Most people can't get enough to eat, but you don't seem to be struggling at all."

"I come from a wealthy family," he said, although he had little to do with them these days.

"Your money could be better spent, but I'm relieved you have not fallen upon hard times, Mr. Magee, because if you had way-laid me to ask for money, I'm afraid I would not give you a penny from my sale."

He almost laughed. "No offence, madam, but I can assure you I do not need your money. I don't want anything from you, except the story behind your ruse. I suspect it might be very entertaining, and I could well use a little excitement and intrigue in my dull life."

She raised her dark, well-shaped eyebrows, and wondered how dull his life could be.

"Please tell me how selling one painting is going to change your life?"

Morna lifted her chin, and looked out of the window, praying they would soon reach Merrion Square. "I don't see why I should tell you anything."

"In that case, I'll tell you what I think I know." Riordan had been putting details together in his mind. His observations, and what she had told him, and his own conjectures about what she hadn't told him.

"Your skin is not lily white, like the ladies who hide themselves indoors playing bridge and taking tea, so I surmise you spend a great deal of time outdoors. This leads me to believe the reason you have not removed your gloves is that your hands are not as smooth as those of a lady accustomed to being waited upon. How am I doing so far?"

She was surprised, and it showed in her tone. "Go on, Mr. Magee," she said, certain he could never guess the truth.

"Although you cuss as well as most men, and there is an element of gentility to you, I believe you have been living with the gipsies. Perhaps you were stolen from a pram as a baby?" Riordan did not suspect she had been stolen, but he was certain Lady Bowers would become defensive and tell him the truth if he rankled her enough.

Morna was impressed. "Very clever, Mr. Magee. I was born into the gentry," she said. "And I have been living with the gipsies, although that's quite untrue about them kidnapping children. They have enough of their own." She remembered not even the gipsy potions and spells had been able to help her conceive. "As a young woman, I ran away with the gipsies." In fact, she'd felt she had no choice, but she did not want to talk about her reasons. "I fell in love with a handsome gipsy," she said, a touch of sadness in her voice. It had taken a year before she admitted she loved Garvie Flynn, even then it wasn't the passionate love she had dreamt about. It was another year before she consented to marry him after the gipsy women convinced her no other man would want her. She expected to see loathing or revulsion in Riordan's features, but instead, he looked genuinely shocked.

His memory had taken him back many years, to the night he had risked his life to find a young woman who had been kidnapped by the gipsies. He'd found her, and discovered she was not in great peril, of which he had convinced himself. She was not even being held prisoner. In fact, it was the gipsies who were held captive by her spell.

"Did your family know you ran away with the gipsies?"

"I'm certain they did. I've not seen them since I left, many years ago."

"Your absence no doubt caused them a great deal of pain," he said, his features hardening. He knew something of that gut-wrenching pain. It had taken him years to get over it.

She turned away and glanced out of the window. "If you don't mind, I do not wish to discuss it further."

"As you choose." Riordan was happy to let it drop and turn his attention to the mystery that surrounded this intriguing lady.

"So where did you get the painting, gipsy lady? Was it stolen?"

Her quick anger surged. "Why do you think I'm a thief, just because I have lived the life of a gipsy?"

"Calm down, gipsy lady. I didn't say 'you' stole the painting."

"Well, I didn't, and no one else did either. And don't call me 'gipsy lady'," she hissed.

Riordan was startled by the vehement tone of her voice. "I'm sorry. I wasn't suggesting you were a thief. I just don't see you as an artist, but perhaps I am wrong. So far, you have proved to have a multitude of talents. Were you the artist of the painting you sold to the gallery?"

Her anger quelled quickly. Riordan was so pleasantly inoffensive. "No. I was the model." She noted Riordan had a stricken look on his handsome face. She couldn't believe he could be so shocked by the idea of her being an artist's model.

"Don't you believe me?" she asked.

He was lost for words; his mind was dragged back to the past.

"The painting I sold this evening was very good," she said defensively. "The gallery owner has one just like it in his private office." She had great pleasure telling him this. "Apparently, he had been searching for more by the same artist, which was very lucky for me." She hadn't found it necessary to resort to the 'grieving widow with a sad story' after all. It had all been surprisingly simple.

Riordan's mouth fell open, and he leant forward, his heart hammering so hard he could barely speak. He had to be certain he had understood her correctly. "Are you telling me… there is a painting of 'you' in the Harcourt Gallery, in the owner's private office?"

"Don't look so surprised," she said, taking offence at his incredulity.

"Merrion Square, sir," the driver called, and the car came to an abrupt standstill, the motor backfiring, which startled them both.

Before Riordan could utter another word, she was out the door.

Still in shock, he called out, "Wait," realizing he had no idea how to contact her.

She disappeared in the direction of St. Stephen's Green, where she had tethered her horse.

"Tara," Riordan called, retrieving the veil she had thrown behind her.

There was no answer. She had vanished into the dark, foggy night. He stared after her, unable to comprehend what had just happened. All this time he had been in the company of the very woman who had haunted his dreams, a woman he felt had betrayed him, and he'd had no idea.

"Shall I light a lantern, sir?" the driver asked. "Whatever could she be thinking, running across the 'Green'? There's all types of deviant characters roaming out there. Just last week a woman was murdered. It is no place for a lady."

"It's no use, Sykes. She's gone and we'll never find her. I have the feeling she knows her way around the "Green", certainly more than we do." Riordan didn't like to say she was 'street wise', and probably knew every trick and con in the book.

Riordan took her headdress to the lights at the front of his vehicle. Sykes watched in surprise, as he lifted long strands of red hair from the material, and examined them closely under the light, in disbelief. "She really is Tara Killain. After all this time, I stumbled upon her." He smiled sadly, thinking of the irony. The only woman who had managed to capture his imagination since 'Tara the gipsy', all those years ago, was in fact, the very same woman. 'Tara Killain.'

CHAPTER THREE

The dawn sky was rumbling and slate grey, heavy with the threat of a thunderstorm, when Tara slipped away from the gipsy camp on the banks of the Liffey. The camp had not yet stirred, but in the fresh morning air Tara could smell odours that had become as familiar to her as the face she saw every morning in the mirror. Warm horseflesh, fresh hay and manure, leather soap, the remains of spit-roasted meat, and stale wine, - and the overpowering perfume from the scented oils the gipsy women used.

As Tara made her way towards her destination, the Mountjoy Prison, she had the oddest sensation that all that had become so familiar over the last few years was soon to become as much a part of her past, as her childhood spent with her family. Although she felt heavy-hearted and had tried to ignore the inevitable, she knew it was time she moved on.

In the past two weeks, she had sensed a growing tension amongst the gipsies. Many of them, particularly the men, had suddenly become cold toward her, and she often caught a hostile glance and noticed them whispering behind her back. One or two of the women, with whom she was normally quite close, had become distant and guarded, but she suspected their husbands were influencing them. Tara had always known the gipsies to be fiercely loyal to their own, and despite her relationship with Garvie Flynn, they'd made her all too aware she wasn't of their blood. But the one thing that irked them the most, was the fact that she brought them no revenue, especially in such hard times.

With Garvie in prison, yet again, Tara had become a burden, a position she had grown to resent, and the very reason she wanted to move on. Normally she was tolerated, but Jake, the acting leader in the absence of Rory, who had taken ill, had been stirring up dissension. Rory was older, wiser, and could always be counted upon to be fair in decisions regarding the group. Jake was the opposite. Very strong in body, and equally as obstinate in mind. In the absence of Rory, no one dared challenge him.

The previous night, while the rest of the camp slept, Jake bailed Tara up outside her caravan. The thought had crossed her mind that he had been lying in wait for her, perhaps watching her movements. She'd even suspected he'd seen her in Grafton Street. Just the memory of the incident sent shivers down her spine.

She recalled the conversation between them. Jake had startled her in the darkness, as she emptied a pail beside her caravan.

"Your husband is in my debt, and I want my money," he said from the shadows.

Even though Tara was taken aback, but she didn't show it. She straightened up slowly, answering him as calmly as she could. "He's owed you money before. You know you'll get it."

Jake stepped forward, out of the shadows and into the pool of moonlight where Tara stood. His black eyes narrowed on her as he slowly perused her body. She'd always hated the way he looked her over, as if she was horseflesh he was inspecting at a fair. His scrutiny was so invasive and degrading. It made her skin crawl.

That Garvie should owe Jake money didn't come as a surprise. She'd heard rumours circulating the camp, and he had borrowed money from him several times before. But Tara wondered why he couldn't wait until Garvie returned, as he usually did. She told him she had nothing of value to give him, yet sensed his impatience, like something tangible, and it troubled her. After all, her husband always repaid his debts when he came out of prison and found work. Why should this time be any different?

"You can dance for me at the horse fair in Cork next week," Jake suggested coldly, "and every other fair, until the debt is repaid."

His arrogance infuriated Tara. She sensed he wanted to seize the opportunity to have her in his power, something she'd never tolerate. "I'll not dance for money," she retorted stubbornly. "And I won't leave Dublin until Garvie is released."

Jake glanced away for a moment, his jaw clenched, as if he was mulling something over. When he turned back, he looked angry. "You'll repay me somehow, girlie, so I suggest you think of a way before I do."

The underlying meaning beneath his barely veiled threat terrified her. She'd heard women were sometimes traded at horse fairs, and wouldn't put anything past Jake. She'd never liked or trusted him. His kind was responsible for giving gipsies a bad name.

Jake reached for her throat. Despite her resolve to show no fear, Tara stiffened. She was still wearing the black widow's gown, but he did not comment. He touched the delicate button at the base of her throat, the colour of creamy toffee, then glanced downwards, following the trail of buttons between her breasts.

"I saw you getting into that fancy automobile earlier this evening," he said, moving his finger down to the next button, then the next. He was standing so close that Tara could feel his warm, liquor-tainted breath, fanning her cheek.

She froze but masked her rising panic beneath a poised exterior. It was her outwardly serene composure that bothered Jake the most. Try as he might, he couldn't ruffle her. He continued to follow the trail of buttons with his index finger. "Is the gentleman who owns that vehicle your rich lover?"

"Of course not." Tara felt colour creep into her cheeks as she recalled Kelvin Kendrick telling her that Riordan had been unable to part with her portrait. Jake took her heightened colour as a sign of guilt, and his eyes narrowed with jealousy. He'd had many, many sleepless nights, tossing and turning, as he imagined making passionate love to her.

Unable to stand Jake's proximity and intimate touch any longer, Tara slapped his hand away, but stood her ground, as his eyes shot up to meet hers, which were cold with rebellion.

"Why would you be getting into his motor vehicle, if he's not your lover?"

"That's none of your business."

"Have you something to hide?"

"You are not my husband, therefore, I owe you no explanation."

Put in his place, Jake baulked. "I want my money," he said between clenched teeth, "so you had better find a way to get it. I don't care how you do it, or how many lovers you take to your bed while your husband's in prison. Just get me my money."

As he strode away, Tara quivered with rage and silently thanked the Lord for the sale of her painting. She'd be damned if she'd give the proceeds to Jake. Although Garvie often borrowed, she had only Jake's word he owed him money. And as far as she was concerned, his word was as worthless as pond slime.

For the first time in her life, Tara knew it was imperative she think of herself and her future. She wanted to leave the gipsy camp, suspecting the gipsies were going to give her little choice. At least she had the funds to buy a cheap cottage as a roof over her head. A small home by the sea, even one that was tumbledown, had always been her dream. She had planned to await her husband's release from prison, and make a home for them both, but was no longer sure that was what she wanted.

When she pictured her future with Garvie, it seemed she would always be alone, awaiting his return from prison. Although she didn't know what she wanted to do with her life, she did know she wanted more from a relationship than awaiting a husband with whom she had little in common. She wanted and needed a strong man, someone dependable, someone passionate about life, and causes. If she couldn't find that man, she would rather be alone.

As Tara neared the outskirts of Dublin, she slowed her tired, old mare to a walk, and contemplated her visit with Garvie, who would be surprised to see her. It was still very early, Tara's favourite time of day, when she felt she had the world and her thoughts all to herself. In her mind, she was going over alternate ways to broach the subject of Jake with Garvie, when a wisp of smoke, coming through the tops of a copse of trees, caught her eye. Curious, she veered off the road, and caught a glimpse of the back end of a caravan, partially hidden by a rambling blackberry bush. She recognized the caravan, painted with animals, - hedgehog, curlew, badger, rabbits, and spotted deer, and the moon and stars, as belonging to Eloisa. The old woman, a gipsy outcast, was considered to be quite bizarre. Many feared her eccentric ramblings, and shunned her, forcing her to lead a solitary existence.

Tara had always felt pity for Eloisa. It was rumoured she had been cursed by a witch, for giving the daughter of a wealthy aristocratic family a potion for morning sickness, which had brought on an abortion, and killed the girl. Although the girl had been allergic to elderberry, the superstitious gipsies blamed her for any bad luck that befell them; even the settlers feared her, but not Tara. Whenever she was alone, and came upon the expatriate gipsy, she stopped to speak to her. Today, for some unknown reason, she felt compelled. As she dismounted, it suddenly occurred to her that she could soon find herself in the same situation as Eloisa, - an exiled gipsy.

The old woman, wearing a bright headscarf, which revealed a small amount of grey hair and enormous hoop earrings, was swathed in a heavy shawl, and huddled beside the fire, drinking tea. Her fingernails, several inches long and painted the colour of dried blood, were wrapped around the tin cup like an eagle's talons, as she absently tapped one of her many rings against the tin, in an hypnotic rhythm. She didn't even notice Tara, as she gazed into the flames, her mind miles away. A cast iron pot containing thick oatmeal was suspended above the heat, the aroma arousing Tara's hunger.

"Hello Eloisa," Tara said softly. At first, she thought the old woman hadn't heard her, but slowly her head turned and her eyes widened, and she gasped.

"It's only me, Eloisa," she said. "Tara Flynn. We've spoken before…"

The old woman dropped her cup, the contents hissing in the fire, and got to her feet awkwardly with the aid of a gnarled stick. She seemed to be looking above Tara's head. Her free hand reached up, towards Tara's face, and she mumbled something unintelligible.

Tara backed away from her 'talons'. "Eloisa!"

Suddenly the old woman stopped and looked into Tara's eyes, and her arm dropped like a dead weight, her 'talons' slashing through the air. "You see, don't you. You see what no one else can see…"

Tara shook her head.

The old woman turned and went back to the fire, and sat down again. Tara stood watching her in confusion. Different thoughts went through her mind. She concluded the old woman must have been thinking about something when she arrived, and she was confused.

Eloisa poured steaming, fragrant black tea into a mug, and turned to Tara. "Will you have breakfast with me?"

Tara was still shaken, but she said, "Yes, thank you."

"Where are you going?" Eloisa asked, seeming to be suddenly coherent, as she spooned the thick, unappetizing oatmeal into a bowl, then sprinkled something resembling bits of fingernail into the mixture, and added a dash of milk.

"To see my husband," Tara replied, suddenly losing her appetite altogether. Eloisa looked at her. "Is he in the Mount?"

Unsure of how to reply, and surprised Eloisa knew Garvie's whereabouts, Tara nodded. The old woman continued to study her with her black eyes. Her nose was large and beaky, giving her a menacing appearance, like a bird of prey. "Something is troubling you," she said.

Tara nodded again. "I'll work it out."

"You will. You know, don't you? You know what is coming?"

Tara stared at Eloisa in shock. "I believe the gipsies are going to ask me to leave the band," she said, relieved to have someone to discuss it with, someone who would understand. "I have no idea what I will do."

"They fear you," Eloisa hissed.

"No," Tara replied.

"Yes, they do."

"Why would they?"

"You are a "Seer"- one of the chosen ones. But your red hair frightens the gipsies. It's a bad omen."

Tara was bewildered. She had never heard such a thing before, and she had been living with the gipsies for nearly eleven years. She was sure Eloisa was rambling.

"They don't like me because I am not one of them, not of gipsy blood," Tara said, trying to make Eloisa understand.

The old woman leant closer, and Tara was wafted with the strong smell of garlic and herbs. "You have gipsy blood, my dear. Royal gipsy blood."

Tara was bewildered yet again, certain the old woman was confused. "No, Eloisa. I am a Killain. My father is a landowner."

"You have gipsy blood, my girl. That is where you inherited your talent as a Seer. Before you came today, I had a vision. When I looked up, I saw an aura around your head. You were the one in my vision."

Tara jumped to her feet, dropping her bowl of oatmeal. "I must go," she said, and turned to mount her horse. Her heart was pounding, but not from what Eloisa had told her, but because she had felt compelled to go to her. She'd had no choice.

As she rode away, she heard Eloisa say, "Ask your mother, my girl. She knows."

Tara rode her mare down the road as fast as the old horse would go, but she couldn't escape the echo of Eloisa's words. Questions with no answers ran through her mind so fast, that she felt dizzy. She had always wondered why her colouring was so different from the rest of the family, but her mother, Elsa had always dismissed her questions with vague references to Mediterranean blood somewhere in the family tree. She had red hair, but unlike Tara's, it was a washed-out colour. Her eyes were light green, her brows so fair they were almost invisible. Tara's hair was a deep, burnished copper, rich in auburn hues. Her brows, over deep, emerald green eyes, were almost black, and arched. But surely she couldn't have gipsy blood? Her mother had always been prejudiced against the gipsies. She didn't even like gipsies to be mentioned in the house. She concluded Eloisa had been mistaken. What she had said was just not possible.

Long ago, Garvie had asked that Tara not attend court when he was being brought before a magistrate, nor visit him in goal. He was normally an easygoing man, but it was the one thing he was adamant about. Gipsies were treated abominably in Irish prisons, and their women were subjected to rough handling and abuse. He had no choice but to endure it himself, but he'd be damned if he'd let Tara suffer the same barbaric behaviour other gipsy women were forced to cope with. She was more refined than the Romany women, although she'd never listen to talk that intimated she was different. It made her feel inferior as if she didn't belong, and that was something she had yearned for desperately, - to be part of the group, who thought of themselves as extended family. It was a yearning that had never been fulfilled.

Although headstrong, Tara had an irrational fear of being confined, so complied with Garvie's wishes, and did not ever visit him in gaol. She hated the thought of going into a prison, even for the shortest time. Early in the relationship, she had missed him terribly, but over time, had grown used to his absences. This day, however, Tara decided she had no choice. She needed Garvie's advice and hoped he could shed light on the reason Jake had become so unreasonable and impatient. She also felt she should tell him of her plans.

Mountjoy Prison overawed Tara. Garvie had been in the Limerick and Cork prisons, but Mountjoy was by far the largest prison in Ireland, housing male prisoners, and those on remand. Female prisoners were incarcerated in the neighbouring Institution of St. Patrick's. Built in the 1850's, Mountjoy had four wings, which radiated from the center like a giant starfish. After signing the visitor's book in the reception area, which was stuffy, and had a fetid atmosphere, Tara was shown into one of three visitor's rooms adjacent.

Each of the visitor's rooms had a full-length table crossing the middle, with a mesh barrier rising from the centre, designed to separate visitors from prisoners. Like the reception area, the room lacked ventilation. The cream paint on the walls was peeling, and the concrete floor had worn grey patches. The only natural light came from one high window, which was heavily barred. Tara decided its atmosphere of cold desolation had nothing to do with the weather. Although she knew nothing of the appalling cramped cells, she was certain if she spent one minute locked inside the Mountjoy Prison; she would never do anything to warrant a return.

Garvie was shocked to see his wife standing on the other side of the table, which served as a barrier. For a few moments, they gazed at each other in bewilderment. Tara had been two hours early for visiting time and had been forced to stand outside in the drizzling rain. A guard had been going to allow her inside, in a waiting room, until he discovered she was there to visit the 'gipsy'. Immediately his attitude became hostile, and she was told she could not come inside after all. It was the kind of prejudice that Tara had never become accustomed to. It made her so angry, especially as she could do nothing to change it. As she stood opposite her husband, she was suddenly self-conscious of her bedraggled appearance and had to forcefully stop her teeth chattering.

"Tara, what are you doing here?" Garvie's expression was pained. "You're soaked through, lass."

"That's a fine way to welcome a visit from your wife. I got caught in the rain," she said, trying to smooth her hair, which always became unruly in damp weather. She moved toward him and lowered her voice. "I had to come, Garvie. Please don't be angry."

"Is something wrong, lass?"

Tara sat down on the hard wooden bench provided, and Garvie did the same opposite, while a sour-faced guard stood watch over them. Their voices carried in the still quietness of the room, making Tara feel acutely self-conscious talking in front of the guard, but her husband seemed oblivious. He was well seasoned to prison life, and the lack of privacy, which shouldn't have surprised his wife, but it did.

"I shouldn't be bothering you with my troubles, Garvie, I know you have enough of your own, but I need your advice."

Garvie was many years older than Tara. In the early part of their relationship, when she'd been so young, he had been a kind of mentor, a father figure, although he was nothing like her own father. For one thing, he never doubted her word. As she had grown into a woman, and matured, the tables had turned, and Garvie often sought her counsel. In the case of Jake, however, she needed her husband's advice.

"What is it, lass?"

All her mentally practiced tactful approaches seemed to vanish. "Jake is pressing me for money he says you owe him," Tara blurted out. "Is it true? I have a little money I could give him." She was loath to part with her funds, but if her husband was adamant, and the sum paltry….

"The limey bastard," Garvie hissed. "Don't give him a penny."

"I wasn't sure he was telling the truth, and I don't understand why he won't wait until you are released. You've always repaid him in the past."

Unable to look into her trusting, green eyes, Garvie looked down, running his broad hands over his shaven head. It was a shock to see him without his thick, wavy hair, which Tara had always loved. He looked like a stranger. His head had been shaved before, of course, but usually, by the time he returned to his wife, it had grown considerably.

"Are you alright, Garvie? I'm sorry I'm bringing my troubles to you."

"I'm fine, lass. And these are not your troubles, they're mine."

Garvie was thankful Tara knew nothing of the degradation he suffered in prison, adamantly believing it was better she remained ignorant. The shaving of bodily hair, and de-lousing, that all new prisoners were subjected to, was just the beginning of a life where privacy, self-esteem and individualism were a thing of the past. The moment a prisoner passed through the gates, they became nothing more than a number.

Mountjoy was the worst of the prisons Garvie had spent time in. Beatings were an everyday occurrence. The food was disgusting, - fish guts day after day for the prisoners whose will the warden wanted to break. Gipsies were considered lower in the chain of life than the cockroaches that shared their cramped cells. The sanitary conditions were non-existent, and while other prisoners were able to bathe once a week, gipsies were granted that privilege monthly, if they were lucky. Garvie had thought Cork Prison was terrible, but at least he'd been able to bathe twice weekly. As if his life were not miserable enough, he'd put a particularly ugly guard offside and was suffering the consequences. His punishment was slopping out the 'shit' buckets from each cell in B block. He'd done it every morning for the past three weeks, with no sign of things changing. The contents of the buckets were barely distinguishable from the disgusting slop they dished up for meals. He was thankful his prison greys hid from his wife how thin he had become in a few short weeks.

"Keep what little money you've got for yourself, Tara," Garvie said. "I can't believe he'd ask you for it."

It was on the tip of Tara's tongue to tell Garvie about the sale of her painting, but she was suddenly hesitant. She felt he was withholding something from her.

"Is that all he said, that he wanted the money?" Garvie frowned, deeply concerned Jake had broken his promise, and even more concerned Jake had crossed him.

Tara could see he looked troubled, and her suspicions grew. "Well... yes. He suggested I dance for the money, but I refused, of course."

"The fecking swine!"

The guard stepped forward, his hand resting on his baton, his callous eyes appraising Tara and Garvie as if they were scum.

"Hush, Garvie," Tara whispered, frightened. She could see the purple marks on the side of his face, and the bruises on his forearms, but she knew he'd never admit he'd been beaten. Breaking the prisoner's 'code of silence' could cost him his life. "I can't help thinking there is something else, something I don't know?"

"If he touches you, I swear I'll call in all the favours owed me and find someone to kill him." Garvie suddenly went white, as his own words reminded him of the reason he'd probably never live to be a free man again, but his thoughts quickly returned to Jake, who'd visited him three weeks ago, and suggested he'd have Tara in repayment of his debt. Garvie had exploded and threatened to have Jake killed if he touched his wife. His violent outburst and outrage had gotten him a week in solitary confinement, tortured by thoughts of what Jake would do to Tara.

Tara noted the change in her husband, and anxiety gnawed her insides. "I'm going to get away, tonight, Garvie." She didn't want to tell him she suspected the gipsies were going to evict her.

Garvie frowned again. "Where will you go? How will you live?" His only comforting thought was that she would be safe from Jake, as long as he had no idea where to find her.

When they were first married, Tara would have been touched by her husband's concern, but the years had made her wise. His concern wasn't enough to keep him out of trouble. She decided to be frank with him, after which she hoped he would be the same.

"You won't believe it, Garvie. I sold the last portrait you did of me to the Harcourt Gallery. They gave me a very good price, so I have enough money to buy a cottage by the sea."

Garvie's eyes widened in surprise, and the prison guard's ears pricked up.

"I can only afford something cheap, which may need repairs, but that doesn't matter, as long as I have enough money to live on until I find work. She had been going to say, 'until your release', but knew becoming a 'settler' would not suit Garvie, just as staying with the gipsies, and travelling, no longer suited her.

The guard, she noticed was smirking, and Garvie gave him a dark look. Tara didn't understand what had passed between them.

"I'm excited about having a little extra living space, and making it homely." She noticed Garvie looked saddened, and knew he suspected she was going to make a life without him. Although she desperately wanted to give him something to look forward to, a new life, she didn't want to give him false hope about a future together. She had 'outgrown' their relationship, which saddened her, but it was the truth. She had often thought he might be different away from the influence of the other gipsies, but he didn't want to change his life, and she couldn't change it for him.

Garvie looked at her as if not a word she was saying made any sense. She thought he was concerned for her.

"Everything will be alright, you'll see," she assured, longing to touch him and give him a little comfort. "I know you always said you'd never become a settler, and I understand. But you must understand I need a roof over my head. I can't live with the constant threat of Jake taking everything I own."

Garvie shook his head, his dark eyes clouding. He knew he had brought her nothing but worry.

"What is it, Garvie?" Tara was baffled. "I've thought it out carefully. I'll be all right. If you don't want to go back to the camp, you can stay with me, but I know you won't be happy staying in one spot. We can't change the way we are…"

"No, lass. You don't understand," Garvie interrupted. "I'm not returning to the camp, or you…"

Tara was confused. "What are you saying? Of course you'll return to the camp, Garvie." When he didn't reassure her immediately, Tara suddenly wondered if his life had been threatened. He'd never kowtow to anyone, particularly an authoritative figure, and that often got him in deep trouble. It occurred to her he may be ill, but he didn't look ill, a little drawn perhaps. A very different idea flashed through her mind. Was it possible he had found someone else? "Have you another woman in your life?" Although Tara was surprised, even shocked, she was startled to feel a small measure of relief. If he had found someone else, she needn't suffer the guilt that plagued her.

His eyes softened, clouding with sadness. "There would never be another woman for me, Tara. I've been no good for you, but I'll never know what I did to deserve you. I'll take the love I feel for you to my grave."

What little colour Tara had drained from her face, and she gripped the edge of the table with both hands. A 'vision' came to mind, but she forced it away, cursing it. "Why are you talking this way? Jake told me you were sentenced to three months for stealing. Poaching game, he said. Isn't that true?"

He nodded; relieved to know Jake had kept his word. "If only that were all, but there's more, much more." Days ago, he'd come to the conclusion Tara had to know the truth. It was the only way to sever the ties between them and make her move on. His heart almost broke with despair at the thought of hurting her, and never seeing her beautiful face again. Losing Tara was much worse than losing his life. "I told Jake not to tell you. I made him swear, lass. I hoped, in time, you'd go on with your life, perhaps meet someone else. I'm relieved you are making plans for a future without me, I just wish I could help you." His dark eyes became bleak with pain, and his head dropped.

Tara's heart wrenched with fear, as guilt swept over her. She had been planning a life without Garvie, not knowing he may be facing a lengthy sentence or worse.

Suddenly her perspective changed, as her plan seemed insignificant, and evaporated. She couldn't desert him now, and leave him alone at such a terrible time. "Don't be ridiculous, Garvie. I'm your wife, for better or worse…"

His hand came up to silence her. "My dear, sweet, loyal, Tara. You are an angel, but you must go on, alone, and be brave. I told Jake I'd get him his money. He obviously doesn't believe me…"

"Why not? You still haven't told me."

"I could be in here for twenty years, if I'm lucky. If not … I'll be carried out in a box."

Tara almost fainted. "No! Surely they're not going to … hang you?"

"Jake paid for a lawyer for me, but you know the judiciary system is prejudiced against gipsies, especially one with a history like mine. I didn't have a hope. I owe Jake near enough fifty pounds, but I swear, if I can, I'll repay him. If you have somewhere else to go, your cottage by the sea, give him the caravan if you must, Tara. Then maybe he'll leave you alone. I know it's old and in need of repair, but he could sell it. I'll settle up with him somehow …"

Tara moved her seat backwards and stared at Garvie as if he was a stranger. For the first time, she noticed his gold hoop–earrings had gone, and so had the chain he always wore around his neck. She'd never seen him without either. He hardly resembled the man she had come to know as her husband. "Forget the caravan, and the money, Garvie. We're talking about your life."

Garvie could see Tara was in shock, and he momentarily regretted telling her the truth. She had so much integrity and compassion, she'd probably try to save his sorry soul, and fret until she became ill. "Don't worry, lass. Perhaps they'll not hang me. I might get twenty years, but I'm not that old that I won't see the light of day again. I beg you, don't concern yourself about me." He tried to smile, but it was unconvincingly wooden.

"How can you ask me not to worry? I could kill Jake for demanding money, and not telling me I might not see my husband again. The man's a low-life swine!'

"Time's up, Flynn," the guard said.

Tara gasped. "Wait. Please. Just a few more minutes." The callous-faced guard shook his head.

Tara reached into her purse and produced a ten-shilling note, just as he knew she would. She discreetly passed it to him. Other visitors were coming through the door, so the guard coughed and snatched the money, sliding it inside his jacket pocket. He then put his hands behind his back, and stared straight ahead, his expression smug.

Tara turned back to her husband, who looked angry that she'd had to bribe the corrupt guards, just so they could spend a few minutes together. He'd not had a visitor for nearly three weeks.

"What have you done … been accused of doing, to be given such a harsh sentence?" Tara whispered. She hardly doubted Garvie was guilty, he'd never been innocent in the past but wanted to appear to be open-minded.

Garvie stared at her, his mind drifting back to the night he first saw her. The memory was as clear as if it was yesterday. She'd been so young, so vulnerable, and bewildered. Her spirit, as pure as the first snowfall of winter, had been shattered into a million fragments of despair. He didn't think she'd ever recover enough to become whole again. Despite the years that had passed, renewed anger surged though him every time he thought of what Stanton Jackson had done to her.

Stanton Jackson! At least he'd not hurt another living soul again. He dropped his gaze to the table and closed his eyes for a moment. "I swear, I had no idea," he whispered.

"No idea about what, Garvie?" Tara was becoming increasingly more frightened. She could feel her heart beginning to thud as if it was in her throat, hear it drumming in her ears, and was suddenly conscious of other visitors nearby.

"Do you remember the night we first met, Tara?" Garvie asked softly, not looking up. "Of course I do," she whispered in surprise. "How …could I forget?"

Garvie nodded again. "You were so distressed. I didn't know how to help you, what to do…"

"You did help me, Garvie. You helped me so much. I don't know what I would've done without you."

"It wasn't enough."

"There was nothing else you could have done. My father was the one who was supposed to make it right, but he didn't." Tara was confused. "What are you saying, Garvie? I can't follow …"

"I've been a miserable failure as a husband, I know, but you have to believe I wanted to do the right thing by you."

Tara couldn't deny what he was saying was true. He had let her down, many, many times. But she'd always known his intention had not been to hurt her. He was just not the man she should've married. It wasn't that he was a bad person, he just wasn't husband material. He had a nose for trouble, and found it, often.

"You are not making any sense, Garvie. I know your intentions have always been good… Why bring up the first night we met?"

Since that night, they had never spoken of what happened. Garvie had always believed it was best forgotten. He had no idea Tara thought of that night almost every time she closed her eyes to sleep, every time he touched her, yet she never spoke of it to anyone. "That night is very relevant to why I'm here," Garvie said, straightening his back and entwining his fingers.

Tara studied his features and waited for him to explain. Terrifying thoughts were running through her mind, but she couldn't voice them, afraid that might make them real. Eventually, she could no longer stand the strain. "Did something happen that night that I don't know about? Did you do something to … You didn't hurt my father, did you, Garvie?"

"Stanton Jackson," Garvie said blandly.

Tara froze. She'd not heard that name for many years and had no idea that Garvie even remembered it. Just hearing it made her feel physically ill, but something else frightened her more. She hoped and prayed Garvie had not avenged her. "What about him?" she whispered.

Garvie looked up, his dark eyes moist with emotion. "I wanted to kill him for what he did to you."

Tara gasped. "No ... Garvie. No!" Tears brimmed her eyes.

Garvie's expression became agonized when he saw the disappointment and despair in his wife's features. Unable to look at her, his eyes dropped again. "I have to tell you this, lass."

"No!" Tara pushed the bench backwards, grating it on the floor.

"I'm sorry, but I fear for your safety," he implored. He glanced at the guard. It was the first time Tara felt he was aware of him overhearing their conversation.

Garvie looked at her, further imploring her for understanding.

The night they first met, Tara's family had hosted a party for her, her debut to society. While getting some fresh air, she had been attacked by a man working for her father. She had run into the forest, her dress torn, blinded by tears and pain, and ended up in the gipsy camp. Garvie had taken care of her until she was calm, convincing her to return to her home.

"When I walked you back to your home, and we stopped on the edge of the forest, I watched you until you went inside the house. I was just about to leave when I saw a man skulking in the shadows by the stables. His behaviour made me think he was likely to be the man who had attacked you. When I saw him go into the end stall, I followed him. I hid in the shadows behind hay bales, just inside the door, and watched him light a lamp and remove his shirt. He began examining marks on his body. From where I stood, they looked like bite marks. I remembered you said your dog came to your aid when you were attacked. Then I saw the scratch marks on his chest and shoulders. You must have put them there when you fought him."

Tara gasped and covered her mouth with her hand.

"When I thought of what he had done to you, I was blinded by rage. I confronted him, and we argued. He was smug about what he had done. He bragged of convincing your father a gipsy had..." He lowered his voice, and Tara felt herself colour with embarrassment, 'raped you'. I hit him, and kept on hitting him, until he fell to the ground. I was exhausted, physically and emotionally, yet rage still burned inside me. As I stood over him, challenging him to get to his feet, I heard voices, people approaching. Knowing the evidence was there on Stanton's body, yet, as a gipsy, I would be the one arrested, I hid behind the hay bales again, hoping whoever was outside would pass by. Two young men, caterers I think, stopped by the stable door. Seeing the light, and Stanton's prostrate body, they came in. They examined him and claimed he was still alive. While one went for help, the other was busy making Stanton comfortable, so I slipped out and ran away. As I made my way towards the forest, I could hear your father shouting somewhere in one of the upstairs rooms. I thought he was angry about what Stanton had done to you, and was glad I had beaten him and rendered him unable to escape. It wasn't until I got back to the camp, that I realized I had lost the chain and medallion I always wore. I thought it must have been broken in the struggle with Stanton. I was going to go back for it when you arrived and told us the police were coming because your father believed one of us had raped you. I was shocked and angry with your father for not believing you. I felt certain he would have examined Stanton and found the marks on his body, and realized what had really happened. If he didn't, it meant Stanton was going to get away with what he had done to you. I wanted to go back and speak to your father, but what you said convinced me no good would come of it. If he didn't believe his own daughter, he certainly would not take the word of a gipsy. All that mattered to you was how your father had betrayed you. I believed taking you away was the best thing. After we left the Watergrasshill Parish, I thought no more of that gold chain and medallion."

Tara shook her head, unable to comprehend what he was saying. Garvie saw the look of bewilderment in her eyes.

"Time's up, Flynn," the guard said again.

"Please," Tara begged. "Just a few more minutes." She opened her purse again and pushed a few coins in his direction. Glancing around cunningly, he took the proffered coins, looking well pleased with himself.

This time, Garvie seemed oblivious to his unscrupulous profiteering. He needed to finish his story, to purge himself to the one person who cared above all others. He prayed she wouldn't be affected by what had happened, but it was possible, so she had to be forewarned.

"The police told me Stanton Jackson died two days later, from a blood clot in his brain. I remember he fell against the wall of the stall, where there was a pitchfork, but I don't remember seeing any blood. The police believe I hit him with the pitchfork, but I swear I didn't. Apparently, they found my gold chain and medallion amongst straw on the floor, and showed it to jewellers in the area. One of them had made it for me and gave them a description. Unaware of what had taken place, I returned to the same jeweller in

Maynooth three months later, and asked him to make a medallion identical to the one I had lost. He did as I asked, charging me an exorbitant fee, but contacted the police when I didn't pay the last installment owed. I was in gaol at the time, and had fines to pay. I had also worked on some of the farms in the area, clearing land and chopping wood. One of the farmers, a neighbour of your father's was able to identify the chain and medallion as mine. The jeweller and the farmer's evidence were all the police needed to serve a warrant for my arrest. As my medallion had my initials on the back, I really had no defense. I was already in custody for poaching, so they had me. They charged me with Stanton's murder."

"Oh, Garvie." Tara began to sob.

"Don't cry, my love."

"It's my fault. If I hadn't run to the gipsy camp that night, none of this would've happened."

"Don't say that, Tara. You are the best thing that ever happened to me. It's me that's no good. Through no fault of your own, you've had to spend most of your married life alone."

"You are misguided at times, Garvie, but you have a good heart."

"Children are misguided, Tara. I'm just trouble. Trouble you could do without."

"I'm going to the police to tell them what happened. If they know the whole truth, perhaps they will withdraw the charges."

"That's typically generous of you, Tara, but nothing will make them withdraw the charges. Whatever he did to you, it was my actions that killed him. If I weren't here for his murder, I'd be here for something else. You know that's true. This way, I'll just save everyone the bother of bringing me to court every few months. I've had a long time to think about what happened, and I believe it's likely Stanton already had a clot on the brain when he attacked you. I remember you talking about him that night, and telling me he seemed in pain and kept putting his hand to his temple. You were trying to make sense of why he did what he did, and thought the liquor he had drunk was giving him pains in his head, but I believe it was something more."

Tara nodded. "You shouldn't be here, Garvie."

"I didn't intend to kill Jackson, but he died just the same. I've accepted my fate, and you must, too."

"But this is such a horrible place. How can you cope with not being able to see the stars at night, or sitting beside the campfire, playing your guitar?"

For a second, Tara thought she saw a flicker of despair in his eyes. She had no idea how much Garvie missed his freedom. In his cell every night, he dreamt of travelling lonely country roads, surrounded by green fields and heather-filled meadows. He imagined sitting beside a blazing campfire, and the breeze off a loch. He loved music, and watching Tara dance filled his soul with passion. He'd give his soul if he could see his wife dance just one more time. But that would never be. He'd have to be content with his dreams and memories, for what short time he had left.

"It's you I'm worried about, Tara. I told the police you had nothing to do with Stanton's death, but I'm not sure they're convinced. They asked me questions along the lines of whether Stanton and I were fighting over you. When they learned you had run away with me, they thought perhaps Stanton was a spurned lover. I'd have peace of mind if you went somewhere and began a new life. You were never meant for the life of a gipsy. I want you to forget you ever knew me, forget the life we shared. You are a real lady. You should have so much more than what I've given you. A grand house, a fine husband, and lots of children. I know you blame yourself for not giving me a child, but it's more than likely my fault. I've never been able to give you any of the things you deserve. You know our marriage was only legal in the eyes of gipsy law. Consider yourself a free woman, and begin a new life."

Tears spilt over Tara's lashes. Even though she'd wanted her freedom, she'd never wanted it at the expense of Garvie's' life. It seemed so tragic.

"Do it for me, Tara. Please. If I know you are safe and happy, that's all I need."

"I won't forget you, Garvie. Don't ask me to. You've been part of my life for nearly eleven years, and my husband for nearly nine of those years. I've never cared about grand houses and all the trappings…"

Garvie could see he wasn't getting through to Tara. "Perhaps you haven't, but you know in your heart I was the wrong man for you. I know it, too."

Tara shook her head. She didn't want to hear what he was saying. All she could think of was Garvie losing his life for avenging her.

His tone became harsh. He was almost certain to be hanged, and he couldn't have Tara wasting her life grieving for him "You forgot your own family, Tara. If you can do that, you can forget someone as worthless as me. We are to have no further contact."

Tara gasped in shock.

"Don't write to me, because I'll not ask anyone to read your letters to me. Don't visit me, because I won't see you. Go, now, and begin a new life, as Tara Killain."

Tara was speechless with shock. Garvie had never spoken to her in that tone before. He stood up, his face impassive, even though his heart was wrenched in agony. He looked at Tara's beautiful face, with tears running down her velvet smooth cheeks, and let her image burn into his brain, to be held in his memory forever. Her sad eyes, shining with tears, were almost his undoing, but he fought to be strong, for her sake. He loved Tara with all his heart, but he had to set her free.

Unable to move, Tara watched him go through the door, back to his cell. He didn't even glance back. She wondered how he could be so cruel, so unfeeling. Her mind refused to face the truth, but in her heart, she knew the answer. He loved her.

Even though Garvie was right, and sure to be hanged, that didn't stop the unbearable pain.

CHAPTER FOUR

When Kelvin Kendrick entered the Harcourt Gallery, it was not yet light, - one of those cold and dismal mornings he dreamt of being somewhere warm, on the other side of the world. As he approached his desk at the rear of the main gallery, he was baffled to see the headdress and veil Lady Bowers ad been wearing the previous day, thrown across his paperwork. Puzzled, he glanced around and noticed the office door ajar. As the gallery was a target for thieves, and Kelvin was the first to admit bravery wasn't part of his make-up, he was alarmed.

Kelvin considered the possibility it was Lady Bowers in the office and thought perhaps she had returned to steal the portrait of the 'gipsy lady'. For some unknown reason, she had seemed preoccupied with it, and her taste in art was quite bizarre for a 'Lady'. He retrieved a pistol kept hidden under his desk, and shakily made his way to the office door. The pistol wasn't loaded, as the thought of seeing blood, even someone else's, made Kelvin's curdle, but he hoped it would terrify any would-be thieves. When he heard no sound, he peered in. He quickly recognized the figure standing in front of the 'gipsy lady' painting, and shook his head in bewilderment, wondering what it could be about that terrible painting that fascinated people.

Kelvin's emotions flickered between relief and annoyance. "Mr. Magee, you startled me. You could have warned me you would were opening up this morning. I nearly had heart failure."

When Riordan didn't answer, Kelvin entered the office.

Riordan had been miles away, in a 'wood' in Tipperary, on a moonlit night. Kelvin could see he was not his usual self. He looked tired and despondent.

"Kelvin, could you package this painting for overseas shipment?" he asked quietly, handing him the portrait of the 'gipsy lady.'

"This painting, sir? Has someone purchased it?"

"I want it returned to its rightful owner."

"I thought you were the rightful owner." Kelvin was confused but thought better of questioning his employer. "Of course, sir, but I purchased another yesterday…"

"I don't want to see it," Riordan interrupted, his tone suddenly harsh. "Send them both to Victoria Millburn, c/o Tambora Station, Wombat Creek, South Australia."

Riordan went behind his desk and picked up some paperwork, a futile attempt to distract himself. Kelvin could see something was upsetting him.

"Is anything wrong, sir? You look… not quite yourself this morning." He thought his frame of mind had something to do with Lady Bowers but did not have the nerve to ask. He glanced at the portrait, propped against the wall, still covered by the brown paper it had originally been wrapped in. He assumed Riordan had not been curious enough to uncover it. He had no idea of the turmoil his employer had been going through, for more than an hour, fighting the desire to unveil it.

"It was a coincidence that Lady Bowers had a painting by the artist of the original 'gipsy lady,' wasn't it, sir?" Kelvin said, fishing for clues for Riordan's melancholy.

"It was not by chance," Riordan replied flatly. "I thought you had a brilliant eye for detail?"

Kelvin was stunned by the criticism. Something was not quite right. He didn't understand how the headdress and veil came to be on his desk, and Riordan certainly wasn't himself.

"I'm sorry," Riordan said, raking his long fingers through his thick, fair hair and sighing raggedly. "You are no more a fool than I, and to be fair to us both, the lady was wearing a veil."

Kelvin could see dark circles around his eyes. It was obvious he had not slept at all.

"Did you notice any resemblance between Ta… 'Lady Bowers, and the gipsy lady in the portrait?"

"Resemblance, sir, between Lady Bowers and a gipsy!" Kelvin was incredulous and becoming more confused by the minute.

"Her features, Kelvin. I know they were hard to see, but did you notice they were similar? I thought you may have, as the light in here is very good."

Kelvin glanced at the portrait. He placed his hand under his chin, the odd, almost feminine pose he held when concentrating on a work of art. "When I said I would purchase the painting, she lifted her veil… I thought it strange at the time."

Riordan studied him, his features suddenly tainted with sadness. "Then you would have noticed the likeness?"

Kelvin scrutinized the portrait more closely. "Now that you mention it, there is a striking similarity, particularly the eyes." He turned to Riordan, his lips pursed in concentration. "I didn't give it a thought yesterday. Her 'attire' was so different. The gipsy woman's clothes are tawdry, almost obscene, whereas Lady Bowers' attire was demure and respectable, - a little outdated, but entirely appropriate for her circumstances. I could not see her hair, but it's unlikely to be the same colour as the 'gipsy lady's' hair. A deep shade of russet," he added, almost as a concession. "Why do you ask, sir? Surely Lady Bowers could not be related to this woman?"

"It's a long story, Kelvin, but Lady Bowers is actually the woman in this painting." Kelvin gasped.

"Do you remember my search for a woman seven years ago?"

The manager nodded, mutely. He was not likely to ever forget that dark period. He'd had to run the gallery single-handed, - buying, cataloguing, selling, all while Riordan had been like a man possessed. No one could make him see sense. He never told Kelvin, or anyone else for that matter, the details, but his search nearly ended in tragedy, when he almost lost his life at the hands of gipsies. None of his friends knew what he had been doing in Chelms Wood, in Tipperary, but they believed the motive for the attack was robbery. The locals, however, were convinced of something more sinister.

"I was searching for the woman in this painting," Riordan said.

Kelvin was incredulous. He couldn't believe Riordan would risk his life for a… gipsy woman. He immediately thought of the portrait he had purchased, and his eyes grew as large as saucers. "Is the painting a … fake?"

"The painting is unimportant, Kelvin."

"Unimportant! I paid her a lot of money for it." Kelvin prided himself on never being taken for a fool, although many had tried. It seemed the 'gipsy woman' had succeeded.

For the first time since Kelvin had come to work for him, almost nine years ago, Riordan realized he was indeed a narrow-minded bigot, just as Tara had claimed. The revelation came as a shock.

"It was me who instructed you to buy any painting by the artist of the 'gipsy lady', remember, Kelvin? The painting is irrelevant. Don't concern yourself about it, or lose any sleep over it."

Kelvin wasn't listening. The thought of being hoodwinked by a 'gipsy woman' appalled him. He wouldn't sleep for days. "I knew the painting was worthless. I cannot understand why you instructed me to pay handsomely for something of such poor quality. Something like that could ruin our good reputation." He remembered her calling him an 'inane imbecile', and felt himself grow warm with mortification. "She has quite a nerve trying to pass herself off as a real 'lady'."

Riordan felt his anger surging but bit it down. "Firstly, Kelvin, Lady Bowers, the 'gipsy lady', is in fact, Tara Killain, a real 'lady'. Ninian Killain was once an avid art buyer, and his sister, Victoria Millburn, is a good friend of mine."

Kelvin's jaw dropped, but Riordan hadn't finished with him yet. "You have been a loyal and capable worker, Kelvin, but perhaps you need reminding that you were born in a two-roomed farm cottage." He watched his employee almost shrink in self-consciousness. "You were lucky an uncle paid for what education you had, and fortunate you have talent and training in the art world."

Kelvin flushed and dropped his gaze.

Sensing his humiliation, Riordan's tone became gentler. "Tara was born into the gentry, and would have had all the privileges that came with it, education, society functions." His eyes closed and he faltered, thinking of the turn her life had taken, and the pain it had caused her family. "She fell in love with a man…who happened to be a gipsy. We have no right to judge her, whether we agree with her choice, or not." Riordan believed himself to be broad-minded and compassionate but realized he was guilty of being neither where Tara was concerned. He wondered if he could make amends, although it was unlikely he'd ever see her again, which was probably a relief, and just as well.

Kelvin thought he'd be damned if he'd be compassionate to someone who had lived as a gipsy. As far as he was concerned they were nothing but savages. Had Riordan forgotten he'd nearly lost his life at their hands? He wanted to voice his opinion, but thought better of it, as he also wanted to keep his position at the gallery.

"Victoria Millburn wanted me to find her niece, so she sent me the painting so I might recognize her." Riordan couldn't go on. Although he had been defending Tara's virtue, he still felt the pain of disillusionment. If he were being truthful, he'd admit it was his own doing and had nothing to do with Tara Killain. He had made the woman in the portrait into a completely fictitious creature, someone who needed him to rescue her, but she existed only in his mind, and now he had to let her go. He was desperate to rid his memory of all thoughts of the 'gipsy lady', something, in the past, he had been unable to do. Sending the painting back to Victoria would be a beginning.

"Leave me alone, will you, Kelvin?" he said softly.

Tara returned to the gipsy camp to find her belongings ransacked by children, and strewn along the banks of the Liffey. Her caravan was gone, along with the gipsies. Quite obviously Jake was not willing to wait for his money, and the gipsies were no longer inclined to support her, especially for the length of time Garvie was likely to be incarcerated. They weren't her family and never would be. Although she had always known how they felt, the rejection still caused her pain.

By the time evening descended upon her, Tara had decided to splurge on a warm bed in a modest Inn, for the night. Just for a few hours she could put her terrible predicament behind her. She had no idea where she would go, or what she would do, and no one to discuss it with, or give her advice. She'd never felt more alone in her life.

Despite the luxury of a comfortable bed, Tara tossed and turned most of the night, thinking about her aunt, and the painting she had found at the gallery. She distinctly remembered her aunt vowing she would never part with it, so knew there had to be a very good reason why she did. They had shared an especially close bond when Tara was growing up. She couldn't go on with her life without finding out what had happened to her.

Riordan was doing paperwork, when he heard a commotion in the gallery. "I demand to know where you got this veil. Where is the owner…?"

"Please leave, before I call a constable and have you thrown out…"

Riordan had just got to his feet, when his office door burst open, and unexpectedly, Tara appeared, dressed as 'Lady Bowers. His heart lurched when he saw her. A flustered Kelvin Kendrick closely followed her.

"I'm sorry, sir. I could not stop her. I shall call a constable."

As surprised as Tara was to see Riordan, she caught the note of disdain in Kelvin's voice and her hackles rose.

Riordan slumped in his chair. "No, Kelvin. I'll see Miss Killain." He leant his head in his hands for a moment, gathering strength.

Tossing Tara a scornful glare, Kelvin left the office.

Tara stared at Riordan, wide-eyed.

He noted she was holding the veil she had discarded the previous evening.

"What are you doing in this office?' she asked, then gasped, as realization dawned. "Surely *you* aren't the gallery owner?" Humiliation washed over her as she remembered her 'cocky' attitude toward him and Kelvin Kendrick the previous day. Why hadn't she sensed he was the gallery owner? Again her *talent* had let her down. Eloisa was wrong, she was certain of it. There was no way she could be a 'Seer.'

"How could you deceive…?"

Riordan interrupted, his tone laced with sarcasm. "Surely you are not going to be hypocritical, and call me a fraud?" Although he had promised himself he'd be compassionate towards her, he couldn't help himself.

Tara flushed with anger and embarrassment. "You called me Miss Killain a moment ago. How did you know who I am, and where did you get the painting I saw here yesterday?" She glanced at the uncovered stack of paintings against the wall. The 'gipsy lady' had gone, but the new portrait she had sold the gallery was still there.

Riordan followed the direction of her glance. "It's been packaged to send back to your Aunt," he said. "I should have done it years ago. You can take the other one back."

Tara's eyes narrowed suspiciously. "How do you know my Aunt? And how did you get the portrait of me? Aunt Victoria vowed to never part with it."

Riordan sighed and looked down at the neat pile of paperwork on his desk, without really seeing it. Tara went toward him, more determined than ever to uncover the truth. When she reached the desk, she stood looking down at the top of his fair head.

"Sit down," Riordan said suddenly tired. "The last thing I want is to have this conversation with you, Miss Killain, but I owe Victoria that much." Riordan hoped that once everything was out in the open, he could go on with his life in peace. Tara Killain had caused him enough torment.

Tara was confused by his change of attitude toward her. "It's Tara Flynn. Mrs. Tara Flynn," she said, suddenly wanting to rankle him, "and the last thing I desire is to have a conversation with you, but I want answers. I think you owe me that much." She perched herself on the edge of the chair opposite him.

Riordan nodded, irritated by the way her proximity made him feel and shocked that she had married. He suspected she'd married a gipsy, which made him doubly angry.

"Begin by telling me how you know my Aunt," Tara demanded. "The last I knew she was going overseas…"

Riordan looked up at her face, into her clear green eyes, and suddenly found it difficult to concentrate. Tara was every bit as beautiful as she had been seven years ago. Visions of her erotic dance swam through his mind, and he had to force himself to think coherently, which exasperated him further, as he felt his body react. "I first met your Aunt in Paris. I was buying for the gallery. By coincidence, we ran into each other in many other European cities and became good friends. We kept in contact after she went to India, where she met her husband, Tom Milburn."

Tara's eyes widened in surprise. She was so pleased her aunt had finally found happiness. Riordan could see she looked delighted and realized Tara must have once been genuinely fond of her aunt. It made it hard to comprehend how she could have callously broken her heart. He fixed his gaze on a paperweight on his desk, a carved sandstone elephant, a gift from a client. "Tom owned a substantial station in the middle of Australia. Apparently, he had lived on the property for a few years, developing it, before going to India. He'd loved it there, and was convinced Victoria would also love Tambora." Riordan's voice softened. "Tom Millburn was one of the kindest men you could ever hope to meet. He made your Aunt very happy."

"You're speaking in past tense. Did something happen to him?"

"Tragically, Tom died five years ago."

"Oh." Tara felt deep sympathy for her aunt. It seemed, like herself, Victoria wasn't destined to find true and lasting happiness. "What happened to my Aunt? Surely she would have wanted to return to Ireland after Tom died."

"You would have thought so, but she decided to stay on in outback Australia, and run Tambora herself. No slight feat, as I believe the property is twice the size of Ireland." Tara gasped.

"I know she encountered many difficulties, but Victoria is an exceptional woman." Tara noted the genuine admiration in Riordan's voice.

He saw her eyes fill with unshed tears.

"She must be getting on in years," Tara said, remembering her aunt had been older than her father.

Riordan nodded. "I remember her as a vital and energetic woman. But the last I heard her health was not the best. If I know Victoria, she won't give in until they're carrying her off the station in a wooden box."

Tara nodded. Riordan's assessment of her aunt's character was quite correct. She had always been very determined, much like herself. "Please explain how you came to have the painting. Did my Aunt sell it to you?" Tara thought that perhaps Victoria needed funds after her husband's death, to keep the station financially afloat. No doubt the Depression had affected Australia.

"Victoria wrote and asked me to find you. She did not have a recent photograph and didn't know whether you had changed your name, so she sent me the painting on loan, so I could recognize you."

Tara was puzzled. "Why did she want you to find me?" She didn't see the glint of anger in Riordan's eyes.

"She wanted you to help her run the station." That was the first reason Victoria gave him, but as time went by, the truth came out.

Tara gasped again. "Me!" For a moment she let this information sink in. It was incredible. "How long ago did she write and ask you to find me? A few months, a year?"

"Seven years ago. Two years before Tom died."

Tara's eyes widened in shock. Her aunt would have needed her more than ever after Tom's death. She jumped to her feet. "Seven years…" That was only about a year after Tara had sent her the portrait. She realized that had she made contact personally, instead of sending a brief note with the portrait, she would have known her aunt was married and planned a life with her husband in outback Australia. "When did you last have word from her?"

"Almost two years ago. I'm probably to blame for that. I haven't kept in contact. I had no news of you…"

Tara did not know what to think.

"Your life could have been so different," Riordan said flatly. "Victoria wanted to teach you all about farming Australian style, which I believe is very different to the way it's done here. Last I knew she was running several thousand head of cattle and sheep on the property. As she had no children, no heirs, she was thinking long term to the day when you would have been mistress of Tambora." A far different life from the one you chose, Riordan thought, feeling a stab of pain and anger.

Tara was unable to perceive what Riordan was telling her. She paced the room, rampant thoughts racing through her mind. She couldn't imagine herself running such a property. It seemed a ludicrous thought when she had been about to purchase a broken-down cottage, just so she could have a permanent roof over her head.

"Do you know if she contacted one of my brothers to help her?" Tara's brothers, twins Liam and Daniel were younger than she was, but they would no doubt have been groomed to run the family estate.

"I doubt it. It was never her intention." Riordan's eyes hardened on her, as he remembered the anguish he had suffered, the same misery felt by her family. Try as he might, he found it impossible to comprehend how she could be so cruel to those who loved her.

"The truth was your Aunt wanted to rescue you from what she believed was a terrible fate. I didn't have the heart to tell her you were happy in your new life."

His tone, and the context of what he was saying, confused Tara. "What do you mean?"

"Your Aunt told me you had been kidnapped by the gipsies."

Tara gasped. "Kidnapped! Why did she tell you that?"

"She could not conceive you would have gone with the gipsies willingly. I know you told her you were happy in the note you sent her with the portrait, but she believed differently. She told me your family gave a lavish party for your eighteenth birthday, your debut to society, and it was the last time they saw you. Apparently, she had been ill, and unable to attend the party."

Tara's gaze dropped. She remembered her aunt had just returned from some foreign country, where she had contracted a fever. "That's true. But I was not kidnapped." She walked towards the curtainless, barred window, overlooking a small allotment at the rear of the building, behind which there was a stable and laneway. It wasn't a pleasant view, but the first snow was falling. It added a softness to an otherwise harsh aspect. She realized that her father might have told her aunt that she had been kidnapped. It would have been easier than admitting what he believed to be true. That she willingly lost her virginity to a gipsy camped on their land, then ran away with him of her own free will. Ninian Killain would have done almost anything to avoid scandal and dishonour. Even turn against his only daughter, Tara thought bitterly.

"Something happened that night. I wanted to tell my Aunt about it. I think she would have understood...." She couldn't go on.

"Perhaps it's better that you did not break her heart and admit you fell for one of the gipsies and ran away with him, without a care for your family's feelings."

Tara became angry. "That is not what happened," she snapped.

Riordan looked at her, his bluish-grey eyes full of scepticism.

"You cannot begin to know anything about my life," Tara spat.

Her 'act' of indignation made Riordan's pain and years of turmoil suddenly erupt like a volcano. "I know you danced for the gipsies willingly, that you had them in your spell." He was equally angry with himself for revealing his true feelings, but he couldn't help it.

Tara gasped. "How could you possibly know that?" she asked vehemently.

"I saw you." There was no stopping the rush of passionate fury that had eaten Riordan up for so many years. "I watched you tantalize the men. I saw the way they leered at you. You enjoyed every moment. It wouldn't be an exaggeration to say you shamelessly thrived upon the lustful attention you received."

Tara went white with anger. Her first impulse was to defend herself, to tell him she loved to dance. She could not sell wares in the street, like the other gipsy women, for fear of being recognised as the daughter of a respected member of the gentry. Surprisingly, she had some talent when it came to foreseeing the future, but she refused to use it at carnivals for money, and her pride would not permit her to beg for a few coins. Her refusal to beg or sell wares in the street made some of the gipsies condemn her as 'uppity', but this couldn't have been further from the truth. Even though she never wanted to see her parents again, she couldn't bring herself to dishonour the 'Killain' name. She had her brother's future to think of.

The gipsies soon realized she was not an asset to the group. She'd had servants all her life. What did she know of cooking or cleaning? She had no experience in looking after young children, much like her mother, who'd always used nannies. She'd also never had to clean up after the animals, which the gipsies expected her to do. She seemed to have no useful skills at all. When they asked her, sarcastically, what she 'could' do, she told them almost in fun, that she loved to dance. The women laughed scornfully, but the men suggested her looks could draw a paying audience, and prompted the women to give her lessons in gipsy dancing. They taught her to move her body in a way she had never dreamt of doing. Riordan could never understand how dancing had restored her sense of worth after her father's betrayal.

"When did you see me dance?" she asked, taking her seat again.

"In Chelms Wood. I went there to …rescue you. I believed, as your Aunt did, that you had been kidnapped, that the gipsies were holding you against your will. I believed you were living a life of degradation at the hands of lustful men. I could not have been more wrong. How on earth could I tell your Aunt what I saw? Tell me that!"

Tara stared at him silently, and then realization dawned. She studied his face, noting a pale scar going from his right eyebrow to below his ear. "You were the man the gipsies beat. I thought they had killed you. My God, that must have been…"

"Seven years ago. They very nearly did kill me," Riordan said angrily. "But the pain and suffering I endured was nothing compared to the disillusionment."

Unable to look at her a moment longer, Riordan turned to the window, remembering the old man, Donaldbain Keefe, who had helped him only because he hated the gipsies poaching on his land. Without the old man's help, he surely would have died.

Stunned by his outburst, Tara watched his back and thought about what he'd said. His attitude confused her. Why should he have been disillusioned? She was nothing to him. She remembered that night as if it was yesterday. Her audience had been a sea of blurred faces, but one person's eyes had caught her attention. Riordan's! His eyes were full of carnal passion, like the rest of the men, but the longing was tinged with what she thought was sadness. What she now knew to be disillusionment. It was something that had troubled her for a long time.

Tara had tried to stop the men from beating him, but the women dragged her away. For months she had yearned to understand why he was there, why he had been looking at her the way he had. She had been tortured with guilt; convinced the gipsies had killed him. It was an absolute miracle he was alive, and for that she thanked God. As she was the reason he'd been at the camp and hurt so badly, she felt she owed him an explanation. It would be very difficult to bear her soul, but the time had come to set the record straight. First with Riordan, and then with her aunt. It was the only way she could move on.

"The night of my eighteenth birthday," Tara began slowly, "I was attacked and…" She tried to be unemotional, but it was impossible. "…. raped."

Riordan's head turned slowly. She could see he was shocked, but slowly his expression turned to contempt. "By a gipsy?"

"No, by my father's estate manager, Stanton Jackson." She immediately thought of Garvie, and her chest tightened with grief. "My father thought highly of him. So highly in fact, he didn't believe me when I told him what had happened." Tara couldn't remain unemotional about her father, try as she might. She choked back tears. She had felt utterly betrayed by him and knew she could never, never forgive him.

Riordan turned to face her, giving her his full attention. She wished he hadn't. It had been easier talking to his back. Forcing herself to concentrate, she let her mind drift back to that painful night, to a time when her innocence had been intact and many handsome young suitors were willing to sell their souls to make all her hopes and dreams come true. "I was having a wonderful time… It was a warm night in June, and the stars were bright… The dance floor had been set up outside in the garden, surrounded by flaming torches, and the perfume of flowers. I danced with every young man… I love to dance.." She glanced up and felt herself blush. Standing, she walked over to the far side of the room, and stood in front of a painting, turning her back on Riordan. She didn't want to see the expression in his eyes. It was like looking into his soul, and she wasn't prepared for that.

"The party almost seems unreal now, so silly and trivial. I can hardly imagine what it would be like to go back to a time when my biggest concern was which young man I would dance with next."

One particular young man had been making a nuisance of himself, Corey Gower. She remembered his awkward ways and clammy hands.

"I slipped away to be alone for a few minutes and walked near the stables. My dog was sleeping in one of the stalls and came out to greet me. We often walked together around the estate, so he bounded off, and I followed. The moon was almost full. I could see the dog up ahead. I called, but he must have seen a rabbit…" Her voice trailed off. When Tara spoke again, it was evident she was trying to keep the emotion from her voice, as her tone was matter-of-fact. "I was grabbed from behind and dragged off the path, behind a hedge. Stanton had been drinking. I could smell the sour odour of whisky on his breath, as I often had before. He told me he'd been watching me. He said I had been tantalizing the men…leading them on." She realized that was exactly what she used to do when dancing for the gipsies… And so did Riordan.

"I tried to reason with him, I even pleaded. When that didn't work, I tried screaming for help, but no one heard me. We were too far from the house and the music was loud. I tried, but …" Her voice cracked with the tumultuous emotion she was fighting. "…I couldn't stop him. Eventually, it was Scully who came to my aid. I think Stanton might have killed me, if not for Scully. He ran off, my dog in pursuit, leaving me bruised and battered in the bushes, like something dirty and discarded. I stumbled to my feet and ran blindly into the wood. I didn't know where I was going. I just wanted to get as far away as I could." Tara began to pace the room, twisting the strap of her purse mercilessly, as the memory of how she felt came rushing back.

"I was hysterical when I reached the gipsy camp. I don't know who was more shocked, them or me, but they were so kind. Some of the men went looking for Stanton. I was too upset to give them more than the vaguest of a description, but the look in their eyes made me almost pity anyone they found. Garvie, the gipsy I eventually married, comforted me like a child. I should have been terrified, after what had happened, but he was so tender. I felt safe. He talked to me for almost an hour, convincing me I had to tell my father what had happened. At first, I wouldn't hear of it. I wanted to keep running and never look back. Garvie gave me one of the women's shawls to put around my shoulders and walked me back to within sight of the house. The guests had gone. I could see the servants frantically searching the grounds for me. I insisted on going the rest of the way alone, as I didn't want to bring any trouble to a man who had been so kind to me." Tara thought of what Garvie had told her, and her heart felt as heavy as lead. If only he hadn't gone after Stanton.

Riordan had moved back to his chair, so Tara went to the window, and stared at the falling snow, remembering how Garvie had believed everything she told him. He was a total stranger, and yet he had not doubted a word she told him. He comforted her, consoled her, and convinced her that her father would have Stanton Jackson brought to justice. It was the opposite of what took place. She understood too well the disillusionment Riordan had felt. It was identical to her own.

Suddenly Tara went cold, as she thought of what happened next. She spoke as if her emotions had been turned off. "I told my father what had happened and…. he called me a… liar." She had loved him so much, and never, ever lied to him. "Apparently Stanton had got to him first, and told him a pack of filthy lies. I couldn't believe my father would take his word over mine. When he saw the gipsy shawl, he went crazy. He locked me in my room and called the doctor. When the doctor confirmed I was no longer a… virgin, my father sent for a constable. My mother looked at me as if I had been sullied. I knew she was thinking no decent man would want 'damaged goods'. Her dreams of a good match for me were in ruins. It didn't matter how I felt."

Tara turned to face Riordan, two tears running down her pale cheeks. "My father wanted the gipsies hunted and hanged. Stanton had told him he had witnessed me making love with a gipsy in the woods." Her tears began to flow freely. Riordan handed her his handkerchief and poured her a glass of water in a state of numbness. He realized he felt ashamed for what he had believed, but her story was so hard to accept in good faith. There were too many unanswered questions going through his mind.

"I persuaded one of my brothers to let me out of my room, and went to the gipsy camp to warn them to leave. I begged Garvie to take me with him. I told him I was going to run away, with or without the gipsies. He relented, but I'm sure it was only to protect me. I knew my life would change forever, but I felt betrayed by my father. It seemed the only solution."

"Where is your…. Garvie, now?" Riordan asked flatly.

Tara dropped her gaze. "That does not matter."

Riordan scrutinized her. Something in her tone made him suspicious. "He's in gaol, isn't he?" His tone hinted at repulsion.

Tara didn't answer. She didn't have to. The look on her face told him everything he needed to know.

Riordan wasn't surprised that her husband was a felon, but from what he knew of the way gipsies were treated in prison, she was not likely to ever see him again.

"Are you still with the … gipsies?" he asked, not able to remain as unemotional as he would have liked.

Having bared the worst of her life, Tara found no use for tactful diplomacy. "No. Garvie owes the leader money, so they have taken what possessions I had, including the caravan, and evicted me from the group. All I have left is a few clothes and my old mare."

Her candidness touched Riordan's heart. "Surely they could not be so pitiless, just because your husband owes them money?"

Tara paused. "I'm not one of them, not of their blood. They only put up with me because of Garvie. Now he's… gone."

Riordan frowned, suddenly all practicality. "What are you planning to do?"

Tara took his pragmatic thinking for cold-heartedness but expected no more. So far, he hadn't demonstrated one iota of compassion.

"I was going to purchase a cottage, somewhere by the sea, perhaps around Devon, but I'm not sure any more." Tara looked at Riordan and frowned. "I would go to my Aunt, but the Depression is making life hard enough, without the added burden of another mouth to feed."

Riordan turned away. Tara sensed something was bothering him, but he was too indifferent for it to be what she had just told him. She suddenly had a shocking thought. "You don't believe anything I have told you, do you?"

"I don't know what to think," he snapped impatiently.

Tara was incredulous. "Do you think I made up everything I just told you?"

Riordan turned to glare at her, angry with her and with himself, but not understanding the reasons. "I know you are capable of concocting wild stories, Tara. Lady Bowers for instance."

"I told you why I did that. I am not in the habit of telling fanciful stories, but I could hardly walk in here as a gipsy. My God, I would not make up something so terrible, so shocking, about myself."

"Then why did your father believe this Stanton fellow? I can't even understand why you left the safety of your family to walk alone at night."

"I wanted to catch my breath. For the love of Holy Mary, why am I bothering to defend myself? It's obvious you've made up your mind."

"Surely there was some evidence this Stanton fellow raped you, especially if you fought him?"

"Evidence?"

"Scratch marks on his face…"

Tara suddenly paled. "Perhaps they weren't on his face, but my word should have been enough for my parents. They knew me better than anyone. I was sometimes willful and disobedient, but never a liar." She glared at him. "As for you, it's not my fault you built me up in your mind as some kind of princess in need of rescuing, so don't blame me if your illusions were shattered."

Her words were like a slap in the face because they were true.

"I didn't betray my father, or you for that matter… " Her voice broke into a sob.

She stormed from Riordan's office in a flood of tears, slamming the door behind her.

Riordan stared after her, his lips pressed together, his face ashen. He had wanted to believe her, but he could not bring himself to trust her. He could not tolerate the thought of believing one thing, only to find something else was true. Not again. He'd seen her dance, seen her tantalize the men into a passionate frenzy. By God, he'd been one of them. He imagined her tripping around the family estate, dressed in flounces of softness, toying with men like Stanton Jackson. No doubt the gipsy men had been watching her, wanting her…

Hell, he didn't know what to think. He'd not seen the innocent, but he'd certainly seen the temptress.

Outside Riordan's office, Tara dabbed her tears and looked up to find Kelvin Kendrick glaring at her, his expression compassionless, his nose tilted upwards.

"What are you looking at?" she hissed.

"Leave the premises at once," Kelvin said coldly. "Your kind belongs in the street." Tara's anger reached unimaginable heights. She stormed towards him. "You effeminate little twirp… You bigoted, unimaginative, toad…."

Kelvin gasped and recoiled. "Showing your true colours, Miss Killain. Leave at once, or I will call a constable."

Looking for something to throw at him, Tara spotted her portrait on his desk. Kelvin had been parcelling it up to send to her aunt. She recognized the name, and the address was Australia. She snatched it.

Kelvin's mouth dropped open. "You can't take that……"

"Why not? It's certainly more mine than yours."

Kelvin glared at her ominously, but Tara stood her ground, her green eyes flashing with temper. She was so angry, she could have faced the devil and not backed down.

They continued to glower at each other for several moments, the painting held securely in Tara's arms, as she dared him to try and take it from her.

Kelvin glanced at Riordan's door, which remained closed. He was thinking Riordan would not know she took it, so what did it matter? He still had the other painting to send. As far as he was concerned, the 'gipsy lady' painting was trash. It belonged with its subject, Tara, the gipsy woman.

Tara paused only a moment longer before she headed for the gallery door, her head held high. She'd deliver the painting herself, and be damned with Riordan Magee.

CHAPTER FIVE

The night sky was glittering with a million stars and the breeze was a balmy north-westerly, - characteristic for late January in the Southern Hemisphere. The 'Emerald Star' was making good time, on the last leg of what had been a blessed, uneventful passage.

After almost two months at sea, the ship made a brief stopover in Fremantle, the southwest tip of the great continent, Australia, where eighty-one passengers disembarked. Forty had been given allotments of land by the government, to try and make a go of farming, and becoming self-sufficient. They had been promised a sustenance rate of sixteen shillings a week for the first six months. After that, they were on their own. The other forty-one were harbouring dreams of finding gold in the western town of Kalgoorlie. Food stocks and water were replenished, before the ship sailed on through the Great Southern Ocean, towards Investigator Strait, and her next port of call, Port Adelaide.

The passengers bound for South Australia were told that if all went well, and the winds were kind, they would be disembarking early the next morning. After the heat of crossing from the Cape of Good Hope, they were eager to put the restrictive confines of the ship behind them.

"I can't believe Eleanor Craddock would give me something so beautiful, Maureen," Tara said, holding the shiny turquoise pendant aloft, in their cramped cabin. "It's my birthstone, you know. That's why she insisted I take it."

Tara had accumulated a box of trinkets, almost enough to open her own shop. She had tried refusing such gifts, but her 'clients' had found inventive ways of making sure she received them. They were placed outside her door, in her laundry, under her serviette at dinner, even in her soup.

"That looks to be worth a small fortune. Whatever you told her must have impressed her."

Tara thought back to her meeting with Eleanor, just after lunch, in her spacious, first-class cabin, six times the size of the shoebox she shared with Maureen and her sensitive, but discerning three-year-old daughter, Hannah. "Her husband has bought into a winery in the Barossa Valley in South Australia, by her account, a fertile area first opened up by the Germans. His business partners are German, and Eleanor has concerns about why they let Roddy invest. Although he's always had an interest in fine wine, he knows absolutely nothing about making it. She also wanted to know whether her son would later join the business. With work so scarce, naturally, she is worried. They don't want to lose the little money they have saved. I laid out the cards, and everything looked good. Her husband's gift is figures, and marketing, something his partners recognise. I told her he should leave the wine-making to them, and take care of that side of the business. It will take time, but I believe the business is an enterprise that will do well in the long-term future, and the partnership will blossom. Eleanor was delighted, but I could tell she had something else on her mind. I have observed her family, so I was sure I knew what it was. I asked her if she was afraid her husband was being unfaithful. She was astounded and thought I had read it in the cards. She confessed she thought he was having a shipboard romance with that American heiress, Lavinia Bliss. She's younger than Eleanor, but in my opinion, unattractive. I'd feel more generous towards her if she didn't always have her nose in the air."

Maureen looked baffled, unable to place her.

"Surely you've noticed her in the dining room? She wears that absurd fox fur every evening, even in this heat."

Maureen nodded and grimaced.

"She's so ridiculous!" Tara added, shuddering.

"And is Eleanor's husband fooling around with Miss Lavinia?"

"Absolutely not. Poor Eleanor was overjoyed when I told her. She really loves Roddy."

"How can you be sure he's not being unfaithful? Was it in the cards?"

"Of course not, Maureen." Tara was determined to deny the truth, something she refused to believe herself. Her feelings about people were just that. Feelings. She put them down strictly to intuition. "The gipsies taught me to be observant. That's their secret, you know. It has nothing to do with potions and curses, and seeing into the future. They watch and observe everything. Hand movements, eye movements. The language of the body. It gives everything away. Roddy is slightly taken with Lavinia, because she's flamboyant, and men notice her. Of course, I didn't tell Eleanor that, but she does not need to worry. Lavinia has her eye on bigger fish. She's been after Theodore Radborn ever since we left Ireland. Rumour has it he made millions in the South African gold mines, so Lavinia can overlook his disagreeable nature and eccentricities."

Maureen was intrigued.

"Haven't you heard? I thought everyone on the ship was talking about him."

Maureen shook her head.

"I've heard he has strange fetishes."

"What on earth do you mean?" Maureen asked, frowning.

"He won't wear the same singlet, or underpants, more than once."

Maureen stared blankly for a moment. "There's nothing wrong with that. I'm always after Michael to change his underwear. Sometimes he'll wear the same pants for three days."

"That's not what I meant," Tara said, thinking that was more information than she needed to know about Michael's habits. "Even after they're washed, he won't wear them again. He throws them away."

"What a terrible waste that is," Maureen blurted out.

"It's said he's used a whole trunk load of underwear on this trip and he wears gloves wherever he goes. The crew says he's afraid of catching something. The gossip, although quite likely untrue, claims he comes from a very poor family and the children had to wear their underwear until it fell off them. If it's true, the poor man is to be pitied. Lavinia must have heard the rumours, but she's blinded by his wealth. The rumour circulating about her is that although she inherited a lot of money, she's almost broke. She's a spendthrift, and although generous with gifts for his lady companions, Theodore is very careful with his money. Lavinia follows him everywhere. This last week, he's taken to his cabin and won't come out. He's not sick, so he must be avoiding her. I told Eleanor about Theodore, and she was so happy, she would have given me the world. That's why I feel guilty taking this lovely pendant from her. I should return it."

"No, you shouldn't. I keep telling you to accept money."

"Maureen, no one has money to spare in the Depression, especially those with families."

"The first class passengers can afford it. You could have made a fortune on this voyage."

"I'll not take money under false pretences."

"We both know you have a gift, Tara, no matter what you call it, or how much you deny it. Look at what happened to Sarah Finlay. You told her to be careful on the stairs, and she slipped and almost broke her ankle. I suppose that was pure coincidence."

"No, Maureen. A drunk on a ship in the eye of a hurricane, couldn't be as clumsy as Sarah Finlay. I only hope the ship's physician can find out what's wrong with her before she does real harm to herself. I wouldn't be surprised if there's something amiss with her balance." Tara looked thoughtful, until she felt Maureen studying her, a meaningful glint in her eye.

Aware of what she was thinking, Tara said, "I'm just guessing."

"Well, she was so impressed by your obvious gift that she's telling anyone who will listen to come and see you. I've heard one young woman wants you to cast a spell on a particular crewman by the name of James O'Brien. I didn't have the heart to tell her he fancies you something terrible."

"He does not," Tara replied emphatically. "And I don't cast spells, Maureen. You'll soon have them convinced I'm a witch. If they begin building a fire on the game deck and calling me Joan of Arc, I hope you have the conscience to come to my rescue." Despite her denials, Tara was blushing.

Maureen's blue eyes sparkled with delight. "What were you saying about the language of the body? I'll take the heightened colour in your cheeks as a sign of guilt."

Tara thought of the smouldering looks that had passed between herself and James, and her blush deepened. "It's not guilt. This whole thing is getting out of hand. Spells indeed!"

Maureen's eyes sparkled with amusement. "We both know James follows you everywhere, Tara. He's definitely under your spell. The man's as lovesick as I've ever seen a fellow. He's always in trouble for being where he shouldn't be, just to be near you. I suggest you make the most of it before we dock in Adelaide."

"Oh, Maureen, you are a hopeless romantic. I'm not interested in a dalliance with a crew member, or anyone else for that matter." She dropped her head.

Maureen knew she still thought of herself as married. Even though her husband had freed her to move on with her life, she was finding it difficult to think of herself as a single woman. That Garvie had been hanged was something she couldn't bear to think about.

Maureen had tried to convince Tara to move forward, and put the past, particularly her bad marriage, behind her. "There's nothing wrong with a little shipboard romance, Tara," she said and smiled wickedly.

Tara couldn't help grinning back at her. "You are shameful," she claimed.

"It's better to be shameful and have a little fun in your life than be bored to death and die virtuous."

"How could I be bored? All day and night I have a stream of people coming to see me, all because you told them I could predict their futures. I feel like such a fraud. No one on board knows what to expect when we land. Absolutely anything could happen."

Her so-called talent, which she thought of as a curse, was unpredictable and unreliable. Every time she wondered where it came from, she thought of the exiled gipsy, Eloisa. She couldn't believe she had gipsy blood. Her mother detested gipsies to the point where no one in the house was allowed to even mention them.

Maureen became serious. "I know, Tara. They probably know it, too. But we've had so much fun, haven't we?"

Tara looked at Maureen's plump, sweet face, and felt inwardly warm. She had become such a dear friend; she thought the world of her. Her husband Michael, was a lovely man, too. He was not classically handsome, tall and dark, but rather short with red hair and a homely face. But he had an inner goodness that drew people to him, - and a love for his wife that had no parallel. Tara had never seen two people who cared more for each other than Maureen and Michael. It was the kind of love that made her envious, a bond so deep and abiding, that nothing could sever it. And their two children, Jack and Hannah, were adorable. Jack was full of fun, a real mischievous scallywag. One of his lopsided smiles, and he had his mother wrapped around his finger. And Hannah, their daughter, was the perfect little girl, sweet, with blond curls and the face of a cherub. Tara knew if not for the O'Sullivan family, the voyage would have been so lonely. Maureen had been the perfect cabin mate, fun and considerate. She couldn't deny she'd had the most fun she'd ever had in her life. The two months at sea had gone by so quickly, and she'd met so many people.

Many of the passengers were from Ireland, but the ship had stopped in Southampton and picked up many more. They were a curious mix, from the lower classes, in steerage, to the wealthy first-class passengers. Amazingly, people from all walks of life had sought Tara out and admired her so-called talent. When she thought of the years in Ireland she'd been shunned for being a gipsy, it was incredible. It had given her faith in the future, something she'd not had when she left Ireland.

At 9 p.m., the ship began to pitch in a fierce wind, and rain lashed the decks. The captain spoke to the passengers over the public address system and told them they had encountered an unseasonal squall, the tail end of a cyclone punishing the western coast.

The wind churned the sea into massive craters and tossed the 'Emerald Star' from one crest of a giant wave to another as if it was made of paper. The storm was so sudden and violent, that three automobiles in the hold broke their chains and crashed through a bulkhead, into the crew's quarters. Leaks sprung in the starboard ash ejector discharge, and the ship began to list. The crew manned the pumps and assured passengers that all would be well, but more bulkheads began leaking and water quickly seeped through the starboard side of the ship.

Thankfully, the storm passed in a few hours, but the damage had been done. Captain Mallory made a judgement call, which, in light of the events that followed, was to prove a mistake. He set the ship at top speed, fifteen knots, and made a bid to reach port. Feeling confident they'd berth safely, he did not send an S.O.S. He retired after midnight, asking to be awoken only in the event of any further catastrophe.

At 3.25 a.m. the crew in the engine room detected a strange odour.

"It's coming through the draft ventilation," the third assistant engineer informed the chief engineer.

There was no doubt about its cause. Smoke!

"Dispatch a fireman to investigate," the chief engineer boomed. "I'll notify the bridge." He was besieged with fears of disaster but pushed them to the back of his mind, and prayed.

Tara awoke from a deep sleep, in a lather of sweat. She had been dreaming about a fire in a storage room. It was so real and terrifying, that she sat bolt upright in her bunk, trying to dispel the nightmare. She would have gone back to sleep, but she was sure she could smell smoke. For a moment she thought she might still be dreaming, but the odour of smoke became stronger.

Opening the cabin door, Tara went out into the corridor. Everything was quiet. The passengers were asleep, but she could still smell smoke. Leaving the door ajar, she followed the odour, her heart pounding. As she passed each door, she felt it. While doing so, she began to recall details of the dream. The fire had been in a room with numerals 1 0 6. But the numerals kept changing order. Room 610 was on the same level as her cabin. The dream was so realistic; she searched and found cabin 610, remembering it was a storage room, as in her dream. She placed her hand on the door, then jumped in surprise. It was scorching hot. She stared at the door, not knowing what to do, then touched it again, just to be sure.

Rushing back to her cabin, Tara woke Maureen and told her to wake Michael, who shared a cabin directly opposite theirs with Jack, and take the children up on deck. As Maureen jumped from her bunk, Tara said, "Take care of each other, Maureen, I have the feeling something terrible is going to happen to you, or Michael and the children. Don't let them out of your sight."

Maureen stared at her blankly for a moment, taking Tara's words deadly serious, her face as white as freshly fallen snow. Without saying a word, she went to awaken her husband.

Hurriedly throwing on a robe, Tara raced upstairs, looking for a crewmember. By coincidence, she found James O'Brien in the stateroom on A deck. She noticed he coloured when he saw her dressed in her night attire, but Tara was too panicked to care. She breathlessly told him about the fire in room 610. He instructed her to stay up on deck.

"I'll go down and check, and then sound the alarm."

"Please be careful," she called after him.

As James O'Brien descended the stairs, he came upon two firemen sent down by the chief engineer to search for the source of smoke coming through the draft ventilator system. They had been unsuccessful.

"A passenger claims there's a fire in cabin 610," James informed them. They had no idea the light had been left burning in the storage room by a crewmember searching for something that morning. The bulb was naked and close to a mattress piled on top of other items, broken chairs and panelling. The mattress began smouldering, eventually catching alight. As soon as James forced open the door, scorching flames leapt out at him. The other two crewmen jumped backwards. James was burned on the hand he used to shield his face.

"My God," he shouted. "We must sound the alarm."

It seemed like forever, but a few minutes later, Maureen, Michael and the children joined Tara, and the alarm was sounded, and the ship's engines shut down. All pandemonium broke loose. Sleepy, dazed passengers began pouring up on deck; most convinced the alarm was just a drill. It wasn't until smoke began rising, and the screams of terror-stricken passengers on the lower decks grew louder, that they realised their lives were in peril.

On C and D decks, it was sheer mayhem. James and the two firemen began pounding on cabin doors to alert passengers. The chief engineer was notified and he hurried to awaken Captain Mallory. Shamelessly, the captain's first thoughts were of his unblemished safety record at sea, one he had hoped to retire with later that month. Two more firemen were dispatched to D deck with buckets of sand and hoses, to do what they could, while passengers were evacuated. It was soon discovered the fire had taken a stronghold, rendering fire-fighting implements ineffective.

On the promenade deck, the crew was filling lifeboats and panic-stricken passengers began pushing and shoving to get themselves and their loved ones aboard. Manners were obliterated, along with practised drills, as first-class passengers claimed to have priority over seats. Tara noticed the fear of going down with the ship brought out the worst in some people.

Suddenly the ship listed thirty-five degrees. The rain had ceased, but the decks were slippery. Screams of panic surged through the passengers, who were running in all directions to find loved ones and friends, slipping and sliding across the decks. In the pandemonium, several people fell overboard.

Tara and the O'Sullivan family were on the port side of the ship. The queues for rafts became chaotic, and Tara found herself on a different line.

"What's happening?" she shouted above the sounds of crashes and booms from deep within the ship.

"The ship has been leaking since the storm," Michael shouted back to her. "The crew said it wasn't serious, but the fire would be burning through the bulkheads below, making the problem worse. Those loud crashes must be cargo shifting in the hold."

Jack said, "Perhaps the seawater will put out the fire, papa."

Michael didn't know which was worse. Drowning or burning to death. Neither was an option he could face for his family. "You and your sister will be safe in a life raft," he said, half smiling to hide the fear taking hold of him.

"We're not going without you and momma," Jack cried.

"Listen, son. We'll all stay together if we can, but we may get separated and find ourselves in different rafts. I want you to watch out for your sister. I'll take care of your mother. Please do as I say. I need you to be strong. If anything happens, I want you to promise to always take care of Hannah." Michael knew it was a big task for a boy of ten years, but he had to do it. Jack glanced at Hannah, her golden curls blowing in the wind, and her sweet face tear-stained, and his own expression became so serious it almost broke his father's heart. He put his arm around his sister and nodded solemnly.

Life jackets, along with rapidly issued instructions, were thrust at the people standing in queues by passing crewmembers. The jackets forced home the reality of finding themselves in the ocean, and panic such as she had never experienced, welled up in Tara, threatening to choke her. Like most aboard ship, she couldn't swim and had an unparalleled fear of deep water. She stole the nerve to glance over the side of the ship. It was so far to the water, which was so black and vast, absolutely terrifying. She thought of sharks... and almost fainted with fright. She desperately fought the desire to lose control and scream with futility at the ill fate that had brought her life to this point but felt herself succumbing.

Tara spun round, teetering on the verge of delirium, and came face to face with an elderly woman, who was watching her with calm, sympathetic blue eyes, filled with moisture. Her serenity, in the face of impending disaster, stopped Tara in her tracks like a thunderbolt. She was dressed in a filmy nightgown, wisps of white hair lifting in the wind like feathers, and clutching what appeared to be a photograph as if it was the most precious thing on earth. Although it was a peculiar thing to do at that moment, given the circumstances, Tara noted the most bizarre things about the woman. The paper-thin skin on her hands, wrinkled with time and worn by a million loving tasks, her beautiful rings, her aura of nobleness. She guessed she was from first class, as she had not seen her among the steerage passengers. The most curious thing of all was her composure amidst the pandemonium around them. It gave the impression she was peacefully resigned to the death she was almost certain she faced. She was an island of poise, in a sea of madness.

As Tara looked into her eyes, brimming with wisdom and colourful history, she could almost read the woman's mind. She had lived a long and full life. Her sympathy and fear were reserved for the likes of Tara and the O'Sullivan family, particularly the children, whose lives should have been an adventure before them. She understood that for some aboard this ill-fated ship, the chance to travel life's voyage might be snatched away. Observing this frail woman facing death with such dignity had a miraculous effect on Tara. Her fears subsided, and a veil of tranquillity settled over her. She wasn't ready to die, or let Jack and Hannah perish. She felt a surge of determination to fight for herself and those around her.

She passed her life jacket to the elderly woman. "Put this on," she said and smiled with a sense of confidence. "We're going to make it," she whispered. "You'll see." Her eyes filled with unshed tears, as the elderly lady nodded with sedate acceptance of her fate, whatever it should be.

The O'Sullivan family was in a raft ready to be lowered, when the crew found the ropes had been recently painted, and wouldn't work with the davits. They were being unloaded, when the crew loading Tara's raft said they had room for the two children and one adult but they must hurry. For Michael and Maureen, the decision was mutual and final. Neither would leave the other, but both insisted the children be given the chance of being saved, as there was a possibility there might not be another raft offered. Tara was not in the least surprised, but all her fears resurfaced. She had a strong feeling she would never see them again. She knew Michael and Maureen loved each other unconditionally, and neither would hesitate to give their lives to save their children, but that's exactly what she feared would happen. Understandably, Jack and Hannah were upset about leaving their parents, as they were hastily put aboard, but Tara reassured them she'd look after them.

"Please come with us, Maureen?" Tara begged as the crew began to lower raft number 13. The children echoed her plea.

Maureen shook her head and glanced at her husband with loving tenderness. He urged her to go, but she refused.

"Take my place, Michael," Tara shouted, standing. "I'll wait for another raft."

"No, Tara." Michael adamantly refused. "Don't worry. We'll see you soon," he shouted. The crew ordered Tara to sit down.

"Look after each other," Maureen resounded, leaning over the railing and blowing kisses to her children, as the raft took them further and further away. "I love you."

"We'll wait for you on shore," Tara shouted back confidently, as frustration and cold dread gripped her heart.

"You'll be safe with Tara," Michael assured his children, who were looking up with terrified expressions on their innocent faces, their worst nightmare realised, being separated from their parents.

Michael's frantic eyes sought Tara's. As the distance between them grew, unspoken words passed between them. She knew, by his earnest expression, that he was relying upon her to get the children to safety. If he didn't make it with Maureen, the children were her responsibility. A lump formed in Tara's throat, choking back a reply. It was a moment that could completely reshape the course of her life, as she knew it would, but there was no time for contemplation.

The helpless passengers were unaware the fire was raging through the ship so fast that the radio operator was unable to transmit a distress message. In desperation, the captain issued instructions for an S.O.S. by use of the Morse Lamp, but within minutes the crew were forced to flee the wheelhouse because of the intense heat. Distress flares were dispatched, some unsuccessful. The captain had also ordered three ballast tanks to be pumped dry, which proved to be another mistake, as the ship became more unstable.

On shore, at Outer Harbour, the orange glow of the burning ship had been seen, and boats were dispatched to come to the rescue of the 'Emerald Star's' passengers and crew. Not far away, a merchant ship, the 'Octavia', had also seen the glow in the sky, and the captain had set his vessel at top speed to reach the stricken ship.

It seemed to take a lifetime to reach the sea below. Tara was grateful to be in a raft that would be taking the children to safety, especially when she witnessed some passengers, too terrified to wait for a seat aboard a raft, jump clear of the burning ship. There was angry shouting, as people queuing feared there weren't enough rafts for everyone, creating frighteningly ugly scenes.

Hannah was sobbing and clung to Tara. The child could not cope with the pandemonium aboard the ship, especially without her mother. Jack was trying to be brave, but Tara could see, like her, he was worried sick about his parents, who were no longer in sight.

As their life raft descended past the lower decks, protruding heads and legs were visible from portholes spewing black smoke. It was a shocking sight, and Tara tried to shield Jack and Hannah. As passengers continued to jump ship, she heard the crew yelling that the water could be shark-infested. This only added to the delirium, as they were sure they were going to be burnt to death.

Just before their raft hit the water, it crashed into the side of the ship, as it listed further. The women and children screamed, fearing they'd be tipped into the churning sea. When they finally touched the ocean and the ropes were cut, water began seeping into the raft where it had sustained damage in the collision. One of the few men aboard removed his nightshirt and singlet and placed them over the damaged area. He then sat on them to stem the seepage.

As the raft moved away from the ship, those aboard realised there was no crewmember with them to take charge. One bear-like Irishman, and his robust wife, decided to man the oars but found one missing, and the raft began drifting. Survivors in the water tried to pull themselves aboard, almost capsizing them. Those aboard were divided about whether to help those in the water, life and death decisions, and arguments broke out.

Tara witnessed the starboard cargo port of the ship opening, and the crew offloading whatever they could, no doubt to slow down the sinking of the ship. It seemed futile, as the fire would inevitably destroy her before she sank. She silently prayed the passengers would be offloaded before that happened. She could only wonder what their fate would have been, had she not dreamt of the fire in room 610. She believed it had been divine intervention and not some kind of mystical power.

As the life raft drifted further away from the 'Emerald Star', time seemed suspended.

They were almost a hundred yards from the ship, when an explosion aboard was followed by fiery flames leaping into the night sky, casting an enormous circle of orange glow on the water. Burning debris rained over the area like a firework display, and then the 'Emerald Star' slowly tuned on her starboard side, creaking and groaning, and spurting air, as she sank.

People in the water, and nearby rafts, gasped in shocked horror, as the ship disappeared to a watery grave, and the area fell into darkness. The sinking ship was a strange sight, but not as surreal as the stunned silence that followed. Tara had wished the screams of panic would stop, but never imagined that silence could be so awful.

All that was left of a ship that had served for seven years, was floating debris and littered bodies. Hannah was unaware of what the sinking ship meant, but Jack was staring at the empty horizon with silent tears rolling down his grimy cheeks.

"I'm sure they're in a raft," Tara whispered, laying her arm across his slumped shoulders. She couldn't, and wouldn't believe she might never see Maureen again, the first real friend she had ever had. Among her numerous good virtues was the ability to listen, without being judgmental, a trait Tara had more reason to appreciate than most, especially when she confessed to having lived the life of a gipsy. She wanted desperately to believe she was alive, and Michael, but she had a feeling of dread deep in her heart.

Her pain was pushed away by a more pressing problem. Their life raft had begun taking on water at an alarming rate, too fast to bale out with shoes or hats, or anything else the passengers were using in desperation. They could see the lights of rescue boats making for them, but they weren't close enough to help.

"We had to get in no. 13," one of the elderly male passengers lamented to his wife. "At least we're in a boat," she commented wearily.

"For how long?" he snapped "In case you hadn't noticed, we're sinking!"

Even though Tara could see the elderly man was afraid, his attitude angered her. She wanted to say, think of those who didn't make it, but she couldn't with Jack and Hannah listening. Jack was worried enough, and Hannah was missing her mother terribly.

The rescue boats could be heard coming closer in the eerie, dark silence that had befallen the wreckage sight. As those who reached the sight first began scanning the water for survivors with lights, the passengers who were able shouted for help. Life rafts number seventeen and twenty-five were nearby but were dangerously overloaded, so kept their distance from those in the water. Before a rescue vessel could reach them, the sea swamped life raft number thirteen.

It was a terrifying moment for Tara, as the raft disappeared beneath them. Holding Hannah with one hand, she lunged for a piece of floating wreckage, taking in a mouthful of salty water. Catching hold of the buoyant timber, Tara insisted the children, who were wearing life jackets, also hang on, so they wouldn't be separated. Tara's insides were quaking with terror she had never before experienced. Outwardly, she constantly reassured the children. Jack tried to be brave, but Hannah was whimpering with fright, her small hand clutching Tara like a lifeline. Her weight was a burden, but Tara didn't object as long as she was close. Seconds seemed like hours, as they awaited a rescue boat. Jack could see Tara was tired and kept calling for a boat. Her arms felt like lead weights, pulling her down. If not for the children, she certainly would have succumbed to the sea. Just when she thought she couldn't last a moment longer, a rescue boat pulled alongside and hooked them to safety.

Their saviours were the crew of the schooner, 'Bella Mia', moored at Port Adelaide. They spoke kindly, in strange accents, and seemed to have an easy 'she'll be right' manner. Tara was relieved to see the elderly woman from the ship was also aboard. They'd been separated in the fiasco of passengers changing life rafts. Both were too drained emotionally and physically to do anything more than acknowledge each other with eye contact.

As they made for shore, Tara stared out to sea. Rescue boats continued to search for survivors amid floating wreckage. It was a desolate sight. She couldn't help thinking Michael and Maureen were amongst the floating bodies being plucked from the water. It was a devastating thought yet she was too numb to cry or dwell upon their fate. The children also seemed to be in a state of shock, which was a strange blessing, as Tara couldn't cope with their grief, as well as her own. She didn't know when that would change. She didn't want to think about the future.

Before daybreak, virtually all of the survivors had been picked up and taken to a passenger terminal at Outer Harbour. Tara searched each boat that came in for Maureen and Michael. When the last one arrived, and they weren't aboard, she screamed that there must be more. James O'Brien was the only person able to calm her. He held her while she cried for her friends. She hadn't wanted to believe they were gone. She kept asking him why they weren't in a life raft or a rescue boat. James, like everyone else, had no answers.

The 'terminal' was a big, draughty shed, with nothing around it. Those that needed immediate medical attention were seen by doctors, before being loaded aboard a train and taken into the town of Port Adelaide, just a few miles away. Those that didn't need medical attention were taken to hotels; The Exchange, The Royal Arms and The Britannia, to rest.

It was just breaking daylight by the time they fell into creaking, iron beds, too weary and shocked to care about their surroundings. The drapes were kept drawn against the outside world. Hannah slept fitfully, while a ceiling fan whirred overhead, and suffered nightmares. Jack lay still, imagining his parents were trapped below water, in the ship. In his mind, he kept seeing them trying to get out, but they were too far down. Tara couldn't sleep either. She watched the children, unable to comfort them. Sometime in the afternoon, they were served a meal of cold meat and salad in their rooms. They picked at the tough, thickly sliced lamb and limp lettuce in silence, then lay down again and closed their eyes, trying vainly to blot out the horror of the shipwreck.

Early next morning the traumatized survivors of the shipwreck were congregated in Customs House, on the corner of Commercial Road and North Parade, Port Adelaide. The pavement outside the building was crowded with curious onlookers who had heard about the fate of the 'Emerald Star.' The story had made the late addition of the local newspaper, and journalists gathered in the hope of an eyewitness account of the tragedy.

The newcomers shunned the attention, too traumatized to cope, and embarrassed by their state of undress. Compared to the tanned onlookers, who all wore wide-brimmed hats to shade their eyes from the fierce sun, they looked like ghosts. A few had attained some colour on the last leg of the journey, but nothing compared to the onlookers, who were almost as brown as the natives, known as aborigines. A small group of aborigines had also congregated, watching the newcomers with dark, fathomless eyes. Having never seen an aboriginal, the passengers stared at them curiously, intrigued by their crimpy hair and broad noses, the children rudely pointing fingers.

While officials talked of reasons for the disaster, Tara sat at the back of the room with Sorrel Windspear, the elderly woman from the ship. Tara had checked the list of survivors taken to the hospital; just to be sure neither Maureen nor Michael were among them. Jack appeared to have accepted the death of his parents quietly. Tara was unaware he was feeling a small measure of relief that they could not possibly be alive, trapped at the bottom of the ocean. Tara wished he would show a little emotion, just so she knew he would be all right. His silent restraint was unnerving, like waiting for an inevitable eruption. Hannah, of course, didn't understand. She constantly whimpered for her momma.

As time passed, weariness and the heat finally caught up with both children. Hannah lay across Tara's lap, asleep, and Jack lay on the bench beside her. Tara stroked Hannah's soft, golden curls, and placed her other hand on Jack's back. His hair was red, like his father's. His skin had a spattering of brown freckles, which had appeared in the last few weeks of their journey, as the sun grew fiercer. All night she had wanted to comfort them, but felt inadequate, a poor substitute for the loving mother and father they had lost.

The officials talked at length about the disaster and listed the causes, which brought it about. They heard mention of the ship being overloaded by two hundred tonnes and claimed the S.O.S. signal was never sent. It was also said, opening the cargo hold had allowed water to flood into the ship, sinking her faster. Tara couldn't understand why they didn't realise the crew had been offloading cargo in an attempt to do just the opposite. Although they did not know the cause of the fire, the crew had alleged there hadn't been enough buckets and bags of sand, and not enough pressure in the hoses to deal with it. It was said many more would have perished if not for early detection by one of the passengers.

Tara and Sorrel, along with the other passengers, listened to all the excuses until finally they'd heard enough. Tara believed laying the blame at Captain Mallory's feet, who himself had perished, was not going to bring more than fifty passengers and crew back to life. It was certain his errors in judgment attributed to the sinking of the ship, but that wasn't going to bring back the parents of the two children, who were now her responsibility.

"In the end," a spokesman said, "A full inquiry will be conducted, but it seems the root of the cause of the disaster lies in human error. Too much faith had been put in modern shipbuilding, and not enough emphasis on seamanship."

Once again the danger of the sea had been underestimated.

While the officials droned on about what they were going to do to help the surviving passengers, all of it amounting to little, Sorrel and Tara began a conversation. Sorrel was in her twilight years, but sharp as a razor, Tara noted. She had a perky twinkle in her eye that gave the impression she didn't tolerate half-witted chumps gladly. She'd steered her course in life, and no matter what, she'd continue to do so. Tara noted her reaction when crewmembers fussed over her because of her age. She sent them scuttling for cover, telling them she wasn't useless or infirm, and they should be helping people who really needed them. It was obvious she believed in speaking her mind. No dancing around delicate feelings, and no dressing up the facts. Her next words confirmed this. "Aren't you the fortune teller everyone was talking about on board the ship?"

Tara smiled wanly. "I don't tell fortunes. I just express my feelings candidly, much like you do."

Sorrel could see Tara felt wary as if she was not comfortable with her ability. "If you can really see the future, you are gifted. I believe in Ireland you would be known as a Seer. Only the chosen are endowed with such a great power."

Tara shuffled in her seat. "I can assure you I don't have that gift. I was just having a little fun to pass the time. No one took it seriously."

"Everyone in first class was talking about you. It's a pity you can't see into the future. The fire was no doubt caused by someone's stupidity. Even so, only Mother Nature could be blamed for the storm, which did enough damage to eventually sink the ship."

Realizing the full impact of what happened aboard the ship, Tara suddenly went pale. "What's wrong, dear? Did you know the ship was going to sink?"

"No, but incredibly I dreamt of the fire. I even saw the numerals that made up the number of the cabin where the fire started, but not in their correct order. Room 610 just happened to be on D deck, near my cabin. I've had dreams before, but never in such detail. It was so real, it woke me up, which is when I smelt smoke. I'm sure the whole thing was a coincidence…." She shook her head as if trying to clear her thoughts. "But if I hadn't awoken, many more on D deck would have perished, me included."

"Then you should be commended."

"Not many people feel that way. Before today, everyone wanted to be my friend. Now that's changed. So many of those same passengers have looked at me like I'm a complete imposter. As if they blame me for not knowing what was going to happen."

"Don't take it personally, dear. They just want someone to condemn for the loss of their loved ones."

Tara appreciated Sorrel's words, but they didn't make her feel any better. "Did you lose someone on the ship?" she asked

"No, dear. I was travelling alone. My husband died four months ago at our home in

Kensington, after a long illness."

"Oh. I'm sorry. I couldn't imagine watching someone I love slowly slip away from me." Tara had not known the death of a family member. Even though she was estranged from her family, and she might never see Garvie again, she couldn't imagine such suffering. Losing Maureen and Michael was terrible enough, especially as she felt she couldn't grieve in front of the children.

"It's not as much of a shock as most of these poor wretches have suffered," Sorrel said. "An illness, particularly a long one, gives you time to adjust to the idea of losing that person. It is, nevertheless, very hard. Robert had a muscle-wasting disease. Watching him whither away was agony. Long before he died, I prayed the Lord would take him, just to end his suffering. He used to be a guardsman at Buckingham Palace. A big, strapping, handsome man. He died a shadow of his former self. I loved him just the same, but it was so cruel."

"Did he die in the hospital?"

"Heaven's, no. I looked after him, with no help, right to the end. He couldn't face the indignity of having a stranger, a nurse…" Her voice drifted off.

"Do you have any family?"

"Just one son, Marcus Robert John Windspear." Tara caught the hint of pride in her voice.

"He's been living in Australia for several years. Ever since the death of his father, he's badgered me to come out and spend the last years of my life with him and his family. They live in a town called Alice, somewhere in the middle of this God-forsaken country. Do you know he trained as a lawyer in England, but he and his wife run a hotel? I find it hard to understand, but they actually enjoy serving a mob of drunken, rowdy patrons, whom they describe as bush characters. They love life in a country town. God only knows what I'll find. I didn't want to leave my home, but I couldn't deny Marcus." Sorrel continually swatted flies, which had been annoying them since daybreak. "Marcus told me the flies in the bush are real pests. If they're worse than this, I don't know how I'm going to cope."

Tara was certain Sorrel could cope with almost anything. She envied her strength. It's what saved her from losing complete control, like so many others aboard ship. She had to thank God she hadn't become hysterical. What would've happened to Jack and Hannah?

"I have to tell you this," Tara said. "It was your composure, in the face of impending danger, that saved my life. I was about to lose control, and may have jumped overboard or done something else equally as foolish, if not for you."

Sorrel looked surprised. "I was absolutely certain I was going to die until you told me we would make it. You seemed so sure, you gave me real hope."

The two women smiled at each other in wonder. Sorrel reached for Tara's hand, which she gave her without thinking. It wasn't until Sorrel squeezed her hand, that Tara remembered how rough her skin was, and the condition of her nails.

Tara watched, as Sorrel's smile waned, and she became fearful about what she was thinking. "What's wrong?"

"Marcus and Irene were going to meet me here," she said. "But I told them not to bother. It's such a long way, and they have little ones, and the hotel to look after. Thank goodness they didn't come. Our landing was far from an auspicious occasion. One could only describe it as an undignified calamity." She reached up and tried to smooth her dishevelled hair, and then shook her head, tears brimming in her eyes. Tara could remember many days when she had been out in the rain, travelling wind-swept roads in the caravan, and looked a fright, but she felt confident Sorrel had never looked so bedraggled in her life. It was really upending her dignity.

Sorrel looked down at the photograph she was still clutching, and so did Tara. Robert and herself looked to be about twenty, and so much in love. He was a very big man, broad, strong, fair and handsome. Probably the way Sorrel wanted to remember him, Tara thought.

"I consider myself one of the lucky ones," Sorrel said. "But I would have gladly given my life to save one of the children aboard ship." A sob rose in her throat, and Tara squeezed her hand, understanding. What they had been through together made them feel as if they had known each other for years. In a few short hours, they had bared emotions normally only ever seen by the dearest of loved ones. They both sensed it was the beginning of a most unusual friendship.

Looking up, Sorrel forced a brighter expression.

"Perhaps you should get word to your son," Tara said. "He might hear about the fate of the Emerald Star in the papers, and think the worst."

"The shipping company have offered to contact him." She raised her brows. "You'd think they were giving me the world. Do you have someone to notify?"

"No. I have an aunt here, or at least I think I do. We haven't seen each other for years. I was going to surprise her." Tara suddenly thought of her suitcase, which contained the painting she had retrieved from the Harcourt Gallery. She doubted it would be recovered. "If I hadn't made it, she would never have known."

"But you did make it, and won't she be thrilled to see you?" Sorrel glanced down at the sleeping children. "What about them?" she asked softly.

Tara frowned. "I don't know." She lowered her voice to a whisper. "I feel responsible for them, but I have no idea what to do. They have no one here. I promised their father I would look after them, but I'm not sure… I'm…" The word 'scared' was on the tip of her tongue, but she didn't feel brave enough to admit it, even to herself.

"It's an overwhelming responsibility," Sorrel said, giving voice to Tara's fears.

"I don't even know if I can legally take them," Tara admitted.

As they spoke, the two women witnessed a scene taking place off to the side of them, at the back of the room. A young, well-dressed woman was clutching a child, while another older woman, dressed in a Red Cross uniform, was trying to take the infant from her. The woman holding the child appeared to be unwilling to hand him over.

"Perhaps they have family back in Ireland?" Sorrel said, referring to Jack and Hannah while keeping her gaze on the two women.

Tara nodded, remembering the hours of conversation she'd shared with Maureen. "They have an aunt. Moryra… no Moyna Conway. She lives somewhere in Derry. Their mother talked about her quite often, but not with any warmth. Apparently, the two sisters didn't get along. Maureen told me Moyna had five daughters, including twins, and two sons. She said her sister virtually treated the girls as slaves. While she lay around all day, they were forced to do all the work on the farm. Her husband worked away, to make extra money. When he returned home, she made believe she'd done all the work. She even kept the girls home from school when her husband was away. As soon as the older girls were old enough, they left home. So the younger girls were worked to the point of exhaustion. Maureen called her a lazy 'tonky pig', amongst other names I couldn't repeat." Tara suddenly looked sad. "Maureen was just the opposite. She'd do anything for her family. I'm certain she wouldn't want the children to go to Moyna, but what other option is there? An orphanage?" Tara shook her head and shuddered. "I couldn't send them to a home for unwanted children. I've come to care for them a great deal."

Sorrel could see Tara was genuinely fond of Jack and Hannah. Her expression became tender every time she looked at them. She wondered why Tara had not had any children of her own. She noticed a pale circle on her finger, where she had once worn a wedding ring. There could have been any number of explanations for why it was no longer there, given the circumstances, but she had not mentioned a husband. From the looks of her hands, and the feel of her skin, she hadn't lived the life of 'a lady', which made Sorrel wonder about her life. She'd always been curious by nature but tried not to be judgemental.

The women were suddenly distracted by the voices of the two women they had been watching, when they became louder, drawing the attention of many others nearby.

"Miss Honeywell, I'll say this for the last time. You are not related to Thomas. I have to take him." The Red Cross woman seemed to be losing patience, but Miss Honeywell still wouldn't hand over the baby.

"And I told you, I'm his nanny. We've never been apart since the day he was born. He doesn't know anyone but me. Have you no heart at all?" The young woman began to sob. Tara realised Thomas' parents must have been first-class passengers, and Miss Honeywell had been their employee. There had been some wealthy passengers aboard, who employed nannies for their children. She suddenly wondered about Eleanor Craddock and Lavinia Bliss. Where were they? Had they survived?"

"Thomas has been through so much, and now he's an orphan," Miss Honeywell pleaded, capturing Tara's attention. "I'm all he's got." Baby Thomas, a chubby child of approximately eight months, clung to her, screaming his lungs out.

"Unless you are a legal guardian or family member, we cannot leave him in your custody."

"How could strangers take better care of him than me? I'll take him back to England, to his family, I promise. Just don't take him away from me now."

Sorrel and Tara glanced at each other, feeling the deep pain of the wretched Miss Honeywell. She had no doubt saved the child's life, and the authorities were callously taking him from her. It was apparent compassion didn't enter the equation.

Sorrel glanced at Tara, and she knew what she was thinking. There was no hope that the authorities would let her keep the children with her. Tara was suddenly frightened, and glanced at Jack and Hannah, then at the almost hysterical Miss Honeywell, as women in uniforms tore the distressed baby from her arms, promising to contact relatives back in England. The heart-wrenching scene brought tears to Tara and Sorrel's eyes. It made Tara wake up to the reality of the situation. She had to pull herself together and do something before it was too late. But what?

While composing themselves in silence, Tara and Sorrel watched the progress of a representative from the Kennard and Rainer Line, who had owned the 'Emerald Star', circulating with customs officials. She smiled with relief when she saw him speak to

Eleanor and Roddy Craddock. Eleanor had her arm in a sling, but other than that, the couple looked unscathed. Their son was nearby talking to another boy.

"Has anyone asked you about the children?" Sorrel whispered, her voice still choked with emotion.

"No, but I am sure they will. They have a list of names and they're slowly getting around to us all. I have to act quickly... But what should I do?"

"Where does your aunt live exactly?"

"Tambora Station, near Wombat Creek. I believe it's many miles north of Adelaide." Sorrel's eyes widened. "I'm sure the 'Ghan' train that goes to Alice passes through Wombat Creek. I have a map..." Her expression changed when she remembered she had no possessions. She had nothing but the nightgown she had been wearing when the ship went down, and a shabby dressing gown kindly given her by the publican's wife at the Britannia Hotel. Nearly all of the surviving passengers were dressed in their night attire. There hadn't been time to get dressed. The Red Cross was passing out parcels of donated clothing to each survivor, but they hadn't reached them yet.

"I had a map. I studied it many times on the ship." She'd spent many hours in her cabin, which was spacious but lonely, with nothing else to do. "I'm quite sure the train goes that way. My son has organized a ticket for me. I'm to pick it up at the ticketing office in the city of Adelaide. You could purchase one there. If you don't have any money, I have. My husband and I travelled a lot before he became ill, so I grew into the habit of keeping my money on me at all times."

"I also learnt that habit," Tara said, not disclosing that all gipsies kept their money on their person at all times. "But thank you for the kind offer. I'd say we are luckier than most. We may have lost our luggage, but we're not penniless." Tara sighed, and looked down at the sleeping children.

"Tambora sounds like a good place for children to grow up," Sorrel said, watching her.

"I'm going into the unknown, with no idea what I'll find. I'm not sure taking them with me is the right thing to do, but I can't bear the thought of leaving them behind."

At that moment, Jack sat up. "You aren't going to leave us, are you?" he asked, his hazel eyes full of fear. He'd obviously overheard the tail end of their conversation at least. Tara wondered if he'd witnessed the scene between Miss Honeywell and the Red Cross representative.

"I don't think... we'll be allowed to stay together because we're not related."

"What do you mean?"

"I'm not part of your family."

"I promised Papa I would look after Hannah, and I won't break my promise. I know Papa wanted you to look after us. You will, won't you?"

Tara could see it hurt the boy's pride to ask her for help. It made his words all the more heartbreaking.

"Of course I will, Jack. I don't want us to be separated. I'm very fond of you and your sister, but what can I do? They'll only let family take you."

"Family? Like Aunty Moyna?"

Reluctantly, Tara nodded.

"I don't want to live with Aunty Moyna. I'd rather have drowned with momma and papa." Jack's bottom lip began to tremble and he looked down at his entwined fingers. Tara's heart almost broke. Fate had dealt the child a cruel blow. She glanced at Sorrel, her expression silently pleading for help.

"There's nothing you can do," Sorrel whispered. She leant forward and looked at Jack. "Tara isn't your mother or aunty, son. If she were, it would be different. I know she promised your father, but the decision will be taken out of her hands."

"Couldn't we just walk out of here?" Jack asked, childishly simplifying his thoughts. "The police would come after you," Sorrel reasoned.

"I'll run away with Hannah before I let them take us back to Aunty Moyna," Jack stated.

"Perhaps that won't be necessary if we can convince the authorities I'm your mother," Tara said, a glint of determination creeping into her green eyes.

A Red Cross worker was making her way towards them, loaded with parcels and a sheet of paper containing names.

"Do you know how to pretend, Jack?" Tara whispered.

He looked confused.

"Have you ever made believe you're a pirate? Or a prince?"

He nodded.

"Could you make believe I'm your mother when this lady coming towards us asks us questions?"

Jack looked uncertain.

"If you could, we might be able to stay together. Right now I can't think of any other way."

A flicker of sadness clouded Jack's hazel eyes, before he bobbed his head. Tara knew he was thinking of his real mother. She was, too.

He linked his arm through Tara's. "Won't she know?" he whispered. "You don't look like momma."

"If they find out the truth, it will be after we're gone," Tara said, suddenly hopeful the plan might work.

"How are you?" a smiling woman in a red and white uniform asked Sorrel, as she glanced at Tara and the children.

"I'm alive, so that makes me in better shape than most," she replied dryly.

Startled, the woman's benign smile faded for a moment. "That's … very good, dear. Being positive and optimistic lifts one's spirits."

Tara could almost see Sorrel cringe under the condescending, but well-meant remark. "My name is Ruby Ashton." She put the clothing parcels on the floor at their feet. Then she glanced at the children and at her list. When she looked up, it was directly at Jack. "What is your name, young man?"

"Jack O'Sullivan," he replied, going suddenly pale.

"I'd say you'd be about nine or ten years old, Jack. Am I right?"

"Yes, ma'am. I'm ten."

Tara squeezed Jack's hand to let him know he was doing well, while Ruby Ashton consulted her list again. "This little sleepy one must be Hannah, your sister?"

Jack nodded. "She's three."

Tara was grateful Hannah was sleeping. If she were awake she would be calling for her real mother.

Ruby picked up two parcels from the pile in front of them, checking labels to make sure they were suitable for the children's ages. They contained items of clothing supplied by the State Relief Committee, which was helping people during the Depression, and a few emergency supplies – soap, combs, underwear etc.

"There are no toys, I'm afraid," she said and glanced at Tara. "Are you the children's mother?"

Tara glanced at Jack apprehensively and forced a small smile. She sat upright, like Sorrel, and tried to copy her dignified demeanour. "Yes," she replied a bit shakily. "I'm … Maureen O'Sullivan."

"Is your husband, Michael, one of the survivors?"

Tara shook her head, fighting genuine tears for her friends. She noticed Jack looked down again.

"I'm sorry, I have to ask I'm afraid… you will…. " She glanced at Jack. "Has anyone taken you to the… the back of the court house, yet?" Ruby Ashton looked uncomfortable.

Tara knew she was referring to the makeshift morgue, where relatives and friends were identifying bodies. Her heart began to thud wildly, and a fine film of perspiration covered her face.

"No. I'll do that now if you like?" She was dreading the task, but there was no avoiding it if she wanted to keep the children. She looked at Jack again and patted his hand reassuringly. "Stay with your sister, son."

He nodded.

Tara glanced at Sorrel, and the old lady could see she was nervous.

"I'll keep an eye on your children, Mrs. O'Sullivan," Sorrel said confidently. "You do what you have to. We'll be just fine."

"Thank you, Mrs. Windspear."

As Tara walked away with Ruby Ashton, she said, "The woman who shared my cabin is among the dead. Would you like me to identify her? There is no one else."

"That would be kind of you," Ruby replied. "I know it's very difficult, but someone has to do it. Only the wealthy may have dental records, so we'd have to wait for relatives from Ireland or England, or try and identify personal items, like rings. As it was the middle of the night…" She shrugged.

Tara glanced over her shoulder. Jack was watching her, his expression reflecting a mixture of emotions, the same jumble of confused feelings she was experiencing.

As Tara was led past rows of bodies, some barely recognizable as human, she almost fainted. The heat was unbearable, the stench of death beyond belief, indescribable. She was sure she would never forget it and was quite unprepared for how difficult the task ahead would be.

A coroner and pathologist were organizing the removal of bodies that had been identified to the city morgue for an autopsy. In most cases, the cause of death was obvious. Crewmembers were assisting with bereaved relatives and friends. As upset as she was, Tara had to acknowledge how wonderful the crew had been. She knew they had also lost many colleagues. She was especially grateful to James O'Brien, who had been wonderful the previous day at the passenger terminal, despite the pain the burn on his hand was causing him.

Tara found Maureen and Michael, lying side by side. As upset as she was, she was relieved that she didn't have to look any further. She couldn't cope with seeing the dead, some she recognized as people that she had given 'readings'. It was especially heartbreaking to see the children.

After the last horrendous hours aboard the ship, Maureen and Michael looked strangely peaceful. Thankfully, they had not been in the water long.

"Thank God they're not burned," she whispered, realizing that had been her greatest fear.

"They were found tied together." The voice behind Tara startled her. She jumped with fright and turned. It was James. He was looking at the bodies with respectful sadness. "Obviously, that's the way they wanted to go."

Tara realized they should be buried together. It was right, and she felt ashamed for what she had been about to do. How could she pretend to be Maureen, and deprive her of eternal rest with her husband, a man she had loved dearly?

As she stared at the still and peaceful form of Maureen, she remembered what a good friend she had been, and what a wonderful mother. It was a double tragedy that her children should end up in an orphanage, possibly separated. Maureen would have hated that idea. What mother wouldn't? This thought drew Tara to the obvious conclusion. Maureen would not want the children to be placed in an orphanage; she'd want them with someone who really cared for them, someone who would bring them up in a loving home, together. That she had no home seemed a small detail in the large picture. None of those arriving in Australia had a home.

Tara glanced at Michael and recalled the way he had looked at her moments before they were separated. He had wanted her to look after Jack and Hannah. If she was to fulfil her silent promise, she had to stick to what she had decided. There was no other way. A legal battle could take years, and she had little chance of winning against a blood relative. If she was going to bypass the legal system, she had to explain her plan to James, who was marking off identified, deceased passengers, on his list. She had no idea whether he would go along with her or not, but there was only one way to find out.

Tara was white as a sheet when she returned to Sorrel and the children.

"We are free to go," she said and embraced Jack and Hannah, who had just awoken. Sorrel looked relieved. James had taken some convincing but finally saw reason. He'd told her he'd spent six years in the Havilah Orphanage in Sydney. He received no education, was made to scrub floors and toilets from morning till night, and received his first pair of shoes from the orphanage at age thirteen. As soon as he was old enough, he went to sea. He loved children and knew Tara would look after the O'Sullivan children well, which, in his mind, was a much better alternative than an orphanage. He also knew how close Tara and Maureen had been. He consented to help all he could and in return, Tara agreed to keep in touch frequently, to let him know how the children were. Of course, Tara suspected he wanted to keep in contact with her, but she didn't mind.

"Most people here are going to stay in Salvation Army Hostels, but I prefer to leave as soon as possible," she said.

"So do I," Sorrel added.

As Tara stood holding the children, she suddenly realised the enormity of the task she had taken upon herself, and it almost overwhelmed her. After many years of praying for a child of her own, she now had two. It was too late to consider how she was going to support them, and the potential problems they might incur. She also knew if the authorities found out what she had done, she would become a fugitive. In the back of her mind, she was concerned about how the children would react when they recovered from the shock and realised they were never going to see their parents again.

Jack moved out of the embrace and looked up at her, his small face so troubled. Tara thought she knew what he was thinking. He wondered what would happen to the bodies of his parents. She had been too upset to ask.

"Mrs. O'Sullivan," Ruby Ashton called.

Sorrel nudged Tara. "Mrs. O'Sullivan, Mrs. Ashton is calling you."

Tara spun around. "Yes," she said, acting a little vague, her heart thudding wildly, as she wondered if she had been found out already.

"I'm sorry to disturb you again, but could we discuss funeral arrangements for your husband?"

She sighed with relief. "Of course."

CHAPTER SIX

Port Adelaide appeared to be a thriving frontier town, with an impressive and varied range of buildings, befitting the Colony's major port. Tara and Sorrel were relieved to find the town wasn't as primitive as they had both secretly imagined. As they wandered the wide streets, lined with shops and businesses, they noticed work in progress on the harbour. A massive reconstruction was underway on some of the wharves in poor repair, and the riverbed was being dredged to accommodate larger ships. The harbour was filled with ships, including a fleet of ketches being loaded by 'burly' wharfies. Tara commented that the town was far more industrious than she had been expecting, as she had been told it was first settled less than a hundred years ago.

"According to one of the crew from the ship, this area was once a swamp," she told Sorrel, as they crossed a wide street, busy with tramcars, motor vehicles and horse-drawn buggies.

"I can quite believe it," Sorrel returned. "The flies and mosquitoes are still here."

As Tara and Sorrel stood on Black Diamond Corner, a busy intersection, and glanced around, everything seemed strange. Even the smells were 'foreign'. The two women missed Irish food far more than they ever imagined. The meals aboard ship had been bland and monotonous. Neither wanted to see porridge again for a very long time.

Their priority, the women decided, after glancing into their bags of donated clothing, was to shop. Sorrel had been given a sleeveless floral ensemble, which left her speechless with dismay. It was cotton and smelt musty, and had huge pink flowers on a lime-green background. Apart from being too tight across her ample breasts, and shorter than she felt comfortable in, it was the most awful thing she had ever seen.

Tara, on the other hand, liked bright colours, so her taste was a little more flexible. Even so, she found her dress positively ghastly. Not only was it polka-dotted blue on a red background, but the skirt was also pleated and matronly, and the blouse was too large. It hung like a sack on her slim figure. She would have swapped with Sorrel, but when the elderly woman saw the plunging back, she gasped with horror.

Tara and Sorrel came across the Sinclair Draper and Clothing Store, where they purchased new shoes for themselves and the children, and a few personal 'necessities'. A handbag and purse each, handkerchiefs, lipstick and rouge, and of course, underwear. Tara followed Sorrel's lead in everything she selected, as she had no idea what a respectable 'society lady' wore nowadays. The gipsy's taste in apparel was so different. Suspecting they were survivors of the 'Emerald Star,' the storekeeper and his wife were very helpful. Cyril Peter's constantly chattered, while his wife, Ella, served the women and offered assistance with whatever they were searching for.

Sorrel quickly found a respectable day dress of a sedate beige colour, which seemed to please her conservative taste immensely. Tara was drawn to dresses in dramatic colours, vivid reds and brilliant blues, which the gipsies loved, but she noticed Sorrel was aghast when she lifted one off the racks. Although Tara much preferred the vibrant colours, she thought if Sorrel disapproved, so might her aunt, and she very much wanted to appear ladylike and tasteful when she arrived on Tambora. Eventually, Tara purchased a fresh pale blue and white dress, for which Sorrel was full of praise. She also found a pretty cotton dress in pale lemon for Hannah, which she thought would be cool, and two new shirts for Jack.

When they had finished shopping, Sorrel suggested they find somewhere to change out of what she referred to as their, 'God awful' clothes. They didn't want to return to Custom's house.

"I must bathe and do something with my hair," she said.

Tara was concerned for Sorrel, who was perspiring freely in the heat, her face flushed as pink as the flowers on her dress. The women rented a room for a few hours in a hotel. A short while later, they were ready to face the world, once again feeling respectable. Tara noticed Sorrel put on nearly all her new underwear, including stockings. Tara couldn't bear to wear stockings in the heat, or petticoats, and noticed many of the women on the streets did not wear them. It was too hot for such formality. Tara didn't know how Sorrel was going to cope, especially as she was feeling the heat so much, but she could see an amazing difference in the elderly woman, once she had dressed. Her head lifted proudly, and her carriage became erect, as she surveyed herself in a full-length mirror inside the wardrobe door. With her hair neatly pinned in a bun, she looked like a new woman.

Tara had pinned her hair up, which made her look more like a modern woman of the times. Shorter styles were more fashionable, but she couldn't yet bring herself to cut her hair.

"Feeling better?" She smiled at the old lady, and her eyes twinkled.

"Infinitely! How about you?"

Tara frowned. "Worried. I think we should leave Port Adelaide as soon as possible."

Sorrel understood Tara was eager to depart before the truth about her identity was discovered.

"We can't leave before…" Sorrel stopped and glanced at the children, who were looking at the town from the hotel balcony. "The funerals," she whispered.

Tara sighed. "I don't think I could attend," she said. "I just couldn't bear it, and I don't believe it would be good for the children."

Sorrel frowned. "How can you avoid it?"

"There will be so many buried the same day. Perhaps we wouldn't be missed."

"That's a possibility," Sorrel acknowledged. "I agree it wouldn't be good for the children, but I'm not sure it would be wise to raise suspicion. Michael was supposed to be your husband. How would it look if you weren't at his funeral?"

"Not very good," Tara conceded. "But seeing Maureen buried as me would be more than I could face. Not only was she one of the dearest friends I've ever had, but I'm frightened Hannah will cry for her mother in front of everyone." Tara turned away; suddenly overwhelmed by the responsibility she had taken upon herself. "Oh, Sorrel. Have I done the right thing? I have no experience as a mother and no income. I don't even know if my aunt is still on the station. What if she isn't? And what if the children don't take to me. What am I going to do then? I can't just take them back to the authorities, and confess to having deceived them. I couldn't do that to the children. If they were fostered out, they might be separated, and that would break their hearts."

Sorrel moved towards Tara and sat her down on the bed, placing her hands on her shoulders. "Calm down, Tara. Don't let the children see you upset. It's only natural you are unsure of the future, but you will be just fine."

"How do you know, Sorrel? I don't feel sure about anything anymore. I can't imagine what ever possessed me to take on the responsibility of two children in my situation." Sorrel could see Tara was panicking. She had the same look in her eyes she had witnessed on the ship when she thought she might perish.

"Take a deep breath," Sorrel said in a serene voice.

Tara looked at Sorrel's face and saw the tranquillity in her blue eyes. She took a deep breath, then another, and began to feel the tenseness leave her body.

"Firstly, if your Aunt is not on the station, and you don't know where she is, you will come to Alice, to me."

Tara's eyes filled with unshed tears. "Oh, Sorrel."

The old lady's eyes softened. "I am sure she will be there, and all will be well, but if not, you are not alone, remember that. Secondly, it will take time for you and the children to bond, and to adjust to the situation. It won't be easy for any of you, but they are fond of you, and you of them, so I'm sure it will work out. Don't expect plain sailing, because that doesn't happen in any growing family. But don't see each little obstacle as a mountain, either."

Tara's head dropped.

Sorrel squeezed her shoulder, gently. "I know it's an overwhelming responsibility, but the very fact that you were willing to take someone else's children, tells me you are a very special person. I know we haven't known each other very long, but I think you have an inner strength that few people possess."

Tara looked at Sorrel hopefully. "Do you think so?"

"Yes, I do, and I don't dish out praise lightly."

This, Tara believed and smiled faintly.

"You are going to be a good surrogate mother, believe me?"

"I'm not usually so despairing. I'm just…"

"Afraid! It's all right to be afraid, Tara. It's perfectly natural under the circumstances. After what we've been through in the last few days or so, we haven't had time to deal with the shock."

Tara realized that was true, and she hadn't been able to grieve for Maureen and Michael. She realized the children hadn't either. Jack was burying his feelings, and Hannah was confused and lost.

Tara was also very frightened the authorities would catch up with her.

"Let's inquire at the railway station about when the 'Ghan' train leaves. If it's later today or tomorrow morning, I say we catch it. The sooner we leave Adelaide, the better I will feel."

At the Port Adelaide Railway Station, they were told the 'Ghan' train, formerly known as the 'Afghan Express' left Adelaide only once a week, from the city. As it happened, it was the next day, the same day the funerals of the dead passengers and crew were scheduled to be held at the Cheltenham Cemetery.

"If we don't take that train, we'll have to stay in Adelaide another week, which might give the authorities time to uncover the truth," Tara said to Sorrel when they had moved away from the ticket office.

"You're right. It looks as if you will have to miss the funerals after all. She glanced at the children. "You'll have to tell Jack something. He may be upset about not attending his parent's funeral. I'm not sure whether it will be a good or bad thing. On the one hand, it might help him come to terms with losing his mother and father, and on the other hand, it might be too much for a boy so young." Sorrel looked at Jack, full of concern. "I don't know what to advise you, Tara. He has hardly said a word, so we don't know what he's feeling. It looks like this will be your first big decision as the children's guardian." Tara, feeling the weight of responsibility, also glanced at Jack. Standing a short distance away, gazing into space, he looked like a lost soul. Although he stayed close to Hannah every minute of the day, he'd hardly said a word to her.

Tara desperately wanted to do the right thing by the boy. If only she knew what it was. "Will you take Hannah to the ladies' restroom while I talk to Jack?"

"Of course."

"If he really wants to attend his parent's funerals, it's his right. Although I could be in a great deal of trouble for taking them under false pretences, I shouldn't deny him, whatever the risk."

Sorrel frowned, afraid for Tara.

Tara asked Jack to sit down on a bench in the station waiting room and explained the situation as gently as she could. For a few moments, Jack said nothing. Tara sat quietly, letting him mull things over. Although he was only ten years old, so much had happened to him. Under the circumstances, it was only natural his feelings were confused. Nevertheless, she wanted him to be aware his opinion and thoughts were of the utmost importance.

"Whatever you decide, I'll go along with you, Jack," she said.

"I should be at Mama and Papa's funeral," he blurted out, close to tears.

Startled, Tara nodded, and neither spoke for a few moments.

"I know Mama and Papa would want me and Hannah to be safe. If that means leaving on the train tomorrow, then that's what we should do."

Tara placed her arm around his small shoulder. "I agree, Jack, but it has to be your decision. Are you sure?" If she had decided for him, he may have resented her doing so.

His gaze dropped and he spoke quietly, the tremor in his voice making Tara aware he was battling with his fragile emotions. "Yes. But I would like to come back one day, to see Mama and Papa's graves. Maybe when Hannah is older, and she can understand."

"Of course." Tara had every intention of renaming his mother's grave. She didn't know how she was going to do it, but she was certain she would do it, somehow.

He looked up, into her eyes, his own so tragically troubled. "Can you promise me we'll never have to live with Aunty Moyna, Tara? It wouldn't be so bad for me, but it would be awful for Hannah. Aunty Moyna was so mean to her girls. I don't think she loved them at all."

Tara swallowed the lump in her throat. "Your mama told me all about Aunty Moyna, and I wouldn't want you or Hannah to live with her. I promise I won't let that happen, Jack. I'm not sure what the future holds, but I'll try my best to make it good for you and Hannah. I know it's hard for you to trust in anything or anyone, after what's happened, and I understand. But it would mean so much to me if you believe I'll do my best for you and your sister. You know, I always wanted children, but…" her voice cracked, and she cleared her throat. "I believe God had other plans for me, and this was his plan. He wanted me to look after you and Hannah."

Jack frowned. "What kind of God would take our parents away from us?"

Startled, Tara faltered. "I don't know, Jack." How could she explain something she had no hope of understanding herself? Michael and Maureen were good people. Why did they have to die? When she thought of all the others, especially the children. There were no answers.

Jack searched her green eyes, looking for answers, and then looked down at his lap again. Feeling his pain and disappointment that she could not answer him, Tara felt hot tears sting her eyes. She knew he was finding it difficult to believe in anything. She could hardly blame him. Aboard the ship, he had been such a happy, fun-loving child. Mischievous, and full of life. Tara wondered if she'd ever see that little boy again. She doubted he'd ever be the same. How could he?

"Sometimes things happen in our lives that are so painful, but we have no way of explaining or understanding why," she said. "If it's any comfort to you, Jack, they happen to everyone, at some time. Tara's thoughts had drifted back to the night of her eighteenth birthday party.

"Has something awful happened to you?" Jack asked, watching her with an expression so much more mature than his ten years. "Are your parents dead?"

"No. But I did have a very traumatic experience. I survived Jack, and so will you. It's hard to believe now, but the pain will become less, as time goes by. You won't forget your parents, and I wouldn't want you to, but your broken heart will heal. Just remember your Mama and Papa will always be watching over you. Not everyone thinks the same, but I believe your parents are in Heaven, with the angels."

"Mama told me about Heaven," Jack said. "She said Grandpa and Grandma are in

Heaven, and they watch over us."

"I believe your Mama and Papa are looking down on you and Hannah, and will always, always, be with you."

Jack seemed to be slightly comforted by that thought.

The train journeyed through the outer western suburbs of Adelaide, towards the city. It was hotter than they ever imagined it could be. Tara could see Sorrel was uncomfortable in her confining undergarments, which were no doubt stuck to her moistened body. Fortunately, some of the doors were open, allowing the air to circulate in the carriages. The wind was hot, which was no relief, but it did help dry their perspiration.

Sorrel and Tara found the neat little cottage homes they passed, with their tiny windows and verandas on the front, so different from the homes in Ireland. They could see the European influence, but the iron verandas made them look strange, although they were quite obviously a necessary inclusion because of the fierceness of the sun. The main contrast between Australia and Ireland was the colour of the landscape. Ireland was always so green, something, up until that moment, the women had taken for granted. The open paddocks they passed were scorched brown under a blazing sun. Gardens seemed to be struggling to grow. The grass was yellow, and the tree's limbs and leaves appeared to have wilted in the heat. Sorrel thought of Alice Springs. If Adelaide seemed so primitive, what would Alice be like? She imagined a dusty, wind-swept town, buzzing with flies, and inwardly shuddered. Although she longed to see Marcus again, she felt terribly home sick for England.

At the Adelaide Railway Station, Tara purchased tickets on the 'Ghan', for her and the children, while Sorrel collected her ticket, paid for by her son. The train was due to depart the next afternoon, at 3 p.m. The conductor told them they must board no later than 2 p.m. They booked into The Grosvenor Hotel, across the road from the railway station.

While Sorrel undressed and lay down to rest in her room, under a whirling fan, Tara took the children to explore the city. They bought ice cream and strolled along the banks of the river, then up the main street, King William Street, and browsed through the shops, where Tara bought them each child a small toy. It saddened Tara that their pleasure was brief, as the pain of losing their parents was never far away.

At 2 p.m. the next afternoon, they returned to the station and boarded the 'Ghan', which Tara was shocked to find was segregated into classes. As well as goods, including a limited selection of fresh produce, and the mail, there was a First Class Sleeper, Second Class, and a native car. A handful of aborigines and several stern-looking easterners in turbans, known as Afghans, boarded the native car.

The first half-hour of the train journey was literally through the backyards of the sparse northern suburbs. Soon afterwards they crossed the Adelaide Plains, a monotonously flat area where migrant farmers had planted grain. Late afternoon they passed the coastal town of Port Germein. They commented on the sight of a wooden jetty, almost a mile long, stretching out to sea.

"Port Germein was meant to be a grain port," Virgil Walcott told them, as he served them afternoon tea. Virgil was the conductor assigned to their car. He hadn't stopped talking since they boarded the train. It was apparent he thought of himself as an unofficial guide, or ambassador, and loved telling travellers all about the train and history of the places they passed.

"It was chosen because it was close to a pass through the Flinders Ranges, which made it a handy shipping point for wheat and wool from the new farms that lay beyond the ranges, which the settlers believed would be prosperous. The port was found to be too shallow for ships to come anywhere near the coast, which meant the jetty had to be built to go out to the ships."

The landscape was mostly brown and very, very dry.

"Drought," Virgil told them, "was not an occasional occurrence in South Australia, but the normal climate. When the rains come, the land is fertile and generous. When the rain doesn't come, that same land brings the reality of hardship and broken spirits."

The ruins of farmhouses in the distance were a testament to Virgil's words. He had told them that European farming methods permanently damaged the fragile soil. Cultivation turned the soil into powder, which was blown away as dust, or washed away as mud by the rare but savage storms. The land was accustomed to the soft padded paws of kangaroos and wallabies but compressed by the hard cloven hooves of sheep and cattle. Crops failed, and the desert advanced.

They were having dinner, when they passed through the town of Port Augusta, beyond which, the conductor told them, was the outback. The Port, he said, drew ships of the world to safe moorings beside her deep water wharves, at the head of a gulf so deeply carved into the coastline that the normal flushing effect of tides was minimized, making the water extraordinarily salty.

"Sailors, who fell off the ships, drunk, believed they would not drown," the conductor said.

"And did they?" Tara asked, noting the twinkle in his eye.

"They're buried in the town's cemetery," he replied, "so I can safely say their theory proved incorrect."

Tara was fascinated by the saltbush, which the conductor told her was a hardy plant, which drinks in the sparse moisture of the night air, providing feed for sheep, where no other plant could survive. The train headed north, but west of Port Augusta, the saltbush ended, and so did sheep farming.

When Jack commented that there were no animals to see beyond the train window, Virgil told him that most of the Australian animals were nocturnal. They appeared in the cool of the desert night, seeking food and moisture to get them through the next day of blazing heat. Jack was delighted when he did see a small herd of wild donkeys sheltering under trees, and as darkness began to fall, kangaroos and emus seemed to appear from nowhere, also delighting Hannah.

As the passengers aboard the "Ghan" slept, the train passed through the Pichi Richi Pass in the Flinders Ranges, then through Hawker, Leigh Creek and on to Marree. When Sorrel had enquired about their expected time of arrival in Alice, she had been told the timetable was more a matter of hope than fact because the elements often conspired against the train. Not only were the hour of arrival indefinite, but even the day, and sometimes the week. Nevertheless, the weekly round trip to Alice was considered a travel adventure. Virgil's next words confirmed this.

"Once we arrived six weeks late."

Tara and Sorrel looked at each other in bewilderment.

"Freak floods washed away the tracks and bridges," he told them.

"Floods! This afternoon you told us South Australia was for the most part in a drought."

"That's right. But sometimes we get freak storms and floods. Once we sat on the banks of a river for two weeks. We ran out of food and the driver had to shoot wild goats to feed the passengers."

"Goats!" Sorrel gasped.

Tara had eaten far stranger things, - badger, hedgehog, and curlew, so she wasn't perturbed.

"This is a dry, hostile country, ladies, for man and machine alike. There is almost no permanent surface water, but as you may have noticed, the country is laced with stream beds capable of rising into a destructive flood, within hours."

As the conductor hurried off to help a passenger who was ill, Tara and Sorrel looked at each other in astonishment.

"There's not a cloud in the sky," Tara said, "so I doubt we have to worry about a flood."

"It's just as well we're not doing this trip in the winter," Sorrel added. "I have a feeling the outback has more in store for us than we could ever imagine."

As if Sorrel's words were prophecy, they awoke the next morning to find the train at a standstill. Thinking they were in a station, they opened the curtain on their window and found they were in the middle of nowhere.

Virgil was hurrying past when Tara opened their cabin door. "Why have we stopped?" she asked.

"The train tracks have buckled in the heat. There's nothing the engineer can do. The line will have to be fixed before we can move on. Fortunately, we're within walking distance of Marree."

"I can't see a town in the distance. There's nothing out there. Absolutely nothing."

"You won't be able to see the town from here. It's about two miles away."

"Two miles," Sorrel said in dismay. "You expect us to walk two miles?"

"That's right. There are railway workers in Marree who can fix the line. There's also a hotel and stores." Virgil smiled as he watched the ladies' worried expressions change to relief.

As the passengers of the Ghan were helped to the ground with a few belongings, their relief was short-lived. The land was flat and barren. They couldn't distinguish where the horizon stopped and the sky began. It all looked the same.

It was early morning, but a shimmering haze blanketed the red earth, dotted with grey bushes, a promise of the searing heat they would experience during the day. A heat from which there was no escape.

CHAPTER SEVEN

"How far do we have to walk?" Jack asked irritably, as he struggled along carrying Hannah. It was still early, but the desert sand burned through the soles of their shoes. By midday, the temperature would soar to unbearable heights. They were glad they had taken Cyril Peter's advice and purchased wide-brimmed hats. Although they could still feel the intensity of the sun's merciless rays beating down on their heads, at least their faces were protected.

Tara was carrying their one suitcase, which was light, but cumbersome. She felt sorry for Jack. "Let Hannah walk for a little while," she gently suggested. Jack seemed reluctant.

"You could manage, couldn't you, Hannah?" Tara asked.

The child pulled a rueful face then turned her head away, still clinging to her brother.

Virgil Walcott was assisting Sorrel and another elderly woman, who was suffering from the effects of the heat. The conductor, who was quite elderly himself, tactfully suggested the women remove some of their restrictive undergarments, which trapped the heat in their bodies, but his recommendation fell on indignant deaf ears.

"We must get into the shade as soon as possible," he said, trying vainly to hurry them along. "We don't want to die of heat stroke."

"My son won't be pleased to hear I had to walk after he paid for my ticket in first class," Sorrel grumbled.

The majority of European passengers, fifteen adults and seven children, were a long way ahead, following the train line into town, but Tara had to proceed slowly with the children, and Sorrel. She noticed the aboriginal and Afghan passengers had simply disappeared into a flat, featureless landscape, something she would never have thought possible. Had she the strength to ask Virgil where they had gone, she would have, but the heat was rapidly draining what little energy she had.

Virgil had provided an umbrella to protect the elderly women from the fierceness of the sun, but Sorrel looked about to collapse. Tara could hear the conductor continually encouraging both elderly women to drink from a water container he carried.

"Dehydration can kill you just as sure as a snake bite," he said.

"Snake bite!" Sorrel shouted. Suddenly the women came to life, watching every step they took.

Tara inwardly groaned when she heard Virgil say Australia had some of the deadliest snakes in the world.

"A healthy-sized Eastern Brown can kill a man in less than an hour. That's how long it takes for the poison to work its way up to his heart. The Death Adder is a clumsy snake, but a bite from a six-foot Mulga can kill a child…"

"Thank you for that, Virgil," Tara called. "Can we talk about something more pleasant, like the rainfall?"

"We don't have enough of a rainfall to discuss," he said. "If you were to get lost out here, believe me, dying of snake bite would be preferable to dying from sun stroke or dehydration. At least it would be quick."

After trudging along for half an hour, Virgil tut-tutting at the state of the train line, he stopped.

"You can see the hotel from here," he said. They all came to a stand still, and shaded their eyes, gazing into the shimmering distance.

"I think I can see something," Tara said wearily. The haze and glare, she noticed, seemed to distort everything. Many times she had seen water mirages and dancing shapes on the horizon, only to see them disappear a few moments later.

Jack put Hannah down, but she began crying, so Tara lifted her onto her back.

"I can't see anything," the boy grumbled, taking the suitcase from Tara, while she fumbled with her hat and the child on her back.

"I think I can see one building," Tara said. "Surely the town has more than one building?" She looked at Virgil and frowned.

"Of course it does," he reassured, puffing under the weight of the elderly woman's cases. Thankfully Sorrel had one very light case, but the other woman had not been a passenger on the 'Emerald Star', so her case was heavy. Nevertheless, he felt sorry for Tara, carrying Hannah on her back.

"The hotel is a double-storey building, that's why you can see it and nothing else."

When the group finally arrived in Marree, exhausted from the growing heat, and as parched as the land around them, they were appalled at the ugliness of the town. It appeared derelict and like everything in the outback, struggling to survive under a thick layer of dust, and a merciless sun. The only vegetation they could see was the grey saltbush in the stony desert, which seemed to be closing in on the town, and one or two Athol trees. Tara imagined, after a windstorm or two, the town would be swallowed up by powdery, red dust, all but The Great Northern Hotel, which effortlessly dominated

Marree, rising in absurdity from the gibber plains, like a monument.

The hotel, thankfully, was relatively cool. The walls were stone, a foot thick, providing good insulation from the heat. After a drink of bore water, which tasted strange, and some sandwiches made with stale bread, the train travellers became bored, and the children were restless, so they decided to explore the town.

A tiny post office squatted in the heat and dust beside the hotel, completely overshadowed. Set back from the train line, were a few fibro railway houses, which looked uninhabited. Only a washing line, with one sun-bleached, dusty towel, draped over it, gave any indication of someone in residence. Beside the houses, were untidy piles of scrap metal. Everything was tinged red, like the surrounding desert.

The group trudged through town on a wide, dusty track, the main street, used only by the odd horse, a few camels, and a herd of goats. The road began nowhere in particular and ended at the railway station. They were heading towards the shopping facilities, which consisted of three incredibly tumbledown stores. The surrounding desert seemed to filter up to the town's door, adding a shimmer along the road, where hardly a scrap of vegetation broke the monotony of the landscape or stopped the dancing haze from scorching the town. The still, quietness, was incredible, magnifying the only sounds that could be heard above their footsteps in the powdery dust, - the buzzing of bush flies, and the occasional squawk from a cockatoo. The lack of trees in which to build nests meant not even the birds wanted to stay in Marree.

Outside two of the shops was a long wooden bench, on which several aborigines were sitting in the sun, seeming to silently contemplate the surrounding desert. Their dark eyes scanned the horizon, searching for something unknown to the Europeans, while they listened to sounds only they could hear. Even the approaching newcomers in town weren't enough to distract them.

Tara, Sorrel and the children entered one of the three stores and found an Indian Hawker ran it. He introduced himself as Mohomet Basheer. His humble shop, a galvanized iron hut, was surprisingly large inside. It would have been stifling hot, if not for a door open either end, a breeze through. There were rows of clothes on racks, mostly brightly coloured shapeless, cotton dresses, in large sizes. Tara was surprised to find such vivid coloured clothes. Sorrel was appalled.

From the few dresses in her size, Tara found three she liked, that weren't too bright. She asked if Mohomet had somewhere she could try them on, as they had been followed into the store by the Aboriginals, who were taking an uninhibited interest in her choice of purchases. Mohomet led her into a small room, tacked onto the side of the shop. It was immediately evident the room was his living quarters, but he insisted she use it. Tara could easily overhear his conversation with Sorrel, while she tried on different garments, including a bathing suit, her first. The passengers on the train had talked about two large lakes further north, Lake Eyre and Lake Eyre South. The heat made the prospect of bathing very appealing. She even hoped to learn to swim.

"Is Alice Springs more populated than Marree?" Sorrel asked.

Tara smiled at the note of hope in her friend's voice and knew she dreaded the answer, fearing it would bring to life all her misgivings.

"Oh, yes. It's much bigger, madam. Too busy for me. I prefer the quietness of this town."

Tara heard Sorrel sigh with relief, yet her own apprehensions were not quelled. She dreaded to think what Mohomet's idea of a bigger town was. A few more stores, a real police station, twenty more houses. She wondered what could possibly attract people to the heart of Australia. Certainly, she found no affinity with this daunting, dusty, red, barren land, and knew Sorrel felt the same.

Sorrel couldn't help noticing Mohomet wore exorbitant jewellery. His neck was adorned with gold chains and medallions, studded with precious stones. Thick gold bracelets hung from his wrists.

"Why do you stay here?" she found herself asking.

Mohomet looked at her in stunned silence.

"Forgive me for saying so, but you appear to be quite wealthy." Sorrel would not normally have been so personal or forward, but the heat was affecting her judgement. It was affecting everything. She felt quite out of sorts.

"I do not need the money, madam. I live simply to satisfy my customers."

He sounded sincere, which confused Sorrel. "Why here?" she asked. "There's nothing here... but dust… and flies."

Tara could hear the repulsion in Sorrel's voice.

Mohomet smiled in understanding, his features softening. "I love the desert climate, madam. I come from the North Western state of Rajasthan in India, which is near the Thor Desert. As for the flies, like everything, they have their purpose."

Sorrel shook her head, and Mohomet realised no amount of explanation would satisfy her. She had to give into the elements and meld with the land before she could understand how the people in the outback not only existed but thrived in their surroundings.

"I used to enjoy hawking my goods between Oodnadatta and Marree, and out to the stations," he said, tidying his racks of clothing. "But I am too old to travel far these days. This," he held up his hands, "is my retirement."

Sorrel stared at him, aghast. She could not understand how Mohomet could love such a desolate place.

"I can see you are sceptical, madam, but I love the wide, open spaces. There is nothing so wonderful than to look across the land, for miles, and not see another living soul." His eyes shone with joy from within, as though the nomadic life of his people, from time immemorial, was a deep, inbred passion. His enthusiasm moved Sorrel and made her consciously re-evaluate her first impression of this God-forsaken country. That done, her opinion did not change.

More than a week passed, and still, the train line was not fixed. Not only had the line buckled in the fierce heat, but also the workers discovered termites had eaten the sleepers. Many miles had to be checked, in case of a derailment. A day after the train came to a standstill, the perishable goods, twenty cases of oranges, fifteen cases of grapes from the Riverland, and an assortment of other vegetables, were loaded onto camels, and taken on to Alice, along with the mail. Up early that morning, Jack saw the camels pass through town, and watched in intrigue, as the string of majestic beasts carried their load into the distance, the rising sun lighting their way. It was a sight the young boy would never forget.

Not knowing when they would be leaving Marree, Sorrel, Tara and the other passengers, were going stir crazy. To amuse themselves, the children, except for Jack, who kept to himself, had befriended the local aboriginal children. Jack had remained quiet, only speaking to lament his hate for Marree. He could usually be found sitting alone on the hotel stairs or a step somewhere in the shade. Sometimes Hannah looked for him. It broke Tara's heart to see Jack grieve and to hear the young girl continually cry for her mother, but there was nothing she could do.

As the days passed, and Hannah refused to eat anything supplied by the hotel, Tara became worried.

"She's so slight," she said to Sorrel, "and she's eaten nothing all day. I can't find anything she'll eat. She doesn't even like the taste of the milk."

"Can you blame her?" Sorrel replied. "The child's not used to goat's milk, and the food is disgusting. We've all lost weight, except for the locals. They seem to eat anything."

"We shouldn't complain," Tara said. "We're in the middle of nowhere, and shortages are a problem everywhere."

"I know. But you'll have to find something Hannah will eat before she becomes ill."

The next afternoon, Tara found Hannah playing with a little aboriginal girl. She was happily munching on something that was making her face around her mouth, and her teeth, black. Aware the aboriginal children ate grubs and snakes, Tara tentatively examined the food. She found it to be some kind of bread, with a hard, black, outer crust. One of the locals explained it was known as damper, a flour and water mixture the aboriginals baked in the hot ashes of the campfire. Tara was so relieved to see Hannah eating that she almost cried.

Tara soon discovered, that most, if not all of the residents of Marree were enamoured by a man known as Ethan Hunter. If all could be believed, this man was almost a living legend in outback Australia. He was a cameleer, of Afghan/English origin, who travelled the interior, to places no one else dared. She heard stories of unbelievable feats of bravery, superb tracking achievements, and unequalled bushmanship. Everyone in town had a tale to tell of a man who went out into an inhospitable, unknown land, unafraid, and made a good life, and a good living, against all odds.

Tara was discussing her concerns about how she was going to get herself and the children to Tambora Station from Wombat Creek, with Sorrel and another train passenger, when the publican of The Great Northern Hotel started singing Ethan Hunter's praises.

"He knows the heart of Australia better than any man alive," the publican said. "He could find his way out of a dust storm, blindfolded. He's the man to get you and the children to Tambora."

Tara's hopes rose. "How do I find him?" she asked.

"He comes and goes. No one knows where or when he will turn up, but he always seems to be here when he's needed."

"Well, that's not much good to me. I need to know how and when I can find him."

"No one runs to a schedule out here," the publican advised her. 'The elements are too unpredictable. But you can bet your life he'll come to town sooner or later. I believe he took the perishables off the train to Alice."

Tara remembered Jack mentioning a camel train, but in all honesty, she hadn't believed him, for which she felt suddenly guilty. She had come to realise, as the publican had said, that schedules were not even considered in the outback. It seemed a strange way to live.

"I wouldn't bet my life on anything out here, especially an enigma," she muttered. "What's an enigma?" the publican asked.

Tara rolled her eyes in frustration. "Something obscure... Never mind. Don't you have any idea when he'll turn up again? A week from now, two weeks..." The thought of staying in Marree or Wombat Creek for that long, appalled her, but what else could she do?

"He's like the wind," a sweaty railway worker suggested, from further down the bar. "He always blows in."

Tara shook her head and sighed in exasperation. "He may as well be a ghost."

The publican and railway worker looked at her strangely, as if she had unwittingly hit upon something. Their suspicious glances made her unsure whether she ever wanted to meet Ethan Hunter. Nevertheless, she still had a problem. She needed to get from Wombat Creek to Tambora, a distance of almost thirty miles, through arid country, and it seemed Ethan Hunter was the man to get her there. But how was she going to find him? Although he sounded more than capable, she sensed there was much to learn about him, and it might not all be good.

The next morning, much to the passenger's relief, the Ghan rolled into Marree. They boarded the train, and a few inhabitants, including aborigines, waved them off. Mohomet was there to farewell them and gave both women a departing gift, which was meticulously wrapped. Tara noticed he lingered with his goodbye to Sorrel, and noted the colour of his clothing was more sedate, which made her smile.

As they left the town behind them, the passengers compared the ugliness of Marree, to the untouched desert, and realised it was man who had created such a monstrosity. The residents, most of whom did not stay too long, thought it a waste of time trying to beautify the town, as the harsh elements were a formidable adversary.

Mid-morning, following the Oodnadatta Track, they passed Lake Eyre South. It shimmered like an enormous body of water, attracting the passengers to the windows of the train, but it was a barren salt pan, - the water was an illusion, a mirage. Tara grimaced when she thought of her newly acquired bathing suit, and her hopes for learning to swim. One thing was certain, she had no fear of drowning in the lake.

Further north, they passed Lake Eyre North, a much bigger salt pan that stretched for miles. As the train journeyed on through the desert, seeming to be going into the 'never

never', Tara began to feel more and more despondent.

At midday, the train rolled into Wombat Creek, and Tara and the children disembarked. It had been difficult saying goodbye to Sorrel, but she promised to write and let Tara know how she was fairing in the town of Alice. Knowing they would keep in touch made the parting easier, and Tara promised to visit her in Alice as soon as she could.

The train pulled away, and Tara and the children stood alone in the unnerving silence, watching it snake into the distance, as dust blew around their legs. When the train had faded from sight, they turned to look at the 'town'.

Wombat Creek consisted of a small, single-storey hotel, screened in along the front with fly netting, one store, and a few tiny homes off in the distance, but absolutely nothing else. Apart from a single tree beside the hotel, there was very little vegetation in the surrounding red desert and not even an inkling of a road. The ever-present buzzing of bush flies was the only sound to break the deafening silence that engulfed them. There wasn't a bird, or any living creature visible, and certainly no people.

Tara's heart sank, and a wall of depression settled over her like a suffocating blanket. She felt tears well up in her eyes. How could her aunt live in such a barren place? How could she farm cattle and sheep out here? How could anything, man or beast, survive in such desolation? It was like the end of the earth.

Tears of frustration and disappointment streamed down Tara's face, unbridled. As the salty moisture trailed through the dust on her cheeks, leaving unsightly, brown streaks, she collapsed in the red dust at her feet. The children watched helplessly, as she fell to pieces emotionally, neither knowing what to do or say.

Everything that had happened in the last few months seemed to pile together, overwhelming her. Garvie's imprisonment and bleak future. The gipsies threw her out of the band and took the only home she had known for years, her caravan. The sinking of the ship. The loss of her dear friends, the children's parents. Although she had come to care for the children, she felt an inadequate replacement for their mother and father, but she was all they had. To top everything off, she found herself in a place even worse than Marree, something she did not think possible. After seeing Wombat Creek, she was too frightened to contemplate what Tambora Station would be like.

It was all too much. Tara wanted to go home, back to Ireland, and the heather-filled meadows, the winding mountain roads, the quaint villages, and the cool, refreshing rain. What she wouldn't give at that moment to see something green, real green, not the varying shades of grey-green she'd seen in Australia. She'd sell her soul to the devil to feel the rain on her face. She closed her eyes and tried to imagine the refreshing droplets, and how the crisp morning air felt on her cheeks, making them tingle. In the dry heat, that burned her skin, it was impossible.

Tara opened her eyes, and almost trance-like, glanced around at the scorched landscape, shimmering in the heat, while the children stood silently beside her. Distant, floating mirages made her head swim. Through the swirling dust, which rose like cones in the wind, she imagined she saw moving shapes. She blinked, and the shapes seemed to come closer. She closed her eyes again, praying it would all go away.

"Are you injured, madam, or in need of help?" she heard a deep, masculine voice ask. Tara opened her eyes and squinted into the glaring sunlight. She blinked several times, unable to focus properly, as her eyes were stinging with salty tears. The merciless rays of the sun, beating fiercely down, made her head throb. She imagined she saw the blurry form of a man, high up on a strange beast. She was sure the sun and heat were playing tricks on her mind, and he was a mirage. She hadn't heard anyone approaching. Nevertheless, she found herself replying.

With her head in her hands, she mumbled, "If I close my eyes, maybe this horrible place will disappear, and then everything will be just fine." All the self-pity in her had risen to the surface, laid bare in the harsh sunlight.

The 'apparition' cocked his head to one side, and his eyes narrowed. "You look healthy enough, and so do the children, but that situation will change very quickly if you continue to sit in the sun feeling sorry for yourself. It is at least 118 degrees in the shade. Were you thrown off the train for not paying your fare?"

Tara was immediately indignant. "Certainly not."

"Then why are you weeping in the dirt, like an infant? You are risking the children and yourself suffering sun-stroke."

Even in her state of distress, she noted the lack of sympathy in his voice. "I ...I am..."

"Well?" he asked impatiently.

"You wouldn't understand," she mumbled defensively. She tried to look at him, but could only open her eyes for a split second because of the glaring sunlight. "Who are you, anyway? And what business is it of yours if I feel like crying, or suffer sun-stroke in this God-forsaken outpost?" She gestured to her sunburned surroundings with a curt flick of her wrist.

"Should you come to grief in this God-forsaken outpost, as you call it, I'll be the first and probably the only person who'll come to your aid. I spend half my life rescuing people from their own stupidity. Quite frankly, I have better things to do."

Tara felt her anger building. Who the devil did he think he was? She owed him no explanation. "Mind your own business. I don't need rescuing."

"Well, perhaps your children do. You appear to be so absorbed by self-pity that you are oblivious to their needs. I suggest they move to the shade of the hotel as quickly as possible. It's sheer carelessness to have them out in the sun with their delicate skins exposed."

Tara dabbed at her eyes with a handkerchief, blew her nose, and tried harder to focus on him. The children were wearing their hats, but quite obviously that didn't seem to be enough for the interfering man who had wandered, unsolicited, into their lives.

Suddenly she heard a deep, guttural growl, and jumped with fright. Hannah squealed and threw her small body at Tara, almost knocking her flat on her back.

"It's alright, wee one," the man said kindly. "Hannibal won't hurt you. He just likes to make loud noises. It's his way of complaining." He dismounted and walked towards them.

Shading her eyes with her free hand, Tara could see Hannibal was an enormous camel, with green slime drooling from his rubbery lips. Huge chunks of shedding fur hung in tatters from his body. He was the most disgusting thing she had ever seen, and the nauseating smell he emitted was made worse by the stifling heat.

"Take that horrible creature away from us," she said, pulling Hannah protectively close. "Can't you see it's frightening the children?"

While continuing to shade her eyes from the glare of the sun, she glanced at the man towering over her. He was glowering at her as if she had just insulted his mother or wife.

"Hannibal is a valuable animal, madam, and I don't think anyone would disagree that he has a more congenial disposition than you do."

Tara gasped. "Are you comparing me.... to that creature?"

"Yes, and right now, he measures up favourably."

Tara was outraged. "He resembles a tatty blanket, only fit for a dog to sleep upon." She glared at him through squinting eyes. Her gaze took in his sweat-stained hat, decorated with feathers, and his sweat-stained clothes, which generated a mental picture of some sort of uncivilized frontier man. Suddenly she had an inkling of who he might be. All the stories she had heard in Marree, about the living legend, Ethan Hunter, sprang to mind. She thought the people of the outback must be desperate for heroes if he was all they could come up with.

Feeling at a distinct disadvantage on the ground, she stood up but found she still had to look up at him, as he was at least a foot taller than she was. Her first impression was of a rugged man who was regarding her with a penetrating glare from eyes so dark, they were almost black.

"You must be the enigma?" she said without thinking, his steadfast gaze for the moment confusing her. She noticed his skin was tanned a rich brown, and he had at least two days of beard growth on his face. His black hair had flecks of grey at the temples, which suggested he wasn't a young man, despite his obvious fitness. He wore moleskin trousers, which were snug over his hips and the taut muscles of his upper thighs. His boots were scuffed and dusty. His shirt, which stretched like a second skin across his muscled chest, had several buttons open, revealing a dark mat of silky hair. He smelt manly, with a hint of animal odour.

"Enigma!" He scowled at her sceptically.

Dragging her eyes from his chest, she said impatiently, "Ethan Hunter."

"That's right. How did you know?" He continued to regard her suspiciously.

Tara was almost overcome by a sudden wave of conflicting emotions. She should have been delighted she had stumbled across Ethan Hunter, or vice-versa, even relieved, but he appeared to be most unsympathetic, insufferably rude, and ill-humoured. It was patently clear he did not possess an ounce of empathy for those who found his environment less than inviting. He appeared to be exercising that impatience, waiting for her to explain herself.

"You fit the description of the living legend I've heard so much about," she said, feeling annoyed that she had to justify herself like a schoolgirl.

A half-crooked smile lifted one side of his mouth. Tara thought he looked more smug than amused and was determined to change that.

"It seems the people of Marree forgot to tell me you were a surly, critical, overbearing man."

His mouth straightened to a thin line, which made Tara feel suddenly nervous.

"Perhaps I should have been warned to look out for a pampered, foolhardy, Irish woman, recklessly dragging two innocent children across the desert, with no concern for their safety, or that of her own. Had either of us been forewarned, maybe we could have successfully avoided each other."

Much to her annoyance, Tara felt fresh tears well in her eyes, and turned away, not wanting him to see he had wounded her. Had she not been feeling so disillusioned with Wombat Creek, and life in general, she may have been angry enough to give him a tongue-lashing. As it was, she felt mentally unfit for anything that required even a modicum of energy.

Feeling contrite for losing his temper in front of the children and unable to suffer a woman's tears, Ethan softened his approach. His dark head cocked to one side again, as he studied her features with unnerving concentration. "What are you doing in Wombat Creek?"

Tara was tempted to tell him to mind his own business, yet again, when she remembered she needed him to get to Tambora. "My Aunt lives somewhere out here." She hiccuped loudly, and Ethan almost smiled. She certainly was a pitiable sight. Even though he was angry with her, her helplessness touched the tender side of his heart. He'd never been able to turn his back on a defenceless creature in distress if only to end its suffering.

"I can't think of anyone disagreeable enough to be related to you," he said with a hint of amusement. "Although there's old Sadie Jennings, she can be as cantankerous as a brown snake if riled. Then there's Nonie Jacob, she goes a bit strange when the moon is full, but I don't think she's got any family..."

"When you've quite finished," Tara interrupted. "I can't imagine my lovely Aunt would know the likes of you."

"I'm sure she does, and it's quite likely she's proud of it." He was treating her to some outback humour, but Tara was in no mood to see it.

"You sir, are a conceited brute, something I will be sure to tell Aunt Victoria when I see her."

"Surely you aren't referring to Victoria Millburn?"

"I certainly am."

"Then you must be... Tara?"

"That's right. How did you know?"

"She did tell me she had a niece with a temper like an old crocodile."

"My aunt would never have said that about me," she said in disgust.

He laughed. "You know, you should lighten up. A sense of humour goes a long way out here."

Tara was lost for words so she gave him a scathing glare.

Ignoring her, his penetrating gaze swept over her breasts and downwards, but her body was concealed by a loose dress in a pale beige colour, quite undramatic compared with the memory that came to mind. "You hardly look like the woman I remember…"

"I'm sure we've never met before. I know I wouldn't forget…" She was going to be rude, possibly vulgar, but stopped abruptly, remembering the children were beside her. As she hadn't been to Australia before, and she was sure his presence in Ireland wouldn't be forgotten in a hurry, she was confused.

"Well, thank you. I have been told I leave an impression."

"Were you told what kind of impression?" His lips moved upwards in a secretive smile, but he didn't enlighten her. "I saw your portrait some years ago."

His words explained the confusion. "Then you have a very good memory." She began furiously dusting off her dress. "I believe my Aunt sent it back to Ireland more than seven years ago."

His eyes slid over her again, this time, languidly. Although he might not have immediately recognised her, he would never forget the portrait. "It was worth remembering," he said in a suggestive tone.

Despite the intense heat, Tara felt her face grow distinctly warmer. "Is my Aunt still on Tambora?"

"She certainly is. We're good friends."

"I find that hard to believe. My aunt was always choosy with her friends." Tara wondered how her aunt could have an association, be it personal, or professional, with someone so arrogant and off hand. Was it likely she had become hardened herself, to cope with life in such an inhospitable land? Tara hoped her aunt hadn't changed so much. She didn't think she cope with any more disappointment.

Ethan was finding it increasingly difficult to feel some compassion for the churlish woman before him. He was not surprised she was alone and thought perhaps her husband had deserted her. He certainly couldn't blame him, but he felt sorry for the children. He took a deep, ragged breath, his lips pressed together, as he studied her for a moment, fighting the urge to bite back. If she were Victoria's niece, he'd ignore her lack of courtesy, for now. Victoria would never forgive him if he let something happen to her.

Tara noted he glanced at the children and thought she knew what he was thinking. Her aunt had never mentioned any children.

Ethan continued to regard the children. They seemed confused, unable to understand why two strangers were being so unfriendly towards each other.

For a few moments, the two adults stood glaring at each other, the children watching them warily.

Tara realized that if she wanted Ethan to take them out to the station, she would have to become more amicable towards him, as difficult as that was going to be. She was about to speak when he turned away.

Realizing he was leaving them, Tara panicked. "Look, Mr. Hunter, I think we have gotten off on the wrong foot. If you are an acquaintance of my Aunts, I think we should be…"

He turned, his features stern. "I told you, your Aunt and I are very good friends, although you seem to find that hard to believe. Rest assured our friendship does not have to flow over to you and I. I'm quite happy for us to remain mere acquaintances. We wouldn't have to go that far, but it would be a courtesy to Victoria."

It was Tara's turn to be astounded. He was the most egotistical, contemptuous man she had ever met. She felt like slapping his arrogant face but fought to control herself. If only there was someone else who could take them out to the station. But there wasn't. She had no other choice but to be amiable to the disdainful man before her. In other words, she had to become an actress, yet again.

To her dismay, he turned away again. With great difficulty, she swallowed her pride and bit down her anger. "Please accept my…. apology for being… a little curt. I've had a rather trying day."

He slowly swung round, his dark eyes narrowing again, as he studied her for a moment, aware her apology was not sincere.

"You want me to take you out to the station, don't you?" He had every intention of doing so but wanted to see if she'd at least show a little civility.

"No," she said quickly.

He looked completely sceptical, and cocked his head to one side again, his strong features hardening. She had the distinct feeling it was not wise to exasperate him further, although doing so gave her a great deal of satisfaction. As much as she wanted to, she couldn't lie under such intense scrutiny. "Well… yes, I do…"

"Why not just say so, instead of pretending to feel regret for your unforgivable rudeness?"

"My rudeness!" Tara decided he was making it almost impossible for her to be nice. "Are you always so …antagonistic?" she hissed.

"Only when someone tries to jerk me around."

"Well, I don't need you. I'll find my own way to Tambora. How far is it, anyway?"

"Almost thirty miles, but I doubt you could find your own way to the hotel from here, so I will take you to Tambora. Before you thank me, I can assure you I am only doing it for the children's sake, and because I have such high regard for Victoria."

"I had no intention of thanking you, but I'm sure my Aunt will be grateful." She was sorely tempted to refuse his offer but knew she could not find her way to the station, and she certainly couldn't risk becoming lost with the children. For that reason alone, she would not argue. Once they reached Tambora, she hoped never to see him again.

He half turned away, contemplating how he was going to get her to the station. "Can you ride?"

"Certainly."

She noted he looked relieved. "I can ride any horse you have." Garvie had taught her to ride like a true gipsy, and she was proud of her skills. At least it was one thing she could do without appearing completely inane.

"Horse!" He made a noise much like a stifled laugh but quickly recognised the glint of hurt flash in her green eyes, and his features sobered. He could feel the children watching him timidly. "I don't have a horse."

"Well surely someone in this God forsaken… " She paused and took a calming breath, also aware the children were watching and listening. In a more rational tone, she said, "Surely someone in this town has a horse."

"No-one in Wombat Creek needs a horse. Not with the train on their doorstep. As you can see there's not much feed around."

Tara gasped. "You don't expect me to ride a … camel, do you?"

"It's that or walk, and I can't see you walking two miles, never mind thirty."

Tara noted his tone held not a hint of understanding for her situation. She was beginning to believe he was truly heartless. If only she didn't need his services so badly.

She glanced at Hannibal, a large sandy-coloured one-humped beast. Even kneeling he was taller than she was. Horrible slime continued to drop in dollops from his mouth, as he chewed on something unseen and watched her with enormous brown eyes, shaded by eyelashes any woman would envy. A low rumbling growl threatened her, and she was wafted with his breath, which she was sure had the power to wilt flowers.

Tara glanced at the children. Hannah looked terrified, but Jack, although a little apprehensive, was clearly fascinated with the prospect of riding a camel. A short distance away, other camels stood in the sun beside the hotel. A turbaned man squatted near them, under the shade of the only tree in town, near a water trough.

Tara knew she had little choice. If she wanted to get to Tambora, she had to travel with Ethan Hunter. That meant riding a camel or walking. The latter was not appealing, but the former was a terrifying prospect.

She tried to put on a brave face, but her legs had suddenly gone to jelly.

CHAPTER EIGHT

Ethan retrieved the bag of mail Vigil Walcott had left hanging on a post beside the train tracks.

"I'm the unofficial mailman, while Rex Crawley is laid low," he said when he saw Tara glance at the bag.

"There's a mail man, out here?" She was incredulous, unable to imagine someone actually delivering mail, when the homesteads must be so far apart, and in so many different directions.

"We may be spread out, but we do have some civilized services," Ethan retorted.

Tara noted a hint of defensiveness in his tone, which she chose to ignore. She glanced around. There wasn't anything resembling a track near the hotel, nothing to suggest anyone came or went anywhere.

"I'll take your word for it, but your only link to civilization appears to be the lonely train line. How often is the mail delivered? Once every other season? Perhaps yearly?"

Ethan's dark brows drew together. "Rex delivers fortnightly. When I deliver with the camels, it takes me a month to cover the same distance." He noted her look of distaste when she glanced at the camels, and grinned, the tanned skin at the corners of his eyes crinkling. "Rex and I have a friendly rivalry between us."

"So horses are faster than camels?"

"I told you there aren't any horses in town. Rex drives an American Packard, so he..."

Tara interrupted. "An auto-mobile, out here?" The thought of an automobile lifted her spirits considerably. Perhaps this country wasn't so primitive after all?

Ethan nodded. "It's as tough as nails, and, as I was going to say, a lot faster than the camels, but not nearly as reliable. Camels don't get bogged in the sand, or caught in a flood."

Ethan's last few words went over Tara's head, as she remembered her ride in Riordan Magee's motor vehicle, which, despite the circumstances, she had enjoyed immensely. She suddenly had an appealing idea. "Perhaps Mr. Crawley could drive us to Tambora?"

It was Ethan's turn to look startled.

Tara thought he had taken offence, and inwardly felt a small measure of delight. After all, he had been insufferably rude. She glanced at the children and noticed Jack watching her. He looked as if he expected her to be more gracious, his glance almost a silent chastisement. She suddenly realised she wasn't being much of a role model for the children. As their guardian, she should be setting an example.

"I'm grateful to you for saying you would take us out to Tambora, " she said, almost choking on the words. "But traveling in a motor vehicle would be more comfortable, and, as you say, a lot quicker. Is Mr. Crawley's automobile in need of repair? Is that why you are delivering the mail?"

Ethan's mouth lazily lifted at one corner. He was amused, but Tara had no idea why. In his mind, he had an image of Rex, bouncing over the dunes in his Packard, laughing like a lunatic. Somehow Tara and the children did not fit into that picture, although he thought it would serve her right if she were to travel with Rex, even for a short distance. Quite obviously she imagined herself riding in sedate comfort, a mistake Ethan had made, only once. He'd been caught in the top end in cyclones and had weathered more sandstorms than he cared to remember, but the trip to Leigh Creek with Rex still remained the most horrendous journey of his life. He decided he'd sooner ride the most unpredictable of wild camels than travel a hundred yards in Rex's Packard.

"Rex is ill with a bout of blackwater fever," Ethan informed her. He didn't like to see Rex ill, but he did enjoy knowing he would be as short-tempered as a wombat digging in a termite mound, just knowing Ethan was delivering the mail on his reliable camels. And of course, Ethan would not let him forget it.

"He'll be out of action for a few weeks yet. And before you ask, I can't drive a motor vehicle, and no one else in town can either." Rex had offered to teach Ethan, but he'd adamantly refused, telling the mailman he'd feel safer swimming with the crocodiles in the Daly River. "There's a petrol shortage out here, anyway," he added almost in delight.

Tara's expression displayed her disappointment. She glanced at the shimmering desert that seemed to meld with the far-off horizon. "How many people live out here?"

"In a five hundred mile radius, about fifty white settlers and twice as many employees, mostly aboriginal roustabouts and stockmen. That number does not include the shearers that pass through or the tribes that wander the area."

"Savages?"

Ethan frowned. "Only if you get on their wrong side. The local clan is the Arabana people, but other clans cross the area, the Kujani and Kokata. Some white settlers have had trouble with them, but mostly it's their own doing. The settlers who have been here the longest have the least trouble. They've learnt not to interfere with tribal law, and not to desecrate their sacred sites."

For the first time, Tara noticed several boxes of groceries and an odd assortment of supplies beside the track, including a wire cage, containing half a dozen young chickens. A label was hanging on the cage with C PRESTON scrawled on it. The chicken's beaks were open, gasping, as the fierce sun beat down on them. Knowing they would quickly die if left with the rest of the supplies awaiting the storeowner, Ethan picked them up. "I'll drop these at the store, then take you and the children into the hotel. I'm sure you are all in need of a drink. I know I am."

"Is there a bath in the hotel? I'd give almost anything for a bath. I had hoped to be presentable when I met up with my Aunt, but the elements are conspiring against me."

A hot wind swirled choking dust around them, and Tara's hat almost flew off. She grasped it with one hand and covered her mouth and nose with her other hand, and coughed. She noticed Ethan glance at the children, and realized, as a 'mother,' they should have been her first priority.

"The children also need a bath, but they don't seem to mind being dirty as much as I do." She placed a tentative arm on each of their shoulders and tried to smile. "This is Jack and Hannah."

Ethan looked down at the children again, nodding and half smiling.

"Say hello to Mr. Hunter, children."

Neither child spoke. Jack looked him over curiously but clamped his lips together tightly. Hannah hid her face. It was an uncomfortable moment for Tara. She didn't blame the children for being withdrawn. How could they possibly act as if everything was normal after all they'd been through? As their mother, she should have been encouraging them to be more cordial, but her relationship with them was as yet too fragile. The best she could do was cover up.

"The children are tired, and ... the journey was so long, and everything is so unfamiliar."

Ethan sensed something was not quite right, but he was not sure what it was. He thought Tara seemed overly tense, and wondered why she felt the need to make excuses for the children. He studied her for a moment, as she continued to cough.

"It takes a while to get used to a place like Wombat Creek," he said gently.

She glanced at him through watering eyes, a scowl marring her features. "I doubt I'll ever get used to it." She detested the outback and was sure that wasn't going to change. Waves of horrible black flies hung around her head, and crawled into the sweaty crevices on her body, sucking the moisture. She swatted at them, but they returned instantly, almost driving her mad. "I can't believe my Aunt came here, and stayed, especially after Tom died." Her eyes filled with tears again.

Ethan's weathered face seemed to soften. "I've known Victoria since she first came to Tambora. The house wasn't even built, so they lived in a shed with open sides. Back then she vowed to keep an open mind, and to her credit, she did just that. Over time, and through hardships that never seem to end, she learnt to appreciate the beauty of this land."

Tara was taken aback. Beauty! She couldn't see it. She certainly couldn't understand why someone would want to live in constant hardship.

Ethan saw the confusion in her features, and read her mind. "In the beginning, I know Victoria felt much as you do now, but she's a woman with true grit."

It was obvious Ethan greatly admired her aunt.

'Everyone who works for her, stockmen, shearers, roustabouts, house staff, all respect her. Don't think it was easy though. She earned that respect the hard way. Out here in a country pioneered by an indomitable breed of man, and which is still largely a man's domain, that's no small achievement."

Tara felt humbled by the genuine affection in his voice.

Squinting against the glaring light, Ethan looked out across the shimmering, gibber plains. Tara wondered what he saw out there. She saw nothing.

"Maybe you shouldn't have come alone," he said.

"Tara squinted up at him and glanced at the children. "I'm not alone."

"I meant, without your husband."

Knowing what she was about to say was probably true, Tara's bottom lip trembled ever so slightly. "I'm a …widow, Mr. Hunter."

He was stunned. He hadn't been expecting her to say that. "That's too bad. Bringing up young ones alone, won't be easy."

"I'm well aware of that, but I'll make a go of it."

He grudgingly admired her resolve. Unfortunately, she was naïve. The outback was one of the toughest places to make a go of it. All he could do was give her encouragement. "Being in a place like this makes you find qualities within yourself that you never knew existed. If you tough it out for a while, you'll know what I mean."

Tara looked at him uncertainly.

Ethan's dark eyes softened. "Just try not to have high expectations, and take each day as it comes."

His words frightened and chilled her. Even with low expectations, she still felt she was going to be greatly disappointed.

Jack was looking at Hannibal wide-eyed, so Ethan handed him the reins and pointed towards the others. Awe struck, the boy led the enormous camel ahead of them. Before they went inside, Ethan stopped to introduce Tara to his assistant, who had been attending the rest of the camels and smoking. Feeling as she did, she would rather he hadn't.

Saladin was a full-blood Afghan. Over baggy pantaloons, he wore a flowing robe of a light, cool material, and his head was swathed in a beige turban. His eyes were squinting and black, his skin very dark, and a beard hid the lower half of his face. Even from the short distance between them, Tara was wafted with the overpowering, spicy scent he wore. She noticed he glanced at the children suspiciously.

"Saladin has been travelling with me for four years," Ethan said. "Since he came to Australia from Peshawar."

Tara nodded, her gaze not leaving the cameleer. Something about him frightened her. He seemed to emanate hostility.

Ethan addressed Saladin. He spoke in English, explaining that he was taking Tara and the children out to Tambora Station. Saladin replied in his native tongue, again looking at Tara and the children resentfully. Then the two men had a rapid exchange in Saladin's native tongue.

Even though Tara did not know exactly what was being said, she was brutally aware Ethan's assistant was not happy about taking them out to Tambora. She knew Ethan was only doing it as a favour to her aunt. After a few moments of heated dialogue, Ethan had the final word, and Saladin threw his hands in the air in a frustrated manner and walked away, to lean against the hotel wall, and brood.

"My presence does not please him," Tara said, feeling embarrassed.

"Don't take it personally. Most Afghans are Moslems, and their customs are very different from ours."

Tara didn't see what this had to do with her travelling with them but thought she would probably find out in good time. "I had been told you are part Afghan," she said. "Do you not live by the Muslim faith?"

"No. My grandfather was part Afghan, but my father was brought up in England, and my mother was English. I understand the Afghans and work well with them, but I do not follow their customs. Saladin lives in a Ghan Town, where the Afghans and their wives remain segregated from the European community. This is partly voluntary, but mostly forced upon them by the white community."

"Does Saladin go on every trip with you?"

Ethan did not miss the disheartened inflexion in her voice. Although he didn't understand it, he had grown used to people feeling uneasy around his assistant. "Mostly. Victoria lets me use some land on the station to breed a few camels. I spend some time there, usually about a week every month. At that time, Saladin goes to Ghan Town to be with his family."

Tara hoped he would do so while Ethan took them out to the station, but she dared not suggest it, as she did not want to put Ethan offside again. Although it went against her independent nature, she needed him for this trip. In the future, she would make her own way to town, as no doubt her aunt did. "Does Saladin speak English?"

"Only a few words. But he understands the English language quite well."

One glance at Saladin, and she realised he had understood what she had said, and was quite aware his dislike of her was mutual. She made a mental note to watch what she said in the future.

"Why is this camel bigger?" Jack asked Ethan. It was the first time he had spoken in hours, or shown any real interest in anything since the shipwreck. Tara was delighted. "Hannibal is the only male," Ethan told the boy.

"Aren't the males stronger?" Jack asked.

"A little, but the females are good weight carriers. If I kept more than one male, they would fight for the females. These females are Hannibal's harem, and like a sheikh, he has his favourite."

Tara walked along the line, known as a 'string'. She heard Jack ask Ethan what a 'sheikh' was, and heard him laugh and reply, "a very happy man." She noticed Ethan spoke in a kind tone to the boy, far different from the cool inflexion in his voice when he spoke to her. She glanced at Saladin, and he gave her another disapproving look, before moving further away.

"This is Layla," Ethan told Jack. "She's Hannibal's favourite amongst the females, and mine, too." He glanced at Tara. "Your mother can ride her with your sister."

Jack looked at Tara, his eyes clouding with pain. She felt a lurch of anguish grip her heart. Ethan's words reminded him of his mother and brought back the sorrow he had forgotten for a few moments.

Ethan took the boy's expression as one of concern. "I assure you, your mother and sister will be safe aboard Layla."

Distracted, Ethan's words did not penetrate Tara's mind for a moment. When they did, she panicked. "Oh, no, we won't," she said. The thought of actually riding a camel terrified her and she could no longer hide it. Seeming to understand, Hannah clung to her legs, her eyes as large as saucers. "I don't care if we have to walk, we will not be getting on that camel, or any other camel for that matter."

Ethan looked startled. Jack looked betrayed.

"Surely someone in town has a horse or even a donkey I could borrow?"

Ethan shook his head. "There are horses on the stations, of course, but I told you no one in town needs a horse. The two miners who live in Wombat Creek take their horses on the train to Alice, and then ride them on to the mines from there. I don't believe I've seen a donkey in these parts for many, many years."

Tara thought he was being facetious about her Irish heritage. "Well, I won't ride a camel. I'll just wait here until someone from Tambora comes into town."

"You may have a long wait."

Although the prospect of being stuck in Wombat Creek was horrifying, Tara's features set in determination. "Didn't you say the people from the stations come into town for supplies if you don't deliver to them?"

"Yes, but not necessarily from Tambora. It also depends on what they're doing on the stations. If they're mustering, we might not see them for a month. If they're shearing, or crutching, it could be a fortnight. Whichever is the case, they don't bring spare horses with them." Ethan felt frustrated. She was certainly a stubborn woman.

"I have a buggy at the back of the hotel, which the camels pull," he said. "I sometimes use it to transport passengers when the train can't get through. It needs some work, and it's rather large for three people, but if you won't ride Layla…"

"I don't want to ride in a buggy," Jack said sulkily. "That's for sissy's."

Tara realized how hurt he was. "I've never ridden a camel before, Jack," she said in a low voice. "I'm afraid Hannah might fall… " Tara pleaded for understanding.

Jack turned away sullenly.

Ethan nodded, but something in his expression conveyed he thought her fears irrational. He went on to tell Jack the names of the other camels, but Tara could see the boy was very upset, and she felt terrible. Nevertheless, even though she was normally fairly brave, her courage had deserted her, and she couldn't face the idea of climbing aboard a camel.

"There's Udo, Mosi, Lilith, Maat, and the youngest is Oma. She's two and half years old, the offspring of Hannibal and Maat."

Despite his frame of mind, Jack was immediately taken with the youngest of the group of seven, a half-grown female.

"Perhaps, Jack, you would like to ride Maat," Ethan said. "Oma stays close to her mother."

Jack nodded enthusiastically, his features brightening.

Ethan dropped the mailbag and chickens in the shade of the store doorway, before taking Tara and the children into the Wombat Creek Hotel, through the back door.

"Ferris must be out checking his traps," he said, as they walked down the central passageway, glancing into empty rooms.

"Traps?" Tara imagined the publican trapping wild animals and noted Jack looked horrified.

"He sets rabbit traps. The rabbits are a pest around here. Not only do they eat what little food is available for stock, but the cattle stumble into their burrows at night, injuring their legs, and then the dingoes get them. Ferris sells the pelts, which brings him a small side income, and the meat is popular because of the shortages. Rabbit stew is always on the hotel menu. Since the Depression, it's quite often all there is to offer unless someone from the station brings in a couple of sheep. Then it's grilled mutton chops. At one time Ferris used to cook wombat a lot, but it doesn't suit everyone's taste."

"Who is minding the hotel while the publican is gone?"

Ethan looked startled. "No one. He wouldn't be expecting anyone until the weekend when the station owners and their families come into town. If shearers or stockmen are due, he always knows. Percy Everett, the storeowner next door, sorts the mail, and Ferris looks after the radio. Between the two of them, they seem to know everything that's going on for hundreds of miles. I'm surprised he didn't know you were getting off the train. He usually greets any visitors."

"I was due more than a week ago. We had no idea when the train line would be fixed, so I doubt anyone else knew. The railway workers in Marree seem to have their own schedule."

Tara followed Ethan down the passageway. "This is the kitchen," he said, opening a swinging door to the left, to show a good-sized room, with big wood ovens. There was a pot simmering on the stove.

"Surprise! It's rabbit stew," Ethan said sniffing the aroma. Tara smiled to herself. Rabbit stew had been a large part of the gipsies' diet, especially when travelling the countryside. She had to admit, the publican's stew smelt good, especially after the terrible food at The Great Northern Hotel, but the buzzing flies hovering over the kitchen table, repulsed her.

Tara couldn't imagine why the hotel needed such big ovens, when there was no one to cook for, and certainly no trees around to supply fuel. Then she remembered two of the camels were carrying wood. She wondered from how far away the wood had been obtained, and if the ovens had been installed in the hope the town would prosper.

Ethan poured them all a glass of water from a pitcher on the counter, then continued the tour.

"There are six guest bedrooms and two bathrooms. One is just outside the back door. It's small and damned hot, day or night, as there's no window. I much prefer the larger bathroom. So do the shearers and stockmen when they come to town."

"Can we see the bathrooms?" Tara asked, barely hiding the enthusiasm she felt.

They followed Ethan out back again, where a small bathroom had been tacked onto the rear of the hotel. He pushed open a door made from wooden slats, with gaps in them, and stood back. Tara peered into the dimness, where she could see a large, galvanized tub, beside which stood a small bench, but nothing else. Flies buzzed in the centre of the room, and insects crawled across the floor. As Ethan had said, there was no window. The gaps in the door seemed to provide the only light, and the roof was low and made of iron, making the room as hot as an oven. Nevertheless, in Tara's mind, any kind of bathroom was a luxury that she had lived without for many years.

The other bathroom was between corrugated iron walls. It had no roof, and the floor was dirt. The tub was enormous, but like everything, dusty.

"We'll use the smaller bathroom," Tara said.

Ethan looked surprised. "Suit yourself. I'll get Saladin to pump some water from the well. You'll have to share the water."

"Of course, but don't trouble your assistant. I can get the water myself."

"It's no trouble." Before Tara could protest further, Ethan shouted orders to Saladin on the other side of the galvanized wall. He was unloading the wood from the camels and stacking it at the side of the hotel.

The thought of a bath thrilled Tara. She mentally damned the persistent hot wind, which stirred up the dust that stuck to the perspiration on her body. When Ethan came back into the hotel, Tara said, "You have no idea how grateful I am to have a bath before heading out to the station."

He looked at her, and his dark eyes seemed to soften. Tara thought the mix of European blood, with just a hint of Eastern colouring, was a very interesting combination. Unexpectedly, his mesmerizing gaze stirred something inside her that she didn't understand, especially as she didn't find him attractive.

"I know exactly how you feel," he said. "I often spend days between water holes and weeks between towns."

"I'm sure you are used to feeling…"

When she saw the look of grievance in his dark eyes, Tara felt suddenly contrite and cursed her lack of thoughtfulness. She didn't know why, but something about Ethan Hunter brought out the worst in her. To be fair to him, going several days in the heat without a bath would be terrible, but she couldn't bring herself to apologize again.

"By the time we arrive on Tambora, you'll be desperate for another bath," he said, again in an offhand manner. "Almost thirty miles in a buggy, across dusty plains and desert, won't be easy."

Tara's spirits sank.

While Saladin put some water in the tub, Tara followed Ethan through the hotel. "Believe it or not, this hotel has become quite an outback attraction," he said.

"That doesn't say much for the outback," Tara said. She couldn't imagine anyone wanting to come to such a small desert town. She imagined Wombat Creek, like Marree, as only a rail stop on the journey to Alice. As far as she could see, there was nothing out here to attract visitors. Nothing but dust and flies, intolerable heat, and more flies.

She noticed Jack slipped outside to see the camels again, and Hannah followed him. Tara went after them and called for them to keep their distance, in case the camels tried to bite or kick them. Saladin was close by, drawing water from a well, but she didn't like to ask him to watch over them. He seemed to be making a point of ignoring their presence.

"We'll be all right," Jack said testily. He seemed to dislike Tara fussing over him, but she knew he had never minded his mother's concern. Not since their intimate talk in the Port Adelaide Railway Station had Jack allowed her to comfort him, or show any form of affection, which kept Tara at arms-length. With Saladin within earshot, she let his testiness go without saying a word.

Ethan looked out the door and issued instructions to his assistant in a foreign language. Saladin jumped to attention but gave Tara another grudging look.

"Don't worry," Ethan said, as they went inside again. "Saladin will watch them."

His reassurances did not wholly quell her fears, but she remained quiet. Not only was she sure Saladin cared little about what happened to any of them, but he was busy filling the bathtub.

As Tara entered the bar, normally strictly a male bastion, she couldn't hide her surprise. The whole room was filled with traveller's mementoes, hats, boots, and photographs of locals from the surrounding stations, shearers, stockmen, aborigines and items of clothing. Even the walls were painted with murals. She thought of the Inn's in Ireland, which were warm and welcoming, but not nearly so personal. The bar was long, with the stools upended on the counter, and the floor was dirty, and crawling with bugs. There was a small ladies lounge off to one side, which had an old sofa and some rickety chairs and a small table in it. It didn't look very inviting.

"Some of the best artists anywhere come from the bush," Ethan told her with a hint of pride in his voice, as he surveyed the murals. He pointed to a photograph of an aboriginal stockman, pinned on a notice board, littered with raggedy-ended notices. "That's Nugget. He's employed on Tambora. He did most of these paintings."

Nugget looked about fifty years old. Even though he was smiling, he appeared shy and self-conscious in front of the camera. Tara imagined him to be a quiet, unassuming man. "He's very talented," she agreed. His work was extremely good, but the paintings made her think of Garvie again, and for a moment she was overwhelmed by sadness, wishing he had taken his gift more seriously. She had always believed he could have done well as an artist, and their lives would have been so different. He would not have had to poach game from landowners, and would not have found himself in prison so often, leaving her to fend for herself. She quickly pushed these painful thoughts from her mind. Nothing could change the past, and she was determined to leave it behind. She had to think of the future, and making a life with the children.

As Tara looked at more of the paintings, her thoughts drifted to the recent past and the Harcourt Gallery, and Riordan Magee. She was sure he'd think the murals were good, and the artists talented. Although she knew virtually nothing about art, in her opinion the murals were better than some of the paintings she'd seen in his gallery. As different thoughts rushed through her mind, she felt Ethan watching her closely, something he seemed to do often, when he thought she wouldn't notice. She had a feeling he missed very little.

"They are very good," she said, wanting to divert his attention. "I don't profess to know a great deal about art, but I've had the opportunity to see works considered quite good."

He nodded, and she sensed he was pleased.

Each mural gave a different account of life in the heart of Australia. Ethan offered no information, so she occasionally asked him a question. When he answered her, it was briefly, but she noted the hint of pride in his voice. One wall depicted stockmen by campfires, boiling billy tea. Another, was a sunset over Ayres Rock, an enormous monolith in the desert, south of Alice Springs, which reflected the colours of the earth and the sun, magnificently. Ethan explained, that as the light changed, so the colour of the rock changed.

A lonely homestead, with a shingled roof, and a sagging timber veranda, caught Tara's eye. Desert sand had piled against the outer walls, giving it a neglected, overburdened appearance. It was how she feared Tambora would look. Even though she tried to fight the emotion, depression crept over her.

Ethan seemed to read her mind. "Are you afraid of what you'll find on Tambora?" he asked, startling her.

"I'm looking forward to seeing my Aunt," she said evasively, trying to disguise her misgivings. She noticed he offered no information to put her mind at rest. In truth, she was more than a little fearful but found herself unable to ask what the station was like. Even if it were worse than she ever imagined, she'd have to stay awhile, for the children's sake, and to help her aunt. She turned her attention to another wall, and paintings of kangaroos, pink and white cockatoos in gum trees, aboriginals hunting with spears and boomerangs, desert flowers, and an emu with chicks.

On shelves above the bar, were an odd collection of bottles, Ethan claimed were from all around the world, and hundreds of beer coasters. There was also an enormous pair of horns over the doorway. When she asked about them, he said they had belonged to a rogue buffalo, that had attacked and overturned a fully laden camel-drawn wagon, before he shot it. Another shelf contained several painted emu eggs, an assortment of aboriginal spears and boomerangs, and even the jaws of a giant crocodile.

"Where did that come from?" she asked, pointing to the crocodile jaws, lined with lethal-looking teeth.

"I'd say the old fella washed down the Cooper in a flood. It's rare, but it has been known to happen."

"Who killed it?"

He paused and said flatly. "I did."

"Why? For sport?"

He looked at her as if he was disappointed that she would think he'd kill just for sport. "He attacked an aboriginal child, a boy aged four before I slit his throat. Luck and good bush medicine was all that saved the boy. His dog wasn't so lucky."

Tara gasped thinking of the horrible injuries the poor child must have suffered in those enormous jaws. She was sure she'd die of fright if confronted by such a fearsome creature. She felt regretful that she had jumped to conclusions.

"Crocodiles live on pure instinct," Ethan went on without looking at her. "He saw the dog and boy as food."

Tara was startled by his way of looking at things. It was obvious he bore the crocodile no malice. He just did what he had to. "I can't believe you killed a monster that big, with just a knife."

"I couldn't risk trying to shoot the crocodile while he had the boy. The crocodile was doing the death roll. I had to wrestle him free."

Tara had to admit she had been wrong about Ethan, and that he wasn't bragging. She was also sure he would be a crack shot.

"You were very courageous," she conceded.

Ethan glanced at her to see if she was being facetious, before brushing off her praise. "I just did what anyone would've done, had they been there."

Tara doubted too many people would wrestle an enormous crocodile, but she kept silent. She was beginning to see why Ethan was thought of so highly in the outback, and how he had come to earn his reputation.

As Tara gazed at the bizarre collection of items, particularly the crocodile jaws, where she could see several broken teeth, a booming voice called through one of the doorways. She jumped in surprise, but Ethan laughed.

"Where have you been, you ugly old bastard?" Ethan's greeting shocked Tara.

"Having a kip down the dugout, where it's not so bloody hot."

She had her back to the man who had just entered the bar but felt herself blush.

Ferris Dunmore caught sight of her and cleared his throat with embarrassment. "For Chrissakes, Ethan, why didn't ye say we had female company?"

Female! Tara grimaced. He made her sound like a species, rather than a woman.

"So you could pretend to be a gentleman? She'd soon have found you out."

The burly Irishman was immediately indignant. "I know how to treat a female, Ethan Hunter. You've been around those bloody camels for too bloody long, but not me. I socialize with real people."

Tara shook her head, not wanting to turn and face the owner of such basic logic. "Obviously, none of these real people are ladies", she muttered.

Hearing shuffling footsteps coming towards her, she felt her blush deepen.

It wasn't that Tara hadn't heard coarse language before. The gipsies were renowned for their colourful language, and, of course, she was guilty of uttering it herself, on many occasions. But there was something about the booming Irishman and the legendary camel driver that made her feel… She mentally searched for the right word. Feminine! That was it. They made her feel more feminine than she'd ever felt in her life. Not the type of feminine where men swooned at her feet, offering their undying adoration. It was more the type of feminine where she was out of her element, unable to cope in her surroundings; too much of a society dame, used to being waited upon by a multitude of servants. A woman she may have become had fate not intervened.

This, of course, was not a good thing. The last thing she needed was to feel incompetent. It brought back recollections of the past, of how useless she had been when she first joined the band of gipsies. Oddly, she felt like history was repeating itself. She had no idea how to cope with the desert heat or the dust and flies… let alone a cattle and sheep station, children, and an ageing aunt. She suddenly wondered how it was she came to get herself into situations that made her feel inept.

"If you don't mind, I'll have a bath before I make your acquaintance," she said, scooting past Ferris with her head down. "I feel just… awful."

The men watched her hurry away in stunned silence. "Was it something I said?" Ferris asked and laughed.

Tara heard Ethan chastise the publican, as she fled down the passageway, towards the bathroom.

"You cuss too much."

She wondered if he even noticed his own profane language.

"I didn't cuss. I only said you've been around bloody camels too bloody long. That's not cussing…"

As she closed the bathroom door, Tara had to smile, deciding Ferris Dunmore had been isolated too long.

It took a few moments for Tara's eyes to adjust to the dimness of the bathroom. As she began arranging her toiletries and towels, and clean garments for Hannah and herself, she suddenly noticed a frightening-looking reptile in the middle of the floor. She didn't know how she had missed stepping on it. As she pressed herself against the back wall, it hissed at her, a darting blue tongue flashing from its mouth. Before she could scream, it scuttled under the tub. Her immediate thoughts were that Saladin had put the lizard in the bathroom. She was certain it wasn't there when Ethan had opened the door only minutes earlier. She contemplated the alternatives, but the more she thought about it, the more she became convinced Saladin was being spiteful, deliberately wanting to alarm her. She'd be damned if she'd let him succeed.

Not telling Hannah there was a lizard under the tub, she called her into the bathroom and quickly washed her, slipping a cool nightgown on her. Then she asked Jack to watch her in their room, while she bathed herself.

Tara lingered in her bath as long as she dared, washing her hair and languishing in the cool water, all the while keeping an eye on the holes in the door to make sure no one was outside. She often glanced at the floor, but the lizard had not come from his hiding place. She felt safe in the tub, as long as it stayed out of sight.

The cool water was a welcome relief from the heat, but the bathroom was as hot as a smokehouse. After dressing, she called Jack, and quietly told him about the lizard, describing it as a small, harmless creature, seeking relief from the heat, rather than a monstrous reptile, almost a foot long, with a darting blue tongue. She told him to bathe quickly and leave it be. Meanwhile she took the little girl into the 'ladies lounge', hoping it would be a sanctuary from the colourful language in the bar. She was wearing one of her new dresses, bought at Mohomet's store, and had pinned her damp hair up, which made her feel cool. Outside the temperature was soaring, but, thankfully, the hot wind had died down.

Ferris came through with a drink for them both and immediately smelt the sweet scent of lilacs, which stopped him in his tracks. Sorrel had given Tara a small bottle of lilac water, to remind her of home. She'd dabbed it behind her ears, a concession to making her feel fresh and sweet-smelling for the first time in several days.

Tara noticed Ferris looked sheepish, as his gaze wandered over her. He seemed to like what he saw. She tried not to feel flattered, as no doubt a female camel would look good to him.

He set their drinks down on a table.

A few moments later, Ethan came through the door mumbling about Jack finding a blue-tongued lizard. He stopped in mid-sentence when he saw Tara. He gave her a strange look, before turning his attention to Ferris.

"Did you say Jack found a lizard?" Tara should have known he'd be too inquisitive to ignore it.

"Yes. In the bathroom. Thankfully you didn't see it. No doubt, your screams would have been heard in Alice."

"Perhaps I'm not a hysterical female," Tara said, lifting her brows.

Ethan's eyes widened. "I think you demonstrated you are capable of hysteria earlier today."

"That wasn't hysteria," she said defensively. "And believe me, I'm not usually so... emotional."

Ethan looked doubtful.

If she had been going to disclose her suspicions about Saladin putting the lizard in the bathroom, she thought better of it. She was certain he would never believe her, and she'd end up sounding ridiculous, like the hysterical female he suspected her of being.

Ethan formerly introduced her to Ferris Dunmore, who, he claimed, had been the publican of the Wombat Creek Hotel for five years. He was a good few inches taller than Ethan, but heavily set, with a booming voice that went well with his bear-like physique. Tara was appalled at his state of undress. He wore a dirty singlet, stretched out of shape, revealing a mat of dark hair on his chest, and no shirt. His crumpled trousers were rolled up to his knees. His enormous feet, void of footwear, were the colour of the desert. Tara didn't know where to look.

"Shouldn't you be dressed, Mr. Dunmore?" she asked. "I know you've been sleeping, but it is the middle of the afternoon."

Ethan tried unsuccessfully to hide his amusement, before excusing himself to bathe.

Ferris glanced at what little clothing he had on, in confusion, then smiled self-consciously. "I am dressed," he said, plonking himself down on the arm of her chair.

"And it's Ferris. No one calls anyone Mr. or Mrs. out here, lass."

Tara thought he smelt like he could use a bath himself, and wished he'd move to another chair,

"Where are ye from, lass?" he asked, taking her by surprise. "I can't quite pick yer accent. I thought it was Dublin, but I'm not so sure."

"I've lived all over Ireland, Ferris, but my family are from Edenderry, in County Offaly."

Thankfully, he made himself comfortable in another chair.

Ferris thought Tara was too young to have lived all over Ireland. "Well isn't that a coincidence? I'm originally from Tullamore, not far from Edenderry."

Tara's heart sank and she fell silent. "What's yer family name, lass?"

Tara was hesitant to divulge personal information. Gossip in country Ireland got around faster than a fever, which meant he might have heard about her past. She had no idea what she was going to say if he mentioned her running off with the gipsies. She craved a new life and wondered how fate could be so cruel. She would always feel she had done nothing of which to be ashamed, in living with the gipsies, but knew from experience, that settlers thought travellers were nothing but trouble. Gipsies were scorned all over the world. That was the plain and simple truth.

Having no choice, she said, Killain, and held her breath. If he knew of her past, she had two options. Plead with him to keep silent. Or pretend he was mistaken. At that moment, she wasn't sure which, if either, she'd choose.

"Killain," he muttered thoughtfully. "I know that name… Is Ninian Killain your father?"

Tara felt her head go light. "Yes," she said, her voice almost a whisper, "Do you… know him?"

"Not personally, but now that I think on it, I believe your aunt may have mentioned her brother having a reputation for breeding the finest sheep. That's probably where she gets her tenacity and good instincts. Mind, even her resolve has been put to the test out here. Over the five years I've been here, many have abandoned their drought-stricken properties, but not Victoria. She's toughened out the hard times, and prospered in the good times, only to suffer more hard times. There's not another like her, man or woman." One glance at Tara and he could see the love shining in her eyes. "Were you close?" he asked.

Tara relaxed slightly. The crisis had passed, for now, and she was eager to hear more about her aunt. "Yes, we were. Does she come to Wombat Creek often?"

"She used to come in fortnightly, like most of the other station owners, but she hasn't been in much in the last year. Her manager, Tadd Sweeney, comes in to get the mail, if Ethan or Rex don't take it out, and pick up supplies. The last time he was here, he said she wasn't feeling so good. I had heard she was having trouble with her eyesight...."

Tara was alarmed. "Is she going blind?"

"Now don't go getting upset. Tadd is a little on the vague side, but I don't think it's that serious. There's a short-wave radio in the office. Give her a call? I'm dying to hear the surprise in her voice when she hears you...."

Tara gasped. "No, thank you. I'd like to surprise her in person." She wanted to speak with her aunt in private and have the opportunity to explain what she had been doing for the past eleven years, and how she came to be with the gipsies. She also had to explain how she came to be the guardian of two children, and she needed to do that in private.

Ethan came back into the lounge, looking fresh in a clean shirt and trousers, and smelling of soap, instead of camels. His dark hair was still damp, and his face smoothly shaven. Tara noticed he had a strong jaw and a well-defined mouth. She couldn't help wondering if he'd ever been married, but she didn't have the nerve to ask him. Although he was a drifter.

"Is Charity visiting her people?" Ethan asked Ferris. "I haven't seen her about and she usually insists on washing my back."

"She went walkabout in the Simpson Desert a couple of weeks ago. I'm expecting her back any day, and it won't be a moment too soon. She used to set the traps for me, and I've got lots of washing and cleaning waiting for her…"

Tara wondered if Charity was his servant or an overworked employee.

Ethan could see she had no idea what they were talking about. "Ferris is married to an aboriginal girl," he explained.

"Married!" He was speaking of his wife. Tara had to sympathize with the poor woman, being treated like a slave. Things were certainly different in the bush if she was expected to wash visitor's backs.

"She goes walkabout every few months," Ethan said. Tara was confused. "Walkabout?"

"The aboriginal's are wanderers, nomads," Ferris explained. "When the mood takes them, they just disappear."

"Oh." Much like the gipsies, Tara thought. Perhaps the people in outback Australia would be more benevolent about gipsies than those from the city. "Charity is an unusual name," she said. 'Peculiar' she really thought.

"It's not her tribal name. I can't pronounce that. I called her Sweet Charity because I thought it was charitable of her to marry an old bast…" He stopped abruptly, but Tara knew what he had been about to say, and hid a smile behind her hand. She cast a glance at Hannah, who was sipping her water, to remind him a child, a little girl was present. Ferris also glanced at the child and bit his bottom lip. "Someone old and ugly, like me," he added, winking at Hannah, who gave him a small, shy smile.

"Actually, I'm hoping she has the baby while she's with the tribe."

"Coward," Ethan said.

"I wouldn't know what to do if she started having it here," Ferris protested, his fleshy, unshaven face going ashen at the thought. "What do I know about birthing…?

"There's nothing to it," Ethan said off handedly. His flippancy made Tara's hackles rise.

"I've seen a bitch have pups, so I suppose it's no different," Ferris agreed.

Tara gasped.

"And I've helped the camel's give birth countless time," Ethan added, as if the two were exactly the same.

"It's hardly the same thing, Mr. Hunter," Tara interrupted, outraged.

Ethan and Ferris looked at each other, and laughed. "Why is it women bite like crocodiles, whenever men make light of child birth?" Ferris asked.

Tara quickly realized she'd been baited, and taken the hook. "Let a man give birth, and the world's population would soon decline." She addressed Ethan, who realised she was not amused by their little joke. "When are we leaving for Tambora?"

He studied her in silence for a moment, sensing her anger hadn't subsided. Tara's eyes narrowed on him. "When? Mr. Hunter," she repeated pointedly.

Aware she meant business, he didn't correct her use of his surname. "That depends on whether you want to camp out one night, or two?"

Tara was cautious. "Is that a cryptic question?"

"No. The answer depends on how practical you want to be. If we leave now, we'll be camping out tonight, and tomorrow night. If we leave early in the morning, when it's cool, we'll be camping out tomorrow night, and arriving on the station late the following afternoon, if all goes well."

Tara understood he wasn't mocking her, so gave his proposal consideration. She had been camping out in Ireland, more or less, for the past eleven years, so she didn't mind at all, except for the snakes, ants, lizards and mosquitoes. Then she remembered Mohomet had given Sorrel and herself a mosquito net and a fly veil each, as a departing gift. She could share the mosquito net with the children, but she wasn't sure how they would cope. Jack would no doubt love sleeping beside a campfire, but Hannah was very young. "I'll leave it up to you. Mr. Hunter," she said, seeming to relax. "It's very kind of you to take us out there."

Remembering he was a poor second choice, and his offer had nothing to do with kindness Ethan tried not to smile. "It's no trouble," he said with a hint of irony. "I have some supplies Victoria asked me to pick up in Alice Springs. I wasn't expecting to be in Alice so soon, so she'll be surprised, and, I'm sure, delighted to see me."

Tara glanced at him with narrowed eyes but did not comment.

"Stay the night," Ferris interrupted. "It will give us a chance to get to know each other. Percy next door can play the fiddle, so perhaps we could dance, Tara? I haven't had a partner for the Irish Jig for so long…."

The thought of dancing with someone as large and uncouth as Ferris, made Tara cringe. She was sure Ethan's camel's smelt better, and certain he would be as light on his feet as a black bear, which he resembled. "I'm sorry, Mr. Dunmore… Ferris, but I'm too tired to dance tonight. Maybe another time."

Ethan decided it was better to stay the night in Wombat Creek, and make an early start the next morning. Tara and the children needed a good rest before tackling the horrendous journey to Tambora.

Ferris dished up his specialty for the evening meal, rabbit stew. It contained only a few small, soft potatoes, and a couple of onions, as vegetables were hard to come by, but it tasted quite good in comparison to what they had been served in The Great Northern Hotel. When Tara told Ferris about the food in Marree, he laughed.

"You'd be sick if I told you what old Harpie cooks up," he said. Tara looked momentarily confused.

"Harpie is Jed Harper, the cook. Didn't you meet him?"

"I don't believe so." She couldn't believe she hadn't met him, as she thought she had met almost everyone in Marree.

"That's not surprising. He keeps his distance from most folk. I shouldn't say this, but he's touched."

"Touched?"

"Not quite right in the head. He spent time wandering about the desert with the Aranda people, so he has a fancy for tribal food."

"I suspected we were eating kangaroo or wombat," she said, pleased with herself, as she thought he believed she'd be mortified if he told her that was the case.

Ferris shook his head, a suspicious twinkle in his eye. "There's nothing wrong with kangaroo and wombat. They're both good eating. I was referring to what we white folk would consider strange."

Tara paled, a stunned expression on her face.

"The vegetables and roots aren't so bad, but he likes termites and sugar ants, and grubs and lizards. Heaven knows what he's been serving you."

"I don't think I want to know," Tara said softly, and hurried outside, where Jack was again patting Oma. "Jack, your dinner is getting cold."

He ignored her.

"What have you done with the lizard?" she asked in a gentler tone.

"Ethan made me let it go," he said.

Tara noticed he referred to Ethan by his Christian name, and felt slighted, as Ethan hadn't suggested she do the same. However, she was relieved he'd let the lizard go, even though he sounded disappointed.

"It could have bitten you," she said.

"Lizards don't have teeth like dogs," he snapped, raising his brows as if Tara had no idea about reptiles.

"Nevertheless, I'm sure it could inflict a nasty bite."

"Darn right," Ethan said from behind her. "If you don't hold them just right, at the back of their heads, they'll latch onto a finger like it's the last meal they'll ever see. You are lucky, boy. That lizard wasn't mean tempered."

Tara glanced at Jack, expecting to see him scowling resentfully, but he was looking at Ethan with an expression of great awe, which made her feel almost envious. She couldn't help wondering if he'd ever look at her like that.

"Tell me about other lizards?" Jack asked.

"Wait till you see a goanna," Ethan said, as he began checking his harness for the buggy, Jack following him. "Some of them are the size of a large dog."

"Cripes! Are there any around here?"

"We'll keep an eye out tomorrow, Jack. I'm sure we'll see one."

Even though Jack hadn't eaten, it appeared food was the last thing on his mind.

An hour later, Tara put Hannah to bed. Ethan was tending his camels, Jack beside him watching everything he did, a plate of rabbit stew in his hand. She noticed Ethan patiently explained anything the boy wanted to know, and appreciated the time he was taking with him. Not wanting to disturb them, she went in search of Ferris and found him in the kitchen.

"Just in time to assist me with the dishes," he said. "I'll deduct the help from your board."

Tara suspected he was serious.

"I would've had them done by now, but I took a plate of food and a drink over to Rex Crawley."

"How is he?"

"As irritable as ever. He knows Ethan's in town, and his mood always takes a turn for the worst when Ethan's around."

"Does Ethan purposely antagonize him?"

"No. They're mates really. Rex just hates Ethan delivering the mail. He can't wait to get back to work, but he has strict instructions from the doctor. He's not to move for several weeks yet. He'd ignore the doctor, but he's too sick. The poor bloke was going stir crazy in his house all day, with nothing to do, so I moved the radio to his house, so he can at least have contact with the homesteads. It gives him something to do, listening to the women gossip."

"Why not give him the mail to sort?" Tara asked. "It would make him feel he's still doing a part of his job."

"We tried that in the beginning, girlie."

"Wasn't he happy doing it?"

"Yes, but he was hoarding the mail away. I found a bag under his bed."

"Do you mean he was stealing it?"

"Not exactly. He intended to keep it until he was well enough to deliver it himself. But the station owners and their staff wouldn't have been too happy getting their mail months late."

While Ferris washed, and Tara dried, he told her about himself. Apparently, he had once owned a pub in County Tipperary, before coming to Australia to make his fortune, mining gold at Timber Creek, in the Territory.

"I lost my fortune gambling," Ferris said, shrugging his huge shoulders. "Then I was speared through the leg by an aborigine, at my hut." He lifted his filthy foot onto the table, which made Tara cringe, and showed her a jagged scar and deep indentation down the side of his shin. It had obviously been a horrific injury. "I'm lucky it didn't go gangrene."

Tara gasped. "Why did the aboriginal attack you?"

Ferris looked sheepish again, an almost absurd expression on a man so large, and dropped his enormous foot to the floor, oblivious to Tara enthusiastically wiping the table clean.

"I had my eye on his woman. Apparently it's customary for the wronged husband to spear the man who wants his wife. He can take three shots, without being challenged, but once was enough for me. No 'gin' is worth getting speared three times for, so I drew my gun and he took off. After I recovered, I went mining again, and made another fortune. I decided to buy the Wombat Creek Hotel before I was tempted to gamble the money away again. My weakness is 'two up'. I just can't resist a game." Suddenly his eyes glinted. "Would you like to learn to play?"

Tara noted the feverish light in his eyes, and knew he really had a problem with gambling. "No, thank you. I don't like to lose money."

He shrugged again "Yer wise beyond yer years, lass." If only that were true, Tara thought.

They finished the dishes and went through to the bar, where Ferris poured himself a beer and Tara a glass of wine she suspected he'd made himself. She didn't like to dwell upon what he might have used. It was very strong, and a little bitter, but palatable.

"Don't you find life out here very lonely?" Tara had felt secluded ever since they left Adelaide. She was sure she could never become accustomed to the isolation in the outback. If was more a sense of solitude, just knowing you were thousands of miles from civilization. That the ocean was so far away seemed inconceivable.

"It takes time, but you get used to it," he said, leaning on the bar. "I could never live in a city again. I married Charity fifteen months ago. With the baby coming, I don't suppose I'll be lonely ever again."

Another man had entered the bar behind Tara, unnoticed, and caught the tail end of their conversation.

"Yer lying old bastard. Lottie made sure you were never lonely, even if it cost you a bob or two."

Tara turned in shock. A slightly built man, aged about sixty, stopped in his tracks.

"Tara, this is Percy Everett," Ferris said, incensed. "The storekeeper, and a bloody liar."

"Fer the love of God, where'd you come from?" he asked her.

"I arrived from Marree today," she said. "Who is Lottie?"

"She's er… a … woman who lives over yonder. How'd you get here?" He scratched his thin, greying hair, perplexed that she should have arrived in town, and he didn't know. "On the train. Where's over yonder?"

"Over… that aways." He vaguely pointed in a northwesterly direction. She wasn't sure whether he meant nearby, or a mile away, or further.

"If there's another woman in town, I'd like to meet her." Tara climbed off her stool. She thought the men would like to talk in private, so needed an excuse to leave them alone. She felt like a walk now the sun was going down, and the chance to talk to another woman was a pleasing prospect.

"You er… can't."

"Why not? I'm sure she'd love the company."

The men looked at each other with mouths agape. "Company is not something Lottie is short of," Percy admitted.

Before they could say another word, Tara went out through the door.

Jack was still with Ethan, helping him feed and brush the camels. She wondered why Percy hadn't seen him.

"You should go to bed soon, Jack," she said. "We have a big day tomorrow."

"I'm not tired," he replied sulkily.

"We'll be finished here in a minute or two," Ethan said. "Jack has been a big help." Tara noticed Jack looked up at him and smiled. She could see he loved working with the camels, and thought a lot of Ethan Hunter.

"Which is Lottie's house?" Tara asked Ethan.

The setting sun had turned the sky a magnificent red, catching Tara's eye. It was almost as red as the desert, she noticed. It was a breathtaking sight, making the surroundings of the town seem even more desolate. A few hundred yards away, in a northwesterly direction, Tara could see three houses squatting in the sandy earth. There was a house much closer, which she assumed was Rex Crawley's.

Looking around, Tara had been too distracted to notice Ethan's look of surprise when she asked which house was Lottie's.

"Lottie lives in the house furthermost away," he said. "Why do you want to know?"

The house looked larger than the others in town, and even from a distance, she could see it was not quite so in need of repair.

"I thought I'd visit her. It would be nice to have a friend in town, and she must be lonely if she lives by herself."

Ethan's eyes widened, and he almost smiled. "Lottie, Charlotte Preston, does not live by herself. She shares her home with Madeline and Corabella."

"Is that what Percy meant by her not being short of company? Are Madeline and Corabella her children, or relatives?"

Ethan fell momentarily silent. "Neither but... I'm not sure you should go over there, Tara."

"Why on earth not? They're friendly, aren't they?"

"Yes. Very friendly, but...."

"There's no 'buts' about it, Mr. Hunter. I'm beginning to think the men in this town are strange. You have not one, but three women, living in a house not a stone throw from the hotel, and none of you seem to want to have anything to do with them."

Ethan shook his head, and looked away. "That's not true, the men... visit, but..."

"I noticed the chicken cage had a card with C. PRESTON on it. I'll take the chickens over. Percy hasn't bothered, and I'm sure they're fed up being in that small cage."

Before he could say another word, Tara had gone.

Ethan watched Tara retrieve the cage of chickens from outside the store and walk towards Lottie's house, off in the distance. He'd always liked Charlotte Preston. She was honest, straightforward and down to earth, and a very successful businesswoman.

Lottie had been a friend to many of the women who found themselves, for one reason or another, in the 'dead heart', with no money, and no prospects. But she'd not found many real friends herself amongst the wider community.

Ethan didn't quite know what to make of Tara. She certainly spoke her mind. As a mother, and a widow, she had a lot to contend with, but something about her told him she wasn't a conventional woman. Even so, he couldn't help wondering how she would react to Charlotte Preston.

CHAPTER NINE

Tara had been under the impression Charlotte Preston was an unmarried woman, but when she saw her home up close, she was suddenly not so sure. Not only was it well preserved, but it was in a far better state of repair than the two cottage homes she had passed to get to it, apparently owned by the miners Ethan had mentioned, who spent little time in Wombat Creek. There were no shingles missing off the roof, or boards missing off the veranda, and the paint, although an unimaginative shade of brown, wasn't blistered and peeling. The two front windows were clean, and had lace curtains behind them, and the veranda had been recently swept. There was a solitary rocking chair at one end, and two large, empty plant tubs stood either side of the front door. In the pots were the shriveled remains of shrubs, evidence of a battle Charlotte had fought and lost with the searing desert heat, and the fiery winds.

Tara knocked and heard a woman call, "Come in." Her voice was inviting, and pleasantly gracious, oddly unexpected in such barren, windswept surroundings, where Tara anticipated the people would be as void in warmth and personality, as the town was in lush vegetation. Up until that moment, no-one had surprised her.

Tara wondered if she'd been seen approaching, or perhaps Charlotte had been expecting someone else. She recalled the attitudes of the men at the hotel, when she told them she was going to see Charlotte. They hadn't said anything specific, but their perspectives had certainly been strange.

Leaving the chickens on the veranda, which faced east, and was relatively cool at that time of day, Tara went inside, expecting to be greeted by Charlotte. Instead, she was startled to find herself in a plushly furnished sitting room, alone. She was particularly surprised, as no one had mentioned Charlotte was well-to-do. Indeed, the last thing she had been expecting to find in Wombat Creek, was someone of means. Someone who didn't have to stay for economical or social reasons, as few as they were.

The sofa and chairs were an unexpected bold red, the audaciousness offset by the cream lace doilies adorning the arms and backs. Several plump tapestry cushions were on each chair and the sofa. A red and blue Oriental rug filled the space in the middle of the floor, also a surprise, as it looked too valuable to tread on. A brass lamp with a tapestry shade, fringed in royal blue, stood in one corner, next to a bookshelf, filled with books.

There was a polished coffee table in the centre of the rug, upon which stood a brass cigarette box and a shiny lighter. Tara looked up at the painting on the wall and gasped. It was of a dancer, a woman Tara thought to be Spanish, but she was definitely gipsy. She wore large hoop ear-rings and a low cut blouse and crimson skirt, exposing coffee-coloured breasts and thighs. It was a beautiful, seductive work of art, but Tara had the feeling it was bought to go with the décor more than anything else. A liquor trolley stood in one corner, but the absence of family photographs or mementos detracted from the homely atmosphere. Overall, it was a lovely room, but the lack of personal items, something to shed light on the personality of the owner, made Tara all the more inquisitive about Charlotte Preston. It was especially strange, as the local hotel was filled with the kind of memorabilia that hinted at the personalities of the talented, or perhaps quirky, inhabitants of the area.

"Hello," Tara called.

A woman appeared through a doorway, a startled expression on her face, as she struggled to remove curlers from her brassy blond hair. Had Tara been feeling charitable, she would have estimated her to be fifty to fifty five years old, but the years had not been kind.

The woman's face was lined and tired, an image made worse by the heavy-handed use of make-up, which looked almost theatrical, especially her crimson lipstick and pencilled brows. She was wearing a filmy nightgown, pale mauve in colour, which not only revealed almost all of her ample bosom; it clashed horribly with her lipstick. A lacy robe, in a deeper shade of mauve, hung over her shoulders. The overpowering, gaudy scent she wore seemed to fill the room.

"Oh! Hello," she stammered, gathering the robe around her in confusion.

"I'm sorry if I'm disturbing you," Tara said, realizing she obviously hadn't been seen approaching. "I brought your chickens over…" She absently pointed in the general direction of the veranda.

"Chickens?" the woman replied vaguely. Tara wondered if she had just awoken.

"Yes. They were left at the store this morning, and it's so hot, I'm sure they could use a drink of water, and Percy hadn't bothered…"

When the woman continued to look uncertain, Tara wondered if the chickens were not meant for her. Perhaps there had been a mistake.

"They had C. PRESTON written on a label attached to the cage. I assumed they were yours…"

Charlotte's mouth softened and her eyes brightened. "Oh, the chickens I ordered from Adelaide. I'm sorry, you must think I'm absentminded, but it was weeks ago. Actually I had given up hope of getting them, with all the shortages…. Thank you so much for bringing them over." She put her hand up to her face, and looked mildly embarrassed. "I ordered them to replace the ones I lost. The snakes were stealing all the eggs and baby chicks, and the damn dingoes picked off the adults. They were good layers, too, and I do like fresh eggs. I had one of the station hands fix me a secure run, so hopefully the dingoes won't get them again. As for the snakes, I've shot as many as I can see around here. There's not much else I can do."

Tara's smile faltered, as a mental picture of Charlotte shooting the deadly snakes Virgil had told her about, came to mind, and she shuddered. If she saw one herself, she'd run a mile. "They're by the front door. Shall I get them?"

"No… dear. I'll take them round the back in a minute."

For a moment they stared at each other awkwardly, both women unsure of what to say next.

Lottie spoke first. "How … er did you…?"

Tara interrupted. "I'm sorry, you are probably wondering who I am. My name is Tara Flynn. I arrived on the train today." She stepped closer to Charlotte and extended her hand, which Lottie accepted, her keen eyes noting Tara's youthful skin, not yet tainted by the parching sun. It looked as soft and velvety as rose petals, and her almond shaped eyes were a magnificent emerald green in colour. She thought Tara striking, and became overwhelmed with melancholy for her own lost youth and beauty. "I'm Charlotte Preston. Folks know me as Lottie."

Tara noted many of her fingers were adorned with enormous, showy rings in amethyst, opal, turquoise and pearl, she suspected to be genuine. "I hope you don't mind me dropping in, but the chickens gave me the opportunity to meet you. It's so… isolated out here…"

Lottie thought she sounded genuinely friendly, a trait she had not seen in strangers for a very long time. "I don't mind at all, dear. Forgive my lack of manners. Please, sit down." She gestured to an armchair. "Would you like a drink? I've got some nice white wine." She suddenly seemed flustered, almost self-conscious. "If you'd rather not…."

"That would be lovely if you are sure it's no trouble, thank you, but only if you will join me."

For a fleeting moment the older woman looked a little overwhelmed. Tara had the feeling she didn't have many friends, or perhaps socialized rarely, which was quite understandable considering where she lived. She thought back to the attitudes of the town folk and wondered why they treated her like an outcast.

"I'd... like that," she said sincerely. "I always have a sundowner."

Tara pictured her sitting alone in the rocking chair on the veranda, surrounded by a barren wasteland of swirling dust in scorching winds. It was a nightmarish insight into her own future, where the thought of such isolation and desolation filled her with dread.

The house was so quiet. There was no sign of Corabella or Madeline, so Tara thought that perhaps Ethan was mistaken about them living with Charlotte. The fact that there was also only one chair on the veranda was perhaps a clue. Then it occurred to her that it was possible she had wrongfully assumed *Corabella and Madeline* were people.

"Ferris gave me something he called 'white wine,' this evening. It was the colour of poached chicken feathers, and tasted like a cross between rotten parsnip and boiled pigs trotter."

Lottie laughed. "You must be a connoisseur of gastronomical delicacies."

"More like disasters! I advise you never to sample my cooking."

"That was a surprisingly accurate description of Ferris' homemade wine. His wife finds him some kind of roots and he makes it from them."

"I imagine wine is hard to come by because of the Depression?" Tara said more seriously.

"It is. I'm fortunate to have a well-stocked cellar. I have a good contact in Adelaide, a... client, related to someone who has a small winery in the Barossa Valley. I've offered Ferris some of my wine, but he won't take it... " Again she looked disconcerted. "He says he doesn't get much call for wine, but I think he'd take it from anyone else..." Her voice trailed off.

"I would have thought in a small town like Wombat Creek, everyone would be close, and help each other. But I suppose living so near can cause other problems, like disagreements, meddling and prying." Tara knew this to be the case in the gipsy camp. The gipsies were fiery, passionate people. Fortunately, they had their own ways of settling things.

Charlotte looked momentarily bewildered. "Yes, that happens in small towns.".

"You mentioned a client. What is it you do?"

Charlotte's expression became blank for a moment. Tara wondered if she had said something wrong.

"Would you prefer red wine, to white? I have both," she blurted out.

Surprised by the question, Tara realized Charlotte was trying to change the subject. "Whichever you prefer. I'm certain it will be much better than what Ferris serves. You are lucky to have a cellar."

"Actually, it's more of a dug out than a cellar, but the temperature is constantly cool, so I keep my wine stock down there, and some foods. But even the butter, when we can get it, still melts. It's a wonder you haven't got a pounding headache from Ferris' home brew."

"To be honest, I didn't finish it."

"Very wise."

While Charlotte poured two glasses of white wine from a fancy decanter on the drinks trolley, and Tara made herself comfortable in one of the armchairs, she wondered what it was she could have said that had upset the older woman. When Charlotte turned back to her, Tara noticed she still looked mildly uncomfortable.

"Are you sure I'm not disturbing you?" she asked, accepting an elegant goblet. "You seemed to be expecting someone, and I've interrupted you dressing…"

"No, dear. I wasn't." She coughed to hide what she couldn't say.

"Are you certain?" Tara wanted to ask why she was wearing so much make-up, if she wasn't expecting company. It seemed highly improbable she belonged to an amateur theatre group in town.

"I'm very sure," she protested. "I'm sorry I'm not dressed for visitors. It's so hot, especially in the afternoons. I wear as little as possible."

It was indeed hot. Even though Charlotte's home was lovely, it was so stuffy." Tara could feel the perspiration trickling between her breasts, and around her neck. She had never felt so hot in her life, and planned to have another bath before retiring.

As if reading Tara's mind, Charlotte opened a window, and a light breeze came in, stirring the filmy curtain. It was like a breath of fresh air from the Gods.

"I was just curious," she said, "how you came to know I lived here?"

"Percy Everett," Tara replied, dabbing at her neck with a handkerchief sprinkled with the lilac water Sorrel had given her. The scent immediately reminded her of her friend, and she couldn't help wondering how she was coping with life in Alice.

Pulling her thoughts back to Charlotte, Tara saw something akin to wariness creep into the older woman's blue eyes.

"What did he tell you about me?" she asked in a slightly shaky voice. Tara could see she almost feared the answer, and decided to be careful with her reply.

"Actually, I was talking to Ferris at the hotel, when we were joined by Percy. I was commenting on how lonely it must be living out here. I've only been here a few short hours, and already I'm feeling the isolation. Ferris was telling me about his marriage to Charity, and the upcoming birth of their child, and how he wouldn't be lonely any more. Percy came in and overheard what he said. He said Ferris had not been lonely because…"

"He visited me," Charlotte finished.

"Yes, that's right."

Lottie's golden skin had turned the colour of cornstarch, but Tara was distracted again, so she didn't notice. She was envisioning Ferris Dunmore at Charlotte's door, in his stretched singlet and rolled up trousers. She didn't even like to imagine his enormous, filthy feet on Charlotte's Oriental rug. In fact, it was near impossible to picture him sitting in Charlotte's elegant living room. Her mind literally boggled trying to imagine how Charlotte dealt with him.

"When I realized there was another woman in town, I wanted to meet you. Percy gave me only the vaguest description of where you lived, so I asked Ethan."

Tara saw Charlotte's expression turn to concern. For a few moments she looked at the woman, realizing something was obviously wrong.

When Charlotte didn't speak up, Tara said, "Ethan wasn't specific, but he gave me the impression I shouldn't come here."

Charlotte looked suddenly stricken, and Tara regretted mentioning Ethan's reaction.

"I should have listened. I must confess I'm impulsive at times. I didn't stop to think that perhaps you don't like visitors, and I am intruding. If that's the case, please forgive me?"

Charlotte straightened her back, and dropped her eyes to her hands. "Ethan was right. You shouldn't have come. It's not that I don't like visitors, I appreciate the company, but really, you shouldn't be here."

"May I ask why not?"

"You really don't know, do you?" she said softly.

Tara shook her head, feeling suddenly naive. What was it she had missed?

"I didn't give Ethan the chance to explain anything. But as far as I can see, nothing needs explaining. You are a woman, living in a lonely place, and I wanted to meet you. Anything else doesn't matter."

Charlotte looked at Tara, as if she wished life was that simple. But she knew it wasn't. "I think I had better specify what I do, Tara. Then you'll understand."

Tara was baffled, but she sat and waited for the older woman to clarify the situation. Charlotte avoided her steady green gaze by staring into the contents of her glass. "This house is ...a bordello."

Tara's eyes widened. Had she heard correctly? Surely not!

The older woman looked up, into her eyes, and saw the bewilderment, the disbelief. "A whore house," she said harshly, her features sombre, her blue eyes glazed with pain. "I am a... prostitute."

Suddenly things the men had said fell into place. Charlotte was never lonely; the men often visited. Tara glanced around the room, realizing it was plushly decorated for a specific purpose. It wasn't meant to be a family sitting room. She couldn't believe she hadn't realized. The clues had all been there. Charlotte's make-up, the fact that she was wearing a nightgown well before bedtime, and the lack of family photographs and mementoes. She thought of the brothels she had encountered in Ireland; dingy rat-infested hovels; the prostitute's diseased, lice-ridden strumpets. Charlotte was certainly a surprise, especially in the outback.

Nevertheless, Tara was annoyed with herself. She was normally very astute, she picked up on things, but she hadn't even suspected. She shook her head, incensed with herself for putting Charlotte in the position of having to explain her situation, and even more upset with the men for not telling her. Since arriving in the outback, her keen senses were way off kilter. In her mind, it was a sure sign she was not meant to live in the bush.

Charlotte took the gesture as one of abhorrence. She stood up, and looked at the floor. "Thank you for bringing my chickens over, Tara." Her friendly tone had been replaced with coldness, a barrier against the pain that seized her each time she was discarded as something repugnant.

"I... I am not here to judge you, Charlotte," Tara stammered.

"You don't have to be polite," she replied, still looking at the floor. "I understand."

"I can assure you I'm not just being courteous." She was hesitant for just a moment. "I know what it's like to be judged and discriminated against."

Charlotte's gaze tentatively lifted to Tara's face. Tara could see wariness and doubt in her expression.

Charlotte desperately wanted to believe her, but she was afraid of being hurt. "Not for the same reasons, I'm sure," she said.

"Not exactly…"

Charlotte turned to look out one of the windows, where she could just see the sun, a blazing fireball, dipping below the horizon. The surrounding sky was a brilliant red, a promise of tomorrow's heat.

She was relieved that such a lovely young woman hadn't had to stoop to selling her body for money. She knew only too well what a degrading existence it was. Girls that had passed through town had told her about some of the unscrupulous madams that ran the bordellos in towns like Darwin and Katherine, and Cooper Pedy, and how ill-treated they had been. Some had ended up very sick, others dead. She had helped as many as she could on the road to a better life, but she had felt it was too late to change her own life. How could Tara possibly know or understand what it was like to be condemned by the community? "The reasons may as well have been the same," Tara added.

Charlotte turned to face her again. She looked sad and very tired. "You are a beautiful woman," she said, thinking Tara could make a good living as a prostitute. She'd certainly attract men. "A blind man could see you come from a good family," she said. "What could you possibly be scorned for?"

Tara considered her position for a moment. She wanted to be open with Charlotte, but she had to be careful. She'd already made that mistake once, opening her heart to Riordan Magee, a humiliating experience that had made her look like a liar and a fool. She vowed she would not do that again. While her thoughts wavered between keeping her secret or sharing it, she looked into Charlotte's eyes, and saw the anguish that lurked in their blue depths. Although her instincts were off-kilter, she felt Charlotte was someone in which she could confide, and maybe sometime in the future she would do so. For now, for her aunt and the children's sake more than her own, she had to remain silent. But how could she be sincere without telling Charlotte the sordid truth?

"Charlotte, I have lived a life that was not unacceptable to the society into which I was born. I wasn't a prostitute…" She faltered, as her emotions threatened to overwhelm her. It happened each time that she thought of her father and Stanton Jackson, and their betrayal, and the consequences. "I'm new in Wombat Creek. I want to leave my past behind..."

"I understand," Charlotte said. "You don't have to explain…"

"I hope you do understand, because I am being as sincere as I dare. I am certainly not going to be a... a fraud, and sit here and judge you. I don't have any right."

Charlotte looked forlorn; as if what Tara had said made little difference. Tara thought she didn't believe her, but Charlotte had noticed the pierced earlobes and the chipped nails and rough skin. She didn't know exactly what kind of life Tara had led, but she did know she hadn't spent the last few years as 'lady of the manor'.

"I know I have no right to ask you to trust me, after all, we've just met. But if you are willing, I'd sincerely like us to be friends."

Charlotte slowly lowered herself onto a chair, in shock, as if she had not heard correctly. "Why? Why would you want to be my friend?"

Tara half smiled. "You can never have too many friends, Charlotte." Her smile waned. "I'm not proud to say, I've had few. This place is so isolated. There aren't many women. It would be nice to have a friend to visit in town."

Charlotte put her hand up to her mouth. "I am sorry. I'm so used to being thought of as trash. I certainly never thought you'd want to be my friend." Tears sprang to Lottie's blue eyes, making them shine. "That is the nicest thing anyone has said to me for a long, long, time."

"I'm serious, Charlotte."

Lottie dabbed at the corner of her eye with a handkerchief. "I can see that. But you don't know what a friendship with me would entail. Even though the stations are many miles apart, you'd be surprised how fast gossip travels, via the radio, and how cruel..." She stopped, and Tara could see the pain she suffered was still raw. "Would you be prepared to have people talk about you?"

"To be honest, I'm used to it." Tara didn't intend to stay out in the middle of nowhere for very long, so what did it matter if people talked about her? Charlotte was a human being, a good woman, as much in need of a friend and acceptance as she was. Tara understood all too well. "In a small community, I know it's only a matter of time before my past surfaces, which means they'll be talking about me anyway. From experience, I know they will eventually tire of it, and move on to something else." This was not necessarily true, but Tara wanted to relieve Lottie of any guilt she may feel about causing her adversity. As a gipsy, the oppression had been endless.

'It has been many years, and they still haven't tired of persecuting me,' Charlotte thought, as she sank backwards into the plush armchair, as if she had suddenly lost all her stamina. Her age and vulnerability were never more evident than in her despondent expression. "In a small town, there's nothing much to move on to, but it would be so nice to have a friend. A real lady." She spoke as if daydreaming about what could be.

Tara laughed. "Don't be too quick to call me a lady, Charlotte. You haven't heard me cuss yet."

The older woman's lips moved in a faint smile. Her face creased into many lines, giving her features a hint of sadness, and wonder. "My friends, few as they are, call me Lottie," she said. "But you have to understand, Tara, we can never openly be friends."

"Why not?" Tara thought she knew what Lottie was going to say, and she was ready for an argument.

Instead, Lottie asked, "Are you going to live on one of the surrounding stations?"

"Yes, God help me. Tambora."

Lottie's face softened. Tara thought she didn't look surprised. "Are you related to Victoria?"

"She's my Aunt. Are you friends?"

Lottie's fragile smile withered, and her eyes seemed to dull. "Heaven's no. Victoria is a real lady, like you. We could never be friends." Real friends, she believed, should be equals. "Your Aunt is one of the finest people around here. She's one of the few people who haven't..." She didn't finish the sentence. Instead, she said, "I respect and admire her immensely."

"I haven't seen my Aunt for seven years, Lottie, but as I remember, she was never a discriminating person. She had many friends, from all walks of life, and she saw them all as her peerage. I'm sure she would never denounce you as a friend because of what other people thought of you."

"She's too nice for that," Lottie agreed, "and a very generous person. But I would not put her in a position where she suffered because of me. And I won't do that to you, either, Tara. Please understand and respect my wishes."

Tara looked at Lottie, and barely nodded. "I'll heed your wishes, Lottie, for now."

Charlotte refilled their glasses. "Come into the other room," she said. "I feel more comfortable there."

Surprised, Tara followed her through the doorway, into a larger room, which served as a kitchen and sitting room. It was immediately obvious this room was where Lottie spent most of her time.

Tara stood just beyond the doorway, her mouth open in surprise. What the first living room lacked in ornaments and knick-knacks, this room more than made up for.

There were pots and ornaments of every description, on shelves, and cupboards, and an old dresser that looked like it had been passed down through the family. There was a comfortable, well worn sofa, over which was a crocheted throw rug, in pinks and blues. Beside the sofa, was a large radiogram. On a side table there was a knitting bag and patterns, and a Singer Sewing Machine stood in one corner. A multitude of utensils and pans hung over the kitchen table. In the centre of the table was a very nice tea set, including a lovely pot, painted with roses. It was the kind of room Tara had been expecting when she entered the cottage. It looked like someone's grandmother's kitchen, homely and inviting. Tara found herself smiling and noticed Lottie watching her.

"I'm sorry," she said. "Earlier, I had been trying to picture Ferris Dunmore in your elegant living room, which, I must admit, I found almost impossible. I still can't see him in this room, amongst all your fragile ornaments."

Lottie visibly winced. "He's so clumsy. Every time he turned around, he broke something, usually something I treasured. Thankfully, now he has a wife, I don't see him, well, not often."

Tara couldn't help laughing. "He showed me the scar on his leg this evening. You know he put his dirty big foot on the table. I was… flabbergasted."

Lottie grimaced. "I insisted he washed in his own bathroom before he came over, but I still made him wash his feet at the back door, so he wouldn't dirty the floor. I can't get close to a sweaty man. I usually let the men use my bathroom, but I made that mistake only once with Ferris. You've never seen anything like the mess he made. If a hundred sheep had been dipped in there, it would have been cleaner."

Tara laughed again. "Judging by the smell of him, he hasn't washed since he was last here, even though he has two bathrooms. Hopefully when his wife returns, she'll convince him of the merits of soap and water."

"I doubt it will be one of Charity's priorities. She's a lovely girl, but that kind of thing wouldn't worry her."

Tara made herself comfortable on the sofa, and Lottie settled next to her, seeming to relax in her own surroundings.

While the women shared another glass of wine, Lottie reached for a nail file and took Tara's hand, and began filing. It was done so naturally, Tara had no objections. Her own nails were filed and painted pink.

"How did you come to…"

"Become a prostitute," Lottie finished.

"I have no right to ask. I haven't been open with you." Tara knew she had no right to ask such a personal question, even though she was a trifle curious. "I was going to ask how you came to be here, in Wombat Creek. If you ask me, it's a terrible place. And surely there's no one here to support your business."

Lottie laughed. "You should be here on the weekend. The town is crowded with people from the stations, and there's always stockmen passing through, and shearers. It's mostly quiet during the week, but you get used to it."

"That's what Ethan told me, but I can't for the life of me imagine myself ever becoming used to it. How did you come to be here?"

Again, Charlotte's smile faded, and Tara almost regretted asking the question. "I was abandoned by my husband in Katherine, in the Territory."

"I'm sorry. That must have been difficult."

"Life with him was difficult. Being left alone was just a different kind of difficult. I'm better off now. I don't have the respect of the community, but I can do what I want, when I want. I have financial security, and the kind of freedom I never had in my married life."

Tara was astonished by Charlotte's story. In some ways it paralleled her own. Having a husband in gaol, and living by the gypsy's rules had been hard for her, but she'd had no other choice, like Charlotte. She hadn't sold her body, but many times it had felt like she had sold her soul, especially when she felt alienated from the rest of the world. Her old friends wanted nothing to do with her, and she couldn't face her brothers, and endure their scorn.

"My husband was a miner," Lottie said. "He worked hard, and had big dreams. I thought those dreams included me, until he struck it rich. He'd always talked about travelling the world. With a pocketful of money, that dream became a reality. Unfortunately for me, he decided his money would last longer if he left me behind."

Tara gasped in shock. "What a selfish swine."

Lottie shrugged her shoulders. "Katherine is a rough town. It's full of desperate men, thieves, murderers, and the greedy. I decided to get out, ironically to avoid being forced into one of the many brothels in town. I decided to travel south, away from the heat and the trouble. I had little money, so this is as far as I got, before it ran out. The hotel was here, but I couldn't afford a room, so I camped outback in a tent." Lottie looked into Tara's green eyes and knew she was curious about how she came to be a prostitute. "Passing stockmen and shearers offered me food, sometimes money. They were lonely, and kind. I know it's a strange thing to say, but I felt better giving them something in return. I've always had trouble accepting charity."

Tara heard the hint of despondency in her voice. Sadly, Charlotte had fallen into prostitution because she was a proud woman. It seemed so unjust.

Tara glanced around the room. "Your home is lovely, and you keep it so nice." Charlotte's eyes shone with pride. She'd finished one of Tara's hands, so Tara gave her the other. "Thank you. I'm quite a handy woman. Being without a husband has a way of making you self-reliant."

Tara immediately thought of her aunt, and the struggle she must have had, running such an enormous station. Then she thought of herself, and her ambitious plans to raise two children without a husband. To achieve that she would have to be very self-reliant. It was just as well that she'd had plenty of practice at coping on her own, with Garvie in prison so often.

"Occasionally I call on one of the local men to do something," Charlotte said, bringing Tara's mind back to the discussion.

"Going from living in a tent, to having such a nice home, is quite an achievement for a woman on her own."

"Someone with a great deal of courage lent me the money to have the house built. I have long since repaid the loan, but it's a kindness I will never forget."

Tara wondered if Lottie was speaking of someone from the area, but felt sure it wasn't someone she had already met.

Over another glass of wine, Tara told Lottie about the shipwreck, and how she came to be the guardian of two children. Lottie didn't ask about the legalities, and Tara didn't offer the details. Lottie was especially interested to hear about the children, particularly Jack. She told Tara she'd once had a son.

"Johnny would have been thirty years old next month," she said, reaching for a photograph, "but the poor little mite died in my arms just three days shy of his fifth birthday, from tuberculosis."

There were other photographs on the shelves, including several of children, but Tara didn't like to ask who they were.

She looked at the sweet little fair-haired boy, standing beside a large, black horse, with a long-handled shovel in his hand.

"He'd been helping his father down the mine," Lottie said. "I wanted another child, but two more pregnancies ended in miscarriage. The years passed, and I never fell again.

I suppose I became too old. It was just Jock and me, until he left me. I often wondered, if we'd had another child, would he still have gone?" Lottie looked up at Tara. "Listen to me. A couple of wines and I'm full of sad stories."

The two women heard a sound in the doorway, and turned to find another woman standing there. She was wearing a filmy nightgown, with no robe. Tara could see the slim outline of her body.

"Sorry to interrupt," she said to Lottie, her voice tainted with a hint of a Welsh brogue, as her eyes slid over Tara. She didn't seem in the least bit embarrassed by her state of undress. "I thought you were talking to Maddy." She looked as if she had just awoken. Her brown hair, which sadly lacked even the slightest kink, was disheveled, and her face was creased on the right side where she had been laying. She was younger than Lottie, somewhere in her late thirties or early forties. She was one of those women about whom there was nothing particularly attractive, but she wasn't unattractive either. Her skin was clear, but lacked a healthy glow. Her eyes were neither brown nor green. Her nose was just a nose, neither cute nor misshapen. She was a woman a man wouldn't look twice at. Tara looked from the younger woman, to Lottie, in confusion. Lottie knew what she was thinking.

"We keep odd hours," she said by way of an explanation, and Tara saw the colour in her cheeks heighten.

Tara guessed the girls had been occupied with customers the previous night.

"Tara, this is Belle. Belle, I'd like you to meet Tara Flynn."

"Hello," Belle said quietly, casually grasping a light robe from inside her bedroom door and throwing it on, almost as an afterthought.

Tara could almost hear the wheels in her head turning. Belle was wondering whether she was being interviewed as a potential worker.

"Ah, Corabella," Tara said, smiling. She glanced at Lottie. "I was told you lived with a Corabella, and a Madeline, and that they weren't your children, or relatives. I was beginning to think they were cats."

"They could be cats. They purr when they're content and sleep most of the day," Lottie said, laughing slightly self-consciously. Tara and Belle laughed too, their raucous awakening Madeline.

"What's all the noise?" she said grumpily, as she stumbled into the sitting room. She had come out of the back bedroom, which went off the sitting room, and had left her door ajar. From where Tara sat, her bedroom looked more like a 'boudoir'. She could partially see a bed with a canopy, draped in red and black netting, and a dressing table with an untidy assortment of powders and puffs, and fancy ornate perfume bottles.

"It's only seven thirty," she mumbled, looking at a cuckoo clock on the wall, then stopped abruptly, for the first time noticing Lottie had company.

Madeline was petite in height, with rounded hips, a small waist, and large breasts. She was far more attractive than Belle. Tara estimated her to be in her late twenties, or early thirties. She had very long, dark hair, almost as long as Tara's. Her skin was fair and quite good, but Tara noticed red lumps on her arms, which appeared to be itchy, as she absently scratched them. Tara assumed they were mosquito bites, as she slapped one of the annoying insects settling on her own hand. Madeline's eyes were a warm sherry brown, and bright and intelligent. Tara did notice she had dark circles around them, a clue that she didn't sleep well in the heat of the day. She was wearing a light blue nightgown, which was surprisingly short, revealing her shapely legs.

"Maddy, this is Tara Flynn, Victoria Millburn's niece."

"Hello," Maddy said, a hint of wariness in her voice. She glanced at Lottie. "I must have been dreaming. I thought I heard a chicken squawking..."

"Oh! The chickens. If there's any snakes still around, they'll soon spot them." Lottie turned to Corabella. "Belle, would you put them in the run and make sure they've got water. They're on the front porch. Tara was kind enough to bring them over from the store."

"Sure," Belle said. "Put the kettle on for me, please," she threw over her shoulder, as she went to retrieve the hapless chickens.

Lottie turned back to Maddy, who appeared somewhat bewildered, as if she was not fully awake. "Remember, I ordered them many weeks ago? They arrived this morning on the train."

Maddy nodded. "We probably wouldn't have got them if it was left to Percy Everett to bring them over," she mumbled sleepily. "He would have given them to Ferris to make chicken stew for a change, and never said a word."

"Ethan would have brought them over," Lottie replied, putting the kettle on the wood stove, and lighting the kindling underneath.

Maddy's eyes lit up; all traces of sleep instantly banished. "Is Ethan in town?"

"Apparently. He told Tara where to find us."

Maddy glanced at Tara again, her eyes sweeping over her, from her head to her toes, before lingering on her face. Her brown eyes seemed to darken with an emotion that could only be described as jealousy.

"Is Ethan taking you out to Tambora?" Lottie asked Tara, as if reading Maddy's mind.

"Yes. Reluctantly, I'm sure."

"Why do you say that?"

"You could say our association got off on the wrong foot. I find him a most difficult man. Arrogant would better describe him."

Lottie laughed. "He's a man who doesn't mince his words, which causes some people to take offence, but he's got a heart of gold."

"Hard and cold," Tara offered.

Lottie smiled. "Just ask Maddy what he's like? She knows him better than the rest of us." Her meaning was not lost on Tara, who glanced back at Maddy, and subjected her to the same scrutiny she had just been treated to.

Maddy, she noticed, was still watching her. Her warm brown eyes seemed to have softened a little. She appeared to have concluded that Tara wasn't the threat for Ethan's affections that she had first imagined.

Tara was thinking she had absolutely no reason to be concerned. He was the last man she would find attractive.

"I had better make myself presentable in case Ethan comes over," Maddy said, turning back to her room and pushing the door to.

"She's fond of him," Lottie whispered, her blue eyes twinkling.

"I can see that," Tara replied, suddenly curious. "Does he visit often?"

"Not often, but he does call now and again. Maddy lives for his visits."

"I heard that," Maddy said, coming to her bedroom door with a hairbrush in her hand.

"It's the truth," Lottie said in her defence.

"I don't deny it. He's one Hell of a man. When a man like Ethan Hunter puts his brand on a woman, she's ruined for any other man."

Tara's eyes widened in surprise. Surely she couldn't be talking about the same Ethan Hunter she knew? He was hardly what she would call a good catch, and certainly no ladies' man. She'd found him to be about as charming as Hannibal.

Lottie glanced at her. "There's not much to compare him to around here, but in Maddy's eyes, Laurence of Arabia couldn't hold a candle to Ethan Hunter."

"He reminds me of Laurence of Arabia," Maddy said dreamily. "Up there on his camel, his strong profile lit by a full moon, shimmering off the white salt lakes."

Lottie laughed. "She reads too many novels," she whispered to Tara, who imagined Maddy taking moonlit rides on Ethan's camels.

"He can take me into his tent anytime," Maddy said winking, "And I won't charge him a penny." She lifted her nightgown and slapped her 'derriere' cheekily.

"Silly girl. I haven't taught you well enough," Lottie said. "Nothing is for free."

"I know. We're sitting on a gold mine. But in Ethan's case, I'd fulfil his every desire in the name of love."

"Maddy," Lottie chastened. "Please remember we have a lady in our presence."

"It's alright," Tara said, remembering the way the gipsy women used to talk about the men. What Maddy was saying was tame in comparison. "I suppose I had better get back to the hotel and make sure the children are sleeping," she said, standing up. "We have a big day tomorrow."

Belle came back into the kitchen. "Would you give something to Percy for me," she asked shyly.

Tara was surprised. "Of course."

Belle disappeared and returned a moment later with a man's watch. "I don't think he realizes he left it here. It was some time ago."

Tara took the watch, and slipped it into her pocket. She wondered why Belle didn't take it to the store herself.

"I have really enjoyed meeting you all. May I call again?"

Lottie looked uncertain.

"Please do," Belle said. "It's always nice to meet someone new in town, other than the men."

"Thank you. I have no idea what to expect out on the station, so I don't know how often I'll get into town, but when I do, I'll certainly call."

Lottie caught the tension in Tara's voice, and realized she was terrified of what she might find out on the station, and with good reason.

"It's not an easy life," she said, "but I'm sure you'll cope if you are Victoria's niece."

Tara thought she sounded like she knew what she was talking about, and realized Lottie's clients probably did just as much talking as anything else. She no doubt knew more about what goes on out on the stations, than the station owners themselves did.

"I'm sure I will," she said with more confidence than she felt.

Lottie walked Tara to the door, and suddenly seemed to feel awkward. Anger towards Percy, Ferris and Ethan, welled inside Tara, for not telling her the truth about the women. Their silence had put Lottie in a terrible position. She decided to teach them a lesson. "Thank you for the wine, Lottie. I really enjoyed it, and our chat."

"I did too."

"I wish I could have been more candid about my own life."

"Enough said, Tara. I understand. Everyone has things they want to keep private. In this game, perhaps more than any other. I just hope your secret remains just that."

"If it doesn't I hope everyone out here gives me a chance, and accepts me for who I am, but if they don't, I'll cope."

"There's no reason they should ever know, especially now you have nice nails."

Tara inspected them. They were the tidiest they had been in years. "Thank you," she said.

"It was really nice meeting you, but remember what I said. We can't openly be friends. If you come back, please, be discreet."

Tara nodded, her green eyes softening. "If that is what you wish. Personally I'd be proud to call you my friend." She turned and walked away, leaving Lottie staring after her.

As Tara made her way back to the hotel, she couldn't help thinking about Maddy and Ethan Hunter. It was quite obvious Maddy was very smitten with the cameleer. What she had said about him putting his brand on a woman, ruining her for any other man, was a complete surprise. Tara presumed Maddy meant he was a good lover, something she found hard to believe. She just couldn't picture him being passionate about anything, other than camels and the outback. Although, it went without saying that Madeline had plenty of experience in the art of lovemaking, and should be able to distinguish a good lover from a bad one. Still, try as she might, she just couldn't picture Ethan making all-consuming passionate love. She blushed at the thought, as she'd only heard about such ardent lovemaking from the gipsy women. She was surprised to find herself imagining Ethan and Maddy in a passionate embrace.

Before Tara reached the hotel, she saw Saladin at the rear, with the buggy Ethan had been working on, and all thoughts of Maddy and Ethan disappeared. A lamp was burning beside him, as it was already fairly dark. The lamp was surrounded by a million flying insects, some quite large. Tara could hear them slapping against the lantern.

As Tara walked near Saladin, she tried not to look at the Afghan, but she could feel him watching her, with his dark, beady eyes, set in brooding features. She was suddenly more certain that ever that he put the lizard in the bathroom. She tried to ignore the sensation of something creepy crawling over her skin, but she couldn't, and glanced at him coldly. He appeared to be cleaning the seat of the open buggy, a large four-wheeled contraption. His actions, short, sharp movements, were filled with hostile resentment. She wished he wasn't going on the trip to Tambora, and silently vowed to watch her step around him.

As Tara walked into the bar, the three men were sitting drinking, their heads together in conversation. She was sure they were discussing her visit to Lottie's house. Hearing Tara approach, they fell silent.

As outside, a light was burning, surrounded by millions of moths, flying in a blind frenzy. She saw small lizards scampering up the walls after a feed, their feet like suction pads. For the first time she noticed the bar had a fireplace, and wondered at the need for it. Then she remembered hearing the desert temperature can plummet to freezing point in the winter.

"Good evening," she said brightly, the sight of Ethan again rousing intimate thoughts of he and Maddy together. With great difficulty, she pushed them from her mind.

The three men looked at her speculatively. Tara noted their anticipation and decided to douse it.

"Are the children asleep?"

"Yes," Ethan said.

"I think I'll go to bed. We have a long trip ahead of us tomorrow. Goodnight." She turned to walk down the passageway, knowing she wouldn't get far before someone commented on her evening. She was right.

"How is Charlotte?" Ethan asked.

Tara turned. "Very well, a lovely lady. I'm really glad I went to meet her." She noticed the men exchange surprised glances.

"I met Maddy and Belle, too." Tara looked directly at Ethan. "Maddy was hoping you'd call this evening, Ethan."

As expected, he looked shocked. Again she wondered how Maddy could find him attractive. He was such a rugged man like he didn't belong indoors. She imagined him more at home around a campfire than anywhere else. Although she had spent almost eleven years around a campfire herself, with Garvie, he was so different to Ethan. At night, Garvie would play his guitar with magical fingers. That, and the way he spoke, in lyrical sentences, made him seem cultured. When he spoke, his words were like syrup, soothing and smooth. Although he had been in prison, and was in reality a thief, he had been charming, and truly believed what he took from landowners belonged to all people. 'If a pheasant can fly, how can it belong to one man?' he used to say when he presented a feast for their dinner.

Ethan was a rough diamond in comparison. He belonged in the desert. "She is? I mean... did Maddy say that?"

"Yes. I got the impression you were quite close friends. She certainly thinks highly of you." Tara was enjoying herself immensely, thoroughly convinced the men had it coming. If she wasn't mistaken, Ethan blushed. Trying to hide a grin, she again turned to go.

"Did er... Were the women ... alone?" Ferris asked.

Tara stopped and half-turned. "That's a strange question. There's no-one here to call on them, other than you men. And you are all here, in the bar. Who did you expect to be over there?"

Ferris half turned away, pretending to wipe down the bar. "I've heard gun shots recently. I wondered..." he mumbled.

"Gun shots? That must have been Charlotte shooting snakes. If you were worried about her, why didn't you go and see what the problem was?"

"His wife's the jealous kind," Percy said, sneering. Ferris gave him a painful elbow in the ribs.

"What about you, Percy? Is there a Mrs. Everett?"

"No," he snapped.

"Aren't you lonely?"

The tables had turned, and now Ferris was grinning at Percy, enjoying his discomfort. "Not that lonely," he said nastily.

Tara's anger was simmering. "Then you don't visit the women?"

"No." He glared at her, his mouth a tight line, his grey eyes hard and challenging, yet fearful the truth might come out.

Tara decided to give him his watch in private, as it was quite obvious the other men did not know he had, on at least one occasion, visited Belle. She couldn't decide whether he was ashamed to admit he was lonely, or ashamed to be associated with the women.

Regardless of Percy, Tara kept up with her needling of the men. "As far as I can see, Wombat Creek must be one of the loneliest places on the earth. Why don't you all get together for dinner, or dances? Personally, I can't understand why the women chose to live in this town in the first place. There's nothing here. But from your point of view, Ferris, and yours, Percy, some population must be better for business, than none." A look of surprise passed between Ferris and Percy.

Ethan was watching Tara closely, trying to work out what was going through her mind. Tara thought she'd give them all something to think about. "Actually, I invited the women out to Tambora for tea. I am looking forward to it."

A smile lifted the corners of Ethan's well-shaped mouth, but Tara noticed Ferris and Percy glanced at each other, agog.

"You can't do that," Percy said.

"I did do that," Tara replied smugly.

Ethan had folded his muscled, brown arms, and was watching her with a twinkle in his eye. He knew what Tara was doing. Yet he was still curious about what she really thought of Lottie, Maddy and Belle. It appeared she liked Lottie well enough to defend her, or her right to be treated fairly, which pleased and surprised him.

"Your Aunt will not appreciate the likes of Lottie and the girls visiting the station,' Ferris declared.

"I know my Aunt well, Mr. Dunmore, and I beg to differ. But perhaps you would like to tell me why you believe she would object?"

"They're…that is…they're not fit to mix with good women."

'And you are fit to make that judgement,' Tara thought, her anger building. She hid her annoyance and said, "Why on earth not? I thought they were all lovely."

"Surely you could tell they're…. prostitutes?" Percy said.

Tara's brows lifted. "Is that something you forgot to mention earlier?"

He pressed his lips together again and dropped his gaze.

"Lost your tongue, Mr. Everett? What about you, Ferris? Did it slip your mind, too?" Ferris stared into his drink, his lips also clamped together.

"I must say, I find your treatment of those women, abominable. When it comes to prostitutes, men can be so hypocritical. Good night, gentlemen."

She turned on her heel and left the bar, which had fallen into silence.

CHAPTER TEN

The sun was merely a quarter sphere on the distant horizon, when Tara experienced the first prickle of oppressive heat, as she roused herself and the children, and headed to the bathroom for what she hoped would be a refreshing wash, her last for at least two days. She was soon disappointed, as even at that time of morning, the bathroom was as hot as an oven, and full of flies and mosquitoes.

The sunlight was dazzling and scorching when the three of them emerged from the hotel. When the air was still, as it was now, Tara noticed the flies descended like a black cloud. When the wind was blowing, stirring up choking dust, it kept most of the flies away. Neither scenario was alluring.

Immediately, Tara knew something was wrong. The buggy had not been hitched to a camel, and Ferris, Percy, and Ethan were standing around idle. Saladin was nearby, tending an impatient Hannibal, who was growling loudly in complaint.

"Is everything alright?" Tara asked, approaching the men with the children in tow. Percy and Ferris turned away. Ethan looked very angry. He cast a piercing glare in the direction of the buggy.

For the first time, Tara noticed all four of the buggy tyres had been ruthlessly slashed. "Holy Mother of Joseph!" she gasped. "How did that happen?"

Ethan was watching her with a steely glare. "I was hoping you could tell me?"

"Me! I have no idea," she said, startled to realize she felt wounded by his insinuation. Ethan's lips clamped together. Tara knew he had spent many hours preparing the buggy for the journey to Tambora, and he had every right to be angry, but she couldn't understand why he was levelling his hostility at her.

"You don't think I... did that, do you?" Even to her own ears she sounded defensive. She just couldn't understand why he would think she'd do something so... pointless.

Ethan looked at her contemplatively. His expression was unreadable in the shadow beneath the wide brim of his hat.

"Mr. Hunter, I want to get out of this..." She stopped herself short, suddenly aware the others were watching and listening. She didn't want Ferris or Percy to be offended by her uncomplimentary opinion of their town. "I thought I had made it quite plain that I am anxious to see my Aunt?"

Ethan nodded, and half turned away in obvious frustration.

Tara studied his profile as he absently kicked a rock in a dusty circle. He didn't appear to doubt her sincerity, but it was evident he was keeping a tight rein on his anger. She had imagined him a man of action, with volatile emotions, and couldn't understand why he wasn't putting all suspects through a grilling cross-examination. After all, there could only be two or three likely candidates in such a small town.

Tara continued to regard him astutely, but Ethan remained grim and silent. She stepped forward and examined the shredded tyres. Whoever had slashed them had been passionate about destroying her only means of transportation to Tambora. There was only one person in Wombat Creek who disliked her so intensely.

Saladin was slyly watching her from a few feet away.

"Jack, please take Hannah inside for a few minutes," she said.

Something in the tone of her voice made Jack do as she asked without question. He glanced at Ethan warily, wondering why he hadn't acknowledged him, then took his sister by the hand and led her inside the hotel. Ferris and Percy tactfully followed.

Tara turned her attention to Saladin. "You did this," she hissed.

The Afghan Cameleer stared at her with a banal expression, but she was sure he had understood her. It was that cold, unemotional detachment that Tara found so unsettling. She was certain staring into the eyes of a snake would be a comparable experience.

"Don't be absurd," Ethan said, jumping to his off sider's defence. "Why would Saladin do such a thing?"

Tara was lost for words. She had no rational explanation for feeling the way she did. "I can't…. I don't know," she admitted.

"You just don't understand the way of the Afghans. Saladin keeps to himself, but he is not a malicious man."

"I certainly got the impression he took an instant dislike to me, and I believe he resents having to take me out to Tambora."

"I can assure you it makes no difference to him. He won't be travelling with us."

"Oh?"

"He's going to the Ghan Town to be with his family for a few days."

Tara felt foolish. "When was this decided?"

"Yesterday evening. I can manage the camels alone with the few supplies I have for the station, so he doesn't need to make the journey."

"Then who slashed the tyres?" Tara asked, folding her arms.

Ethan looked uncomfortable for a moment. "I believe ... Jack did it," he said quietly. "Jack! That is absurd."

"He was very angry when you refused to ride a camel."

"Yes, he was, but he got over it when you said he could ride Maat."

"I don't believe he did. I think he's very troubled. I realize he has recently lost his father, so I will make allowances, but I intend to keep a close eye on him. I can't afford to have my possessions destroyed."

Tara couldn't help feeling protective of Jack, and wary that Ethan was examining their lives so closely. "I realize that," she said, genuinely sorry for the damage to his property. "But spending time with my son does not make you an expert on his personality and problems, Mr. Hunter. It will take time to get over the loss of his father, but that's not reason enough to do something so destructive." A niggling doubt popped into her mind. Jack had lost both of his parents, and she began to consider the remote possibility that his grief could destructively manifest itself. Despite her slight doubt, she continued to discount possibilities. "Jack doesn't have a knife."

"I gave him one yesterday."

Tara was shocked. "You did what?"

"I realize I should have asked your permission, that was my mistake, but he admired it."

"I don't approve of a ten-year-old boy being in the possession of a dangerous knife."

"You must understand that out here a knife is a necessity. There may be an occasion when it could save his life."

Tara didn't want to think about what that meant but decided having the means did not make Jack guilty. "Perhaps so, but nevertheless Jack was asleep when I went into the room last night, and Saladin was still working on the buggy. Percy and Ferris would have nothing to achieve by such senseless mutilation, and neither would the women. That leaves Saladin." She glared at the Afghan cameleer, but he appeared unmoved. There was something about him that made her uneasy.

Ethan shook his head and looked up at the sky, uttering an oath under his breath. "We're not going to agree on this, but that doesn't change the fact that the buggy is no longer usable." He issued orders to Saladin in his native tongue.

Tara was immediately wary. "What are you doing?"

"I'm having a camel saddled for you and Hannah, unless you have decided to stay in Wombat Creek?"

Tara opened her mouth to speak, but shut it again. She knew she had no choice, but she felt panic rising inside her.

"If your riding skills are as good as you claimed yesterday, you will have no problem riding a camel," Ethan stated.

It was clear he was throwing her a challenge. It was in the cocky angle of his head, and the flashing glint in his dark eyes.

Tara looked directly at him, her green eyes smouldering with conflicting emotions, wavering between pride and fear.

Ethan sensed her quandary. "Riding a camel is hardly any different to riding a horse," he said softly. "The ride on a camel is perhaps a little rockier, as they have a different gait, and the reins are a little longer, but you should have no problem at all."

Tara was still not wholly convinced. In her mind, a horse and a camel were as far apart as a dinosaur and a Shetland pony.

"Victoria had planned to enter the Alice Springs Camel Cup on Hannibal when Tom had his accident."

Tara's mouth dropped open. "I don't believe you."

"I swear it's the truth."

Tara remembered her aunt had been wary of horses, and often joked about it. Ninian had kept a carriage and driver at her disposal at all times. If Victoria had been game to ride a camel, then she had no excuse.

She turned to the now saddled Layla, who was kneeling quietly and patiently, and decided she didn't look too foreboding after all. Perhaps riding a camel would not be so different from riding a horse? Her willingness to try might even bring her closer to Jack.

"We had better get going," she said. "I'll call the children."

"I have to warn you," Ethan said, "it's going to be a difficult journey, and I am going to push hard to cover the distance. Is that understood?"

Tara felt apprehensive, but she nodded.

In less than thirty minutes, they were on their way to Tambora. Ethan led the group of seven camels on Hannibal. Once in motion, Hannibal settled into his position like a regal sheikh, leading his harem. Jack, aboard Maat, with baby Oma at her side, followed, then Tara and Hannah, on Layla, and finally Udo, Mosi, and Lilith, who were carrying supplies. Tara noticed when Ethan packed for the trip, he took every precaution to have everything they needed, from extra water, to a first aid box and snakebite anti-venom.

That he was so competent gave her confidence in him. She knew in her heart, she would never have felt so reassured in the desert with anyone else.

As they moved across the gibber plains in a majestic line, Jack turned to smile at his sister. Tara fleetingly considered the possibility of him doing something so damaging as slashing the buggy tyres but dismissed the thought as ludicrous. Although Jack was trying to restrain his emotions, it was obvious he was childishly excited about the trip.

The view from more than ten feet off the ground was amazing. Tara pointed out different things of interest to Hannah, an eagle, a red kangaroo, a lone dingo, a thorny lizard, and an emu. They were surrounded by Mulga scrub and red sand, with only the occasional Acacia Tree, so there was not a lot to see. The journey may have been pleasant, but the flies seemed to hang around the camels in the thousands.

Tara watched Ethan's broad back, as he rode so masterfully, envying the ease with which he handled Hannibal. The male camel was headstrong and powerful, and for the first half-mile or so, he took some strong persuasion to keep his mind focussed. Ethan told Tara he sensed Lilith was coming into season, or what they referred to as musth. Discussing the camels mating habits made Tara wonder whether Ethan had been to see Maddy. She was surprised at how curious she was, and spent the next half an hour trying to think of a way to broach the subject, without sounding like she was prying. Finally she decided to skirt the topic.

"Do you deliver supplies to Lottie and the girls?" she asked.

"I deliver to everyone in the area, from Marree to Alice Springs?"

"Lottie was concerned that people would talk about me if I visited her home."

"That is inevitable. The women out on the stations are lonely. Their husbands spend days, sometimes weeks away at a time, mustering sheep or cattle. The radio is their only link to the other stations, so a lot of gossiping goes on. It's up to you whether you want to live your life worrying about what other people think, or do what pleases you."

Tara had the feeling Ethan always pleased himself. "I liked Lottie, and the girls." Ethan made no reply, but he was glad.

"Lottie told me about her scoundrel of a husband deserting her. Do you know if Belle or Maddy have ever been married?"

Ethan's lip moved upwards. "I can't believe you spent so much time over there, and didn't find out for yourself, Tara. That is so unlike a woman."

Tara felt her cheeks grow warm.

"What you would really like to know is if I visited Maddy last night."

Feeling acutely embarrassed, Tara said, "That is typically conceited of you to think I am that interested in your personal life, Mr. Hunter." She turned away, pretending to take an interest in the passing scenery. If she wasn't mistaken, Ethan laughed.

They ate and drank while moving. By late afternoon Ethan could see Tara and the children were exhausted, but he insisted they keep going. Hannah had been complaining for some time about being saddle sore and constantly shuffled restlessly, but it wasn't until the sun began to set that Ethan decided they make camp.

While he unloaded the camels for the night, Tara and the children collected wood and she made a campfire. Ethan prepared damper, a doughy mixture, which he baked in a camp oven. When it was ready, they spread it with jam. Ethan said he usually cooked lizard or snake for himself and Saladin but thought they might not want to eat bush tucker. Jack insisted he would have tried it. Tara wasn't so sure.

The children fell asleep soon after eating, but Tara wanted one last mug of tea before she retired. Ethan sat on the opposite side of the campfire listening to the night insect's symphony. As tired as she was, Tara couldn't help noticing the stars in the sky. She had never seen so many.

"The sky back home is nearly always cloudy," she told Ethan, when she saw him watching her. "It's either raining or drizzling somewhere in Ireland every day. Drying washing was a never ending dilemma."

"Water shortages are always a problem out here, but your clothes are dry literally minutes after washing them. I can't remember the last time it really rained. It was either late last year or the year before."

Tara was shocked. "That long ago? I never thought I'd say this, but I miss the rain." Even though the sun had gone down, it was still so hot. She longed to lounge in a bath and soak the weariness from her aching muscles.

Ethan drained his mug and slapped a mosquito on the back of his hand. "Where did you live in Ireland?"

She was surprised by his question, and hesitant to answer. "My family are from Edenderry, in County Offaly."

"Is that where you lived with your husband and the children?"

"Not exactly. We moved around quite a lot."

"How did your husband make a living?"

Tara's mind flashed to Garvie, a musician and tinker-come-thief. He'd worked on farms, on fishing boats, and at horse fairs. There wasn't anything he hadn't tried, but he never stuck at anything. Even his art had been pushed by the wayside by his many terms of imprisonment. The children's real father had been a stable man, with a trade.

"Michael was a coachbuilder. He had been offered a position at the Islington Rail Yards, in Adelaide. Did Jack tell you the ship went down just off the coast?"

"Yes."

Tara wondered what else Jack had told him.

"That must have been terrifying. Did the ship hit a reef?"

"No. There was a storm and a fire." Tara became emotional. She really didn't want to talk about the sinking of the ship. Not only was it still too painful, but she didn't want him to guess the truth about the children.

"You build a campfire like a stockman," he said, startling her again. Tara felt her face grow warm.

"You made the Billy tea as if you've been doing it all your life. But that hardly seems possible. That's why I asked where you had lived. I imagine you had a home, yet you know your way around a campfire like a… gipsy."

Tara stared at Ethan wide-eyed, for a moment literally stumped for words. "I learnt from the gipsies. They used to camp on my father's land. I found them fascinating." She hoped her feeble explanation satisfied him.

He noted her heightened colour. She was lying and yet, the children were definitely middle class, and not of gipsy blood.

His next words shocked Tara even more. "You are not the natural mother of these children, are you?" He'd noticed there was no emotional attachment between Tara and the children. She was fond of them and protective, but they did not respond as they would have, had they been her own children. He'd not heard Jack call her momma, although he had heard the little girl calling for her momma. He'd also noticed a mark on her finger where a wedding ring had been. Had her husband just died, surely she wouldn't have removed the ring so soon.

Tara didn't know how to answer him, so continued to stare mutely.

"Were both their parents drowned when the ship sank?"

She had no alternative but to admit the truth. There was no doubt Ethan was perceptive, which meant there no point in lying. She'd look foolish, and he'd soon find out the truth. It was only a matter of time before Jack slipped up.

"Yes, they were," she said softly.

Ethan nodded, but made no reply. No allegations, no accusations. Tara was relieved.

She was far too exhausted to combat any judgements.

Ethan realized his first impression of Tara was way off the mark. It took a special person, someone selfless, to take on the responsibility of someone else's children. And yet he felt sure there was something more to her story.

"There was no room in the life raft for them," Tara said in a whisper. Those few words brought everything rushing back. She turned to stare out into the darkness, as her mind returned to that fateful night. The surrounding blackness reminded her of the cold, dark sea, and despite the heat, she shuddered and wrapped her arms about herself. "Maureen and I had been cabin mates. She was so much fun." Tara choked back tears. "When the ship was going down, Michael put the children in the life raft with me, in case there wasn't room in one of the few left. It was sheer bedlam on the decks, people pushing and shoving. Maureen could have come with us, but she wouldn't leave her husband. I offered to give Michael my place, but he wouldn't hear of it. I should have made him take my place."

"Don't feel guilty, Tara. I'm sure the situation was traumatic for everyone. Imagine how Michael or Maureen would have felt if you had perished?"

"Not worse than I do. What if one day the children blame me?"

"They won't."

"I'll never forget the way Michael looked at me, as the raft was lowered. Never!" Her eyes filled with tears. "He was beseeching me to take care of the children if anything happened. No matter what, I won't let him down." She glanced at the sleeping children. They looked so tragically innocent. "I'm not claiming to be some sort of martyr, I'm very fond of Jack and Hannah." She glanced at Ethan. "Was it my ineptness as a mother that gave me away."

"Your situation is extraordinary, and very difficult. Give it time."

Tara was unable to comprehend his change in attitude. He could have said she was incompetent, but he seemed sympathetic.

"It is the most difficult challenge I have ever faced."

Ethan knew there were far more difficult challenges ahead.

"I want to learn to be a real mother to Jack and Hannah," she found herself confessing.

"All parents make mistakes, Tara. Don't be so hard on yourself."

"It's difficult to admit this, but I envy your naturalness with Jack."

"I was an only child, but I had many young cousins and spent a great deal of time in their home, so I pitched in. Didn't you have siblings?"

"I have brothers, but we were virtually raised by nannies."

"Then you have a privileged background."

Tara made no comment. After an awkward silence she said, "I appreciate the time you have given Jack. He has been so withdrawn."

"That's only natural under the circumstances."

Tara knew he still thought Jack had slashed the buggy tyres, but she still believed Saladin had been the culprit. Time, she imagined, would prove her right.

"Jack seems to really like the camels." Tara didn't realize she sounded mystified by his fascination with the dromedaries, until one corner of Ethan's mouth lifted again.

"Almost as much as you hate them," he said, trying not to laugh. She half smiled. "They're not so bad," she said.

His eyebrows lifted.

"I still think they're smelly creatures." She sniffed at her clothes and wrinkled her nose. "And they make horrible noises, but I suppose I'll get used to them."

"Well, that's progress." Ethan's smile broadened. He looked into the glowing embers of the crackling fire, and seemed to become lost.

The next day passed much as the day before. Ethan said they were heading for a ridge, which appeared to be miles in the distance. The red desert seemed never ending, as did the company of annoying flies, some of which bit very hard.

"Does the lake ever have any water in it?" Tara asked Ethan, daydreaming of a vast expanse of cool water.

Ethan turned in the saddle. "Lake Eyre?" His tone held surprise.

"Yes. Would you believe I purchased a swimsuit in the hope I might finally learn to swim?"

Ethan laughed. "If you are patient, you might be lucky. But there's only been water in the Lake once since European settlement. Floodwaters from Queensland flowed through the Diamantina and Warburton Rivers, and Cooper Creek, into Lake Eyre. I was told it took many weeks to fill, and was very exciting for the few locals. I wasn't here at the time, but some of the old timers still talk about it. Apparently the wildlife that appeared was remarkable. All sorts of migrating water birds and fish, and an abundance of wildflowers. Of course, snakes and dingoes also flourished, because there were more mammals, like hopping mice and longhaired rats. I hope I live to see it happen again. It would certainly be a sight to behold. Inland Australia is not the perfect place to learn to swim? Not unless you go further north, where there are some natural springs. Where did you buy a costume?"

"Marree."

"Let me guess, at Mohomet Basheer's Store?"

"That's right."

Ethan laughed.

It was dusk when the exhausted 'caravan' came upon Ethan's small cabin. Tara pleaded with him to stop and make camp. He had pushed them all day, but she was too exhausted to go another yard, and so were the children.

"How far are we from the station?" she asked, disappointed that they hadn't made it.

"As the crow flies, less than half a mile," Ethan said. "The trouble is, you have to go more than a mile out of your way to get to the bottom of the ridge." Ethan gave the command for the camels to drop to their knees, and Tara and the children dismounted. "You can see the homestead from here," Ethan said, noting Tara's surprise.

Although afraid to see Tambora for the first time, Tara struggled to the edge of the ridge carrying Hannah, and looked down, her heart pounding. At the bottom she could see a ramshackle home that made Ethan's cabin look like a palace. Her heart plummeted like a stone. It was far worse than she ever imagined, but she hadn't the energy to cry. Had she not been holding Hannah, she may have thrown herself off the ridge.

Ethan came up to stand beside Tara, and noted her stricken expression. He followed the line of her gaze, and understood. "Look, over there." He pointed in the direction of some tall, shady trees off in the distance. In the fading light, Tara could just make out an enormous white house between the trees.

She gasped. "Is that Tambora?" It looked so grand.

"Tom had it built in the image of their home in India. It took more than a year to finish the outside. At every stage, they'd slaughter a steer and throw an enormous barbecue, and invite everyone. A lot of the locals pitched in, but tradesmen were brought from as far away as Adelaide and Melbourne for the more difficult tasks."

The house was two-storey, with arched balconies all the way round on both floors. It was so magnificent; it would have suited a Rajah. A light burned in an upstairs room, probably her aunt's, but otherwise the house was in darkness. There were several outbuildings and cottages, one lit up, and several fenced yards, some containing horses, all surrounded by shady trees. There were no lawns or flowerbeds, understandable in the drought, but Tara could just make out potted palms on the verandas.

Tara's smiled broadened, then she began to laugh until tears ran down her grimy cheeks, her emotions a jumble of relief and fatigue.

"Look children," she said, "that is our new home."

Jack's expression was a mixture of mild curiosity and apprehension, but Hannah was too tired to have cared less.

"What were you expecting?" Ethan asked, watching her closely. He suspected he knew.

"The worst," she whispered. She glanced in the direction of the dilapidated homestead below them. Looking at Tambora again, she said, "This is the nicest surprise I've had since I landed in Australia." It's just a pity it's out here in the middle of nowhere, she thought.

Ethan turned to look at Tambora, and spoke softly. "Remember, I told you not to expect too much, and you won't be disappointed."

At first Tara thought he meant she'd had low expectations, and had been pleasantly surprised, but when she noted his concerned expression, she became worried. She looked again at the enormous white house, and her happiness began to ebb. It appeared grand, but when she thought about it, how could her aunt be living such an illustrious life, in such a hostile environment? Surely it was impossible. The drought had decimated the area. She'd seen that for herself. Surely that would have affected her aunt's stock, and in turn, affected her life, and then there was the Depression.

CHAPTER ELEVEN

Before making camp and settling for the night, Ethan unloaded the camels, and with Jack's help, gave them feed and water. Tara found some tinned food in the cabin and put together a quick meal. She then built a fire. While the baked beans and corned beef were heating in a skillet over the coals, she pumped water from a well for a wash, and filled the Billy for tea.

As expected, Jack was more interested in the camels than in food, or a bath. Ethan had his breeding stock in a fenced paddock not far from the cabin. Several of the females had young, two of which were only weeks old. With soft woolly coats and innocent brown eyes, they were certainly adorable, and Jack was drawn to them immediately. While Ethan carefully inspected the animals condition, Tara heard him tell Jack that he sold camels to other cameleer's travelling the interior of the vast continent, but sometimes he was called upon to ferry a large shipment of supplies to mining corporations in areas inaccessible by horse or bullock wagons.

After a refreshing wash, Tara felt almost human again. As darkness descended, they ate their meal around the campfire. Tara noticed Hannah picked at her food, and seemed lethargic. She was wondering whether the child was ill, perhaps suffering heat stroke, when she noticed Ethan watching the little girl.

"I think she's exhausted," he said. "It's been a very difficult couple of days for one so young." He looked directly at Tara. "Actually, you've all done well."

Tara could see he meant what he said, even though he had pushed them. "I'm disappointed we didn't make it to the station," she admitted. "I know we slowed you down."

"Considering you've never travelled such a distance in this climate or on camels, you should be proud you got this far."

Tara appreciated his words. She'd never felt so exhausted; she was literally bone weary. The journey had been hard for Hannah, but she thought Jack had coped exceptionally well. "I'll put Hannah to bed," she said, taking the little girl into the cabin.

When Tara came out of the cabin, Ethan was grooming Hannibal, something she found ironic after she had called the camel a tatty blanket. For all his efforts, Hannibal didn't look any different. Jack was by his side, brushing Oma.

Tara thought Ethan was a complex man. He obviously needed very little in the way of possessions and almost no company to make him feel contented. He travelled light, and kept his life simple. Perhaps that explained his friendship with Maddy. His physical needs were met without any emotional involvement or attachment. He lived an uncomplicated life, which Tara could almost envy for its simplicity. And yet she knew she could not cope with a life of solitude. She needed people around her, and yearned for the kind of love and passion she had not yet found. Above all else, she had always dreamt of having her own family.

In her heart, Tara knew that was why she had taken on the role of the children's guardian. For one reason or another she had been denied the prospect of being a mother. The gipsies had blamed her, but Garvie had blamed himself. Her life with the gipsies had cheated her of many things, including friendships outside the band, and the respect of the community. It had taken her many years to realize approval of her peers, and a family of her own, were two of the most important things to her. She also wanted the love of a man who would allow her to be herself, someone with whom she could feel safe and protected. Although Garvie had meant well, he had been incapable of providing any of these things.

While Ethan and Jack settled the camels for the night in a fenced yard, Tara cleared away their dishes and tidied up; thinking of how grateful she was that Ethan had taken Jack under his wing. Once he went on his travels, she had to learn to cope with the boy by herself, which she knew wasn't going to be easy.

Before retiring, Tara found herself drawn to the edge of the ridge once again, to take another look at Tambora. It was late, and the house was in darkness. A full moon cast its pale illumination over the landscape, making the ghost gums surrounding the house look like unearthly figures standing sentry. The moonlight shimmered off the white walls of the house, and cast gloomy shadows under the arches of the verandas. Again, Tara thought the house was magnificent, but in the glow of moonlight it seemed to have an aura about it, giving the sense it held many secrets and stories. She couldn't believe her aunt lived in such an impressive home, surrounded by arid desert. It was a far cry from her parent's home, a country manor house on a sprawling estate.

A thrill of excitement ran through Tara at the prospect of seeing her aunt for the first time in over seven years, but it was quickly followed by apprehension. She hoped Victoria would be as glad to see her, but the last thing she wanted was to be a burden. That was something she feared, especially as she had the children with her.

Tara went back to the fire and poured herself tea. Soon after, Ethan joined her.

"Jack has finally gone to bed," he said. "He was exhausted to the point of collapsing, but he insisted on helping me."

"He enjoys your company," Tara said, handing him a mug of tea.

"I think it's the camels he's fond of. Not many people take to them like he has."

Tara noted the faint look of pleasure in his features, and his mouth moving upwards at the corner. She fell silent for a few moments, Ethan watching her.

"What is day-to-day life like on a station?" she suddenly asked.

"A difficult struggle, nothing but hard work, day in, day out, year in, year out. But it can be rewarding. There have been very profitable seasons, but droughts can last for years, so the good seasons are few and far between."

Tara shook her head, unable to understand how her aunt had coped. "I'll do whatever I can to help, but surely my aunt has staff? You mentioned a manager."

Ethan knew he had been right. Tara imagined a grand lifestyle came with an imposing house, the very reason he had not told her about Tambora before she saw it. "In years gone by there were many staff, particularly when Tom was alive, but the last few years have been tough, and these days the staff are much fewer. There's something you should know about your Aunt, Tara. Victoria was always a very hands-on person. She was never the boss lady, who gave orders. She'd get out there and do what she could herself. These days, Tadd Sweeney seems to keep things going, but Victoria wouldn't be happy anywhere else but on Tambora."

"Is the station making any money?" she suddenly asked.

Ethan seemed surprised by her directness.

"I know that is a blatant question. The only reason I am asking is because I am curious about whether my Aunt is suffering financial hardship. The Depression is making life difficult for everyone. I was hesitant to come here because I didn't want to burden her."

Ethan could see her concern was genuine. "I honestly don't know. Since Victoria's sight has deteriorated, Tadd keeps an eye on the books. She's never seemed concerned, so he must have assured her the station is still viable."

"What's he like?"

Ethan caught the edge in her voice. "Victoria trusts him and she knows him better than anyone."

"Ferris mentioned her failing eyesight. Do you think the problem is serious?"

"I'm not sure. To be honest I haven't seen her for awhile. I've only seen Tadd or Nerida the last few times I've called. These last few months I've only been home briefly, which is unusual."

"Where was my Aunt when you called?"

"Tadd said she was asleep. She usually lies down in the afternoons."

Tara wondered why Victoria hadn't had her eyes checked. It could be she just needed glasses. She suddenly had the awful feeling something was not right, and became anxious to see her.

"What is that?" Tara asked, pointing west. It was very early in the day and they were travelling towards the homestead on the camels when a cloud of red dust ascended from the horizon and began moving towards them. Tara thought it was some type of weather phenomenon, a cyclone, or a tornado, and she became frightened for the children.

"It's a bit hard to tell from this distance whether it's sheep or cattle, but it's almost certainly a herd on the move," Ethan replied.

Tara gasped. "Is that all?"

"What did you think it was?"

"I… I had no idea. A tornado perhaps."

"You mean a willy-willy."

"What's that?"

"A swirling wind that causes the dust to spiral in cones, sometimes hundreds of feet in the air. They remove valuable topsoil from farms, but don't generally cause too much harm to people or property out here."

Tara remembered seeing something on a smaller scale from the train window, and near Lottie's home.

An hour later, they met the herd not more than half a mile from the homestead, and Tara was being introduced to Nugget, an aboriginal stockmen who worked for her aunt. Ethan and Nugget greeted each other enthusiastically, and exchanged news about the camels. From their brief conversation, Tara gathered Nugget looked after the camels while Ethan was away.

Tara remembered seeing Nugget's photograph in the Wombat Creek Hotel. Face to face, she got a similar impression of a modest man, with a down to earth approach to life and an easy manner. In worn moleskins, and a loose fitting shirt with the sleeves rolled up, dusty boots, and a broad brimmed hat trimmed with crocodile teeth, which partially hid his dark, unfathomable eyes, he was very much a product of his harsh surroundings. Tara assessed his age from the few clues visible to her, a couple of days of beard growth, tainted grey, smooth cheeks and deep lines around his smiling eyes. His seat in the saddle suggested he'd probably spent every day of his near fifty years on a horse.

"Nugget," Ethan said. "This lady is Victoria's niece, Tara."

Nugget touched his hat. "Please to meet ya, Missus. You'll be one big surprise." He smiled broadly, revealing the loss of his two front teeth, which explained his slight lisp.

Tara liked him immediately. There was no pretension. "I've seen some of your artwork. It's very good. Where did you learn to paint?"

Nugget beamed proudly. "My father was one of the best, Missus. He showed me how when I was just a little tacker."

"This is Hannah and Jack," Tara said.

Nugget grinned at the children. "You piccaninnies will have much fun out here. Maybe I can teach you to throw a boomerang, hey lad?"

"What's a boomerang?"

"It's an aboriginal weapon, used for hunting," Ethan explained.

"Can knock a roo's head off," Nugget grinned. When he saw Jack frown, he added, "A boomerang is a curved, flat piece of wood. You throw it right way, and it come back to you."

Jack's eyes lit up. "I'd like to see that, but not a kangaroo's head being knocked off." Nugget laughed. "He make good tucker, lad."

"Where's Tadd Sweeney?" Ethan asked the stockman. He couldn't see him with the herd.

"Back at house no doubt," Nugget replied flatly, "sitting in the shade."

Ethan often had the impression Tadd was lazy. He liked to play boss, giving orders, but doing little himself.

"Better get back to work, and get these sheep to the home paddock," Nugget said. "No feed over west. Bloody locust plague eat everything. They be coming this way. Lot more sheep to herd before the week is out."

"Locust plague?" Tara said aghast.

"They've had rain over west," Ethan explained. "Perfect conditions for locusts. They eat any new shoots that appear, leaving the cattle and sheep with nothing. At least the lizards and snakes will get a good feed of locust."

As they circled the herd, giving them a wide berth to avoid the choking dust, Tara observed that at least three other stockmen were keeping the sheep together with the aid of four dogs. Two were a reddish-brown colour, like the desert. The other two were black and white collies, which moved around the perimeter of the thin, dusty sheep like professionals.

"The reddish-brown dogs are Kelpies, and mainly used with cattle," Ethan told her. "Some of the first pioneers brought over Scottish collies, which were crossed with dingoes. The other two dogs you probably recognise as Border collies, from the English-Scottish borderlands. Fergus, the larger of the Border Collie's, is a prize stud dog. He's sired nearly all of the Collies for hundreds of miles around. To watch him work sheep is a pleasure."

As they left the herd behind, and the clouds of dust, Tara asked Ethan about the wool from the sheep. He told her he usually carted the wool bales on the camels to Wombat Creek, where they were loaded on the train to be taken to Port Adelaide for export. The Depression meant the wool was almost worthless, and transporting it barely worth the trouble.

As the camels dropped to their knees between the trees near the house, Tara's excitement nearly overwhelmed her.

"I'll see if I can find Nerida, the house girl," Ethan said, observing her sudden nervousness. He'd no sooner spoke, than a girl appeared on the front veranda, a broom in her hand. Nerida was a young aboriginal, perhaps no more than sixteen. As Ethan led Tara and the children towards the shady veranda, tiled in mosaic, Tara noted the girl had the shapeless body of pubescent teenager. Her legs were like twigs, protruding from a loose cotton dress. Her flat feet were unusually large. She wore a colourful scarf, securing a shock of wild hair, and her eyes were bright, contradicting her demeanor, which was shy and awkward.

"Nerida, this lady is Victoria's niece, Tara Flynn."

Nerida's already large eyes widened, showing the whites, and she wiped sweat from her face self-consciously. To Tara's surprise, she curtsied awkwardly.

"Welcome to Tambora, Missus Flynn," she said in a small voice.

"Please call me Tara, Nerida, and thank you. There's no need to curtsey. I am not royalty." She'd no sooner said the words, than Eloisa's words, 'You have royal gipsy blood,' flashed through her mind, and she shuddered, as if cold.

Nerida looked embarrassed. "Yes, Missus." She bowed her head. Tara thought she was either extremely shy, or they had few visitors on Tambora. "I am so happy to be here. I just hope my Aunt appreciates the surprise and is pleased to see me."

"She be surprised alright. Missus Victoria not had a visitor for a very long time."

Tara was astounded, and felt pity for her aunt. She must be terribly lonely if she didn't have visitors and didn't get to town, such as it was. Although there was only a handful of people in Wombat Creek, Ferris had said the town was actually crowded on the weekends.

"Where is Victoria?" Ethan asked, ushering them inside the yellow and green tiled foyer, which was cool and dim, after being in the blazing sun. They were greeted by the loud squawk of a white parrot on a stand, which made the children jump with fright. "Hush up, Zac. You crazy bird," Nerida said, and its yellow crest shot upwards.

"Hush up," the bird squawked back.

"Missus Victoria still upstairs," Nerida said. "She be dressing."

"I'd like to go up," Tara said.

"I'll stay down here with the children," Ethan suggested. "Nerida, this is Jack and Hannah. Can you organize them something to drink? I'm sure they are very thirsty." "Sanja in the kitchen." Her brows raised, and so did Ethan's, hinting that Sanja was something of a tyrant.

"We go through," Nerida said.

Tara caught the faint aroma of something unfamiliar and spicy cooking. In the alcove under the stairs, a beautiful grandfather clock chimed ten o'clock. Tara glanced up the grand staircase to the first landing, where she saw a large porthole shaped window of stained glass, mainly in yellow's and green's, which distorted the colour of the blue sky beyond. It was obvious Tambora had once been a very grand home. Tara would have liked to have seen it when Tom was alive.

"First door to the right, Missus Tara," Nerida called, already forgetting she had been asked to drop the "Missus."

Tara stood looking around for a few moments, in utter amazement, letting her senses absorb the ambience of her aunt's home. The house was cool and spacious, with lofty ceilings, but had a sad air of neglect. Potted palms stood everywhere. If they hadn't been in need of attention, a leaf trim and a good watering, they would have given the feeling of a lush oasis after travelling across a desert with very little grey foliage. The entrance foyer was tiled, but needed mopping; the other rooms beyond had polished floors, walls papered in floral, and an excess of lovely old furniture, again in need of a dust and polish.

There were ornaments and knick-knacks everywhere, even a gramophone. Exotic fringed rugs were scattered across the floors. The staircase was polished wood, with a rug down the centre. Tara wondered how often Nerida cleaned a house so large, and whether she had any help, because she would certainly need it.

As Tara stood still for a moment, and closed her eyes, she felt overwhelmed with excitement and happiness. In all her dreams she had never imagined Tambora, although neglected, would be anything so wonderful. She had envisioned a run down homestead built in timber, with one or two small windows, and had dreaded the thought of opening the front door each morning to be greeted by the encroaching desert, a hot, barren wasteland. Although the desert did surround the station, her aunt and her husband had tried to create an oasis. Tara imagined being able to shut the front door of the house, making the dusty plains beyond the trees seem non-existent.

As Nerida led Ethan and the children down a passage, towards the kitchen, Tara climbed the stairs. She paused on the landing to look out of the window, where she got a view of the grounds at the rear of the house, and the outbuildings. She could see stables and a long building, which she supposed was a bunkhouse, surrounded by more shady trees. Behind the bunkhouse there was an overgrown vegetable garden. The corn had gone to seed, and the other vegetation looked like hardy drought toughened weeds. Further away there was shearing sheds and what looked like a cookhouse if the chimney was anything to go by. Off to the right, she could see dog kennels, where there were several pups. She smiled when she thought of how happy the children would be to see the pups.

As Tara watched the pups, a man approached the kennels. Her smile vanished when she saw him raise his hand in a threatening gesture at the pups, which were jumping on the wire. They cowered when he opened the gate, and threw in some food, hunks of raw meat, dark in colour. The puppies had knocked over their water bowl, but she noticed he didn't refill it. Even from where she stood, she could see the kennels needed cleaning. He was not a tall man, and of a wiry build. Tara made a mental note to report his conduct to the manager. With a name like Tadd Sweeney, he was bound to be a fellow countryman. If he was as good to Victoria as Ethan claimed, she was sure they could have an affable friendship.

Tara continued up the stairs, and found the first door on the right, which was slightly ajar. She tentatively walked towards it, her heart thumping so wildly she thought she might faint. Through the door, she could see a dressing table, and part of a rug on the polished floor. Taking a deep breath, she knocked softly, and pushed the door open a few more inches. She could see a woman sitting on the bed. Her profile was familiar, but her hair was tainted grey and untidily pinned in a bun. She was looking towards open French doors, and the veranda beyond, seeming to be thinking about something, or perhaps only daydreaming.

"Aunt Victoria," Tara said, her voice weak to her own ears. The Aunt was barely audible. She was about to try again, when her aunt turned.

"Is that you, Nerida?"

Tara's heart lurched. Her voice was the same, but she was shocked to see her aunt had aged quite dramatically. Tara had worked out that she must be in her late fifties, so she hadn't expected her to look so vulnerable. Her skin was lined and weathered. Even from the distance separating them, Tara could see the light in her eyes, which had always been so bright, had faded.

"You're not Nerida." Victoria seemed confused. "Who…. are you?"

Tara felt tears spring to her eyes. Her aunt didn't recognise her. "It's me, Aunt Victoria," she said, choking back a sob.

Victoria frowned. "Come closer," she said in an unsteady voice.

Tara ventured nearer, her hands wringing something imaginary, her knees weak. For months she had been waiting for this moment and hadn't imagined how nervous she might feel. And her aunt didn't even know her. She was devastated but tried to put on a brave face.

"It's Tara. Surely you haven't… forgotten me, Aunt Victoria?" She inwardly fought the emotion threatening to overwhelm her, but lost the battle and tears began streaming down her cheeks. It was as if the bottom had dropped out of her world.

Victoria slowly stood up and stepped closer. She was wearing a printed cotton dress that needed washing and ironing, and worn slippers on her feet. Tara looked down, watching her tentative steps. Through her tear-filled eyes, her feet appeared to be swollen. Her first steps were a little wobbly, but then she steadied. Her carriage was still erect, and her demeanour proud, that hadn't changed. Tara went forward to meet her. As they came face to face, Victoria placed both her hands on her shoulders, and looked at her closely, at her hair, and her eyes. Her expression changed, her eyes lit up, and her bottom lip began to tremble. "Tara, …is it really you?"

Tara caught the hope in her voice. She hadn't forgotten. "Yes, aunt. You don't know how happy I am to see you." Her words were choked off by a sob.

Victoria enfolded her niece in her arms, and cried tears of happiness. "Tara. Tara. I can't believe it's really you. I have prayed you'd come one day. I've prayed so hard, and now my prayers have been answered."

"I thought you didn't know me."

"I'm sorry. It was such a shock to see someone other than Nerida standing in the doorway. I haven't had any visitors for such a long time, and my sight is not what it used to be. I thought I was imagining things... but how could I forget you? Where did you come from? How did you get here?"

"That's a long story, Aunt. I have so much to tell you. But first I want to know if my being here will be a burden on you?"

"A burden?" Victoria frowned. "Whatever gave you that idea?"

"The Depression has made life difficult for everyone, and life out here must be even harder. I don't want my presence to put a strain on the household."

Victoria shook her head. "What nonsense, my girl."

Tara felt relieved to hear her aunt say otherwise, but a niggling doubt lingered in the back of her mind. She wasn't sure her aunt would admit it if she were a burden.

"I know the Depression has made life difficult for a lot of people, but it's been little more than an inconvenience to us. Tambora isn't thriving, we've had better seasons, but we're by no means struggling. I have excellent help."

Tara was confused. From what she had seen and from what Ethan had told her, it was not possible that Tambora was prospering. She loved her aunt for her kind generosity; it was so typical of her, but she did not know the full story. She did not know that her niece had two children with her, two more mouths to feed. "Aunt Victoria, I have so much to tell you," she said a little apprehensively.

"You must be tired, Tara? Do you want to lie down?"

"No. I'm too excited to rest."

Victoria smiled. "I'll order tea, and we'll have a long chat." She pulled a sash beside her large bed, canopied with mosquito netting, and led Tara out onto the balcony. The view was surprisingly lovely, and the balcony shady, although the faint breeze was very warm. Nearby tree branches almost touched the house, giving the impression they were perched in the foliage, which looked far from lush. White Cockatoo's squawked from the top limbs of the trees, where they were chewing the finer branches. The bird that was in the entrance hall screeched a reply. A crow cawed from a tree further away.

"This is lovely, Aunt," Tara remarked, noting the cobwebs under the eaves, and animal droppings on the ledges.

"If you don't mind having a family of possums run riot in the house, and climb over you at night. They're not native to the area, but Tom brought a pair out here years ago, and the family has grown considerably. Sometimes they wreak havoc."

"Possums!"

"They're nocturnal, and very cute, but unfortunately not housetrained."

Tara moved away from the droppings. "Do they bite?"

"They can, but they're quite tame now. Nerida would like to cook them, but I won't let her."

"Possum stew real good tucker," Nerida said, as she came in carrying a tea tray.

"Can you bring tea?" Victoria asked, just as the girl put the tray on a table. "Oh, you read my mind," she said.

Tara noticed her Aunt's sight was much worse than she had been led to believe. She hadn't seen the tray in Nerida's hands; she'd heard the rattle of cups and saucers.

"You see, Tara. I am well looked after," Victoria said, then turned to the aboriginal girl. "Have you met my niece, Nerida?"

"Yes, Missus. You be surprised?"

"I certainly was. We're going to have a lovely chat and catch up on things. See that Tadd does not disturb us. He wanted to discuss selling off some sheep this morning, but I don't want to talk shop for an hour or so."

Tara watched her aunt as she spoke. There was something different about her mannerisms and speech. Although Ethan had described her as a hands-on person, she played the part of the lady of the house very well. If she wasn't mistaken, it was as if Victoria was re-living her days in India, under Colonial rule. Whether it was the house, and the servants that made her almost oblivious to the real world around her, the flies, the heat, the dust, the drought, the economic battle all the station owners had on their hands, or a state of mind, Tara did not know. Had Ethan not made her aware of how harsh life was, Tara might have been deluded by her aunt's carefree manner. She couldn't help wondering if it was all an act for her benefit.

As they relaxed on the shady veranda, amidst potted greenery, which drooped in the heat, Tara felt able to go into depth about her past life. It was like purging herself of a great pain. Victoria listened, and sometimes asked questions, but was never judgemental. Tara had little difficulty telling her about Stanton Jackson, and the rape. As expected, Victoria never doubted her innocence.

"Aunt, my father didn't believe me. He chose to take the word of an employee. His lack of faith in me broke my heart. I had to run away with gipsies. I couldn't stay at home." Victoria shook her head sympathetically. "My dear, your father is my brother, and I love him dearly, but his one failing is his lack of insight into people. He could tell a champion ewe from an imposter at a hundred yards and had an exceptional eye for a thoroughbred horse, but with people, his vision was impaired."

Tara knew her aunt was referring to her mother. Her father had never been able to see her faults.

"Aunt, I wasn't kidnapped. I believe my father told you I was, but the gipsies were very kind to me. You have to believe that."

"I wasn't sure, Tara. The note you sent me with the portrait was so vague, and your father wanted to believe they had kidnapped you. You have to understand it made it easier for him and your mother." Victoria suddenly looked sad. "He did you a great injustice, and in the process lost you. He was a fool, and I'm sure there's not a day he doesn't wake up and feel regret." She looked out over the scorched land. "Even so, I do miss my brother. We had some wonderful times together."

"How is he?" Tara found herself asking in a small voice.

"I was going to ask you the same question."

"I do not know, Aunt, but I thought you would have kept in contact."

"I haven't heard from him since I came to Tambora. I wrote many times when we first came out here, but he never answered my letters."

Tara went quiet for a moment, while Victoria sipped her tea. Even though she would never forgive her father for his lack of faith in her, she still felt concern for his welfare. He was her father, after all.

"How did you know where to find me?" Victoria asked. "Riordan Magee must have made contact with you?"

"We met under strange circumstances." Tara told her aunt the story of how she went to the gallery to sell her painting, and how she found the portrait of herself.

"I was in disguise, so Riordan did not recognise me at first."

"Why were you trying to hide your identity?"

"A gipsy cannot walk into the prestigious Harcourt Gallery to sell a painting, Aunt. I would have been thrown out on my derrière."

Victoria almost smiled. She'd always had trouble imagining her beautiful niece as a gipsy. "Of course, I had forgotten..."

"When Riordan finally realized who I was, he told me you had been trying to find me."

"I remember receiving a letter in which he said he thought he knew where you were. He said that he felt sure he would soon have good news. I was so excited. I then received a vague letter saying he had made a mistake, but would keep looking. I think I only received one other letter, which was terribly evasive. I didn't know what to think. Finally I came to the conclusion he had lost interest, or been too busy. I didn't like to push him. He did say he would send the portrait back, though, but I never received it."

"I know he was going to send it back, Aunt. He had it packaged and addressed, but I took it from his gallery. That's how I found out where you were."

"I'd sooner have the real thing."

Tara smiled, but it waned as she remembered the portrait went down with the Emerald Star. She decided to tell her aunt what happened when Riordan found her. "The letter you received from Riordan, saying he would soon have good news, must have been sent when he found the gipsy band I was living with."

Victoria gasped in surprise.

"Before he had a chance to speak to me, the gipsy men discovered him in the camp. They are very protective of their women. He didn't get a chance to tell anyone who he was, or what he was doing there."

"What happened?"

"I am afraid they beat him mercilessly."

Victoria gasped again. Tara could almost read her mind. She blamed herself for what had happened to Riordan. Although she had decided against it, Tara had to tell her aunt the truth about Riordan's fixation with a woman who existed only in his mind.

"I've had months to think about it, and I believe it wasn't your fault, Aunt, or mine. From what Riordan himself told me, I've come to the conclusion he was obsessed with 'Tara the gipsy". He thought of himself as her knight in shining armour. When he saw me dancing, entertaining the men, and realized I wasn't a prisoner at the gipsy camp, it shocked him so much he became careless. Unfortunately, it almost cost him his life. The whole ordeal seems to have made him bitter. When I tried to tell him the truth, he was very cynical. I tried to explain how I came to be living with the gipsies, but he

...couldn't accept my story."

"I'm terribly sorry to hear that," Victoria said. "I always found Riordan to be a compassionate man. Maybe there's something we don't know about that made him so embittered."

Tara was relieved her aunt didn't think his preoccupation with "Tara the gipsy" was the cause of his bitterness. She didn't want to believe she, or an illusion based on herself, could almost destroy a man. It was too much of a cross to bear.

Tara went on to tell Victoria about her friendship with Maureen and Michael, and the sinking of the 'Emerald Star.' "My friends drowned, Aunt," she said.

'That is so tragic, dear, but thankfully you were spared. What became of the children? Don't tell me they perished, too?"

Tara paused, suddenly fearful. "No."

"Thank goodness."

"I have them, Aunt. I couldn't leave them to be put in an orphanage and possibly separated."

Tara watched Victoria's reaction very carefully. She appeared to be shocked, but not displeased.

"Of course not," she said. "You are a wonderful girl. You were always so giving."

"You don't mind, Aunt?"

"Mind? I'm delighted."

Relief washed over Tara, but she had to tell her aunt how she really felt about taking on the responsibility of Jack and Hannah, her innermost fears. "I may have acted hastily. I know raising them is going to be an enormous responsibility and I have no way of supporting them. I'm not at all sure I did the right thing."

Jack stood just inside the bedroom doorway and heard Tara's words, and his heart sank. A moment earlier he had been exploring the house. For the first time since losing his parents, he had contemplated a happy future, in a wonderful home. Nerida had been kind, and while Sanja was a little strange, he seemed to like children, and he liked Ethan. He thought Tara had wanted him and Hannah, but it was clear she regretted taking them. He turned and fled down the stairs and out the front door.

"Tara, what on earth are you worrying about?" Victoria said. "Tambora will be your home. You can raise the children here. You will make a wonderful mother. Everything will be just right and dandy, you'll see."

Tears filled Tara's eyes again, and she was suddenly lost for words. 'Just right and dandy' was something her aunt had always said whenever she had been worrying about something. "Just hearing you say everything will work out makes me believe it. You are so kind, Aunt."

"Kindness has nothing to do with it. You have no idea how happy I am to have you here."

Tara could feel the love emanating from her aunt. How could she tell her she wasn't sure life in the outback was what she wanted, especially when she had no other options? She wanted what was best for the children, and being homeless certainly wasn't a preference, especially if the law was hunting her. "I have come to really love the children."

"I know. I can hear it in your voice. You are family, Tara. That makes them family, and I'm sure I'll love them, too."

Tara noticed her aunt's expression suddenly changed, and she panicked. "What is it, Aunt?"

"I was just thinking about Tadd. He's been like family since I lost Tom. Now I am lucky enough to have you, and the children. I can't wait to meet them."

"Would you like me to bring them up here, Aunt?"

"No, dear. We'll finish our tea, and go down."

Tara noticed the breakfast tray beside her aunt's bed and wondered if she usually spent most of the day in her room. "I'm sure Jack is anxious to meet you. Poor Hannah is so young, she hardly knows what's going on."

"They'll soon settle. It's going to be wonderful to have children in the house."

Tara went quiet, and Victoria wondered why she'd never had children of her own. She hadn't yet mentioned her husband.

"I always wanted a family," Tara said, as if reading her mind. "I just never fell pregnant. The gipsies gave me potions, and herbs, and I tried all the tricks they knew, but I just never conceived."

"There could have been all sorts of reasons for that, Tara. Sometimes it takes time. I left it too late, but it's not too late for you."

Tara's eyes widened. "I don't have a husband, Aunt. We parted before I left Ireland." "Oh. That must have been very difficult for you, but in all honesty I'm not sorry to hear it. I never really believed living as a gipsy was the life for you."

"You're quite right, it wasn't. And Garvie was not the right man for me."

Tara went on to explain that her husband was in prison, but she did not go into detail.

As they finished their tea, Tara thought of how wonderful her aunt had been. She'd asked few questions about Garvie, for which she was relieved.

"Aunt, I am hoping to begin a new life out here," she said. "I want to leave my past with the gipsies behind."

"Of course, dear. As far as anyone is concerned, you are a widow with two children. Anything else is your own business, and it shall remain that way."

"It didn't take Ethan long to work out that I was not the natural mother of Jack and Hannah, so I'm sure others will quickly come to the same conclusion."

Victoria looked thoughtful. "We'll say you adopted them after their parents died. After all, that is near enough to the truth. Does Ethan suspect you may have lived an … unconventional life?"

"He has an inkling I lived with the gipsies, but I did not confirm it."

"He won't breathe a word. Ethan has always been the soul of discretion."

"I hope so. I've almost forgotten what it's like to be respected."

Tara was not comfortable with having her peace of mind in the hands of Ethan Hunter, but she had no alternative.

"Wait until all the single men in the area here about you," Victoria said. "We'll be beating them off the doorstep."

Tara shook her head. "I have enough to think about, for the time being anyway." Victoria knew it was too soon, but one day, Tara would change her mind.

As the two women descended the stairs, Tara remarked on Victoria's beautiful home. "It's a white elephant, really," Victoria said, taking the stairs slowly. "Tom had it built to replicate our home in Delhi on the Jumna River, but apart from being cool, it's quite impractical. For one thing, there is so much cleaning. The dust never stops blowing out here. Poor Nerida is run off her feet, and I'm not much help these days. She's been marvelous though. Her mother used to work for me, so Nerida's been helping out since she was about twelve."

"What happened to her mother?"

"Cissie died of a snakebite. She went to Mellie's aid when she was just a pup, and the damn thing literally chased her. Mellie is one of our best sheep dogs. She's not long had a litter."

As Tara thought of the children playing outside, she went lightheaded, but her aunt didn't notice.

"You've no idea how hard it is to train the aboriginal women to work around the house. Their lives in the bush are so different. Things like dusting seem totally irrelevant to them, which of course makes perfect sense. Even watering the palms seems a strange thing to do. Life in India was so much easier. We needed such a large house to accommodate all the staff we employed. This house was of course much too big for just Tom and I. Nerida and Sanja have a room each downstairs, but the other staff, jackeroo's, roustabouts, and shearers, have their own quarters out back. Tadd has the manager's cottage. I think Tom anticipated a family. At one time, he had up to ten aboriginal children running about the place. He sorted of adopted them."

"Where are they now?"

"The Australian Government has a policy of taking them from their aboriginal parents and raising them in white families."

Tara was appalled. "Whatever for?"

"I think they want to wipe out the aboriginal race. It's tragic. Anyway, the end result is a lot of heartbroken aboriginal women, and children who grow up not knowing their real family units. The women with babies try to keep moving, hoping the Government won't catch up with them. If any officials come this way, I lie to them." She didn't like to say that Tadd hadn't liked them around, and he was agreeable to the Government's actions. Tara felt panic rise in her. She wondered if any Government officials would come looking for her and the children. She knew she would have to fully explain the situation to her aunt, and soon.

Victoria thought Tara looked shocked, so she changed the subject. "You won't have seen too many homes out here, but the first settlers built European style homes, instead of homes built to withstand the heat. They're nearly all single-storey, but thankfully some had the sense to put on verandas."

"I saw some paintings of homes on the walls of the Wombat Creek Hotel. I much prefer this house."

Victoria laughed. "Tom would have liked you."

"I was so sorry to hear you lost your husband, Aunt Victoria. It took you so long to find him."

Again, Victoria laughed. "You make me sound like I was desperate."

"I didn't mean that." Tara blushed when she realised what she had meant to say came out quite differently.

"I know. You're as candid as I remember."

As they reached the foot of the stairs, Ethan approached and he and Victoria greeted each other heartily. If Tara wasn't mistaken, Ethan seemed a little taken back when he first saw Victoria. She remembered him saying he hadn't seen her for a few months.

"You look very happy," he said. "Having your niece here agrees with you."

"It's simply wonderful," Victoria claimed. "Thank you so much for bringing her out to the station. I didn't ask Tara how and where you two met?"

Ethan looked at Tara, his dark eyes glinting with amusement. He could see she looked a little unsettled. "She had just gotten off the train in Wombat Creek, and was suddenly overwhelmed with the stark beauty of the area."

Tara's eyes narrowed, daring him to say he found her sobbing in the dirt outside the hotel.

Victoria laughed. "I remember when I arrived here. I was overwhelmed too, but stark beauty had nothing to do with it. I hated the outback and trying to hide my feelings from Tom was near impossible. I cried myself to sleep for weeks."

Tara was surprised, and her eyes widened. "But you are still here," she said in a small voice.

"We're Killain's," Victoria said, putting her arm around her niece. "We're a tough lot."

Hannah came down the passageway with Nerida. "Look, Missy Victoria," Nerida said. Tara could see Nerida was fascinated with the little girl, particularly her golden curls, which she kept touching. She thought again of the aboriginal children being taken from their parents. It was madness.

When Hannah was close enough for Victoria to see, she said, "Oh, Tara, she is absolutely adorable."

The little girl appeared confused by all the new faces.

"Where is Jack?" Tara asked, trying to keep the panic from her voice as she again thought of the snakes.

"He must be outside," Ethan said. "I know he went off to explore."

Tara's eyes widened in alarm. "I'll see if I can find him." She hurried outside.

Victoria went through to the spacious living room and sat down in her favourite chair, beckoning Hannah to her side. The little girl was shy and hesitant, but Victoria produced some candy from a tray beside her chair, and Hannah was soon by her side.

"Tell me all the local gossip," Victoria said to Ethan. "What is Sadie Jenkins up to? And how are Ferris and Percy? The radio is playing up and I haven't spoken to a soul for weeks."

Ethan was alarmed that Victoria should be cut off from the rest of the world, especially now she had Tara and the children with her. He made a mental note to look at the radio and see if he could fix it before he left.

Tara found Jack by the dog kennels. Her heart was thudding with fear as she made her way toward him. "I've been looking for you," she said breathlessly, glancing around to see if any snakes were near. When she finally looked at Jack, she could see he was upset. "My Aunt is anxious to meet you," she said.

Jack ignored her. He had his fingers through the wire, and the puppies were licking them. The bitch, she noticed, kept her distance at the back of the kennel. She was a border collie and very thin and timid. Tara noticed a nameplate on the kennel gate, which read, "Mellie". She remembered her aunt had mentioned Nerida's mother had gone to Mellie's aid when the snake bit her. Tara thought the bitch and pups must be vulnerable in the kennels. The snakes could get to them any time.

"Why are these dogs in cages?" Jack asked, not looking at her.

"I don't know. It doesn't seem right, but they are working dogs. Perhaps it's for their own good." Tara scanned the ground for anything that moved. What looked like a tree branch lay in the dust a few feet away, and she found herself studying it for any sign of movement.

"How could it be for their own good? They hate being locked up."

Tara caught the angry inflection in his voice, and it puzzled her. She sensed his anger wasn't just about the dog's predicament. She had thought Jack would be pleased to have such a nice home, and be a little happier.

"I don't know, Jack. Like you, I am new to life on a station. There is so much we have to learn. It'll take time." She watched Jack, but he showed no emotion. He seemed to have retreated back into his protective shell. She supposed he was thinking of his parents. She realized it was insensitive of her to think a nice home could replace what he had lost. "What do you think of our new home?" she asked nevertheless curious.

He shrugged.

"You know you can talk to me about anything, Jack. I can't replace your mother, but I want to know how you are feeling."

He gave her a scathing look. "Why do you pretend to care?" he asked.

Before Tara could reply, he had run off, around the front of the house. For a moment she was still, in shock. She wondered what had brought on his sudden change of mood. Different thoughts ran through her mind, but nothing made sense. After a few moments, Tara felt she was being watched, and turned her attention to Mellie, cowering at the back of the filthy kennel.

"Come here, girl," she said gently. The dog was hesitant, but wagged her feathery tail. "Come on, I won't hurt you." The pups were already eagerly clawing at the wire of the kennel, longing for freedom. Slowly their mother made her way to the gate. She was very timid, her tail between her legs, her soft brown eyes lowered. Tara put her hand through the wire, and she cowered again, but Tara spoke soothing words of encouragement, and she raised her head to be stroked, almost disbelieving that someone would show her kindness. Her three pups took advantage and began suckling her, draining her already thin body. Tara thought it was high time they were feeding independently, which would allow Mellie time to recoup her weight and strength. She didn't appear to find the raw meat on the floor appetizing, especially with all the flies crawling over it. Tara thought it would soon become maggot infested. She could hardly wait to speak to Tadd Sweeney. Maybe he was not aware of how the dogs were being treated, perhaps too busy with the station to notice.

Tara found her aunt in the living room, with Hannah beside her, happily munching on candy. The walls of the living room were wallpapered in a rose print, which, for the moment, made her feel oddly homesick for the family home in Edenderry. As she turned, Tara was shocked to see one wall consisted entirely of a cabinet filled with guns, which quickly reminded her of where she was, in outback Australia, an uncivilized frontier.

Victoria had a tin on her lap, filled with old photographs she was showing Ethan and the little girl. Jack was no-where in sight.

"Did you find Jack," Ethan asked, when he noted she was alone.

"Yes. He was by the dog kennels, but he's run off to explore some more." She kept her tone light, not wanting to worry her aunt.

"Let him explore," Victoria said.

Ethan could see the concern in Tara's features, but of course, her aunt couldn't. "He's probably with the camels. I must go and give them a drink, so I'll look for him."

"Thank you," Tara said, again grateful that Ethan had taken such an interest in the boy.

"Tara, will you look at this," Victoria said, holding up a picture. "Tell me if it's me in a yellow dress and a big sun hat?"

Tara took the worn photograph, realizing her aunt could not see the detail in the picture. "Yes. You are sitting on a deck chair, under a shelter."

"A shed open on three sides?"

"That's right. You are saluting the photographer with a drink. His shadow is caught on the ground in the late afternoon sun, and there are two nanny goats off to one side." Tara thought Victoria looked much younger, and fitter. What she could see of her hair beneath the hat was still brown, and her face was full and healthy.

"The photographer is Tom. He was always taking pictures, but he hated having his own taken. Would you believe that shed was my home for the best part of year?" Victoria said. "We were blown out in dust storms, and flooded out after it rained for three days straight. We shared our living space with horses, ants, flies, snakes, lizards, even termites."

Tara was shocked. How could her aunt have tolerated such a terrible life?

"That was my initiation into life in the outback."

Tara thought her own initiation paled in comparison. At least she'd been able to stay in the Wombat Creek Hotel.

"Tom said if I could tough that out, I could survive anything." Her tone became wistful. "As long as I was with him, I would have lived on Planet Mars." She smiled sadly. "I can look back now, and laugh. But they were hard times. Nothing, not droughts nor losing stock seemed hard in comparison." Victoria held the picture up close and squinted while she examined it. "That shed is still on the property. It's used for storing feed now, when there is any. The house was a long way from finished when we moved in. The floors weren't covered, and there were no windows, but I couldn't get out of that shed fast enough. I remember begging Tom to let me sleep in the house long before it was ready. He always gave in to me. He couldn't deny me anything. That was why when he said he wanted to live out here, I couldn't refuse, no matter how apprehensive I was. He'd never asked anything of me, but it was obvious he loved this country. At first I wondered why he was bringing me to the end of the earth. There was nothing out here. Only a handful of European settlers, and they all seemed to me to have been touched by the sun. But Tom wanted to prove something to me." Victoria glanced around the spacious room. From a distance, she could no longer see more than shadows, but she could feel all her precious belongings, filled with happy memories, around her. There were carvings of elephants, and wooden statues, woven trays and bowls, brass ornaments, shelves and shelves of books, even a gramophone, and many framed photographs of their lives in India.

"I soon came to love this place as much as he did, but I bet you think I'm crazy."

Tara wasn't sure how to answer her diplomatically, yet still tell the truth.

Instinctively, her aunt knew what she was feeling. "Keep an open mind, dear girl. In time, you'll get a feel for the land. It's a spiritual place. The aborigines taught me that, just as they taught Tom all those years ago."

Tara couldn't imagine herself ever feeling the same affinity for the vast land around them.

A few minutes later, a man walked into the room. Tara looked up from the pile of photographs in her lap, and gasped. It was the man she had seen from the porthole window on the landing.

For a moment, he looked equally shocked to see her, then he smiled, his expression friendly and welcoming. He removed his sweat-stained hat, showing thinning grey hair. His complexion was ruddy, and his hands well worn. He had blue eyes, and bushy brows, and his legs were bowed. Tara thought he was about fifty-five to sixty years old.

"I didn't know you had visitors, Victoria?"

"This is my beautiful niece, Tara, all the way from Ireland."

Tadd laid his hand on Victoria's shoulder. Tara was surprised by the intimate gesture. "Tara, this is Tadd Sweeney, my manager."

Tara went to stand up but realised the photographs would spill onto the floor. Tadd held up his hand to stop her.

"I am pleased to meet you, Mr. Sweeney," she said, trying to keep the shock from her voice. "I've heard so much about you."

"All good I hope," he said grinning. Victoria snorted good-naturedly.

Tara was briefly hesitant. "Of course, Mr. Sweeney." She had the strangest feeling, hardly able to acquaint the man before her, with the man she had seen at the kennels. Unless Tadd Sweeney had a twin brother, he was two people, living in the same body. One was surly and unfeeling, the other friendly and jocular.

"Please, call me Tadd. No-one is formal in the outback. Here for a bit of a holiday, are you, Tara?"

She caught the hesitancy in his voice, almost as if he dreaded the answer.

"She's here indefinitely if I have anything to say about it," Victoria answered. "Tara has come to live with us, and she has two children. This little darling is Hannah."

Tara was watching Tadd while Victoria spoke, and thought she caught a glimpse of surprise in his features, and just the briefest flicker of displeasure, then he was all smiles again. "That's wonderful," he said enthusiastically. "I hope you like the heat, and flies, and dust." He was obviously trying to be lighthearted, but there was an edge to his voice.

"Not particularly, but I'm sure I'll cope," Tara replied. She wasn't at all sure she could handle living in the outback, or even wanted to, but she didn't want to voice her uncertainty to her aunt, especially as she had been so generous in accepting them all, without question.

"There's not much out here for nippers."

"Nonsense, Tadd," Victoria said. "Station life is a wonderful learning experience for children, especially boys. Just think of all you can teach young Jack. I wish I was mobile." She suddenly looked vulnerable again and Tara's heart wrenched, so she didn't notice Tadd looked slightly annoyed.

Victoria addressed Tara. "A teacher from the Presbyterian Mission in Beltana visits the stations where there are children, and leaves lessons, so maybe Ethan could get in touch with the Reverend Guthrie and let him know Jack and Hannah are here. If our radio wasn't on the blink again, we could contact him ourselves."

"No," Tara said sharply. She didn't want anyone to know the whereabouts of the children until she was sure the authorities weren't looking for them.

Victoria looked startled, and Tara could feel Tadd also watching her. "Don't trouble Ethan. I'll give the children lessons myself, and see how I go. Maybe sometime in the future we'll see about lessons from the teacher."

Before Victoria could agree or object, Ethan came through the door with Jack, whose eyes remained downcast. Tara was beginning to worry about him.

"Here he is," Ethan said. "Victoria, this is young Jack, the best apprentice cameleer a man could have."

"How wonderful," Victoria said.

"Now maybe Nugget can concentrate on the livestock," Tadd added.

Ethan glanced at the station manager in surprise, but Victoria ignored his comment.

"Come here, lad, and have some candy before your sister eats it all." Victoria was teasing Hannah, whose face was sticky and pink.

Jack reluctantly came forward and accepted a piece of candy.

"Jack likes dogs," Tara said to Tadd. "He noticed you have kennels at the back of the house."

"That's right, but those dogs are working dogs, not pets."

Tara thought hardness had crept into his eyes, a glimpse of the man she had seen outside by the kennels.

"If you will excuse me, I have some chores to do before lunch," he said, again patting Victoria on the shoulder.

As Tadd left the room, Tara glanced at Ethan who was watching him, and frowning slightly.

"The children can play with the puppies, can't they, Aunt?" Tara asked.

"Of course they can. It's bred in the dogs to round up sheep and cattle. No amount of spoiling them will change that, but Tadd has other views. He breeds the dogs, trains them, and sells them. It's a good side earning for the station. Our kennels are renowned in outback South Australia. Mellie throws the best pups in the state, nearly all champions. Tadd attends all the sheepdog trials. Tom used to enter them with Mellie's mother. He won a trophy every year before he died."

Tara suspected Tadd was breeding poor Mellie to death, but said nothing.

Nerida entered with a tray of cold drinks and some rice cakes for morning tea. In the background loud clanging could be heard coming from the kitchen.

"Sanja very upset," she said to Ethan. "He unpacked the supplies, and say you brought the wrong brand of Turmeric, and you forgot his bay leaves."

Ethan raised his eyebrows, muttering an oath under his breath. "You can tell Sanja I don't know a bay leaf from a gum leaf, and Turmeric is bloody Turmeric. What the Hell does it matter what brand it is?"

"Hush, Ethan," Victoria said. "There are children present. Ignore Sanja's tantrums. I don't want to lose him."

"And he knows it, so he rides roughshod over you, and you take it."

"I certainly don't, but no-one cooks a Beef Vindaloo like Sanja."

"A what?" Tara said.

"It's a blazing hot curry," Ethan said, "and by the smell of it, he's making one for your lunch."

"But I don't eat curry," Tara said aghast.

Ethan laughed. "Then you are going to starve because Sanja curries everything, and I mean everything!"

Tara glanced at the children. If they weren't all going to starve, she had better brush up on her cooking skills.

She suddenly had an alarming thought. She didn't have any cooking skills!

CHAPTER TWELVE

Just before noon, Riordan Magee slipped into the gallery with the morning paper tucked under his arm and made straight for the sanctuary of his office. Kelvin Kendrick was busy with a client but caught a glimpse of him disappearing into his office, and felt his face grow warm with shame, grateful the client had his back to him. With his hair uncombed, and wearing a soiled raincoat, Riordan looked more like one of the dishevelled vagrants that meandered down the lanes off Grafton Street, searching for food scraps and shelter, than the owner of the prestigious Harcourt Gallery.

It was a depressing day, bitterly cold, drizzling and windy, which suited Riordan's morose mood perfectly. He ignored the pile of paperwork and mail on his desk, and slumped into his chair, removing a half-full flask of rum from his top draw and taking a mouthful, before turning to stare at the rivulets of water running down the windowpane.

A few minutes later, Kelvin came in, barely disturbing Riordan's state of despondency. "We've just sold the 'Cherubs on Ice'," he said. It was a prized Stuart MacDowel painting, but Kelvin's excitement was quickly tainted with disappointment when he noted the physical and mental state of his employer. Each day he seemed to deteriorate more.

"Who bought it?" Riordan asked with barely veiled disinterest. A few months ago he would have been suggesting a celebration lunch with Kelvin accompanied by a bottle of his favourite Bergerac Rosé or Merlot/Cabernet Franc from his own private stock. Now he could barely arouse a response.

"Ronald Cavan purchased it on behalf of Lord Richard Grantland of Sussex, England. He didn't even quibble about the price." Kelvin studied Riordan to see if he was even listening. It was evident his curiosity was minimal. "The sale and subsequent healthy profit means we won't have to close our doors this month," he said flatly, growing irate that Riordan showed no curiosity in their financial dilemma, leaving him to shoulder all the worry.

Despite his forlornness, Riordan recognised Kelvin's tone and brand of satire. Clearly, he was worried about his own position.

"Should it become necessary, Kelvin, I'll supplement the gallery with my own funds," he said dejectedly. "Rest assured, you won't have to stand on the unemployment queues just yet."

Kelvin picked up on the irony of Riordan's words and felt a mixture of grief and exasperation. How long could that go on?

The gallery had been losing money for several months; a fact that apparently hadn't registered in Riordan's altered state of mind. For quite some time Kelvin had been vetting the mail, particularly correspondence from the bank. He was more aware of the Gallery's financial position than it seemed Riordan was, but he couldn't say anything without disclosing he had opened mail that was deemed private. The loss of sales subsequently meant Riordan's fortune had been dwindling too, although he seemed to be suffering the delusion that it was infinite. What really angered Kelvin was that Riordan had no idea of the sacrifices he'd already made to save the gallery, Riordan's reputation, and his own position. As far as Kelvin was concerned, his penances were far more costly than Riordan would ever know.

Ronald Cavan was well connected in the society world. He'd worked as a broker for some of the more influential of the English and Irish aristocracy. Although he was well respected for his work, he was not liked personally amongst those few that detected something queer about him. However, others had eagerly sought his services, and asked him to discreetly solicit sexual partners for a select group of acquaintances that could only be described as warped. In Kelvin, Ronald Cavan had recognised traits that made him perfect prey, greed, a yearning for sexual excitement, and an unhealthy dose of ambition. In return for Kelvin's cooperation, Cavan was willing to recommend affluent clients for the gallery. For several weeks, Kelvin had been attending clandestine meetings Cavan had arranged. Now, as he looked at his employer's emotionless expression, as he wallowed in self-pity, Kelvin became furious. Riordan had no idea how deviant some of the so-called elite could be, nor did he have any knowledge of some of the distasteful acts Kelvin had been coerced to perform.

Riordan was, however, aware that Kelvin was no martyr. Had he known of his manager's sacrifices, he would have had cause for concern in regard to his ambition and high aspirations. Kelvin saw himself ultimately rewarded as the future owner of the illustrious Harcourt Gallery.

Riordan sighed raggedly, and Kelvin felt his elation at the big sale evaporate. It was patently clear that Riordan had absolutely no interest in the business whatsoever, and quite frankly, Kelvin was fed up with his melancholy. Apart from his extra-curricular activities, he'd been doing all the work at the gallery himself, as if Riordan wasn't there at all, and he might well not have been for all the input he'd given, or the few hours he graced the gallery with his presence. The fact that Riordan hadn't even bothered to shave today, and his shirt looked as if he'd slept in it, was further proof that his mental state was taking a further downward slide. He was becoming a liability to the gallery. Kelvin was tempted to ask him if he'd been at the gaming tables all night, but knew that was not the case. He'd even lost interest in cards, something Kelvin had never imagined would happen. He also knew the gipsy woman was the reason Riordan had lost his stamina and will to succeed, just as he had years ago when in search of her. He almost wished he'd find her, and get her out of his system, once and for all.

As Kelvin stood watching Riordan, he thought it seemed almost ironic that what he had in his pocket could be the key to ending his employer's pain. Removing an envelope he had planned to conceal from him, he slid it amongst Riordan's other mail.

"There's an obituary notice in the paper today that might be of interest to you," he said, his tone a mixture or resignation and sarcasm. He left the office in a huff.

For a few moments, Riordan continued to stare out of the window. "An obituary notice? Whatever was Kelvin on about? Why would he be interested in an obituary? He suddenly thought of his family but quickly dismissed the notion that one of them had passed away, as he would certainly have been notified if only to be told he had been disinherited. He knew Kelvin was a gossip, so decided it must be one of the gentry that had expired. No doubt Kelvin knew all the ins and outs of the family history, and who was going to inherit what, and who was to be left penniless. At times he seemed to revel in other's misfortune, spitefully enjoying their downfall. Riordan had always felt he was a very jealous person, assuming it was because of his own humble beginnings.

Several minutes later, out of mild curiosity and habit, Riordan opened the paper in the hope the deceased would have some valuable art he could obtain at a bargain price. He perused the list of names of the recently deceased and gasped when he came to 'Killain'. Ninian Killain had passed away at his home in Edenderry ten days ago. He was only fifty-two years old. Riordan scanned the names of the bereaved family members, desperately searching for one in particular. He found a notice that mentioned Tara and her brothers, Daniel and Liam, and Ninian's wife Elsa, but even amongst the numerous other mourners and family members, Victoria was not mentioned.

Riordan realised it was unlikely Victoria would yet know her brother had died. It would take months for a letter to reach her, although there was an overland telegraph line across Australia, it was unlikely it took in the small town of Wombat Creek. He knew he should contact her, had known it ever since Tara had appeared at the Gallery several months ago. He just didn't know what to tell Victoria about her niece, or how to tell her Tara was not a captive, and he had no idea of her whereabouts. He was pondering this quandary as he sorted through his mail, and an envelope with eloquent writing caught his attention. He turned it over and saw that by a strange twist of fate, it was from Elsa Killain.

Kelvin looked up from his paper work to see Riordan hurriedly leave the gallery. He hadn't any doubt his departure had something to do with Elsa Killain. His anger was peppered with relief that at least Riordan was doing something other than sitting brooding and drinking himself into a stupor.

Riordan barely had time to go home and change his clothes and shave, before his meeting with Elsa in the tearoom at the Green Acorn Hotel. Since reading her short letter, he had been wondering why she had chosen such an unlikely hotel to meet him. As it was, he arrived barely moments before she did.

Riordan and Elsa Killain had met once, briefly, many years ago, when he had personally delivered a valuable painting to her home in Edenderry. At the time, his business had been at a precarious stage of development, and Ninian had held promise of being a very good client. On that visit, Riordan was barely aware that Elsa and Ninian had a daughter. They made fleeting mention of her, as he remembered, saying she was on a sojourn with an indulgent aunt, but Ninian spoke at length about their sons. It was soon afterwards that Tara went missing, about the same time, he now realised, that Ninian Killain lost interest in buying valuable art.

From Riordan's brief contact with Elsa, he had gained the impression she was pretentious and aloof, her main concern being the observance of proprieties, and remaining unscathed by gossip. As she came through the hotel dining room door, dressed in a plain black dress and heavy coat, a single strand of peals at her throat, he was overwhelmed with an entirely different assumption. The woman who approached him with a faint smile on her pallid lips, and noticeable strain in her gaunt features, was a far cry from the woman he had met years ago, who had been confident and remote. He couldn't help feeling sincere empathy for her loss. In his opinion Ninian Killain had been a true country gentleman.

"Hello, Mrs. Killain." Riordan accepted her outstretched, gloved hand, as he looked into her watery green eyes, shadowed by dark circles, which suggested many sleepless nights. It struck him immediately that her colouring was a washed-out version of her daughter's. What he could see of her hair beneath her stylish but conservative hat, was a blanched orange, whereas Tara's was a rich coppery hue. Her skin looked as if someone had dusted it with cornflour. Tara's skin was the colour of honey kissed by the sun, her cheeks rosy and vibrant. "Please accept my condolences. I've only just read about your loss in the paper this morning."

"Thank you, Mr. Magee," Elsa said, as Riordan pulled out a chair for her. Once seated, she struggled to remove her gloves. He considered the possibility she was bereft to the point of being barely able to function, but when she spoke, her voice, although shaky at first, soon steadied. "I do appreciate you being able to meet me on such short notice."

"The postal service is appalling of late. Your letter arrived this very morning."

Odd, she thought. She'd posted it more than a week ago. "Then I am very lucky indeed, and must apologize if I have caused you any inconvenience."

Riordan's impression of Elsa completed its transformation. Her tone was warm, not at all reticent, and her simple attire and lack of flashy jewelry banished all thoughts that she was ostentatious. In fact, although she seemed fragile, he sensed they were going to have a very candid conversation.

"In your letter you mentioned the desire to sell some works of art."

"I'm afraid it's necessary. I must apologize for being so cloak and dagger, but I didn't want to come to the gallery and give the gossip's fuel. We've suffered their wrath long enough, and even now there seems to be so much speculation about Ninian's sudden death."

"I understand," Riordan mumbled as an automatic response, when in fact, he didn't. He presumed they had suffered being the substance of gossip, in view of Tara's indiscretion, but he couldn't help wondering why there should be so much conjecture about Ninian's death.

"I know this hotel is a little out of the way, and..." She glanced around, "a little down market, but they do serve very reasonable.... nice afternoon teas. I hope you don't mind meeting me here?"

Riordan was becoming more inquisitive by the minute. Elsa looked embarrassed that she had all but admitted she was watching her pennies. Riordan wondered how things could be so bad that she had to resort to selling art works and finding value for money places to take tea. "Not at all, Mrs. Killain."

"Please, call me Elsa, if I may refer to you by your Christian name, Riordan, isn't it?"
"Of course." Riordan ordered Devonshire teas for two.

They discussed different works of art that Elsa owned. It was clear she was undecided about which to sell. It would have been easier if the paintings had been purchased as an investment, but this was not the case. Ninian had genuinely loved fine art. It appeared to Riordan that Elsa felt she was somehow dishonoring his memory, by selling them off, so he tried to make the decision as painless as possible. He gently explained which would fetch a good price and attract a buyer. Unfortunately they were her most valued treasures, purchased by Ninian in Europe.

Pulling herself together, Elsa knew what had to be done. She was keen for a quick and discreet sale, preferring, if possible, that the paintings go back overseas, to avoid further rumor. Riordan explained that is was quite likely only someone aristocratic in Europe could afford the paintings, and suggested they be auctioned at Nickleby's Auction House, or Sotherby's, or even Wolf's, for a hasty sale.

"I feel it is necessary to explain my unfortunate predicament, Riordan," she said.

"It is not essential. You've just lost your husband…"

"I lost him years ago," Elsa replied dryly.

There was an awkward moment of silence. Riordan didn't understand her remark, but didn't like to push her for reasons for making it.

"Eleven years ago, we lost our only daughter…"

Riordan's chest tightened. "Tara," he said softly.

Elsa was no longer surprised that almost everyone knew of her family's shame. "That's right. I'm afraid that's when we lost Ninian, too. I'm sure you've heard snippets of gossip, but in case you haven't heard the truth, our daughter ran away with a band of …gipsies." It almost tore her heart from her breast every time she thought about the 'gipsies'.

Riordan remained silent. He didn't feel right about telling her that Tara had told him a far-fetched story herself, or that she had been bitter that her parents hadn't believed her 'account' of a farm manager raping her.

"Ninian told our friends she'd been kidnapped. He couldn't face the … shame. If I were telling the truth, I'd admit he could have faced it, but he knew I couldn't. From that point of time, he took no interest in our property or livestock. The boys tried to help, but they were too young and inexperienced, and neither was gifted with their father's business acumen. After years of agonizing over the future, Liam decided to go to sea. Daniel married an English girl and lives in Cornwall. He's a …tin miner, I believe." A look of anguish crossed her face. It seemed inconceivable that one of her sons was now a miner. "Both boys felt they were deserting me, but I couldn't see them suffer, trying to deal with Ninian's seemingly never ending melancholy."

Riordan looked down at his tea, understanding all too well. He wondered if Tara had any idea how much her family had suffered because of her foolish, impulsive actions.

"Ninian died a long and slow death, from a broken heart," Elsa said. "He never understood that it wasn't really his fault that Tara ran away..."

Riordan's gaze shot up and he frowned. "His fault...?"

Elsa's expression was pained. "He blamed himself." She could see that Riordan was baffled, and looked mildly uncomfortable for a moment. "You have to understand that Ninian and Tara had always had a special bond. She and I were never very close, she was her daddy's girl."

Riordan felt the blood drain from his face. "But why would he blame himself for her running away? How could it possibly be his fault?"

Elsa looked down into her cup, as if searching the tea leaves for answers. She suspected Riordan had heard sensationalized stories, partial truths. "Something terrible happened the night of Tara's eighteenth birthday. It's very difficult to discuss." She glanced around the quiet tearoom, with it simple décor of blue and white tablecloths and old cutlery with yellowed ivory handles, composing herself.

Riordan's thoughts raced. He knew what she was going to say, but he didn't understand why. They hadn't believed Tara's story years ago. What could have changed?

"Our farm manager at the time ... attacked Tara that night. No one knew the truth, except our daughter. I'm ashamed to say we didn't believe her."

Riordan noticed Elsa's eyes became bright with tears, and he had a sickening feeling in the pit of his stomach.

"I thought she was covering a romance with a gipsy. Her father thought she was lying outright because she'd been caught in a compromising position with a man highly unsuitable. I could blame the shock, but there is really no excuse..."

"No one could blame you for doubting her story," Riordan said, echoing his own rationale. When he saw Elsa frown, he rushed on. "I mean, you must have trusted this man, the manager."

Elsa looked down. "To be honest, Ninian was on the verge of firing him for drinking during working hours, which makes our mistake all the more unforgivable. It's tragic that Tara ran away before Ninian found out she had been telling the truth. We should have trusted our daughter, Riordan. That we didn't... was unjustifiable. Ninian's suffering came from knowing that the vicious assault she suffered, and the shame, were not the reasons she left. He believed she ran away because he had doubted her, in a sense, betrayed her. He'd taken an employee's word over hers, something he never forgave himself for. I'm ashamed to say my first concern was for her reputation, and worse, ours."

Riordan felt his heart thudding like a leaden weight. Elsa was right. That was the reason Tara had run away. She felt her father had betrayed the special bond between them. "How did he find out the truth?"

"The man... Stanton Jackson, was killed by one of the gipsies. The police discovered the gypsy's identity and searched for him for years. Quite by chance, they found they had him in custody earlier this year for another matter. I believe he is to be hanged."

Riordan gasped. He hadn't been aware of the murder. Surely it hadn't been Tara's husband.

"We assumed Stanton had died from pitchfork wounds to the head and body, and that he had no other injuries, but when the autopsy results came back, it was reported his back, and the backs of his arms, were covered in dog bites. They were matched to our dog's teeth."

Riordan tried to recall Tara's words. She had mentioned the dog coming to her rescue, in fact, she had said it was possible the dog had saved her life.

"At the time he was found dead in one of the stables, he was lying on his back. When he was moved, it was assumed the blood on his back came from the pitchfork wounds, as the pitchfork was nearby. Ninian knew the dog would never have attacked him unless he was harming Tara. He was shattered when he found out the truth. He went in search of Tara, but couldn't get close to any of the gipsy camps. He paid several gipsies for information, but nothing ever came of it. I think they took his money, but ignored his pleas for news of her. He hoped and prayed that one day she would return home. Each day she didn't, a small part of him died. I prayed she'd return before it was too late, but my prayers weren't answered. I doubt she will ever come back now." She sniffed, holding back tears. "Anyway, it's quite likely there will be no home to return to. I'm afraid I am going to have to sell the farm and lands, although God only knows who will have the money to purchase property, even at a bargain price."

For a few minutes they sipped their tea in silence. Riordan's emotions were floundering. He too, had judged Tara incorrectly. She had been telling the truth, and he hadn't been able to bring himself to believe her, all because he had been afraid of suffering the same gut wrenching disillusionment he had suffered the night he went to the gipsy camp. For the past few months, since he last saw her, he'd known deep down in his soul that she had been telling the truth. It had been killing him to ignore it.

"A few months ago, Tara came to the gallery to sell a painting," he said quietly.

Elsa looked up in surprise, not sure she had heard correctly. "What did you.... Did you say you've seen Tara? My Tara? How can you be sure it was her? You've never met her, have you?"

"I hadn't met her personally until earlier this year, but I had a portrait of her."

Elsa looked confused.

"I should start at the beginning. Many years ago, Victoria asked me to find Tara."

"Victoria? The last I heard of her, she was in some far off...uncivilized country, where there are wild natives and no neighbors for hundreds of miles." The crinkle of Elsa's nose gave just a hint of the pretentious landowner's wife.

"Australia."

"That's right."

"Have you been in contact with her?"

"We haven't heard from her for many years. She wrote to Ninian from ...Australia, but he never answered her letters. He loved his sister, but he wasn't in a fit state to deal with her or anyone else. I knew she travelled a lot, so I assumed she had moved on. That is why I never wrote myself." She glanced down at her hands, and whispered, "Victoria doted on Tara. I didn't know... what to tell her." She glanced away, fighting tears. "Do you know where Victoria is? I should notify her of Ninian's death."

"I have an address."

She nodded. "Tell me what you know of Tara, Riordan, and don't spare me the details." Riordan realized Elsa thought the worst, and he could hardly blame her. "When Victoria last came home on a visit, Tara sent her a gift, a portrait of herself. Victoria sent it to me so that I might recognise Tara if I came across her."

Riordan watched Elsa digest this news, anxious to see her reaction to what he had to say next. "It had been painted by Tara's... gipsy husband, and Victoria thought he might try to sell others at the gallery."

"Husband! She's married?" Elsa's eyes filled with tears. "Has she ...children?"

"No." Riordan didn't want to tell Elsa her daughter's husband was in prison, possibly for the murder of Stanton Jackson. "She told me she planned to leave the gipsies, and ... her husband."

Elsa was surprised, and secretly relieved. Although she didn't wish her daughter any pain, she was comforted that she had come to her senses and left the gipsies. "Do you know where she is?"

"No. She said something about buying a cottage by the sea."

"Oh. That's positive news, isn't it?" Elsa's features lit up, taking years from her face. "I must find her, Riordan. Will you help me?"

He gazed at her softened features, filled with hope, and knew without a doubt that he would do anything to find Tara now. He prayed she would forgive him his doubt in her. "Yes, of course I will."

"Oh, Riordan. You don't know what it will mean to me to have my daughter back." She hoped it didn't sound like she didn't want to spend her life alone, although that was true. The last ten days had been the loneliest of her life.

"I think I do," he said softly. He wasn't sure Tara would ever forgive her mother, as she had made it perfectly clear she would never forgive her father.

Elsa studied Riordan, sensing her daughter had made quite an impression on him. This pleased her, as she felt sure he would leave no stone unturned to find her. She couldn't help feeling regret that Tara hadn't married someone like him. They would have been perfectly suited, he was handsome and successful, and although Tara had sometimes been a little willful, she had been poised and very beautiful. Elsa shuddered to think what she would be like after spending several years with the barbaric gipsies.

She stood up. "We must begin at once, Riordan."

For the next four weeks, Riordan searched each and every village along the East Coast of Ireland. He recruited the help of two private investigators, a retired police officer with a dubious record and severe case of gout, and an almost blind but talented would-be Sherlock Holmes, who enlisted the 'sight' of a young protégé. They searched the Northwest and the South coasts, but not one positive sighting or lead materialized.

"Elsa," Riordan said, when they met again in the tearoom at the Green Acorn Hotel, "I have uncovered nothing. It's as if Tara vanished into thin air."

"She can't have," Elsa said despairing. "You don't think she went back to living with the… gipsies, do you?" The thought clearly appalled her.

"No. One of the investigators I hired has a connection to a source amongst the gipsy community, and he said she is not with the gipsies."

"Is this source reliable? The gipsies are very secretive. Ninian could find out nothing."

Riordan nodded, knowing all too well what the gipsies were like. "I believe his informant is very dependable." Riordan remembered the exorbitant fee that had to be offered for the information, but deemed it worthwhile. He only wished he'd known of the source the last time he had been searching for her. It would have saved him a lot of pain and suffering.

"Then what could have happened to her?"

Riordan looked reflective.

"Have you an idea?" Elsa asked. She could see Riordan looked uncertain. "Even if it's only a hunch, it's better than nothing."

"It's far fetched, but I am going to try and find out if she left Ireland."

"Left Ireland? Where do you think she would go?"

Riordan looked at her thoughtfully, and Elsa's mouth dropped open.

"Do you think it's possible she went to …Australia, to be with Victoria?"

"I believe it's a distinct possibility. I am on my way to the shipping office now. Would you like to accompany me?"

Elsa nodded. "How would Tara know where to find Victoria?"

"Do you remember I mentioned she came to my office?"

Elsa nodded.

"That day I had my manager parcel up the portrait Victoria had sent me, to be shipped back to her. As I have had no word from Victoria, it may be safe to assume it didn't get there. I think Tara may have taken the parcel from my office. Victoria's name and address were on it."

"Maybe Victoria is no longer there," Elsa suggested, becoming disheartened. She couldn't believe Tara would travel all the way to Australia, alone.

"I believe Victoria is still on the station in Australia. I have no reason to think otherwise. If she had come back to Ireland, she would have tried to contact Ninian. From her letters, I gathered she loved the life on the station, and was committed to staying there. In fact, after her husband died, she wanted Tara to help her run it."

Elsa was clearly astonished. She couldn't imagine the Victoria she knew living amongst livestock and dust, in a country so vast. She had always been a society belle.

"I understand Victoria's husband was very wealthy, and they built an extraordinary home, which Tara would someday inherit."

Elsa was pleasantly surprised. This news certainly changed things.

"My manager claims to know nothing about Tara seeing the address on the portrait, but he is a little intolerant of ... gipsies, and Tara was rather defensive and hostile towards him, so his word in this matter is questionable." Riordan was certain Kelvin would try to cover up any helpful clues, but believed it was highly likely Tara may have seen the portrait and the address. "I know it's a slim chance, but I have no other leads."

By late evening, Riordan and Elsa had the information they were seeking, but obtaining it had been far from an uneventful course. The Depression meant wheels didn't turn unless they were greased, and there were many bureaucratic wheels to oil to get the information they needed. Eventually they were told at the shipping office that Tara had left Ireland, bound for Australia, on October 6th. Their emotions had suffered a full gamut when they learned the Emerald Star had gone down off the coast of South Australia, and many had perished. It took two agonizing hours to find out a copy of the list of those that did not survive could not be located. They spoke to a former crewman working in the shipping office, who thought Tara Flynn was on the list of the deceased, but when he saw a photograph of her that Elsa tearfully produced, he was almost certain she was one of the survivors.

As they walked away from the shipping office and climbed into Riordan's Model T Ford, Elsa made a decision.

"Riordan, I believe my daughter is alive, and I want to go to her. Will you take me?" Riordan was stunned. "I have the gallery, Elsa. I can't go to Australia." If he were being honest with himself, he would admit that the thought had already crossed his mind, but he'd dismissed it as implausible madness.

"Surely business is very slow, Riordan. Couldn't your manager look after things for a few months?"

Riordan didn't want to admit Kelvin had been running the gallery single-handed for many months. He knew if he hired an assistant for him, Kelvin could really concentrate on lifting the business. Since his thoughts were more sober in the last few weeks than they had been in months, he realized Kelvin would do better without him, at least until he could give the business his full heart. As it stood now, it was in a far off land, in the hands of a beautiful gipsy girl.

CHAPTER THIRTEEN

Tara and the children jumped with fright when Nerida hit an enormous gong in the dining room, and the sound reverberated through the entire house, like a deafening echo.

"Lunch is ready," Victoria announced, casually getting to her feet. "I hope you are going to join us, Ethan?"

"As much as I like your company, Victoria, you know that curries are not to my liking," he said.

"You like Dhal, and Naan bread. I had Sanja make some just for you."

Tara could see that Ethan wanted to get back to his camels, but he was unable to refuse such a gracious host.

They followed Victoria into the dining room, where an enormous table had been laid with fine cutlery and bamboo place mats. It was the middle of the day and stifling hot, despite open doors and windows. The last thing Tara felt like was a hot lunch. She had an unquenchable thirst, but her appetite had completely deserted her.

Several bowls and platters containing a variety of steaming foods, which Tara could only describe as completely foreign, had been placed in the middle of the table. As they were about to sit down, to her surprise, Tadd Sweeney appeared from nowhere. She was startled to see him pull Victoria's chair out for her, and then take his place beside her, as if it was the most natural thing in the world to do.

It was obvious the cook had gone to a lot of trouble. The centrepiece was a silver bowl containing dark, spicy meat, the 'Beef Vindaloo'. Even the aroma of the dish smelt hot, if that were possible. Another large bowl contained steamed rice. There was also a plate heaped with flat Indian 'Naan' bread, several small bowls of various condiments to be eaten with the curry, and a bowl of green mush which Nerida was serving the children.

"What's this green stuff?" Jack asked, his freckled nose crinkling in distaste, as Nerida spooned the thick mixture onto his plate.

Tara held up her hand to stop the aboriginal girl giving him too generous a serving, as she was afraid he would leave it. Waste was almost a crime in the Depression, but Tara was especially wary of wasting food in her aunt's home, however well she claimed they were doing.

"Jack, please mind your manners," Tara said, feeling her face grow warm with embarrassment. The boy hung his head, and sulked. Tara had no idea what was the matter with him.

Thankfully, Victoria was unaware of the boy's mood, and only laughed. "That's Dhal, Jack. It's made with lentils and spices. It's really delicious."

"It looks like something from Hannibal's mouth," he mumbled, and Tara glared at him. Stifling her anger, and forcing a vivid mental picture from her mind, she turned her attention to Hannah on the chair beside her, wondering what she could give the child to eat, other than bread, and her eyes widened in dismay. Hannah was flicking the 'Dhal' and rice from her plate, onto the table and floor, making a horrible mess. Tara snatched her spoon from her and looked at Nerida helplessly, as she reached for serviettes.

"Hannah, that's naughty," Tara whispered, as Nerida retrieved more serviettes from a sideboard drawer. Tears welled in the little girl's eyes. Tara was fearful she was going to make a scene, so she gave her a piece of Naan bread to occupy her while she helped Nerida clean up the mess. She was on her knees under the table with Nerida, when something darted between the legs of the chairs, and she almost screamed.

'It's just a mouse," Nerida whispered. "There's a plague out here." A moment later, the sound of a trap could be heard behind the sideboard, and Nerida grinned. "Got him!"

When Tara composed herself and returned to her seat, she was horrified to see Hannah had shredded the bread and was eating the rice with her fingers, but more was going onto her clothes and chair than into her mouth.

"Perhaps you should feed her," Ethan whispered.

Tara blushed. She hadn't realised the little girl was probably not used to feeding herself at the table. So far on their journey, she hadn't eaten much at all, or just wandered around nibbling something in her hand.

Victoria seemed oblivious to what had taken place, which made Tara almost ashamed for thinking her shortsightedness was a blessing in disguise. She stood up and leant over the table, and explained to Tara what some of the accompaniments were, as she put a generous helping of rice and Beef Vindaloo onto her plate, then added a small spoon of each of the condiments.

"This is hot tomato sambal. It's made with dried tomatoes, garlic, onions, tamarind sauce, chillies, and coconut milk. Of course, Sanja uses dried coconut milk and tomatoes. We order some of the spices from the markets in Darwin. They are sent down to Alice Springs, which can take months. Ethan either picks them up in Alice, or they are put on the train to Wombat creek, and he picks them up there for us." She glanced at Ethan, as

Nerida spooned some chutney onto the side of her plate. "Your timing today was a Godsend, Ethan. We had completely run out of most of these condiments."

Tara put as small an amount of each of the foods onto her plate that was politely acceptable. "How is it you have an Indian cook, Aunt? Don't you yearn for some Irish food?" She couldn't hide the longing in her voice for a stew made with a drop of stout.

"Heaven's no, I love Indian food. Sanja was once in our employment in Delhi, so when we were settled, Tom contacted him to see if he would come out here. We'd both missed Indian foods so much. Quite frankly all they serve on stations is mutton chops, grilled, roasted, stewed, every way they can think of. After a while you begin to look like a mutton chop."

"What about the cows? Don't you eat them?"

"Yes, of course, but if we kill a cow, we usually share the meat with neighbours because there's too much to keep without it going off. Anyway, it was fortunate for us that Sanja was unemployed at the time that Tom contacted him, and he's not a Hindu."

"Why is that fortunate?"

"Hindu's won't eat beef," Tadd interjected, his tone condescending. "Imagine living on a cattle station and not eating beef?"

"Cows are sacred to Hindus," Victoria added patiently. "Sanja's not a Moslem either, but that wouldn't matter, as we don't keep pigs. He was delighted to come here."

Tadd laughed derisively. "He wasn't so delighted when he arrived. He thought Tambora was a terrible place, and threw tantrums nearly every day. I'd have soon shipped him back."

"The house wasn't finished and the droughts take some getting used to. But mostly he hated the isolation," Victoria said, "and he was disappointed he couldn't shop for his cooking ingredients himself, something he was used to doing in Delhi. The markets there are absolutely amazing, but you wouldn't believe some of the strange things they sell."

"What kind of things?" Jack asked in a sulky tone. He was pushing the food around on his plate, but hadn't tried a morsel.

For a moment Victoria wasn't sure what to say. "Well..."

"Goats eyes, and the testicles of tigers and sheep's intestines," Tadd answered.

"Tadd, stop telling tales. You've never even been to India!" Victoria admonished. She looked at Jack. "They eat very exotic foods, things we would call strange."

"They eat some rather odd things here, too, Aunt," Tara said. "Ferris was telling me some of the foods Jed Harper, the cook at the Great Northern Hotel, serves up. Termites, sugar ants, grubs, and lizards."

"That not strange food," Nerida said, as she refilled glasses with water. "That what my people call good tucker."

"It's strange to us, girlie," Tadd claimed.

It wasn't the first time that Tara had noticed the disapproval of something Tadd said in Nerida's dark eyes, but Tara hadn't meant to offend the girl. "I suppose every culture eats foods that other cultures would think are strange. Look at the English, with their Toad in the Hole."

Nerida began giggling. "I not know the English eat toads. They poisonous…"

"It's not actually a toad at all, Nerida. It's a sausage cooked in pastry," Victoria explained.

"And black pudding is not a pudding at all. It's a sausage made from blood," Tara added. "And then there's tripe, which is part of the stomach of a cow, and chitterlings, which are part of the innards of a pig."

Nerida looked startled and Jack glanced at his meat even more suspiciously.

Tara placed a small mouthful of the "Beef Vindaloo" into her mouth, to reassure him. A moment later her expression changed. Her mouth felt as if it was on fire. She chewed and swallowed quickly, then gulped at her glass of water, her face going red. Hannah and Jack watched her, mesmerized. Jack then pushed his small portion of curried meat to the side of his plate.

"Oh Aunt, this curry is so hot," Tara said gasping, her eyes watering, and perspiration breaking on her forehead and the bridge of her nose. She knew Jack would not be able to eat it, and thankfully Hannah did not have any on her plate.

"You get used to it, Tara. I remember having my first curry. I never thought I'd eat it again, but I love it now, and so does Tadd. Have some of the Dhal with it. It will take away the heat."

Tara made a mental note to speak to Sanja and suggest some less spicy food.

"Sanja has managed to grow a few of the different herbs and spices he uses," Victoria said. "His chilli bushes are actually a huge success. They need little water, and make a colourful show in the garden with their bright red, yellow, and green chillies."

Tara couldn't remember seeing any chillies growing in the garden, certainly no colourful healthy bushes, but supposed they might not have been visible from the landing window. "I think he used far too much chilli in this curry," she said, draining her glass of water, which Nerida immediately refilled. Despite several more gulps of water, the fire in her mouth wouldn't subside.

As Victoria chewed her food, she looked at Nerida. "This is lamb, Nerida," she said.

The aboriginal girl looked slightly embarrassed. "There was no beef in the cool house, Missus, so Sanja had to use lamb."

Victoria turned to Tadd. "Why is there no beef in the cool house, Tadd?"

He looked uncomfortable. "Charlie hasn't had time to kill a steer," he said.

Victoria looked puzzled, but refrained from comment.

"My Aunt tells me you have been with her on Tambora for a number of years, Mr. Sweeney," Tara said, when she'd got her breath back. The curry had burnt the back of her throat, and she noticed her voice had changed pitch.

He looked up smiling, and swallowed a mouthful. "That's right. We're practically family."

"Tom bought this land from Tadd's father," Victoria said. "He's been with us ever since."

Tara noticed Tadd glanced at Victoria fondly, and patted her hand. She thought he was reinforcing his position, and was perhaps too familiar for an employee.

"I don't know what I would've done without him after Tom died," Victoria said, looking suddenly vulnerable.

"You'd have managed," Tadd replied, his tone just a touch disingenuous, Tara thought.

"Not these days," Victoria said. "You virtually run the station by yourself."

Tara could see the pain in Victoria's eyes when she spoke, but she could hear it more in her voice, and her heart wrenched. It wasn't hard to see how much her Aunt missed being 'in the saddle'. Tara watched Tadd, and wondered if he'd deliberately made Victoria dependent on him. She cast a glance at Ethan, who was watching Tadd and Victoria intently. She wondered if he was thinking the same thing she was, that her Aunt was not the person she used to be, the independent, strong willed woman who had earned the respect of the community for hundreds of miles around.

"I'm sure you'd have managed, Aunt," Tara said softly, hoping to bolster her confidence. "Everyone I have met speaks highly of your ability to run such a vast station. I don't think you have any idea how much you are admired, do you?"

Victoria looked startled. "I'm sure you are exaggerating," she said, but Tara could see she was pleased.

"No one could do it alone, Tara," Tadd said, and Victoria's fragile smile evaporated like campfire smoke on a windy day.

"I realise that," Tara replied testily.

"You have to have good employees behind you. I have been fortunate," Victoria added.

"I'm sure you do, Aunt. But leadership is very important."

Again, Victoria smiled with pleasure. "I'm not much of a leader. I used to love getting out there amongst the sheep and cattle."

"Aunt, you've certainly changed since the days when all you thought about was going to society parties."

Victoria laughed self-consciously. "I know I have changed, I've let myself go. But what you look like hardly matters when you're covered in dust and stepping in sheep dung. Working out here gave me so much satisfaction, far more than any trivial party made up of shallow gossips. When I was able, I felt I was doing something worthwhile, and I always slept so well after a long day in the saddle. If only my sight wasn't letting me down..." She looked wistful, obviously longing for the return of those days, but Tadd, Tara noticed, shrugged his shoulders as if it hardly mattered.

"None of us are getting any younger, are we?" he said with forced cheerfulness. "Thankfully I have a few more years, but the day will come for me too, when I can't do what I used to do. The bones start creaking, and, as in your case Victoria, the sight goes."

"My Aunt is not blind, Mr. Sweeney," Tara said.

"No...she's not... I didn't mean..."

Tara turned her attention to Victoria. "When did you last ride, Aunt?" she asked gently.

"It's been almost a year now."

"But you still can?"

"You never forget how, but my sight..."

"Tara could take you out," Ethan suggested. "Your faithful old mare would not lead you astray."

Victoria's eyes brightened. "Could you, Tara? Tadd doesn't have time to molly coddle me, and I'd love to ride around the station."

"Of course. I'd enjoy it."

A glance in Tadd Sweeney's direction disclosed he was not all that pleased. She couldn't work out whether he was concerned for Victoria's safety, or unhappy that she would be mobile again. Her suspicious mind had her wondering whether he had something to hide.

"Ethan introduced me to Nugget this morning," Tara said to her aunt. "He was moving sheep, and said something about a locust plague."

"Nugget is a good worker," Victoria said smiling, her mood more jubilant than it had been in a very long time. "If the locusts are on their way, we'll soon be sweeping them out of the house by the bucket full."

Tara's eyes widened in dismay as she pictured the grass hopper invasion.

"You have to keep on his back," Tadd added, referring to Nugget. "Abo's can be a lazy lot."

Tara glanced at Nerida and saw the hurt and embarrassment in her features, and she became angry at Tadd's insensitivity. She remembered when Ethan had asked Nugget about Tadd, and he'd said he was probably at the homestead, sitting in the shade. He'd all but said 'he' was the lazy one.

"How many men do you employ, Aunt?" Tara asked, trying to keep the conversation flowing and on a safe topic.

Victoria glanced briefly at Tadd, who was shoveling curry and rice into his mouth. "Usually about ten stockmen and roustabouts, but when we're shearing or crutching...."

Tadd looked up from his almost empty plate, as he reached for his third piece of Naan bread to mop up the remaining curry sauce. He cleared his throat, interrupting Victoria. "We haven't had the need for that many men for some time, Victoria. At the moment, there's Nugget, Bluey, Charlie, and his son, young Karl." He looked at Tara. "We hire shearers on contract."

Victoria seemed embarrassed that Tadd had corrected her. "You didn't mention Howie Dunn?" she said.

"Of course I didn't."

"Why not?"

"I fired him several months ago." Victoria looked astonished. "Remember, I told you?" Tadd added.

"No, you didn't. I think I would remember you firing our head drover. I might be losing my sight, but I'm not losing my memory!"

Tadd glanced at Ethan and Tara, and deliberately gave Victoria an indulgent look, which angered Tara. "We discussed his dismissal, Victoria. Do you remember I told you he lost twenty four head of cattle on the drove to the southern markets?"

"For Heaven's sake, Tadd, we've lost two thousand head in a drought. Twenty four is nothing. You shouldn't have fired him for that, and you should have discussed it with me."

Victoria glanced at Tara and Ethan. She seemed flustered and angry, as if she was losing her grip on the station, or worse, her mind. Tara wondered if her Aunt's memory was going, or whether Tadd had been deliberately taking matters into his own hands, without consulting her. She suspected the latter was true.

"If you'll excuse me, folks, I have work to do." Tadd stood up, pushed his chair in, and turned to leave.

"Before you go, Tadd, see that Ethan is paid for the supplies he brought," Victoria said. Tadd stopped in his tracks, a blank expression on his face. "You'll be around for awhile, won't you, Ethan?"

"Yes, There's no hurry, Victoria," Ethan said coming to stand beside her. "I'll be here for a few days. I must get the camels back to my place and turn them loose for a well deserved spell. Thank you for lunch."

"You'll come over tomorrow, won't you, Ethan?" Victoria said, taking his hand. He glanced at Tara and the children. "Of course."

Jack jumped to his feet. "Can I come with you, Ethan?"

Ethan looked at Tara again, and so did Jack, his lips tightening. "I think you should settle in here," he said.

Tara appreciated his support. She wanted to talk to Jack. She wondered what had changed his mood so drastically. She could understand his grief, but not why he was being so hostile towards her.

"I tell you what, Jack, why don't you ride over to the abandoned mining hut below the ridge after breakfast tomorrow. Bring a spare horse. I'll meet you there and show you the path up, the short cut."

Jack's disappointment faded somewhat. At least he knew he could be with the camels the following morning. Giving Tara another resentful look, he ran from the dining room. Ethan gave Tara a look that suggested she give Jack time to adjust. "I'll see you tomorrow," he said.

Addressing Victoria, he said, "I'll have a look at the radio before I leave."

"Thank you, Ethan. Tadd doesn't seem to have time."

Ethan thought Tadd Sweeney should have made time. It was their only link with the outside world. In the case of a bush fire warning, or an accident, it was essential.

"I'm sorry I blew up, Tara," Victoria said, when Ethan had gone. "Perhaps I am losing my memory."

"I doubt it, Aunt. It's probably just a… communication mix up. Station life must be terribly busy." Tara noticed Nerida was still upset, as she busied herself clearing the table. Her lips were pursed, and her actions erratic.

"Nevertheless, I should apologize to Tadd," Victoria said. "He does shoulder most of the responsibility for the station. I don't want to appear ungrateful, I just get so… frustrated."

"I understand," Tara said. "Maybe when you've had a ride around the station, you'll feel better."

Victoria nodded. "I can't believe Howie's gone, and I didn't know."

"Maybe Tadd had forgotten to tell you about Howie Dunn. I'm sure his memory is not perfect." Again Tara noticed Nerida was clanging the dishes. She sensed the young girl didn't like Tadd Sweeney, and wondered whether she'd tell her why.

"He seemed so sure." Victoria looked confused. Tara wondered how often this sort of thing occurred.

Victoria squeezed her niece's hand. "Are you tired, Tara? You've had a long journey."

"A little."

"I think we should have a lie down. I usually have an afternoon nap these days. The heat can be so draining. It must be 115% in the shade already."

"If you don't mind, Aunt, I'd like to go and meet Sanja," Tara said.

"Oh! Would you like me to come with you?"

"That won't be necessary. You go up and rest."

"Are you sure?"

"Of course, Aunt. Why the concern? Should I be expecting Quasimodo?"

Victoria laughed, but it quickly faded. "No, dear. Just…. Never mind. Come up when you're ready." Victoria headed for the stairs with Nerida, who was glancing over her shoulder anxiously at Tara.

"Would you like some milk, Hannah?" Tara asked the little girl. Hannah shook her golden curls.

"Are you tired?"

She rubbed her eyes, but again shook her head. Tara found her baffling. She called to Nerida to take Hannah upstairs with them for a sleep.

Tara was on her way to the kitchen, when she came across Tadd Sweeney in the hallway. She didn't want to talk to him, so stepped aside for him to pass, but he stopped.

"It must be hard to see your Aunt has changed so much," he said.

Tara felt her hackles rise. "I don't believe she has," she replied defensively.

Tadd's features softened, as if he understood. "She doesn't always remember things I tell her. I'm afraid she lives in the past a lot."

Tara had had the same feeling when they chatted on her veranda. Nevertheless, she wanted Tadd to know if he was taking liberties, it had to stop.

"Although her health is not the best at the moment, not being consulted about decisions in regard to the station probably makes her feel resentful, as if she no longer has control." She wondered if that was what Tadd had been doing, taking control.

"I do involve her in decisions, lass, but…quite often she's indecisive when something has to be resolved. Just this morning, I needed to discuss selling off some sheep, and she avoided it. What can I do? Things have to get done."

Tara remembered her Aunt wanting to dodge the discussion and wondered if she had judged Tadd incorrectly. She wondered if it was possible that what he was saying was true?

"I'll have a talk to her later," she said.

"I doubt it will help, but thank you, lass." He patted her arm in a comrade spirit, which annoyed Tara. She didn't want him to feel she was siding with him against her aunt in some conspiracy. It made her feel disloyal.

Tadd went to walk away, but Tara stopped him. "May I ask you something, Mr. Sweeney?"

"Of course, and it's Tadd, remember?"

Tara didn't want to be on a first name basis with him. She didn't really understand why she disliked and distrusted him, but she couldn't help it.

"I know I've only been here five minutes, but in that time my aunt has given me the impression the station is doing very well. With the drought, and the Depression, I find that hard to believe."

Tadd's eyes narrowed. "No one is doing very well," he said.

Tara thought he sounded mildly defensive. "I am only commenting because I am concerned about whether the children and myself will be a burden on my Aunt, and I think she's too kind hearted to tell me the truth."

His expression softened. "Things are not so good, but your Aunt is a generous person. She would never turn anyone away, especially kin."

"So my Aunt has been... lying to me, and we are a burden?"

His eyes dropped. "She hasn't exactly been lying...."

"What do you mean?"

"I haven't been telling her the truth, well, not the whole truth."

Tara had been right, but she was still stunned that he was admitting it. "Why would you do such a thing?"

"Victoria would be heartbroken if she knew the reality of the situation. I've been trying to protect her. There's no sense in her worrying about something she can't change."

"I understand you think you are doing what is right, but I don't agree keeping the truth from her is in her best interests, Mr. Sweeney. My Aunt worked hard for years to make the station viable, and she employed many people. Lying to her seems... disrespectful of all her years of hard work."

"You are right of course, but I'm very fond of Victoria. I don't know how she'd take the truth, lass. She's not been herself for some time. I thought things would improve if the drought broke, but that hasn't happened, and doesn't look likely to in the near future. I've done what I can, but I'm not a miracle worker."

Tara was appalled. Even though Tadd appeared to be sincere in wanting to spare Victoria anxiety, she couldn't help worrying about what would happen when she found out the truth, which was inevitable.

"It would be best if Victoria sold the station," Tadd said. "She'd not get much, but if she waits much longer, it will be completely worthless. Perhaps you could convince her to move on. I'd miss her, but I think going back to Ireland with you would be the best thing for her."

Tara was stunned. Although that had originally been her intention, she'd already come to see how much her Aunt loved her home. "I doubt she'd ever do that, Mr. Sweeney. She loves Tambora."

"It's no use being sentimental, lass. That's not good business practice. The station has to pay for itself, and she's no longer fit to do the work she used to, which breaks her heart."

"I came here prepared to work hard, Mr. Sweeney."

"Your intentions are honourable, lass, but I'm afraid you're too late."

"Are things really that bad?"

"Well, we're not in good shape. Because of the Depression, the sheep and wool have become almost worthless and we have so few cattle left. Your Aunt is a good woman, one of the best, and I'd work for nothing, but the men have to be paid… If I owned the station, I'd sell. I know it's a hard call, but sometimes the tough decisions have to be made." He turned to walk away.

Tara quickly gathered her thoughts. While she had the opportunity, there was something else she wanted to say to Tadd Sweeney.

"Mr. Sweeney, I wanted to discuss another point while we're alone?"

He turned, looking slightly exasperated, but seemed to force himself to be cheerful. "Yes, lass."

"Have you noticed Nerida gets upset whenever you make negative comments about Aboriginals?"

Tadd looked at her as if she had just said the moon was made of cheese.

"No, lass," he said, quite obviously restraining his impatience. "I can't say that I have, but I wouldn't put too much stock in her moods."

"I'm sure I don't have to point out that as Irish people, we are proud of our culture."

"Aye, that we are."

"I think it would be more appropriate to be a little more sensitive to Nerida's culture. It's never wise to generalize when talking about people." Tara remembered all the disparaging remarks the gipsies had had to endure from settlers. She knew what it was like to be on the receiving end of bigotry.

Tadd's eyes narrowed. "Surely ye can't be comparing the Irish with the Aborigines, lass?" He was incredulous, which angered Tara. "Abo's don't have any culture," he said.

"I don't know how you can say that?"

"Because it's true."

"Whatever a person's race or creed, they should be judged as individuals, and not lumped together."

"Look, Tara, you've just arrived out here and don't know much about the Abo's and how things are done in the outback. You have to be firm with them, show them their place. Sometimes they just wander off and do their own thing."

"I was told they are nomadic people."

Tadd's eyes widened. "If they are employed by us, they should stay put. I'm certainly not going to watch everything I bloody well say for fear of offending them. Now if you will excuse me, I have to get back to work."

Tara was flabbergasted. She had hoped to get along with Tadd Sweeney, but as far as she was concerned, he was 'bloody narrow minded', and she had the feeling they were going to lock horns again in the near future, no doubt when she mentioned the condition of the dog kennels.

Tara took a moment to compose herself before her confrontation with Sanja. She hoped, for the sake of the children as much as herself, to get on-side with the cook, but if he was anything like Tadd Sweeney.

When she entered the kitchen, she found Sanja at the sink with his back to her.

He heard someone come in, and assumed it was Nerida. "Look at all this food come back," he shouted. "Missy Victoria's family eat like sparrows. Waste is not good. They get it back for supper." He turned, scowling, and appeared startled.

"Hello," Tara said intrepidly. "I'm Victoria's niece."

Sanja's mood completely changed. "Ah, Missy Tara."

Tara smiled, thinking this was a good start. He seemed happy to meet her.

The first thing to strike Tara about Sanja was his stature. He was small, with thin, neatly combed dark hair, and a pleasant round face. Tara had expected the man who seemed to strike fear in the heart of Nerida and rule his employee with threats and tantrums, to be much larger. As she walked towards him, she noted his eyes were a warm sherry brown, and his skin was a lighter shade of the same colour.

"You not eat very much, Missy Tara?" he said, taking her by surprise, as he wiped his hands on a cloth. "You tired from long journey?"

"That's what I've come to see you about, Sanja" she said, noting, to her disgust, that she felt a little apprehensive. She gave him her friendliest smile, hoping to win his cooperation. "Although your curries look absolutely delicious, we've never had spicy food before."

"Ah, curry is very, very good for you," he said, not catching her intention. "But you must eat more, keep strong, yes?"

"No, I'm afraid not. You see, Sanja, we can't eat curries."

The cook looked perplexed.

"They are too hot," Tara explained, hoping to make him understand.

For a moment Sanja continued to stare at her blankly. "Too hot!" he exclaimed in annoyance.

"Yes, I'm afraid so. Do you think we could have some less spicy food? I don't suppose you do an Irish stew?" The words had no sooner tumbled out, than Tara could see Sanja had completely overlooked her tentative effort at lightheartedness.

He picked up a pan he had just washed, and banged it down on the sink, making her jump. "Sanja Naidoo no can 'do' Irish stew," he said, his eyes blazing with fury.

"That's fine," Tara said, trying to remain calm. "I can do it myself."

He looked horrified. "Missy want to cook …in Sanja's kitchen?"

Tara glanced around and noted the 'kitchen', unlike the rest of the house, was spotless. It was the epitome of neatness and order. Even his white apron was pristine. She was tempted to point out it was her Aunt's house, and kitchen, but dared not cause an argument on her first day on Tambora. She had the feeling she might come off second best if her Aunt was asked to choose between her or one of Sanja's 'Beef Vindaloo'. She had plenty of time to sort him out. "If you don't mind…?"

"Sanja mind." He pointed through the door. "You cook outside, Missy, in shearers quarters."

Tara was livid, but she held her temper. "Very well. One kitchen is as good as another."

He shook his head, leaving her in no doubt the kitchen in the shearers quarters could not possibly compare to his. "Children eat Sanja's cooking," he said, as if challenging her.

"No, Mr. Naidoo. They won't."

"They eat," he said, crossing his arms. He cocked his head upwards, and jabbed his finger at her. "You good cook, Missy?"

Tara lied in the face of his impudence. "Of course." If she wasn't mistaken, he snorted derisively.

"You cook for shearers and men at mustering camp, Missy?" It was more a statement than a question. "Me…?"

He laughed, as if he had proved his point, and folded his arms again, puffing out his chest.

There seemed to be little left to say, so Tara turned to leave. She wondered what had happened to cooks who served what they were told, and tried to imagine what her mother would do under these circumstances. For the first time Tara could appreciate that her mother had always managed the staff so effortlessly, and wished she had paid more attention to her methods.

At the door, Tara glanced back and gave Sanja Naidoo a look that said she would speak to her Aunt about his uncooperativeness.

He glared back at her confidently, leaving her in little doubt she would be wasting her time.

CHAPTER FOURTEEN

Loud screeching awoke Tara from a restless sleep. Bathed in perspiration, she sat up in fright, her heart pounding. For a few moments she was disorientated. She'd been dreaming of the Mountjoy Prison, and the gallows. In her subconscious mind, the screeching had become the swinging rope, with a faceless heavy weight on it. She shook her head to dispel the horrible images.

Feeling strangely unsettled, she turned to the balcony, where, through the gauzy mosquito netting surrounding her bed, she could see the sky. It was the most brilliant red she had ever seen. It literally took her breath away. It was almost as if the clouds were fluffy balls of fire. In her confused state, she didn't know whether it was a sunset or a sunrise, but of one thing she was certain, Ireland and the Mountjoy Prison were a long, long, way away.

The screeching broke the tranquil silence again, this time from further away. As Tara moved to get off the bed, she realized Hannah was asleep beside her, her arms flung out in careless abandon, her curls soft and damp. The bed was enormous; plenty of room for two, but Tara couldn't remember her being there when she retired.

Out on the balcony, Tara discovered the screeching raucous was being made by white cockatoos in the gum trees. Their weight shook the branches, but there was only the faintest breeze to stir the crispy leaves on the trees.

"They'll awaken you every afternoon and morning before sun up," Victoria said from behind her.

Tara groaned. "Why ever do they make such a fracas?"

"At this time of day, they're squabbling over a roost. I have no idea why they do it in the morning. I suppose they are just greeting a new day, and the chicks are hungry. One thing is sure, you don't need an alarm clock."

"A gun would be handy," Tara said, then smiled when she saw Victoria's eyes widen in surprise. "Just to frighten them away, Aunt."

Victoria laughed. "Tom used to say that, but his intention was far more sinister. You'll get used to them. After a time, you won't even notice them. You might want to close the balcony doors if you don't want the possums waking you during the tonight. Did I mention they are nocturnal?"

"Yes, but it's too hot to close the doors, Aunt. Do you think there will be a breeze tonight?" She dabbed at her neck with a handkerchief, silently praying for rain.

"Most nights there is."

"I'd sleep naked, but it seems Hannah doesn't want to stay in her own bed."

"She's no doubt used to having her momma close by, poor mite. Give her time."

Tara smelt the aroma of food, and knew it was curry again. Then she remembered Sanja saying they were getting the leftover lunch for their supper. She was thankful she wasn't hungry. The heat had completely ruined her appetite, but she didn't want to admit it to her aunt.

"Dinner is generally around seven o'clock," Victoria said. "Sanja runs to his own schedule, but you'll hear the gong. I'm going downstairs, dear. Come down when you are ready."

Leaving Hannah to sleep, Tara decided to take a walk on the grounds before joining her aunt in the living room. With the fiery ball of the sun almost completely gone below the western horizon, the twilight air was verging on pleasant. She found herself near the kennels again. The uneaten meat Tadd Sweeney had thrown in smelt awful, and the dogs still had no water. There were four more dogs in two other kennels, the Kelpies and the Border Collies she had seen earlier in the day working the sheep. They looked tired. Disgusted at the state of the kennel containing the bitch and pups, Tara opened the cage door and let them out. Although her stomach was practically heaving at the smell, she rolled up her sleeves and got to work cleaning up the mess. Half an hour later, after vigorously scrubbing with a brush and a bucket of water, the kennel was clean, the water bowls refilled, and the rotting meat buried. She placed a rock in each of the water bowls to keep them from being knocked over.

"I'll see if I can find you something better to eat," Tara said to Mellie, who seemed to appreciate her brief freedom. She noticed they had no bedding, not anything at all for the bitch and her pups to lie on.

Tara reluctantly returned the dogs to the confines of the kennel and turned back to the house. She stopped when she caught the aroma of meat cooking. She glanced in the direction of the shearers quarters, and saw smoke drifting above the chimney and decided to see if Nugget had any scraps for the dogs.

Looking in the open doorway she found the shearer's quarters empty, but she could hear voices nearby. She went around the back and found Nugget with two other men, and an adolescent boy. They were sitting around a campfire, talking and smoking with their feet up.

"Hello, Missus," Nugget said in surprise, when he saw her.

"I hope I'm not disturbing you," Tara said, glancing appreciatively at the meat sizzling in a skillet over the fire. She was amazed at the sudden rush of nostalgia that washed over her, and astonished to realize that despite her initial queasy stomach, she had worked up an appetite. "Have you by any chance some leftover scraps for the dogs?"

"We'll have some fat bits and bones in a while, Missus, but Tadd Sweeney not like us feeding his dogs. He say it spoil them."

"To Hell with him, Nugget. I've never heard such rubbish. They can't be expected to eat rotting meat."

"Too right, Missus," one of the other men said. "They don't like roo meat anyway, but he won't give them anything else."

Tara shuddered, realizing that was why the meat smelt so 'strong'. It was kangaroo. "I'm Victoria's niece, Tara Flynn," she said.

"I'm Charlie, and this here is my boy, young Karl." The gangly boy nodded, but quickly dropped his gaze. Charlie appeared to be half-caste aboriginal, but his boy could have passed for a white lad.

"I'm Kevin O'Donnel. My mates call me Bluey," the other man said. "Pleased ta meet ya, Missus. You stoppin' out here long?"

Bluey, or Kevin O'Donnel, had reddish brown hair and a freckled face, but his broad nose and dark eyes made him look part Aboriginal, too.

"I'm not sure how long I'll be here," Tara said truthfully.

"Fancy a mutton chop, Missus, or will you be havin' some of that curried stuff Sanja serves up every day?" Nugget seemed to be feeling awkward about offering her a portion of his simple meal.

Tara had to admit the sizzling chops smelt very good. "I'd like one, if you have any spare, but please don't go short yourselves."

His eyes lit up in delight. "Plenty here, Missus."

"If you're sure, Nugget. I can't stomach spicy food and Sanja won't cook anything else. I told him I'd do some cooking, but he said I had to use the shearer's quarters."

"You go right ahead, Missus. I know Sanja not like anyone in his kitchen. He can be right strange fella at times. Don't know how the Missus put up with 'im."

Tara nodded in agreement. She felt apprehensive when she thought of the old black oven inside. She had never even attempted to cook in an oven, and wondered if she'd set the shearer's quarters on fire. "Actually, Nugget, I'd be happy to put something in a pot over a fire out here, if you don't mind?"

Nugget looked astonished. "You don't want to be making a fire out here, Missus. You use the oven inside. It much cleaner, better for you."

Tara was dismayed, but decided to let it drop, for now. "I did ask Sanja to cook a stew, but he refused. My children certainly can't eat the spicy food he serves up, but he insists they will."

"Always plenty of mutton chops to go round, Missus, but not much else."

Tara glanced at the other men. "Have you had a hard day?"

"No different to any other. Hot, dusty, and enough flies to last a lifetime. How are you coping with the heat?"

"It's draining, but I suppose I'll get used to it. I doubt I'll ever get used to these pesky flies." She swatted them from her face. "…and the dust…."

"Even the crows fly backwards to keep the dust out of their eyes out here, Missus," Charlie said, and Tara laughed.

"Bit different to Ireland, aye?" Bluey added. "Not many flies over there."

"With a name like O'Donnel, you'd have to be Irish?"

"Not me, Missus. I'm an Aussie. My father was an Irish prospector, but my mother is aboriginal, from the Kujani clan. I was born out here in the Mulga scrub. Never been anywhere else. Not like Charlie here, he's been all over Australia, and most of the world, too. Young Karl was born in South Africa."

"Cape Town," Karl added with just a hint of an Afrikaner accent.

"Really?" Tara said. "How long have you been out here?"

"Since I was seven."

"Nearly eight years," Charlie added. "His mother was murdered for a pair of shoes. After burying her, we travelled around a bit, then came out here. The climates are similar, but even with the Depression, the living is better."

"I'm sure my… son would like to meet you," Tara said to young Karl. She still found it unnatural referring to Jack and Hannah as her son and daughter, and a fraud, but hoped that would change with time.

"If you don't mind me asking, where's your husband, Missus?' Bluey asked.

Tara felt fraudulent again. "We had some bad luck on the crossing from Ireland. The ship went down… he was drowned."

"That's terrible luck, Missus. You're too pretty to be left alone."

Embarrassed, Tara addressed Karl. "I think Jack would be happy to know there's another lad on the station. He's a bit younger than you, but he seems to love the outdoor life and Ethan Hunter's camels."

"I hate camels," Karl said. "They stink, and bite, and spit and kick. I won't go near them."

"Oh. Well, perhaps you could show Jack how to round up sheep."

Karl grunted. "I hate sheep, too."

Charlie rolled his eyes. "He'd like to live in the city, but he's too young to be on his own just yet."

"I'd like to go back to Cape Town," Karl stated. "At least I'd get paid for any work I do." He went inside, and Tara looked at Charlie, puzzled.

"Things have been tough out here. I keep telling him everyone is suffering. It's not the Missus' fault she hasn't been able to pay us."

Tara was shocked. Tadd Sweeney hadn't mentioned the men hadn't been paid. "How long since you had wages, Charlie?"

"A couple of months, but even then it wasn't a full wage. But that's not so bad. Nugget hasn't had any pay for much longer than that. Tadd Sweeney says we'll get paid out of the next sale of sheep, but I won't hold my breath. Even if he can sell them, he won't get much. Nobody can feed them, and nobody has the money to buy the meat. It won't matter soon, as Tadd says the Missus will sell up before long. I never thought I'd see the day."

Tara was shocked. Tadd Sweeney had not told her things were that bad, and he had no right to tell the men Victoria was going to sell up.

"I can't believe she'd do that, Charlie. My Aunt loves Tambora. Even so, it's very loyal of you men to stay here and work when you are not being paid." Tara was in awe of their devotion to her aunt, especially Nugget's allegiance. She glanced at him, and he shrugged his broad shoulders.

"We got work, somewhere to sleep, and food. And Missus Victoria is a good boss lady," he said.

"Nevertheless, I can't imagine many employees would stay on under those conditions." Tara felt terrible that her aunt didn't even know these men weren't receiving wages. Something had to be done.

"I bin here long time, Missus," Nugget disclosed. "This land is my home. But one day Tadd may tell me go."

Tara wondered if Nugget had been threatened by Tadd Sweeney, but didn't like to ask. Nugget put two enormous chops on a plate for her. It seemed he expected her to take them away, so was pleasantly surprised when she sat down on an upturned oil tin, to eat with them.

" My Aunt will be wondering where I am," she said, licking her lips appreciatively.

"You don't have to stay, Missus," Nugget said awkwardly. "You maybe like to eat in comfort."

"Of course I'll stay if you don't mind. I'm quite comfortable."

He grinned, showing the gap where his front teeth should be, and his eyes shone in the fading light. "I'll get you a chair from inside, Missus."

"This will do just fine, Nugget."

"You'll hear that wretched dinner gong," Charlie said, and she laughed.

Tara felt more comfortable than Nugget and the others would ever know. She had felt strange at lunchtime, sitting in her aunt's formal dining room, complete with candelabra and silverware. It would take some time to adjust to eating under such ceremonial circumstances again.

Nugget produced some damper from a black pot with a lid and broke it up with his fingers. He threw a handful of flour in the fat and juices from the meat in the pan, added a little water, and stirred it into a gravy. The men grabbed a hunk each of steaming damper and bit into it. They ate the meat with their hands but offered Tara a knife and fork. She noticed they liberally sprinkled salt on the meat and mopped up the gravy with the bread. It was a simple, inelegant meal, but she thoroughly enjoyed it. The meat was a little tough but tasty. She collected the left over bones, gristle and fat, and took it to the dogs. They relished it and looked for more. She wondered if she dared ask Sanja for meat offcuts.

When she returned with the plate, Tara asked the men who used to tend the vegetable garden.

Nugget shrugged casually, but Bluey said, "No time, Missus. Years ago was different. The boss give work to many fellas, lots of lubras about the place to help the Missus. All gone now."

"I thought Sanja might do the garden. He needs the ingredients for his cooking," Tara said.

The men laughed. "Don't be telling him that, Missus," Nugget said.

"My aunt said Sanja grew chilli bushes. Where are they?"

"Boss lady got bad eyes, Missus. She not see, there no more chilli bushes."

Bluey and Charlie glanced at each other, grinning. They did not want to tell Tara that they used to urinate on Sanja's chilli bushes until he caught them. There was such an uproar, after which Sanja let the bushes die.

The dinner gong sounded, the noise sending the cockatoos in the gum trees into flight.

"I had better go and tell my Aunt I have eaten," Tara said, handing Nugget the empty plate.

Nugget gave her another tin plate containing several more chops. "For the piccanninies," he said. "Bring them over any time, Missus."

"Thank you, Nugget. I really enjoyed having dinner with you. I'll probably see you all in the morning." She turned to Charlie. "Please say goodnight to young Karl."

'Good night, Missus," Bluey and Charlie echoed.

When Tara had gone, Nugget said, "New Missus all right. She not got nose in the air, like Tadd said."

"Reckon she'll be good company for Missus Victoria," Bluey added.

With Victoria's approval, the children enjoyed their mutton chops out on the veranda, where the insects, particularly the mosquitoes were a pest, but it was a little cooler, and it didn't matter so much if Hannah made a mess. Jack ate in silence, but he appeared happy when Tara said he could give the leftovers to the dogs. She told him she had cleaned out the kennels and how much the dogs had enjoyed the food scraps she had given them earlier.

They were standing beside the kennels when Tara saw something move from the corner of her eye. Her heart jumped, as she thought it was a snake. It was Tadd Sweeney bearing down on them. Knowing what was coming, she inwardly groaned.

"What do you think you are doing?" he balled.

"Feeding the dogs," Tara said. "They are enjoying it, too."

Tara noticed he was surprised the kennels were clean, although he did not comment. "I've already fed them today. You can't overfeed working dogs."

Tara thought this statement was nonsensical, as Mellie was virtually skin and bone. "If you are referring to that rotten meat, I buried it," she said.

"You did what?"

"You couldn't expect them to eat it. It stunk to high Heaven and was no doubt maggot infested."

"I shot the roo myself early this morning."

"I'm not a fool, Mr. Sweeney. That meat smelt several days old, at least."

He gave her an impatient look. "It's the heat. Nothing stays fresh for long."

Tara suspected he was lying. "They hadn't touched it, and it didn't look as if they were ever going to."

"If they were hungry enough, they would've eaten it. You can't waste meat out here."

"They didn't even have water, Mr. Sweeney. Surely that's neglect in this heat."

"It's not my fault they knock it over."

"Haven't you a heavier dish somewhere? They can't go without water for long. And the kennels were filthy. Who is supposed to clean them out?"

He looked angry. "Whoever has time. There is so much to do around here and not enough hands to do it."

"Well there's more hands here now, Mr. Sweeney, and we intend to pull our weight. We'll look after the kennels, and feed the dogs, won't we Jack?"

The boy looked startled, but nodded. "On one condition," Tara said.

Tadd's eyes narrowed. He wondered who she thought she was, setting conditions down. "What's that?"

"The dogs are allowed out of the kennels for several hours a day, and not just for training."

He frowned. "I told you before, they are not pets."

Tara could see Jack and Hannah were delighted at the prospect of the puppies running around, so she softened her approach. "I know that, but they need exercise and you are busy. I'm only trying to allow you more time to do important things."

Tadd seemed to contemplate her proposal. Although he felt she was being pushy, he did need more time to take care of other matters.

"Very well," he said. "As long as they don't show any signs of being soft during training. The pups are due to be sold in a few weeks."

"We'll also look after the other domestic animals. Hannah can feed the chickens and collect the eggs, and I'll show Jack how to milk a cow."

"You can't take over Nerida's work. You'll have her turning lazy like the rest of them."

Tara felt her anger rise, but fought to control it. "It's quite obvious that the house is too much for her by herself. The vegetable garden also looks neglected, so I'll tend to it.

The children can help me." Tara knew almost nothing about growing vegetables. In fact, she didn't know a weed from a potato plant, but she didn't want Tadd Sweeney to know that. She'd only recognized the corn plants because they were so tall.

Tadd nodded, although he seemed to be torn. Tara knew he was used to running things, and handing over the reins for some of his responsibilities was no doubt difficult. She had no idea he was thinking she wouldn't last five minutes digging in the vegetable garden, especially in the heat.

While the children were busy feeding the pups through the wire of the kennels, Tara led Tadd a few feet away, and lowered her voice. "I am going to have a talk with my aunt later this evening, Mr. Sweeney. I think it's time she was made aware of the true situation in regard to the station's finances."

Tadd scowled at her.

"Why didn't you tell me the men haven't been paid for months?" she asked.

Tadd looked startled, then lowered his gaze. "We've all had to make sacrifices. As long as they get their tobacco ration, some meat, tea and flour, they're happy."

"They're entitled to wages, Mr. Sweeney. They are not slaves."

Tadd looked shocked. Tara suspected it wasn't because she was suggesting the men were being treated unfairly, but rather because she was actually defending them.

"I can't give them what I haven't got," Tadd snapped.

Tara understood he was in a difficult position, and he had been shouldering a great deal of responsibility. "Have you been getting wages?" she asked, feeling a little repentant for thinking the worst of him. After all, it can't have been easy managing the station during the Depression, while suffering a never-ending drought.

"I'd hardly take wages myself if the men aren't being paid."

She softened her tone. "Of course. I'm sorry. But my Aunt shouldn't be kept in the dark any longer. Surely you realize that?"

He looked skeptical. Again, Tara's suspicions rose, and she wondered if he was concerned for her aunt, or his own position. She hated being so mistrustful of his motives, but she just couldn't help it.

"I'll be gentle with her," she said. "But she must be told the truth."

"Do you think you could convince her to sell the station?"

That hadn't been Tara's intention, and again she felt a prickle of suspicion. "When she knows the facts, I'm sure she'll come to a decision. You are under no obligation to stay, Mr. Sweeney. Although you've been a great help to my Aunt, I know she wouldn't want you to feel beholden."

His jaw clenched, making him look angry. "I'll not leave Victoria in the lurch. Whatever you think of me, I have been good to her."

Tara saw the hurt in his eyes. It seemed genuine, and again she wondered if she had misjudged him. "I know that, I didn't mean to sound ungrateful for all you've done. But you seem to be pushing for her to sell up, and I know that would break her heart."

"It would break mine, too, lass. I've been here a long time." He glanced around, then turned to go. Tara realized Tambora had also been his home for a number of years, and she remembered her aunt had said his father once owned the land. She regretted her insensitivity.

"Perhaps we can come up with something to save the station, Mr. Sweeney. My Aunt has been through difficult times in the past and survived. It's possible this time won't be any different."

Tadd shook his head.

Tara thought he had lost all hope, and her heart sank. "I'd like to see the accounting books tomorrow morning."

He was clearly astonished. "Whatever for?"

"So that I can explain things in more detail to my Aunt. I'm sure she'll want to know exactly where we stand, especially as I understand she always took care of the books herself."

"That's right, she did, but I'm afraid I have been neglecting them. We've been so short-staffed."

"I realize that, but I'd like to take a look at them anyway."

He nodded, and walked towards his cottage with his head hanging, leaving Tara feeling more confused than ever. She honestly did not know what to make of Tadd Sweeney.

CHAPTER FIFTEEN

After her bath, Tara went in search of her aunt. She found her sitting on the upstairs veranda outside her bedroom, wearing a thin cotton nightgown, and worn slippers. She looked so contented. Tara watched her for a few moments, unobserved. She felt saddened that the discussion she had planned would destroy her aunt's fragile peace of mind, which tempted her to postpone it.

As Tara came out onto the balcony, Victoria turned and smiled "Are the children asleep? They've had such a big day."

Tara noted the faint weariness in her voice, and again felt hesitant about causing her any anxiety. "Hannah fell asleep the moment her head touched the pillow, but when I looked in on Jack, he was still awake." She didn't mention that he was withdrawn to the point of being hostile towards her. She had gently tried to broach the subject of his anger, but he'd turned his back on her, flatly refusing to answer any questions. Although she felt hurt by his coldness and outright rejection, Tara decided to give him time to settle before attempting to discuss his feelings again. If he wouldn't talk to her, she hoped he might talk to Ethan. Anything was better than bottling up his grief.

"You sound a little weary yourself, Aunt," Tara said. "I hope you haven't been waiting up just for me? I lost track of time languishing in the bath. I must confess I feel guilty using the water when there is so little to spare."

"Nonsense, Tara. I know it was the first real bath you've had for a week."

"The children used it first." This was not quite the truth. Jack had refused to bathe, and no amount of cajoling would change his mind. She didn't know what she was going to do with him.

Victoria looked up at the sky. "I like to sit here and enjoy the evenings. It's so peaceful, but I am getting tired. I was too excited to sleep for more than a few minutes this afternoon."

"It's been a very long day, for all of us." Tara looked out over the surrounding land. A faint breeze stirred the leaves on the trees, and the stars shone down like millions of fireflies. The moon was full and seemed so near she could reach up and touch it. It's light softly bathed the grounds around the house, disguising the parched earth in serenity and coolness. With a little imagination, some of the areas shadowed by trees gave the illusion of pools of water. But it wasn't water. It was dust. She could hear insects now, but in the daytime, it was so silent. Tara didn't know how her aunt could truly feel at home in such a place.

"Don't you miss Ireland, Aunt? At the oddest moments I feel terribly homesick. I'd give anything to see Loch Derg, or the Silvermine Mountains, or a country road through Edenderry, and a heather filled meadow and wild hops. I even miss the rain…"

Victoria caught the yearning in her voice. It brought back memories long forgotten. "When I first came here, I used to miss home dreadfully. But then I would remind myself of how much I hated the winters, - the long bouts of illness I used to suffer, the snow and sleet, and chilblains and frostbite. I couldn't imagine living anywhere but on Tambora, now."

"You've replaced those miseries with mosquitoes, snakes, flies and dust."

Victoria laughed. "I suppose I have, but I love to hear the kookaburra's laughing in the trees, and when it rains, the sound on the iron roof is so comforting. Almost overnight, the dry grass turns green and the birds flourish. And to see a new lamb or a calf born, and know I helped to bring it into this world, there's no feeling like it. Do you know Australia is two thirds desert, and this area used to be an enormous Inland Sea?"

Tara was surprised, but a movement in the grounds caught her attention. Someone was lurking near the trees.

"Aunt, I think I saw a woman down there, an aboriginal," she said. "I'm sure it wasn't Nerida."

"You probably did. The local aborigine's come and go. You can't stop them. They've been rather absent since you arrived because they probably thought you were a government official come to take the children. Nugget or Bluey or Charlie would have assured them this wasn't the case, but they will still be cautious for awhile. When they are not going walkabout, they sometimes make camp not far from here. Can you see smoke just above the trees? That would be their campfires."

Tara could just distinguish gray smoke against the ink black sky above the trees. She hadn't noticed it before. She'd been able to smell smoke, but thought it was the stockmen's campfire behind the shearers quarters.

"The woman you saw might have been visiting Nugget, or perhaps Bluey. I don't really understand their family structure, it's rather complex, but don't be surprised to see children pop up once they know you are not to be feared."

"Theirs?" Tara asked, referring to Nugget and Bluey.

"Perhaps, who knows. The lubra's always seem to be pregnant. The children keep out of Tadd's way, but they still come. I think Nerida feeds and clothes them. Now and again I find an item of my clothing missing. Mostly it's something old and unwanted, but not always. I usually pretend I don't notice." She laughed. "Once I saw an elderly lubra in one of my best evening gowns. Tom had bought it for me for a New Years Eve celebration in New York. It was silver lamé, and low cut, back and front. She looked so comical, with her breasts hanging down to her waste, and her frizzy hair with streaks of white, that I began laughing hysterically, and couldn't stop. I was literally in agony, with tears rolling down my face. The poor woman ran away screaming, and I never saw her again."

"Did you get your gown back?"

"No, but it didn't matter. It was foolish of me to bring it out here, but I plead ignorance on the grounds that I didn't know what I was coming to. Actually, I brought enough clothes out here to open my own store, and they were nearly all impractical for this way of life. Ethan often teases me about having to use extra camels just to transport all my suitcases."

Tara looked for the woman in the grounds again, but she had disappeared. She was delighted to see the silhouettes of kangaroos moving near the trees, and other nocturnal creatures, but not so pleased to notice some looked suspiciously like rats. A rustling in the nearest tree startled her.

"It's the possums," her aunt said. "Mind you don't step in their droppings."

Tara stepped back gingerly, noticing large round eyes shining from a branch above her.

"How have you enjoyed your first day here?" Victoria asked.

"It's been wonderful, Aunt." Tara sighed, her feelings a complex mixture of happiness and overwhelming concern for the future. "But tomorrow we intend to begin earning our keep."

"Oh! What are you going to do?"

"I'm going to tend the vegetable garden."

Victoria looked genuinely astonished. "I didn't know you knew anything about growing produce, dear."

"I don't, Aunt, but surely it can't be that difficult."

"Strangely enough, getting plants to grow is not the most difficult part of having a vegetable garden out here, although that's near impossible with the terrible soil and lack of rain. Keeping the roos, cattle and sheep from eating what you've grown is the challenge."

"I'll get the men to build a fence for me."

"We've tried that, Tara. I believe the remains are still surrounding the garden. The rabbits and wombats dig under the fence, and the sheep and cattle push it over, and the roos jump it."

"Then we'll have to make it strong and high."

Victoria marvelled at her niece's optimism. She wondered how it would survive the test of time. "We have plenty of seeds you can use, and they are labeled."

Tara was relieved. At least she would know what was what. "Hannah is going to feed the chickens and collect the eggs," she said. "By the way, how many laying hens do we have?"

"I'm not sure. The dingoes take them whenever they can."

"Then we shall get some geese. It'll be a foolhardy dingo who'll challenge a flock of geese, and their eggs are wonderful."

"How do you know about such things, Tara?"

"You'd be surprised at what I've learnt from the gipsies, Aunt. Not necessarily practical things, like cooking," she laughed, "but useful tricks about surviving and living well off the land. I should be able to put some of it to use out here. By the way, I noticed the kennels were neglected, so Jack and I are going to take over looking after the dogs. I've discussed it with Tadd, and he agrees he doesn't have time with so much else to do. He's even relented about letting Mellie and her pups run around for a few hours each day, a prospect that delights Jack and Hannah."

"That's wonderful. I won't ask how you changed his mind. I always thought Tadd was a typical Irishman, stubborn."

"When it comes to stubbornness Aunt, he's met his match."

"Obviously! I must admit I always feel safer when Mellie's running around. She's the best snake catcher we've ever had on the property. She can sense a King Brown at a hundred yards, and kill it in seconds."

Tara was appalled. "What if she gets bitten? I was told King Brown's are venomous." "They are, but she's too quick for them. I've lost count of how many she's killed. She rips their heads clean off. I hope all this work you plan to do won't be too much for you, Tara? You are not used to this heat."

"I'll be fine, Aunt." Just the thought of snakes was sending involuntary shudders through her. She knew she was going to jump at everything that moved. "I have no intention of being idle. I came here to help you, however I can. I believe contributing will be good for the children, too. It will give them a sense of belonging, and they need that so much. If needs be, I'll help the men round up the sheep and cattle. You'll be surprised to know I'm very competent on a horse these days, something else my gipsy husband taught me."

Victoria was curious about Tara's life with the Romany's, but she knew her niece would talk about it in her own good time. "Droving is hot, dusty work, dear. But I used to love it."

"Is it true you've ridden Ethan's camels?"

Victoria laughed at the disbelief in her niece's voice. "I was rather good, too. I won three races on Hannibal and came second on Layla. I had planned to enter the Alice Springs Camel Cup when Tom had his accident. The prize money is usually very good."

"I didn't know whether to believe Ethan or not, when he told me. At first I thought it was a ploy to get me on a camel, especially when I remembered how frightened you were of horses."

"Frightened! I was terrified. Tom couldn't convince me to go near a horse, but Ethan has a way of making you feel safe; as if anything is possible. He used to break horses for a living and still competes in rodeos. He can get an animal to do anything for him. They seem to instinctively trust him. We'd only been here a few weeks when Tom went away mustering. Ethan could see I was lonely, so he offered to teach me to ride. I never thought I'd do it, but I wasn't afraid of failing because Tom wasn't here to see it. Once I'd mastered horses, I was game for anything, so Ethan suggested I ride the camels. Tom was so surprised when he saw me aboard Hannibal for the first time. The expression on his face was pure disbelief. Ethan is a wonderful teacher, so patient. He'll be a marvelous tutor for Jack and Hannah."

"You admire him a great deal, don't you?"

"Very much. He's such an amazing man. If you take the time to really look, he's quite handsome beneath all that ruggedness, and he has a magnetizing quality. Have you noticed his extraordinary presence?"

Tara frowned. "I can't say that I have."

Victoria's eyes widened when she caught the edge in Tara's voice. "Surely... you don't dislike Ethan?"

Tara thought her aunt sounded incredulous, and inwardly groaned. Wasn't there anyone who didn't think of Ethan Hunter as some kind of hero?

"In all honesty, he's been wonderful with Jack, but we did get off on the wrong foot when we first met. I thought he was the most arrogant, overbearing man, and so rude. After hearing so much about him in Marree, I was expecting a prince. But Prince Charming he wasn't."

"He has his own brand of charm, I'll admit, but it's very attractive."

"I wouldn't call his strange wit, charm, but I must admit I didn't have any qualms about going into the desert with him."

"You couldn't have been in safer hands."

"He seems very competent. I did meet someone who shares your appreciation of his unrefined brand of charm, in Wombat Creek."

"Oh?"

"I visited Lottie and the girls."

"Ah, then you are referring to Maddie. She's in love with Ethan. Everyone between Darwin and Adelaide knows it."

"Are her feelings returned?"

"I really don't know. Ethan is the type of man who hides his emotions. I don't believe in all the time I've known him, he's ever spoken of his feelings for a woman."

"Surely he's had one relationship… a woman in his life at some time?"

Victoria noted Tara's curiosity, and suspected he intrigued her, despite her claims to the contrary. "I'm sure he must have, but he's never mentioned anyone specific."

"I suppose he couldn't expect a wife to sit at home and wait for him. From what he told me, she'd only see him a week every month."

"That's a normal way of life out here, Tara. Shearers, stockmen, station owners, all spend a great deal of time away from home. I was lucky to see Tom two days in a month when he was droving sheep or cattle to the markets. Once he was away for eight weeks taking cattle to the railhead in Port Augusta. The trip should have lasted four weeks but flash floods prevented him getting home. I didn't know what had happened to him. Luckily Ethan got through, and sent word to say he was still alive. I had been nearly out of my mind with worry."

Tara was astonished by what her aunt was telling her. At least she'd always known where Garvie was, which prison. She hadn't had to worry whether he was dead or alive.

"I was so grateful to Ethan," Victoria said. "Over the years he's done so much for us...."

Tara was baffled by her aunt's admiration for someone like Ethan Hunter. It seemed to go much further than appreciation for all he'd done for her.

"Aunt, Ethan is so uncultured, even by gipsy standards. He's like a wild frontier man. He's not the sort of man I imagine your Tom was." She visualized Tom Milburn as a real gentleman, like her father.

"You are quite right. Tom was nothing like Ethan. Not only were they complete opposites in appearance, but in almost every other way. Tom was softly spoken, and always insisted on dressing for dinner, even in this heat. He loved the property and the livestock, but he couldn't kill anything, bless him, not even a snake. I loved Tom dearly, and I wouldn't have changed him for the world, but he wasn't an exciting man, like Ethan. Ethan is a real manly sort of a man, if you get my meaning. He's perhaps rough around the edges, but those broad shoulders and deep chest, and those muscular thighs..."

"Are you trying to say he possesses some kind of sexual appeal, Aunt?"

Victoria's eyes sparkled in the moonlight. "He certainly does. Don't tell me you don't see it?"

"Certainly not! You sound as if you're in love with him." She also sounded like Maddie!

"I love him, yes, but not the way you think. But if I was a few years younger it would be a different story."

"I can't believe I'm hearing this, Aunt."

Victoria laughed. "There's a bit of life left in the old girl yet. By the way, I've asked Sanja to tone down his curries so you and the children can eat them."

"Oh, Aunt! Was he upset?"

"He's an employee, Tara, even though you may have gotten the impression he holds us to ransom."

"I met him after lunch, remember, Aunt?"

"Oh, that's right." Victoria smiled sheepishly. "Well, he didn't actually consent, but I hope he'll do as I've asked. He was in fact quite put out that you didn't come to dinner. And when he found out you and the children had eaten mutton chops, cooked by Nugget, he was outraged. I explained that you are not used to eating chilli and if he put less in the curries you'd be able to eat them. We can't have you living on those dreadful mutton chops."

"The children enjoyed them. I must admit, I did, too. I especially liked eating with the men around a campfire. It was like old times." Tara laughed at her aunt's scandalized expression. "Actually, it gave me a chance to get to know them a little better."

"They're good men. As I told you at lunch, it's so hard to get loyal employees. I have been blessed."

Tara couldn't agree more. She thought it must be rare to find men who would work for nothing for so long, especially with Tadd Sweeney riding their backs. It would be impossible if they had families who relied on their wages. This train of thought made Tara curious. "Hasn't Bluey or Nugget ever been married?"

"Nugget once had an Aboriginal wife, but she died many years ago. Unfortunately, the aboriginal mortality rate is very high. Bluey has had several different women, mostly aborigines. I'm sure you saw one of his women tonight. A lot of them are of mixed blood. It's common place out on the stations."

"Young Karl looks European. Was his mother South African?"

"Yes, a Boer Descendant. It was a terrible tragedy for Karl and Charlie when they lost her. Charlie doesn't say so, but I believe her murder was racial."

Tara looked confused.

"Charlie's half-caste aboriginal. Some of the whites in South Africa are very intolerant of inter-racial relations. That's why he came out here. With the odd exception, the Australian's are a more relaxed lot, especially out in the bush."

"I think Tadd Sweeney would have to be the odd exception. He gives me the impression he's very bigoted towards the aborigines."

"Tadd! You don't want to take much notice of what he says, Tara. He sounds harsh, but he's really as soft as butter."

Tara thought Nugget and the boys would disagree, but she didn't say so.

Tara had been contemplating how she was going to turn the conversation to finances, when she suddenly had an idea. "Aunt, I have asked Tadd if I can see the station ledgers tomorrow. I know he doesn't have time to do them, so I might take over, if you don't mind?"

Victoria looked up in surprise. "No, dear. I don't mind at all. Actually I was going to ask you to do it. I'd like to know our financial status in more detail. Tadd is so vague."
"He has told me the ledgers are not up to date, so I hope I can work out exactly where we stand."

"I wish I was still able to do it myself." Victoria looked momentarily uncomfortable.

Tara suspected she felt valueless, and knew it was especially hard for her as she had always taken such an active role on the station. The sooner she got her back in the saddle, the better.

"You'll have to guide me, Aunt. I haven't any experience in bookkeeping."

Victoria nodded, but she looked miles away.

Tara took a deep breath. "I was talking to Tadd this afternoon. He told me things are not so good, Aunt."

Victoria stared at her for a moment in bewilderment. "Tadd said that? Why?"

"Because it's true. I'm so sorry, Aunt."

Victoria lowered her head. She remained quiet for a minute or two.

Tara could see she was shocked. "Are you alright, Aunt? We don't have to discuss this now, if you are too tired."

"You must think I am a stupid woman?" she said, taking Tara by surprise.

"Of course I don't, Aunt. Why do you say that?"

"Apparently I don't even know the financial state of my own property."

Tara knelt beside her. "It's not your fault, Aunt," she said softly. "Tadd told me he hasn't been telling you the whole truth. He probably only told me a partial truth, but I'll see what I can find out."

Victoria frowned. "You suspect we're in bad shape, don't you?"

"It's probable, but if we know where we stand, we can try to do something about it."

"What do you know, Tara? Tell me the truth, please."

"Of course, Aunt. As I said, I don't know all the facts yet, but apparently there are few cattle left, and the men haven't been paid for quite some time."

Victoria gasped. "Oh, dear." She put her hand up to her mouth. "That's not good." She looked out over the station. "I don't understand why Tadd kept this from me."

"He said he wanted to spare you the worry."

"All this time I've been thinking we're all right. He should have told me the truth."

"I agree, but he thought he was doing the best thing."

Victoria didn't seem to be listening. "I've been through hard times before. One bad year, we lost over two thousand sheep. Only two hundred survived the drought. Nearly all the property owners for hundreds of miles walked off their land, but not me. It was the year after Tom's death, and believe me, it would have been so easy to give up. Tadd knows all this. He worked for me at the time." She shook her head. "I don't want to lose Tambora, Tara. I've worked so hard to keep it. If it wasn't for my failing eyesight, I would die trying to save this property."

Tara was angry with Tadd. In her mind, he'd done more harm than good in keeping the truth from Victoria. "I'll help however I can, Aunt. You know that."

Tears welled in the older woman's eyes. "You're a Godsend, Tara." She suddenly frowned. "I wonder if Ethan has been paid for all the supplies he's brought us?"

"I don't know. If he has, there may be an entry in the ledger."

"If he hasn't, I'll pay him out of the little money I have put away. I can't tolerate the idea of being in debt to him. He has to pay cash for the goods he picks up, so it wouldn't be right." She sighed. "I suppose I shouldn't be so hard on Tadd. He's tried so hard to talk to me, but…"

"But what?"

"He always wants to sell off sheep or cattle, but that is not always the answer. He's hinted often enough about selling the station. In the old days, if times were hard, we found new ways to do things, diversified ideas. Over the years we've tried different crops, even date palms; we've farmed goats, we've even shot rabbits to make ends meet. Tom thought breeding camels was an excellent idea. Australia has the only disease-free camels in the world. That's how Ethan came to keep his camels on the property. They were going to be partners. Tadd's a good man, but he never wants to listen to new ideas."

Tara thought Tadd seemed very keen to sell the station, overly so, in fact. She wondered about his motive; felt sure he had one.

"Can anything save the station, Aunt?"

Victoria was quiet for a few moments. "Did Tadd tell you how many sheep we have left?"

"No, but the men were moving a sizable herd this morning. Why do you ask?"

Victoria lowered her voice. "Tadd does not know this, but some time ago, when my sight was not so bad, I wrote to an old acquaintance of mine in India, with whom I corresponded from time to time. He has a rug-making business and had told me he was soon to begin making woollen rugs. He once mentioned the idea of exporting my wool to him. It was about the time Tom died, and I was too grief-stricken to give it serious thought. But last year I made some discreet inquiries. As you probably know, wool is almost worthless here, but the economic situation is a little different in India. For one thing, labour is dirt cheap, always has been. I wrote and told him I thought it was feasible, and asked if he was still interested. About two months ago, I received a reply, but the combination of my failing eyesight and William's shocking handwriting meant I couldn't read his letter. I couldn't ask Tadd to read it to me. I didn't want him to think I didn't trust him to manage my affairs. He can be so touchy about things. I would've asked Nerida, but she can't read, and Sanja can't read English. Ethan would've read it for me, but until today, I hadn't actually seen him for a few months."

Tara felt suddenly excited. "Where is the letter, Aunt? I'll read it to you."

"In the top drawer of the bureau beside my bed. His name is on the back. It's William Crombie."

Tara began searching while Victoria kept talking. "William bought the rug making business about ten years ago, as an investment. He's never been short of a rupee. He owned several hotels when Tom and I lived over there. Apparently the rug business proved to be quite a boon. William always had the Midas touch. Last I heard, he was employing nearly two hundred workers, and was exporting his rugs all over the world." Victoria could hear agitated rustling. "What's the matter, Tara, can't you find it?"

"No. Are you sure you put it in this drawer, Aunt?"

"Yes. I'm certain that is where I put it." Victoria got up and followed Tara into the bedroom.

"Is there anywhere else it might be?" Tara asked.

"No. That's where I keep my correspondence."

Tara kept searching, but the letter was nowhere to be found. "There's only one thing left to do, Aunt. I'll have to write another letter."

"It would take months to receive a reply, and we don't have time on our side."

"I know, but what other choice do we have? Meanwhile we'll keep searching for the reply you received. Maybe Nerida has been tidying up and put it somewhere else."

"I don't think so." Victoria looked confused. "She doesn't usually touch my personal papers."

"Don't worry. I'm sure we'll find it."

Victoria suddenly brightened. "Perhaps we could send a telegram?"

"Where from? There's no telegraph line near here, is there?"

"Yes, it runs right through Wombat Creek. Percy's store is a post office. He'd send a telegram for us."

"That's great news, Aunt. We'll either get Ethan to take a message into Wombat Creek next time he goes, or I'll make the trip myself."

"I'm sure Ethan wouldn't mind doing it for us."

"We'll ask him in the morning. William Crombie could reply to Wombat Creek, and we'd have an answer in no time." Tara took her aunt's hand. "I don't want you to worry, Aunt. Together we'll save the station, no matter what we have to do. I promise." Tara had no idea how she was going to achieve the impossible, but she couldn't bear to see the pain in her Aunt's eyes. She prayed William Crombie came through for them.

"In my prayers tonight, I'm going to say a special thank you to the Lord for sending you here," Victoria said.

Tara smiled wanly. "I should be me thanking the Lord for having an Aunt kind enough to take me and the children in. But while you're speaking to him, see if he has a miracle to spare. Goodnight, Aunt. Try not to worry."

When Tara had gone to her own room, Victoria went back out onto the balcony and looked over the land she loved so passionately.

"I won't lose Tambora," she whispered. "Not while I still have a breath in me." Tears ran down her cheeks, and she brushed them away impatiently. "It's not only my home now, it's Tara's and the children's. We can't lose it. We just can't!"

CHAPTER SIXTEEN

The screeching parrots roused Tara just before daybreak. She'd snatched little more than a few minutes sleep at sparse intervals, as the possums had begun invading her room soon after she retired. They'd scampered over her dressing table, knocking things over, climbed the bedposts to the top railing, from which the mosquito net hung, and even squabbled under her bed. Thankfully they had kept off the bed, but when she lit her lamp to chase them out, she was dismayed to see their 'calling cards' scattered around the room. When they returned to the trees, and she thought she could finally sleep in peace, Hannah had crept into bed beside her, and tossed and turned for the remainder of the night.

Tara was in no mood to admire the streaks of vivid colour that flushed the dawn sky, as she made her way towards the overgrown vegetable garden, equipped with a pitchfork and spade, swatting the loathsome flies and cursing the noisy birds under her breath as she went. Trampling through knee-high dry grass and weeds, she suddenly remembered the snakes, and decided to let Mellie and the pups out of the kennels.

The collie bitch was delighted with her freedom. She scouted the area surrounding the vegetable garden with her tail in the air and her nose on the ground, while the puppies made a nuisance of themselves around Tara's feet. Within seconds Mellie began barking furiously at something in the grass about twenty feet away. Tara tried to call her away, but she wouldn't come, and there was no one about to help. Terrified Mellie had found a snake, and she would get bitten, Tara tentatively ventured near enough to see, while keeping far enough away to be able to make a quick escape. She gasped in shock when she saw the culprit was a lizard the size of a small crocodile. Surrounded by the barking collie and her inquisitive pups, and faced with a nervous woman wielding a long handled spade, the lizard made an ungainly retreat. This time Mellie came when called, but two of the more boisterous of the pups pursued the lizard.

"Good morning, Missus," Nugget said, startling her. Somehow he'd approached unheard through the dry grass and crisp leaves, but Tara was too flustered to fathom how.

"Did you see that lizard, Nugget?" she asked breathlessly. "It was enormous. I'm afraid it might eat the pups."

Nugget regarded her as if she had sunstroke; his dark eyes seeming to be full of age old wisdom. Shaking his head, he said, "Him just a goanna, Missus. Make good tucker."

"A goanna? Are you saying… that creature is actually harmless, despite its size?"

"Yes, Missus. Tribal piccanninies and lubras hunt him for tucker."

Women and children! Tara felt foolish and bent to examine the foliage of what she suspected was a weed, so that Nugget wouldn't notice her discomfort.

"You up early this morning, Missus."

"I've hardly slept, Nugget." She wiped perspiration from her brow, wishing she could strip naked and lounge in a cool bath.

Nugget could see she was tired. "Too hot for you, Missus?"

"It is, but possums wreaking havoc in my room kept me awake most of the night."

He grinned and Tara saw his pink tongue where his front teeth should have been.

"Possum stew real good tucker, Missus."

It seemed Nugget thought of everything as a potential meal. "So Nerida says, and after last night I'm tempted to suggest you cook them up, but my aunt is fond of them, so we had better leave them be."

"You know what yer doing here, Missus?" He gestured to the overgrown patch, which barely hinted at its brief history as a constructive garden.

"I haven't a clue."

Nugget's eyes crinkled at the corners.

"It would help if I knew which of these plants were weeds," Tara said. "I don't want to pull the vegetable plants out."

"Plants not same where you come from, Missus?"

"No, Nugget." Tara was pleased to have any excuse for her ignorance. "Nothing looks familiar, other than the corn plants, which have gone to seed. Even the trees are different. Back home we had Ash, and Oak, and Elm… I haven't seen anything like that out here."

Nugget looked at the surrounding gum trees, with their smooth trunks, and far reaching limbs, not really understanding, then squatted and pointed out the different weeds, explaining that some of them were edible, some thorny and others medicinal or poisonous. Typically the weeds looked to be the hardiest and healthiest of the growing vegetation. Everything else looked parched and lifeless.

"Missus should not do hard work out here," Nugget said.

"We need fresh vegetables…"

"Locusts coming. They eat everything."

"When, Nugget?"

He shrugged, and gazed off into the distance, as if listening for something.

Tara prodded at the ground, and her pitchfork hit a rock. "I should at least get the garden ready for cultivation. The first thing I need to do is clear these rocks."

"Sorry cannot help, Missus. Got plenty sheep to muster before sun down."

Tara could see horses saddled in a yard nearby. "That's all right, Nugget. Jack will be helping me later. I wanted to let him sleep this morning."

"Young fella not sleep. He saddled two horses, Missus."

Tara was taken back. "I thought he was still in his room."

"He bin up long time, before sun up. Had damper and tea with us, then go over yonder." Tara was quite astonished. Jack wasn't supposed to meet Ethan until after breakfast. She hoped he wouldn't try to climb the ridge before Ethan showed him the way.

"Is Tadd going out with you today," Tara inquired.

"No, Missus."

"What does he do, Nugget?"

He shrugged. "Not know, Missus. That something only white fella God know."

Tara laughed, although she sensed Nugget wanted to say much more, but was either afraid to, or didn't believe he should be talking behind Tadd Sweeney's back.

"You don't like him, do you, Nugget?"

Nugget shrugged again. "He not easy man to know, Missus. He keep to hisself. Spend much time with Missus Victoria."

Tara sensed Nugget didn't trust Tadd Sweeney, which was exactly how she felt, although she wasn't sure why. For the first time she seriously considered the prospect that he may be in love with her aunt. She wasn't sure how she felt about that, either.

Tara toiled for an hour under the blazing sun, with only a small pile of stones to show for her effort. The ground was sandy on the surface, but underneath it was as hard as iron. By the time the breakfast gong sounded, she already had blisters on her hands, and her back ached. She was ashamed to realize her determination had waned in the growing heat, and her frustration with the flies almost drove her to screaming.

Soon after she had begun work, Nerida came outside to do some washing in a trough, and Hannah made her way over to Tara. Nerida said the little girl had collected the eggs from the chickens, and broke four, which Sanja was cooking for their breakfast. Tara made a game of putting the rocks in a pile, but Hannah soon tired of it, and played with the puppies instead. Mellie stood watch over them.

Tadd and Victoria were already seated at the table when Tara and Hannah came into the dining room. Sanja was serving some sort of flat bread. He gave her a disdainful look, before he defiantly plonked down a bowl of what looked like scrambled eggs. Tara was annoyed to see they had been curried.

"Have we any jam, Aunt?" she asked loudly and cheerfully.

"I think we have a jar, dear. Sanja, will get it for you."

The cook gave Tara a haughty look but went off to the kitchen, leaving her pleased with her small victory.

"You had an early start in the garden, Tara," Victoria said. "I could hardly believe it when Nerida said you were working outside, and I wasn't even out of bed. How is it going?"

Tara was tempted to say it was bloody hard work, and she detested it, but instead forced herself to sound positive. "I've made a start on getting the area ready for cultivation, but Nugget suggested I wait until the locust plague has passed before planting. He said the locusts will eat everything, including the weeds, which might save me some work."

"Who's to say they are going to come this way at all," Tadd said offhandedly.

"What makes you think they won't?" Tara asked curiously. "Surely nothing can stop them."

"They are not always predictable. Sometimes they suddenly change direction for no apparent reason. Other times the wind carries them away. You could hold back your vegetable garden for weeks, only to find they don't appear at all."

"Nugget seemed sure they were heading this way. He's moving hundreds of sheep to an area where there's more feed."

Tadd cocked his head to one side and smirked. Tara tensed, sensing he was going to say something derogatory about the Aboriginals.

"Nothing is as it seems out here, Tara. For instance, it often looks like it's going to rain, but it doesn't. We have to move livestock all the time, because with no rain, there isn't much feed around. I don't want to be saying anything against the Abo's, but if you think about it, what makes Nugget an expect on the behaviour of grasshoppers?"

Tara noticed Nerida's lips compressed tightly, as if she was holding her tongue, as she passed a jar of jam to her and hovered over Hannah.

"I ... I don't know, but it seems to me that would be just the sort of thing he would be an authority on, being Aboriginal."

Tadd laughed. "Nugget was brought up on a mission, run by the Presbyterians. He's used to having his food given to him, just like you and I."

Tara was astonished. "He seems to think of almost everything as a potential meal, things I wouldn't consider."

"Maybe so, but he eats lamb everyday. Being black doesn't make him tribal or an expert at living off the land."

"That's not quite true, Tadd," Victoria intervened. "Nugget is a good tracker, better than any white man I know, with the possible exception of Ethan. And don't take this to heart, but I'd put my money on him surviving in the desert before you." Victoria addressed Tara. "It's true Nugget lived on a mission up north as a boy. His father was Aboriginal but his mother was only part Aboriginal. The missionaries had converted her to the Presbyterian faith. I'm sure Tadd is aware that Nugget spent most of his adolescence, a time of tribal initiation or coming of age for boys, with the Arabana people, after his mother and father died. That was where he married his tribal wife, who later died from what I believe was an appendicitis attack."

"Well, maybe I'm exaggerating to make a point, Victoria," Tadd conceded, "but if the Abos's know that Tara believes every word they say, they'll play on it. I just don't want her to assume whatever they tell her is fact."

"Are you advising her to plant her vegetable garden?" Victoria asked.

"I'd take the chance if it were me."

Tara wasn't sure what to believe, but she knew it would take a few days to have the garden patch ready for planting. If by then the locusts hadn't appeared, she would sew her seeds. She felt some responsibility for contributing to the food supply.

"What are you doing today, Mr. Sweeney?" Tara asked, more curious than ever about his activities, especially as he had so much to say about what others did and thought.

"I'll be chasing up the stragglers that the men miss…"

Victoria cut in. "There won't be many of those. The dogs are too good."

Tadd looked annoyed. "Well there's stock yard fences to be fixed, and, if I have time, I'll check the bores. I doubt I'll be in for lunch today. Sanja is packing me something to take with me."

"Where's young Jack?" Victoria asked Tara.

"He was up even earlier than me, so I suspect he's already gone to meet Ethan. He's so enchanted with the camels."

"Perhaps Ethan could take him on as an apprentice cameleer," Victoria suggested.

"Didn't you say the lad would be doing chores around here," Tadd asked frowning.

"Yes, he will, but I'm not going to press him for a day or so."

"There's plenty to do that won't wait," Tadd added.

"Moving here has been quite an upheaval for him." Tadd frowned again.

"The boy needs to find his feet," Victoria said. "Especially after the trip out. Give him a week or so to settle," she added, glancing at Tadd cautiously.

Tara realized her aunt hadn't told Tadd anything about her situation, and was sure he was speculating. She also suspected he thought Victoria and herself were being too soft on Jack. Just in case he was tempted to say something to him, she decided to make him aware the boy was grieving.

She glanced at Hannah, who was fidgeting and tired. Tara knew when the little girl was tired she usually called for her mama. She didn't want anyone, other than her aunt and Ethan, to know she wasn't the children's mother.

"Nerida, would you take Hannah upstairs and see if she will have a nap?"

"Yes, Missus."

Tara kissed the little girl and Nerida took her away. She was thankful the aboriginal girl was always willing to take care of Hannah. It was easy to see she had grown very fond of her in the short time they had been on the station.

When they had left the room, Tara said, "There is a reason I am being lapse with Jack, Mr. Sweeney. He recently lost his father."

The manager looked shocked.

Tara glanced at her aunt, before turning her full attention on Tadd Sweeney. "The ship we came out on went down off the coast and he drowned. As you can imagine, it's been very traumatic for the children, but especially Jack. For that reason, I am overlooking behaviour that is out of the ordinary. You may have noticed he's even been very distant with me."

Tadd had been wondering where the boy's father was, but hadn't had a chance to ask Victoria. He'd also noticed Jack was acting strangely towards her. "I'm sorry, lass. I didn't even suspect you were widowed. That is a tragedy."

His words were like a knife in Tara's heart. Losing Michael and Maureen was terrible enough, but she couldn't bear to think Garvie had been hanged. She fought tears that were stinging the backs of her eyes. "It's not something I want made public. I just want to get on with life with the children as best I can."

Tadd nodded. He thought Tara brave, and admired her resolve to pick up the pieces and go on, especially with young ones.

After breakfast, Tadd left Victoria and Tara alone for a few moments, while he went to the kitchen to get a packed lunch.

"Would you like to go for a ride, Aunt, before it gets too hot?"

"Yes, but aren't you busy with the garden?"

"I can get back to it later, perhaps when the sun is going down, and it's a little cooler."

Tadd came in to say goodbye. His lunch looked enough for three people.

"My Aunt and I are going riding this morning, Mr. Sweeney, so if you could show me where your tack room is, I'll saddle two horses."

"For the love of Holy Moses, call me Tadd, Tara. This Mr. Sweeney business is making me feel like a banker, and you know how popular they are at the moment." His tone was friendlier than it had been since they first met, and his eyes twinkled at her.

Tara couldn't help responding. "Alright, Tadd it is."

"Come on then. I'll show you Lori. She's Victoria's mare."

"This is wonderful," Victoria said, sitting tall in the saddle on Lori, as they passed through the dappled shade of gum trees surrounding the house and outbuildings. "I can't believe it's been so long since I was last out riding."

Tara certainly felt more at home on a horse than she had done on a camel. "When did you last visit town, Aunt, or have any visitors?"

"I haven't been to Wombat Creek for more than year, and I haven't had a visitor for months. I used to keep in touch on the radio, until it went on the blink."

"The isolation must have been very lonely."

"I must admit it was lonely. I do love the solitude and the peace of living out here, but it's nice to talk to people, and find out what's going on in the world."

"Wombat Creek is a far cry from the world, but we'll make a trip to town in the next week or so. Ferris tells me the hotel actually gets crowded on the weekends. I'm not sure I believe him, so I want to see it for myself." She laughed. "You should have seen Ferris and Percy's face when I suggested they get together with Lottie and the girls for a dance."

Victoria laughed, too. "You've always been full of the devil, Tara."

"It's awful the way the men treat them, Aunt, and so hypocritical. Ethan visits them, and Ferris was a regular until he married Charity. I suspect Percy visits too, because Belle gave me a watch to return to him."

Victoria was astonished. "What a fraud that man is! He'd have everyone believe he is a monument to virtue."

"All three of them knew I was going to visit the women, and none of them had the courage to tell me they were prostitutes. It made no difference to me, I still would have gone, but it put Lottie in the embarrassing position of having to tell me herself. Her humiliation made me so angry, I decided to have a little fun with the men when I returned to the hotel."

"What did you do?"

"I told them I had invited the women out here for afternoon tea. I think Ethan knew what I was up to, but you should have seen the indignity on Ferris and Percy's faces. It was priceless."

"I can imagine, but even though Lottie is a good woman, with a heart of pure gold, I doubt you'll change their attitudes."

"I asked her if you and she were friends, but she said no."

"That was Lottie's choice, Tara. I like her, and I admire her courage. As far as I'm concerned, she is just as good as anyone else, certainly more honest than the likes of Percy Everett. She provides a service, but how she makes her living is of no concern to me. When she first came to the area, she camped at the back of the hotel in a tiny tent."

"She told me. It must have been horrible."

"Unfortunately for her, that year we had a record rainfall. I felt so sorry for her. I even asked her to come and live out here, but she wouldn't hear of it. She's such a proud woman, but had the shoe been on the other foot, she'd have dragged me kicking and screaming into her home."

"She told me someone lent her the money to have her home built."

Victoria nodded. "Did she say who it was?"

"No." Tara suddenly wondered.

"It was Tom and I, but no one suspected. We had just finished building this house when Lottie arrived in Wombat Creek. Our enormous home seemed so indulgent when she was living in such appalling conditions. Despite what she had to put up with, Ferris was no help. The old scrooge charged her a fee to use the hotel bathroom, and for drinking water. If she didn't have the money, she went without." She sighed, remembering how angry she had been. "We had a difficult time persuading her to accept the money to build her own home, especially as we didn't want it returned. When she finally relented, it was on the condition that the money was a loan, which she insisted she repay with interest. After much haggling, we compromised."

"I didn't think Percy or Ferris loaned her the money, but I had wondered about Ethan. Even though he looks penniless, I had heard he's made good money as a cameleer."

"He has, but no doubt he's suffering like everyone else at the moment. I've always suspected he was the chief benefactor of the mission, and donated to other charities when he had the money. I'm in no doubt he would have given Lottie whatever she needed, willingly, if Tom and I hadn't. But Percy and Ferris, no, never, and yet, even though they publicly shun her, both of them know her business attracts a lot of people to Wombat Creek, mostly men of course, but they drink in the hotel and shop in the store. I doubt the town would exist without Lottie and the girls."

"Did you talk to them on the radio, when it was working?"

"Sometimes, but always on the pretence of something innocent. Other people can listen in, so you have to be careful what you say. It doesn't bother me, but they give Lottie a hard time, especially the jealous wives."

"Which way shall we go?" Tara asked, once they cleared the trees.

"Out towards the ridge," Victoria replied. "It's shady that way at this time of day. If I can find them, I'll show you where there are some aboriginal drawings that are supposed to be thousands of years old."

Lunch was cold lamb, which had been smeared with a hot pickle so Tara couldn't eat it, Sanja's revenge, and Indian 'Roti' bread. When they were finished, Victoria and Tara examined the books. Over the last few months there were few entries, but it appeared that Ethan had not been paid for quite some time. The last entry for wages to Nugget was almost a year ago, and the other men had not been paid for several months. In Tadd's defense, he hadn't had wages for almost as long as Nugget.

"Did Howie Dunn have severance pay?" Victoria asked. "It looks like only a week's wages."

"What about Nerida?"

"There's nothing here for Nerida for the past year."

Victoria was devastated. She went to the drawer containing the cash box, but found the box empty.

Tara thought her aunt was going to faint, but she seemed to pull herself together.

"I have a little money put away upstairs," Victoria said. "Tom always made me keep it for emergencies. This situation certainly qualifies." Tears finally overwhelmed her.

Tara put her arms around her. "We're going to be all right, Aunt, I promise. Just remember we're Killains. We're a tough breed."

"You're right." She sniffed. "I've survived worse, and so have you. But now we have the children to think about. They need a home, and food on the table."

"The children will be all right, Aunt. We won't starve, even if we have to go native ourselves. I just don't want you to lose Tambora."

"Thank God I don't owe the bank any money, and we have the emergency funds. They should see us through until we find a way to get back on our feet."

The two women went upstairs, where Victoria instructed Tara to look for a small silk bag, hidden amongst her clothes in the wardrobe, which she said contained her emergency funds. Tara found the bag and gave it to her aunt. Victoria took it over to the bed and emptied the contents.

"How much is there?" she asked Tara.

Tara counted the money. "Twenty seven pounds, and some change."

Victoria gasped. "That can't be right. There should be almost three hundred pounds."

"Are you sure, Aunt?"

"Of course I'm sure. I haven't touched those funds for … it must be two years. We had a lean season, and I had to use about a hundred pounds to buy feed, but I was able to put it back when we sold some cattle." Victoria slumped onto the bed.

"Surely you haven't been robbed?"

"No. Tadd must have used the money and didn't tell me."

"Would he do that?"

"There was a time when I wouldn't have thought so. But I suppose he couldn't ask for money without telling me what he wanted it for. He knew I had the money, and vaguely where it was, but it's never been necessary for him to ask for it. There's usually a cash flow of two thousand pounds in the tin downstairs, and several thousand in the bank. It costs a lot of money to keep a place this size going." She glanced at the notes and coins on the bed. "I don't think twenty seven dollars and some change is going to do it."

Nerida came into the room. "Little Miss is sleeping," she said to Tara, then looked at Victoria, her small face full of concern. "Ethan is downstairs, Missus."

"Thank you, Nerida. I must go down and talk to him. I'm dreadfully sorry you haven't been paid for such a long time, Nerida. I had no idea…"

"It not matter, Missus. I like being here with you."

"Bless you, girl," Victoria said, close to tears. "But as soon as we're back in the black, I'm going to pay you everything I owe you. That's a promise." She took a deep breath and scooped up the few pounds on the bed.

"How much do we owe Ethan, Tara?"

"Almost twenty pounds, not counting what he brought yesterday."

"Then we may have enough to pay him."

Tara nodded, her expression grim.

Victoria put on a bright face when she came downstairs with Tara.

Jack looked happy, until he saw Tara, and his expression completely changed. He turned and went outside before she could ask him how he had enjoyed his morning.

"Ethan, come through and sit down," Victoria said. "I wish to settle our account with you."

Ethan looked puzzled. He followed Victoria into the sitting room. Tara noticed he hadn't shaved, and he smelt of livestock. As her gaze ran over his muscled chest and thighs, she thought again of what her aunt had said about him having sex appeal. She supposed that if you liked the wild frontier man type, his physique would certainly fit the bill. But attractive....

"I told you yesterday, there is no hurry," Ethan said to Victoria.

Victoria looked solemn. "And I said I wish to settle up, now."

Ethan frowned. "Why now?"

"Why not now, Ethan? Tara has taken over doing the books and we're getting them straight. How much do we owe you?"

Ethan looked glum. He glanced at Tara, who was watching him with a serious expression. When she lowered her eyes, he knew something was very wrong. "I really have no idea what you owe off the top of my head. I would have to check my own books."

"You're beating around the bush, Ethan. You've always been an uncanny business man, so don't pretend you have no idea."

"What's this all about, Victoria, and I want the truth?"

"I told you, we're getting the books up to date."

Ethan could see Victoria was fighting tears. "Has something happened?" he asked gently.

Tara glanced at her aunt, who had begun to shake. "Excuse me," Victoria said. "I'm going to get a drink."

"I'll get it, Aunt."

"No," she said more sharply than she had intended. She shuffled from the room, calling over her shoulder, "Would you like one?"

"No, thank you," Ethan and Tara echoed.

When she was out of earshot, Ethan turned to Tara. "What's going on? Tell me the truth. I've never seen Victoria this shaken."

"Tadd has been keeping secrets from her. He told me he has been hiding the fact that the station has been losing money. Apparently it's been going on for quite some time. She had no idea how bad things were until today. The men haven't been paid for months, and the cash box was empty. She had an emergency supply, but Tadd has been tapping it, and there's not much left."

Ethan cussed under his breath. "How could Tadd do this?" He wondered why the wires on the radio had been disconnected. Now he had his answer.

"I think his intentions were good. Despite all this, my aunt really wants to settle up with you. It's important to her, so please take the money. Let her salvage what's left of her pride."

"Pride is no substitute for food, Tara."

Victoria came back into the room with a glass of water in her hand. She seemed to have composed herself.

Ethan stood up and paced the room in front of the fireplace.

"I have told Ethan the situation, Aunt," Tara explained.

"Do you think you are the only one in this predicament, Victoria?" Ethan asked. "Everyone out here is suffering. Some are in far worse shape than you."

"I doubt that, but we've come back before, and we'll do it again. I won't give up."

"I know you have survived far worse, and if anyone can come through the tough times, you can. So please stop worrying about what you owe me. I thought we were friends. Friends help each other out."

"Friends don't take advantage of each other. And that is what we're doing to you. I want to settle our account. I have the money."

"Christ, Victoria, everyone else is at the bartering stage. I have been given chickens, a violin, preserves, tinned foods, and radio parts. At one time I even had an unexploded Japanese bomb from Darwin, which Wally Macintosh convinced me I needed. Fortunately, the government confiscated it for a museum before I blew myself up. They compensated me with food rations, but no cash. Surely that tells you something. Tadd may have been sheltering you from the truth; I suspect he disconnected the radio so you wouldn't hear the bad news from someone else, but now I want you to talk to other station owners. Speak to Jock Wilson, and Sadie, find out how they are managing. None of them have seen a pound note for months."

Victoria sank back in her chair, in shock. She couldn't believe she'd been living in some kind of make believe world, and had not known what was going on around her.

"Do you know of anyone with geese they don't want?" Tara asked Ethan.

He looked momentarily startled. "Yes, Lester Eaton from Emu Creek has some geese he wants to get rid of. But I'm surprised you're interested. They can be hard to handle."

"That's true, but their eggs are much larger, and in Ireland they keep the foxes away, so I'm hoping they'll do the same with the dingoes. Could we trade something for them?"

"I'm sure you could. Lester has been wheeler-dealing all his life."

"What is considered tradable out here?"

"Surprisingly, ladies stockings are high on the list of things to trade…"

"I bought two pairs in Port Adelaide, and I certainly won't wear them in this heat."

"They'll come in handy, but not for the geese. Lester Eaton isn't married."

"Will he take chickens?"

"I doubt it. He breeds poultry."

Tara racked her brain. "It would be best if we asked him what he wants for the geeses?"

"I'll radio him now if you like." Ethan went to the radio room down the hall.

Tara glanced at her aunt. "I've done plenty of bartering in the past, Aunt. It can be challenging, but often rewarding when you trade well. We're going to be fine. I know it." Victoria could tell she was excited. They could hear the crackle of the radio, and then Ethan came back.

"If you had cash, he'd take two pounds for eight geese. If not, he wants three bottles of wine, or a soup pot and some bowls, or, don't be shocked, a chamber pot and some potatoes. He'd also like some darning done if anyone is willing."

Tara looked from Victoria to Ethan. "I'm afraid I'm not very good at sewing, and my aunt can't see to darn." She imagined Lester's smelly old socks, and inwardly cringed.

"But we have nearly all of the things you've mentioned," Victoria said, getting caught up in the spirit. "Tom collected wine. There's some rather good bottles in the cellar." She suddenly had a thought. "If Tadd hasn't sold them. Would you go down the cellar, Ethan, and see what's there?"

"Of course." He left.

"I dug up a few old potatoes in the garden this morning," Tara said. "They weren't very good, so I turned them in, but if we could trade them for something…"

Ethan came back. "There are about twenty five bottles of wine down there. Do you know what you should have?"

"Not exactly, but I thought Tom had at least seventy or eighty bottles. Please tell Lester Eaton we'll trade two bottles of very good wine for the geese, as long as they're young and healthy. I'm sure he wouldn't know the difference between a good bottle and a bad one, but we won't give him three that are probably worth quite a bit. If he has two ducks, a female and a drake, or a turkey for eating, I have a chamber pot he can have. And Ethan, we must come to a mutually satisfactory agreement about settling our account."

"I haven't paid Nugget for taking care of the camels for me while I'm away. That would cover at least half of what you owe me."

"That's between you and him. He took care of them in his own time. I know you give him tobacco and whatever else you can lay your hands on. Tadd said he's seen him wearing your shirts, and showing off new socks."

Ethan grinned. "I have to compensate him for being bitten by Hannibal." He glanced at Tara and saw her eyes widen, and winked at her, a hint he wasn't serious. But she wondered.

Tara was digging in the garden when she saw Jack near the kennels. She was hot and tired and her hands hurt. She straightened her aching back, and watched him for a few minutes. He looked lost in thought, and unhappy. She had hoped he might help her in the garden, but he'd avoided her ever since he returned with Ethan, which was several hours ago.

Jack didn't hear Tara approach. "The kennels need cleaning out," she said, startling him. "I thought you might do it. I've been trying to get the vegetable garden ready for planting seeds, but it's damn hard work…"

"It wasn't my idea to look after the dogs," Jack interrupted.

Tara was in no mood for disrespect or thoughtlessness. "We all have to do our bit," she snapped.

He didn't reply.

She softened her tone. "Hannah has been collecting the eggs."

"I help Ethan. That's all I'm doing." He looked her up and down with such contempt, Tara recoiled.

"I'm not helping you," he said, and ran off.

Tears were running down Tara's cheeks, as she trudged back to the garden. She couldn't understand why Jack hated her so much, or what had changed since they arrived on Tambora. He'd been reserved on the journey, but not hostile.

Venting her frustration, Tara tackled the garden with such fervour that the handle of the spade broke in her hand. She cussed in anger and threw it as far away as she could.

"Now see what you've done," Ethan said, startling her.

She whirled round. "Don't you start on me," she snapped, not noticing the twinkle in his dark eyes. A huge splinter had imbedded itself in her palm, and it hurt like Hell.

Ethan looked startled by her fury. He'd been shoeing horses in the stable, when Jack had run past, ignoring him. He'd thought it strange, but now realized there was a connection. "Did something happen between you and Jack?"

Tara slumped to the ground in defeat. Ethan came to kneel in front of her and took her hand and examined the palm. He was shocked to see the raw blisters. He produced a knife from a sheath on his belt. "Hold on, I'll get that splinter out before it gets infected." She tried to pull away, but he held her hand firm.

"Are you squeamish?" he asked gently.

Tara shook her head and he began to gently dig with the sharp point of the blade. She winced, but in less than a minute, the splinter was out.

"Your hands are in a terrible state. You should have worn gloves."

Tara mumbled, "It's too hot." She took a deep breath to compose herself. "Has Jack said anything today?"

"About what?"

"Me."

"No."

"Has he told you what has made him so angry?"

"He hasn't been upset today, at least not while he was with me. He has his quiet moments, which I expect under the circumstances, but we've had a very good day."

"Then it's me he's angry with. I didn't want to believe it, but something is wrong. It began the day we arrived here, but I don't know what brought it about. I was hoping he would confide in you. He certainly won't talk to me."

"Maybe he'll tell me something, but I don't want to push him. He enjoys being with the camels. It makes him happy for a little while. I did think he looked tired, though, but there again, I could say the same about you."

Tara rolled her eyes. "Possums! I'll be shutting the balcony doors tonight. I've also had Hannah creep into my bed, and she's a very restless sleeper. I suppose her mother was used to her, but she keeps me awake. I imagine the nights are bad for Jack, too, especially as the ship went down in the middle of the night. He probably has nightmares, I do. I just wish I knew why he was being so aggressive towards me. It's so frustrating. This business of being a mother is very difficult. Maybe I'm not cut out for it." She leant her head in her hands, and felt like sobbing, but held back.

"You've had a hard day," Tara, "and you're tired. Tomorrow will be brighter. Now go and rest, and put some iodine on your hands." He leant forward and gently lifted her to her feet by her arm.

"Did you make arrangements with my aunt about payment for the supplies?" she asked.

"Nothing she is agreeable to. Apparently, she has something she wants me to do for her in Wombat Creek, so I'll hold her to ransom." He smiled, and his dark eyes crinkled at the corners.

Tara thought again what an unusual and complex man Ethan Hunter was. He was a hard-line, rugged bushman, with a soft heart, who for some unknown reason aroused the sexual appetites of women of all ages. Tara couldn't work him out, and wondered if she ever would.

CHAPTER SEVENTEEN

Tara was digging in the garden when Mellie started barking excitedly.

Victoria popped her head out of the back door and shouted, "I think the geese have arrived."

Tara dropped her spade and wiped perspiration from her forehead, as she watched Ethan round the corner of the house on Hannibal, with Mellie yapping at the camel's heels. Three camels followed behind with two large wire cages on each, that were shaded by lightweight covers

"If I had to go any further, I don't think they would have made it," Ethan called to Tara. "I've had to throw water on them to keep them alive."

Tara sympathized with the poor creatures. They'd endured one day's train journey from Emu Creek and two days on the camels, cooped in small cages, in the unbearable heat. Tara could hear them hissing above the growls of protest from the camel's, as they dropped to their knees.

The chickens had been moved to a smaller pen in readiness for the arrival of the geese and ducks. One side of their new home was shaded by an acacia tree in full blossom, and Tara had raked up all the chicken muck, which she intended to use as fertilizer on her garden, and put fresh hay in the roost, and clean water in the trough.

The three women watched as Ethan unloaded the cages and set the ducks and geese free. They wobbled on their feet and one or two dropped to the ground.

"Are they dying?" Tara called in alarm.

"They're suffering mild heat stroke," Ethan said. He picked up one goose at a time, and dunked them in the water trough, and then sat them down in the shade. The two ducks he left in the trough, where they splashed and dunked their heads, making Hannah laugh.

After a minute or two, the geese got to their feet and shook their feathers, before making an indignant inspection of their new living quarters.

"I think they'll all survive," Ethan assured. "It's been a long trip for them, and the train was late, again." He accepted a much-needed drink offered by Nerida and downed it in seconds.

"Thank you for fetching them for us," Tara said, doing a quick head count. "We appear to have one extra goose."

"Lester was so pleased with the wine, he threw in a gander, for breeding or eating."

"Oh. That's wonderful." Tara turned to her aunt. "We'll keep him for breeding, but why don't we have roast chicken for dinner tonight, as a treat?" She hadn't eaten anything but bread and jam for lunch and mutton chops for dinner, for days. Chicken would be a nice change. "We could also roast the few potatoes I found in the garden."

"That's a good idea. I'd like something different from lamb, myself. It's extravagant, but we'll open a bottle of wine, too." She frowned. "I know Sanja won't kill the chickens. He doesn't mind plucking them, but I usually get Nugget or Charlie to do the deed." She gestured to imply the cutting of their throats. "And they're not back yet."

"I'll do it," Ethan said.

"Oh, thank you, Ethan. What would we do without you? You must stay for dinner, of course. We'll kill three and give one chicken to Nugget and the boys. I'm sure they'd also like a change from damper and mutton chops."

"Aunt, be sure Sanja doesn't find some way to add even the tiniest bit of curry to the chicken, please."

Ethan shook his head. "That'll be a feat.

"I'll see that he doesn't," Victoria assured, "even if I have to sit in the kitchen all afternoon, and watch him."

Sanja had toned down the curries, but not enough for Tara to eat them. Jack had begun eating a little though, which the cook saw as a victory, and Hannah had come to like the Dhal and rice.

Ever since Tara had begun working in the garden, almost a week ago, she'd had the feeling she was being watched from nearby trees. She hadn't seen anyone, but she could sense his or her presence.

Several times when Nerida had brought her a glass of water, Tara had noticed she glanced towards the trees.

"Who is out there?" Tara finally asked. Nerida looked startled and wary.

"I know someone is watching me," Tara said, continuing to dig. "I just wish they would come and give me a hand." She had relented, and worn cotton gloves after the first day of digging, and her hands had begun to heal, but her back ached so much, she could barely straighten up. The garden was coming along slowly, but there was still so much to do.

"The tribal women are curious, Missus. They not want trouble. They like your hat and dress."

"Do you think they would help me, Nerida? I can't pay them, but I could give them something. Some eggs perhaps."

"They not want eggs, Missus? They find bird eggs…"

"How about something more personal? A ribbon for their hair, or a scarf, or some pretty jewellery?" She had something inexpensive in mind, beads or the like. Unfortunately, she'd lost all of the pretty gifts she'd been given aboard ship for her readings when the ship went down. They could have been put to good use now.

Nerida smiled. "They like pretty things, Missus."

Tara kept working while Nerida went off to speak to the women. She returned soon afterwards with three shy lubras. They were much older than Nerida, and looked to be full-blooded, with very black faces, broad noses, and frizzy hair. Their legs and arms were as skinny as Nerida's, but their tummies and breasts were large. They were wearing soiled shifts but no shoes.

"Could you show what you give them, Missus? Then they work."

"Of course." Tara went inside and found some ribbons she had bought for Hannah and two scarves Victoria said she didn't want. Victoria had very little jewellery, as it had been sold over the years to make ends meet, but she found some beads, old bracelets, and two broaches that she didn't mind parting with. Tara brought them out to the women, who were chatting amongst themselves in their language.

"If I give you these, will you help me dig the garden?" Tara asked, offering the bribes. The women talked amongst themselves excitedly.

"Do they speak any English?" Tara asked Nerida. "Can they understand me?"

"Not lot, Missus. Yani spend some time on a mission, but not lot."

"What are their names?"

Nerida said, "Mona, Yani and Mumu."

"Are they going to work for me?" Tara asked, while smiling at them, and demonstrating how to wear the items she had given them. She thought they looked absurd, but it was obvious they didn't think so.

"They work, Missus."

"Could you explain what I am trying to do, while I find some more garden tools?"

"Yes, Missus."

Tara returned with the tools, and Nerida left them to work. The women spoke to each other, and often glanced at Tara but did not try to communicate with her. Mona put the ribbons in her hair and two bracelets on her thin arms, and Yani and Mumu wore the scarves and beads around their necks and broaches on their dresses. They had worked for less than an hour when Tara told them she was going inside to get them all a drink. She thought if she kept them happy, they'd work harder. She wasn't sure whether they understood or not, but she tried to convey her intentions with hand signals. The women stopped work and watched her go. As she went inside the back door, she smiled and waved, and said she'd be back shortly.

When she returned with glasses of water, the women had gone.

Tara could have screamed in frustration. She sent Nerida after them, but she couldn't find them.

"If they come again, they won't get anything until the work is done," Tara said angrily.

Tara heard shouting when she came back into the house. As she went down the hallway, Victoria came out of the kitchen. "Sanja is refusing to roast the chickens," she said. "I'm sorry, Tara."

"You're sorry! For goodness sake, Aunt, he works for you. He should be doing what he's told."

"He wants to curry the chickens," Victoria said, sounding almost sympathetic.

"I'm sure he does."

"To be fair to him, he hasn't cooked a roast dinner the whole time he's been here."

"That's no excuse, Aunt. He should do as you ask him."

Tara was frustrated and hot, and felt like venting her irritation on someone. Despite her aunt protesting, she marched into the kitchen to confront the recalcitrant cook.

"If Missus Victoria asks you to roast the chicken's, then that is what you will do," she said. "In case you have forgotten, she employs you."

Victoria touched Tara's arm gently, and she spun around.

Dropping her chin, Victoria whispered, "Do you think we should be giving orders to the staff, Tara? They haven't had any wages for so long."

"That's beside the point, Aunt. Sanja seems to think he runs this house."

Tara turned back to the cook and shouted, "If you want to stay here, I suggest you roast those chickens."

The cook's eyes narrowed in defiance. "Sanja no roast chickens. You ask black fella roast chickens."

Tara knew he was having a dig at her for eating with Nugget and the boys. "All right," she said, "I'll do just that. And you'll have your pay docked one day."

Sanja snorted. "What pay?"

"You'll get it, and you can be sure it will be short."

Tara turned to her aunt, who looked mortified, and lifted her chin. "Nugget can roast the chickens over a spit, Aunt. They will taste incredible, certainly better than curry, day in, day out. Sanja will have us all turning yellow, like him." Tara knew it was a bigoted remark, but she thought he had it coming, after referring to Nugget as a black fella.

The cook gasped in shock.

Tara snorted derisively, as he had done to her, and left the kitchen with her aunt in tow. As they went down the hallway, they could hear pots and pans clanging and angry shouts.

"I hope he doesn't leave," Victoria whispered. "I do love my curries."

"He won't leave, Aunt. No one else would put up with his tantrums, and he knows it. Anyway, he probably hasn't got the money to go anywhere." She laughed, and Victoria shook her head, whispering, "You're a wicked woman."

While Bluey and Charlie plucked the chickens, telling hilarious anecdotes about their days as crocodile catchers in Darwin, Nugget built a fire at the back of the house. When the coals were hot, the chickens were spit roasted. Tara had Jack and Karl bring chairs outside, and they all sat around the fire, sharing two bottles of Tom's finest wine. Bluey and Charlie continued to recite stories about their misspent youths that made everyone laugh, while Jack and Karl chatted about the local kids, and Hannah amused herself by throwing twigs into the flames and playing in the dirt. Tara could see her aunt was really enjoying the evening, and so was she. The smoke kept the mosquitoes away, and the night sky was a magnificent spectacle of twinkling stars and a shimmering silvery moon.

Tara didn't know whether it was the evening, the company, or the wine, but the chicken was absolutely delicious, the best she had ever tasted. At one point she noticed Sanja watching them from the back door. She hoped he had learnt a lesson. They could get by without him.

"Tadd's late," Victoria commented. "I hope he's alright."

"I'm sure he is," Ethan assured. "You know he often loses track of time. He's probably on his way."

Tara glanced at Nugget, who had that faraway look in his eyes. Again she sensed he knew more about Tadd's activities than he was telling.

Even though Tadd was often late, Victoria knew there was always a chance of an accident in the bush, a fall from a horse, the accidental discharge of a gun, a snake or spider bite. Some hostile aborigines may have even speared him, although that was unlikely. Still, she was worried. She decided she'd give him no longer than another hour before sending the boys out to search for him.

"Garden looking good, Missus," Nugget said to Tara.

"It's been hard work, but it's getting there." She didn't mention the lubras abandoning her. She felt it was humiliating.

"We put up fence on Sunday for you, Missus. Keep roos, rabbits, wombats and stock out."

"Thank you, Nugget. Hopefully I'll be able to cook you goose eggs for breakfast." Nugget smiled. They all noticed an emu had wandered between the bunkhouse and the stables, and the aboriginal stockman turned to Tara, a grin on his face.

She read his mind. "Now there's a good bird to roast," she said. "He make real good tucker, hey Nugget?"

Nugget laughed. "If you want, I cook him up for you, Missus. Make oven in the ground."

Tara's eyes widened at the thought. "I don't know, Nugget. I don't fancy plucking him."

"No need pluck him, Missus."

"Oh." She wrinkled her nose in distaste. The thought of eating meat with singed feathers on the outside was most unappealing.

The men all laughed.

Ethan stood up. "I had almost forgotten, I brought a present for Hannah." He went to the saddlebags on Hannibal's back, and pulled something out.

When he returned, Tara could see it was a Teddy Bear.

"It might help her sleep," he said. Lowering his voice he added, "in her own bed." Hannah was clearly thrilled with the bear. Her little cherub face lit up as she took it and held it close. She glanced at Tara, and the expression in her young eyes almost made Tara cry.

"Thank you, Ethan," Tara said. "That was very thoughtful of you." He never stopped surprising her. "Where did you get it?" She could see it had once belonged to another child. Its ear had been stitched back on, and it had buttons for eyes, but it made no difference to Hannah.

"From one of my customers. Her daughter had long outgrown it, and I thought Hannah might like it."

She wondered if it was in payment for goods. "I can tell she loves it."

Tadd suddenly came around the corner of the house. He looked startled to see everyone sitting together around a campfire.

"Hello, Tadd," Victoria called. "You're back late. I was just about to send out a search party."

"What are doing out here?"

"Dining on roast chicken. It's delicious. Think yourself lucky we saved you a leg."

"Why are you eating outside, with...?" He frowned, and glanced at the men, as if they should not be sitting with Victoria and her family, when it was obviously the other way around.

"Nugget cooked for us, and the meal was wonderful; we even had a couple of bottles of wine with it. I think we should eat out here more often. Come and sit down, and have yours."

"No," Tadd snapped and went off towards his cottage.

Tara looked at her aunt, who didn't seem surprised by his reaction, and neither did Nugget or the other men. Embarrassed, they stood to go.

Tara suddenly realized why they kept out of the way, behind the bunkhouse. "Sit down, please," she said. "It's too early to go inside."

Nugget looked unsure. He glanced at Victoria. She motioned for him to be seated.

"I want to talk to you all," she said. "This is the first chance we've had to be together for days, because you've been so busy." Victoria stood up. "A couple of days ago I found out you men hadn't been paid for quite some time, especially you, Nugget. I was shocked, and upset, but mostly ashamed. This may be hard to believe, but I honestly had no idea the station was in such bad shape. I know how hard you all work and I can only say I am very sorry that you haven't had any wages."

"It not your fault, Missus," Nugget said.

"I have to take the blame, Nugget, but thank you for being so generous. I want you to know I will pay you what you are owed, even if I have to sell up, but I'm hoping it won't come to that. I know Tambora is your home as much as mine, and you have all been so loyal. You'll never know how much I appreciate you." She faltered, fighting tears. "I am going to do all in my power to save the station. I don't know how I'll do it yet, but I want to offer you all the opportunity to bail out. I won't think badly of you. I know everyone out here is suffering, but you might have ideas of going to the city or somewhere else, and I certainly wouldn't blame you."

"This my home," Nugget said. "I stay here."

"Before you commit, Nugget, you must realize I can't pay you. I virtually have no money, and I'm not sure when that will change."

"Not need wages, Missus."

"There's no work in the city," Bluey said. "We've got a roof over our heads out here, and food. I want to stay on and see it through until we're back on our feet again. The rains will come, Missus. Everything will be right." He glanced at Charlie.

"I'll stay, too, Missus." Charlie glanced at young Karl, who said nothing.

Victoria looked at the lad. "I know you do the work of a man, Karl, and I should be paying you for it. If none of the other men have any objections, as soon as we're back on our feet, you are due for a pay increase."

The men nodded in agreement.

Karl looked up. "You mean it, Missus? You are gonna pay me a man's wage?"

"I believe in paying my men what they're worth." She almost laughed. "Usually." The men laughed, too. "We know, Missus."

Karl's face lit up. "Gee thanks, Missus Victoria. I'll work damn hard." He turned to his father. "Did ya hear that? I am going to get a man's pay packet."

"That's mighty generous, Missus," Charlie said.

"I'm assuming things will work out, Charlie. If they don't, and I have to sell up, I'd sooner give this land to all of you, than to anyone else for a song." Ethan had sent their telegram from Wombat Creek, but Victoria didn't want to mention anything to the men, until she heard back from William Crombie.

Victoria looked at Nugget. "I am going to talk to Tadd for a few minutes. Tell Tara about your time with the Arabana people. I used to love to hear aboriginal stories."

Nugget looked pleased to have the opportunity to share his spiritual 'Dream time', his creation, with Tara and the children.

Tara knew her aunt was going to confront Tadd about all the missing money. For the past few days, he'd kept out of the way, going off early and coming back late, so she'd had to delay confronting him. But he certainly had some explaining to do.

Victoria went down to Tadd's cottage and knocked on the door, which was slightly ajar. He opened it with his boots in his hand.

"I want to talk to you, Tadd," she said.

He noted the solemness in her features and tone, and felt dread wash over him. He knew it had been obvious he'd been avoiding her, and he felt cowardly. Placing his boots outside the door, he said, "Can this wait, Victoria? I was just going to get cleaned up."

"No, Tadd. It's been waiting too long as it is."

"As the Mistress, you shouldn't be eating with Nugget and the boys, Victoria?"

She heard the displeasure in his voice, and for the first time seriously wondered if Tara was right about him being bigoted towards the aborigines. "Why not? They've been working for me for months for nothing. I respect that kind of loyalty."

Tadd reeled. "Are you saying I've been disloyal?"

Victoria heard the pain in his voice. "No, of course not. I'm sure your intentions were good but...."

"But what?"

"You should have told me the truth. All of it."

"You've checked the cash box, haven't you?"

"Yes. I know it's empty. I also know you've taken most of the emergency money, too. I'm disappointed you didn't ask me for it, Tadd. When were you going to tell what was going on, when we were penniless?"

Tadd dropped his head. "I know I've done wrong, Victoria. I was afraid to tell you. Afraid I'd break your heart."

"Well you've succeeded in doing that." She could see he looked ashamed, and felt sorry for him. "I wish I had found out sooner, Tadd. Perhaps this mess could have been avoided."

"I doubt it, Victoria. Everyone is in the same predicament."

"We are going to have to take rash action to save the station."

"Wouldn't it be simpler to sell up and go back to Ireland?"

Victoria gasped, as if he'd slapped her. "Go back to Ireland!"

"With your niece, and the children."

"I have no intention of going back to Ireland, Tadd. I want to live my life out here, on Tambora. It's Tara's home now, too, and the children's. No matter what I have to do, I'm going to save the station. I'm here to ask if you are going to help?"

Tadd frowned. "You know I will, Victoria. I'll do whatever I can." He sounded defeated, Victoria thought, certainly not enthusiastic.

"I've always appreciated your loyalty, Tadd. You know I've always felt we were far more than employer and employee."

"I know, lass, and I've let you down."

"There'll be no more said about it, Tadd. We'll do whatever we have to, to save the station. I've a friend in India who has a rug-making factory. He once suggested exporting our wool to him. I did look into it some time ago, and it was a viable proposition. I've had Ethan send him a telegram from Wombat Creek. If the reply is favourable, we have a chance. With you and Tara by my side, I'm sure we'll succeed."

"That's wonderful, lass." Tadd said.

Victoria turned to leave. "I'll have young Jack bring your chicken over."

"Thank you," Tadd said, although he had lost his appetite.

CHAPTER EIGHTEEN

"I'm not leaving here until you tell me where my sister is," Moyna Conway panted. She heaved her ample bosoms, which were like two over ripe melons, onto the counter of the shipping office in Dublin. Her abundant weight had made the endeavor to get to the office an enormous effort, leaving her face flushed and her dirty hair dishevelled. She also had three whining urchins clinging to her voluminous skirts.

Another child, an adolescent boy with protruding ears and teeth, was trying to pick the pockets of people in the waiting room.

"I told you yesterday, madam, we do not have that information," Magnus Stewart said. He was a highly-strung, painfully thin man, prone to gastric attacks if upset. Consequently he had spent most of the previous night in the bathroom. "If we did, I would certainly give it to you." He would've done anything to avoid seeing her, or her pilfering progeny, again. "Were the Red Cross of no help?" he asked, feigning interest. "They were not, which will come as no surprise to you, I'm sure. I didn't come all the way from Londonderry, a calamitous trip, to be pushed from pillar to post…"

Magnus did not doubt the journey had been horrendous. The five of them were a walking debacle, and a prime example of the very reason he had avoided the state of holy matrimony.

"I cannot afford to stay in digs another day, so I may be forced to camp out in this office if I don't get any satisfaction," she threatened.

Magnus felt his thin legs almost buckle beneath him, and braced himself on the counter.

"Surely you can tell me something?" Moyna moaned, changing tact. "My sister can't have disappeared into the wilderness, or whatever it is they have in that isolated outpost no decent Catholic would call home." Since reading about the disaster in the paper, Moyna's mind had been working overtime. An official had informed her of Michael's death, which raised the barest of emotions until she read that the Kennard and Rainer Line were paying compensation after losing a court battle that claimed negligence. Maureen was bound to get a good pay out, Moyna thought, as Michael had been a tradesman. She'd decided, after very little contemplation, to offer her sister and the children a home to return to. It was the least she could do. That she needed the extra help on the farm after three of her daughters had selfishly left home, was inconsequential.

"It appears, Mrs. Conway, there is no record of your sister providing anyone with a forwarding address when she left Port Adelaide."

"Surely someone would be knowing something of her whereabouts," Moyna shouted. "I'm inclined to believe you could be more helpful if ye put ye mind to it."

Magnus felt his innards rumble.

"I don't know what I can tell you, Mrs. Conway. Some records were lost in the transition between here and Australia. As ye can imagine, the situation over there was chaotic. I believe many of the bodies were burnt beyond recognition, which made identification almost impossible. Most of the people in the waiting room," he gestured behind her, "are going over to identify the personal belongings of kin, a terrible task."

If Magnus had been hoping for empathy, he was denied it. Moyna was losing patience. "Lost records are not my problem, Mr. Stewart. I have to find my sister. It seems your shipping line's negligence has cost more than fifty lives."

Magnus was aware of heads turning and ears pricking. "We're doing our best, but some circumstances are beyond our control."

"Yer dishin' out a lotta blarney, and I'm not buying any of it. Did my sister have a cabin mate aboard ship? Perhaps her or her family would know something?" She thought it likely that someone had taken Maureen in, perhaps her cabin mate's family? Maureen had always aroused kindness in folk, and, unlike herself, she made friends easily.

"If she wasn't a first class passenger, then she would certainly have been sharing. I'd have to check records, even then it's unlikely I can tell you whether her cabin mate perished or not."

"Check yer records, Mr. Stewart. If her cabin mate gave her destination, it would be a place to start."

"I'm afraid I can't give you the personal details of a passenger you are not related to. That is against company policy, madam."

Moyna inwardly groaned. Now he was quoting company policy. She was going to have to get seriously troublesome, something of which she was more than capable.

Magnus watched in horror, as her bulbous eyes widened so much that he thought they might pop onto the counter like two corks from rum jugs, then suddenly she began wailing.

"Please, madam, stop," Magnus begged, covering his ears. But there was no stopping Moyna. She wailed at the top of her lungs, and her girls joined in. The din was horrific.

"Please, madam, I'll try to find something," Magnus shouted, feeling the urge to run to the bathroom. "I beg you, stop that God awful keening."

Moyna stopped in mid breath, her face almost carmine from lack of oxygen. "Hush up, brat," she said, cuffing one of the girls on the ear with blind accuracy. "Did I hear ye right?" she asked Magnus. "Ye said you'd help me?"

He nodded in resignation and went through to his office. After several minutes of rifling through records, he came out again. Speaking in hushed tones, he said, "I've found a form filled out by a Mrs. Tara Flynn, the woman who shared a cabin with your sister and her daughter. She lists her destination as Tambora Station, c/o Wombat Creek, South Australia, but this particular address is not on anything else. As some of the records have been lost, I am not sure whether Mrs. Flynn is a survivor or not, so if you make contact with relatives, I urge diplomacy."

"It's going to take months to find out whether my sister is all right," Moyna moaned, thinking of the urgency of her own predicament.

Magnus was desperate to be rid of her as quickly as possible. "I know many of the relatives of passengers have been sending telegrams, perhaps you should, too."

Moyna immediately thought of the expense. "Only the wealthy can afford the likes of telegrams."

Magnus was tempted to give her money, anything to see the back of her. "If you are really concerned you could keep the message brief."

Although incensed that he was questioning the depth of her concern, Moyna considered the idea. "I might just do that, Mr. Stewart." She left the office, dragging her whining offspring behind her.

Magnus Stewart sighed with relief. He'd sooner be on a sinking ship, heading into a war zone, than endure another visit from Moyna Conway and her brats. He rushed off to the bathroom.

"Missus," Nerida shouted. "Come see... Come see..."

Tara opened her eyes, squinting in the glaring sunlight streaming through the open balcony doors. "See what? What time is it, anyway?" Her head felt fuzzy, reminding her she had never been accustomed to drinking wine.

"Eight o'clock, Missus."

"In the morning?" she asked in a state of confusion.

"Yes, Missus. Yanyi, Mona, and Mumu workin' in the garden."

Tara was shocked, and sat up. "Are you saying the women came back, of their own accord?"

"Yes, Missus."

Tara couldn't believe she had slept through the raucous from the parrots. She hadn't even heard the possums and she had forgotten to close the balcony doors when she went to bed. A quick glance around and she saw their calling cards.

"Where's Hannah?" she asked, noticing she was not beside her as she got out of bed.

"She sleep, Missus."

"In her own bed?"

"Yes, Missus."

Tara couldn't believe she had slept all night, in her own bed. The Teddy Bear had obviously made her feel secure.

"Where is my Aunt?"

"She downstairs, Missus, in room with box make chatter-chatter."

Tara laughed at Nerida's interpretation of the pedal radio.

In the last few days Victoria had spent a lot of time catching up with neighbours on the radio. She'd also gotten into the spirit of bartering and was keeping Ethan busy taking traded items between stations. She had been doing quite well, too. She'd swapped Sanja's homemade chutneys for tinned fruit and condensed milk, which the children enjoyed. She'd also swapped an extra butter churn for three sacks of flour and a tin of cooking oil. But her best trade of all was three bottles of wine and a smith's forge for a prized Peppin Merino Ram that had won ribbons in the Royal Adelaide Show.

"We have to begin breeding again," she told Tara optimistically, "so another good ram will come in handy."

"Has Missus Victoria mentioned anything to you about a letter we can't find, Nerida?" Although Ethan had sent a telegram to William Crombie, the mystery of the missing letter intrigued Tara. She'd had the strongest feeling there was something behind its disappearance. Ever since coming to Tambora, she had felt an underlying current of a hostile nature, although she couldn't quite put her finger on its origins, as yet.

"I not see letter, Missus?"

Tara believed Nerida. Her enormous brown eyes were as expressive as an open book. "Do you suppose anyone could have taken it?" she asked.

Nerida looked back at her blankly.

"Like Mr. Sweeney? Could he have taken the letter, perhaps by mistake?"

Nerida looked down and shuffled her feet. "I not know, Missus?"

"You do not like Tadd very much, do you, Nerida?"

The aboriginal girl lowered her eyes.

"Do you clean his cottage?" "Yes, Missus."

Tara contemplated an idea. She put her hand on the girl's thin shoulder. "If you ever need someone to confide in, or just to talk, I'll be happy to listen, and I'm the soul of discretion." She put her finger to her lips to indicate what she meant.

Nerida looked up shyly. "Thank you, Missus," she said awkwardly.

When Tara came outside with Nerida, the aboriginal women were working and chattering. They looked up, and waved. Mona was still wearing the ribbon in her hair, and the bracelets, and the other two women were adorned with their broaches and scarves. In fact, they were wearing the exact shifts from the previous day, only they were dirtier. Knowing water for washing was always in short supply, Tara did not feel badly about them.

"Why did they leave yesterday?" she asked Nerida. "We'd only been working an hour."

"When you go inside Missus, they thought work finished for the day."

Tara remembered waving and realized they had misunderstood. She fed Mellie and her pups leftovers from the previous night's meal, and let them out of the kennels. She was delighted to see the women had made considerable progress in the garden. They chattered away in the Arabana language while working, until the breakfast gong reverberated through the still air, and the women laughed. Tara called for Nerida to bring something outside for all of them, but when Nerida spoke with the women, they declined any offered food. They told Nerida they would eat at the tribal camp, just beyond the trees, and asked if Tara would join them. Nerida encouraged her to go, but although she felt honored, Tara was a little apprehensive, mostly about what they would give her to eat. Finally, she accepted.

As they walked towards the tribal camp, followed by Mellie and the pups, Tara discovered Yani spoke and understood a few words of English, but the other two women did not. As they approached the campsite, Tara saw two elderly men squatting under a shady tree. One had white hair and a bushy white beard. He was painting a lizard on a piece of bark. Yani said his name was Jabba Jurra. The other man, Jackie Kantji, was obviously completely blind. His eyeballs had turned white. Tara remembered her aunt telling her a lot of aboriginal's suffered with a disease of the eyes, which left them blind.

There were also three girls at the camp. They seemed no more than ten or twelve years old, but Yani tried to convey that the girls were waiting for their husbands, who were hunting. Tara felt sure she had misunderstood, and thought that perhaps Yani meant the girls were awaiting their betrothed, as in some cultures, young girls were promised from as early as birth. She was absolutely sure this was the case, until she was shocked to notice one of the girls was pregnant.

There were also at least five scrawny dogs scrounging for food around the site. They saw Mellie and her pups as competition for the few scraps there was, and began growling at them. Mellie, protective of her pups, growled back. Jabba Jurra picked up a stone and threw it at the dogs, hitting Mellie. She ran back to the kennels, yelping. Tara was horrified. She knew Mellie was Tambora's prize bitch, and Tadd would be very angry if she was injured. She scolded Jabba Jurra for throwing stones, but he only smiled at her.

The women, who seemed unflappable and unhurried in their actions, sat down on the ground near the fire and gestured for Tara to sit with them. Tara noticed the dirt and the smoke didn't seem to bother them, but her eyes were streaming. Yani poked at some damper in the ashes, fishing it out. It was as black as soot on the outside and looked unappetizing, but the women seemed to excitedly contemplate their meal. While it cooled, Mona made tea using some strange leaves. Mumu passed around the remains of the previous night's meal, a type of meat, which Tara couldn't distinguish. She was dismayed to see it was only half cooked.

"What is this?" she asked Yani, tentatively chewing a tiny piece, thankful there were no singed feathers on it. The meat looked like chicken, but tasted a little stronger, and it had dried out. She tried not to think about all the flies that had no doubt crawled over it, for fear of retching.

"Perenti," Yani said, smiling broadly.

"Oh! What is Perenti?" Tara thought it might be an aboriginal word for wild turkey, or bustard.

Yani smiled broadly again. "Him goanna, Missus."

Remembering the lumbering goanna from the day before, Tara felt suddenly ill. Although he'd looked fierce, he had in fact been quite shy and harmless. That he had been killed for a meal appalled her. She spat the meat into her hand, and slyly threw it to one of the starving dogs.

"I'm not very hungry," she said. "It's the heat. A little damper and tea will do just fine." It took a great deal of will not to be sick.

While they sat around the fire, Jackie Kantji began talking to Tara. He told her hundreds of aborigines up north were dying from scurvy. Because of the drought, their natural food had died, and the rations they received from the mission did not have the nutrients they needed. The old man seemed very sad. Life as he knew it had changed so much. Tara did not know what to say to him.

By late afternoon, the vegetable garden was ready for the seeds to be sown. Tara was pleased, as her aching back couldn't take any more digging. Nugget and the boys had removed the remains of the old fence, ready to put up the new one the next morning, and she'd spread the chicken muck fertilizer, which attracted millions of flies. Tara decided she'd wait one more day to see if there was any sign of the locusts, which as yet had not appeared, much to Tadd's delight. He seemed to revel in proving Nugget wrong.

Tara waved goodbye to Yani, Mona, and Mumu, and headed to the trough at the back door, to wash her hands. She was exhausted. While she splashed water around her neck to cool off, Sanja came outside and threw a bowl of dirty dish water in her direction. She was sure he'd done it deliberately, and shrieked in indignation, as the water and dirt spattered her, but he made no apology. Tara cursed him with all the fury and colourful language of a gipsy, but the cook only gave her a contemptuous look, and went back inside.

"There's plenty more cooks need a job," Tara shouted after him. "I'll get Ethan to spread the word that Tambora is looking for someone."

Sanja popped his head out the door. "None work for free, Missus."

Tara had to annoyingly concede he had a point, but that would change one day in the near future.

Late that afternoon, Tara sat on the balcony after her bath, resting her aching back before dinner. The strong odour of curry drifted to her. Normally she'd be shaking her head, irritated with Sanja, but at this time her thoughts were centered on Jack, whom she'd hardly seen all week. He'd spent most of his time up at Ethan's cabin, tending the camels. Ethan had told her he was particularly fond of the youngest camels, which pleased her, but she couldn't help feeling dismayed that their relationship hadn't improved. She also couldn't help noticing whenever Ethan was away, a time when Jack was forbidden to go near the camels, he seemed to deliberately cause mischief.

Several days ago he'd lit a fire in the bush, which thankfully the aboriginals had contained and extinguished before it caused any real danger. Victoria had spoken to him and tried to make him understand how devastating a bushfire could be. The very next day, Tara had nearly had heart failure when she'd found him on the roof of the house. He'd climbed from the balcony into the tree, then up onto the roof. Tara didn't want to imagine what could have happened if Hannah had tried to follow him, as she often did. When Ethan returned from Gundawindie Station, where he'd picked up a repaired stock saddle for Tadd, she spoke to him about it, expressing her concern. He immediately took action, cutting down the branch that came closest to the house, making it impossible for Jack to get into the tree from the balcony. Even though Ethan spoke to Jack at length, he seemed to think the cutting of the tree branch was Tara's idea, and that she was just being spiteful, and his resentment heightened.

Tara stood up to stretch her legs. The sun was beginning to set, flushing the sky a myriad of warm colours. A temperate breeze rustled the gum leaves, through which the sunlight filtered, creating dappled patches of light in the afternoon shadows on the ground. For the first time, Tara really appreciated what a peaceful place Tambora was. She was contemplating this change of heart, when movement in the grounds below caught her attention. Victoria was walking with Hannah. As Tara watched, her aunt stopped and pointed up into the trees, to the magpies and the kookaburra's. Tara smiled at what a charming picture her family made. As she continued to watch, Victoria squatted beside Hannah, and whistled, as she did to the dogs. Her action puzzled Tara, as the dogs were locked in their kennels at the back of the house.

Twenty feet beyond where her aunt and Hannah stood, another movement caught Tara's attention. An animal moved from where it had been standing, partially hidden by the wide trunk of a gum tree. At first Tara thought it was a small kangaroo, but as she realized what it was, she gasped in horror. Victoria whistled again. With her poor sight, she obviously thought the animal was a dog. But Tara could see it was one of the most feared animals in the bush, a wild boar, with enormous tusks, capable of ripping open anything that threatened it, intentionally or otherwise. Tara wanted to call out, but she felt paralyzed with gut twisting fear. The boar had lowered its head, ready to charge.

Tara remembered the guns kept downstairs. Although she didn't like guns, Tadd had given her instruction on how to use one of the rifles. It was kept loaded at all times, in case of an emergency. But for safety reasons, with children in the house, it was stored in a locked cabinet. Tara was sure there was not enough time to unlock the cabinet and retrieve the rifle, and get outside, all before the boar attacked.

The next few moments seemed to happen in slow motion. The boar began charging towards Victoria and Hannah. Tara, with her heart pounding like a black smith's hammer, opened her mouth to scream out a warning. A gunshot shattered the tranquility of the bush, sending birds into flight, and the wild boar fell, dead.

Moments later, Ethan was beside Victoria, a rifle in his hand.

Tara ran down the stairs and outside, passing a frightened Nerida by the front door. When she reached her aunt, she was shaking like a leaf in the wind, but Victoria appeared calm, unaware of how close she had come to being severely gored, or worse, killed. She had Hannah in her arms, comforting her, as the little girl sobbed with fright.

"Aunt, are you hurt?" Tara gasped. "Is Hannah all right?"

"I'm just fine," Victoria said, unsure of what all the fuss was about. "But the gunshot frightened Hannah. Why did you shoot the dog, Ethan? Was it a dingo? I'm sure it wouldn't have harmed us. They're inquisitive..."

"It wasn't a dingo, Victoria, or any kind of dog," Ethan said gently. "It was a wild boar, possibly the one that's been causing havoc with Sadie's pigs. She'll be pleased to know we got him." He strode off to examine the boar, which he'd killed with one clean shot to the head.

"I thought it was Shelby or Fergus. How could I make that mistake?" Victoria put her hand up to her mouth, as she contemplated what could've happened to Hannah. "I thought it strange that it didn't come when I whistled. My God, Hannah could have been..."

"She's fine, Aunt, but this time you were lucky." Tara almost collapsed with the thought of what might have happened. "You realize we can't risk this sort of thing happening again. You are going to have to see someone about your sight. It's quite likely you only need glasses."

"I can't afford glasses," Victoria said despondently.

"We'll find the money, Aunt, even if we have to sell something. We can't have you risking your life over something that might be easily rectified."

"Fancy roast pig for dinner?' Ethan asked. He had the pig's legs hog-tied, and was carrying it over his shoulder.

"It looks disgusting," Tara said, eyeing the boar's dirty tusks and deadly razor sharp teeth. It smelt awful, too.

"You can't eat them in the wet season, because of worms, but this fella will be just fine. Won't Nugget be thrilled, Victoria?"

"Yes. He loves a bit of roast pig."

Ethan gutted the pig and hung it in a tree, before spit roasting it over an open fire. It's outer skin was crackling nicely when Nugget and the boys returned from mustering sheep. Apparently they'd smelt the aroma of roast pig a mile out.

"Him make good tucker," Nugget said with an enormous grin on his face. Tara had to laugh.

When the men went off to wash, Ethan approached Tara. She told him about Jackie Kantji, and what he had said about the aborigines dying from scurvy. She hadn't been able to stop thinking about it.

"It's been a terrible problem," Ethan admitted. "But the missionaries are now bringing in whole wheat flour and oranges, when they can get them. It's helping."

Tara was relieved.

"I heard you tell Victoria you wanted her to see someone about her eyes."

"That's right, Ethan. I can't contemplate what might have occurred if you hadn't shot the boar. I saw what was about to happen from the balcony, and literally froze with fear. We just can't risk something like that happening again."

"There's a resident doctor in Alice Springs now, but more specialized doctors are in the city, where Victoria has always refused to go. A doctor and a district nurse pass through here from time to time, but they're not due in Wombat Creek for at least a month."

"We can't wait that long. I've been thinking about it. I know she'd prefer to go to Alice, rather than the city. I have a friend in Alice, Sorrel Windspear. We travelled out here together. I'll send her a telegram and ask if she'll look after Aunt Victoria for a few days. I'm sure she will."

"I'm going into Wombat Creek tomorrow," Tadd said from behind her. "Did you say you want a telegram sent?"

Tara spun round. "Yes, Tadd?"

"Then I'll send it for you, lass. Victoria has just told me what happened this afternoon. Thank goodness you were here, Ethan. Your action averted a tragedy." Tadd headed off to his cottage.

"There's just one more problem to solve," Tara said. "What's that?"

"If my Aunt needs glasses, we'll have to find the extra money?"

Ethan's gaze dropped. "I wish I could help…"

"It's not your problem, Ethan. Besides, Sadie Jenkins told my Aunt you have just given a very generous donation to the Mission to keep it going. My Aunt claims the Mission wouldn't survive without you."

Ethan shrugged off the praise. "We have an annual Gymkhana in Wombat Creek to raise money for the town, or any other cause deemed worthwhile at the time. In the past, the money raised has been donated to all sorts of worthy causes, a bushfire relief fund, or believe or not, a flood relief fund. Once it was donated to a sick child who needed treatment in the city. Another time it went to purchase a wheel chair for a stockman's son, who had been trampled by a steer. I don't see why it can't be for Victoria's glasses this year. With a little extra organization, we could bring the date forward."

"Are you serious, Ethan? That would be wonderful."

"I'll have a talk to the folks in town and let you know what's decided, but I'm sure it won't be a problem. So far, there's nothing specific in mind for the funds to go to this year. I would suggest we don't tell Victoria what the money raised is for until the last possible moment."

"You're right. She's a very proud woman, and she might not accept it." Tara suddenly looked mystified. Ethan noticed her change of mood.

She was thinking that Ethan always seemed to be there when he was needed. He was there for Jack, and he'd been there for her aunt today, and from what Victoria had said, many other times, too. He was also the lifeline between the stations and the towns. Despite his seemingly nomadic lifestyle, he was quite obviously dependable. She realized that in the past she had never thought that was possible.

Tara had always blamed the gipsy lifestyle for Garvie not being dependable, or there when she needed him. It had been easier than facing the truth, which, for the first time, glared at her. He was an irrepressible rascal, the drawer of misfortune, and a defender of the right to flout the settler's laws, which he often did, with dire consequences. She thought of Rory, and Jasper, and some of the other gipsy men, and realized they had always supported their families, providing them with as much security as the life of a traveller could ever hope for, and wondered why it was that she had never seen it before.

"What's going through your mind?" Ethan asked, watching her intently with his dark, mesmerizing eyes.

Tara half turned away from him, suddenly overcome with unfamiliar emotions. "I was just thinking, and realized something that I never have before."

"What would that be?"

"I'm surprised at myself," she said self-consciously, "but I think being out here has enabled me to see the truth about someone back in Ireland."

For a few moments Ethan didn't say anything. Tara turned to look up at him, but he was gazing out over the vast land surrounding them, with its Spinifex grass, and Mulga scrub, in much the same way the aboriginals did, listening, sensing, feeling.

Tara remembered that Ethan had told her this vast land would open her eyes and change her perception of life. She hadn't believed it, but it was happening. But she wondered, was it the land, or was it the man?

"This land is very spiritual, the perfect place to find truth," Ethan said. His dark eyes crinkled at the corners. "In your case, I honestly thought it would take longer."

Tara's eyes widened in astonishment, and he laughed.

CHAPTER NINETEEN

"Good morning, Aunt," Tara said, as she came into the dining room. "Where is everyone?"

It was only six thirty in the morning, and the house was as quiet as a church. As it was Sunday, Tara had told the men to sleep in for at least an hour, before beginning work on the vegetable garden fence. She'd told them she'd cook them breakfast about eight o'clock, but she wondered where Tadd, Nerida and the children were.

"Hannah has gone with Nerida to collect eggs from the geese and chickens, and I believe Jack is with Tadd, watching him training the pups. At least we know he'll be occupied for a little while and not getting into mischief. I heard Sanja scolding him this morning. I think he caught him coming out of the cellar with a spoonful of treacle."

"I noticed a lock on the door. I thought perhaps you were concerned about more wine going missing."

"Tadd won't touch it now he knows I'm aware of what's going on." She suddenly looked concerned. "Don't say anything to Jack, Tara, but I noticed Zac is in a tree outside."

"Do you suspect Jack set him free?"

"I know he couldn't undo the chain securing him to his perch, himself."

"I'm so sorry, Aunt. I know you've had him for many years. Could we catch him?"

"I'm not upset about it, Tara. Zac should be free. I would have freed him myself, but I was concerned he'd die in the drought. He hasn't flown away yet, so I put water and seed on the balcony outside my room."

Tara agreed Zac should be free, but she could see Victoria was worried. Although Zac had been terribly noisy, especially in the mornings when he could hear the wild parrots in the trees outside, he was part of the family.

Tara sat down and smeared a pancake with jam. Since the goose eggs were so wonderful, Sanja had begun baking. Unfortunately his cakes were flavoured with far too much ginger and five spice.

"I'm sorry Jack is being so much trouble, Aunt. I was hoping he would settle down, but whenever Ethan is away, and he can't go near the camels, he seems to become even more rebellious."

"He's just being a typical boy. Your father was no angel when he was Jack's age. I remember him tying me to a tree that had a hive of wasps in it. My father rescued me and got stung several times. I thought he was going to kill Ninian. He had to hide in the stables for two days, until father cooled down." Victoria laughed. "Another time he took one of father's most expensive Havana cigars and smoked it. He was so sick, and a horrible shade of green. Mother didn't have the heart to tell Father. She was sure he'd been punished enough."

Tara wasn't so sure Jack was being a typical boy. She thought he was deliberately trying to goad her. It was as if he was testing her dedication to being his new mother.

Using a magnifying glass, Victoria perused the advertisements in the Outback Gazette, the Alice Springs paper, which was more than a week old.

"Anything interesting?" Tara asked, pouring herself a cup of tea.

"Actually, yes, there is something here I want to show you. I am not sure I'm reading it correctly. It sounds almost too good to be true."

"What is it?"

"You read it, dear, and see what you think."

Tara took the paper and read the notice. It was an advertisement asking for accommodation for orphaned and foster children. It said the government was trialling a scheme where a remuneration of two pounds per week, per child, was given to carers in a suitable home. There was an article alongside the advertisement that claimed government run homes were overcrowded because so many destitute families had been forced to place their children in care, while their search for work took them far from home, often in different directions.

"My goodness," Tara said, looking up at her aunt. "They are paying well."

"That's what I thought."

Tara caught the excitement in Victoria's voice. "Aunt, are you considering the possibility of applying to take these children in?"

"It crossed my mind. We have all this room, enough for at least a dozen children."

"That would be twenty four pounds a week income." Tara's eyes widened. "That much money would solve a lot of our problems," she added.

"It would indeed, at least until we hear from William Crombie, but it would also be such a lot of work caring for that many children."

Tara considered the idea. "It says rural foster families would have to provide schooling, as well as meals and accommodation."

"Reverend Guthrie, from the Presbyterian Mission in Beltana, would provide us with lessons. I'm sure that would satisfy government officials."

"And the children could help with chores. We have a cook, if you can get him to prepare something other than curry. Actually, it sounds like a really good idea, in theory."

"Do you think so, Tara?"

"Yes, I do, Aunt." Tara glanced back at the article on the opposite page, and she frowned. "It says here, potential homes have to be inspected and found to be clean and free of vermin." She looked up. "Nerida told me there is a mouse plague out here, and I've seen evidence of it myself."

"We have it fairly well under control, but there is always a problem with mice in the country."

As if on cue, the mousetrap went off behind the sideboard, and Victoria laughed. "Tom never liked cats, but I think we should get a couple."

Tara looked back at the article. "It also states that applicants backgrounds must be checked for suitability."

"I know, but we have nothing to hide and I'm sure our home would be perfect for children. We have so much room, and surely Jack and Hannah would love having playmates."

Tara frowned and sighed. "What's wrong, Tara?"

"I'm afraid of what might happen if government officials start delving into my background. I'm not legally the children's guardian."

Tadd Sweeney stopped outside the dining room door. He'd caught the tail end of the conversation and wondered if he'd heard correctly. He thought Tara had said she was not the legal guardian of Jack and Hannah. But how could that be, if she was their mother?

"I don't think you have anything to worry about, Tara, " Victoria said. "The children have no relatives out here, do they?"

"No, but..."

The floorboards creaked outside the door. Tara's head snapped round. "Is that you, Sanja?" Victoria called.

Tadd came in. "If you are looking for Sanja, Victoria, I think he's outside. Shall I get him for you?"

Tara and her aunt glanced at each other, both wondering if Tadd had overheard their conversation, but he showed no sign.

"No, it's nothing important, Tadd," Victoria said. "Are you about to leave for town?"

"Yes. I have that information you gave me, Tara. I'll be sure and send that telegram."

"Thank you, Tadd. Could you give this to Percy Everett?" It was the watch Belle had asked her to give to him. "Tell him he left it in the hotel bathroom, and I meant to give it to him, but it slipped my mind."

Tadd took the watch. "I'll see you both when I get back."

In the passageway, Tadd paused, but he dared not risk trying to overhear any more of their conversation, as much as he wanted to.

Victoria looked at Tara. "I'm not so keen to go to Alice, dear."

"I know, Aunt. But it's only for a few days. I'd go with you, but I wouldn't feel right about leaving the children. Hannah is only just beginning to feel a sense of security and I have no idea what Jack will do next."

"I understand, Tara. The children need as much stability as they can get at the moment."

"You'll like Sorrel, Aunt." Tara smiled remembering Sorrel's poise and kindness. "She's a real lady, but she speaks her mind with such candidness, you can't help but admire her."

"Did you become friends on the trip out here?"

"No. She was a first class passenger, so our paths didn't really cross until we came face to face, when the ship was sinking. Actually, it was her braveness and composure that stopped me from completely losing any self-control I possessed." She shuddered at the memory.

Victoria was intrigued, and curious. "What is she doing in Alice?"

"Her son and his wife have taken over the lease on the Stuart Arms Hotel. After Sorrel lost her husband, her son insisted she come out and live with them. I don't think she was keen on living out here, but she didn't want to disappoint her son."

Victoria understood how she felt. "Tara, under the circumstances, I shouldn't be taking this trip. We really can't afford glasses, if I need them."

"Don't worry, Aunt. We'll have the money. I promise."

"How, Tara?"

"I don't want you worrying about it, Aunt. Have a little faith." Ethan had gone into Wombat Creek to pick up mail to be delivered, and promised to speak to Ferris, Rex and Percy about moving up the date of the annual Gymkhana and donating the proceeds for Victoria's glasses. He was going to radio her when he had a firm decision.

Victoria wanted to find out more, but she'd caught the hint of determination in Tara's voice, and knew better than to question it. Nevertheless, she hated the idea of leaving Tambora, even for a short while.

"I suppose I could make discreet enquiries into the prospect of taking in children while I'm in Alice, but I don't think we should mention it to Tadd just yet. If I think the authorities will dig too deeply into your background, Tara, I'll abandon the idea. But I can't imagine what you are worried about."

Tara lowered her voice, and glanced at the dining room door. "I didn't tell you this, Aunt, but I took the children under false pretences. I told the authorities I was Maureen O'Sullivan. They think Tara Flynn perished on the ship."

Victoria's eyes widened in astonishment. "How did you get away with that?"

"I identified the bodies, and one of the crewmen went along with it. James O'Brien had been an orphan, and had awful experiences, so he was more than willing to help. It was the only way I could leave the Port of Adelaide with the children."

Victoria was shocked. "Was it really that necessary to go to such extremes, Tara?"

"I was desperate, Aunt. While we were waiting at Customs House, Sorrel and myself witnessed officials tearing a baby from his nanny's arms. Both of his parents had perished. The poor nanny was beside herself with torment. She'd looked after baby Thomas since he was born, but the authorities were heartless. She even offered to take the child back to England, to relatives." Just the memory of the nanny's anguish brought tears to Tara's eyes. "It made me realize I had no hope of keeping the children with me, even though I am sure that is what their parents would have wanted. I couldn't let them put Jack and Hannah into an orphanage. The only relative Maureen spoke of was a sister back in Ireland, whom she detested. Apparently this sister treated her own children as slaves. I had no choice but to pretend I was Maureen O'Sullivan. Unfortunately, the authorities may have found out the truth by now. For all I know, I'm a wanted woman."

Tadd found Percy Everett in the hotel, having a drink with Ferris and some of the station owners and stockmen who had come into town.

"How's that woman coping with station life?" Percy asked sarcastically, referring to Tara. "I didn't think she'd last five minutes out there."

Tadd noticed the men's ears pricked up. They'd heard about Tara on the radio.

"She's doin' all right," he said begrudgingly. "Better than I expected, but I really don't think she's cut out for outback life in the long term." He remembered the watch in his shirt pocket. "She gave me this to give to you. Said something about you leaving it in the hotel bathroom."

Percy went pale when he saw the watch. He knew exactly where he'd left it, and it wasn't the hotel bathroom." Humiliation washed over him.

"You all right, Percy? You've gone the colour of sour butter milk."

"Yeah, I'm just feeling the heat today. Let's have a drink."

"Business first, Percy. I have a telegram to send for Tara."

"That's a coincidence. There's a telegram there for the station. It came about an hour ago, and just missed Ethan, so I put it aside."

"Has Ethan taken Tambora's mail? I usually pick it up."

"Yes."

Tadd was concerned. He had been expecting something he didn't want Victoria to see. "Which way did he go?"

"Out to the MacDonald's and then on to Sadie's place."

Tadd relaxed. He'd get back to the station before Ethan, and sort the mail himself when it arrived.

Percy lowered his voice. "Between you and me, the telegram is about Tara Flynn."

"Oh! Is it addressed to her?"

"It's addressed to the relatives of a Mrs. Tara Flynn, so that would be Victoria. It came all the way from Ireland."

In the store, Percy gave Tadd the telegram and then sent one to Sorrel Windspear for Tara. Ethan had already spoken to Percy and Ferris, and some of the other men, about the proceeds of the Gymkhana being donated to Victoria for her glasses, so he wasn't surprised at the context of the telegram.

"Are ye coming for a drink?" Percy asked, when they'd concluded their business. "Yeah, sure. I'll be there in a minute. I want to have a look at one of my horse's shoes. He seems a bit lame."

"Don't be long. I'll have Ferris pour you a coldie." Percy went back into the hotel and Tadd went around the side, where he opened the telegram and read the contents.

TO THE RELATIVES OF MRS. TARA FLYNN STOP I AM LOOKING FOR THE WHEREABOUTS OF MY SISTER MRS MAUREEN O'SULLIVAN AND HER TWO CHILDREN JACK AND HANNAH STOP I BELIEVE SHE SHARED A CABIN ABOARD SHIP WITH A MRS TARA FLYNN STOP IF YOU COULD GIVE ME ANY INFORMATION REGARDING MY SISTER I WOULD BE GRATEFUL STOP

YOURS SINCERELY. MRS MOYNA CONWAY

The return address was Londonderry, Northern Ireland.

Tadd was confused. He'd heard Tara say she wasn't the legal guardian of the children, and the telegram stated that Maureen O'Sullivan was the mother of Jack and Hannah. But where, he wondered, was Maureen O'Sullivan? He remembered Tara becoming upset when she spoke of losing her husband. Had that been just an act? If this was the case, she was a devious woman, and perhaps Victoria should be warned. The only conclusion he could draw was that Maureen had died on the ship, and Tara had taken the children. But surely that was illegal? He couldn't help wondering why she would do such a thing, and how she had achieved it? More importantly, what was her motive in coming out to Tambora? After all, she hadn't seen Victoria for many years. One thing was sure, he had no intention of letting her interfere with his plans.

Lottie watched Tadd from her front window. He'd caught her attention when she saw him skulking around the side of the hotel. When she saw him open something resembling a letter, she became really curious. It was unlikely whatever he was reading was meant for his eyes, or he wouldn't be reading it where he thought no one could see him. As he'd no doubt visit her after a few drinks, she felt sure she might learn what was going on.

Checking that Percy was still in the hotel, Tadd went into the store and quickly sent a reply to Moyna Conway. He knew how to work the telegraph machine, as he'd worked in the store before Tom Milburn stocked the station.

In the telegram, he urged Moyna Conway to come to Tambora Station to reclaim her kin, who were in the custody of a woman calling herself Mrs. Tara Flynn. He claimed he did not know the whereabouts of Maureen O'Sullivan, but stated that the children were unhappy in their present situation. He signed off the telegram as a Reverend Jim Malally from the Hermannsburg Mission, and stated that he was opening up a Mission in a remote part of the Territory, where he was unlikely to be contactable for up to two years. He finished by wishing her every success in her endeavour to find her loved ones.

CHAPTER TWENTY

While the men worked on the vegetable garden fence, Tara cooked them goose eggs in the shearing quarters. To ensure the breakfast wasn't a total disaster, she'd enlisted Nerida's help in setting the fire under the stove and preparing the damper.

The fence was well under way by the time Tara served breakfast, two undercooked runny eggs, and four slightly burnt eggs. Fortunately the men were very hungry, and Nerida had done an exceptional job with the damper. Nugget had laid wire about a foot below the ground to stop the rabbits and wombats from digging under the fence, and put wire strands at one-foot intervals, up to eight feet high, to deter the roos from jumping into the garden. The wooden posts and railings were mostly recycled fencing posts.

"We stop 'em hungry buggers, Missus," Nugget told Tara proudly.

She smiled. "I hope so, Nugget. I want to plant the seeds as soon as I can. There is still no sign of the locusts."

"They be comin' this way soon, Missus." He gazed off into the distance.

"Are you sure, Nugget? Tadd said they might not come this way. He said sometimes they change direction or the wind blows them away."

Nugget shook his head. "You plant seeds, Missus, but locusts comin'."

Tara decided she'd ask Ethan what he thought when he returned from the mail run.

While the men finished the fence, Tara decided to have a look at the seeds, and see what there was. Victoria had told her that Tadd had stored them in a cupboard on the veranda of his cottage, but she didn't know if the ants had gotten into them, like they did everything else. As Tara headed for the cottage, Nerida came out carrying a bundle of washing, which she took to the trough at the back of the main house. Tara soon found the seeds, and the ants hadn't ravaged them, as Tadd had put them in sealed jars and wrapped them in a cloth soaked in kerosene. Some of the seeds were labeled, as Victoria had said they would be, but some were not. Tara was considering what to plant, when she glanced through the open door of the cottage, and felt an overwhelming compulsion to go inside. Even as she fought it, it reminded her of the time she was passing Eloisa's campsite, and she'd felt compelled to stop.

Tara had to admit she was curious about Tadd Sweeney. Sometimes she felt she trusted him, usually when her beliefs were swayed by her aunt's opinion, but more often she had an uneasy feeling about him. It was a gipsy fortune-teller concept, that handling a person's personal possessions gave a sense of who they were, and Tara had found it sometimes worked for her. She decided to see what Tadd's home revealed about him.

The cottage consisted of three main rooms, the living room, a kitchenette, and one bedroom, all furnished with basic items with essentially no personal touches, a typical bachelor's quarters, Tara thought. She glanced into the bedroom, which was the first door to the right. The iron bed had been stripped and the wardrobe door was open. Since Nerida had collected Tadd's dirty washing, the room was basically tidy. Tara opened the drawer in a chest beside the bed. Inside she found personal items, a very old watch that didn't work, quite possibly his father's or grandfather's. Whichever, she had a sense of a hard working man. There was also a pipe, which looked old, a bottle of Californian Poppy hair oil, nail scissors, and a compass and other bits and pieces. She looked through the living room, where she found a few books on cattle breeding and sheep dog trials, and some old newspapers. The kitchenette was obviously rarely used. The counter was covered in dust, and the oven looked like it hadn't been lit for years. As Tara headed back to the front door, feeling strangely dissatisfied, she felt herself drawn into the bedroom again.

As her gaze wandered around the room, Tara noticed two boxes on a shelf inside the wardrobe. She lifted one down and put it on the bed. It was very heavy, which made her curious, especially as it was tied up with string. When she removed the lid, she found it contained a metal box, which was locked. Remembering another gypsy trick, Tara felt inside a jacket pocket in the wardrobe, and sure enough, found a key that fitted the lock. Smiling to herself, she opened the box. Expecting to uncover something of value, she was surprised to find the box contained about twenty coloured stones, that were smooth and highly polished, in blues, greens and whites, some with flecks of red. Tara thought they were rather beautiful, but she'd never seen anything like them before. Inside the other box, which was the larger of the two, she discovered pieces of rough stone.

Tara put everything back the way she found it, and glanced out of the window. She could see Nerida at the wash trough near the back door, and the men were putting the finishing touches to the fence. She knew Tadd wouldn't be back from Wombat Creek until late afternoon at the earliest, and yet she felt guilty for rifling through his personal belongings, and invading his privacy. Then she remembered that Tadd had searched for and found her Aunt's emergency funds, and spent most of it, with seemingly no conscience at all. And there was still the mystery of the missing letter.

Tara looked under the bed, where she found a small suitcase. She opened it and discovered it contained his correspondence and personal papers, a birth certificate and passport etc. She was about to close the case when she noticed an envelope stuck down the side. She pulled it, but it was partially wedged under the bottom.

"How did that get down there?" she mumbled and pulled it harder. Suddenly, the base lifted, and Tara gasped. Underneath, she was shocked to find at least twenty letters, which baffled her. Why were they hidden under the base of the case? She turned the one in her hand over, and got her answer. It was addressed to her aunt. She was not surprised to see it was from William Crombie.

Tara was livid. Tadd had obviously stolen the letter from her aunt, and here she was, just moments ago, feeling like a criminal for invading his privacy. Rampant thoughts ran through her mind. If the news was good, why hadn't Tadd shared it? She considered the possibility that William had declined Victoria's offer, and Tadd had wanted to spare her disappointment, as he claimed to have done in the past. Tara wanted to believe this was true, just as Victoria did, but something didn't ring true. There was only one way to find out if Tadd Sweeney was the man Victoria thought he was, a loyal and trusted employee, and that was to read the letter.

Tara quickly scanned the contents of the letter, and tears filled her eyes. In essence, William Crombie was very pleased to have the prospect of doing business with Victoria. He requested a sample of wool to show the manager and foreman of the rug factory, but expected no problems and was looking forward to a long and happy business association. Tara felt a sinking feeling in the pit of her stomach. All these months William had been waiting for Victoria to send him that sample of wool. Perhaps all their financial problems could have been avoided. If only Tadd had been honest with Victoria.

Tara went numb. Time and time again, she had doubted Tadd, only to convince herself she was wrong. She felt no comfort in knowing her very first instincts had been right. He did have ulterior motives for wanting the sale of the station. But what could they be? What did he have to gain? As far as she could see, if the station was sold, Tadd would lose his home, his place as manager, and Victoria. Surely that was a high price to pay?

The feeling of numbness was slowly replaced with building anger and resentment, as Tara sifted through the other hidden letters, hoping to find answers. They were all addressed to Victoria, and mostly from the Leigh Creek Branch of the Adelaide Bank. But even before she opened the letters, she knew they contained bad news for her aunt.

The first letter Tara opened was a bank statement. In disbelief, she stared at the bold red print at the bottom of the page, the debt Victoria owed the bank, - several thousand pounds. She felt her chest tighten with anguish, as she remembered her aunt telling her only days ago how relieved she was that she was not indebted to the bank, and therefore under no threat of having Tambora taken from her. Tara had certainly been given the impression that Tom and Victoria had never had to borrow from the bank, even in hard times. How then did Victoria owe the bank so much money? She must have, at some time, applied for an overdraft, unless Tadd had forged her signature? Tara closed her eyes; unable to believe Tadd would stoop so low?

Tara's anger was replaced by shock, as she opened one letter after another. Some were statements, others threats of legal action if an interest payment wasn't made by a certain date. It seemed the interest was compounding and the debt mounting. As some of the letters were backdated up to three years, Tara dreaded to think what their current position was. The most recent letter was a threat of the bank foreclosing on the loan by Christmas. That only gave them a matter of weeks to come up with thousands of pounds.

Tara kept the letter, intending to contact the bank herself. She put everything else back the way she found it. She was so angry with Tadd, and so disappointed that her aunt had virtually no chance of keeping Tambora. How could she tell her this news? It would shatter any illusions Victoria had about Tadd being a trusted friend and loyal employee. He had committed the ultimate betrayal. But even that would not compare to the heartache she'd feel at losing her beloved Tambora.

Tara was fighting tears of despair and frustration when she came out of the cottage, and so preoccupied with how she was going to keep this terrible news from her aunt, that she almost walked into the path of a horse. Jack was aboard with Hannah in the saddle in front of him.

"Where are you going?" Tara snapped, shading her teary eyes from the glaring sunlight as she looked up at the children.

"Just riding around," Jack replied broodily.

Tara was in no mood to be patient with his unwarranted bitterness. "Don't go far from the homestead. I don't want you getting lost," she said. "And be careful with Hannah."

"I won't get lost. I'm not a baby," Jack bit back.

"Anyone can get lost out here, Jack, so don't think you are so clever or that you know everything. And don't cause any more mischief. We know you set Zac free this morning, and my Aunt and I have enough to worry about without fretting over what strife you might cause next."

Jack was defiant. "It was cruel keeping Zac on a chain. Birds should be able to fly." Deep down Tara knew this was true, but the anger and grief she was feeling resulted in her lacking empathy. "Whatever you feel, it wasn't your place. My Aunt reared Zac from a hatchling. Did you consider the possibility that he might die because he can't find food and water for himself?"

Tara hadn't meant to vent her anger and disappointment on Jack, but she couldn't help it. She hardly noticed he was stricken at the thought of having done more harm than good for Zac.

From Jack's point of view, it was all Tara's fault. He gave her a resentful look. "I don't know why you brought us out here. You don't want us," he said.

Tara was startled by his remark, and slow to react in her present state of mind. "That is not true," she mumbled when she gathered her thoughts, but Jack had galloped away.

Tara stumbled towards the veranda, past Nerida at the wash trough, and burst into tears. Nugget was watching her from the vegetable garden, as she slumped into a wicker chair, and covered her face with her hands. She fought desperately to pull herself together. She couldn't risk her aunt seeing her upset and asking questions.

Nerida approached and stood silently before her for a few moments. "All right, Missus?" she asked shyly.

Tara shook her head and blew her nose. She noticed Nerida glanced towards Tadd's cottage suspiciously, but didn't notice that Nugget did the same. When the aboriginal girl looked back at her, Tara said, "Tadd has many secrets."

Nerida's reply was barely audible. "Yes, Missus." She glanced in Nugget's direction, then looked at the ground.

Tara wondered what the girl knew, although it hardly mattered any more.

"Unfortunately, his secrets are going to destroy someone I love very much, my Aunt."

The aboriginal girl looked up in concern. It was only when Tara saw the innocence in her dark eyes that she remembered how young she was.

"Is there anything you'd like to tell me, Nerida?"

The aboriginal girl dropped her gaze again. "No, Missus."

Tara hadn't expected her to say anything. It was obvious she was frightened of Tadd.

Before she went into the house, Tara made up her mind not to tell Victoria about the debt owed the bank, at least not for a little while. She also decided not to tell Tadd she'd found out he'd been keeping more secrets. She wanted him to go on feeling a false sense of security, for the time being anyway. She was determined to find out what he was up to, and what those colourful stones were, and if they were of any real value. She was also curious where Tadd had got them.

Tara planted the seeds in the garden and gave them just a little water, day and night. Although it seemed a pointless exercise, it kept her mind off more pressing problems, - problems she was powerless to solve. On the third day she could see shoots popping out of the ground. She felt a curious mixture of delight and despondency. She'd planted onions, carrots, cabbages, seed potatoes, corn, and tomatoes, and some unlabeled seeds, which she called vegetable surprise. All she needed now was a good soaking of rain, and to find a pot of gold at the end of the rainbow, and all her problems would be solved. "I suppose the locusts will turn up next," she muttered despairingly.

Day and night, Tara watched Tadd's movements. She began to notice a pattern in his behaviour. He worked around the homestead for a day or two, and then disappeared for a day or two, but never with the men. She was so determined to find out where he went, that she'd tried to follow him on two occasions, but he seemed to know, and doubled back. She also noticed he had suddenly taken an interest in the children. He spent time talking to them, and trying to gain their trust, particularly Jack's. He was up to something, Tara was sure.

Tara was stood by the vegetable garden one evening, when Ethan came to her.

"Congratulations. You've done well," he said, glancing at the neat rows of healthy green plants. He turned to look at Tara when she didn't reply, but she seemed far away.

A minute or two passed in silence.

"I come out here every morning expecting to find an animal has devoured everything," she eventually said. "I just chased a curious kangaroo away."

Ethan wondered why she wasn't happier. "Nugget and the boys built a good fence." He pointed to tracks around the perimeter. "A wombat has been here in the last few hours, and the rabbits have been digging, but the underground wire has stopped them, for the time being, anyway. The top wires look secure, so I'd say the roos haven't tried to jump over, yet."

"We should have quite a crop by Christmas, if the locust don't come. Do you think they will, Ethan? Tadd says they probably won't, but Nugget seems so sure they will."

"I'd be inclined to believe Nugget," Ethan said.

Tara frowned. "To be honest, I did believe him, but I was hoping for a miracle. As time went by, and there was no sign of locusts, I thought they may have changed direction."

"You have to realize that a locust plague covers hundreds of miles, Tara. There are literally millions of them. When they pass through an area, they don't leave a shoot or blade of any vegetation. Pastoralists have tried spraying them with poisons, and even burning them out, but nothing stops them."

"Then all my efforts have been for nothing," she said, feeling dejected.

"Maybe not. I was going to suggest you cover the plants if the locusts appear."

"Cover them, with what? We have nothing large enough to cover the entire garden, unless I pull down the curtains, and I don't think my Aunt would appreciate that."

"I have some large canvas sheets up at the cabin. I use them when I'm transporting Lucerne bales up north in the wet. I'll bring them over in the morning. You may still lose some plants, but I think it's worth a try."

"Thank you, Ethan. You always seem to be coming to our rescue." Tara felt herself blush under the gaze of Ethan's dark eyes, and looked away for a moment. "By the way, how are the plans for the Gymkhana coming along?" No matter what happened, Tara wanted her aunt to get her glasses.

"Very well. The planning committee, Ferris, Percy, Rex and myself have agreed to bring the date forward. It's to be held Saturday week."

Tara smiled with happiness, but it faded quickly, Ethan noticed. "That's wonderful, but it must have taken some hasty organization."

"Mostly everyone has been notified by radio, mail, or word of mouth. Rex is taking down the names of entrants. So far, we have a fair expression of interest. Entrants are coming from as far away as Coober Pedy and Alice Springs for the horse and camel races."

"I've heard my Aunt mention Coober Pedy. It's a mining town isn't it?" He nodded.

"Gold?"

"No, opal. Coober Pedy looks like the world's largest rabbit warren, with holes everywhere, but in fact it's the world's largest opal mining town. It's so hot, most of the population live underground, in dug outs."

Tara was intrigued. "What does opal look like?"

"Coloured stones, basically. The most common colour is blue and green, sometimes with flecks of other colours through it, but good white opal is worth a fortune."

Tara's eyes widened in surprise. Now she knew what the stones were that she'd found hidden in Tadd's cottage, - opal. And some of them were very light in colour. But where had it come from?

"Was Tadd ever an opal miner?" she asked casually.

"Not that I know of. Why do you ask?"

"I thought…. I heard him talking to Jack about it."

"As far as I know, he's been working on stations most of his life. I believe he once mentioned having mates in Coober Pedy, though." Ethan studied her and frowned. "Is something other than your Aunt's failing sight bothering you, Tara?"

"Why do you ask?"

"You've seemed very tense the last few days."

Tara was hesitant. "There is something, Ethan. I want to mull it over for a few days yet, but sometime soon I would like someone to discuss it with, and I had you in mind."

"Can't you talk to Victoria?"

"No," she said sharply.

"Is it about Jack or Hannah?"

"No."

Ethan was curious, but his mouth lifted at one corner and his dark eyes crinkled at the corners. "I'm a good listener, and an agony aunt for most of the lonely women for hundreds of miles, so my advice must be good."

Tara half smiled, and shook her head. "Don't be getting a big head. Their only other alternative is a sheep," she said, enjoying wiping the grin from his face.

Ethan suddenly looked thoughtful. "Seriously, I know we didn't get off to a good start, but if you want to discuss something…" He looked awkward. "I'm always willing to listen, and if I can help, you know you can count on me, and not just because you're Victoria's niece."

"Thank you." She smiled up at him. "I've changed my opinion of you, too."

Pleased, he smiled back at her. "By the way, I do have some news that might cheer you up."

"I could do with some. What is it?"

"Victoria asked me to tell you Percy Everett radioed her. He received a reply to your telegram from Sorrel Windspear."

"What did she say?"

"She'd be happy to have Victoria stay with her for as long as she needs to. She was disappointed you weren't coming, but she understood."

"I am so pleased. I must admit I'm really curious about how she is coping in Alice. She wasn't too thrilled about coming to the outback."

"Percy had another message, too, but Victoria couldn't quite get it because of static interference."

"Did she say what it was about?"

"Something about visitors coming out to the station tomorrow."

"Really! We're not expecting anyone. Didn't Percy say who it was?"

"I gather he did, but Victoria couldn't understand him because of the interference. I suppose we'll find out soon enough."

"Surely it must be a neighbour."

"No one mentioned they were coming out here when I delivered the mail."

A piercing shriek awoke Tara. For a few moments she wasn't sure if she was dreaming or not. She glanced at the dawn sky through the open balcony doors. It was flushed a rather strange shade of pinky-gray, and the wind had come up. When she heard the shriek again, Tara realized it was Hannah, and sprang out of bed. She was alarmed to find the little girl's bed was empty. She heard more shrieking and went out onto the landing. Hannah was at the bottom of the stairs, and she was hopping about in sheer panic. Nerida was coming down the passageway. Although Tara only glanced at her, she could see the aboriginal girl looked off colour.

"What's wrong, Hannah?" Tara called.

The little girl was still in her nightgown and clutching her teddy bear. She began climbing the stairs backwards, one at a time, while keeping her focus on the entry foyer floor. From where Tara stood on the landing, she couldn't make out anything on the tiles, other than blowing dust and leaves, but something was terrifying the little girl.

"Is it a mouse?" Tara asked, as she began descending. "It won't hurt you, Hannah."

It wasn't until Tara reached the lower steps that she noticed hopping insects all over the floor. It took a moment for her mind to register what they were.

"Oh my God," she shouted. "The locusts are here!"

CHAPTER TWENTY ONE

"Please take Hannah upstairs, Nerida," Tara called, as she grabbed a broom from behind the front door and tried in vain to sweep the grasshoppers outside before they invaded the entire house. She soon discovered the futility of her efforts, and slammed the door shut in an attempt to keep them at bay.

"Fer the love of Holy Jesus," she muttered angrily, when she noticed they were still coming under the door.

Wondering why Nerida hadn't yet sprung into action, Tara turned to look at her. For the second time she noticed the young aboriginal girl looked off colour.

"You're not looking a bit like yourself this morning, Nerida. Are you unwell?" Tara scooped Hannah into her arms. The little girl wrapped her small arms around her neck tightly, clinging in terror. "It's alright, Hannah," she whispered. "The locusts won't hurt you."

Nerida clutched her stomach. "I am feeling terrible sick this morning, Missus."

"Well, for goodness sakes, girl, go back to bed. I'll have Sanja get you some stomach salts."

"I be fine, Missus." The aboriginal girl took the near hysterical child from Tara's arms and hurried upstairs, closely followed by hopping insects.

Victoria came out onto the landing. Jack was behind her. "Tara, what's going on down there?" she called. "I heard Hannah squealing like a banshee."

"The locusts frightened her," Tara shouted back. "I must try and save the vegetable garden." She suddenly remembered that Ethan hadn't yet brought over the canvas sheets, and panicked.

"You can't, Tara, and get dressed dear, before you do anything," Victoria said, but Tara didn't appear to hear her.

Opening the front door again, Tara gasped in disbelief. For as far as she could see to the West, and North West, which was miles of flat Mulga country, the ground appeared to be alive and moving, like a rolling ocean wave. It was the strangest sight she had ever seen, peculiarly beautiful, except for the fact that the millions and millions of ravenous locusts were literally consuming everything in sight. Tara glanced towards her vegetable garden in dismay, praying the wire mesh on the lower railings might stop some of the voracious insects, even though she knew it was certainly no impregnable defense.

"I have to do something," she whispered.

Running upstairs, Tara passed Jack, who was coming down to investigate the locust plague with undisguised glee. Dashing from room to room, she literally ripped sheets from beds, while Victoria watched her niece's illogical behaviour in astonishment.

"Ethan said if we cover the plants, we might save them," Tara shouted to her aunt, who quite obviously thought she had gone stark-raving mad.

"You can't do anything," Victoria called after her. "You are wasting your time and energy. The locusts will be gone in a day or two. We just have to wait it out, and clean up the mess afterwards."

"You can't expect me to stand idly by and watch those creatures eat the vegetable plants."

"Tara, believe me, there is nothing you can do," Victoria pleaded, afraid for her niece's peace of mind.

"Bollocks!" Tara said angrily, startling Victoria who'd never heard such language from her before.

With her arms full of bundled sheets, and with Victoria looking on dumbstruck, Tara raced down the stairs and out the front door. She barely noticed Jack was chasing grasshoppers with three aboriginal children and Mellie and the pups. The children were all laughing as if they were having the time of their lives.

Tara hardly heard the rumble of thunder above the wind, as she tried to lay the sheets over her vegetable plants, stamping on as many locusts as she could while doing so. She placed rocks on the edges of the sheets, but the wind was fierce. As fast as she covered the young plants, it lifted the sheets, hurling the ineffective rocks into the air as if they were made of paper. Tara called for Jack or Nugget to help her, but no one answered. She felt like screaming in frustration, as the insects landed on her time and again, and dust blew into her eyes and mouth. Shrieking with horror, she plucked the locusts from the plants and threw them as far as she could. Waving her arms like a mad woman, she tried to hit them as they slapped into her face, but it was futile. The young vegetable plants were literally disappearing before her eyes.

When she turned, Tara saw Ethan at the far end of the garden. Near him she could see a pile of canvas sheets. He was placing leftover fencing rails on the edges of the canvas sheets, which were heavier than the bed sheets. Unfortunately there wasn't enough spare railings to cover the entire garden. Tara continued working at her end of the garden, not noticing that large droplets of rain had begun to fall, quickly turning the powdery red dust into rivers of mud.

Before long, Tara was covered in mud and weary with the effort of re-covering the young vegetable plants as fast as the wind took the sheets away. Suddenly the hopelessness of it all overwhelmed her. She'd been trying to pretend there was a chance of saving the station, and that preserving her garden was somehow a small step towards that success. But it was impossible. The odds were too great. Like the locusts, the bank couldn't be defeated.

"Why am I bothering," she shouted in disappointment. "Everything will be lost." She clambered to her feet and let out an agonizing scream of frustration. As if challenging her right to be angry, the rain began to pelt down, hard and straight. It was something Tara had never before experienced, but she barely noticed it. Her drenched nightgown, which she'd forgotten she was wearing, was smeared in mud and stuck to her body like a second skin, leaving very little to the imagination, but she was too despondent to care. She had never felt so downhearted in her entire life, not even when the gipsies had evicted her.

Ethan was watching her, but she was oblivious to the effect she was having on him. Trying to remain unaffected by the sight of her breasts and thighs, outlined by her wet nightgown as clearly as if she were naked, he came to stand beside her and placed an arm around her sagging shoulders.

"I'm sorry I didn't get here sooner, Tara. The locusts took me by surprise, but I think we'll save a few plants." He avoided looking into her stricken face for fear she'd see how unsettled he felt. "This sort of thing happens out here. It's not the end of the world."

"You don't understand," she cried passionately. "It's all going to be lost. Absolutely everything!"

Ethan could see Tara was devastated, but the depth of her despair confused him. He'd thought she was stronger than she now appeared, especially after all her hard work in preparing the garden, with virtually no complaint.

"I wouldn't call a few plants, everything, Tara. These seedlings only took a few days to come up. I'll help you plant more. After this rain, they'll be up in no time."

As distraught as Tara was, she could see Ethan was elated about the rain, and with good reason. After years of drought, any fall was a joyous event, although its timing couldn't have been worse. But what Ethan didn't realize was that nothing was going to save Tambora.

The wind had eased, but the rain continued to tumble down by the bucket full. Tara looked about her at the devastation the garden had suffered. Even the sodden sheets, which were holding pools of water and supposed to protect the young plants, appeared to be crushing them. She fell to her knees in the mud, and began to cry, great sobs of despair that racked her whole body.

Ethan felt helpless, and yet strangely stirred as never before. He wanted to stay and comfort Tara, but for the first time in his life, he wasn't sure he trusted himself. He decided it was best he walk away while he could, but he didn't get more than a few steps, when Tara lifted her head to gaze at him helplessly. Taking a deep breath, he knelt before her and tentatively pushed a strand of wet hair from her face, while trying desperately to remain immune to her, and yet give her consolation.

"Out here, Tara, we're at the mercy of nature and the elements, and they can be savage." He tried to sound unemotional, but she was looking at him with watery eyes, and he could see her heaving breasts clearly through her wet nightgown.

"Christ," he muttered. Did she not know how she was affecting him? He knew if he took her in his arms, it would be his undoing, so he cleared his throat and looked away. "You have to learn to roll with it. When you get knocked down, you just get up again. If you take this sort of thing to heart, this place will destroy you."

Tara was staring at him as if he was imparting the gift of age-old wisdom. Raindrops ran down his face, and dripped from his black hair. Even though he was frowning and trying to be serious, she could see sympathy and compassion in his expressive dark eyes, and something else that was warm and indistinguishable. He'd worked beside her to save her plants, and even though they had been unsuccessful, she felt an enormous wave of appreciation wash over her. She felt so grateful, she was momentarily overcome with the urge to kiss him. Her gaze came to rest on his well-shaped mouth, but she saw him tense, and noted his dark eyes half closed and his fists clenched, so she resisted the compulsion. "I wasn't referring to the garden …when I said everything was lost, Ethan." She turned away, and gazed about her despondently. "Everything just seems so pointless."

"Things look bleak now, but trust me, in a few days you'll wonder why you were so upset."

Tara shook her head, and for the first time, Ethan realized there was something more to her sense of hopelessness than the locusts eating the vegetable plants.

"I know you've been troubled about something, Tara," he said softly. Feeling his emotions slide again, he tried to adopt a collected, professional approach. "If you tell me what it is, maybe I can help?"

Tara had wanted to find out what Tadd was up to before saying anything, but now she understood how impossible that was. Tadd was canny and shrewd, and she was afraid he was working on the children to find out all he could about them, and her. If he knew the truth about her taking them illegally, she quite possibly faced a goal sentence, which meant her aunt would confront the loss of Tambora alone. It was all too much to bear. She had to talk to someone.

"A few days ago I found out my Aunt owes the bank a great deal of money," she said. Ethan looked shocked, and baffled.

Tara closed her eyes for a moment. "And what's worse, I don't believe she knows."

"How can that be?" Ethan was confused. "Did Tom mortgage the property before he died?"

This hadn't occurred to Tara, but none of the letters dated back to the time before Tom's death. "I think Tadd has been borrowing money behind her back over a long period of time. I know that sounds impossible, but only days ago my aunt told me how relieved she was that she didn't owe the bank any money." A sob rose in her throat. "The debt is now so large, and the interest is compounding. There is no hope of ever paying it back, and the bank is going to take the station by Christmas."

Just saying the words out loud somehow made the situation more of a reality, and Tara sagged forward in the mud again. Utter helplessness washed over her, leaving her weak and vulnerable, but she had no more tears to cry.

Ethan took her by the arms and gently lifted her up to face him. "How do you know all this, Tara? Did Tadd confess to doing such a terrible thing?"

She shook her head again. "I found a letter from the bank in his cottage. I didn't intentionally go there to snoop. I went there to get the vegetable seeds, but something I can't explain, a compulsion, made me go inside. I know it was wrong but I've had this strange feeling about him ever since I came here, and my aunt was missing a letter that I found. I suspected he had taken it and I was right. It was hidden in a suitcase with a lot of other mail that was addressed to my Aunt, mostly letters from the bank." Suddenly fresh tears came again. "How am I going to tell my Aunt she has no hope of ever keeping Tambora. Tell me how, Ethan?"

Tara fell into Ethan's arms, which closed around her like a comforting blanket.

"We can't tell her," he said feeling angry with himself for not protecting Victoria or suspecting Tadd. "We have to find out the facts from the bank first. If Tadd has done something illegal, maybe Victoria won't be responsible for the debt. Certainly stealing mail is an offence." Ethan knew he was clutching at straws, but he wanted to give Tara hope. He couldn't bear to see her so devastated. He also knew Victoria couldn't take losing Tambora. It would literally kill her.

"I'll think of something, Tara. Plenty of people out here owe me a favour. If I have to call them all in, I will."

A few moments passed, but Tara was reluctant to leave the comfort of Ethan's arms. She felt him relax; not realizing he had given in to the pleasure of holding her close, something he had been struggling to deny himself. She clung to him, letting his strength infuse and console her. For the first time in her life, she felt truly safe and secure. If anyone could put things right, it was Ethan. She was barely conscious of something stirring between them, until her wet skin sliding against his simultaneously sent a sensuous shiver through them both.

Tara felt Ethan's powerful arms tighten, pressing her breasts against his muscled chest. She was aware of his heart hammering against her own fluttering heart, as the mud on his shirt and her nightgown, riveted them together. Her hands slid over his upper arms, where his muscles felt solid and reassuring beneath her fingertips. She felt his large warm hands move over her back, hungrily kneading her skin, which felt naked through her wet, silky nightgown. It was the most stimulating sensation Tara had ever experienced, and she quivered violently in response.

Ethan had never before experienced such an erotic sensation and knew he was on the brink of no return. Tempting thoughts of laying Tara down in the mud and ravaging her went through his mind. His hands slid upwards and he entangled his fingers in her wet hair, tilting her face up to his. For a lingering moment, he looked into the pools of her green eyes. She recognized the longing in his; it matched the desire burning in her. A moment later, his lips were moving over hers tenderly, and a lightning bolt of pleasure shot through her. The kiss became urgent, as he hungrily devoured her moist mouth with unleashed passion, and she felt overwhelmed with a desire so powerful that it ripped through her senses. As the rain pelted them, she lost all conscious thought and responded to the pressure from his lips with an all-consuming passion, that burned through her with the heat of fire. Her fingernails dug into his powerful shoulders. She heard Ethan groan, and from somewhere deep inside her, she answered him. Her senses were reeling, her mind incoherent. Reasonable thought was banished with the need to be closer to the man whose arms encased her, whose lips abolished all reasoning.

Suddenly Ethan pulled away, leaving her shaken, breathless, dazed, and strangely bereft. "What's wrong," she whispered, opening her eyes, which were a smoky emerald green with desire. She was extremely shocked that he could arouse such a strong reaction from her, when she had not for one moment consciously thought of him in the capacity of a lover.

Ethan's mind waged a battle of wills. "I… thought I heard the engine of a motor car, but I must have been imagining it." The rain was falling so hard it seemed to drown out all sound, and yet he could hear his heart drumming in his ears.

If not for the breathlessness of his words, Tara would have thought she had imagined his desire for her. She had no idea how hard Ethan was trying to restrain his emotions, and finding it almost impossible. As his hands released her, Tara noted they were shaking. "I'm so sorry, Tara. I shouldn't be… taking advantage of you while you are in such a vulnerable state." He got to his feet and lifted her to hers.

"Don't apologize, Ethan," she said standing close. "I think we are both surprised, shocked, by what just happened. I… never expected to feel…" Her gaze was drawn to his mouth again, and his to hers, and they swayed toward each other, like moths to a flame. "Tara… Is that …you?"

Stunned, Tara turned to see a man and a woman standing just a few yards away, under a shawl that was ineffectively keeping the rain off them. An automobile was parked behind them. Ethan recognized it as Rex Crawley's, but the rain on the windscreen was making it difficult to see if it was Rex behind the wheel. Tara crossed her arms self-consciously over her breasts, blinked and wiped rainwater from her face, unable to comprehend what she was seeing.

With his mouth agape, Riordan Magee was staring at her as if she was a ghost. And beside him, was her mother, Elsa, who, apart from appearing appalled at her surroundings, looked noticeably older and far more vulnerable than Tara remembered her. Her face was white with shock, as she cringed under the assault of the locusts and the tumultuous rain.

Ethan was curious about the visitor's identities, especially as Tara seemed to be shocked to see them. Watching them warily, he retrieved a bed sheet from where it had been hanging over the fence, and wrapped it around her shoulders.

"What …are you doing here?" Tara asked her mother in bewilderment, glancing at Riordan in disbelief.

Ethan noted the displeasure in her tone.

"I… had to come, Tara," Elsa replied, her gaze going from her daughter to Ethan Hunter, whom she looked over with undisguised distaste. "What are you doing in the mud, Tara?"

Tara heard the familiar tone of disapproval, and sadistically gained pleasure from it. All the frustration she was feeling suddenly erupted. "You had to come. Why, in Heaven's name?"

Elsa didn't want to blurt out that she was widowed and alone and had lost her home. "You are my daughter... and I love you." She suddenly let out a shriek, startling everyone, as a locust landed on her skirt. She disgustedly brushed it off.

"What shenanigans, mother. You love your good name far more than you ever loved me."

Elsa gasped. She was shocked by the degree of hostility in Tara, especially as nearly twelve years had passed.

For the first time, Riordan spoke up. "Please, Tara, let your mother explain."

Tara was surprised by his almost humble attitude. It was certainly far different from the man who had looked down at her from lofty heights the last time she saw him.

"I shouldn't be surprised you two formed an alliance. You certainly have common traits. I thought I had made it abundantly clear than I never wish to see either of you again."

Ethan was listening with undisguised curiosity. He realized Elsa was Tara's mother, but he was particularly interested in who the gentleman was. His clothes were expensive and well-cut, so he presumed he had means. Tara certainly hadn't greeted him with any warmth, so he felt confident in assuming they were not related, but had he once been her lover? He found the thought strangely unsettling.

"You have every right to be angry, Tara," Elsa stated calmly. "I deserve your wrath. I know I was wrong, and there hasn't been a day gone by that I haven't regretted what happened. I know you were innocent of any wrong doing, and I'm here to beg your forgiveness."

Before Tara could reply, Victoria called from the upper balcony. "Bring our visitors inside, Tara."

Elsa looked up with tearful eyes, and waved.

At first Victoria didn't recognize her, as she couldn't make out her features with any clarity. "Who is it?" she asked.

When Tara said nothing, Elsa called out. "Victoria, it's me, Elsa."

"Oh my goodness," Victoria said, over come with surprise and delight. "Elsa! How wonderful."

She left the balcony and Elsa knew she was coming downstairs. She turned to Riordan, a look of anguish on her face. Tara caught her expression and immediately knew something was wrong. She'd also noticed her mother hadn't mentioned her father.

Rex Crawley got out of his car. "Can a man not get a cup of tea after driving for hours?"

"You are not supposed to be doing any driving," Ethan chastised.

"I had an offer too good to refuse." He raised his brows in the direction of Riordan and Elsa, who had no doubt paid him handsomely to deliver them to Tambora. "Besides, I'm sure the people out here are anxious for a decent mail delivery again."

"Their mail is delivered with haste and competency and they don't even have to put up with any demands for cakes and tea, or something stronger."

Rex scoffed him good-naturedly. "They are more than willing to offer refreshment for such a speedy and efficient service."

"They often need sustenance themselves, after rescuing you and your vehicle from the sand dunes. Typically, your passengers look a little worse for the experience of travelling with you."

Elsa, who looked offended at Ethan's remark, appeared shaken, but Ethan wasn't sure if her discomposure had been caused by Rex's erratic driving, or the fact that she was disconcerted with the lack of a warm welcome from her daughter. The gentleman beside her also seemed disturbed, but Ethan suspected that seeing Tara in the arms of another man was the reason.

Ethan turned to Tara. "I think we had better get cleaned up." She nodded.

Victoria called out from the shelter of the back door. "Come in for goodness sakes. What are ye all standing about in the rain for?"

CHAPTER TWENTY-TWO

Tara deliberately took her time bathing. Knowing the rainwater tanks were benefiting from the continuing downpour, she didn't feel quite so guilty about using the water. She did, however, feel emotionally unprepared to face her mother, and unwilling to dredge up painful issues that she had buried for the past eleven and a half years. She certainly wasn't ready to forgive her mother for not believing Stanton Jackson had raped her, no matter how many times she said she was sorry. It was just not that simple, and with everything else that was happening around her, it was all too much to deal with.

As for Ethan, she couldn't get the eruption of passion that had ignited between them, out of her mind. Just reliving those few moments sent an infusion of colour from her head to her toes. She was literally in a state of shock that someone she considered so unlikely could arouse such intense, overpowering emotion in her. Although it was unlikely to ever reoccur, she knew she would never look at Ethan Hunter in the same way again.

Tara shook her head, trying to clear her thoughts. She'd come to a decision. "Riordan and my mother simply have to go, and that's all there is to it," she muttered, climbing out of the tub.

When Tara finally appeared in the living room, she was surprised to find it deserted. Apart from locusts hopping all over the floor, the house was strangely quiet. Even Nerida seemed to be missing, and so were the children. Tara checked all the rooms on the ground floor, including Nerida's room, but the aboriginal girl was nowhere to be found. She tried to ask Sanja if he knew where everyone was, but he'd barricaded himself in the kitchen to escape the locusts, and, in his usual uncooperative fashion, refused to open the door. At least she knew where Ethan and Rex were. They had gone to the shearing quarters, where Ethan was going to bathe.

Tara went upstairs in search of Jack and Hannah. She was hurrying past her aunt's room, when Victoria called out to her.

Reluctantly, Tara stopped by the open doorway. Her aunt was sitting on her bed, Elsa beside her. They had both been crying.

"There you are, Tara," Victoria said, dabbing her eyes. "We came up here… to escape the locusts." She glanced at Elsa and Tara suspected they had come upstairs for her benefit. The locusts would not have worried Victoria.

Tara could see her aunt was having difficulty containing her emotions, and for the second time she noticed her mother looked unusually vulnerable, something she had never imagined possible. It was in the roundness of her shoulders and the quiver of her lips. Elsa had always been so poised, so capable, even when the world around her was in chaos. To see her look fragile was a great shock, especially after Tara had spent her entire childhood thinking her mother was almost immune to human emotions.

Tara was wearing a loose cotton dress, but she still felt warm, as the rain and the heat had combined to make the air very humid. Victoria always wore loose-fitting dresses, but Tara could see her mother was suffering in the simple but elegantly cut suit she was wearing, which looked ridiculously out of place in the outback.

With her damp hair tumbling loosely down her back, Tara was unaware of how young and impressionable she looked, or that she reminded her mother of happier times, when she had been an innocent adolescent girl with the world at her feet. As Elsa thought of the years that had passed, she could hardly believe so much had happened, or that Tara barely looked any different. It wasn't until her mind flashed back to just an hour ago, when she had found Tara in a passionate embrace with a coarse looking man, that she had to face the realization that her 'little girl' had changed dramatically. She couldn't bear to think about the life she had led, the type of existence that had changed her perspective so vividly that she could find such an unsuitable man attractive.

"Come and sit beside us," Victoria said softly.

Tara was hesitant. "I prefer to stand, Aunt," she said coldly. She glared at her mother. "I really don't understand why you are here?"

"I wanted to see you… and…" Elsa glanced at Victoria, and both women lowered their gaze.

"I think you should go back to Ireland," Tara said inhospitably. One glimpse of her aunt, and Tara knew Victoria was not pleased with her attitude. In fact, she looked disappointed.

For the first time Tara noticed Riordan was out on the balcony, watching the steady fall of rain. He turned and came to lean on the architrave's in the open doorway, and looked at her with a strange expression on his handsome face. Tara noted he looked leaner than when she last saw him, and a little tired.

Riordan, too, thought Tara looked young and unsophisticated in the shapeless dress she was wearing, a stark contrast to the temptress who had titillated lustful gipsy men around a blazing campfire. Now he knew her reasons for running away were valid, he was deeply ashamed of how he had treated her. He'd had a long time to understand she was a victim of tragic circumstances, and that being beautiful, vivacious and alluring, were not a crime. But would she forgive him for his ungracious and unwarranted behaviour? If the way she was looking at him was any indication, he had little hope.

Tara was glaring at Riordan scathingly. She thought he was about as welcome as king brown snake in a stockman's swag, but Tambora was her aunt's home, and he was her friend, however much she loathed him.

Riordan dropped his gaze to the floor and turned back to the balcony. She hadn't needed to tell him he was not well received. He'd got the message, loud and clear. Feeling no remorse, Tara turned to leave.

"Wait, Tara," Elsa said. It was hard to hear her soft voice above the sound of the rain pelting the iron roof on the house. "I have… something I have to tell you."

Tara turned and mentally braced herself. She suspected bad news was coming, and she knew it was about her father, but she tried to mask her emotions. Visions of him swam in her mind, images in which he was ill and feeble, so unlike the strong man she had left behind. She made a conscious effort to push them aside. If he wanted her to come home, she would refuse.

"You have nothing to say that I want to hear," Tara said, flatly.

"Please listen to your mother," Victoria pleaded.

There was something about her tone of voice that frightened Tara. It was so earnest. "Your father…" Elsa faltered, and Victoria took her hand and squeezed it.

"If my father is ill and wants me to return home, mother, I won't go."

Elsa looked sad, bereaved in fact, and suddenly Tara feared the worst. Not wanting to hear what her mother had to say, she turned to flee.

"He's not ill, Tara," Elsa said quickly. Tara stopped near the railing on the landing, her back to her mother; her eyes squeezed tightly shut. As angry as she was with her father, she didn't want to hear that he had…

"He passed away a few months ago." Tears filled Elsa's pale green eyes as she walked toward her daughter, stopping short of touching Tara's frigid body. "He knew he had been wrong about you, Tara, we both did. He was never the same after you left. If only you had come home…"

Tara felt physically sick. "Are you blaming me … for my father's death?" Keeping her back to her mother, she fought the tumultuous emotions that threatened to erupt in a violent outburst. She wanted to lash out at her mother, and say it was not her fault that her father had suffered. She'd suffered too. But at the same time a small part of her, the little girl buried within, wanted to have her mother take her in her arms and comfort her. But Elsa had never been the demonstrative type. Physical contact had been limited to nannies.

"Of course I'm not blaming you." Elsa barely touched Tara's arm, but she flinched as if a white-hot poker had burned her. "He grieved as if you were…" She couldn't say the word, but it had been as if Tara had died, for both of them. "It was his dying wish… that you know how sorry he was for ever doubting you. I had to find you, to tell you…"

Tara was shaking as she slowly turned. "If you want my forgiveness, mother, I can't give it to you," she said, fighting tears. "I just can't…"

Elsa nodded, and swallowed the lump in her throat. "I understand… it's too soon. But, perhaps one day." She looked hopeful, but Tara dropped her gaze to the floor, not willing to commit.

"We have to talk, privately," Tara said in a restrained tone. She looked through the open doorway, at her aunt. "We'll use another room, down the hall."

Victoria nodded. "I'll see if Nerida will bring tea up."

"I don't know where she is," Tara said. "I couldn't find her downstairs and Sanja has barricaded himself in the kitchen."

Victoria half smiled. "He's always been terrified of locusts and beetles." They'd had an invasion of stinkbugs the year Sanja came out from India. For weeks he had found the foul smelling beetles in cupboards in the kitchen, in pots and pans, drawers, in sacks of flour, rice, even in their tealeaves. The beetles had almost driven him mad. Since then, he became almost frenetic at the sight of anything crawling in the kitchen.

"You go and talk," Victoria said. "Riordan and I can fend for ourselves."

The two women walked down the hall in tense silence. As Tara came to Hannah's bedroom door, which was ajar, she peered inside, hoping to find Nerida. Hannah was sitting on her bed, partially covered by a sheet, which, it appeared, she had been hiding beneath. She looked nervous, and kept glancing warily at the floor, searching for the invading grasshoppers. Jack had an open storybook in his hands. It looked as if he had been reading to his sister. Tara was touched by his thoughtfulness. He was a complex boy, but there had never been any doubt about his devotion to Hannah.

"I thought Nerida would be here," Tara said.

"She left," Jack replied sullenly. He seemed to put up a protective emotional wall every time Tara was near. She still had no idea why.

"What do you mean, left? Where did she go?"

"She just said she had to go, and asked me to stay with Hannah."

Tara was confused. She wondered if Nerida had gone to the aboriginal camp to seek help for the sickness she was suffering, perhaps some kind of tribal medicine, but surely not in this deluge?

"Who do these children belong to?" Elsa asked, peering over Tara's shoulder.

Startled, Tara turned to her mother. She hadn't given it any thought, but had assumed that her aunt would have told her mother about Jack and Hannah. Evidently, she hadn't.

"They are my children," Tara said, maliciously relishing the shock on her mother's face. Elsa gasped, her hand coming up to her mouth. As she looked at Jack and Hannah, her eyes became glassy with moisture. "Yours... I had no idea..."

Tara said nothing. She had expected a negative reaction, anything from a hint of disapproval, to outright condemnation, but her mother looked genuinely moved, as she valiantly fought tears.

"They are beautiful, Tara," Elsa whispered. She appeared so vulnerable, and overcome with emotion, that Tara almost weakened and told her the truth.

"How old are they?" Elsa asked, as she walked past Tara into the room. Tara frowned, but did not reply.

"I am your... grandmother," Elsa said to the children

Jack looked at Tara uncertainly, as Elsa perched herself beside him on the bed. Hannah looked bewildered and pulled the sheet over her face.

Tara gathered her thoughts. If she weakened, and let down her defenses, she'd be hurt again. "Mother," she said sternly. "Please come with me. I want to talk to you, and it can't wait another minute." The last thing Tara wanted was her mother embedding herself in their lives, in any capacity. She certainly wasn't going to let her endear herself to the children, forming an emotional attachment that would be difficult to break.

Elsa had a stricken expression on her pale face. "I'd like to get to know my ... grandchildren?"

"Not now," Tara said coldly.

Elsa glanced at the children again, stood up, and pressed her lips together.

Tara could see her mother was terribly hurt, but she remained outwardly unmoved. Inside, she was trembling. Being spiteful didn't come naturally.

The two women entered a spare bedroom several doors from Hannah's room. Tara closed the door to ensure privacy, while Elsa opened the balcony doors, and stepped outside. They were on the far side of the house, a long way from the children or Victoria and Riordan.

Holding the balcony railing so tightly her knuckles turned white, Elsa took a deep breath, and looked out over the land that Victoria, and now Tara and her children called home. The gum trees appeared to be lifting their branches to the welcome rain, which had slowed the locust plague from moving on. The ground was literally saturated with insects.

"You can't stay here, mother," Tara said.

Elsa slowly turned. "Victoria said Riordan and I could stay for as long as we wished, and I think we need time to resolve our differences, Tara."

"I don't know how you can think it's that simple, mother."

"Surely, if we spend time together, we can become close again."

"I don't ever remember us being close."

Elsa's head tilted to one side, and she looked every day of her fifty years. "Tara, why are you being so cruel?"

"I could have asked you that question nearly twelve years ago."

Elsa's gaze dropped to the varnished timber floor of the veranda. "I hadn't meant to hurt you. At the time I didn't know what to think… but I was wrong, and I am so sorry. Give me time to make it up to you, Tara, please?"

Tara shook her head, and walked back into the room. Elsa followed.

"You shouldn't have come here, and I wish you hadn't brought Riordan Magee with you. I detest the man."

"He's been so good to me since your father's death. I'm sure I would never have found you without his help. He even hired private investigators."

Tara snorted angrily.

Elsa was mystified by her hostility towards Riordan. "I understand he nearly lost his life trying to find you several years ago, Tara? Under the circumstances, I think you could be a little more gracious."

"Thank you for the criticism mother, but he should have known better than to come to the gipsy camp, especially at night. The gipsy men are very protective of their women and children."

Elsa visibly flinched. It was apparent to Tara that her mother still could not bring herself to talk about the gipsies. For this reason, she found it impossible to conceive she would have royal gipsy blood, as Eloisa had claimed.

"Why do you dislike Riordan so much?" Elsa asked, changing the subject. "I believe he genuinely cares for you."

Tara thought of the way he had treated her when she last saw him. He'd all but called her a liar. If that was his idea of caring, she could do without it.

When Tara didn't reply, Elsa said, "I think he's a wonderful man, so charming and handsome."

Tara recognized her mother's tone. Riordan Magee was the type of man she would have wanted her to marry. Tara suddenly wondered if her mother had matchmaking in mind. She remembered the way she had looked at Ethan Hunter, like he was a detestable gipsy. Quite obviously she had been horrified to see her daughter in his arms. Perversely, Tara decided her mother's dislike of Ethan made him more attractive.

"If you think Riordan Magee is so wonderful, mother, why not marry him, yourself?" Elsa gasped in dismay, but Tara frowned, outwardly unrepentant. Inwardly she was feeling churlish, but she could hardly control her rampant emotions.

As both women took stock of their feelings, a few minutes passed in silence.

Tara was the first to speak. It was quite obvious from her tone that she was losing patience. "Mother, I have no idea why you would want to stay out here."

"I told you…"

"But have you really taken in your surroundings? The nearest form of civilization is the town of Wombat Creek, with its one little store, a hotel, and four houses." She wanted to mention the bordello, but out of respect for Lottie, she refrained. "There are no neighbours for miles…"

"I stayed in the Wombat Creek Hotel for a short while, Tara," Elsa said. "So I know what the town is like."

It had taken Riordan several hours, and a great deal of money, to persuade Rex Crawley to drive them out to Tambora. The man literally took the opportunity to legally rob them.

Those few hours in the town were the longest hours of Elsa's life. Ferris Dunmore had regaled her with his life story, a bizarre and sordid tale of one mishap after another. And his wife…a wild native girl, named… Hope or Charity, or something, had roamed about half naked, and only moments away, it seemed, from giving birth. She'd even had the nerve to suggest Elsa help her skin dead rabbits which left her with no appetite for lunch. And the wine… it was the same colour she imagined the water used to wash Ferris Dunmore's discarded singlets would be. And she found it appalling that he didn't wear socks, or shoes. She'd thought Wombat Creek was a shocking place, surely the forgotten end of the Earth, a dusty hole…

Elsa had foolishly imagined the journey out to the station would be a respite, but it had proven to be horrendous. She was sure Rex Crawley lacked any good sense. Driving at break neck speed, he'd chased kangaroos down the 'track', and then suddenly he'd veered off, flying over sand hills after emus, all the while locusts smashed into the windscreen, and flew in through the open windows on burning winds. Elsa had even accused him of being drunk, but Rex claimed he was having the time of his life, and even had the gall to remind them he was being paid handsomely for it.

"You couldn't cope out here," Tara told her mother. "I didn't want to stay myself, when I first arrived. I'm not even sure I do now, but at least I was half prepared after living as a gipsy for several years. The outback is the harshest environment, and given to vast extremes. How would you contend with choking on dust and flies, surrounded by thousands of sheep and cattle, and foul smelling camels?

"Tara, are you forgetting I was the wife of a farmer?"

"Oh, mother. You were the wife of a landowner, one of the gentry. I doubt you've ever gotten within a hundred yards of a sheep. You've led a pampered life, waited upon by servants. Your idea of exercise was strolling around a rose garden and attending flower shows and tea parties. There's no social life out here, just hard work. If you want proof, just look at my hands."

Tara held up her calloused hands for her mother to inspect.

Elsa tried to hide her reaction, but Tara could see she was shocked. Her nails were filthy, and her skin, dry, rough and chapped. A scullery maid in Ireland had better hands, even a gipsy woman.

"I have spent days digging ground that is as hard as iron, in the hope of growing some fresh vegetables. After all my efforts, the damned locusts are the only ones who've had a feast."

"Why on earth didn't you get the gardener to do it, or at least help you?" Elsa asked.

Tara looked exasperated. "What gardener? Haven't you been listening, mother? There aren't any servants out here. Nerida, the house girl who usually looks after Victoria, seems to have gone walkabout, and the cook… he runs the house."

"You mean the kitchen, surely?"

"No. I mean the house. He cooks what he wants, when he wants, and how he wants, and it all amounts to one thing. Curry!"

Elsa looked startled, wrinkling her nose. "Curry!"

"Aunt Victoria won't dare challenge him. She's terrified he'll pack his bags and leave."

"Whoever heard of a cook running the house?"

"I've tried speaking to him, but he practically threw me out of his kitchen."

Elsa's eyes widened. She'd never heard of such a thing.

Tara sat down in a chair, and sighed raggedly. "Mother, even if I was foolish enough to consider the possibility of us spending any time together, there are other factors that prevent it from being practicable for you to stay here."

"What factors, Tara? There is certainly plenty of room. This house is absolutely enormous." Elsa glanced around the room, noticing the cobwebs and dust. It certainly needed cleaning, but properly run, Tambora could be quite a showpiece, and fabulous for entertaining, although goodness only knows who the guests would be. She absently wondered if there was a ballroom?

"I'm referring to our current financial situation, which is dire to say the least."

"The Depression has made life difficult for everyone, dear."

"Our problems go beyond any the Depression have caused."

"Are you saying Victoria is in a financial bind? Riordan told me she had married a wealthy man."

"Tom was a wealthy man, but he died some years ago, and the drought has been devastating. As it is, we are bartering for food, and what little sheep we have left have been dying of hunger and thirst. At least they will have water now, but there's not much feed about. But that's not the worst of it. I just recently found out the station manager has been borrowing money from the bank against the property, and Aunt Victoria doesn't know about it."

Elsa went pale, and dabbed perspiration on her forehead with a lace handkerchief.

"He's got the station into so much debt…it's quite likely we'll all be homeless by Christmas. So you see, mother, I'm afraid you have to go."

Elsa was distraught. "Tara, I have a little money."

"No, mother." Tara stood up and began to pace the room.

"Tara, please, hear me out. I had to sell the family home after your father died, and all of the antiques and art works he had collected. I didn't get what our assets were worth, and some of the money went to pay debts, but whatever is left, is yours."

Tara thought her mother was being uncharacteristically generous, but realized if she was penniless, they couldn't ask her to leave. Besides, the station was in so much debt, a small amount of money would only keep them going for a few days.

"If I can buy you a little time, Tara, let me do it."

"Would it ease your conscience, mother?"

Elsa flinched. "All I ask is that you allow me to spend some time with you, Victoria, and the children. After that, well, I'll go home. I certainly don't want to be a burden."

Tara sighed, undecided.

"Wouldn't four hundred pounds help?"

Tara gasped. It certainly would help. It wouldn't touch their debt, but it would keep the bank off their backs for several months, and she could use a reprieve, if only to postpone the inevitable, breaking Victoria's heart.

"I could look after Hannah for you, too, if Nerida doesn't return."

Tara knew Nugget and the boys needed help to round up the sheep for the next few weeks, so that they could be sheared, and she couldn't trust her aunt to watch Hannah. After spending several minutes warring with her pride and the practicality of accepting her mother's offer, practicality won out.

"Very well, mother, you can stay, but only until Christmas, and I won't accept all of your money and leave you penniless. As far as you and I are concerned, our relationship is damaged beyond repair, so don't expect miracles, because you'll be disappointed." Elsa was satisfied to be over the first hurdle. As far as she was concerned, just being able to stay with Tara and the children, for any length of time, was a minor miracle.

Tara walked out onto the balcony again, and Elsa followed. "I have something else to tell you, mother. I didn't give birth to Jack and Hannah."

Elsa flinched as if Tara had struck her. "You lied..." Elsa thought that was the cruelest thing her daughter could have done. She'd dreamt of the day that Tara would make her a grandmother.

"Their parents drowned on the ship coming out here. We were very close..." She felt her throat tighten. "I intend to raise Jack and Hannah as my children."

"Oh, Tara, that is so very generous of you. They appear to be lovely children."

"No one, apart from Aunt Victoria and Ethan Hunter, knows they are not mine. I especially don't want the station manager to know. He can't be trusted."

"Of course," Elsa said. She was curious why being the children's guardian required secrecy, but she didn't want to say anything to jeopardize her tenuous situation.

Tara was curious about her brothers, Liam and Daniel. She wondered if they had children, but she could not bring herself to ask her mother.

Tara looked out over the land. The rain had eased slightly, but she could hear water running from the roof into the rain water tanks. "You have to realize everyone must pull their weight out here, mother. Even more so with Nerida gone."

"Of course, I'll do whatever I can."

"Are you prepared to work, mother, because the house needs a good clean, and the cook certainly needs taking in hand?" Tara was testing her mother, sure she'd fail.

Elsa was only momentarily hesitant. "Yes, of course."

"Are you sure you're up to it? It's not like you've ever had to do anything physical before." Tara knew how useless she had been when she joined the gipsy band, and she'd been young and willing, but it made no difference.

"I'm sure I'll surprise you." Elsa had had to do many things for herself in the last few months when she didn't have any money to pay servants, nothing like cleaning such a large house, but she had done a little cleaning and cooking.

Tara caught the uncertainty in her mother's voice, and seriously doubted she would last a week, but she refrained from saying so.

As they walked down the corridor, Elsa asked in a small voice, "How many rooms in this house?"

"Enough to keep you busy cleaning for a week before you get back to where you started," Tara said. She intended to help, of course, but she didn't say so.

Elsa looked daunted.

"Mother, if you can get Sanja to cook something other than curry, and especially an Irish stew, I'll… I'll…"

Elsa hoped she was going to say 'I'll forgive you'

"I'll be most surprised."

Elsa put on a brave face. "I'll consider that a challenge."

Tara's expression made her mother quake. It was obvious she thought she had absolutely no chance of succeeding, which made Elsa more than curious, and a little apprehensive about the rebellious cook.

CHAPTER TWENTY-THREE

Leaving her mother with Victoria, Tara excused herself and hurried to her room. The moment the door was closed and locked, she burst into tears. Like an opening floodgate, her emotions poured forth in a tumultuous jumble of pain, sorrow, frustration, anger and tragic loss.

With her father gone, Tara could freely admit just how much she had missed him. She could also finally acknowledge that she had harboured a secret hope that one day they would reunite. Now that hope was lost forever. That her father regretted his actions made her pain even more acute.

After crying for almost an hour, Tara was drained of emotion, but she had come to a decision. The past should be buried with her father, and forgotten, even if bitterness left her unable to forgive. For the children's sake, she had to concentrate on the future. She had to move forward.

Drying her eyes, Tara went back to Hannah's room. From the open doorway, she could see the little girl had fallen asleep, but Jack was still sitting on the bed beside her, his back propped up by pillows. He appeared to be day dreaming, as he gazed out through the open balcony doors. The forlorn expression on his face made Tara's heart ache. She suspected he was thinking of his parents. For the first time she fully understood his pain.

Tara sat down at Jack's feet, and he turned his head to look at her. He could see she had been crying, and wondered if she had been arguing with her mother. As young as he was, he had noticed the tension between them.

"I see Hannah finally fell asleep," Tara commented in a small voice.

Jack nodded.

Tara noticed how like his father's his eyes were, a pretty corn blue and kind, sometimes older and wiser than his tender years.

"My mother is staying here for awhile, at least until Christmas," Tara said.

"Why don't you like her?" Jack asked.

His direct question took Tara by surprise. "We have... a complex relationship," she said, not really knowing how to sum up years of differences in opinion and resentment. "She believes spending time together will help us better understand each other, but I'm not sure I agree with her." Her father had understood her, but her mother had resented their closeness. How could Elsa now expect to take his place in her heart?

Jack continued to watch Tara. She could see he was curious, and she wanted to be as honest with him as possible. Since hearing the news of her father's death, she'd come to the conclusion that being truthful and open with Jack and Hannah was the only way they would ever truly bond, and she wanted that more than she ever conceived.

"You've been crying," Jack said.

Tara nodded. "My mother has just told me my father passed away a few months ago. It was a ... shock." On the verge of tears again, Tara looked away for a moment.

"Were you close to your father?" Jack asked.

"We were very devoted when I was growing up, but something happened years ago that made me angry with both of my parents."

"What was it?"

Tara was hesitant. "I think you are too young to understand just yet, Jack, but maybe one day..."

Almost instantly, he seemed to shut down emotionally. The curiosity and life that had danced in his eyes just moments ago had gone, snuffed out like a flame. The thin thread of a bond that had barely existed between them had been broken by her lack of regard for his feelings. Tara sensed he needed her to trust him, to open up to him if he was ever going to open up to her. He'd also made it abundantly clear that he hated being treated like a child, and wasn't that exactly what she had just done? After all he'd been through, she knew he deserved better. And if they were ever to have a good relationship, it had to be something different to that which he'd had with his parents. She could never take their place.

Taking a slow breath, Tara endeavored to explain the violation she had suffered in a way that Jack could understand. "On the night of my eighteenth birthday, a man who worked for my father attacked me," she whispered, staring at her hands clasped in her lap. She glanced at Jack briefly, not wanting him to see the pain in her eyes, and noted his renewed curiosity was tinged with surprise. "He wasn't a very nice man. I always thought he was strange, kind of creepy, and he drank too much." She shuddered. "He was drunk that night, and hurt me badly. Then he lied to my parents. I tried to tell them my version of what had happened, but they chose to believe his account."

"Why would they do that?"

A very good question, Tara thought, one she had tried to answer a million times. "I honestly don't know, Jack. My mother always worried about what other people thought.

She was terrified of scandal, and my father was highly respected in the community. In my mind, there was no excuse for the way they treated me. I felt betrayed. I ran away from home, and never went back."

"Where did you go? How did you live?"

Tara considered her answer. "Some people took me in. They were kind, but my life was never the same, as different as yours is now. Sometimes it was difficult and I wanted to go home, but I was too hurt and far too proud to go running back, and I truly believed I wasn't welcome. My mother told me that soon after I left, she and my father realized I had been telling them the truth, but it was too late." Tara noticed Jack looked as sad as she felt.

"I think I wanted them to find me, to put things right, but it never happened. The years passed, and my bitterness grew." Tara stood up and walked toward the open balcony doors, where she stood looking out with her arms folded.

"Will you forgive your mother, now?" Jack asked. His voice became small. "I would, if she said she was sorry."

Tara turned to face him. He looked sad again. "I don't know if I can, Jack. I've been resentful for so long, forever it seems. I know my mother needs my forgiveness, and it would be easy to say the words, but in doing so, I wouldn't be true to myself if that's not what I felt in my heart. I've tried to explain this to her, so she will just have to be patient. In all honesty, it may never happen." She walked toward him again, and sat down on the bed. "My father's death has made me appreciate how precious life is, especially relationships. I can't change the past, but I want to make plans for the future, with you and Hannah."

Jack frowned. "What kind of plans?" In his young mind, he thought she might want to send him away, perhaps to Auntie Moyna, or boarding school.

Tara could see he looked apprehensive. She hoped he would be pleased with her idea. "Very soon, Aunt Victoria is going to Alice Springs to see a doctor about getting some glasses. She's going to stay with Mrs. Windspear. Do you remember her? We travelled together on the train?"

Jack nodded, his apprehension growing.

"Mrs. Windspear's son, Marcus, runs a hotel in Alice, but he's a lawyer. I am going to ask Aunt Victoria to speak to him about making our relationship formal."

Jack was still scowling, and Tara realized he did not understand.

"I want to legally adopt you and Hannah. If that's not possible, I want to see if I can at least be considered your legal guardian. What do you think about that, Jack?"

Jack looked skeptical. Although he understood what adoption meant, for weeks he had believed she didn't really want him. He also suspected she didn't want the authorities to catch up with her. "Why would you want to do that?"

Tara was surprised by his question. She thought he'd be happier if he felt more secure. "Because I want us to be a real family, but only if that's what you want, of course."

Jack jumped off the bed and stood glaring at Tara. His bottom lip was trembling ever so slightly. She didn't know what to think. His reaction was so unexpected.

"I thought…" He stopped, evidently on the verge of crying.

"What, Jack? What did you think?"

His gaze dropped to the floor.

Tara watched him. "I wouldn't have taken you and your sister if I didn't want you, Jack. You believe that, don't you?"

"I heard you tell Aunt Victoria that you weren't sure, that you thought taking us was a mistake.." He stared at Tara as if he dared not trust her.

Tara tried to remember when she had said that to her aunt. It was the day they arrived on Tambora. She realized that Jack must have been listening, and heard at least part of their conversation. No wonder he had been misbehaving.

Tara's expression softened with understanding. "I'll be truthful, Jack. I've had my doubts about whether I did the right thing in taking you and Hannah." She saw the flash of pain in his eyes.

"But not for a moment have I questioned my feelings for you. I just wasn't sure I could look after you properly because I didn't have a home for us, or any means. To be really honest, I was scared. I'd never had the responsibility of a child before, let alone two, but it didn't take me long to realize that none of those things mattered, as long as we're together." They could quite likely find themselves homeless, but Tara couldn't imagine her life without the children.

Tears welled in Jack's eyes.

"I love you and Hannah, Jack. I want us to be a real family."

Jack sprang into her arms, and Tara held him tightly, as they both cried tears of happiness.

"I've done some terrible things," he admitted, clinging to her.

Tara thought of the slashed buggy tyres. She still couldn't believe he had done that.

"It doesn't matter, Jack." She looked into his troubled face, covered in sun kissed freckles. "You've had so much to deal with, far too much pain. I know you feel responsible for Hannah, and you want to look after her, but there'll be time enough for that when suitors come to court. Promise me you won't grow up too soon. I want to enjoy your childhood."

He smiled, and Tara caught the relief in his blue eyes, as if a ton of weight had been lifted from his small shoulders. "All right," he said. He suddenly looked shy and glanced at his sleeping sister. "If you do adopt me and Hannah, would that make you our... mother?"

"Yes, but I don't want to take your real mother's place in your heart. I hope there's enough room for both of us."

He nodded, and sadness shadowed his eyes. "Could I... Would it be all right if I ... called you momma?"

Tara fought tears of happiness. "I'd like that, Jack, very much."

He looked relieved. "Would your mother be our grandmother? She said she was."

"Yes, she would be your grandmother." That was a daunting thought.

Jack looked pleased. "I've never had a grandmother before. Momma said they both died before me and Hannah were born."

Tara smiled cautiously. "My mother has been waiting for grandchildren, so look out..."

In the early evening, when the kookaburra's and cockatoo's were at their noisiest, they went down to the dining room. Tara and Jack had spent an hour sweeping up locusts in the hallway and entry, but more had appeared, which meant Tara had to carry Hannah because she became hysterical at the thought of them jumping on her.

Riordan and Victoria were alone at the dining table. Tara was surprised to see Riordan tucking into an enormous plate of lamb curry. Just the aroma of chilli made her eyes water. Since Tara had threatened Sanja with dismissal, he'd been even more heavy handed with the use of spices, just to spite her.

"Would you believe it, Tara?" Victoria said. "I think Riordan loves curries as much as I do. Of course, like me, he's travelled to the exotic East."

Tara didn't reply. She glanced at Riordan warily, as he wiped perspiration from his brow. "Can we have lamb chops with Nugget?" Jack asked Tara.

Tara was thrilled to see him smiling at her again. "All right? You don't mind, do you

Aunt?"

Victoria caught the change in the tone of Jack's voice, and it pleased her. "Of course not, dear. Your mother is still asleep, but Ethan and Rex have opted to eat with Nugget. I believe he's cooking a stew, as well as chops."

"Has Nerida returned?" Tara asked, not trusting herself to think about Ethan.

"No. She must have gone with the tribe. They would have fled, thinking your mother and Riordan were government officials, come to take the children."

Riordan looked perplexed. "They've no need to fear me. I'm really not very fond of children, let alone a tribe of them."

Victoria laughed.

"That doesn't explain why Nerida went," Tara said, thinking it was strange not to like children. "She didn't run away when I came here."

"I know," Victoria said. "I am worried about her, especially as she wasn't feeling herself. The aboriginals don't like to take our remedies for any ailment. They prefer to use their own cures, which they make themselves, so it's not uncommon for them to just disappear. I just wish Nerida had told me she was going. She's usually so reliable."

"She probably felt confident in leaving you, with mother and I here," Tara said, casting a cold glare at Riordan. "We'll see you later, Aunt."

When Tara and the children had gone, Victoria glanced at Riordan. "She's still very angry with you. I can hear it in her voice."

"I don't blame her, Victoria. I'm hoping she'll grow accustomed to my being here, and then I'll talk to her. For now, I'll give her the space she needs to establish a new relationship with her mother."

Victoria patted his arm. "You are a very understanding man, Riordan."

He smiled wryly. "I doubt your niece would agree with you. Had I been understanding seven years ago, and several months ago when Tara came to see me, things might be different. Unfortunately my judgement was clouded by my obsession with her. I think I've come to terms with that now. At least I hope so."

"You still find her attractive, don't you?"

"Yes, God help me, I do."

Ethan and Rex Crawley were sitting in the shearers quarters with Bluey, Nugget, Charlie and young Karl. The rain had almost ceased, but the grounds were covered in puddles of muddy water, polluted with drowned locusts. It would have been almost impossible to light a campfire. Nugget had a pot of stew simmering on top of the stove and several lamb chops on a tray in the oven, which smelt appetizing.

As soon as Tara appeared in the doorway, her eyes were drawn to Ethan, and her heart began to hammer. She smiled self-consciously.

"Do you have any lamb chops to spare, Nugget? The curry smells very hot this evening."

"Of course, Missus. Come out of the rain."

Tara stepped inside with Jack and Hannah. "The rain seems to be easing, but what a mess out there." There was a moment of uncomfortable silence. "Does anyone know where Nerida has gone?"

"Gone walkabout, has she?" Rex asked.

"I don't know," Tara replied. "She's usually dependable, but she said she didn't feel well this morning. I just hope she's all right."

"She must have gone off with the tribe," Ethan suggested, looking directly into her eyes with the kind of intensity that turned her legs to jelly. "If she didn't feel well, she would have gone to see Kitty Koko. She's a kind of nurse to the aborigines on the mission lands. She's bush-trained and a real marvel."

Ethan looked clean and freshly shaven. Tara imagined his arms around her, and his lips on hers, and she felt herself growing warm all over.

"You must be Tara Flynn," Rex said. "We haven't been formally introduced. Nobody around here has any manners." He glanced at Ethan.

Ethan said. "Tara, this is Rex Crawley."

Rex added, "I'm the official mailman in these parts."

Tara noted Ethan's eyes went heavenward, and she tried not to smile.

"I've heard all about you on the radio, Tara," Rex added. "Anyone new in the area is a hot topic for discussion."

Tara wondered what was being said, but she couldn't bring herself to ask. "I'm pleased to meet you, Rex." She extended her hand.

"Have a seat," Rex said offering his, but Ethan had already produced a chair for her, much to his annoyance. It was clear their rivalry extended to everything.

"You're a legend out here in the outback, Mr. Crawley," Tara said, winking at Jack. Rex's delight illuminated his tired features. "Do ya hear that, Ethan Hunter?" he said, nudging him in the ribs.

Ethan gave Tara an exasperated look. She bit her bottom lip so she wouldn't laugh. "Let Tara try your stew, Nugget," Ethan said.

Suspecting he was up to something, Tara's features sobered. "What kind of stew is it?" she asked sceptically.

"Good tucker," Nugget said grinning, which usually meant it was something she'd consider strange.

When Tara glanced again at Ethan, he was looking out the door at the sodden ground, a grin lifting one side of his mouth. Jack was also smiling.

A horrible thought came to mind. "Surely you haven't been cooking … locusts, Nugget?" The stockman grinned, and stirred his pot. "They make real good tucker, Missus."

Tara grimaced. "Don't ye be thinking I'm eating any of that," she growled and the men laughed.

Tara steered well clear of the stew, which, although Nugget denied it, did look suspiciously like locust. It even crunched when the men chewed it. She enjoyed her lamb chops, as did the children. After their meal, Ethan moved to sit beside her. He and Rex had been verbally sparring to amuse Jack. He'd laughed so much, his stomach hurt, but now the men had turned their attention to a serious card game, with high stakes.

"How has your mother settled in?" Ethan asked Tara casually.

"It's too early to tell," she said. "She wants to stay, but I can't imagine her getting through the first week, let alone lasting until Christmas."

"I didn't think you'd last a day when I found you sitting in the dust, outside the Wombat Creek Hotel," he said, grinning at her. "But you're still here."

"My mother has led a far more pampered life than I have," Tara said, looking away for fear he'd see how much he affected her. If only they hadn't kissed. Now she found trying to have a normal conversation with him almost impossible. She couldn't stop thinking about being in his strong arms, and the feelings he aroused in her.

"Who is the man with her?" Ethan asked, evidently quite capable of thinking of other matters.

"Riordan Magee. He's a long-standing friend of my Aunt's.

"And yours?"

"Certainly not."

Her reaction was rather too defensive, Ethan noted. "You seemed to know him. I thought perhaps he was an old acquaintance." He tried to keep his tone light, not wanting Tara to suspect he was experiencing something akin to jealousy.

"We met… briefly, on two occasions, but that does not make him an old acquaintance." She lifted Hannah onto her lap, as several locusts came through the open door. Jack's attention was taken with the card game, and the rapid exchange of matchsticks.

Ethan was more curious than ever about Riordan Magee. "How long is he staying?"

"I have no idea, but he can't leave soon enough for my liking."

Riordan lowered his voice. "He looked distraught this morning when he saw you and I, together."

Tara couldn't help smiling, even though she was blushing. "He didn't look nearly as horrified as my mother."

Ethan noted how pleased she sounded that his unsuitability irritated her mother.

Tara could see he was embarrassed. "We must have made a rather strange sight, standing in the rain, covered in mud and surrounded by locusts." She watched his expression, which was thoughtful. That they were kissing had certainly made an impression.

"I imagine your mother would find this Riordan Magee fellow a far more appropriate companion for you, than me," he said quietly.

"My mother and I have always had different views on what's right for me. She can certainly forget any notion about a match between myself and Riordan Magee."

Ethan watched her closely for a minute. "Admit it, Tara, you are every bit as astounded as your mother, by what happened between us."

Tara's blush deepened, and she found she couldn't look into his dark eyes. "I was surprised, especially considering we've barely been friends since our first meeting, but you were surprised, too."

He agreed. They were so different, but perhaps that was the attraction. He'd certainly never felt so drawn to a woman. "It was an emotional time, especially for you…" he said, trying to downplay what happened. "And we just got carried away."

Tara felt humiliated by his words. He obviously didn't feel as drawn to her, as she did to him. "That's right. We got swept up in the moment. I'm sure nothing like that would ever happen again…"

"No… You're right, of course."

"I'm off," Rex said, slapping Ethan on the back, distracting them both. "This lot has left me skint. I'll see you all in town on Saturday for the Gymkhana. I'm one of the judges for the races, so beware. I'll be watching for any dirty riding." He laughed. "Keep in mind, I'm corruptible. Bribes will be gratefully accepted, especially cold beer."

Tara smiled. It seemed the Gymkhana was not a serious affair.

"Watch how you go on the journey back to town," Ethan said, quite obviously genuinely concerned, despite their rivalry. He knew the roos could be treacherous at night. The lights of the car mesmerized them. "Be sure to radio through in the morning to let us know you got back to town."

"I could find my way blindfolded, Ethan," Rex insisted.

"Why not stay the night and make the journey in the morning?" Tara suggested.

"I've already suggested he stay with me," Ethan said. "But he's as stubborn as the day is long."

"We have plenty of room in the house," Tara said. "You are perfectly welcome, Mr. Crawley." She turned to Ethan. "And you too, of course, Ethan."

"Thank you, Tara," Rex said, for the first time noticing the tension between them. "But you already have guests, and I think they are going to be a bit of a handful, especially your mother." He grinned conspiratorially, and Tara took no offence. She could well imagine the journey he'd had out to the station with her mother. She'd have given him quite a tongue-lashing.

"Another time, I'd be honoured." Rex lifted his bushy brows at Ethan. "It would be a nice change from sharing sleeping quarters with a man who smelt like camels."

Ethan glared at Rex, but he only laughed.

CHAPTER TWENTY-FOUR

"Momma, momma. Help me."

"Where are you, Jack?" Tara called. "I can't see you."

"Over here, momma. Get me out."

His voice seemed to be coming from a long way away, and echoed in the stillness of an almost moonless night. Tara stumbled through the bush, ripping her skirts on thorny acacia shrubs, while ghost gums stood watch in apparent judgmental silence. Kangaroos and Emu's crossed her path, stopping to stare curiously, before making a hasty retreat into the darkness.

Tara sensed a need for urgency. "Jack, I can't find you," she called anxiously. She felt blinding pain in her ankle as she tripped over a rock and lurched forward, just stopping herself from falling into a pitch-black hole. From its murky depths she could hear the sound of slopping water.

"Jack," she called, her heart thumping with paralyzing fear. "Are you down there, Jack?" Her words reverberated to haunt her from the hollow blackness of the abyss.

Tara heard Jack cough and choke. "Momma, help me, help me. I can't swim, momma. Please get me out."

Suffocating panic welled up inside Tara, closely followed by a sense of overwhelming helplessness. She tried to think of a way to rescue Jack, but quickly realized she couldn't do it alone.

"Jack, hang on, I'll go for help," she shouted. She heard a gurgling sound, as Jack sank below the depths of the water, and then silence, - terrifying silence.

Tara screamed, and sat bolt upright, her arms flaying. It took a few moments to realize that she was in bed, with perspiration trickling down the sides of her face.

"It was only a nightmare," she reassured herself, covering her face with her hands. It was the third night in succession she'd had the same horrifying dream, and each time it had chilled her to the bone. Her heart was racing as the images remained in her mind, so terrifyingly clear. She knew it was no ordinary dream; it was far too real, but she tried desperately to convince herself otherwise.

Bathing her face in cold water, Tara rationalized that subconsciously she was scared of losing the children, and that was the reason she was having the dream. "Thank God there is no such hole in the ground around here," she told herself. She'd asked Bluey,

Charlie, and even Tadd, if they knew of such a hole somewhere, but they'd all said no.

At the bottom of the stairs Tara was confronted by her aunt, who was the most excited she'd ever seen her.

"I've just been on the radio with Percy Everett," she said breathlessly. "A telegram came late last night from William Crombie. He wants a shipment of wool sent to him in India as soon as possible. Isn't that wonderful, Tara?"

Still traumatized by the nightmare, Tara could only nod her approval.

"Apparently, in the letter William sent me months ago, he had asked for a sample of wool, but he said to disregard that request, and just send a shipment of one hundred bales of Merino wool as soon as possible."

"That's wonderful, Aunt," Tara managed. She was almost tempted to confess that she'd read the letter, but knew if she did, she'd have to disclose so much more.

"It's the best news I've had for a long, long time, but my goodness, there is so much to organize. There is still at least a thousand sheep to herd, and then I must contact the shearers, and a wool classer. We had no hope of selling the wool here, but now we might just get through the next season. With this good news, and the rain we had yesterday, which will provide feed for the stock, I'm feeling far more optimistic about the future. I do believe you brought good luck with you from Ireland, Tara."

Tara thought of the debt owed the bank, and her heart ached. How could she tell her aunt there was virtually no hope of keeping the station, no matter how much wool they exported to William Crombie?

"What's wrong, Tara?" Victoria asked, frowning at her. "You don't look yourself this morning."

"I'm fine Aunt, just a little tired."

"Are you sure? You're rather pasty."

"I had another nightmare last night, that's all."

"Oh, dear. They must be a legacy from your shocking experiences aboard ship. I'm sure they'll pass, in time. At least you are not ill. You don't want to miss the Gymkhana. It's the only social event on the calendar out here, and for some reason they've brought the date forward this year. Nugget and the boys have already left for town. As competitors in the races, they claim that they want to give their horses a good overnight rest so they'll be fresh for tomorrow morning. My guess is they don't want to miss the two-up games that will start this afternoon. Actually, considering all the work that needs to be done over the next week or so, I'm pleased they are having this time to socialize with our neighbours. There'll be some serious drinking done tonight, and some sore heads tomorrow. We'll be leaving for town ourselves, soon after breakfast, and arrive there by late evening, all being well. I am so looking forward to catching up with everyone."

"Aunt, have you seen Jack," Tara asked, as she came into the dining room half an hour later. Strangely, her ankle hurt for no reason, which made her nightmare seem all the more real. She and Hannah were dressed, but she hadn't been able to find Jack. "He didn't go with the men, did he?"

"No dear, I'm sure he didn't. I wasn't going to say anything, but I believe he was in trouble with Tadd first thing this morning. I heard Tadd shout at him. He has a terrible Irish temper. Jack may have gone off to be by himself for a while. He's such a sensitive boy."

"What did Jack do that upset Tadd?" Tara had not had any trouble with Jack since their talk a few days earlier, in fact, quite the opposite. He'd been polite and obedient and insisted on helping with the chores, including salvaging vegetable plants and planting more seeds after the locust invasion. Tara assured him he didn't have to make up for his earlier lack of enthusiasm, but he seemed to want to.

"I'm not sure of the details, you'd have to ask Tadd, but he did say something about Jack spoiling Mellie and the pups. Apparently Tadd had been training the pups early this morning, as he's hoping to find a buyer in town tomorrow, and he claimed Jack was distracting them. I know Mellie has become particularly fond of Jack. She follows him everywhere."

"Surely that's not a bad thing, Aunt, for either of them? Mellie was starved of affection when we came here, and I know she's been good for Jack. He just loves her."

"I agree with you, Tara, but Tadd wants Mellie to return to work now the pups are weaned. He'd have worked her before now, but her milk would have dried up."

"Where is Tadd? I want to ask him what happened."

"I'm not sure. " Victoria heard footsteps behind her. "Oh, here he comes now."

Tara turned to find Tadd coming down the hallway, and she felt herself tense. "Do you know where Jack is?" she asked brusquely. Since she'd found out what he'd been doing behind her aunt's back, Tara found it difficult to be civil to the station manager.

At the mention of Jack, Tadd looked irritated. "He rode off when I scolded him."

"Rode off… And you let him go?"

"I couldn't stop him."

"Why didn't you say something to me? He hasn't returned."

"He'll cool off and come back." Tadd went to pass her by, but Tara wasn't ready to let the matter drop.

"What did you say to upset him?"

"I told him he's ruined the pups, which is true. They won't do a thing I say."

"What nonsense!"

"Nonsense, is it? They won't even come to me when I call them. They follow the lad everywhere. Dogs can only have one master."

"Dogs respond to kindness, Tadd, and nobody could accuse you of being humane to animals. Is it any wonder they prefer Jack?"

Tadd's loose jowls flushed with anger. "Those dogs are working dogs, not pets. I knew if I let you have your way, they'd be ruined. They won't fetch a decent price untrained, and we need the extra funds."

Tara was almost furious enough to shout out the truth, that it was his fault that the station would be lost. For her aunt's sake, and with great difficulty, she held her temper in check. Victoria stepped between them. "Arguing isn't finding the boy," she said. "Riordan has just told me that he saw Jack riding off in a southwesterly direction. We should be organizing a search, but with the men all gone to town, that just leaves us."

"Perhaps he followed the men to town," Tara said, as the thought crossed her mind. She noted that Tadd suddenly looked preoccupied.

"They left before first light," Victoria replied. "He'd never catch up with them."

"My horse is saddled, so I'll go and look for him," Tara said.

"You won't know which way to go," Tadd said harshly.

"That's right, Tara," Victoria said, catching her arm. "We don't need you getting lost, too. If only Nugget or Ethan were here. They're both excellent trackers."

Victoria didn't notice that Tadd took offence at her remark.

"What if Jack doesn't come back, Aunt?" Tara was beginning to panic. "We'll never find him out there." She thought of the hundreds of miles of open country, and her heart sank like a stone in a millpond.

"I'll radio town. Ethan arrived there yesterday to organize things. He'll know what to do."

"I'll head out in the direction Riordan said he saw the boy go," Tadd said. "I know that country pretty well, and I'm perfectly capable of tracking."

"There's no answer," Victoria told Tara, after trying to get Percy, Rex or Ferris on the radio for the third time.

"They must all be outside where they can't hear the radio," Tara said in dismay. "What about Lottie or one of the girls? They're bound to be home, although they might not be up at this hour. One of them could take a message to Ethan."

"Good idea," Victoria said.

A moment later, Lottie's friendly voice crackled over the airwaves.

"I didn't wake you, did I, Lottie?" Victoria asked.

"No. The girls won't be awake for hours… they were busy last night. But the slightest noise wakes me, and there's plenty of it around today."

Victoria explained the situation, and Lottie said she could see Ethan from her front window. "He's setting the racecourse. I'll take a message to him immediately."

Victoria could hear the raucous of people in the background through Lottie's open window, and she felt a thrill of excitement.

"Tell him that Tadd has gone out searching for the lad," Victoria shouted. "But we need his advice."

"It sounds as if it's Tadd's fault the boy ran off," Lottie replied. "I've noticed he's been acting very strange lately."

"What do you mean?" Tara asked suspiciously.

"A few days ago I caught him skulking around the side of the hotel, reading something. He obviously didn't want anyone to know what he was doing. He came here later that evening, after he'd had a few beers, but he was in a very peculiar mood."

Tara was puzzled. She wondered what Tadd had been reading, and how he could afford to visit Lottie when he hadn't had any wages for so long? The only conclusion she could draw was that he'd ambushed another letter from the bank, and that he was selling the opals to pay for his visits to Lottie. "Did he say anything to indicate what he'd been doing, or why?" she asked.

"He was restless, and unable to… well, you know… preoccupied, if you get my meaning."

Victoria blushed. It was obvious to Tara that her aunt hadn't known Tadd visited the bordello. "I don't know what that's about," Victoria said.

Sensing she'd disclosed too much, Lottie said, "I'll get your message to Ethan right away. I'm sure you are anxious to find young Jack."

"Thank you, Lottie," Victoria said. "Over and out." A few minutes later, Ethan radioed them.

"I'll come straight back to the station," he said. "But I won't get there until late afternoon at the earliest." Ethan intended to borrow a fast horse, but knew no one would be keen to lend him one with the races taking place the next day.

"I'm terribly sorry," Tara said. "I know you are needed in town, but we've searched everywhere around the station, and Jack can't be found. I wouldn't have bothered you, but I'm really afraid something terrible has happened."

"I understand, Tara. I'm very fond of young Jack." Ethan was seriously considering asking Rex to drive him to Tambora. Although he dreaded the journey, it would be fast, and Jack's life could be at stake.

"Do you think Jack could be up at your cabin?" Tara asked.

"Saladin is there, tending the camels. I've just radioed him, but he said he hasn't seen Jack. I've told him to come down to you, and help search for the boy until I get there." Tara panicked. She did not want to see Saladin. "There's no need," she said.

Ethan caught the anxiety in her voice. "He's a very good tracker, Tara, and time is crucial. I don't want to frighten you, but the longer Jack is wandering around, the less chance he'll survive."

"But Tadd has gone out searching…"

"It's a big country, Tara. A hundred men might not find Jack, and if he isn't found within twelve hours, it may be too late. I've told him to never go out without water, but if he was upset, it's very unlikely he stopped to fill a canteen."

Tara knew he was right. She had to put her personal feelings aside. Jack's life depended on it. "I'll do whatever you say, Ethan. We've got to find him before it's…" Her dream was still haunting her, and she felt her throat constrict with fear.

"I'm on my way, Tara," Ethan said. "If he's not found by nightfall, I'll radio town and we'll get everyone out looking."

Tara wished he was already on Tambora, but knew even Ethan couldn't be in two places at once. She found just his voice so comforting. He wouldn't let anything happen to Jack, she was sure of it.

"Don't let anyone cover tracks that might help Saladin. He will get to you as soon as he can."

Tara insisted that Victoria, Riordan, and her mother, go into town for the Gymkhana. She'd barely seen Riordan in the few days he'd been on the station, for which she was grateful. Victoria had told her he wasn't coping at all with the heat. When he wasn't complaining, he spent most of the time lying down. Tara gathered, from what Victoria had said, that Riordan also detested the flies and mosquitoes, had no interest in livestock, felt uncomfortable around children, and wasn't even inquisitive enough to see the aborigine's art. Tara didn't know why her aunt didn't just ask him to leave. She'd pointed out that he was of no use to them, and just another mouth to feed, but Victoria magnanimously insisted he would soon become acclimatized, and when he was feeling himself, could be quite entertaining company. She was also encouraged by the fact that he intended to make the trip to town for the Gymkhana.

Tara knew her aunt was looking forward to the Gymkhana, and it would serve no purpose if she stayed at the station. Victoria was reluctant to leave, but Elsa told her it was futile that they all wait for news. Tadd was out searching and soon Saladin would be there to help, so Jack was sure to be found, safe and well. Victoria seemed to have great faith in the Afghan cameleer, almost as much faith as she had in Ethan.

"We'll go then, Tara," Victoria eventually agreed. "You follow on with Tadd when you've found Jack." She turned to her sister-in-law. "Are you ready, Elsa?"

"I'm going to stay with Tara," Elsa blurted out.

Tara turned in surprise. "There's no need for you to stay, mother."

"My mind is made up," Elsa said stubbornly. "You need someone to take care of Hannah. The journey into town will be too tiring for her."

Tara was grateful. They had originally planned to leave Hannah with Nerida, but the aboriginal girl still hadn't returned.

Tara and Elsa watched from the veranda, as Victoria and Riordan set off for town in a buggy. Tara almost smiled at how ridiculously Riordan was dressed, in a cream linen suit and a Panama hat. Amongst the stockmen, drovers and shearers in town, he would look as out of place as a goat at a Merino sheep sale, and no doubt provide fodder for their amusement. If she hadn't been so angry with him, she would have suggested he dress more like the locals.

After the buggy had faded from sight, Tara walked to the far side of the house, and looked out over the plains from the shade of the veranda, in the direction that Jack had gone. Elsa followed her with Hannah, who was playing with her Teddy Bear. Almost overnight, the rain had given the yellow spinifex grasses that covered the plains, a green tinge, but apart from the odd noisy bird in a tree, the house and surrounding area seemed as quiet as a cemetery. There was no sign of the locusts that had plagued the area. They'd disappeared almost as suddenly as they had appeared.

"For three days I've had the same awful dream about Jack," Tara said softly, when Elsa came to stand beside her. "What if it comes true, mother?"

"Tell me about it?" Elsa said, hoping to calm Tara. She could see she was on the verge of hysterics.

"Jack is calling me. I'm searching for him in the bush at night, but I can't find him. I trip and nearly fall into a very deep hole in the ground. It's half full of water, and Jack is down there, drowning."

"It's only a dream, Tara," Elsa assured, thinking the nightmare was inspired by the events that took place aboard The Emerald Star.

"But it was so real. What if it's a warning or some kind of prediction? I've had this happen before."

Elsa stared at Tara in amazement. "Are you saying you've foretold events that have taken place?"

"Aboard ship I did it for fun, but the night the ship went down, I dreamt of the fire. I even knew the numbers on the cabin door where it started, although not in the right sequence. I found the cabin on D deck, down the passage from my cabin. It was a storage room. I was able to alert passengers and the crew, or many more on the lower decks may have perished, including myself and the children."

Elsa gasped and swayed. She reached for a railing to steady herself.

"What is it, mother?" Tara asked. "You look as if you've seen a ghost."

"I think the heat… is affecting me…" she lied.

Tara turned to stare off into the distance again. She was clutching the railing so tightly, her knuckles had turned white. "I have a terrible feeling about this, mother." Her voice rose. "I have to do something. In my dream, Jack drowns because I can't get to him."

"Is there such a hole on the property, Tara? A well, or a shaft perhaps?"

"I haven't asked Nugget or Ethan, but Tadd, Bluey and Charlie say there isn't such a hole. I'm probably just being foolish, worrying for nothing. I'm sure my dreams don't mean anything, but…" She shuddered and wrapped her arms about herself. "Why can't I shake the feeling of impending disaster?"

"Tara," Elsa said in a solemn tone. "It might be wise to trust your instincts."

Tara was puzzled by her mother's shift of attitude. "Why, mother? You have just said it was only a dream."

"Just to be on the safe side. If there are any clues in your dreams, have someone check them out, or do it yourself. Some people have a gift for seeing the future."

Tara turned away, and scanned the land off in the distance for any sign of movement. She hardly noticed her mother suddenly looked anxious.

"An old gipsy woman told me I had gipsy blood," Tara said softly. She was thinking aloud, running thoughts through her mind. "Of course, it can't be true...."

Elsa sank into a wicker chair. "Eloisa," she whispered so softly, Tara barely heard her. Surprised her mother knew the old gipsy woman, Tara turned to look at her. She was shocked to see how torn, distraught, and agitated she appeared to be.

"Do you know Eloisa?" Tara thought that surely it couldn't be the same woman, the exiled gipsy.

Elsa didn't reply.

Tara was suddenly suspicious. "Mother, Jack's life may be at stake. If you have something to tell me, tell me now, before it's too late."

Elsa closed her eyes, trying to block out the truth about a past she had been scrupulous in covering for so many years.

Tara stood in front of her, staring at her intently. "Is it true, mother? Do I have gipsy blood?"

Elsa moved her head from side to side. Tara exhaled the breath she had been holding. She didn't realize that Elsa hadn't meant a negative reply to her question, she was just trying to mentally dispel the truth.

For a moment longer, Tara watched her mother, who appeared on the verge of a breakdown.

Suddenly Elsa began to sob. "It is true, God forgive me."

Tara fell back against the railing, her eyes wide, and her mouth agape. Not for a moment had she ever considered the possibility it could be true. She was stunned.

Elsa looked up at her with stricken features that seemed to have aged ten years in minutes. "I never thought I'd admit this... if not for Jack being in danger... wild horses couldn't have dragged it from me." That they were in the middle of nowhere gave her the necessary courage to admit the truth.

Tara was too dumbfounded to speak. She'd lived with the gipsies for all those years, but not for a moment had she considered herself to be one of them.

"My mother was a... gipsy Seer," Elsa whispered, as if the words were being dragged from her by an invisible force. "She died when I was ten years old. My father's mother, the sister of the Earl of Bradford, raised me."

"You told me your mother was related to a Countess…"

Elsa stood up and braced herself on the veranda railing. "That was a fictitious story… invented by grandmother. I learnt from a very early age never to speak of my real mother, although I didn't understand for some time why I couldn't mention her."

Tara was too dumbstruck to say anything.

"When I was about fifteen, a gipsy, who told me she was my grandmother, approached me in the garden of the Bradford Estate. She told me her name was… Amorita. Her sister was Eloisa. Amorita had beautiful burnished copper hair, just like yours. She was also a gipsy Seer. She told me about my mother, Celena, and gave me this ring, which had belonged to her." It was a ring Elsa had always worn; a delicate filigreed gold band. Tara had believed it was her grandmother's, even though she had seen similar rings worn by the gipsies. "We talked for a few minutes, until the gardener chased her away. I never spoke to her again, although I sometimes caught her watching me. She died about thirteen years ago."

"How do you know?"

"Eloisa got word to me."

"Why didn't you tell me this before? You've always given me the impression you hated the gipsies."

Elsa closed her eyes again, struggling with her precarious emotions. "I was taught to be ashamed of having gipsy blood. My grandmother told me if anyone knew the truth, I would never have a good life. I'd be shunned by good folk, and spat upon in the street… it broke my heart that you chose to live that life when I had kept the truth from you for all those years."

Elsa's grandfather had paid Amorita and Eloisa a handsome sum for their silence. After Amorita approached Elsa and told her who she was, an assassin murdered her. The killer was never found. Elsa suspected her grandfather was responsible, but she couldn't bring herself to ask him until he was dying. Even on his deathbed, he denied having any part in Amorita's murder.

"I didn't want you to ever feel inferior," Elsa said.

Tara closed her eyes. Ironically, that was exactly how she had felt while living with the gipsies because she wasn't one of them. "Did father know?"

"No," Elsa said emphatically. "If I had told him the truth, or anyone for that matter, he wouldn't have been allowed to marry me, if he had wanted to." Elsa suddenly looked contrite. "I know I was selfish, thinking of my own needs, but I did love your father,

Tara. He was a good man, kind and generous, perhaps too good for me. I tried to cover my shame by being overly pretentious, and in the process made his life a misery. I thought if people thought me uppity, it would never occur to them that I was a class below them."

Tara didn't know what to think. "Why bring this up now?"

"Because you may be able to help Jack."

Tara drew back. "Are you saying you believe I have the ability to foretell the future, Mother? That what I dreamt might… come true." She was horrified and terrified at the same time.

"I never had the talent, but it seems you do. Trust your instincts, Tara, but speak of this to no one."

Tara couldn't believe that her mother was still worried about her reputation, when Jack's life was at stake. She panicked. "I must find Jack… before it's too late."

Tara happened to glance out of the corner of her eye, and caught sight of Saladin. Like a ghost in flowing robes, he'd silently appeared. He'd startled her, but she tried not to show it. Elsa screamed when she saw him, startling Hannah.

"It's alright, mother. Saladin works for Ethan. He's been sent to help search for Jack."

Without speaking a word, Saladin suddenly turned and disappeared around the side of the house. A moment later, he was back again, aboard a camel. Elsa gasped when she saw the beast, which was growling noisily in complaint.

"I'm going with you," Tara said. "I'll get my horse." In reality the thought of being anywhere near Saladin appalled her, but she had no choice. When Jack was found, she was sure he'd need to see a friendly face.

Saladin shook his head, but Tara ignored him and went to get her horse, which was saddled and ready, at the front of the house. In moments, she was aboard and back beside the Afghan cameleer. She was going with him, like it or not, and it appeared he did not, if his hostile glares were any indication.

"Tara, are you sure you should go?" Elsa glanced warily at the foreboding figure that Saladin made aboard the shedding camel, and clutched Hannah to her. The Afghan looked back at her with barely disguised insolence.

Ignoring her mother, Tara said, "We have been told the boy went that way." She pointed in a southwesterly direction.

Without a word, Saladin set off, and Tara followed.

Elsa watched them go, and then took Hannah inside.

The little girl said she was hungry, and Elsa realized it was already mid morning. Hannah usually had something to eat, and then a nap. For days, Elsa had felt absolutely fatigued. She blamed the long journey to Tambora, and the heat. She'd been unable to face the cook and the challenge of getting him to diversify his meals. But now seemed as good a time as any, and it might take her mind off Tara being with that strange man, and Jack wandering, lost in the bush.

Taking a deep breath, Elsa entered the kitchen with a flourish. When dealing with staff, confidence was of the utmost importance, but dignity and poise were a close second. She'd also found that respect, if given, was usually returned twice fold.

"Good morning, Sanja," she said. "I'm Elsa Killain, Mrs. Millburn's sister-in-law."

"Good morning, Missus," Sanja said, his defenses immediately aroused.

"Would you look at this kitchen? It's so clean, and tidy." Elsa wasn't acting. She hadn't expected to find such a pristine kitchen, especially when the rest of the house needed a good clean. "I'm most impressed, Sanja."

"Thank you, Missus. I not like dirty kitchen."

"Standards are so important, Sanja, but lost on some of the chef's of today." She thought if she referred to him as a 'chef', instead of merely a cook, he'd be more willing to impress her with an exciting array of dishes. "But I can see you have the highest ideals. Now I know why Victoria and her late husband went to the trouble and expense of bringing you out here. They certainly knew what they were doing."

Sanja looked pleased with himself.

"As you probably know, Sanja, Victoria has gone to town, and left me in charge of the household for a couple of days."

Sanja's brows raised in question, but Elsa pretended she didn't notice.

"She's told me so many good things about you." While talking, Elsa wandered around the kitchen, a look of admiration pasted on her face. Sanja followed her progress curiously. "As she's travelled so much, and eaten in so many aristocratic homes and countries, I can hardly wait to taste your culinary delights. I've barely touched a morsel since I came here. The journey was horrendous, but now my appetite is returning. I must shamefully confess I'm renowned for my healthy appetite. Thankfully it doesn't show on my waistline. I understand there's a shortage of foods and condiments out here, but could you give me a repertoire of the cuisine you prepare, which I might select from?"

Sanja's sherry brown eyes narrowed. "No repertoire, Missus. Not enough ingredients out here. I just cook what is available. Lamb or beef." He folded his arms defiantly, but

Elsa didn't falter.

"I understand, Sanja. But I'm sure you're as creative as you are modest. Even someone like me knows there are so many ways to cook lamb or beef. Beef Stroganoff is one of my favourites, and Lamb Ragout is simply delicious. Lamb roasted with rosemary is also tasty. Of course, I've no need to tell you about Stroganoff and Ragout. I'm sure you could prepare either of them better than any of the European chef's. You've heard of Maurice Rycroft?" Elsa gave Sanja no time to reply. "Of course you have," she said, waving her hand in a dismissive gesture and laughing surreptitiously. "Maurice is one of Europe's finest chef's. He stayed with my late husband and myself for a short while, while the Earl of Aberdeen had a new kitchen built for him at his castle in the Scottish Highlands. They say the kitchen was better than those in Buckingham Palace. He cooked us some exquisite meals. My late husband didn't go much for spices and the like. He much preferred good country fare, and I must say I became accustomed to it myself. I simply long for an Irish stew, cooked with a drop of stout. I suppose that is out of the question, with no stout…"

"I not cook…"

"Listen to me," Elsa said interrupting. "I am going on, when you have meals to prepare. Could we have cold cuts for lunch today, Sanja? There'll be just Hannah and myself, and perhaps a simple lamb casserole for dinner. You don't want to go to any trouble just for us. Again, let me compliment you on one of the cleanest and best-organized kitchens I've ever seen. Trust my sister-in-law to find such a treasure…"

Elsa breezed from the kitchen, leaving Sanja somewhat bewildered. He didn't know whether to feel pleased with himself, or outwitted.

CHAPTER TWENTY-FIVE

To avoid seeing Saladin's face, or disturbing any tracks on the ground ahead of them, Tara rode behind the Afghan. She almost felt a sense of relief that he was ignoring her, as she didn't feel she could deal with his hostility and worry about Jack at the same time.

As they proceeded at what seemed to Tara, a snail's pace, Saladin watched the ground intently. She desperately wanted to hurry him along, as the sense of urgency she had felt earlier was building within her. Jack needed her help, she was sure of it.

"Hang on, Jack," she whispered. It took all her willpower not to gallop ahead of Saladin; only the fact that she did not know which direction to take prevented her from doing so.

Now and again Saladin stopped to examine something on the ground more closely. As it had recently rained, tracks were clearly visible in the soft earth, even to Tara. Ethan had often pointed out different tracks to her, so she had come to recognize some of them. Kangaroo, emu, wombat, goanna, sheep and cattle tracks, - all crossed each other, even the snakes left a telltale trail in the damp earth. In which direction they were going, or how long ago they had passed through the area, still mystified her.

"Tadd Sweeney headed out in this direction more than an hour ago," Tara offered, when Saladin seemed confused by several sets of horseshoe prints going in different directions. The Afghan cameleer ignored her comment, which incensed her, but for Jack's sake, she held her temper in check, even though her stomach was churning with anxiety.

Saladin studied the two sets of tracks, and drew his own conclusion.

Tara watched him. "How do you know which are Jack's tracks?" she asked. "One horse is much the same as another?"

"Boy's horse carry less weight," Saladin said. It was the first time Tara had heard Saladin speak English, and she was surprised by how slowly and articulately he spoke. His voice also sounded mellower.

"Dog follow boy," he added. Tara was alarmed. "A dingo?" The Afghan shook his head.

"Then it must be Mellie," Tara whispered. Knowing Mellie was with Jack gave her a small measure of comfort. At least he wasn't alone.

They came to the base of an escarpment that stretched for more than ten miles in an east- westerly direction, and Saladin stopped and looked up.

"Did Jack go up there?" Tara asked anxiously. The rocks looked steep and dangerous. Saladin's expression gave nothing away.

"Tell me," Tara shouted, losing patience. She had a sickening feeling in the pit of her stomach, certain they had little time left to save Jack.

Saladin glanced at the rocky ground and then upward.

"Do you think Jack could have climbed up there? It looks so perilous."

Saladin shook his head.

"Oh, Jack, where are you?" Tara whispered. She closed her eyes in despair. If she had any talent as a Seer, as her mother had suggested, then surely she should know where Jack was. But she didn't. She could have screamed with frustration.

"I obviously don't have the gift," she muttered. Suddenly she had the strongest sensation that she was as near to Jack as she'd been all day. It overwhelmed her.

"Jack," she called, dismounting. "Are you up there, Jack?" She whistled for Mellie.

Tadd Sweeney was bent over the mineshaft, when he heard a woman's voice shouting and then the whistle. He was sure it was Tara.

"Bloody meddlesome woman," he muttered angrily.

"Momma, help me," Jack called from the darkness of the shaft, his voice noticeably weaker. In his mind he could see his real momma reaching out to him from the murky depths of the ocean. In the last hour or so he had become confused, imagining he was aboard ship, and the cabin he shared with his father was filling with water. He'd been holding onto a groove in the wall of the shaft he'd made deeper with his knife, for what seemed like hours, but he was tiring, physically and mentally.

Tadd left the shaft and went to the rocky ledge at the edge of the escarpment, and looked over. He gasped when he saw the top of Saladin's head on a camel, more than fifty feet below, and a saddled horse nearby. He heard someone trying to scramble up the escarpment, and rocks sliding away, and knew it was Tara. Saladin appeared to be searching for tracks on the ground. It was only a matter of time before they found a way up.

Tadd was in a quandary. Should he let the boy die, or save him? He had been going to let him die, and then leave his body to be found somewhere miles away in the opposite direction, thus diverting attention from the mine site, but it was too late for that. If Tara was close, she was sure to find the mine, and he'd lose everything, especially if Mellie was still hanging around. He'd chased the dog off, but she may not have gone back to the station. If Tara found her, the dog would lead her straight to the mine, and Jack. "Damn," he muttered. He had no choice.

Going back to the mine, Tadd threw a rope down. "Tie the rope around you," he called only loud enough for Jack to hear.

Jack was too weak to do as he was asked. He knew if he let go of the groove in the shaft wall, he'd drown.

Tadd cussed. He would have to go down and get him.

Tara was unable to get up the rocky incline of the escarpment, and Saladin was animatedly shaking his head, trying to tell her it was too risky. She noticed whenever he got excited he reverted back to his own language, which prevented her understanding him. From his frantic hand movements, he indicated that they would have to go around the base, and then ride up where the ground had a gentler incline. As there was no time to argue, Tara mounted her horse and followed him.

Half a mile from where they had stopped, Tara and Saladin reached an area where it was possible to ride up. The ground was more sand than rocks, and Saladin could see tracks, although he couldn't make out what they were. They were both concentrating on the tracks, and the direction in which they went, when Tadd Sweeney suddenly appeared above them. He had Jack in front of him on his horse. Mellie was trailing a discreet distance behind.

Tara was so relieved to see Jack safe and well, that she leapt from her horse and covered the distance between them in seconds.

Jack appeared to be in shock, as Tara gently lifted him down from Tadd's horse, into her arms.

"Where did you find him, Tadd?" she asked joyously.

Jack pressed himself against her. He was wet, and had scratches on his face and arms. Tara noticed he was holding one arm against his body, which was swollen near the elbow.

"His horse had thrown him into a ...rock pool up there," he said, pointing west, instead of east, where the mine was.

"You're hurt, Jack?" Tara said, looking into his eyes to find evidence of a concussion, confusion or a lack of focus. She noticed a red welt on his neck, and a bump on the side of his head.

Jack dropped his eyes and pressed his face into her.

"We must get him back to the station," Tara said, for the first time noticing Tadd's trousers were also wet. "How did you find him, Tadd?" she asked.

"I followed tracks to the base of the escarpment, and then Mellie led me to Jack." He'd heard Mellie barking half a mile from the mine.

Tara didn't notice Saladin's dark eyes narrow suspiciously "Did you find his horse?" she asked.

Tadd was hesitant. "No."

Tara turned to Saladin. "Will you look for his horse?" she asked.

"He's most likely headed back to the station," Tadd said quickly "We didn't see him."

"I'm sure he'll be there when we get back."

Tara suddenly had a strong mental picture of Jack down a hole in the ground. It was so vivid it left her shaking. She pressed Jack closer to her.

Jack didn't say a word on the trip back to the station. Tara was concerned about the vacant expression in his eyes. It was as if he'd lost all hope for the future, when only the previous day he'd been laughing and joking for the first time in weeks. Something had deeply traumatized him, and she didn't think it was the fall from his horse.

Before Saladin departed, Tara thanked him for finding Jack. He did not reply, nor did his dark eyes disclose any emotion, which left her feeling slightly foolish.

"I believe I have been wrong about you," Tara said shyly. "I hope you will forgive me?" Saladin barely nodded in reply, and then left, his white robes flowing behind him, as he rode majestically across the desert. Tara watched him, and thought he made a striking picture. She also realized Ethan had been right about her lack of understanding about the ways of the Afghans.

At the station, Tara bathed Jack's wounds. His arm didn't appear to be broken, just badly sprained, but he was covered in cuts and bruises. She intended to question Tadd more closely about where he'd found Jack, and how he could have gotten so many injuries from a fall into a rock pool. Since she knew Tadd was deceitful, she would never take anything he said at face value again, but hoped he'd trip himself up lying.

"My Aunt told me Tadd scolded you for spoiling the dogs," Tara said gently, as she sat on the edge of Jack's bed after making him comfortable. Mellie was lying beside the bed. She'd refused to leave Jack's side, and watched his every move with her gentle brown eyes, full of concern. "Is that why you ran away, Jack, because Tadd shouted at you?"

Jack turned his head away.

Tara was concerned that he was retreating into himself again. The last few days had been so wonderful. They'd been closer than ever, and she didn't want that to change.

"I'm not angry with you, Jack. If showing an animal love and kindness is spoiling them, then I am far more guilty than you."

"The pups were only being playful," Jack said quietly. "But Tadd hit Shellie." She was the smallest and the only female of the pups, and Jack's favourite, Tara had noticed. "I told him not to, so he raised his hand to… hit me."

Tara gasped, and anger rippled through her. How dare Tadd …

"Mellie growled at him. She was just protecting me, but Tadd was very angry. He was going to kick her, so I called her away. He tried to call her back, but she wouldn't listen. He got even angrier." Jack began to cry.

"Oh Jack, it's going to be alright, I promise," Tara vowed.

"Don't say anything to him," Jack sobbed, lifting himself up. "He'll be angry with me again."

Tara had every intention of saying plenty. She pressed her lips together, trying to restrain her anger.

"Please," Jack pleaded, his hazel eyes full of anguish.

Tara didn't want him further upset. He'd been through enough. "Alright, Jack. I won't say anything, for now."

"Promise?"

"I give you my word."

Jack sank back onto the pillows and turned his head away, closing his eyes.

Tara's heart ached for him. She was furious with Tadd. He knew that Jack had lost his father, although he didn't know he'd also lost his mother, and that being with Mellie and the pups had given him a small measure of happiness, and yet he was still cruel to him. It took all her willpower not to go downstairs and take a stock whip to him. Tadd certainly had a lot to answer for.

"I'll bring you up something to eat, Jack, and then you can rest, " Tara said, forcing herself to sound cheerful.

"I'm not very hungry."

"Maybe later, then." Tara left him to sleep.

Tara was fighting a losing battle against her tears as she came downstairs. "How is Jack?" her mother asked.

Tara shook her head, and dabbed tears that were sliding silently down her cheeks. "I could strangle Tadd Sweeney with my bare hands," she said, thankful he was no where in sight, or she might be tempted to break her promise to Jack.

"But he found Jack, didn't he?"

"Yes, by a strange coincidence. I wonder how it was that he knew exactly where to look?"

"I suppose he followed the boys tracks, like that strange Afghan man did."

"He said he did, and that when he got close, Mellie led him to Jack."

"Well, there's your answer."

"I'm not so sure, mother."

Elsa was confused. "Do you know why Jack ran away?"

"Yes, because Tadd upset him. He was training the pups and one of them was not doing as it was told, so he got angry and hit it, and Jack intervened. Tadd raised his hand to Jack, and Mellie growled at him."

Elsa got the picture. "Which made him even angrier, because he saw her defense of Jack as a betrayal."

"I gather he stormed after them, and Jack took off, and Mellie followed."

"Are you going to have words with Tadd?"

"I would dearly love to have words with Mr. Sweeney, but Jack begged me not to. I've agreed to let it drop, for now. But believe me, mother, Tadd has a lot to answer for."

Tara was sitting on the veranda outside Jack's room, with Mellie beside her, when she heard a motor vehicle. It was Rex Crawley's car. By the time she came downstairs, Ethan had alighted from the vehicle. It was the first time Tara had ever seen him less than composed.

"Jack has been found," Tara blurted out.

"I know. We passed Saladin. It's wonderful news. Is he alright?"

"He's got some cuts and bruises, but thankfully nothing more serious. I radioed town as soon as we got back here, but you'd already left."

"Rex was kind enough to give me a ride out here," Ethan said, looking at him oddly. Tara glanced at both men. "You got here in good time. I wasn't expecting you for hours."

"My old Packard can get up some good speeds, even over the sand hills," Rex claimed slapping the car door in fondness. It was obvious he was delighted to have every opportunity to demonstrate the car's merits and establish supremacy over Ethan's camels.

"I don't mean to sound ungrateful for the lift out here, but a camel with three legs would provide a smoother ride," Ethan retaliated. "I've felt less bone jarred after breaking in a hundred wild brumbies."

"You're getting soft, Ethan," Rex insisted, barely containing his amusement. He turned to Tara. "I hope you've got the Billy boiling. I'm dying of thirst."

Tara and Ethan glanced at each other. Ethan raised his eyes to the skies, and rubbed his sore back.

"I really appreciate you trying to get back here as quickly as possible," Tara said.

"It seems I'm no longer needed."

"Yes, you are, Ethan," Tara said softly. "Something is not right."

Elsa had Sanja serve afternoon tea in the dining room. Tara noticed the cakes were freshly made, nicely presented, and there was the distinctive 'lack' of a ginger spice aroma about them. Her mother thanked Sanja, praising his efforts. When she exclaimed that she could hardly wait to try his cinnamon tea cakes, which smelt delicious, Tara noticed Sanja looked pleased with himself, and if she wasn't mistaken, almost humble.

Tara took Ethan up to see Jack, who was asleep. Ethan looked at his head and arms, but Jack was so fatigued, he didn't want to wake him. Tara led Ethan out onto the veranda, where she would be certain Jack wouldn't overhear their conversation if he awoke.

"His arm is very swollen," Tara said, "and he has so many cuts and bruises on his back, and his legs.. I can't imagine they all happened from falling into a rock pool. He was soaked with what looked like muddy water."

Ethan frowned. He had noticed the red mark on Jack's neck, which looked like a rope burn, and he thought he should have been sunburned, if he'd been lying in the sun for hours, injured, but he wasn't. Saladin had told him he believed Tadd had deliberately tried to cover the boy's tracks, and that he thought Tadd was lying about where he found the boy. Ethan could hardly believe it was true, but after what Tara had already said about him stealing Victoria's mail, and borrowing money against the property, he was beginning to think anything was possible where Tadd Sweeney was concerned.

"For the last three nights, I've had the same terrible nightmare about Jack," Tara said. "I dreamt Jack was down a hole in the ground, which was half full of water, and he was drowning. The dream was so real and terrifying. When Jack was missing this morning, I was sure my dream had come true."

"But it didn't, Tara. Jack is safe." He reached for her arm and rubbed his fingers on the skin above her elbow. Tara shivered and moved away, fearing he'd see how much his touch disturbed her.

"I didn't tell you this before, Ethan," she said, "but the day I found the stolen mail in Tadd's cottage, I also found a box of coloured stones. I didn't know what they were at the time, but I now believe they're opal."

"Opal? Where would Tadd be getting opal?"

"I have no idea, but I think his behaviour is sometimes quite odd."

"Does Victoria feel the same?"

"I think she's used to his strange ways, but Lottie commented on it this morning."

"What does he do that you think is odd?"

"Every few days he disappears and no one knows where he goes. I've tried to follow him twice when he's left the station, but he seems to know and doubles back. He always has an explanation for where he's been, but nothing that makes any sense. I haven't confronted him about the opal because I don't want him to know I was in his cottage looking through his things. I know it will eventually have to come out, but my aunt is so optimistic at the moment, and we haven't yet made contact with the bank."

"Jack's injuries do seem consistent with him falling down a mineshaft or a well, although I don't know of any on Tambora. But surely he would have told you."

"I'm sure he would have unless it was a mine." The thought was shocking. "… and Tadd threatened him."

Ethan's eyes narrowed. If Tadd had in any way threatened Jack… "Perhaps there's a way I could question him about an opal mine without letting on about you finding opal in his cottage, but first I want to radio Mohomet Basheer. If anyone is buying or selling opal between Port Augusta and Alice Springs, he'll know."

Not wanting to be left alone with Elsa, Rex excused himself from the dining room, and took his tea and cakes outside on the veranda, where it was cooler. He'd sooner contend with the flies, than a woman who constantly criticized him. Elsa went to the kitchen to tell Sanja there would be extra people for dinner, so the dining room was empty when Tadd came in. He was pouring himself a cup of tea when Ethan and Tara found him. "You did a good job finding the boy," Ethan said.

"I'm just glad he's alright," Tadd replied without looking at them. Tara stiffened, thinking he was such a fraud.

"It's almost a miracle, considering he'd gone so far," Ethan claimed.

"You're not the only one around here who can track," Tadd replied defensively. Ethan ignored his remark. "The rain we've had would've made it easier."

Tadd cast him a malicious look, and turned back to his tea.

"I've just been to see Jack, and he has some rather nasty cuts and bruises," Ethan went on. "I know you said you found him in a rock pool, but his injuries are consistent with someone falling down a well, or a shaft."

Tadd looked up, clearly startled. "You're an expert on injuries now, are you? I believe his foot got caught in the stirrups and his horse dragged him. You know there's no wells or shafts around here."

"I don't know of any," Ethan said. "But I haven't covered every inch of this country. That would be impossible. Speaking of shafts just reminded me that someone in Marree told me you've been selling opal?"

Tadd's face went blank with surprise. "Who said that?"

"Is it true?"

Tadd looked away, composing himself. He felt like telling Ethan to mind his own damn business, but knew that would arouse his suspicions even more, and he'd keep digging until he found the truth. "I have a very small interest in a mine in Cooper Pedy. My partners asked me to sell a few opals for them. I don't see that it's anyone's business but my own."

"There's no need to be defensive, Tadd. I was just curious."

Tadd stood up and picked up his cup of tea. "Everyone is secretive about opal, Ethan, you know that. If my partners knew someone had got wind of their find, they wouldn't be too happy with me, and I get a small enough share as it is." Tadd left the dining room, hoping he'd dampened Ethan's curiosity.

Ethan and Tara looked at each other.

"When I return from Wombat Creek, I'll go back to the area where you found Jack with Saladin and have a look around. I have the strongest feeling I'll find an opal mine. If it's on Tambora, Tadd has no claim on the opal he's found."

CHAPTER TWENTY-SIX

The dinner gong sounded at seven o'clock, awakening Jack with a start. He sat up screaming, "Momma!"

Tara rushed into the room from the veranda, where she'd spent the unbearably hot afternoon dozing in a chair, pestered by flies, while he slept.

"I'm here, Jack," she said, enfolding him in her arms. She noticed he was perspiring, and his hazel eyes were wide with fear. "It's alright. You're safe," she whispered. "I won't let anything happen to you."

After a few minutes he became calm, and released his agitated grip on her.

"Are you hungry?" Tara asked, smoothing his damp, red hair back from his freckled face.

"A little," he said, dropping his gaze.

"Would you like to come down to the dining room for dinner, or would you prefer me to bring something up?" She suspected he might not want to see Tadd. She didn't particularly want to see him herself.

Jack seemed reluctant to answer. Tara sensed he was afraid, and again she wondered if Tadd had threatened him. She decided now was not the time to ask. He was too traumatized.

"Hannah may have already eaten, but I'm sure she'd love to sit with you...."

The door opened and Elsa came in carrying a tray. "I thought you and Hannah might like your dinner in your room this evening," she said to Jack. Hannah was trailing behind her, carrying her Teddy Bear.

Tara noticed Jack looked relieved, and she felt sure Tadd was responsible for his unease. "Thank you, mother," she said, touched by her thoughtfulness. She couldn't ever remember her mother being so attentive when she was a child. She barely took notice of Tara or her brothers when they were ill, let alone bring them a tray.

"It's lamb casserole, but as we haven't many vegetables as yet, they've been substituted with dumplings."

The casserole smelt delicious. "I can't smell curry," Tara said.

"Lamb casserole doesn't have curry in it," Elsa said smiling.

"Sanja's does," Tara and Jack said at the same time, and both smiled, which made Elsa laugh.

"How did you get Sanja to cook without using curry spices or chilli?" Tara asked her mother, as they descended the stairs.

"I appealed to his sense of pride as a chef," Elsa proclaimed. "And so far it's working a treat."

Tara remembered the first time she'd met Sanja, he'd practically thrown her out of his kitchen. "I've tried being polite," she said, "and assertive, even hostile, but nothing has worked. There have even been many times over the last few weeks when I've wished I had your aptness for handling staff." Her mother had always made it look easy.

"It took years for me to appear even slightly competent, Tara. When I first married your father I hadn't a clue about running a house. I learnt the hard way, and believe me I made mistakes. I do remember one old cook who took absolutely no notice of anything I said. I thought he was deaf until he heard me making an offensive remark about him under my breath. He literally scared the wits out of me, leaving me a bumbling, fumbling, incompetent ninny. One day, when I was about ready to pack my suitcases, the housekeeper took me aside and gave me some sound advice, which still serves me to this day. It boils down to one thing, mutual respect. Be firm, but respectful, and always appreciate what is done for you. Demanding this and that may work for some, but I found it never worked for me. I've also discovered a few choice compliments can go a long way to a good relationship."

"Did the old cook change his ways?"

"No. I eventually persuaded him to retire gracefully by threatening to fire him if he didn't. Once he knew I was serious, he took the gracious way out, and left. For a short while I was not too popular with Ninian, as that particular cook had worked for the Killain family for two generations. I was very careful with my choice of a replacement, and in the end, the situation worked out very well."

Elsa stopped and turned to her daughter, her expression suddenly earnest. "I know you wanted me to clean Tara. I intend to do it, but it's taken me a few days to get used to the heat which is so draining."

"I don't think you ever get used to the heat, mother, or the flies and mosquitoes… you just have to cope as best you can."

Elsa didn't reply. If not for Tara, she would not have stayed another minute in the bush. She wished the house girl Nerida would return. If she was to clean Victoria's enormous house, she needed all the help she could get.

Ethan and Rex left for Wombat Creek in the afternoon, while they still had a couple of hours of daylight. Rex claimed they could be back in town soon after dark, as long as they didn't get bogged in any sand hills. Tara could tell Ethan was dreading the return trip, but he was looking forward to finding out how the Gymkhana had progressed in his absence, and he wanted to catch Victoria before she headed for home.

"I wish I could be there to see you tell Aunt Victoria the money raised was for her glasses," Tara said.

"Then come with us," Ethan suggested. Tara was hesitant. She wanted to go, but…

"There's lots of station owners and their stockmen curious to get a look at you," Rex informed her. As if realizing too late what he'd said, he flushed. "…What I mean is, there's plenty of folk in town dying to meet you." He glanced at Ethan for support, but there was none forthcoming. Ethan was scowling at him.

"They're always curious about newcomers," Rex explained feebly.

"I can't leave Jack and Hannah," Tara said, "and Jack isn't well enough to travel."

When Tara radioed Lottie around lunch time that day, to say that Jack had been found, Lottie said the races had been a great success, and they'd had a larger than usual crowd in town. She claimed word had gotten around that there were two new women in the area, and that every man for a five-hundred-mile radius, single and otherwise, had come to look them over.

"Not since Brahman Bulls were introduced to the area, to cross breed with shorthorns, have the station owners and stockman had their interest so aroused," Lottie said. She didn't say that was not all that was aroused. Business had been booming.

"I hardly find that a compliment," Tara replied, indignant at being compared to livestock, but Lottie only laughed.

Lottie went on to tell her that they were all disappointed that neither woman had attended the Gymkhana, but Belle had heard some of the men planning a trip to the station on the pretence of looking for work. She didn't mention that the single men were taking bets as to whether the women were suitable for breeding purposes.

Tara was a little bewildered that her mother and herself had piqued their curiosity so much. She wondered how they'd all feel if they knew they had gipsy blood.

Elsa and Tara ate alone in the dining room. Tadd had requested that Sanja take his meal over to his cottage, where he could brood alone, and Tara was thankful.

Candelabra stood in the center of the table, and Elsa had laid out place settings for five, using Victoria's best silverware, china, and linen.

"It looks like it's just the two of us," Elsa said, a little flustered as she cleared away three place settings.

Tara did appreciate her mother's efforts, but she felt awkward sharing a meal alone with her after so many years apart, and the conversation was at first, stilted.

"The table looks very nice," she said.

"Thank you," Elsa replied. "Victoria has some nice dinnerware and cutlery." There was an awkward silent pause.

That Tara was expected to forgive her mother for thinking she had taken a gipsy lover and made up something so terrible about Stanton Jackson, hung between them like a pea soup fog.

Finally Tara plucked up the courage to ask about her brothers. "What are Liam and Daniel doing? Are they married, with children?"

"After you left…"

Tara visibly tensed, and Elsa realized her mistake. "After your father passed away Liam went to sea."

Tara couldn't hide her surprise. She wondered if her mother was blaming her for Liam leaving the farm.

"Don't you remember how curious he was about anything to do with the sea?" Elsa asked.

"I do remember him loving books about the sea," Tara said. "Particularly Herman Melville's 'Moby Dick.' He read it every chance he got."

"He tried to please your father and myself by taking an interest in the farm, but his heart wasn't in it. As he grew into a young man, he often talked about life as a merchant seaman. After your father died, I encouraged him to follow his dream. He was reluctant because he thought I needed him, but I insisted." She didn't say there was no way they could hold onto the farm after Ninian's death. Things had gone too far.

"And what of Daniel? He loved farming."

Elsa smiled. "Yes, he did, but in all honesty, he was never very good at it."

"What is he doing?"

"He's married to an English girl, and lives in Cornwall. Aileen is expecting their first child."

"Oh." Tara smiled, trying to imagine Daniel as a father. He'd been barely an adolescent when she left home, and always mischievous. It was hard to picture him with a family and responsibilities. "How is he making a living?"

Elsa looked awkward for a moment. "He works with Aileen's father and brothers … mining tin."

Tara's mouth dropped open.

"I believe he's happy, Tara, and that's all that really matters."

Tara was taken back by Elsa's statement, and it must have shown in her expression.

Elsa put down her knife and fork. "You never thought you'd hear me say that, did you? That being happy was more important than holding a position of high esteem. But that's how I feel these days."

Tara shook her head. "It has been a day for revelations, hasn't it, mother?" They both knew what she was talking about.

"How do you feel about knowing you have gipsy bloody, Tara?"

"I'm not sure. I lived as a gipsy for years, so I suppose I don't feel any different. Ironically, I was thrown out of the band before I left Ireland because I wasn't really one of them."

Elsa looked mortified. "It would be best if we kept this to ourselves, Tara. People can be so …intolerant." She looked ashamed. "I suppose I don't need to tell you that?"

"No, mother, you don't. I know exactly what you mean."

"May I ask why your husband didn't protest at you being ostracized?"

"He couldn't… he was in prison."

Elsa tried unsuccessfully to mask her shock. Tara could almost see the multitude of questions running through her mother's mind.

"I may as well tell you, mother. He may be hanged for Stanton Jackson's murder."

Elsa's eyes widened. This time she didn't even try to hide her dismay. "You married a … murderer!"

"No, mother. Garvie was a loving and kind husband. He did fight with Stanton on the night I ran away, but he didn't kill him. He didn't even know he was dead until the constabulary questioned him. Stanton must have fallen and hit his head, although both Garvie and myself believe he was having some kind of seizure when he attacked me. He appeared to be suffering pain in his head when he…." Tara couldn't say the word.

Elsa looked uncomfortable. "I'm so sorry that happened to you," she said.

Tara ignored her words. "I wanted to stay in Ireland and protest Garvie's innocence, but he sent me away to begin a new life. That was the type of man he was, mother, unselfish. Sometimes he was misguided, and often a bit of a rascal, but always kind and generous. He never doubted anything I told him."

Elsa dropped her head, and Tara realized she had made her point.

"I do not want to ever speak of this again, mother. We can't change the past, we must move forward."

"How can we do that when you can't forgive me, Tara?"

"I don't know," Tara said honestly, "but I intend to try."

When Sanja came in to serve them desert, a creamy rice pudding with raisons in it, Elsa praised the meal lavishly, but Tara remained silent.

"You've outdone yourself, Sanja," Elsa concluded. "The lamb was absolutely succulent, the best I've ever tasted."

"Thank you, Missus Killain," Sanja said, clearly basking in her praise. "I only have dried fruit and milk for the pudding, but I hope you like."

Tara noticed he gave her a disdainful look.

"It smells wonderful, Sanja," Elsa commented. The cook bowed his head and left the room.

Tara turned to her mother, her mouth agape. "You've certainly turned him around. He's usually so contemptuous. I threatened to have him fired just a week ago for throwing a bowl of dirty dish water at me."

Elsa hid a smile behind her hand. "I'm glad you didn't. If this casserole is anything to go by, he's an excellent cook." She laughed wryly. "I couldn't boil water, but I always had the knack of spotting a good cook from a bad one, even before they lit the fire."

"I really must be heading back to Tambora," Victoria said.

It was mid morning the following day. Ferris had persuaded Victoria and Riordan to spend the night in the hotel, as Ethan had radioed to say he was on his way, and would be back at the hotel by eight o'clock in the evening. When neither he nor Rex had returned by ten o'clock, Nugget, Bluey, Charlie and young Karl went out to look for them.

"You can't go," Ferris told Victoria when she looked about to leave. "I think Charity is going into labour, and I don't know what to do."

"I haven't had any children, Ferris, so how much help do you think I'd be? Call one of the tribal women."

"They've all gone walkabout."

Victoria was beginning to become suspicious. Since breakfast, Ferris had been coming up with one excuse after another to keep her in town. Firstly, he'd claimed he needed help behind the bar, because his leg was hurting him. Victoria had served for more than an hour when she caught him whirling Charity around the kitchen. Then he said he felt ill, and she found him wolfing down an enormous plate of rabbit stew. Then he said Riordan was drunk which was partially true, as the men kept shouting him drinks. He had been asked to judge the races the previous day, as Rex had gone with Ethan to Tambora, and nobody else wanted the task, and the men had found him partial to a bribe. As he accepted bribes from nearly every entry in the numerous events, he was blind drunk by midday, but he'd made many friends with his affable nature and riotous sense of humour, which appeared when intoxicated. Victoria had enjoyed herself immensely, and surprisingly, so had Riordan; who hadn't had the chance to sober up, but Victoria was eager to get back to Tambora.

"What's going on, Ferris?" she finally asked.

"Nothing, Victoria. Why are you always so suspicious?"

Victoria glanced at Percy, who quickly looked away. "Ferris, I know when I'm being manipulated. If you won't tell me the truth, I'm off."

The door opened and Ethan and Rex blew in with the dust and flies. Victoria noticed that Ethan seemed relieved to see her.

"Where've you been?" Ferris asked.

"The axle of Rex's reliable motor vehicle broke," Ethan said, casting Rex a smug look. "We hit the only fallen tree between here and Tambora."

Ignoring him, Rex headed straight to the bar.

"I don't know what's wrong with Ferris today, Ethan," Victoria said. "He's coming up with one excuse after another to keep me in town."

"We love your company," Ferris said, throwing his enormous arms up in the air. Victoria shook her head, and Ethan grinned. He downed the beer that Ferris had just poured in a matter of seconds. Not only did it quench his thirst, it settled his nerves after the harrowing night he'd spent in the bush with Rex, before Nugget and the boys arrived.

"I'm to blame, Victoria," Ethan said. "I wanted Ferris to keep you here until I got back. I thought I'd be here last night." He gave Rex another reproachful look. "Had I been on a camel I'm sure I would've been. At least they have the sense to go around fallen trees."

Victoria became worried. "Is something wrong on Tambora? Is Jack all right?"

"Jack is fine. He'd fallen from his horse, so he has a few cuts and bruises, but now he's enjoying being pampered by Tara and her mother. Everything else is just as you left it."

"Then what is going on? I don't understand why you are all being so secretive."

"As you know, the money we raise from the Gymkhana goes to a worthy cause every year."

"That's right. But nobody has told me where it's going this year."

"For a very good reason."

"What's that?"

"I think everyone will agree, that this year the cause is exceptionally worthwhile."

Victoria frowned. "Well, what is it?"

"Your new glasses."

Victoria gasped. "Surely you are not serious? There are far more worthy causes…"

"We're very serious." Ethan glanced at the cheque presented to him by Percy. He was startled by the amount. "There's enough here for your trip to Alice and your new glasses, and probably a nice meal at the Stuart Arms Hotel." He handed Victoria the cheque, noticing her hands were shaking. "Please accept this on behalf of the people of Wombat Creek and the surrounding areas."

The bar, which was still half full of patrons from the previous day, erupted in applause, and tears rolled down Victoria's cheeks.

She turned to Riordan. "I can't take this…"

"Yes, you can," he said.

"I don't know what to say…"

"How about thank you?" Ethan said, laughing.

Victoria turned to face the crowd of people watching her with smiles on their faces, her neighbours and friends. "Thank you so much, everyone. I'm really honoured, and a little taken aback. I can think of many causes far more worthy. Sadie needs a new rainwater tank…"

"Bob Reynolds patched it, and it doesn't leak anymore," Sadie said from the corner where she always sat in the Wombat Creek Hotel.

"Nonie Jacob's roof is breaking up…."

"That's been fixed, too," Sadie added, grinning widely to reveal her one tooth, which was the same shade of grey as her hair.

Riordan put his arm around Victoria's shoulder.

"Does Tara know about this?" Victoria asked Ethan.

"Yes, she does."

Finally Victoria knew why Tara had been so confident they'd have the money for her trip.

Tara was sound asleep when she heard Jack scream out. She leapt from bed and went to his room.

"Jack, I'm here," she said, holding him while he sobbed. He clung to her frantically. "I had a ... nightmare," he said.

She wanted to ask what it was about but dared not. "Would you like to sleep in my room?" she asked. She felt a little awkward but knew as a mother, it was the right thing to do.

Jack nodded. Tara took him through to her room and put him on the other side of her enormous bed. "I'm right here," she said, climbing in the other side. "If you feel frightened, just reach out and touch me."

Jack nodded, and curled up.

"I'll leave the lamp burning," Tara added and closed her eyes. She vowed she'd speak to Tadd Sweeney in the morning and find the truth.

CHAPTER TWENTY-SEVEN

"Rex has just radioed," Tara called up the stairs to her aunt, who was standing on the landing. "He's on his way."

Victoria was in a panic. The train was due in William Creek at two o'clock in the afternoon, and she didn't want to miss it. Sorrel Windspear was meeting her at the station in Alice, and despite initially not wanting to go, she had become quite excited about the trip.

As Victoria came down the stairs with her small suitcase in her hand, Tara noted the frown on her face. She took the case from her and put it by the front door, smiling to herself. "You have at least an hour and a half to wait before he gets here, Aunt."

"All being well," Victoria grumbled. "He should have been here at six o'clock this morning."

Tara could see she was agitated. "You know he had trouble getting the spare axle for his car brought up from Port Augusta. It only arrived yesterday, so he's done rather well to have the car fixed. Apparently, he and the men in town worked on it until well after dark last night." Rex had made a point of telling her so.

Victoria's frown-lines softened. She knew everyone in town had been doing whatever they could for her benefit, and she appreciated their kindness more than she ever hoped to express, but that didn't stop her from agonizing over every detail of the trip.

"Stop fretting, Aunt," Tara said gently.

"I can't help it. I'd hate to miss the train and have poor Sorrel not know what happened to me."

"You won't miss the train."

"What if the axle breaks again? They may not have fixed it properly. We could be stuck between here and Wombat Creek and no one would know. If only Ethan was here, and not somewhere between Marree and Leigh Creek. I'd feel so much better." Tara had come to understand that her aunt relied on Ethan Hunter more than anyone else.

"Nugget told me Ethan and Saladin have taken feed and water to an exploration expedition stranded on the Strzelecki Track. It was an emergency, or he wouldn't have gone."

Tara had given Ethan a payment for the bank, which he was going to visit in Leigh Creek while he was in the area. She'd told him to find out all he could about their debt and to see if somehow they could come to a financial arrangement with the bank whereby Victoria could keep Tambora. She prayed his mission was successful, but although Ethan seemed confident, as he knew the bank manager personally, their debt was enormous, and it was likely his hands were tied.

"Now Tara, I've organized the men to keep rounding up the sheep and I'll get in contact with the shearers when I return. I've had Tadd send a telegram to the Port Adelaide shipping office regarding the wool shipment, so we should get a reply shortly. I should only be gone a few days, but if anything comes up you can phone me from Wombat Creek or have Percy send a telegram to the Stuart Arms Hotel."

"You've told me all this ten times, Aunt. Do you think I'm forgetful?"

"No, of course not, dear. I just don't want you to worry about anything, and I know you do."

"I won't worry, Aunt. We'll be fine for a few days, or however long it takes. I just wish you'd stop fussing." Tara understood that it had been a very long time since Victoria had been away from Tambora. She hoped the trip would be successful. She was certain it would be good for her.

Victoria had no sooner left with Rex, who promised to drive cautiously despite her nagging him to hurry when Percy radioed Tambora.

"I've just had a telegram from India," he said.

"What does it say?" Tara asked as the radio crackled.

"It's addressed to your Aunt," he said tersely. "I have to speak to her. It's a matter of confidentiality."

Tara could tell Percy was just being difficult. "Where did you learn such a big word, Percy?" she asked sarcastically. Without waiting for a reply, she shouted at him to be heard over the static airwaves. "My aunt isn't here. Rex has just picked her up, and she's flustered enough about her trip to Alice, without you giving her anything else to worry about. So tell me what William Crombie has to say, and don't pretend you haven't already told Ferris and Charity what's in the telegram. I'm sure half the people in the area are listening."

Tara thought she heard gasps of shock, but Percy sighed with exasperation. "Very well," he said. "But if Victoria is upset about this, I'm blaming you."

"You do that. Now what does the telegram say?"

"It's from a Mr. William Crombie."

"That much I know, Percy. For goodness sake, what is the message?"

"He wants the wool shipment urgently. If it doesn't arrive by the end of next month, his new partner is going to sign a contract with a sheep farmer in New Zealand, who has a shipment standing by."

Tara thought she heard a few mumbles, as those listening assessed the news. Any of the other station owners in the area running sheep would have jumped at the chance to export their wool.

"Oh dear," Tara thought. "We had better speed things up at this end."

"You'll never round up a thousand sheep in a week with those four lazy abo's…" Percy said.

Tara gasped in shock. She also thought she heard someone sniggering. "I hope you are not referring to the stockmen on Tambora?" she said irately. "They work exceptionally hard considering they haven't been paid for so long." Tara realized she shouldn't have been giving out so much personal information over the air, but her anger had made her jump to the defence of Nugget and the other men.

"I'm just saying… you won't get that wool shipped off in time."

"You seem to know a lot about our business?" Tara snapped.

Percy stumbled over his words. "Victoria told me her plans when she was in town."

"Well, she can't know about this, Percy. I want her trip to Alice to be worry-free. Do you understand? When she gets to town, you are to say nothing. And that goes for everyone else listening." This time Tara was sure she heard gasps of surprise.

"Very well," Percy said, noting her ominous tone. He knew if Tara mentioned anything about his watch being left at Lottie's place, everyone in the area would know. Just the thought made him tense and in desperate need of a drink. It was the only reason he was giving in to her demands.

"As for us not getting the wool shipped off in time, we'll do it if we have to work day and night."

Tara desperately wanted to speak to Nugget, and tell him the urgency of rounding up the sheep and getting them sheared, but he'd already left for the mustering camp with the men. She searched for Tadd, who'd been there to see Victoria off, but he seemed to have disappeared. She went to his cottage, the kennels, and the stockman's quarters. The stables were the last place she looked, and his horse was missing. Back on the veranda of the house, Tara gazed out over the landscape, in the direction she imagined Tadd had gone, southwesterly, where Jack had had his so-called accident. He should have been helping Nugget and the boys. They needed all the help they could get. She was so lost in thought that she barely heard footsteps behind her.

"Is something wrong?" Riordan asked, startling her. He thought she looked deeply concerned.

Tara turned and looked him over with one hostile sweep. He was wearing a clean white shirt and cream linen trousers. He'd obviously just washed and shaved, and his fair hair and moustache were neatly trimmed. He hadn't looked so good in days. He even had a bit of colour from his trip into town. "Nothing I can't handle," she snapped haughtily.

Riordan paused, a frown marring his features. "Now that we're alone, Tara, I think we should talk."

"I don't understand why you're here, Riordan. You've seen my aunt, and no doubt caught up on old times, so why don't you go back to Ireland? You and I have absolutely nothing to discuss."

His twinkling grey-blue eyes seemed to dull with pain, but Tara barely felt a tinge of regret.

"I know I was wrong about you, Tara," he said. "I treated you appallingly. I can't tell you how sorry I am, or how much I regret what happened at the gallery. If you will let me explain, then possibly you'll understand."

"You're apology means nothing to me, Riordan," she replied coldly, determined to hurt him as much as he'd hurt her.

She noticed he flinched, as if she'd slapped him, and his handsome face seemed to pale. "Surely, Tara, you have some forgiveness in your heart, if not for me, for your mother."

Tara found his concern for her mother touching, but it did nothing to dampen the anger she felt towards him. "What happens between my mother and myself is private, Riordan, and no concern of yours."

He looked contrite. "You're right, of course, Tara." He paused again. "I do have something I want to say to you, though. After you've heard me, I'll leave if you wish."

"I'm really not interested in anything you have to say." Tara turned her back.

After a moment's hesitation, he said. "I came all this way to see you, so I'm going to tell you what's on my mind."

Tara made no comment. She wanted to walk away, but decided she'd listen to him because he promised to leave Tambora afterward, and it couldn't be soon enough for her. Riordan moved to stand at the veranda railing a few feet from her, where he looked out over the Mulga scrub, now a faint shade of green. Tara glanced at him out of the corner of her eye. For a few moments there was silence and she wondered if he'd changed his mind. She was about to walk away, when he spoke.

"When your Aunt sent me your portrait, I thought you were the most beautiful woman I had ever seen." He glanced at Tara self-consciously, but she turned her head away from him.

If he thought flattering her would soften her heart, he was mistaken, she thought.

Riordan turned again to the harsh landscape of the Australian bush. As he gazed at the shimmering haze on the distant horizon, he let his mind go back … back to Ireland and a time when he was hopelessly captivated by "Tara the Gipsy". He felt the anguish of the obsession he'd felt for her, and the agony of unrequited love ripple through him, torturing him all over again.

"You were barely a woman," he whispered. "Young, vulnerable, fragile, and yet the most sensuous woman I had ever seen." Those qualities were an irresistible combination, Riordan thought. "And yet, when I gazed into your eyes, you appeared … lost. I imagined you needed me to take you away from a life that…" He couldn't say what he felt about her life. It caused him too much pain.

Tara was shocked by his grasp of how she had felt at the time the portrait was done. She had felt lost between two worlds, belonging to neither. She didn't feel she should be with the gipsies, and yet she couldn't go home. Garvie didn't even know how she felt, and yet Riordan could see the truth just by looking at her portrait.

"I was wrong, of course," Riordan said. Tara didn't correct him.

"I know that now, but I believed you really needed me. It's sounds ludicrous, but I fell deeply and hopelessly in love with the woman in the portrait."

"You didn't even know me," Tara said incredulously

"But it wasn't you, that is what I'm clumsily trying to explain. The woman in the portrait only existed in my mind."

Tara frowned in confusion.

Riordan endeavoured to explain. "The portrait was of you, but the woman I saw was someone else. I became obsessed with someone who didn't exist. My business suffered; my personal life suffered, but I was oblivious to everything but the woman in the portrait. I didn't know you, not the real you, but I convinced myself I did. As you know now, I was told you had been kidnapped. It tormented me that the woman in the portrait, the woman in my mind, was being held by the gipsies against her will. I thought I was letting her down by not finding her, and rescuing her."

Tara glanced at Riordan, but he was looking straight ahead. She could see the pain in his features and it seemed genuine, although she couldn't fully understand his obsession with a woman he claimed didn't exist.

"When I found her, you, I was captivated, but also devastated, as my illusions crumbled. At first, I thought the gipsies had drugged you, and were forcing you to entertain them, but it soon became apparent that wasn't the case. Even though you stirred something inside me, - something so powerful I was almost hypnotized, I felt utterly betrayed."

Tara felt heat rise from her neck to her face, and she was glad he wasn't looking at her.

"It wasn't your fault, I know that now, but when you came to see me, I still hadn't come to terms with reality."

He turned to face her, his expression earnest, and Tara lowered her eyes. "I want you to know I have conquered my obsession. I know you are completely blameless for everything I imagined, and for what happened with the man who worked for your father. I'm really very sorry that your husband had to pay for what he did to you…"

"How did you know that?" Tara asked.

"Your mother told me one of the gipsies was to be hanged for murdering Stanton Jackson. I assumed it was your husband, Tara." He could see he was right by the pain in her eyes.

"It was an accident, Riordan. Garvie didn't even know Stanton was dead."

"It's a tragedy, Tara, but it's you who has paid the highest price of all."

Tears filled Tara's eyes and spilt over her cheeks. She brushed them away impatiently. "Garvie is going to lose his life. There's no higher price than that."

Riordan stepped toward her and took her in his arms while she cried. She hadn't realized how much she needed a comforting arm around her.

"I'm sorry I don't have a handkerchief this time," he said, and despite her pain, Tara smiled.

Riordan looked down into her watery green eyes, his own softening with compassion. "I know I have no right to ask this, but if you will forgive me, I would like to begin our friendship all over again. I'd like to get to know the real you."

Despite her resolve, Tara was moved by his words, which were said with such heartfelt sincerity. "I don't know, Riordan."

"Think about it, Tara. When I'm not being an obsessed lunatic I think you'll find I'm really quite a nice fellow. Victoria always thought so." His grey-blue eyes twinkled at her, and the memory of their first meeting flashed through her mind. She had found him to be so charming and witty, and devilishly handsome.

She heard herself say, "I will think about it, Riordan, but I can't make any promises."

He smiled that devastating smile and her heart fluttered. For a moment she wondered if he knew the power of his charm? But when she saw the twinkle in his eyes, she was sure he did.

"That's all I ask. Now getting back to where we started when I found you here looking deeply troubled about something. If I can help, and you'll let me, I'm more than ready."

Tara smiled at his naive willingness. "Can you round up sheep?" she asked, then laughed at the shocked expression on his face.

"I haven't actually ridden a horse for some time, although I'm sure I'm still capable. As for rounding up sheep, they're as foreign to me as... Yak's."

"I've never mustered sheep either, but we have a thousand sheep to bring in for shearing. Nugget and the boys are going to need all the help they can get. I'm willing to give it a try. How about you?"

Riordan looked taken back. "Well if you're game, then so am I," he said.

As they turned to go inside the house, Riordan felt his heart ache with bitter-sweet pain, and he knew falling in love with the real Tara would be as easy as falling off a horse, which no doubt he'd do more than once in the next few days.

HAPTER TWENTY-EIGHT

"I can't spend hours in the saddle today," Tadd said to Tara, when she asked him to help muster the sheep.

"Why not? Surely it's your job as manager to be overseeing such a big undertaking." Tara knew Nugget had already tried to discuss the muster, and that Tadd had simply shrugged, told him to get on with it, and walked away. She couldn't help being suspicious of everything Tadd said and did. She still hadn't found out what his motives were for getting the station into debt, and hiding Victoria's mail, but it seemed as if he didn't care that the station was to be taken by the bank.

"It's my back," he complained, grimacing as if in pain. "It plays up sometimes, and it's giving me Hell at the moment. I'll have to stay behind and do what I can around the homestead."

"We can't let Aunt Victoria down, Tadd. She doesn't know that William Crombie has brought the date forward for the delivery of the wool. We have as little as two weeks to round up a thousand sheep, and get them sheared, if we are going to meet our shipment commitments."

"I understand, and I wish I could help, but.... I simply can't."

Tara was sure he was not at all sorry for their predicament, and she didn't believe his back was giving him grief. In her opinion, if he really thought as much of Victoria as he said he did, he'd work, bad back or not. He could at least have the decency to help get the station out of debt, but this obviously wasn't on his agenda.

Frustrated, Tara and Riordan set off with Nugget, Bluey, Charlie and young Karl. Jack had wanted to help, but Tara had insisted he have one more day of bed rest.

Elsa gave Jack and Hannah their breakfast, and was taking a tray of dirty dishes back to the kitchen when the back door opened, and an aboriginal girl appeared. Elsa gasped in surprise, but the girl seemed equally startled to see someone strange in the house.

"Who you?" Nerida asked, when her eyes adjusted to the dimness of the hall after the glaring sunlight outside.

"I'm Elsa Killain," Elsa said. "Tara's mother. Who are you?"

Sanja appeared from the kitchen when he heard voices. "Where you bin you lazy girl?" he admonished, wagging his finger at her. "Go back to bush," he shouted. "Missus much cross with you."

Elsa suddenly had an inkling of who she might be. "Nerida?" she queried, and the girl nodded, her large eyes welling with tears. Elsa saw her as her salvation in regards to cleaning the house. "Don't take any notice of Sanja," she said, handing the cook the tray of dirty dishes and leading her down the hallway. "Missus Victoria will be very glad to see you, and so will Tara." I for one am terribly relieved you're back home, she thought. "Let's go through to the sitting room." Elsa led the shy girl through the house, away from Sanja's prying ears and eyes.

"Where Missus Victoria?" Nerida asked, glancing up the stairs as they passed them.

"Victoria has gone to Alice Springs to see a doctor about some glasses, and Tara has gone out with the men to muster sheep."

Nerida looked at her blankly.

"I've been left to look after the children and …clean the house. Now that you're back, you can help me."

"Yes, Missus." Nerida kept her eyes fixated on her clasped hands, which gave Elsa the chance to look her over. She was appalled that the aboriginal girl wasn't wearing any shoes. The soles of her feet looked like sun baked leather strips, and between her spread out toes the dirt was as red as the desert. She was wearing a loose shift that could have done with a good wash, and her hair stood out from her head in a wild halo.

"The house is so big, Nerida," Elsa said. "However did you manage to clean it on your own?"

"I do what I can, Missus, mostly look after Missus Victoria. She not worry about the house so much."

"I can see that," Elsa thought, glancing at the dust on the furniture and the cobwebs in the corners.

Nerida stood up. "I go now to my room, Missus."

Elsa also stood up. She didn't know what Nerida's intentions were, but there was work to be done. "I want to start cleaning upstairs this morning," she said. "Will you meet me in Victoria's room?"

The girl nodded reluctantly, but Elsa intended to get her working.

"Bring a broom, dusters, and a bucket of water, some lye soap and cloths."

"Yes, Missus."

Elsa thought Nerida sounded downhearted, or troubled. "Are you all right?" she asked in concern. She had no idea Nerida had walked ten miles to get back home.

"Yes, Missus." With her head hanging, Nerida walked down the hallway to her room.

By mid morning, the sun was fierce out on the plains. Riordan had managed to stay on his horse, but found rounding up sheep quite a mystery. He'd go one way, and they'd go the other, and then they'd split up, going in two or three different directions, and he didn't know which way to go. He tried to follow Nugget's lead, who, to his credit was being patient, while Charlie and young Karl gave Tara instruction on keeping the sheep moving in a group.

By mid-afternoon, Riordan and Tara were doing far better. They'd stopped at lunchtime for a quick 'Billy of tea', in which time Nugget gave Riordan tips and encouragement.

"To be honest," Riordan admitted to Tara. "Mellie is making me look better than I am." She was chasing all the sheep that got away from him, and it looked as if it was wearing her out. As they stood around the campfire, she kept a careful eye on her charges, with her tongue lolling out the side of her mouth, and her sides heaving as she panted furiously in the heat. Riordan was full of admiration for her and the other two dogs, Shelby and Fergus. He thought they were absolutely marvelous with the sheep. Nugget had given Shellie to Jack to keep him company for the day in place of Mellie. Tara had explained the situation to him, and Jack understood that Mellie was needed.

Elsa and Nerida took more than two hours to clean Victoria's room. It was the hardest Elsa had worked in her life. Her back ached and her hands were red and chapped from scrubbing the floor. She thought Nerida would be efficient at cleaning, but she found her to be painfully slow and somewhat lackadaisical. Elsa was still convinced the girl didn't feel well, either that or she was bone idle.

"Are you ill?" she finally asked Nerida when she sat down for the umpteenth time.

No, Missus," Nerida replied with her head down.

Elsa thought that perhaps she was depressed about something. "Victoria told me you were sick, and that you went to get help from someone in the tribe."

"I not sick, Missus. Please, you not send me away?"

"I have no intention of sending you away. In fact, I was going to ask if you knew of any women who could help us clean the house. There's so much to do."

"Tribe gone walkabout, Missus."

"Walkabout! Do you mean they've gone away somewhere?"

"Yes, missus."

"When will they be back?"

Nerida shrugged and got back to work.

By the time Elsa and Nerida had moved to Tara's room, where the bed was stripped, the floors swept and washed, the cobwebs removed, and everything dusted, Elsa was exhausted, perspiring profusely, and felt like she was suffering mild heat stroke. She could hardly believe they'd only done two rooms, and it had taken them nearly all day. She knew Tara was right in her estimation of how long it would take to clean the entire house, a week if they were lucky, and then they'd have to begin all over again.

The western sky was scarlet, and the parrots screeching in the gum trees, when Tara and Riordan returned, both so exhausted they almost fell off their horses. Elsa met them on the veranda with tall glasses of water. She noted their filthy clothes, and the grime and sunburn and on their faces. She'd felt exhausted, until she saw the state of them.

"Tara, this is too much for you," she said when her daughter collapsed into a chair, almost too fatigued to drink, and stinking of horses. "Couldn't Tadd Sweeney hire some more men to help muster the sheep?"

"We can't afford it, mother, but even if we could, we haven't got the time to spare to find more stockmen."

Elsa shook her head. "Look at you, Riordan. I've never seen you so… dirty. No-one from Dublin would recognize you."

"I doubt I'd recognize myself if I looked in the mirror, but I must say, although I'm tired, I thoroughly enjoyed myself today."

Surprised, Tara turned to look at him, and smiled wearily. "You did seem to get the hang of it, eventually."

Riordan laughed. "I didn't fall off my horse, either, although I came close a couple of times."

"I think Nugget said we mustered about one hundred sheep, but we have to do better tomorrow," Tara said. Turning to her mother, she asked, "How are the children?"

"Fine, and you'll be pleased to know Nerida has returned."

"Wonderful, we certainly need her. Is she alright?"

"As far as I can tell. I thought she looked ill, but when I queried her, she denied it. She seems more worried about me sending her away. Why, Heaven only knows? I appreciated her help today. Although she was slow, and a little… slap-dash, I'd still be doing Victoria's room without her help."

"What did Tadd do all day?" Tara asked. He was nowhere in sight and there was no evidence of any work that had been done, mended fences or mucked out stables.

"I haven't seen him," Elsa said.

"What about lunch time? He seems to have a knack for knowing just when lunch is being served."

"He didn't come in for lunch. I haven't seen him in or around the house at all today."

Tara sighed with exasperation. Of one thing she was sure, he'd lied to her, again.

The next day seemed even harder for Riordan and Tara. It was extremely hot, and the sheep were less co-operative, when they could find them. Tara had a fall after her horse tripped chasing three ewes down a steep gully to what had once been a riverbed. She landed hard, and hurt her shoulder. Soon after, Riordan and Jack's horses collided, and Riordan hurt his ankle. It was windy and dusty and they only succeeded in rounding up about seventy sheep.

At the homestead, Elsa was becoming frustrated with Nerida. The girl worked for just over an hour and then disappeared. Elsa eventually found her lying down in her room. "For goodness sakes, Nerida, what is the matter? And don't tell me nothing!" Elsa demanded from the open doorway, in her severest tone. She couldn't handle the cleaning by herself, but she also couldn't handle Nerida's lethargy. When Nerida suddenly burst into tears, Elsa was startled. She ventured into the room and sat on the end of her bed. "I didn't mean to shout," she said. "I just wish you'd tell me if you're sick. Perhaps I could help you?"

Tadd Sweeney walked into the General store in Wombat Creek. Percy was serving Lottie, and having a joke with her until he saw Tadd, when his features suddenly became sober, and his manner off hand, but Lottie understood. The men were always different when they were alone with her.

"G'day, Tadd," she said, as she left the store. He didn't reply, but she knew she would almost certainly see him later, after a few drinks.

"I'm glad you're here," Percy said in hushed tones. "I've just had an urgent telegram from Victoria."

Tadd turned and waited until Lottie was out of earshot. "You didn't tell Lottie, did you?" he queried.

"No, I didn't say a word."

"Then give it to me," Tadd said brusquely.

"You're in a right grumpy mood this fine morning," Percy said. "What's up? The women out on Tambora giving you a difficult time?"

Tadd snorted.

"Perhaps they're bored. Find them something to do," Percy suggested.

"I wish they would do nothing. They're trying to run the place. Yesterday, that niece of Victoria's was trying to tell me my job, and today she was asking what I did while she was out mustering sheep with the men."

"I knew she'd be trouble the minute I saw her," Percy said, giving Tadd a sympathetic look as he handed him the telegram, which ironically was addressed to Tara.

"I'm going for a drink," Tadd said despondently, and left the store.

Around the back of the hotel he opened the telegram, unaware Lottie was watching from her front window. She'd heard Percy say there was a telegram from Victoria, and was almost sure Tadd would read it. She knew he'd be drunk when he came over later, and hoped there would be an opportunity to find out what he was up to.

When Tara, Riordan and Jack returned from the muster, they were all feeling sorry for themselves. Elsa watched from the veranda as they walked toward her from the stables. Riordan was limping, Tara was holding her shoulder and Jack looked dog-tired.

"What happened to you?" Elsa asked shading her eyes from the afternoon sun, as Tara lowered herself gingerly into a wicker chair.

"I'm going to have a wash," Riordan said, and he went off to the wash house out back.

"I fell off my horse," Tara said to her mother.

"Oh, Tara, how badly are you hurt?"

"My pride is more bruised than my shoulder. It wasn't a very dignified fall." Tara noted a letter on the table between them. When she turned it to face her, she read her name on the front. "Where did this come from?"

"That camel man," Elsa said, crinkling her nose in disapproval.

"Saladin?"

"No, the other one. The wild frontier man…"

"Ethan?"

"Is that his name?"

"You know it is." Tara sighed with exasperation. She was in no mood for games. "Where is he?"

"He went with the robed one on camels, in that direction." She pointed southwesterly. Tara realized Ethan was going to explore the area where Jack had been found, to see if he could find a mine.

"I have something to tell you, Tara," Elsa said, moving forward to sit on the edge of her chair. Tara had begun opening the letter.

"What is it?" Tara asked, only half interested. She thought her mother was going to tell her something fairly insignificant, like Sanja was cooking a stew, or there was a mouse in the house.

"Nerida… is pregnant."

Tara's gaze shot up to meet her mother's. "What? How do you know?"

"She told me, although I had to practically force it out of her. The girl is painfully shy. I noticed she was acting strangely, but she was not suffering an illness, as I had suspected, it was morning sickness. Apparently, a woman named Kitty, whom I gather is some kind of bush nurse or missionary, confirmed it."

Tara blinked several times in astonishment. "Who is the father?" She'd never seen Nerida with a man, other than those who worked on the station, but even then there was nothing to indicate a romance. She thought the father must be someone from the tribe. "That much I don't know. She won't say a word."

"I wonder what Aunt Victoria is going to make of this bit of news?"

"I don't know. Nerida is terrified she'll be sent away. You don't think Victoria would get rid of her, do you?"

"No. Aunt Victoria thinks the world of her." Tara opened the letter from Ethan, and scanned the contents. The news was not really a surprise, and it certainly wasn't good. Ethan's friend at the bank had confirmed that Tambora had been heavily mortgaged. He said they had papers signed by Victoria, which Tara was certain Tadd had forged. The loan repayment Ethan had made on their behalf had delayed the repossession by a month, but that was the best they could do.

Tara shook her head in dismay. Perhaps, she thought, with the wool shipment and the possibility of taking in children, they could delay the inevitable long enough for a miracle to eventuate.

After Tara had bathed, she went to lie down, and fell into a deep sleep. Three hours later, she was being violently shaken.

"Wake up, Missus," Nerida said.

"What's wrong?" Tara asked in a daze, her first thoughts of the children. "Someone speak on box make chatter-chatter. They ask for you," Nerida said.

Tara rushed downstairs and into the radio room, where she picked up the receiver. She was surprised to find Lottie on the other end.

"How nice to hear from you… Lottie."

"I can't talk for long, Tara. A telegram came for you from Victoria this afternoon."

"Oh, thank you for letting me know. I'll radio Percy…."

"No," Lottie snapped. "Don't do that."

"Why not?"

"Tadd picked up the telegram. I don't want him or Percy to know I know about it. Tadd was here a few hours ago, and he'd been drinking. While he was with…. Belle… I took the telegram from the pocket in his trousers and read it without his knowledge. I know that was wrong, but I believed he had no intention of telling you about it. He was in such a foul mood when he came in."

Tara felt her anger rise. "What did the telegram say," she asked.

"Victoria said that she'd been to see about the matter you discussed regarding homeless children and that someone from the government was coming to inspect the house in the next day or so. She's due back late the day after tomorrow, but she thought they might come meanwhile, and she wanted you to be prepared. She also said she'd left your name out of it, whatever that means."

"Oh," Tara gasped.

"Do you understand the message?" Lottie asked.

"Yes, I do. Thank you for letting me know, Lottie."

"You're welcome. I'm sorry for calling you so late, but… there'll be no one listening at this time."

"I appreciate it." Tara thought of all they had to do in the next two days, and felt overwhelmed. She could just imagine how her mother was going to react.

Tara found her mother lying down in her room with a wet flannel on her forehead, fanning herself with a paper.

When Tara explained the situation, Elsa paled. "I can't possibly clean the whole house in less than two days, Tara," she said. "It's taken me that long to do a few rooms.

Nerida only worked for an hour today."

"You'll just have to do the best you can, mother, perhaps just an overall tidy up, a flick with the duster and the removal of cobwebs. We can only hope the inspectors won't be too thorough. I can't stay and help because the men need all the help they can get mustering the sheep. We only have another day or so, before the shearing will have to begin."

Elsa sat up. "Did you hear that, Tara?"

Tara was preoccupied. "I didn't hear anything."

"I thought I heard someone shouting, outside."

"Are you sure?" Tara went out onto the balcony, where she could hear what sounded like a heated argument, but it seemed to be taking place somewhere at the back of the house.

"That sounds like Ethan, and Tadd," she said to her mother. "I'm going down to investigate."

Tara rushed over to Tadd's cottage, but even before she reached the door, she heard angry shouts.

"What the Hell are you up to, Tadd? Jack is a ten year old boy, and Victoria has always been good to you, and this is how you repay her, by betraying her and threatening her family."

"I've worked hard for Victoria, and nobody can say any different. She would never have kept the station after Tom died, without me."

"Only because you purposely made her dependant on you. She worked just as hard as Tom, and harder than most men in the area, including you."

"That's rubbish…"

"What's going on?" Tara shouted as she went inside. "I could hear you upstairs in the house." Ethan looked more furious than she'd ever seen him.

"This piece of scum has been lying to all of us," Ethan said. "And what's worse, he threatened Jack not to tell us about his mine, which incidentally, I found today."

Tadd looked mutinous.

"You swine!" Tara hissed. "How could you threaten a young boy like Jack?"

"I did no such thing," Tadd declared indignantly.

"He told me himself, and I'd believe him any day before I'd take the word of scum like you," Ethan said.

Tara noted his fists were clenched, and Tadd's bottom lip looked swollen. A chair in his living room was also broken, and the bookshelf had been knocked over. Ethan had obviously well and truly lost his temper. Tara could only wonder why?

"Where is Jack?" she asked in a panic.

"He's upstairs in his room," Ethan said. "He was waiting for me when I returned this afternoon, and he was in a terrible state. Apparently Tadd had found him down the mine. Jack believes he was going to leave him there… to drown…"

Tara gasped with shock, her eyes widening.

"That's not true," Tadd said vehemently, casting her a cautious look.

"Eventually he got him out, no doubt when he thought you'd find the mine, and then Tadd told Jack he'd hurt Hannah or you, if he didn't keep his secret. Jack has been living with this fear, but he couldn't take it…. Apparently he was having nightmares about you, and Hannah."

Tara was incredulous. She had noticed a change in Jack. Now she understood. "Poor Jack. Hasn't he been through enough?" She wondered why Jack hadn't said anything to her, fright she supposed. He obviously saw Ethan as someone who could protect them. "My God, Tadd, what kind of monster are you?" she asked.

"That's all lies. You know the lad is trouble. Look at what he's done since he's been here?"

"Don't even try to deny it, Tadd," Ethan raged. "He had rope burns on his neck."

"How dare you try to make out Jack's at fault," Tara said, glaring at Tadd. "We know you've mortgaged Tambora to the hilt. You obviously forged my Aunt's signature, because she believes the station is debt free. What you've done will break her heart." Tadd looked momentarily startled. He wondered how they knew about the debt. Had Ethan bumped into the Bank Manager in Leigh Creek?

"What are you talking about?" he asked, feigning innocence.

"Donald Blair told me everything," Ethan said, confirming Tadd's fears. "And now we know you've been mining opal," he added. "And the mine is on land belonging to the station."

Tadd's eyes narrowed. "I haven't found anything much," he said, determined to keep his haul, which had taken more than a year of hard work to obtain.

"Then why go to so much trouble to hide it, and make up stories about being a partner in a mine in Coober Pedy?" Ethan asked.

"You're such a liar, Tadd Sweeney," Tara said, before Tadd could come up with an excuse. "I'm sure you don't have a bad back, and how is it, if you found nothing, that you're not short of money like the other men on the station? You're able to drink in the hotel and visit the girls in town."

"I'm entitled to spend a little on myself. I work hard enough."

Tara snorted in derision. "Not around here, you don't. I'll see you are fired when my Aunt gets back," she said angrily. "I suggest you start packing."

Ethan and Tara walked toward the open door of the cottage, but Tadd followed.

"Victoria won't fire me," he said in a snide voice. "There's no-one else to take my place, no one that knows the station like I do."

Tara turned, her green eyes flashing in temper. "Oh yes, there is. Nugget! He'd make a far better station manager than you've ever been, and I'm going to see he gets your job."

Tadd was absolutely enraged at the thought of Nugget replacing him. "You must be joking. That lazy, good for nothing…"

Tara saw red. "You're the lazy one. As far as I can see, Nugget and the boys do all the work around here. My Aunt may not have been able to see that, but I intend to make her aware of everything. Until she gets here, I don't want you in the house or anywhere near my children."

"They're not your children, are they?" Tadd said, unable to hold his tongue.

Tara's mouth dropped open.

"Not legally," he added. "I'd be careful if I were you?"

Ethan launched himself at Tadd and grabbed him by the scruff of the neck. "You low life swine," he hissed drawing back his fist. "If that's any kind of threat Tadd Sweeney, you won't live long enough to act upon it."

Tadd was alarmed. "It's the authorities she should be worrying about, not me," he said, wriggling to get loose from Ethan's steely grip.

"Let him go," Tara said, and Ethan almost flung him away. "He's not worth any trouble. As for the authorities, forging my Aunt's signature is a very serious offence, Tadd. I'm sure the local constable in Leigh Creek would be interested in speaking to you about that."

Tara turned and left the cottage with Ethan. Tadd watched them, feeling humiliated. They're not your children, he thought to himself. And I don't think you'll be keeping them for long. He hoped Moyna Conway had taken some action to retrieve them. He couldn't wait to see the day they were taken from Miss High and Mighty Tara.

Outside the cottage, Tara turned to Ethan almost in a state of shock. "I must tell my Aunt everything now," she mumbled.

Ethan nodded solemnly, watching her closely. "Don't worry about what Tadd said, Tara. If he makes trouble, it will be the last thing he does."

Tara appreciated his support more than she could ever hope to express. She stared out over the vast plains, which were almost blanketed in darkness. "My mother was right," she said, thinking of the mineshaft and all the fears she endured. "I do have the gift..."

"What gift, Tara?"

Tara looked up at him. "I dreamt about Jack falling down a hole in the ground, that was half full of water. I dreamt it three nights in a row, and it came true. When I told my mother, she confessed something to me that she had hidden for years."

"What was it?"

Tara was hesitant. Her mother had told her not to tell anyone, but Ethan already knew the truth about the children, and he had not judged her. Although this was different, she had to tell someone, and she felt she could trust him. She needed his help with Tadd; there was no way she could cope alone, so he should know the whole truth. "She said I had gipsy blood. My grandmother and my great-grandmother were gipsy Seer's. They could foretell the future."

Ethan looked taken back.

"Are you shocked?" Tara asked fearfully.

"Surprised," he said. "But if you have a gift, then nurture it for the good it can bring." Tara could have cried with relief. Ethan certainly was an extraordinary man. She realized she couldn't have tolerated the thought of him looking down on her. She had come to respect him too much.

"I have the overwhelming feeling that Tadd is going to cause me trouble about the children."

"Perhaps you should seek to have them legally."

"I've already taken steps to do so. I had Aunt Victoria talk to Sorrel Windspear's son in Alice Springs. He's a lawyer, and I asked her to find out from him if I could adopt the children legally. As it is now, I could be in a lot of trouble with the law for the way I took them."

"I don't understand why you were allowed to take them. You are not a blood relative.

Surely there should have been some legal procedure."

Tara dropped her head. "I deceived the authorities," she whispered. "I told them I was the children's mother. They think I'm Maureen O'Sullivan, and that Tara Flynn perished aboard ship."

Ethan was clearly shocked, and shook his head. "It's a miracle you haven't been found out yet. Does Tadd know about this?"

"I'm not sure, but as for the authorities, there would have been no reason for them to suspect I was lying. Jack went along with it, and as some of the bodies were burnt beyond recognition, they did not delve too deeply into the survivor's identities. I had to do it, Ethan. Jack was terrified he'd be put in an orphanage and possibly separated from Hannah."

"I understand. It must have been horrific for him. Let's hope Victoria has some good news when she returns."

"There's something more you should know, Ethan. Aunt Victoria has answered an advertisement in the paper, a request for people to take in orphaned children."

"Why would she do that? How could she support them?"

"The government is trialling a new scheme where they are paying two pounds per week/per child, to people willing to care for them because the government run homes are overcrowded. She thought it was a good way to get some money coming in, and we certainly have the room. Lottie radioed this evening to say Victoria had sent a telegram, only Tadd intercepted it and she didn't think he was going to give it to me."

"My God, that man has a lot to answer for. Why didn't you say something to him about it?"

"I didn't want to get Lottie into trouble after she was good enough to risk finding out what he was up to."

Ethan understood. Lottie was a good woman.

"The telegram was to warn me that someone was coming to inspect Tambora to see if we could provide suitable accommodation. I think that would give Tadd the opportunity to make trouble for me, and he's in just the frame of mind to do it."

"You could be right. Perhaps you shouldn't be here, Tara."

"I can't let my Aunt down, Ethan. Nugget and the boys need all the help they can get mustering the sheep. We have a dead-line to meet."

"You can't risk going to goal, either. Where would that leave Jack and Hannah? They're just settling in here."

"I know. I just don't know what to do. I don't want Tadd to get away with what he's done, but I don't want him making trouble for me, either. I suspected he may have overheard my Aunt and I talking."

"I have an idea, Tara," Ethan said, looking thoughtful. "Perhaps you could still help the men, but have Tadd believe you have left the station, and taken the children."

"I'm listening."

CHAPTER TWENTY-NINE

"Lottie, it's me, Tara." It was eleven o'clock at night, so Tara was almost positive no one would be monitoring her call.

"Hello, Tara. Is everything alright?"

"I want to ask a favour of you, Lottie, and I wanted to be sure it was between us."

"Of course, anything I can do."

"You know the visitors we're expecting?"

"Visitors? Oh, yes…"

"They will no doubt arrive on the train from Alice Springs in the next day or so, and I would like you to radio me, or my mother when they get to town?"

"Of course. Forewarned is forearmed they say."

"Exactly. Thank you, Lottie. It's even possible they will be on the same train as Victoria."

"Will Ethan be picking them up?"

"No. He's going to make arrangements with Rex to bring them out to the station."

"Rex is here now…"

Tara was startled. "Really?"

"We often share a late night cup of tea. He has trouble sleeping in the heat, and I'm up…." Tara could hear the smile in her voice.

"Ethan is here," Tara said, feeling herself blush. "Could he have a word with Rex? It will save him radioing him at his place."

"Of course."

"Thank you, Lottie, and not a word about that other matter."

"I understand."

"I'm glad that's all arranged," Tara said to Ethan, as she walked him out onto the veranda. She was still a bit shocked about Rex sharing 'late night cups of tea' with Lottie, although she was sure Lottie would be good company for anyone. "It's good of you to offer to help with the muster."

"Saladin can look after the camels for a few days, and make any necessary deliveries. I noticed Riordan Magee is still here."

"Yes, he's been helping us with the muster."

Ethan looked startled. "I can't quite picture him working with sheep. Wouldn't he get his cream suit dirty?"

Tara saw the white flash of his teeth in the darkness, and knew he was poking fun at Riordan. Ironically, she felt it was her duty to defend him.

"Neither of us really know what we're doing, Ethan, but we're willing. Actually, Riordan was enjoying himself until he hurt his ankle today. Jack's horse collided with his horse. Now that I think about it, Jack had seemed preoccupied, now we know why." There was silence for a moment. Tara had the feeling Ethan wanted to ask her something of a personal nature.

"You seem to have changed your opinion of Riordan," he said.

There was something in his tone that made Tara feel defensive. "We've settled some of our differences, and tentatively agreed to a new beginning, and Nugget and the boys need all the help they can get with the muster if we're going to meet the deadline with the shipping company. I think it's good of Riordan to help out."

Tara glanced up at Ethan, but she couldn't read the expression in his dark eyes in the shadows of night.

He was wondering what their differences had been, and intended to observe them together in the hope he'd know whether they had ever meant something to each other. That he was so curious came as a surprise to him, but then so many of his feelings for Tara astonished him.

"I agree," he said, and I'm sure Victoria will appreciate his help. I'm staying in the bunkhouse tonight, so I'll see you in the morning. Good night, Tara."

Ethan turned to walk away, leaving Tara feeling a little confused. As she watched him lead Hannibal around the side of the house, to a yard near the stables where he kept a horse, she wondered if he was jealous of Riordan, but decided that was too ridiculous to contemplate. Ethan didn't form attachments, Victoria had said so. And in her opinion he was too self-assured to ever feel envious of another man. As Tara climbed the stairs to her room, she wondered what the next day would bring, and prayed Ethan's plan to keep her safe, worked.

Elsa was awakened at dawn by shrieking parrots and blow flies buzzing outside the mosquito net that hung over her bed. She dragged herself from between crumpled sheets, believing she must be the first one up, until she heard the men in the stable yards saddling horses, and smelt the aroma of freshly baked damper mingling with the distinctive odour of burning gum leaves. Downstairs, she took one look at Nerida, and knew she would be of no help to her, so she set to work cleaning by herself, dreading the long day ahead.

With Ethan's help, the rounding up of the sheep took on a different dimension. Riordan and Tara were both completely in awe of his skill. Although Nugget and the other men were good stockmen, it was not inconceivable to see why Ethan was considered a legend in the outback. Man and horse were one, as his palomino responded to the softest whistle or the slightest pressure from his knees. They moved together in a fluid motion that Tara and Riordan found hypnotic to watch. Before lunch they had mustered over two hundred sheep, twice as many as on previous days, and penned them in the only fenced holding yard on the station, at the back of the shearing sheds.

"You much better today," Nugget told Tara and Riordan, when they stopped to boil the Billy for tea at lunchtime, while Charlie and Bluey pumped water from a bore for the sheep and horses.

"I was beginning to think so, but Ethan makes us look even more like amateurs," Riordan said sincerely. The two men had warily kept a respectful distance from each other, but Riordan felt he had to give credit where it was due. Although he thought Ethan uncultured, not the sort of man worthy of Tara, he was perfectly suited to life in the outback.

Ethan looked up from the rope he was winding. He'd been discreetly observing Riordan all day and was certain he had deep feelings for Tara. Whether his feelings were returned or not, he couldn't tell. "I was practically born in a saddle," he said, "and Nugget's father tied him to a stockman's saddle before he could walk, much like Charlie, Bluey and young Karl," he said. "Nugget is right. You've both done very well today, considering you are novices." One side of his mouth lifted at the corner.

"Another day as good as this, and we'll have enough sheep and fleece to meet the quota for Victoria's shipment."

"Ethan," Jack said shyly. "Karl told me a boy about my age won three camel races at the Gymkhana."

"Matt Lewis," Karl added. "But he wouldn't have beaten Ethan on Hannibal if they'd been competing."

"I'm not so sure about that, Karl. Hannibal and I are starting to feel our ages, and young Matt is a good rider."

"Did you teach him to race camels?" Jack asked.

"I gave him a few lessons, but that was two or three years ago, and he has his own camel now."

Riordan could tell that Jack greatly admired Ethan, although he wasn't sure Ethan was a good role model for the boy. He led an odd lifestyle, roaming the country on camels, with no home to speak of. Riordan also thought the children were too great a responsibility for Tara. In his opinion they would be better off with relatives in Ireland.

Ethan had thought Jack was about to say something more, but he held back, looking anxious.

"Would you like to race camels one day, Jack?" he asked.

The boy's face lit up. "Would you teach me, Ethan?"

Ethan glanced at Tara. "Of course, if it's all right with your mother."

Tara felt dubious, but she could see the idea gave Jack immense pleasure, so she put her misgivings aside. "If you're careful, Jack, and listen to Ethan's instructions precisely."

Jack nodded and his eyes blazed with joy. He was so different from the previous day, Tara thought, when he'd had the weight of the world on his young shoulders. Although at odd moments he still looked haunted by what Tadd had done to him, knowing that his grandmother and Nerida were caring for Hannah gave him comfort, especially as Tara had told him that Tadd was no longer allowed in the house, and Ethan had given him his word he'd protect him, and Hannah and Tara.

Tara, Riordan and Jack had just returned to the house at dusk, when Lottie radioed. At first Tara wondered who was calling, as Lottie was disguising her voice. Tara had only spoken to Charity once, briefly, but she thought Lottie sounded a little like her, or what Tara imagined she'd sound like under the influence of Ferris's homebrew.

"I've been trying to reach you for three hours," she said.

"Oh," Tara knew her mother had been working upstairs, where she may not have heard the radio. Tara was about to ask who it was, when Lottie rushed on.

"The train came through late this afternoon from Alice, and that package you asked about… was on it."

"Package?" Tara was momentarily confused. Her head ached from being out in the glaring sun all day. "Oh! That package." She panicked, realizing it was Lottie, and the 'package' was the government officials. "Will Rex be bringing them… it … out straight away? We're not in any hurry to receive it, you know." They weren't prepared and she wondered if the officials would want to stay the night on the station. She certainly hoped not.

"Rex has been in the bar… drinking with… Ferris and Percy …for most of the afternoon, celebrating the birth of Charity's…. the baby…"

"Oh, wonderful. Was it a boy or girl?"

Lottie forgot her ruse and dropped the accent in her excitement. "A boy, and I believe he's lovely, although she hasn't showed him to me yet. I've made some little gowns…"

"Did ya hear that, Mabel?" a strange voice asked.

"I did. As if Ferris' wife would want anything from her…"

Tara and Lottie were silent for a few moments, both feeling humiliated. Lottie for herself, and Tara for her. Tara wanted to say something biting, but she thought she'd only make things worse.

"Anyway," Lottie said. "I'm sure Rex won't be driving anywhere until the morning."

"Oh, well, tell him that suits us. There's absolutely no hurry." Tara couldn't emphasize this enough.

"I will."

"Thank you. Over and out."

Tara felt Lottie's pain, and anger welled inside her. She gathered the children together with a few belongings, and under the cover of darkness, went over to the bunkhouse, where their accomplice met them.

Elsa dragged herself out of bed early the next morning. Every muscle and bone in her body ached, making her feel nothing shy of a hundred years old. She'd had not more than an hour's sleep, but she dressed herself in one of her prettiest frocks, and ordered Nerida to get out of bed and put on a clean dress, and a pair of her shoes. Nerida had to squeeze her broad feet into the shoes, and walked most awkwardly, her heels clattering on the polished and tiled floors, but Elsa insisted. She also made her put a scarf on her head, to contain her wild hair.

Sanja was always up early, but Elsa asked him kindly to bake teacakes for important guests. At eight o'clock, Rex radioed to say he was leaving town with the 'visitors', a man and a woman, and that they would be arriving in just over an hour, all being well. Elsa couldn't help feeling nervous. She had been left to face the music alone. Her performance could make the difference between a successful outcome and abject poverty, but she knew Tara and Victoria were counting on her.

By the time Rex drew up outside the house in a cloud of dust, half an hour late, Elsa was reclining on the veranda, giving the impression of complete composure. The same could not be said for the passengers who alighted from his vehicle. Rex immediately departed to deliver mail to neighbouring stations, shouting that he would return at lunchtime. Elsa noticed that he always seemed to time his arrivals at meal times, which she was sure wasn't a coincidence.

Herbert Quinlan and Mrs. Blythe Horton seemed momentarily dazed, as they gazed around them at the surrounding vast desert, while a layer of dust from Rex's departing automobile settled over them. Elsa heard the woman comment distastefully that they were literally in the middle of nowhere, and the journey back was bound to be just as horrendous as the journey out, worse if they had another flat tyre. When they turned to look up at the house, they appeared even more astonished.

"What an amazing house," Elsa heard the man comment. "It looks quite out of place out here, but I wish we'd come out last night. The hotel in town was one of the worst I've ever stayed in. I don't know which was more disgusting, the food, or that drunken lunatic, Ferris Dunmore. I can't wait to go home."

Having the feeling things were getting off to a bad start, Elsa stood up. "Good morning," she called to them cheerfully. "Welcome to Tambora. Please come in. The sun is terribly fierce this morning." And every God damned morning, she said under her breath, as she felt perspiration trickle between her breasts.

"Oh," Blythe gasped, straightening the skirt on her matronly dress. "Forgive us, we didn't see you. We were just... admiring your home."

"Thank you. I'm Elsa Killain, Victoria Millburn's sister-in-law. Victoria hasn't arrived back from Alice Springs yet, so I'll have to give you the Royal Tour of the property myself."

"I'm Blythe Horton, and this is Herbert Quinlan," Blythe said. "As you probably know, we're from the Department of Children's Services."

"Yes, do come in. Victoria told me to expect you, but I didn't think you'd be here so soon."

"As a rule, we don't get out to the rural areas very much, but we had business in Alice Springs," Blythe explained.

It was easy to imagine that Herbert Quinlan was normally the epitome of neatness, but an hour and a half travelling with Rex Crawley, over a rough track and sand hills, had made the difference between neat and tousled, glaringly obvious. He was a tall gentleman, possibly in his late fifties, with spectacles and thin grey hair. He wore pinstriped trousers held up with braces and a shirt that had an hour ago been crisp and white, but was now crinkled and stained with rubber and dust from the tyre that Rex had convinced him to change. His bow tie was also askew, and Elsa could tell Mrs. Horton was longing to straighten it.

Despite her abundance, Blythe had a pinched face that would scare the bravest child. Noting Elsa's poise, she self-consciously patted her once neat brown hair into some kind of order. Elsa's first overall impression of Blythe took in legs that looked like sticks out of a potato body, and biceps that appeared capable of giving any tattooed sailor a run for his money in an arm wrestle.

As only a woman can do, Blythe swept a look over Elsa that took in an astonishing amount of detail. She noted her floral summer printed dress, with white collar and cuffs, white court shoes, lace gloves and a single strand of pearls, and decided she looked nice, but somewhat out of place in the outback. Her opinion did an about-face, however, when she stepped into the elegant tiled entrance hall of the house. She thought Tambora was magnificent, and Elsa looked every bit the lady of such a grand home.

"Oh, my, what a wonderful home, Mrs. Killain," she exclaimed. She'd never seen anything like it. She could see her reflection in the tiled entrance floor, and the stair banister and furniture gleamed. The mirrors and windows sparkled, and the potted palms lent an air of coolness.

"Thank you. We find it comfortable. Do come into the living room and sit down. I'll have our house girl fetch you something cool to drink, or would you prefer a nice cup of tea?"

"Tea would be wonderful, wouldn't it, Herbert?"

"Yes, yes, tea will do nicely. The drive out here was hair-raising to say the least. I don't think our driver had sobered up since last night." His spectacles bobbed up and down on his nose, as he dabbed the back of his neck with a handkerchief.

Elsa didn't have the heart to tell him Rex always drove like a lunatic. "Wombat Creek is a small town, so it's a big event when there's a birth. I think we're so lucky to have such an efficient mail service, though. Rex will bring almost anything out here for us."

The officials didn't look impressed so Elsa called Nerida, and a moment later they could hear the echo of clopping shoes coming across the entrance hall.

Blythe and Herbert turned to look at the living room door in expectation, as Nerida appeared. To Elsa's horror she was standing pigeon-toed, and she looked about to vomit.

"Nerida, could you bring tea for us, and some of Sanja's tea cakes?" Elsa said in her politest voice.

"Yes, Missus." Nerida did one of her awkward curtsies and turned to clop, clop down the hall again.

A few minutes later, while discussing the number of rooms needed to accommodate twelve children, they heard a mighty crash.

Elsa excused herself and found Nerida had dropped the tea tray in the hall outside the kitchen. Tea, sugar and milk had splashed the walls and floor, and Sanja's delicious cakes were crumbled amid smashed pieces of Victoria's china cups and elegant tea service.

"Girl can't walk in shoes," Sanja said accusingly, as he hastily cleaned up the mess while Nerida cried.

"Oh my Lord," Elsa exclaimed. "Pull yourself together, Nerida, and bring more tea. I'll take our guests on a tour upstairs."

"What they here for, Missus Killain?" Sanja asked. He'd come to the conclusion they were not ordinary guests.

"If they like the house, Victoria has plans to take in orphaned and homeless children, about a dozen of them I believe."

Sanja straightened up. "Who cook for all these children?"

"You will, of course."

"Sanja no cook for that many children. Too much work."

Elsa fought the urge to scream in frustration, and thought quickly. "The government will be paying rather well, Sanja, which means you'd receive wages, good wages. I'll even ask Victoria to give you a raise. Whatever you like, within reason."

Sanja thought for a moment, then nodded and smiled. "Can't be too hard cooking for children. Children eat anything."

Elsa knew Sanja had just called her bluff, but she couldn't worry about that now.

As Elsa made her way upstairs with the officials, Blythe paused on the landing.

"In the notes we were given, Mrs. Killain, it says you and Mrs. Milburn are widows. Is that true?"

"Yes, that's right."

"I'm afraid I will have to point out that as single women, you are at a disadvantage."

"I don't understand?"

"At least half the children we are trying to place are boys, very boisterous boys. They really need a man around to keep them in line. I'm sure they'd play havoc with you and Mrs. Milburn out here." She imagined them literally running wild.

Elsa thought of the money they needed so desperately. "Surely Victoria told you how many men she employs, Mrs. Horton."

"No, she didn't."

"Obviously she didn't think it was of any consequence. She's been running this station for years since her husband died, and has done a marvelous job for a woman. Every man in the area agrees. But not counting the chef, five men work for her full time. I understand, that before the drought, there were many more. Tadd Sweeney, the station manager, is considered practically family. The other workers are station hands, who've been with Victoria for years. They live on the property and sleep in the bunkhouse out back. I think I should also point out that I raised twin boys, so I fully understand the meaning of boisterous."

Blythe smiled insipidly, but Elsa did not feel reassured.

Elsa was showing Blythe and Herbert the bedrooms, when suddenly Tadd appeared at the open doorway of Jack's room, startling her.

"Where's Tara and the children?" he hissed.

Elsa could see he was in an ugly mood, and tried to draw him out into the hall, but he wouldn't budge. Blythe and Herbert were on the far side of the room, near the open balcony doors, but Tadd had their full attention.

Elsa tried to smile reassuringly. "They've returned to Ireland, Tadd. I thought you were told?"

Tadd scowled at her. "No one told me." It was obvious he seriously doubted Elsa was telling the truth. Ignoring the visitors, he glanced about the room. He was looking for Jack's belongings, but he could see none. He went down the hall and looked in Tara's room, and then Hannah's. Their personal belongings had gone also. Elsa followed him.

"When did they go?" Tadd demanded to know, finally believing she had told him the truth. He thought Tara must have known she'd be caught out, and she was running scared.

"Yesterday," Elsa lied. "She thought it best if she took the children home, to their Aunt." Elsa glanced at Jack's bedroom door, where she could see the bottom of Blythe's skirt protruding into the hall. She was obviously eavesdropping.

Elsa could tell Tadd was ropeable because Tara had thwarted his plans. It was no use telling the government officials about her and the children now, if she wasn't on the station. He stormed down the stairs. Elsa watched him go. As he passed Nerida, Elsa noticed the girl put her head down in fear.

"Who was that ...man?" Blythe asked when Elsa came back into the room.

Elsa was hesitant to reply. She was trembling and her nerves were ragged. She hadn't expected Tadd to come into the house after Tara had told him not to. Obviously Tara had been right about his intention to make trouble for her. Thank goodness Ethan had come up with the idea of her going bush with the children and some tribal members.

"Tadd is the... station manager. He was away working... when a guest of ours left to return to Ireland with her children."

"He didn't seem to believe they had gone," Herbert said, clearly suspicious and thinking Tadd was a typical surly Irishman. In his opinion, he didn't behave like one of the family.

"He became very fond of the children... while they were here. He has none of his own, you see, that is why it will be lovely to have children on the station. Tadd intends to spend a lot of time with them, teaching them all about farming sheep and cattle." Blythe and Herbert gave each other a dubious look, and Elsa wondered if she'd said the wrong thing. Tadd's lack of manners and mistrusting nature weren't exactly appealing qualities for someone in whom you planned to place the care and trust of children.

"Who would be giving the children their formal schooling?" Herbert asked.

Elsa tried to remember what Tara had told her. "I, that is Victoria and I were planning to do that. We'll get lessons from a local mission, and give the children at least two hours a day of reading and writing, and sums. The rest of the time they can learn to shoe horses, and shear sheep and the like. If any of them are interested in cooking, we have an excellent chef. I was also thinking of tutoring them in painting. There are some excellent landscapes around here"

The officials frowned in confusion, thinking that surely she wasn't referring to the Great Victoria Desert. West of Lake Eyre the plains were sandy and Mulga-clad, with low tablelands, certainly nothing that captured the eye.

"How nice. I'd like to see the kitchen," Blythe said. "Sanitation is very important when raising children."

"Of course," Elsa said, confidant that the kitchen was always in order, even when the rest of the house was in chaos.

Elsa should have known something was amiss when she took Blythe and Herbert down the hallway, and found a trail of flour leading from the cellar door, which was wide open, to the kitchen. Shouts of hysteria could be heard coming from the kitchen, and the thumping of something hitting the floor. Shrieking in terror, a shoeless Nerida ran past them to her room, leaving white footprints in her wake, and almost slipping on the remnants of the hastily cleaned up morning tea. Elsa's first thoughts were that Sanja had been attacking the girl, and she was mortified.

Elsa went to the kitchen door, closely followed by her guests, and peered inside, and her jaw dropped. An open sack of flour stood leaning against a cupboard door with its contents spilling out over the floor. Sanja was running around the kitchen like a mad man, chasing at least three enormous cockroaches with a broom. For a moment Elsa stood watching the small Indian man in disbelief. He was almost beside himself with hysteria, shouting at the top of his voice, while clouds of flour wafted in the air to settle over his normally pristine kitchen.

Elsa was only barely aware of Blythe and Herbert standing beside her. "Sanja," she shouted. "What on earth are you doing?"

Suddenly Elsa was elbowed aside, as Blythe entered the kitchen. With the precision of an expert and lightning speed for one so large, she stamped her foot on one of the loathsome cockroaches, and then another. Sanja got the third one with the broom, and the two stood looking at each other triumphantly.

"They're vile creatures," Blythe said. "I detest them."

Sanja glanced at Elsa's now colourless face. "Roaches in my flour, Missus. Mice make hole, and then they get in."

Elsa nodded mutely. Mice! Cockroaches! Oh, God! She felt her head go light. Could things get any worse?

A moment later she found her voice and said the first thing that came to mind, - something completely ridiculous under the circumstances, but she was desperate to give the impression everything was under control, even though that couldn't have been further from the truth. "How … is lunch progressing?" she asked breathlessly, then collapsed.

Ten minutes later Elsa came round, and found herself on the sofa in the living room, with Blythe Horton standing over her. "What happened?" she asked, sitting up quickly. Her head swooned, and she fell back against the cushions.

"You fainted dear," Blythe said, patting her hand.

"Oh, no. I'm terribly sorry."

"My sister used to faint at the sight of a mouse. It seems you're not partial to cockroaches. Don't worry about it. Mr. Crawley has returned early, so we are heading back to town."

"But lunch…" Elsa said, barely thinking coherently enough to realize they probably wouldn't want lunch from a kitchen where mice and cockroaches were running rampant. "Sanja has lamb cold cuts and pickles and boiled goose eggs…"

"Never mind, dear. Herbert is keen to catch the afternoon train to Adelaide."

"But… what shall I tell Victoria?"

"We'll notify her of our decision in a few days."

Although Elsa wasn't feeling herself, Blythe's tone left her in little doubt that the decision would be a negative one.

"We'll see ourselves out," Blythe said, and left with Herbert.

Elsa struggled to her feet. "I can't believe I worked like a slave, and all for nothing," she sobbed. "I've got blisters and raw skin…" She glanced at her hands, expecting to see gloves, and her heart plummeted. Blythe had removed her gloves, revealing hands that made a scullery maid's look like the hands of royalty. She felt utterly humiliated. She had to explain herself to the Blythe and Herbert, for Tara and Victoria's sake. They were depending on her, and she just couldn't let them down.

Out on the veranda Elsa could see Blythe and Herbert disappearing into Rex's automobile. Rex had a mouthful of teacake, so he couldn't call to her. He also had a cake in the hand he was waving with.

"Wait," Elsa shouted.

A few moments later they were gone. If not for the trail of dust snaking into the distance under a vast blue sky, Elsa would have thought she had imagined their visit.

CHAPTER THIRTY

Jabba Jurra's favourite place in the late afternoon was the shade of a gidgee tree. Using ochre, he was painting traditional dot patterns on bark, with Jack and Hannah beside him, imitating his work on rocks. Tara and Nugget were seated by the campfire, deep in conversation with Jackie Kantji. Using Nugget as an interpreter, Jackie was telling Tara stories about his days as a horse-breaker. Nugget claimed that Jackie was the best horse-breaker in the Broken Hill/Wilcannia area, where there were thousands of wild brumbies, some of which were broken in for stock horses for the big stations up there.

"White men up that way always bet on Jackie," Nugget said proudly. "Them make lots of money."

"How long has Jackie been blind?" Tara asked him. She could see the old man enjoyed reliving his glory days as a famous horse breaker. "It's so tragic that he can't see anymore."

"Darkness bin comin' long time, Missus, but Jackie still sees everything, in here." He pointed to his head. Tara thought he was referring to his memories, until Jackie turned toward the bush, pointed, and said something to Nugget.

"Ethan is coming, Missus," Nugget said.

"How do you know?"

"Jackie told me." He gestured to the bush behind them. Tara turned, but she couldn't see or hear anything beyond the Mulga scrub. She thought Jackie was imagining things, and felt sorry for him. But he sat waiting patiently, and three minutes later Ethan appeared.

"How did Jackie know he was coming?" Tara asked Nugget in utter surprise. Ethan was on Hannibal. Compared to a horse, a camel treads quietly through the bush, so it would have been almost impossible for Jackie to hear him coming from any distance.

Nugget grinned but didn't reply.

Tara couldn't believe Jackie had known Ethan was coming. There were so many distracting noises in the bush, insects, birds, and animals crunching through the dry Mitchell and spinifex grasses. In fact, the noises were so noticeable at night, with kangaroos, emus, rabbits and wombats coming and going through the campsite, as well as the symphony of insects, that Tara had been unable to sleep.

"The visitors have been and gone?" Ethan said as he poured himself a fragrant mug of tea from the Billy.

"Is everything all right? Did Tadd try to cause trouble?"

"I haven't spoken to your mother, but I think it's safe to return to the homestead. Charlie saw Rex drive away with the visitors when he went back to the homestead about lunchtime for fresh horses." Ethan glanced at the children. "Have Jack and Hannah enjoyed camping out?"

"They've loved it. Jabba Jurra has been showing them all sorts of interesting things. They found sugar ants and witchety grubs..."

Ethan smiled. "Did they eat them?"

"Jack has surprised me. He's been game to try anything, but Hannah would only eat damper. She did enjoy hooking the grubs out of the ground with a stick, though."

"What about you? Have you tried witchety grubs?"

Tara wrinkled her nose. "Certainly not, but I did try snake last night. To be honest," Tara grinned at Nugget, "it was good tucker, but I was so hungry, I would've eaten the bark off the trees."

Ethan laughed, but then he became serious, his gaze intent on her. Tara remembered the kiss they had shared and was sure he was doing the same, especially when his gaze came to rest on her mouth and she felt herself grow warm.

"I've enjoyed being out here, Ethan, and so have the children, but I can't help wondering if Tadd bought the story about us going back to Ireland. I've been worrying about my mother having to deal with him."

"I'm sure she's all right, but we'll head back now if you're concerned."

Tara and the children said goodbye to Jackie Kantji and Jabba Jurra and thanked them for their hospitality. Both men expressed that they had enjoyed having company. Nugget said the old men had been lonely, as they hadn't been able to go walkabout with the rest of the tribe because Jackie wasn't well enough. His knees and one of his hips were giving him a lot of pain, and the tribal medicines were of no help.

"No medicine can cure old age," Nugget told her matter-of-factly. "Jackie is ready for the spirit world."

"Tell me how Jackie knew Ethan was approaching the camp?" Tara asked Nugget on the journey back to the station. "I didn't hear or see him."

Nugget grinned. "He just know, Missus."

"There's a lot about Aborigines we can't explain or understand," Ethan added. "They have an indigenous sense of the land, the seasons, and everything living, the plants, the animals, even the insects."

Tara had been wondering whether Jackie had an acute sense of hearing, or whether he was possessed with a type of extraordinary sixth sense, like a Seer. Whichever it was, it made her talent seem insignificant.

Tara and the children arrived back at the homestead with Nugget and Ethan at dusk. At the same time, Rex's car pulled up. Tara was alarmed, and hid behind the stables with Jack and Hannah, thinking the government officials had returned on Tadd's advice.

"It's Victoria," Ethan said looking out for her, "and she has another woman with her. She's elderly but very dignified. I've never seen her before."

"Sorrel," Tara squealed. A moment later she was running toward the house with the children.

"Sorrel, how wonderful to see you," she shouted excitedly.

Standing beside the car, Sorrel and Victoria looked at her with their mouths agape.

"What's the matter?" Tara asked, then realized she must look a fright. Her hair was unbrushed; her clothes were filthy, as were the children's, who also had ochre smeared on their faces.

"What on earth have you been doing?" Victoria asked. She was wearing dark-framed glasses, which didn't suit her in the least, but Tara was just pleased she could see.

Tara laughed. "Can you see me clearly, Aunt?"

"Not perfectly. These glasses are temporary, thank goodness, they're awful. Mine will be ready in a few weeks, but I can still see how dirty you are. Surely you haven't been doing more gardening?"

"No, we've been camping."

"Camping?"

"Yes, I'll explain everything in good time."

Sorrel laughed. "I do believe you've gone native, Tara," she said, embracing her. "And Jack and Hannah have grown so much in a few short weeks, and they're so brown, or is that dirt?" She touched the freckles on Jack's nose with her finger and examined it.

"It's dirt and paint," Jack said grinning.

"I brought you all presents," Sorrel said, and the children's eyes lit up. "But first, Victoria has promised me a good strong drink, and believe me, I need it." She cast Rex an accusing glare.

"You need a drink?" Rex said in disbelief. "It's my second journey out here today. One thing's certain, this time I'm staying the night."

"I suppose they've all got hangovers in town," Ethan said, as he approached.

"You're not wrong. Ferris is as grumpy as a bear this morning. The baby has been crying all night, which did nothing for his bad head."

While introductions were made, Tara and the children got cleaned up quickly and joined everyone in the living room. As they came in, Tara heard Elsa talking about the government official's visit.

"I don't think they were very impressed," Elsa said despondently, after telling them about the disaster in the kitchen, which made Rex and Ethan laugh. "I'm terribly sorry, Victoria. I feel as if I've let you down."

"You can never tell with these things, Elsa, so don't worry about it," Victoria said. "It's no use pretending that catastrophes don't happen out here in the bush, because they do. You did your best, and from what I can see, the house looks absolutely wonderful."

"The house does look really nice, mother," Tara said. "I can't believe you did it all in just two days. You must have worked from dawn till dusk."

"And half the night," Elsa said, "but it made little difference in the end."

"Didn't Nerida help you, Elsa?" Victoria asked. "Sanja told me she came back a few days ago, but I don't know where she's hiding."

Elsa flicked a glance at Tara. "She's still not well, Victoria," she said.

"Oh. What's wrong with her? Maybe she should see a real doctor. The bush nurses are darn good, but they don't know everything."

"It's nothing serious, but we'll talk about that later, Aunt," Tara said. "How did you like Alice Springs?"

"It's grown since I was last there. There are too many people now, at least three hundred, and shops, a boarding house and a garage… but Sorrel was a marvellous host, and I had a wonderful time. By God, I missed this place, though."

"How do you like Alice, Sorrel? And how is your son?"

"Marcus is very well, and the hotel is doing nicely. They've expanded it recently and insisted I work in the bar for the first week or so, to get to know the locals. That was an experience I can tell you. Some of the locals are a rough bunch, but I must admit people from the outback have a great sense of humour."

"And the town?"

"At first I absolutely detested Alice. The heat and flies were unbearable and the dust never stops blowing, and not a green tree in sight. But since I've been helping the governess at Adelaide House and The Inland Mission Hostel, I've been too busy to think much about the weather, or the dust and flies. I suppose you could say I've adapted."

"What do you do?"

"I teach drama and give music lessons, and I love it. It takes me back to the days before I married, when I used to work in theatre."

Tara could see Sorrel was fulfilled, and it made her happy. "I had to drag her away," Victoria said.

"That's not true," Sorrel admonished. "If you wouldn't come to Alice, Tara, then I had to come here and see how you were doing."

"I'm really glad you did."

"Tell us why you went bush," Victoria asked, as she served drinks from a tray that Sanja had just brought in.

Tara glanced at Ethan. She was about to speak up when Tadd walked in. He spotted Tara straight away, and his eyes narrowed viciously.

"I knew you hadn't gone back to Ireland," he hissed. He glared at Elsa, who managed to look unrepentant, even though she was quivering.

"Back to Ireland?" Victoria said. "What on earth are you talking about, Tadd?"

"I can explain," Tara said.

"I bet you can," Tadd growled.

"Allow me," Ethan interrupted. He stood up and glared at Tadd. "I think we should talk privately, though, Victoria. Will you come through to the dining room?"

"Whatever for, Ethan? I don't understand."

"Please, Aunt," Tara said.

"We'll go out onto the veranda, where it's cooler," Elsa said. "Come on children, Riordan, Mr. Crawley, Mrs. Windspear?"

"Call me Sorrel, please Elsa. Mrs. Windspear makes me feel like someone's eccentric Aunt. No offence, Victoria." She got to her feet and followed the others out.

Victoria barely heard Sorrel's remark, although she had become used to her dry sense of humour. She was preoccupied with trying to work out what Ethan was going to tell her.

"Now what's this about?" Victoria asked. She had realized that Tara would not want to see the government officials, but she intended to explain to her in private that she had not listed her as an official carer, therefore no questions would be asked about her personal circumstances. She also had bad news from Marcus in regard to her legally adopting the children, which they needed to discuss when they were alone.

"Aunt," Tara said, "I have to tell you some news about the station, and it's going to be a devastating shock for you."

Victoria's eyes widened. "What is it?"

Tara glanced at Tadd, hating him for the pain she knew her aunt would feel. "Tadd has been borrowing money from the bank against the station, a lot of money."

Victoria turned to Tadd, who was standing behind her. "Surely that's not true, Tadd?"

Tadd dropped his gaze to the floor and sighed. "I'm afraid it is true, Victoria. But I didn't want you to know until I'd sorted it out."

"He's also been mining opal on the property," Ethan added. "That's where Jack was when he couldn't be found. He'd fallen down the mine."

Victoria gasped.

"And I got him out," Tadd said. He could see Victoria was stunned. He came around to her, and sat beside her on the sofa, taking her trembling hands in his.

"I had to borrow money to keep the station going, Victoria," he said. "I know it was wrong, and you were always against it, but if I hadn't done it, we would've lost this place over a year ago."

"That's still going to happen, Tadd," Tara said angrily. "But not only will my Aunt lose the station, she'll be in debt for the rest of her life. I'm going to see you go to jail for what you've done."

"Now hold on Tara," Victoria said, fighting tears. "I'm sure Tadd can explain..."

"You won't lose Tambora, Victoria," Tadd said quietly. "I promise you that..."

"I know how much debt there is," Ethan said. "I've spoken to the bank manager. No matter what you do, you can't put off the inevitable. I'm really sorry, Victoria."

"Is it that bad?" Victoria asked, tears running down her cheeks. "Couldn't the money for the wool we're going to export get us out of trouble?"

Tears filled Tara's eyes. She knew how much her aunt was suffering. "I'm afraid not, Aunt, and instead of working to save the station, Tadd's been trying to fill his own pockets," she said "He wouldn't even help us round up the sheep when we found out the deadline for the wool to be exported had been moved forward. I've been helping Nugget, so has Ethan and Riordan, even Jack, but not Tadd."

"I wanted to work the mine…"

"We know. You don't think you fooled us with that bad back story, do you?"

"Why didn't you tell me about the mine?" Victoria asked Tadd in disbelief. "I've trusted you all these years. My God, Tadd, I thought of you as family."

Tara was holding her breath, waiting for Victoria to fire Tadd.

"Victoria, I know this looks bad, but I did what I did for you. I was mining the opal to pay back the debt to the bank. I thought that was more important. I hoped I'd find a good vein and we'd never have to worry about money again."

"What lies," Tara spat. "You told Ethan and myself that you found virtually nothing, but that's not true either, is it Tadd? You intended to keep all your riches for yourself."

A strange look crept into Tadd's eyes. Tara could only describe it as menacing. She suspected he was wondering if she knew about his opal stash. He could hardly deny the truth if she did.

"I have found a substantial amount of opal, which is none of your business, Tara." He looked at Victoria, who was staring back at him as if he was a stranger. He knew he had to do something drastic, or he'd find himself out of a job and a home. The last few years he'd virtually ruled the roost, but since Tara had come, Victoria's confidence was returning to what it had once been. "It's enough to cover the debt, and I intend to pay off the loan in the next few days. All the months I've worked secretly were so that you need not have the worry of ever knowing how close to the bone we've gone over the last year or so. This drought has been devastating, and we couldn't have survived without that extra money. I know more than anyone what Tambora means to you, Victoria, and I swear I only had your best interest at heart."

Tara and Ethan glanced at each other in shock. Somehow Tadd was making himself look more like a hero than a villain.

"Are you sure you've got the debt covered, Tadd?" Victoria asked.

"Yes. I've checked out what the opal is worth, and there's enough to cover everything I've borrowed. I hope you can forgive me for deceiving you. I just didn't want you to worry."

Victoria sighed with relief. "I'm not pleased you didn't discuss this with me, but it seems there's no harm done."

"No harm done… Aunt, he forged your signature on bank documents," Tara said. "That's illegal."

"Out here, Tara, a drought can make a person desperate. As long as we've still got

Tambora, and we can export wool, I'm sure we'll be all right. From now on, I'll be looking after the books."

Tara thought of telling her Aunt that Tadd had threatened her and the children, but she held back only because she didn't want her further upset. She could also have told her why she went bush but knew it would do no good. In her aunt's eyes, Tadd was a loyal and trusted friend and employee. She wondered if Victoria knew he had stolen the letter from William Crombie, would she still think he had only her best interest at heart?

"I'm going to the bank with you, Tadd," Ethan said determinedly. "I'm sure that won't be necessary, Ethan," Victoria said.

"It's all right," Tadd said. "I don't mind the company, even Ethan's." Tadd looked at Victoria again. "I'm rather exhausted, Victoria. If you don't mind, I think I'll retire?"

"Of course, Tadd. Good night."

"It's good to have you home lass, and I'm glad we have everything out in the open." Tadd stood up and gave Tara a sly look of triumph, and left the room.

Tara heard her aunt mumble, "Poor Tadd," and shook her head in disbelief. She had hoped her aunt would fire him, but it was obvious he could do no wrong in her eyes.

"Your mother looks so dispirited, Tara," Victoria said. "I think we should throw a party to celebrate the birth of Ferris and Charity's baby. That would cheer her up, and everyone loves to toast a new baby. We certainly don't have many in the area."

Tara didn't know what to say. She'd thought they would've been having a wake, but instead they were going to have a party. It was too much for her.

Elsa was coming through the door and heard the last few words Victoria said. "Did you say we're throwing a party, Victoria?" The thought of entertaining in such a grand home thrilled her.

"Yes. It's about time we had some fun out here. We've had enough worry to last a lifetime. It will also give Sorrel the chance to meet the locals."

Elsa's face lit up. "Oh, how wonderful, Victoria."

"I'll get on the radio first thing in the morning and spread the word," Victoria said. "There's actually another new baby on the way," Tara said, thinking now was as good a time as any to tell Victoria the news, especially when they were getting everything out in the open.

Victoria looked astonished. "Oh! Who is expecting?"

"Nerida!" Tara said.

"That is why she's been ill," Elsa added.

"My goodness. I go away for a few days and ...Who's the father?"

"We don't know, and she won't say. She's actually terrified you are going to send her away, that's why she'd hiding."

"I wondered where she was. What nonsense! Nerida is part of the family, and I love her. I'd never send her away."

"I think she'll be relieved to hear that."

"Thank goodness I've got glasses," Victoria said. "Now maybe I'll be able to see what's going on right under my nose."

True to her word, Victoria was on the radio bright and early the next morning. By lunchtime, the word had spread like a bushfire on a windy day, Victoria was throwing one of her famous parties on Tambora, and everyone wanted to come. The lavish parties of years gone by were still talked about by the locals.

Late that night, Victoria and Tara got on the radio and called Lottie and the girls, and invited them. The invitation was sincere, and Lottie was touched to receive it, but it came as no surprise to Victoria and Tara when she declined.

"Thank you so much for asking us," Lottie said, and they heard the emotion in her voice. "You'll never know how much it means to me."

"Thank you for everything you've done for us," Tara said. "You've been a very good friend, and we'll always be in your debt."

Lottie barely said 'over and out' before she was crying.

The next morning a package arrived on the train from Adelaide. It was addressed to Victoria. Tadd was in town picking up supplies. He'd been to the bank in Leigh Creek with Ethan, and he was in a very surly mood. It had taken all of his opal to pay off the debt and the interest he'd incurred, and he'd had some good pieces. In his mind, that meant all his hard work had been for nothing. He knew if he'd denied having it, Ethan would have found it and turned it over to Victoria, because legally it was hers. If only Jack hadn't fallen into the mine, it would never have been found. He cursed the day Tara and the children came to Tambora.

Tadd's initial plan had been to use the opal to buy the station from Victoria, when she'd had enough, and it was virtually worthless. Then one day Victoria told him she'd left the station to him in her will, so it was only a matter of time... and meanwhile he could treat it as his own. Then Tara arrived, and quite by accident, while he was searching for her emergency money he found Victoria's will, and she'd changed it. Tara was to inherit the station.

"Perhaps I should marry Victoria", Tadd thought, not for the first time giving the idea serious consideration. "Then Tambora would be mine and there would be nothing Tara could do about it." He had asked Victoria to marry him after Tom had died, but she'd refused him, saying it was too soon to think about marriage to someone else. Perhaps now she might seriously contemplate the idea, he thought

"Someone from Ireland has sent Victoria a painting," Percy told Tadd when he came in. Tadd only grunted with disinterest.

"I know it's a painting because the wrapping is torn on the corner."

Tadd wasn't listening. He was selecting items from a poorly stocked shelf.

"I wonder if it's worth anything?" Percy mumbled to himself. "It's from a Gallery." As Percy lifted the painting over the counter, the torn paper caught on the corner of the counter, and ripped open. "Oh, Hell," he said, turning the painting over. "Now look what I've done." When he looked at the face revealed, he gasped in disbelief. "It can't be…" he said. "My Lord, it's… Tara."

Tadd turned from the shelf, with the extra tins of food that Victoria had ordered for the party.

"What's Tara?" he asked, coming over to the counter, and dropping the tins. He tore what was left of the paper from the painting and looked at the portrait, and his face lit up. Suddenly he felt a whole lot better. "Fancy a drink in the bar, Percy? I'm shouting."

When Tadd arrived back at the station with the portrait, he had a bounce in his step. He found Victoria talking to Tara in the living room, and could barely contain the excitement he felt.

"I've contacted the shearers, and they have promised to be here bright and early in the morning," Victoria said to Tara. "So we're all set. It should only take five of them two days at the most to shear one thousand sheep, even less if Wally Sherbourne comes, so we should have no trouble meeting our deadline." Victoria looked up and saw Tadd standing in the doorway.

"Oh, Tadd. You're back. Did you get the extra supplies I wanted?" With her temporary glasses, Victoria could see Tadd had been drinking. His eyes were bright and he had a small smile on his lips. She thought he had been celebrating paying off the loan.

"Yes, but you won't be needing them any more."

"What on earth do you mean?"

"No-one's coming to your party."

If Tara wasn't mistaken, he didn't sound displeased or upset for Victoria. She wondered what he was up to now.

"What are you talking about, Tadd? Everyone I have spoken to has accepted my invitation."

"Well they've changed their minds."

"Why would they do that?"

"Because of the 'gipsy'." He glared at Tara, who'd lost all colour in her face.

"This," he reached for the painting which he'd stood behind the door, "arrived on the train today." He turned the painting around and held it up. "Percy said to apologize for the wrapping getting ripped on the counter in the store."

The portrait was the one Tara had sold to the Harcourt Gallery before she left Ireland. She'd always thought it was one of Garvie's finest works, but she'd never been more displeased to see it. In the portrait, she was dancing around the campfire with her full skirts held up to reveal shapely legs, and her back arched and her head thrown back. The firelight was playing on her long legs and full breasts, making her skin look like golden silk. Her mouth was slightly open, her lips moist and full, and her emerald green eyes half closed. Her hair was like burnished copper, the firelight shining through it. She looked seductive, a real gipsy temptress.

Tadd was still holding up the painting when Riordan walked into the living room.

"Where did you get that?" he asked him.

"It came on the train today."

Riordan looked at Tara's stricken face before she buried it in her hands. "Kelvin must have sent it," he said. "I had forgotten I asked him to return it to Victoria."

"Oh, Aunt. I'm so sorry," Tara said before she ran from the room in tears.

"I'm afraid Percy saw the painting before I could do anything about it, Victoria," Tadd said. "There was no stopping him telling everyone in the hotel about it. You know how loose-lipped he becomes when he's had a few… The men were so… shocked. I tried to defend Tara, but you know how people are."

"Yes," Victoria said. "I know how people are."

Another portrait of Tara had hung in the dining room for a year before she'd sent it to Riordan. The men who saw it had admired her beauty, but Victoria had known the women sniggered behind her back about her having a gipsy for a relative. Fortunately, no one had recognized Tara when she came to the outback, except Ethan. Now everyone would know she'd lived as a gipsy.

Victoria didn't mind what they said about her, and Tara claimed she was used to being vilified by people who looked down on her, but Victoria was certain the gossiping would destroy Elsa.

CHAPTER THIRTY-ONE

Nugget was up before daybreak to give feed and water to the sheep. He was pumping water from the bore, when he heard the shearers arrive. They were always a noisy bunch, especially the gun-shearer, Wally Sherbourne, a big man in his late thirties, with a mat of dark hair on his back and shoulders, and almost none on his head. He could shear one hundred and fifty sheep a day, in temperatures sometimes over one hundred and forty degrees in the sheds, but the sweat would 'leak' from his body as if he was a bucket full of holes.

After filling the troughs with water for the thirsty sheep, Nugget went over to the sheds to greet the men. He usually prepared damper and tea for them before they started work, but Tadd had told him that the men wouldn't be arriving until after nine o'clock. Nugget thought this was odd, as they always started at first light, but Tadd hadn't given him a reason why today would be different. Before Nugget got to the open door of the sheds, he heard Tadd's voice, and stopped.

"I'm surprised to see you boys here," Tadd said in a cocky tone, which confused Nugget, as the shearers were expected.

"Victoria said she needed the job done urgently," Wally said, sharpening his shears on the boards with the precision of an expert.

"Where's Nugget with our tea and damper," Wonky Warburton asked. He was a slight man, but as tough as an old shoe. He'd lost one eye when he was hit in the face with a flying piece of paper bark swirling in a Willie Willie, and wore a patch, but he was still one of the best shearers in South Australia.

"To be honest, I told him not to bother to come down this morning. I thought for sure you wouldn't be coming."

"Why did ya think that?" Wonky asked.

"You mustn't have heard the news getting around town," Tadd said. "Maybe it's just as well."

"What news is that?" Wally asked. The other four men were intrigued and stopped what they were doing to listen to what Tadd had to say, but Wally kept working.

"Well, I probably shouldn't be saying anything, but I suppose you have as much right to know as anyone else. Victoria's niece is living here, and everyone in town has just found out she used to live with the gipsies in Ireland."

"Percy mentioned that last night, but so what, I say?" Wonky said. "I used to live with a woman who's grandmother was supposed to be a gipsy. Bloody lovely she was, and a darned good cook, but she left me. She said I was as stupid as gallah when I got a few drinks in me, and I couldn't argue with that."

"Not everyone is as liberal minded as you, Wonky," Tadd said. "I'm not judgmental myself, but apparently Tara used to dance for the men for money. Anyway, no one wants anything to do with her, or it seems anyone that associates with her, including Victoria. And you know, if they'd turn on Victoria, they'd turn on anyone. I'd say you're risking future jobs just coming out here."

Nugget was shocked. Tara had told him about the gipsy painting when he'd noticed she wasn't her usual bright self, and commented. Although he couldn't see any problem with her having shared her life with the gipsies, and he told her so, he understood all too well about white folks being bigoted. What he didn't understand was why Tadd was telling the shearers about it.

"I doubt it will affect us," Wally said, getting back to his work. As a shearer touring the country from Kangaroo Island in the south, to the high country in New South Wales, he'd seen and heard almost everything. Nothing surprised him, and he made it a point not to get mixed up with station problems or politics. He just sheared the sheep and got out. He had actually heard the men talking in the Wombat Creek Hotel, but he'd turned off and gone outside for a game of 'two up' with Ferris. He was heading south in the next week or so, to the Flinders Ranges, and he didn't want any trouble meanwhile.

"Victoria had planned to hold a big party this weekend. Everyone was coming until they found out about Tara. Not one of them will show up now. But it's up to you whether you want to take the risk of getting work or not. I know some of you have families to feed and work is scarce at the moment. I just wanted to put you in the picture." Tadd could see the men were not wholly convinced. He thought he'd let them moll over what he'd said, and went to walk out of the sheds, but suddenly had an inkling of an idea and hesitated. "Aren't you going to Bill MacDonald's after you've finished here?"

"Yes, that's right. Like most folks out here, he's selling his wool to the Wool Board. They don't give a good price, but the station owners have to recoup their loses."

"Well, I won't let on you came here. You know how Bill is? He barely puts up with the abo's. I don't think he'd be too pleased to have anyone around who sympathizes with gipsies, especially as he comes from Wimbledon, one of those 'toffee' areas in England where they have no time for the likes of tinkers."

"This is the first work we've had for weeks, Tadd. We can't afford to knock it back. Les has got a girl pregnant, and her father's after him with a shot gun, and Jock's missus has another bun in the oven."

Tadd was becoming frustrated, but he still had one hand he hadn't played. It was underhanded, but he was desperate. "I understand, Wally. By the way, I suppose you know Victoria is exporting this wool to India, so you won't be getting paid for some time."

"She didn't say anything about us having to wait for our money. We've never had to before."

"Well, I'm sorry, but things are a bit different now. She's got a house full, with Tara and the children, her sister-in-law, and a Gallery owner from Ireland, and now another visitor from Alice."

"I'm not risking losing a paying job on MacDonald's Station for money I won't be getting for months. I have five kids to feed and we all have debts to settle."

The other men mumbled in agreement. Their debts were mostly tabs at hotels, including the Wombat Creek, where they'd run up quite a debt the previous night. Wally also owed Ferris a few pounds on 'two up' bets he'd lost.

"I'm sorry, Tadd, but we'll have to go," Wally said.

Nugget heard the men packing up to leave. He wanted to stop them, but he couldn't. Knowing how upset the Missus would be, he shook his head in frustration.

"I understand, Wally," Tadd said. "You have to do what you think is best." Nugget turned and walked away in disgust, his heart heavy for the 'Missus'.

Tadd walked out of the sheds, a satisfied smirk on his face. He just caught sight of Nugget disappearing around the side of the building.

Following Nugget, Tadd called angrily. "Wait up, fella."

Nugget stopped and turned. Tadd noticed the aboriginal man was looking at him strangely, and knew he'd overheard their conversation.

"What are you doing here?" Tadd snapped. "I told you the shearers wouldn't be needing breakfast."

"I was giving the sheep water, boss."

"The sheep are out back in the holding yards. What you've been doing is snooping."

"No boss… but you makin' trouble for the Missus?"

"That's none of your damned business."

Nugget dropped his gaze to the dust at his feet. "Missus Victoria counting on the wool, boss. What you do is no good." Victoria had helped them muster the previous day, so he knew exactly how anxious she was that the wool be exported on time.

Tadd was furious. "You've got too damned much to say for yourself, fella. I suggest you find work somewhere where they want a black fella with a big mouth."

Nugget had been expecting Tadd to fire him for some time. Even if he hadn't, he knew he couldn't stay on the station and not say anything to the Missus, who'd always been good to him, so he nodded.

"You say anything to Victoria and I'll track you down and shoot you," Tadd said, as if reading his mind. "Now get off Tambora."

Nugget glared at Tadd in a way that made him nervous, but he'd sooner cut off his arm than show it. He'd always found the aboriginal's to be unpredictable, and knew he'd have to watch his back.

Without another word, Nugget turned and walked away.

Victoria had been waiting on the veranda since six in the morning for the shearers to appear, and it was almost lunchtime.

"I can't understand it," she told Tara when she came out with a drink for her. "I radioed town, and Ferris said the shearers left well before sun up. They should have been here hours ago. Will you ask Nerida to bring Nugget to me? He might know something."

"I'll fetch him, Aunt," Tara said. "Nerida is lying down. She's feeling terribly sick this morning."

"All right, dear. I'll get Nerida some Andrews Salts to settle her stomach. It's driving me crazy sitting here waiting."

"Aunt, you won't believe it," Tara said. "Tadd fired Nugget!"

"He did what?"

"It's true. Apparently he's already gone bush. Charlie and Bluey just told me. They're very upset. I don't think they're happy to work under Tadd anymore."

"Where is Tadd?" Victoria barked angrily. She just couldn't understand him lately. But this time he had gone too far.

"I don't know. In his cottage I suppose." Their paths hadn't crossed for the past few days, for which she was grateful.

Victoria met Tadd at the front door of his cottage. He was just coming out, and slammed the door shut behind him."

Victoria didn't mince her words. "Tadd, is it true you fired Nugget?"

"Yes."

"Whatever could you be thinking? He's been with us for years. I wish you would consult me before you do such impulsive things."

Tadd tried to keep his patience. "Victoria, you made me station manager years ago, and told me it was my place to hire and fire our station hands. I caught Nugget in my cottage, stealing. What should I have done, said it was alright?"

Victoria gasped. "Nugget is as loyal as they come. He'd never steal from us. I'm sure you must be mistaken."

"I think I know when someone is stealing from me. There's no excuse for him being in my cottage, none whatsoever."

"Did you ask him what he was doing?"

"He had a bottle of wine in his hand that Ferris gave me, and some loose change, so I'd say the evidence spoke for itself."

"Are there any witnesses?"

"If you are referring to the other men, they'll back Nugget up, you know that. He was probably going to share the wine with them." Tadd thought about declaring that his word should have been good enough, but knew that would be pushing it.

Victoria would never believe Nugget had stolen anything. Never! On the other hand, she knew Tadd had been deceitful of late. With her lips clamped together so she wouldn't say anything she regretted, she turned and walked back to the house.

"Is it true, Aunt," Tara asked when Victoria came inside. "Did Tadd fire Nugget?"

"Yes," Victoria said angrily.

"Whatever for?"

"He claims Nugget was in his cottage, stealing. But I don't believe it for a minute, no matter what Tadd says."

"Then give Nugget back his job. You have the final say."

"In time, Tara. In time." Victoria knew Nugget wouldn't have gone far. He'd be in the bush nearby. Tambora had been his home for too long, and he was born not far away by Aboriginal standards, in the heart of the Simpson Desert. He'd been on stations since he left the mission, which was all of his adult life and part of his youth, and he'd made it known many times that Tambora was where his heart and spirit were.

Frowning, Victoria went down the hall towards the radio room, her mind in turmoil. First the shearers hadn't turned up, and now Tadd had fired Nugget. Something was going on, she was sure of it, and she intended to find out what it was.

Victoria stopped in the doorway of the radio room. Elsa was sitting by the radio, her expression stricken and her eyes brimming with tears. The receiver was on, and she could hear the conversations taking place between the women out on the stations.

"Oh, Elsa, don't listen..." Victoria said. Elsa held up her hand to silence her.

"Fancy Victoria having a gipsy for a niece...

"They're dirty thieving scoundrels. We used to chase them off our land in England all the time...

"I heard that this niece of hers used to dance naked for the men... for money... "And who knows what else she did for money...

The women laughed spitefully. They'd heard their husbands say Tara was beautiful, so they were relishing being malicious.

Tara could see Victoria standing by the open door to the radio room and wondered what she was doing. She walked up behind her and looked over her shoulder. She was shocked to see her mother sitting by the radio in a state of distress. Tears continued to roll silently down Elsa's cheeks, but far from crumbling, she looked as if anger was building inside her, and it was about to erupt into rage. Victoria was concerned. She'd been afraid Elsa would snap.

Tara's hand went to her mouth. She didn't care that the women were saying horrible things about her, but she could see the pain in her mother's eyes and knew she was the cause. Elsa was barely aware of the presence of Victoria or her daughter. All she could hear was the women sniggering about gipsies ... and it reminded her of the reason she had tried to hide her true identity all her life. Her worst fears had become reality.

Had the women just been talking about her, Elsa might have gone away and pretended it had never happened, but the back-biting guttersnipes were talking about her daughter and it raised all her maternal instincts to protect her child, even though she was a grown woman.

"How could Victoria have a gipsy living out there with her... I don't understand... Thank God Tom isn't alive to see it. He had standards..."

Victoria recognized the voices of Eva and Clara Vine, two spinster sisters who spent their lives breathing life into scandal. They lived over a hundred miles away, so they didn't get into town regularly, but they spent hours a day on the radio ruining reputations.

"I don't know. No decent person would put up with it... but I've heard Victoria has been a bit strange lately... perhaps the gipsy is rubbing off on her..."

Tara put her arm around her aunt's shoulder, and Victoria squeezed her hand to say it was all right, she didn't blame her.

"She was probably going to read our fortunes at the party," they snickered.

"I'd like to read their fortunes now," Tara whispered, and Victoria glanced at her and smirked.

"Not for free I'm sure...
"I wonder if she has a crystal ball... "And cooks frogs legs and spiders...

Suddenly Elsa could take it no more. "Now you listen hear, you sniping gossips. Tara Killain has better blood running through her veins than you'll ever have."

"Who is that?" Eva asked haughtily.

"Elsa Killain. Tara's *mother*."

Most of the women gasped, but one woman, Mildred Gower's, bit back. "How dare you speak to us like that. We're good women, from good backgrounds. My husband pioneered this country..."

"My husband was a fine country gentleman, one of the English gentry, and my paternal grandmother was the sister of the Earl of Bradford, but I am just as proud of my mother and maternal grandmother, who were gipsies, royal gipsies, and I'm equally as proud of my daughter. As far as I'm concerned, people who gossip and rip other people's lives to shreds have no more class than a litter of mongrel pups. My daughter is beautiful, kind, unselfish and noble. How many of you can say that about your daughters? And if I hear you say one more nasty remark about my Tara, I'll personally be out to see each and every one of you, and I'll cut out your gossiping tongues with a blunt knife. Now get back to doing something useful, like cleaning your houses and looking after your husbands and children."

For a moment there was utter silence on the other end, and then Elsa flicked off the receiver almost violently, so the women had no chance to retort once they'd gathered their wits.

Victoria and Tara looked at one another in astonishment, and then applauded. Elsa turned in surprise, and took a deep calming breath.

"Oh, mother," Tara said emotionally. "You certainly told them." Tara knew what it had cost her mother to admit she was a gipsy, - virtually everything that made up her character. She knelt at her mother's feet and embraced her. "...and I love you for it." Elsa had her daughter back, and that was all she needed to make her happy.

"Good for you, Elsa," Victoria said. "Those Vine sisters certainly had that coming, but I never knew you had that much gumption."

Elsa shook her head, smiled and wiped away her tears. "Neither did I. I'm glad those women aren't coming to our party. I don't want them here."

"We don't need them to have a party, do we?"

"No, we don't, Victoria. We don't need anyone. We'll have a party by ourselves, and celebrate... being here, together. We can do whatever we like, dance naked if we want to. Who's to stop us?"

"Oh, dear," Victoria said, laughing. "That would give them something to talk about."

"Tara, your Aunt told me about your idea to legally adopt the children. I'm sorry Marcus couldn't help, but your situation is very complicated." Sorrel was sitting in the dining room having a cup of tea when Tara came in. She was reading a week old paper from Adelaide that Ethan had left for them.

"It's all right, Sorrel. I should have known nothing could be done, especially as I took the children illegally. I've discussed it with my Aunt, but my options are limited. If I contacted the children's real Aunt in Ireland, she might want the children back. I couldn't risk that. Jack hates her, and Maureen told me she was a terrible mother. Even if Moyna didn't want the children, the authorities would take them off me and put them in a home. I'll just have to leave things as they are for now. I hope Jack understands. I haven't told him yet."

"Where are Victoria and Elsa? I haven't seen them this morning."

"They were upstairs when I last saw them, giggling like school girls over the idea of having a fancy dress party."

"Oh, Lord, no," Sorrel muttered. "They are not getting me in some silly costume."

"I wouldn't worry about it, Sorrel. There won't be any guests to see us."

"Has Victoria found out why the shearers didn't come?"

"A woman in town radioed late last night to say they were in the Wombat Creek Hotel. She's going to radio us tonight if she can find out why they didn't come."

"Maybe the town's people influenced them."

"That's possible. But the hotel publican did tell Aunt Victoria that they actually left town to come here. If the people in town had influenced them, they wouldn't have left the hotel in the first place. I'm wondering whether Tadd sent them away? I wouldn't put it past him."

"Why would he do that?"

"I know it sounds far-fetched, but nothing he's done so far has been in Aunt Victoria's best interests, despite his claims to the contrary. Look what he did to Nugget?"

Tara heard a crash as the back door swung violently open and hit the wall. Then she heard Jack sobbing.

Rushing out into the hall, she found Jack almost hysterical. "What's wrong, Jack?"

"It's... Mellie... I think she's dead."

CHAPTER THIRTY-TWO

"Oh, Mellie," Tara whispered, fighting tears. She knelt in the dust where Mellie's still body lay. Her lifeless eyes were open and so was her mouth. Ants were beginning to crawl over her, and bush flies were buzzing around. Tara instinctively knew she'd had a terrible death.

"A snake must have bitten her," she said to Jack.

"No," he shouted, startling her. "Mellie was too quick for the snakes. Tadd killed her."

Tara was shocked and horrified by his remark. "What makes you say that, Jack?"

Jack began to sob. "He tried… to call her… and she wouldn't come. She wanted to stay with me."

"I don't understand. When did this happen?"

"Last night. Mellie didn't want to be locked in the kennels. She likes to sleep beside my bed. I knew by the way Tadd looked at her… so hatefully, that he was going to do… something terrible to her." He buried his face in his hands, as great gasping sobs racked his body. Tara found it heart wrenching to watch him.

"I wish I was a man," he sobbed in frustration. "I'd do something terrible to Tadd."

Tara picked Mellie up and carried her to the veranda, where Nerida stood in the shade.

"Will you find something to cover her with, Nerida?" Tara said, placing the dog on a two-seater wicker chair. She brushed the ants from around her mouth and eyes.

Jack knelt beside Mellie and stroked her black and white fur, and cried. His bewildered expression broke Tara's heart. He'd lost so much in his short life, and Mellie had become his constant companion and friend. The pups, now three months old, began sniffing around their mother. The two males, Rusty and Duke, sat beside her still body in confusion. Shellie placed her head on her mother. The little bitch was so like her, in looks and spirit. Beside the shipwreck, it was the most heartbreaking scene Tara had witnessed.

Tara glanced at Tadd's cottage, and thought she saw the curtain move in the front window. She could barely contain the fury coursing through her. How could Tadd do something so … despicable, simply because Mellie preferred to be with Jack?

Marching over to his cottage, she pushed open the door without knocking. Tadd was stood on the other side, further evidence, she thought, that he'd been watching them from his window.

"Tadd Sweeney, you are the lowest creature I've ever had the displeasure of knowing. How could you do something so contemptible to an innocent dog, just to hurt a small boy?"

"What are you ranting about, woman? Has something happened to one of my dogs?"

"You know damn well something has happened to Mellie, because you did it," Tara shouted, pointing an accusing finger at him.

"I don't know what you are talking about? What has happened to Mellie?"

"You poisoned her," Tara raged. "You're a lowlife swine…"

"Are you completely mad? Mellie is my best breeding bitch. Where is she?" Tadd pushed past Tara and headed towards the veranda.

"Don't you go near Jack," Tara said, chasing after him.

After hearing shouts, Victoria and Elsa had come out onto the veranda. "What happened to… Mellie?" Victoria asked Nerida.

"That's what I'd like to know," Tadd boomed as he stormed toward them, frightening Nerida, who retreated behind Victoria.

When Tadd reached the veranda, Jack stood up. He wasn't a tall boy, but he stood as straight as he could. "You killed Mellie," he yelled at Tadd.

Tara rushed past Tadd and pulled Jack into her arms protectively.

"Of course I didn't," Tadd said, examining the bitch. "If she'd been locked up last night, maybe this wouldn't have happened."

"That's not fair, Tadd," Victoria said. "You know as well as I, that a snake could just as easily get her in the kennels as anywhere else."

"There's nothing can be done," he said coldly. "I'll get one of the men to bury her." He stepped back. Tara thought his attitude was rather callous for someone who'd just lost a dog that was supposed to have been his 'prize bitch'. If he thought so much of her, he'd have wanted to bury her himself.

"No," Jack shouted. "Don't you touch Mellie."

"We'll bury her," Tara said with such conviction Tadd had no answer.

After giving her a caustic glare, he walked away. Jack's flash of bravery deserted him and he collapsed, crying over Mellie again.

"I'm sure it was snake bite, Tara," Victoria said softly. "Mellie's bred us some of the best dogs in the state, champions. Tadd would never poison her."

"After all he's done lately, Aunt, how can you still have so much faith in him?"

Victoria lowered her gaze to Mellie and Jack. She had no answer to that question.

"Where are we going?" Jack asked Tara as they headed into the bush on horseback. Tara had Mellie's body over her saddle.

"To find Nugget. Charlie said if we head in this direction, we'll find his camp. I'm sure Nugget will be able to tell us what happened to Mellie."

A short while later, Tara saw campfire smoke rising above a woodland of bimble box and acacia trees.

As Tara had suspected, Nugget was camped with Jabba Jurra and Jackie Kantji. They were surprised to see Tara and Jack.

"Nugget, I need your help?" Tara said dismounting. She greeted the other men. Jabba Jurra was cooking a kangaroo tail in the campfire, and Jackie Kantji was sitting under a gidgee tree, otherwise known as a stinking wattle or acacia, carving a boomerang with all the skill of a sighted man.

"Is Missus Victoria all right?" Nugget asked.

Tara could see he was really worried. "Yes, Nugget, she's fine. Jack is not so good. He found Mellie dead this morning."

Nugget glanced at Jack sympathetically. "Did a snake get her, Missus?"

"That's what I'm here to find out, Nugget. Can you tell the difference between snakebite and poisoning? Charlie and Bluey said you probably could."

"Maybe, Missus. But who would poison Mellie?"

"Jack thinks Tadd did it."

Nugget glanced at the boy, and Tara got the distinct impression that he agreed with Jack.

Tara and Jack gently lifted Mellie from her horse and unwrapped her. Under the shade of a gidgee tree, Nugget examined her body, carefully looking over every inch of her, even between her toes.

"No snake bite on her, Missus." Nugget smelt Mellie's mouth. "Can't smell poison either, but maybe it happen before sun down yesterday, and she be sick."

"I don't think that is possible, Nugget. She slept beside Jack's bed."

"If she had poison today, I can't smell it."

"So you don't think she has been poisoned?"

"I can't say for sure, Missus, but there is no snake bite."

Tara didn't know what to think.

"You want me bury dog for you, Missus? Some nice spots around here."

Tara glanced at Jack. "I think Jack would like her buried under the balcony nearest his bedroom, Nugget, so I'll get one of the other men to help us, but thank you."

Nugget nodded. "Missus, did Tadd say… why he sack me?"

"He did say something to my Aunt, Nugget, but she didn't believe him, and I don't either."

Nugget looked at the ground and Tara suspected he couldn't tell her the real reason. She felts certain Tadd had threatened him.

"I have to go, Nugget, but I want you to know my Aunt has complete faith in you. She has a few things to sort out, and then she wants you to come back to work for her. I think she's doing some investigating into why the shearer's didn't turn up. When she finds the answers, things will change, so please have patience."

Nugget looked sad. "I can't work for Tadd, Missus," he said. "You be careful, and watch out for Missus Victoria."

Tara nodded.

When Tara got back to the station, she had Charlie dig a hole for Mellie under the balcony nearest Jack's room. Young Karl made a cross and put Mellie's name on it, which Jack really appreciated.

As they stood over her small grave together, Tara whispered, "She'll always be with you, Jack." Shellie sniffed around the pitiful mound of earth covering her mother, and then lay down beside it.

"I think Mellie will live on in Shellie, don't you?" Tara said. "She's so like her."

Jack reached out and stroked Shellie, but he never took his eyes from the cross bearing Mellie's name. "I heard Tadd tell Aunt Victoria that Shellie's going to a station in New South Wales."

Tara caught the despair in his voice, and it nearly broke her heart.

When Tara went inside, Victoria confronted her. "Tara, where have you been? We were so worried about you."

"Jack and I went to see Nugget, Aunt. We took… Mellie with us."

Victoria was taken back. "Whatever for?"

"I wanted Nugget to examine her to see if he could tell us why she died, poisoning or snakebite. He looked her over very carefully, but he found no snake bite."

"Are you telling me she was poisoned?"

"Nugget couldn't be sure."

Victoria's expression saddened. "We'll probably never know the truth, Tara. I know

Tadd has done some odd things lately, but I just can't believe he'd do something so terrible to Mellie."

Tara didn't know what to think, but it was clear her aunt still couldn't bring herself to believe Tadd had an agenda of his own. "We've just buried her. Jack's gone upstairs with Shellie."

Victoria looked distressed. It was bad enough losing Mellie, who was like one of the family, but she hated to see Jack so upset.

"Aunt, can I ask you to stop Tadd selling Shellie? I know we need the money, but she's so like Mellie, and she seems attached to Jack."

"If she makes Jack happy, Tara, she's staying here. Tadd can't argue with me, because we'll have to replace Mellie."

Tara was relieved. She hadn't been sure Victoria would back her up.

As they went through to the living room and sat down, Victoria said, "I have some rather surprising news. Lottie radioed while you were away, and she said the shearers were in town."

"You knew that, didn't you, Aunt?"

"Yes, but it seems one of the men had been with Maddy the previous night, and he'd claimed they weren't coming to Tambora for the same reason the rest of the town have turned against us…"

"Because I lived with the gipsies…."

"Yes, but wait till you hear this." Victoria was clearly astounded. "Lottie apparently became so angry, she threw the shearer out of the house before he could get his pants on, and called a strike. Can you imagine that?" Victoria's eyes widened. "Lottie and the girls have gone on strike!" She laughed. "I've never heard of such a thing. The single men from the stations will go crazy, especially the shearers and stockmen. They always call in Lottie's place when they're in town. Not Wally Sherbourne, he wouldn't dare because Dixie would kill him if she found out, but I know the others visit." Victoria clasped her hands together. "Good for Lottie, I say. She said she's not calling off the strike until the shearers have come out here and sheared our sheep."

"Do you think that will work?"

"Only time will tell."

"But we don't have time, Aunt. Charlie, Bluey and Karl said if the shearers aren't here by first thing in the morning, they're going to take up the shears themselves."

Victoria looked surprised, and touched. "We've only got a few pairs of old shears, and the men, God bless them, can't shear very well."

"They admit they are slow, and they haven't got very good shears, but they are willing to give it a go, and even teach me. If Riordan and Ethan will help, we might still make the deadline for exporting the wool."

Victoria brushed a tear from her eye. "I'm so lucky to have all of you," she said. "But if the shearers don't come, Tara, we have virtually no chance of making the deadline."

Riordan came out onto the veranda and sat down beside Tara. She was having a drink before heading over to the shearing sheds, where Charlie and Bluey were going to give her a shearing demonstration. She'd barely seen Riordan in two days, and thought he looked slightly uncomfortable as he settled in a chair beside her. She wondered if he blamed himself for the portrait arriving in Wombat Creek, or whether he was embarrassed that it was now common knowledge that she'd been living the life of a gipsy.

"You don't belong out here, Tara," he said. "No more than I do. Your mother agrees with me." He'd enjoyed mustering the sheep, but he missed the art world, and the thrill of obtaining something rare and valuable.

"To be honest, I don't know where I belong, Riordan, especially now, but I came out here for a new beginning, and to help my Aunt. I admit I hated the outback at first; I still don't like the heat and the flies, but this country has a strange way of growing on you. I am beginning to see how my Aunt came to love it."

"Don't take this the wrong way, but at the moment I think your Aunt would be better off if you weren't here."

Although Tara felt hurt by his remark, she had to admit he was speaking the truth. "I ran away from my family years ago, and from my life in Ireland, but I don't want to run again. If my past can catch up with me here, it can catch up with me anywhere. Besides I have the children to think about now."

Riordan looked down at the ground, and Tara noted his jaw clenched.

"They're not your children, Tara. It was kind of you to take them, wonderful in fact, but I don't believe you were thinking clearly."

"Riordan, I love those children, and although it was a very traumatic time when the ship went down, and there was really no time for contemplation, I knew what I was doing."

"Don't you think they would be better off with blood relatives, their own kin?"

"The only relative I know of is their mother's sister, and Jack has practically begged me not to send him to her. Maureen wouldn't have wanted that either. She told me her sister was awful to her children. She virtually treated them as slaves. I really believe Jack and Hannah could have a good life here."

"If your Aunt manages to keep Tambora. But even if she does, you shouldn't stay on the station if the people out here are going to treat you so badly."

"Where would I go, Riordan?"

He was hesitant for a moment. "Back to Ireland, with me, as my wife."

Tara was startled. She searched Riordan's grey-blue eyes for a sign he was wasn't serious, but to her surprise, he looked earnest. "Now who's not thinking clearly? How would your clientele react to you having an expatriate gipsy for a wife?"

"You were never meant to be a gipsy, Tara."

"But that's exactly what I was, Riordan, for eleven years."

"No one in the circles I mix in would ever know."

"Kelvin knows."

"He won't make trouble."

"You know he will. He hates gipsies, and me."

"I could sell the Gallery."

"And do what? The Gallery is your life."

"I do love art, and I've always wanted to open a Gallery in Paris, or Rome. This would be a perfect opportunity."

"Riordan, you can't turn your life upside down for me. That wouldn't work for either of us."

"Tara, you are my life. I love you…"

"Riordan, you've explained how you felt. You were obsessed by Tara the gipsy…"

"I know, but I've come to love the real you. I've watched you since I came here, and you are everything I imagined you'd be. That you are beautiful goes without saying, but you are so much more. You're kind, loving and generous. You always put others before yourself, and you are willing to stand up for what you believe in." His arms encircled her, and before she knew what was happening, his lips found hers. His mouth was soft, and warm, and his moustache tickled her nose. His kiss held longing and pent up passion, but his lips did not evoke those feelings in her. When he finally drew away from her, she was neither breathless, nor was her heart racing. But as she gazed into his handsome face, she could see he really did care for her.

"Riordan... I don't know what to say."

"Say you'll marry me, Tara, and come back to Ireland with me. I'll do whatever it takes to give you a good life. I can't imagine living without you."

Tara was lost for words. "Excuse me!"

Riordan and Tara turned in surprise. Ethan was standing just outside the dining room doorway, and he looked far from pleased. In fact, his dark eyes were blazing.

Tara wondered if he'd overheard their conversation, and seen them kissing.

"Charlie and Bluey are waiting for you in the shearing sheds, Tara," he said. "Shall I tell them you are ... otherwise engaged?"

Tara felt herself blush. "No, Ethan. I'm coming." She stood up, and looked at Riordan. "Charlie and Bluey are going to show me how to shear a sheep. If the shearers don't turn up, we are going to have to do it ourselves."

"Could you use another pair of hands?"

"Certainly. The more the better."

Lottie looked out of the window when she heard a knock on the door. "What do you want, Jed?" she called to the man on her doorstep. "Open up, Lottie. You can't keep this up."

"Has Wally Sherbourne and the other men been out to shear the sheep on Tambora?"

"No, and they're not going to."

"Then I'm not opening my door."

"You'll starve to death."

"Not in your life time."

Jed sighed in exasperation. "Lottie, come on. What's Victoria Milburn got to do with you? That's not your argument."

"Well I'm making it my argument. What Victoria's niece did in Ireland is no one's business but her own. If you men want to make that your business, then I'm not having any of you at my place. Now go away and tell the men not to come here until those sheep are sheared, and that's my final word."

Belle and Maddy were standing behind Lottie. They all heard Jed Hanson walk away, cussing as he went.

"How long are we keeping this strike going?" Belle asked.

"As long as it takes."

"I don't think that will be very long. I've had men knocking on my bedroom window all night."

"So have I," Maddy added. "I hardly got any sleep."

Lottie looked thoughtful. "Girls, put on your prettiest dresses," she said. "We're going to a party."

Belle and Maddy looked surprised. "Where?"

"Tambora. I don't think Victoria and her family will mind having us for a few days, and it will get us away from here."

"How wonderful," Maddy said. "I haven't seen Ethan for weeks, and he's bound to be there."

CHAPTER THIRTY-THREE

The men began drafting the sheep at dawn, separating the lambs from the ewes and rams. They held little hope the shearers would turn up, so were ready to begin the task of shearing the sheep themselves. As usual, when there was hard work to be done, Tadd Sweeney had disappeared.

The men decided, after a valiant effort on Tara's part, that she was too petite to be throwing around a fifty-pound sheep. She was better suited to being a roustabout, or shed hand, which involved picking up the fleece from the boards and throwing it over a table, and then skirting it, - which was trimming the shabby edges. In normal practice, the classer may skirt the fleece, but on smaller jobs, one of the shearers or a shed-hand would do it. As the wool was going to William Crombie for rugs, Victoria said it didn't matter that it wasn't classed. Jack had been made tar boy, which involved tarring any nicks and cuts on the sheep, and sweeping the boards. To keep Hannah happy and make her feel included, Tara had given her a poddy lamb to bottle-feed. Its sick mother had been easy pray for a dingo, but Nugget had managed to save the lamb.

Although he found shearing hard going in the hot sheds, and it was backbreaking work, Riordan did his best to help. He'd come to the conclusion that the Australian outback man was one of a tough breed, and realized that in comparison he'd led an easy and privileged life. At times he was overwhelmed with homesickness, but he vowed he wouldn't return to Ireland without Tara.

Unfortunately Ethan had been called away on an emergency, and couldn't begin work in the sheds. A search party had failed to find two children who were lost on Emu Plains Station, one of the largest stations south of Wombat Creek, and Ethan was their only hope. He'd left with Saladin in the small hours of the morning so that they could begin searching before the searing sun rose in the sky. Tara had noticed when the call for help came over the radio, that he was momentarily hesitant to go, and was curious why. She was certain he'd never refuse to assist someone in need, so there had to be a good reason why he'd wavered before committing. Bluey told her later that since their neighbours had turned against Victoria, Ethan had made himself unavailable to them, something he'd never done before.

"Had lives not been at stake, I'm sure he wouldn't have made an exception," Bluey said. Although Tara felt Ethan's loyalty was strictly for her aunt, she was surprised and touched. Ethan hadn't said a word about it, but then she instinctively knew he wouldn't.

The day dragged interminably. The men worked hard, but by sundown they'd only sheared sixty sheep between them, and they felt miserable and disillusioned.

"A gun shearer could shear sixty sheep before his morning cuppa," Charlie said, throwing his shears across the shed in frustration.

"You'll do more tomorrow," Tara said. She was dog-tired herself, and drained from the heat.

"We won't meet the deadline for the Missus," Bluey said despondently, "Especially without Nugget and Ethan to help us." Tara knew the men resented the fact that Nugget couldn't help, especially as they weren't being paid. She intended to speak to her aunt about it.

"Come up to the house tonight for the party," Tara said. "It will cheer us all up."

When Tara, Riordan and the children got back to the house, they were surprised to see Rex Crawley's automobile.

"It looks like Rex has decided to come to the party after all," Tara said. "I wonder if he brought anyone with him?"

They were going inside when they heard women's laughter.

"Who could that be?" Tara asked aloud. She glanced at Riordan, who shrugged.

When Tara and Riordan came into the sitting room, followed by the children, they were surprised to find Lottie and the girls with Victoria and Elsa.

"Oh, my goodness," Tara exclaimed. "How lovely to see you all here."

"Thank you, Tara," Lottie returned.

"Isn't it wonderful?" Victoria added. "And don't they all look fetching in their party gowns? I especially like yours, Maddy. Where did you get it? It certainly doesn't look like something from Mohomet Basheer's store."

Maddy swept a haughty glance in Tara's direction. "An 'admirer' bought it for me," she said, pretending to be coy, and Victoria pursed her lips and said. 'Ooh!'

Tara wondered if Maddy was hinting that her suitor was Ethan.

The gown was a deep purple, which contrasted starkly with Maddy's porcelain skin. It had a plunging neckline, revealing a great deal of her ample bosom, and a tight bodice. It was drawn in at the waistline, emphasizing her hourglass figure, and had a full skirt. Overall, she made an eye-catching picture, and Tara self-consciously tried to wipe a smudge of wool fat from her nose, only succeeding in smudging her right cheek. She turned to glance at Riordan, to see if he was also feeling uncomfortable, but it was apparent that he was too taken with Maddy to feel anything remotely resembling self-consciousness. When Tara glanced back at Maddy, it was obvious the feeling was mutual.

"Riordan," Tara hissed. "Perhaps we should wash and change before joining our guests?"

"Yes, yes… of course."

"Hurry back," Maddy said flirtatiously. A few moments earlier she had been quite downhearted when she'd found out Ethan had gone away, but her mood had changed the instant she realized there was a handsome gentleman in residence. Even covered in dust and grime, she thought Riordan was appealing, certainly more so than the majority of the men between Marree and Alice Springs. Although he looked 'soft' in comparison to Ethan, Maddy found him an attractive man. She also saw the fact that there was no wife in tow as an added bonus.

Belle was wearing a cream gown with a demure neckline, which did nothing to enhance her straight, mousy brown hair, or ordinary features. Lottie, on the other hand, was wearing an aqua-blue gown and a colourful sequined shawl around her shoulders, which brightened her up. It reminded Tara of the vivid shawls the gipsies wore. She'd also toned down her make-up, and piled her brassy blonde hair on top of her head, which lifted her features. She looked very happy to be amongst people who accepted her without judgement.

"It's just terrible that you are having to shear the sheep yourselves," she said to Tara. "We should thank you for trying to… persuade the shearers to come out here," Tara said blushing.

"It's like being on holidays," Belle said laughing, which made Tara laugh, too, and the awkwardness passed.

"I was just telling Lottie I think going on strike is marvellous," Victoria said. "I wouldn't be surprised if it made the papers."

"Do you think so?" Lottie asked. "I didn't know what else to do. I detest injustice." She suddenly looked anxious, reminding Tara of the first time they met. "I've asked Victoria if we could stay for a few days. I hope you don't mind, Tara?"

"Of course not. I think it's wonderful."

Lottie looked relieved. "For the last two days the men have been knocking on our windows, day and night. We've hardly had a wink of sleep." They could have coped if they'd had to, but Rex Crawley had told Lottie that Victoria's party was being boycotted because of Tara's gipsy past, and Lottie felt they could use a little moral support.

Tara noticed the expression on her mother's face, as she stood at the back of the room. She didn't look pleased that the women were staying.

"If you don't mind noisy cockatoos first thing in the morning, I'm sure you'll sleep peacefully out here," Tara said. "If you'll excuse me, I'll bathe and change. I'm sure I smell worse than sheep dung."

"You don't smell as bad as Ferris Dunmore's feet on a hot afternoon," she heard Lottie say, as she left the room.

"Thank goodness for that," she called.

"I'll bath Hannah," Elsa said, grasping the little girl by the hand and leading her out of the room. Jack had gone with Riordan to the outside bathroom the men used.

Tara was sure her mother just wanted to escape. As they mounted the stairs with Hannah, she asked her what was wrong.

"Nothing," Elsa replied.

"Are you upset about the guests?"

"This is Victoria's house, so she can have whomever she likes here."

"Lottie and the girls striking to support us is incredible, mother," Tara whispered.

"I know," Elsa said. "I've just never been in the company of … women like that."

"I don't suppose you have," Tara replied dryly.

"I don't know how to… act, or what to say." If Elsa had been truthful, she was more afraid of what the women were going to say, and how they were going to act.

Tara smiled. "You don't have to act at all, mother. They are just like any other women. In fact, Lottie is one of the loveliest women I have ever had the pleasure of meeting. I visited her in her home the day I arrived in Wombat Creek…"

"Tara, whatever made you go to a bordello?" Elsa asked in shock.

"I didn't know it was a bordello. There was no sign outside advertising the fact, and even after meeting Lottie, I still had no idea she was a prostitute, until she told me. As far as I was concerned she was just a woman, a potential friend in an isolated town. But it made no difference when I found out the truth. I liked her immediately. I've since learnt that she's candid, generous and thoughtful, and I feel privileged to call her a friend. You'll really like her when you get to know her."

Elsa wasn't so sure. "What were you planning to wear tonight, Tara?" she asked, tactfully changing the subject.

"I don't know. I lost everything I owned when the Emerald Star went down. I bought a couple of dresses, ironically at Mohomet Basheer's store, but I have nothing that can compete with Maddy's gown."

"I may have the solution to your dilemma."

"Oh! Have you something I can borrow?"

"Not exactly. When I heard about the ship sinking, I bought some gowns for you. I wasn't even sure you had survived, the records were in chaos, but buying the gowns made me feel more optimistic. "

Tara's eyes widened in delight. Her mother had always had exquisite taste. "I have been waiting for the right moment to give them to you..."

"Oh, mother, this is the perfect moment."

Elsa smiled. "There's one that is just right for this evening."

By mid-evening, several bottles of wine had been opened. The party was being held in a reception room upstairs that could double as a ballroom. It was equipped with a piano that had rarely been used in the last few years, and an enormous buffet table. The balcony doors were open, which allowed a cool breeze to cross-ventilate the room.

Lottie and Victoria took turns playing the piano and singing at the top of their voices. When they weren't singing, the conversation became risqué, but Tara had never laughed so much in her life. She also caught her mother laughing behind her hand, especially when the women began discussing past clients and their strange habits and fetishes. For confidentiality reasons, they didn't mention names and claimed the particular men they were referring to were their clients before they came to Wombat Creek. They claimed one man loved them to rub dripping into his skin, particularly his bottom, and another liked to wear women's underwear, especially Lottie's brassieres. Another man, Belle said, insisted on wearing his dead mother's wig when in bed with her. Victoria, Tara and Elsa were shocked, but couldn't help laughing when Belle described how he looked in the wig, in her words like someone's ugly grandmother.

Maddy told them a story about when she was sixteen and a friend of her father's, an undertaker, had tried to rape her.

"That's terrible," Victoria said, the smile leaving her face, as Riordan filled her glass with wine. The other women also looked horrified.

"My father was so incensed," Maddy said earnestly, "that he had the man charged. But when the matter came before the court, the judge proclaimed there was no such thing as rape."

The women looked at each other in astonishment.

"My father demanded to know how he came to such a conclusion," Maddy said, "and the judge said it was because… a woman can run faster with her skirts up, than a man with his pants down."

For a moment, Tara, Elsa and Victoria looked at Maddy dumbfounded, but then Maddy burst out laughing, and although the matter wasn't an amusing one, they couldn't help joining her, as she obviously saw the funny side of it.

Riordan danced with all the women, but Maddy succeeded in monopolizing him. Bluey and Charlie sat out on the balcony telling stories. They enjoyed the view and the breeze from the height of the treetops almost as much as Victoria's wine. Young Karl and Jack played cards in an adjoining room, and kept sneaking sips of wine when no one was looking, until eventually they fell asleep. Rex had been reluctant to join in the festivities, even though he'd finished his mail run. After apologizing to Victoria, he drove back to town long before the party got going. Victoria understood that he didn't want to be ostracized by the people in town. After all, he had to live amongst them.

When Tadd returned to the station about nine o'clock, he heard laughter and glanced up at the balcony. He wondered who Victoria's guests were, as the laughter sounded strangely familiar. As he stood watching the house, he saw Riordan come out onto the balcony with a woman, and his mouth dropped open when he recognized Maddy.

Tadd had been in town most of the day, drowning his sorrows at the hotel. Lottie and the girls were the hot topic of conversation, but he never imagined they'd be out on the station. The men knew they had left town, and thought they may have caught the train to Adelaide, but no one had seen them board. They insisted that the women would soon return, as they needed the money more than the men needed them.

Tadd shook his head. "Wait till they find out," he thought. He watched for a while longer, then went off to his cottage in a huff. He'd made up his mind he would not join Victoria or her guests, or help them in any way, and he was sticking to it. But it still irked him that they were having so much fun.

Just after eleven o'clock, Tara went down into the grounds for a walk. The party was still in full swing, but she needed a little time to herself. She wandered between the gum trees and looked up at the stars and moon, and thought about Riordan's proposal. Even though he'd been dancing with Maddy most of the night, she noticed he kept watching her, and when she'd danced with him, he held her very close. But as for marrying him… she'd already made the mistake of marrying for the wrong reasons. She didn't want to do it again.

"What are you doing out here all alone?"

Tara turned in surprise to find Ethan standing behind her. She was unaware that he'd been watching her for several minutes. She was wearing a red gown in a silky material that draped over her body in a gossamer film. With her hair piled on top of her head in curls, she looked like royalty, with just a hint of exotic gipsy. She literally took his breath away.

"I was just getting some air. When did you get back?"

"A short while ago."

She noticed his damp hair was glistening in the moonlight and he smelt of soap. There was no denying he exuded 'manliness' more than any other man she had ever known. "Did you find the missing children?" she asked.

Ethan was thinking Tara was the most feminine woman he had ever known. Her facial features were delicate and her skin looked like satin in the moonlight. "Yes, and just in time. They were dangerously dehydrated. I doubt they would have lasted another hour."

"I'm sure their parents were grateful."

Ethan declined to answer. Being praised always made him feel uncomfortable, especially when he was just doing someone a good turn. Tara recalled what Bluey had said about him keeping his distance from the people who had turned against Victoria.

"Bluey told me that you have been refusing to do so much for the people who have turned against my Aunt. She doesn't know, but I'm sure she would appreciate such loyalty."

"No one has the right to judge you for the life you lead in Ireland, Tara. Christ, anyone would think they were saints."

Tara was surprised and mystified that their behaviour offended him, especially as he knew virtually nothing of the circumstances that led her to live with the gipsies. She felt herself grow warm when she recalled the things the women on the radio were saying about her. "Not many people would take a stand… especially for someone they've known for only a few short weeks."

"I don't know about that… Lottie did."

"Yes, she did, but I knew the moment I met Lottie that she was a very compassionate woman and that she'd be the type to defend someone like me." She suddenly realized Ethan had done exactly the same, without question, and she was amazed. He continually surprised her. "She and the girls are here, you know." She tried to gauge his reaction in the darkness.

"Oh." He smiled. "I wondered where they were?" He suddenly heard wicked laughter and recognized Maddy's voice.

"Had you been to their home and found them missing?" Tara asked.

Her tone held just a hint of accusation, which Ethan found slightly amusing. One side of his mouth lifted again. "No, but everyone for hundreds of miles is speculating about where they went. I doubt anyone suspected they were on Tambora. I certainly didn't."

Tara turned away and tried to keep her tone even. "Maddy has spent most of the evening dancing with Riordan." She wasn't envious, but she had noticed Maddy had a way of charming a man, even someone who hinted at being reluctant, as Riordan had.

Ethan was silent for a moment. He knew Maddy was an outrageous flirt, and could quite imagine her being attracted to someone like Riordan. "So that's why you're out here. Your *fiancé* has a roving eye." He was mystified why Riordan would want to look at another woman, especially tonight. Tara was a vision he'd never tire of looking at.

Tara spun around. "Riordan is not my fiancé, and he doesn't have a roving eye. Maddy is just hard to … ignore… I'm sure you know what I mean."

"Yes, I do." He knew Maddy could be quite the little vixen." He smiled for an instant, but then his features sobered. "Are you saying you… turned down Riordan's proposal?"

"Not exactly." Tara didn't like the idea that Ethan wasn't immune to Maddy. "I'm giving it consideration."

Ethan's gaze dropped to the ground, and Tara found herself looking at his well-shaped mouth in the pale moonlight, as she thought of Riordan's kiss. It hadn't thrilled her, like Ethan's kiss, but then she considered the possibility that had been a 'one-off'. 'An 'emotional time' Ethan had called it. If he kissed her again, it was likely that she would not feel the same.

"I'm sure your mother would approve of a marriage between you and Riordan," Ethan said, watching her closely. He found the idea pierced him like a spear.

Elsa had hinted as much on many occasions. "I told you, I rarely do what pleases my mother."

"Kissing me certainly didn't please her." He'd wondered if that was the reason that she had responded so passionately, but realized she couldn't have known her mother was watching.

Again, Tara found her gaze drawn to his mouth. She remembered how breathless she had become when he kissed her, and the ache in the pit of her stomach, and wondered why she had never felt like that when Garvie had kissed her, or Riordan....

"It pleased me," she found herself whispering. She hadn't meant to say it aloud, but several glasses of wine had made her careless.

Leaning on the trunk of a gum tree, Tara closed her eyes, and let her mind wander back to the day of the locust plague. The wine had relaxed her, so it was easy to let her thoughts drift.. The faintest breeze stirred tendrils of her hair, and lifted the lilac scent from her skin, to float away. Ethan watched her, the lilac scent tantalizing his senses. He felt his heart begin to thud in his chest as he gazed upon the alluring vision she made in the moonlight. He thought she was the most beautiful woman he had ever seen, and fought the urge to take her in his arms. When her lips parted, as she remembered the kiss they had shared, and her tongue flicked across her lower lip, he felt himself succumb to the desire coursing through him.

Strong hands took Tara's upper arms and pulled her towards a warm body, and she shuddered but didn't open her eyes. She imagined she felt Ethan's breath on her cheek, as his lips brushed against hers provocatively. She felt herself respond with a small shiver, as she swayed toward him and thought she heard her name whispered on the breeze.

Suddenly Tara found herself encircled in arms like steel bands. Ethan's lips moved hungrily over hers, and her legs went weak. An all-consuming passion surged through her like a lightning bolt, and she moaned softly, gripping the powerful muscles in his back with needy fingers. She heard an answering groan from somewhere deep and distant and felt her body crushed against his hard physique. She hardly trusted herself to think coherently, let alone object ...

"Tara," she heard her name whispered hoarsely, as he trailed kisses over her throat, and right shoulder. "Oh, Tara!"

Just when she felt at the point of no return, Ethan let her go. She felt herself sway unsteadily and opened her eyes to see Ethan step away from her.

"I shouldn't be doing this," he whispered, his voice thick with emotion. Something caught his eye, and he glanced up to the balcony of the house, where Riordan had appeared. Dazed, Tara looked over her shoulder and saw Riordan standing on the balcony above them. She wasn't sure he had noticed them in the shadows by the trees. Maddy stepped up beside him and handed him a glass of wine.

Tara turned to look back at Ethan, but she couldn't read the expression in his dark eyes. She longed to be back in his arms, to feel his lips on hers, but she tried to pull herself together. She certainly had the answer to her question. His kiss had affected her in exactly the same way as it had the day of the locust plague. It mystified her, as she didn't know exactly what it meant. She wondered if she had subconsciously fallen in love with Ethan, or was he just a master at the art of arousing a woman beyond sense? Both seemed unlikely prospects.

"I should go inside," she whispered.

Not trusting himself to speak, Ethan nodded.

"Are you coming? I am sure everyone will be glad to see you."

"No... I don't think so... will you ... will you tell Victoria I have left a telegram for her on the bureau in the dining room? It may be something important."

"Of course."

He turned to walk away.

"Ethan, you're back..." Maddy called excitedly. "Come up."

Ethan looked at Tara. He thought she looked vulnerable and irresistible...and he longed to take her in his arms again. The last person he wanted to see was Maddy at that moment, but without being extremely rude, there was no way he could avoid it.

"You don't want to disappoint her," Tara said, taking his arm and willing her heart to stop racing.

From the moment Ethan walked into the room, he became the center of Maddy's universe. It was as if Riordan no longer existed. The transformation was astonishing to watch, and Tara thought Maddy a fickle woman. Riordan did not comment Tara and Ethan kissing, but she thought he had looked at her strangely when she came into the room with Ethan.

"I've always preferred a woman to be a little more subtle," he said when Tara commented on how quickly Maddy had transferred her affections.

Tara's brows shot up. "What do you mean?"

"The things she says are ... well... to the point...."

"What sort of things?"

"She's very ... suggestive. I can imagine men find her ... exciting."

"That would be a bonus, given what she does…"

"Victoria told me." Riordan looked uncomfortable.

Tara looked back at Maddy, and blushed with humiliation. She was thinking she must seem like an inexperienced schoolgirl in comparison. Suddenly, she had never felt less 'womanly' or desirable in her life.

Riordan glanced at her and saw the shadow of doubt in her eyes. "That sort of excitement is short lived, Tara. A woman with a little mystique, particularly one in a fetching red gown, is far more alluring to a man."

Tara tried to smile, but Maddy was whispering something in Ethan's ear, and she saw the slow smile come to his mouth, and the twinkle in his eyes. As she watched him, he looked up at her. The expression in his dark eyes became strange and indefinable.

"Would you like to dance?" Riordan asked.

"Yes, thank you," Tara said, grateful for the distraction.

As they waltzed around the room, Tara heard her mother telling Lottie that they made a lovely couple.

"I agree," Riordan whispered in her ear, and she smiled.

She also heard her mother telling Lottie and Belle about Riordan's Gallery in Dublin. She tried to imagine herself at the gallery, as Riordan's wife, but far different images kept coming to mind, images of the desert, the stars, and a dark-haired man with lips that could make her senses reel.

Victoria slipped out of the ballroom to check on Nerida. She hadn't seen her all evening, and was concerned about her. As she went down the dark hallway towards her room, she noticed Nerida's door was slightly ajar. It appeared a lamp was burning low. As she got closer, she thought she heard muffled noises. Pausing outside the door, Victoria wondered if Nerida had company, perhaps one of the children. She slowly pushed the door open…

"Nerida…' Victoria said softly, and then gasped. For a horrifying moment she couldn't believe what she was seeing. Tadd was on top of Nerida, ripping at her dress. The aboriginal girl was crying and fighting him, but clearly she was no match. Neither of them were aware Victoria was standing in the doorway.

"Keep still… you little bitch," Tadd hissed, as he fought to penetrate her, but Nerida continued to squirm.

"Tadd!" Victoria shouted. She entered the room and picked up a stone doorstop, the nearest heavy object she could lay her hands on.

Tadd turned, his eyes wild with shock and animal passion. Nerida looked absolutely mortified. As Tadd stumbled off the bed, Nerida pulled her dress down over her naked and slightly swollen body and curled up, crying.

"You swine!" Victoria hissed, hurling the doorstop at Tadd. He barely moved in time, as the rock crashed into the wall behind him.

Victoria had never been so livid in her life. She could barely think coherently.

"What are you doing, Victoria? You could have hurt me."

"Nerida's…. pregnant," she shouted. She suddenly realized why no one knew who the father of Nerida's baby was. Tadd had been raping her. It was too shocking for Victoria to contemplate. While she'd slept upstairs, completely unawares, Tadd had been downstairs molesting poor Nerida.

"Pregnant!" Tadd shouted, his face turning carmine. While Tadd fumbled with his trousers, he looked at Nerida as if she was the vilest creature on the earth. "You stupid bitch!" he shouted. "You'll not have my child." He lashed out at her.

Nerida wailed in anguish, burying her face in her hands.

"Tadd," Victoria shouted, stepping closer. "Get out of my house and never come back."

Tadd turned to her in astonishment. "She's been leading me on, Victoria. She wanted me to marry her."

"Don't lie to me, Tadd Sweeney. Nerida is little more than a child. Think yourself fortunate I don't call in the law. I want you to go and never set foot on Tambora again. Never! Do you hear me? Now get out of here, before I succumb to the urge of taking a stock whip to you."

There was nothing Tadd could say. He knew Victoria meant business. He'd never seen her more determined.

Victoria slammed the back door behind Tadd, and took a moment to compose herself before going back to Nerida. She felt like crying, and screaming, and smashing something, but gradually, with a few deep breaths, she gained self-restraint.

"You poor girl," she said to Nerida. "I am so sorry this happened to you."

Nerida continued to cry.

Victoria was thinking of Nerida's mother, Cissie. As she'd lay dying in her arms of snakebite, Victoria had promised Cissie she'd look after Nerida. "I know I've let you down, Nerida, but I swear I'll look after you and the baby." She took Nerida in her arms.

"I wish you had told me what he was doing. I'd have fired him a long time ago."

"I was 'fraid, Missus," she sobbed. "Tadd said you'd... send me 'way."

"I can't believe I've been so blind to his faults," Victoria whispered, finally letting the tears come. "Tara was right all along. Tadd is a terrible person."

An hour later, Victoria went back upstairs. She found Tara out on the balcony, alone. Riordan had gone to fetch drinks, and Ethan and Maddy were at the far end of the balcony, talking. Belle and Lottie had Charlie and Bluey up on the dance floor. If Victoria hadn't been so upset, she might have laughed at the sight they made. Charlie was about as coordinated as a drunk caught in a Willie-Willie, and Bluey thought he was Fred Astaire.

"You know where Nugget is, don't you, Tara?"

"Yes, Aunt, if he hasn't moved camp." Tara could see her aunt looked upset. "Will you go and fetch him first thing in the morning?"

"Of course. Has something happened, Aunt?"

Victoria closed her eyes, trying to shut out the horror of the scene she'd witnessed between Tadd and poor Nerida. "I just caught Tadd ...trying to rape Nerida."

"Oh, my God. Where is he?"

"He's gone."

"Then... surely he's not... the father...of her baby?" Tara found the thought appalling.

"I'd say so. Nerida is too upset to tell me much at the moment, but I doubt tonight was the first time he's been interfering with her."

"He's a despicable man." Tara thought of all she hadn't told her aunt, but nothing compared to Tadd ... raping Nerida.

"I've fired him. If he ever sets foot on Tambora again, I think I'll shoot him."

"Oh, Aunt. I know you are disappointed in him, but I'm sure it's for the best." Tara thought the timing was right to tell her aunt the whole truth about Tadd Sweeney. "I didn't tell you this before, Aunt, because I thought you had enough to deal with, but I found William Crombie's letter in his cottage."

Victoria looked momentarily stunned, but then she seemed resigned to the truth.

"He'd also kept all the correspondence from the bank, so you wouldn't know about the loan. I'm so sorry Aunt."

"I just wish I had listened to you, Tara, when you had doubts about him, but I thought Tadd was my friend, my confidante. My God, I remember a time when he wanted to marry me."

Tara wasn't surprised. She had suspected they'd been more than friends. "I believe he wanted Tambora, Aunt. It seems he was willing to go to any lengths to achieve his goal." Thinking of the will she'd made in his favour, Victoria said, "He'll never know how close he came to getting it."

CHAPTER THIRTY-FOUR

"You wanted to see me, Missus."

It was six thirty in the morning and Nugget had his hat in his hand as he stood in the shade of the veranda, where Victoria was waiting for him.

"Thank you for coming, Nugget," Victoria said, briefly glancing at Tara, who was standing behind the aboriginal stockman looking anxious. "Did Tara tell you …I fired Tadd last night?"

Nugget's eyes widened. "No, Missus." He glanced at Tara, waiting for her to confirm what Victoria said, just so he could believe it. He never thought he'd see the day.

Tara nodded, and looked at her aunt. "I thought I'd let you explain." She hadn't known how much information her Aunt wanted to give the men.

Victoria looked out over the plains surrounding the house, already hazy and dusty from the glaring sun and the scorching winds. "I didn't want to believe he was no good, Nugget. Even though the evidence was mounting, I suppose I had to see it for myself." Victoria turned to a chair and sat down wearily. "Last night… I caught Tadd trying to …rape Nerida. It was the last straw."

Nugget's eyes dropped. He'd suspected Tadd was forcing himself upon Nerida, but she wouldn't tell him anything. She secretly feared the tribe would get involved, and she didn't want any harm to come to Victoria. When he heard she was pregnant, via the bush telegraph, he offered to look after her, but Nerida was too proud to accept, and too timid to express how she felt. But Nugget sensed her shame, and her fears that her tribal family would shun her for carrying a white man's child. He had even hinted that she confided in Victoria, but she must have felt she couldn't.

"Nerida has been under my protection since Cissie died several years ago, and I feel I've let her down," Victoria said. Tears filled her eyes when she thought of how long Tadd might have been molesting Nerida.

"Nerida is shamed, Missus, but she not blame you."

"I blame myself, Nugget. I hope you know that had Tadd consulted me, I would never have let him fire you. I'm very sorry."

"You always treated me real good, Missus, but I could not stay after I heard what Tadd tell the shearers."

Victoria frowned. "Are you telling me the shearers came here?"

"Yes, Missus."

"Why didn't you tell me?"

Nugget shuffled uncomfortably, and Victoria and Tara realized Tadd had threatened him. Even after everything Tadd had done, they were both horrified.

"Tadd sent the shearers away, Missus. I heard him telling them 'bout Missus Tara living with the gipsies."

Tara closed her eyes as humiliation washed over her.

"… and him saying they wouldn't get any more work if they sheared on Tambora. Him no good, Missus."

Victoria felt like a fool for being the only one blind to Tadd's evilness. "Well, he's gone, Nugget, and he's never coming back. I asked you to come this morning because I need a new station manager, and I was hoping you'd be willing to fill the position."

Nugget looked startled. "There's plenty good white station managers looking for work, Missus."

"I know, Nugget. But why should I hire one of them when the best man for the job is right here. I may have been blind to Tadd's faults, but I wasn't blind to the fact that you and the other men have been doing most of the work around here. You know the station, and what I expect, and you've certainly earned the position."

Nugget was speechless. He felt choked with emotion. He'd never dreamed that one-day he'd be the manager of a station like Tambora. There weren't any aboriginal station managers in South Australia that he knew of.

Tara smiled broadly. She hadn't told her Aunt that she thought Nugget would make a good station manager, but she was certainly glad they agreed. "You'll accept, won't you, Nugget?" she said.

The aboriginal man grinned broadly. "I be crazy not to, Missus."

Victoria looked happy. "Then it's settled. You can have the manager's cottage, and a pay rise, as soon as we sell the wool."

"I'm happy to stay in the bunkhouse with the men, Missus."

"Well the cottage goes with the position, but it's up to you."

Tara's expression sobered. "Speaking of the wool, I had better get over to the sheds and help out."

Nugget turned to go with her, but paused. "Thank you, Missus," he said. "It's real good to be back home."

Victoria nodded and smiled at Nugget. She knew she'd done the right thing. Nugget deserved her confidence. "There's plenty of work to be done before tomorrow afternoon if we're to meet that deadline, so I'll get changed and join you in the sheds. Elsa can look after our guests for a few hours."

"Oh, Aunt, with all the commotion last night and this morning, I forgot to tell you Ethan left a telegram on the bureau in the dining room. I hope it wasn't something important."

"I'll take a look, and see you in the sheds."

Tadd Sweeney arrived at the hotel in William Creek just after nine o'clock in the morning. He hadn't slept a wink all night. He also hadn't shaved or changed his clothes and looked as weathered and rugged as the men had ever seen him. When he walked in and threw down his scuffed and dusty suitcase containing a few clothes and personal possessions, Ferris and Percy knew something was not right.

"What's all this, then?" Ferris asked, "Going on holiday?"

"I need a room," Tadd said grumpily.

The men glanced at each other quizzically. "For how long?" Ferris asked.

"Dunno yet, but what does it matter? You all booked out?" He was being sarcastic, but Ferris was too curious to notice.

"The shearers are still here. Have you left home, Tadd?" Ferris and Percy sniggered, but Tadd cast them a hostile glare that wiped the smile from their faces in an instant. "This is a flamin' hotel, isn't it? How can you explain a man dying of thirst?"

Ferris poured Tadd a drink, which he drained in one gulp. Refilling his glass, Ferris knew it was only a matter of time before the booze loosened Tadd's tongue.

Overall it had been an interesting morning in the Wombat Creek Hotel. As it was a Saturday, the bar was crowded. As well as the shearers, stockmen and roustabouts had come from as far away as Oodnadatta in the north and Hawker in the south. Dirk Dolan, an Irish/aboriginal dingo hunter had dropped in for a few drinks. His thirteen-year-old son was coming in on the afternoon train from Adelaide, to join him for the Christmas break. Dirk was always loud and usually drank far too much, but the men knew he had the loneliest job in the world. He travelled 'the dog fence', all three thousand two hundred and ninety seven miles of it, from Ceduna in South Australia, right up into the heart of Queensland. He was fond of reminding everyone that the dog fence was three times longer than the Great Wall of China.

By lunchtime, Tadd was leg-less. Ferris had propped him in a corner on a barstool, out of harms way. He'd been babbling for hours, but Ferris and the other men had been too busy and disinterested to listen. When he finally confessed that Victoria had caught him in Nerida's room, and fired him, Ferris's curiosity was aroused.

"That don't seem right," Ferris said suspiciously, as he poured Tadd another drink. "Nerida was willing, wasn't she?"

"Of course she was. You don't think I need to force myself on a woman, do ya? How was I supposed to know she was bloody well in the family way." He still couldn't believe the girl had gotten herself pregnant. "I thought abo women knew how to prevent unwanted babies."

"You got her pregnant?" Percy said incredulously. "Christ, Tadd, you should know better at your age."

"It wasn't me, you bloody fool. It was... Nugget."

"Nugget. He's always been sweet on Nerida," Ferris said.

"Has he?" Tadd hadn't realized.

"If he'd have gotten her pregnant, he'd have married her."

"She doesn't want to marry 'im, cause she's got bigger fish to fry."

"Oh yeah, and who would that be?"

"Me, of course."

The men smirked and Tadd became angry.

"I've got a cottage and a good position, and I've told you before, I was supposed to inherit Tambora before that gipsy tramp turned up."

"She's kin, Tadd. You can't argue about that. Besides, you haven't even got a job now, let alone a cottage."

"It's all her fault. Victoria and me were real close before she came along, putting ideas in her head. We might have married one day."

This time the men grimaced. Not one of them had ever believed Victoria would marry Tadd.

"Messing with Nerida sure spoiled your chances," Percy said, laughing.

"Yeah," Ferris said. "If you needed a woman, you should've come to town to see Lottie."

"You think you know so much. Lottie's not in town. She's out on Tambora with the girls."

"What?"

Tadd felt pleased with himself. "That's right."

"Do ya hear that, men?" Percy said. "Lottie and the girls are out on Tambora."

"What are they doing out there?" Wonky Warburton asked.

"Last night they were partying with Victoria and her guests," Tadd said, slurring his words. "You should have seen them. flamin' dancin' and laughin' they were, as if they were toffs. Drinking all Victoria's best wine and singin'. Dressed up like right fancy women they were."

Most of the men regretted not going to the party. At least half of them were 'in the dog house' with their wives, although they'd never admit it to each other. The women had wanted to go to the party. Even though they were doing all the gossiping, they'd all been looking forward to getting dressed up for one of Victoria's soirees and were certainly curious to meet Elsa Killain after she'd scolded the Vine sisters and Mildred Gowers. It would have been the first real social occasion in the area since the beginning of the Depression, not counting the Gymkhana, which was more fun for the men. But the women couldn't go to the party without the men, and the men were adamant they were boycotting it.

"When are the women coming back," one of the men shouted from the back of the bar.

"Dunno," Tadd said. "Maybe they'll stay out there."

"Well Victoria will soon go broke, because Wally and the boys aren't shearing her sheep."

Tadd scoffed. By now he was leaning on his elbow on the bar. "They're doin' that themselves."

"What? Shearing?" Wally said incredulously, pushing his way through the crowd to get to Tadd.

"Yep. They're all having a go, Charlie, Bluey and young Karl, - even that pretty boy Irishman. They've even got Tara as roustabout, and the lad as tar boy."

"Nugget's not there, is he?" Wonky said. "He could shear a hundred a day when he was young."

"You can bet yer life he's back by now. Tara was talking about makin' him station manager. Can you imagine 'im as station manager? Bloody criminal it is."

The men weren't concerned with Tadd's minor grievances, especially as they all respected Nugget.

"This is your fault, Wally," Des Brown said. "If you'd have sheared Victoria's sheep, we wouldn't all be as frustrated as roosters locked out of the hen house."

"That's right," Fred Wilcox said. "I've just spent a month branding cattle at a stockman's camp in the Simpson, with only sweaty men and cows for company. I was really looking forward to this weekend, then I get to town and have to spend my time looking at your ugly mugs, when I could be tucked up between the sheets with Maddy and those magnificent breasts of 'ers. No offence, but I'd much prefer to be with 'er right now."

"Yeah, and I have a regular Saturday night booking with Belle," another man mumbled.

"This isn't our fault," Wonky protested, his good eye wide with indignation. "We thought we were doing the right thing."

Wally Sherbourne shook his head. "I can't believe they're trying to shear the sheep themselves out on Tambora. You've got to hand it to Victoria and the men out there, even that Tara woman. They've got real guts."

The men went quiet.

"Tara! Tara, the children are coming." Victoria was practically running as she came into the sheds with the telegram in her hand and a look of pure shock on her perspiring face.

Tara threw a fleece over the table to be skirted. She was so tired she could hardly think straight. "Children!"

"Yes, the children, all twelve of them, aged between five and fifteen. Five girls and seven boys."

Tara suddenly realized what she was talking about. "Oh, my Lord. When will they be here?"

"Tomorrow. The telegram Ethan brought is from a Mrs. Blythe Horton. Elsa said she's the woman who came here to inspect the place. She apologizes for the short notice, but apparently they've got so many children in the government run homes, they don't know what to do with them. Elsa is numb with shock. She was sure we'd be turned down, but Mrs. Horton says the house met all the standards required, and that it was obvious every effort was being made to ensure the children would be properly cared for in a homely, but gracious atmosphere."

"That's wonderful, Aunt. But are we ready for the children? There's beds to be made … I don't even know if we have enough food."

"We don't have to worry about that for the time being. Apparently, due to the short notice, Mrs. Horton is sending five days food rations with the children."

"Then I suppose we're all set."

Lottie, Belle and Maddy suddenly appeared behind Victoria. Tara and her Aunt were surprised to see them all in men's dungarees, borrowed from the store in the bunkhouse. "We're here to earn our keep," Lottie said, her blond hair covered by a scarf. "We've left Elsa and Sorrel making twelve beds."

"That's good of you," Tara said gratefully. "We need all the help we can get."

At ten o'clock, Sorrel and Elsa came over to the sheds with trays of cinnamon cakes freshly baked by Sanja. Nugget had the Billy boiling for tea. The men had sheared sixty-five sheep between them. Even Riordan was getting the hang of it, but his back felt like it was breaking in two.

"We'll do better when Ethan gets here," Nugget said. Ethan was helping Saladin load and deliver a shipment of supplies for the children at the mission. He'd promised to return to the station shortly after lunch, and said they'd work through the night if they had to, to get all the sheep sheared. Victoria feared they'd never make the train in two days, despite Lottie helping Tara, and Belle and Maddy stitching the wool into bales. She felt more dispirited than she ever had in her life. Not only did she not want to disappoint William Crombie, but she wanted the money to pay the men and Nerida all she owed them. She wouldn't feel right until they were square.

As the men were about to get back to work after a brief break, they heard the engine of a car. A minute later they looked up to find the best shearers for miles around, - Wally, Wonky, Dave Barnett and Mitch O'Connell at the door of the sheds, with Rex Crawley behind them.

"What are you doing here?" Victoria asked coldly.

Wally looked as contrite as a man his size could. "If you lot have got the guts to try and shear a thousand sheep yourselves, then I take my hat off to you," he said, literally removing his hat.

"If you came all the way out here to take your hat off, Wally Sherbourne, you wasted your time," Victoria snapped.

"We came here to shear sheep, Victoria. I'm sorry we listened to Tadd. What your niece did before she came out here is no-ones business but her own."

"Not many agree with you."

"As we were getting ready to leave town, Ethan turned up at the pub. He reminded the men that not many of them are eligible for the priesthood. I think they got the point. If your Tara is half as gutsy as you, and from what I hear she is, she's alright in my books."

Victoria was silent for a moment. She was tempted to smile, but she fought the urge. Glancing at Tara, she could see the relief in her green eyes. "Are you willing to work all night, because that's what it's going to take if I'm to meet my shipping deadline."

"We won't stop till the job's done."

As there were more than eight hundred sheep to shear, Victoria was impressed. She looked at the men and women in the sheds with her. They all looked relieved to see the professionals. The work was killing them, but they'd never know how grateful she was for their loyalty and devotion.

"Then you had better get started," Victoria said to Wally.

Wally walked to the back of the sheds and looked out at the pen of sheep they had sheared, and smiled to himself. The poor sheep had plenty of nicks and cuts, but overall they hadn't done a bad job for amateurs. Victoria was watching him, so he dared not comment. Nevertheless, it was time to show them how it was done professionally.

By the time the job was finished, and the shearers had laid down their shears, it was 2 a.m. Victoria had put several oil lamps in the sheds so they could see what they were doing, and the men had actually found shearing in the cool of night easier going, despite their weariness. Two hours later the wool was all stitched into the bales, Sanja had fed the men and they had retired exhausted to the bunkhouse.

"I think we're going to make the deadline," Victoria said to Tara, over a cup of tea in the dining room. It was the first time she'd felt confident.

"I hope so, but I do wish the children weren't arriving today, Aunt. I'm so tired I could sleep for twenty four hours, even in this heat."

"I know what you mean." Victoria was almost asleep in the chair.

As Tara went to mount the stairs, she noticed suitcases by the front door. "Are those Sorrel's?" she asked her Aunt. "I thought she was staying for another few days."

"They belong to Riordan. He told me he's going back to town with Rex Crawley this morning, so he can catch Monday afternoon's train to Adelaide."

Tara was shocked. "Why? I knew he'd be leaving sometime, but why now, so suddenly?"

"I honestly don't know," Victoria said. "But I suspect it has something to do with you."

Tara knocked softly on Riordan's door, which was slightly ajar, but there was no answer. She pushed the door open and saw his silhouette on the balcony.

"Riordan?" she whispered, as she came up behind him.

He turned in surprise. "I thought you'd be asleep," he said, his expression pained. "You must be exhausted." After a brief rest, Tara had gone back to the sheds to skirt the wool for the shearers. She was more fatigued than she'd ever been in her life.

"I was going to bed when I saw your suitcases. Were you going to leave without saying goodbye?" Tara knew Rex was leaving after breakfast with the shearers.

Riordan turned to look out over the moonlit landscape. It would be light in just over an hour. "I hate good-bye's, and saying goodbye to you is something I didn't want to face." Suddenly emotional, he turned away. He couldn't bear the thought of never seeing Tara again.

Tara did not know what to say. Since Riordan had asked her to marry him, he had not mentioned his feelings again, and Tara hadn't given him a definite answer, so she didn't understand why he was suddenly leaving. "Why are you going so abruptly? Is it the work, or the heat? It does take some getting used to."

"The day I arrived with your mother, I saw you kissing Ethan Hunter."

Tara blushed.

"It was the most passionate kiss I had ever seen. When I kissed you, you did not respond in the same way, yet I foolishly hoped… until… I saw you kissing Ethan again the night of the party. I knew then that you would never come with me to Ireland."

Tara was confused. "Riordan, I … don't understand that myself…"

"If you kissed me like that, Tara. I would be the happiest man in the world."

"Surely you are not suggesting that Ethan has feelings for me, or I for him. We are so different, worlds apart in fact."

"Perhaps that is the attraction, Tara, for there certainly is one, even if you refuse to admit it."

Tara did not know what to say, or how to respond. That she didn't deny there was an attraction almost broke his heart.

"He's a nomad, Tara, a drifter. Surely, you don't want that life again?"

"No, of course not..."

"We could have a good life together, a nice home... even a family if that is what you really want."

Tara remembered Riordan telling her aunt he was not fond of children.

Riordan could see Tara felt torn. "I'm leaving in a few hours, Tara. Come with me..."

"I have Jack and Hannah to think about, Riordan. They are my family."

"You know they are not your responsibility, Tara. You should be having babies of your own."

Tara recoiled. It was suddenly clear to her that Riordan would never understand her feelings for Jack and Hannah, but Ethan understood. He seemed to understand everything about her.

"I can't go with you, Riordan." Tara walked to the door, where she turned to look at him. He was still out on the balcony, his back toward her, but she could feel his rigid pain. "Good bye, Riordan. I will never forget you." She turned to go.

"Tara."

"Yes."

"If you ever change your mind, you know where to find me."

Tara closed the door behind her.

CHAPTER THIRTY-FIVE

Tara was awakened by a commotion downstairs. The sun was high in the sky, searing all beneath it, which meant it was the middle of the day. In the few befuddled moments that follow wakefulness, it registered that Riordan would be long gone. A small part of her was going to miss his clever wit and boyish charm, but their lives were destined to be at cross-purposes.

Tara knew Riordan thrived on mixing with the colourful characters and socialites in the art world. Buying and selling rare pieces, and holding exhibitions to unveil new talents were what he lived for. He spoke about it constantly. The only thing missing in his near-perfect world was a decorative wife on his arm, a dilemma, as he could only imagine Tara in that role, and she wanted something entirely different, a quiet life in a happy home with Jack and Hannah.

When Tara looked over the stair banister, the drowsiness she was suffering, induced by the heat and lack of sleep, evaporated. The entrance foyer was full of excited children of varying ages and sizes. They were mostly poorly dressed, with unkempt hair, some without shoes, and the little ones were flushed from their journey in the heat. A bewildered Victoria was standing amidst them.

As Tara came down the stairs, she could see through the open front door. Rex Crawley was making an uncharacteristic hasty retreat in the Packard, leaving Nugget to stack the haphazardly dropped boxes of food rations on the veranda.

Victoria was clamoring to get the attention of the rowdy children, to no avail. They were full of questions, and shouting to be heard above their own din.

"When can we go riding?"
"Are there any creeks or dams to swim in?"
"Are there any lambs or calves to feed?"
"Can we climb the trees?"
"I'm thirsty... I'm hungry..."

Tara groaned as she took the last few steps to the ground floor.

Suddenly a gong reverberated through the house, and a hush fell over the group. Elsa and Sorrel were standing by the gong, which was just outside the sitting room doorway.

"Now listen, children," Elsa said, her voice cracking with nerves. "I'm sure you are all thirsty and tired from the long journey out here, but there will be no refreshments served until you are quiet and orderly. My name is Mrs. Killain, and this is Mrs. Windspear. Your hosts are Mrs. Milburn, and her niece, Mrs. Flynn."

"Tara, please," Tara said. 'Mrs. Flynn' made her feel old, and worse, - matronly.

"The house girl is Nerida, and the cook is Sanja. There is more staff on the station, whom you'll meet later. Please be patient over the next few days, while we learn your names." Suddenly lost for words, Elsa glanced at Sorrel and Victoria.

Sorrel took the lead. "While we organize who will have which room, you will be required to go quietly to the dining room with Nerida, where Sanja will serve drinks and cakes he baked this morning."

"You can leave your suitcases in the entrance hall for now," Victoria added. To her surprise the children dropped their small, and in most instances, battered cases that hinted at an unsettled life, and followed Nerida quietly to the dining room. Victoria turned to Elsa. "I wish I had thought of hitting the gong," she said.

"I didn't know what else to do to get their attention," Elsa replied.

"You were marvelous, mother," Tara said. "And you too, Sorrel. You both sounded so... in charge."

"Thank you. I can assure you it was a sham," Elsa whispered.

"Wasn't there a chaperon with the children?" Sorrel asked.

"No, which is very odd indeed," Victoria said. "But I doubt there was room. There were three youngsters in the front of the car with Rex and the other nine children rode in the back, amidst the mail and the supplies he was delivering, which included a young turkey to add to Sadie's menagerie. I couldn't imagine a lady climbing in there."

"Excuse me, Missus," Nugget said from the front doorway. "Rex said a lady name Missus Horton was on the train with the children, but she ... very big lady, and could not fit in his automobile with children." Rex had actually described Blythe Horton as a *'fat sheila' with arms like a wrestler,* but although Nugget had had a good laugh, he sensed as 'manager' discretion was called for.

"She probably hasn't yet recovered from her last trip out here with Rex," Elsa said diplomatically, her thoughts running along the same lines as Rex's comments to Nugget. She certainly couldn't imagine Blythe Horton scrambling into the back of Rex's battered Packard with a turkey and several children.

"Rex give me this letter to give to you, Missus, and this," he held out a bigger envelope, marked CONFIDENTIAL. "He said this is medical and background information on some of the children."

"Thank you, Nugget. Let's see what the letter says." Victoria opened it and scanned the brief contents. "Mrs. Horton apologizes for leaving the children with Rex, but says she couldn't squeeze in his vehicle with them, and that Rex assured her he would get the children safely to Tambora."

Victoria raised her brows. "Did you notice he couldn't get away from here quick enough?"

The women nodded, each wondering if they'd feel the same by the end of the week.

"That's about it really. Mrs. Horton has supplied a number where she can be contacted with any questions about particular children, or problems. Our first payment of twenty- four pounds will be in the bank by the end of the week." Victoria looked up at each of them. "For better or worse, we're on our own with the children." She sighed wearily. "I hope we can make it work, - Heaven help us."

It took two hours to organize the children into rooms and get them settled, which left the women exhausted. If they'd had more than a few hours sleep they may have coped better, but as it was they were feeling short tempered and unable to contend with the children's questions and idiosyncrasies.

They struggled through the rest of the day, and dinner, which was a noisy and messy affair. Sanja had looked over the food rations that came with the children in disgust. The tinned meat he described as 'rubbishy', and the 'bush' biscuits, bags of oats and corn meal, he shook his head at. He then made Dhal and Roti bread, and plenty of rice to go with his version of a stew, - a milder version of a curry.

The children devoured the meal, pleasing the cook immensely. By evening they were all ready for an early night, but it seemed to take forever to settle everyone. To Victoria's surprise and delight, Lottie and Belle told bedtime stories to some of the group.

The youngest of the orphans was to share Hannah's room. Mary had turned five but was emotionally and physically scarred by the many traumatic twists and turns in her brief life. She could barely speak coherently, or undress herself, and ate with her fingers. In the history supplied, the women discovered her mother's battered body had been found beside a canal in Manchester, soon after Mary was born. Her drunken father was the prime suspect, but nothing was proven, and he kept one step ahead of the law by moving incessantly, which meant Mary had more than thirty addresses by the time she was four, when her father brought her to Australia. After a drunken binge, he set his bed alight while smoking, and was horrifically burned. With no other relatives in Australia, and nobody in England willing to take Mary, she was placed in an orphanage for her own safety. That Mary was withdrawn, or backward, was of little consequence to Hannah, who was thrilled to have another little girl to share her room.

Early next morning, Tara was again woken by the sound of Rex Crawley's automobile. If the wind was blowing in the right direction, it was possible to hear the engine of his car long before a snaking cloud of dust rising in the air was visible. This morning, however, the sound was partially drowned out by children's voices, which led Tara to conclude that the silence of the outback was a thing of the past on Tambora.

Tara went out onto the balcony, and saw a woman leap from the front seat of Rex's car as if she'd been sitting on an ant nest. Her first impression was of a large, slovenly person, but in all fairness, everyone who alighted from Rex's automobile looked dishevelled.

"Fer the love of Holy Moses! We're lucky to get here in one piece, you raving lunatic," the woman shouted, and slammed the automobile's door shut on Rex's retort. "You must have paid someone from an asylum fer yer driving license."

Tara recognized an acute Londonderry accent.

Rex opened the driver's side door, and stuck his head out. "I'm the mail man, not a flamin' taxi service. You can walk back to town for all I care. Better yet, I'll send a relative of yours to pick you up. A bullock!"

The woman shrieked in horror, a sound to rival a tree full of screeching parrots, but before she could say another word, Rex was reversing at break neck speed. He spun the car around in a cloud of dust, and headed off, leaving the woman coughing and choking in his wake.

"Can I help you?" Tara called from the balcony when the woman had gotten her breath back. Tara was mortified by what Rex had said to her, and yet curious. It crossed her mind that she might be related to one of the children now in their care.

The woman looked up, squinting in the morning sun light, while furiously swatting the bush flies that had descended upon her. Her puckered face reminded Tara of a twisted gumshoe. She certainly couldn't match that face with one of the children's in the house. "Oh, but it's good to be hearing an Irish accent out here in this God forsaken country, that no good Catholic would call home. That crazy man was no assistance whatsoever. He claimed to be a local of ten years, and yet he hadn't heard of the Reverend Jim Malally from the Hermannsburg Mission, or my sister."

"I've heard of the Hermannsburg Mission, but not a Reverend Jim Malally, but I'm a relative newcomer out here myself. Perhaps my Aunt knows of your sister. What is her name?"

"Maureen O'Sullivan," the woman said. Tara almost fainted.

"I was told in Port Adelaide that my sister left Customs House with her children, and now you are telling me that she perished on the Emerald Star, with her husband. How do I know this is true?" Moyna Conway was sitting opposite Tara in the sitting room, her expression more one of hostility than despair, and yet she dabbed at invisible tears.

"I identified Maureen and Michael's bodies," Tara said emotionally. "They had tied themselves together… and drowned… I'm terribly sorry, Mrs. Conway. I know this is a shocking way to find out the truth. I was Maureen's cabin mate, and she was a wonderful mother to Jack and Hannah, and the first real friend I ever had. I loved her dearly. You can ask me anything that will prove I'm telling the truth."

"How can you expect me to take the word of someone who stole my sister's identity?"

Tara felt her heart sink. "I know it was despicable, but the circumstances were… extraordinary."

Although Moyna was upset to hear her sister had lost her life, her sole purpose for this trip was financial gain. With Maureen dead, and herself as the children's legal guardian, the compensation offered the relatives of survivors had virtually fallen into her lap. To think, she almost hadn't made the journey, but then her husband had broken his back at work, becoming a liability, and his devoted sister, a woman Moyna detested, had come to help look after him. It was an opportunity too good to pass up, so Moyna left her children with her sister-in-law and husband. She was thinking of the future. She would not live like a pauper, or work like a slave.

Tara lowered her head. "Moyna, you have to understand I was afraid the authorities would put Jack and Hannah in a home and separate them. Jack was afraid, too, and poor Hannah was bewildered. I know I did a terrible thing, but I felt I had no choice. I'm very fond of the children."

"Bollocks! You were after the compensation the shipping line is paying."

Tara was startled and Victoria looked shocked.

Elsa was standing behind Tara. She placed her hands on her shoulders. "My daughter would not do such a terrible thing," she said.

"That's right," Victoria added. "We have not heard about any compensation."

"You are probably all in on it," Moyna said, leveling her attention on Tara. "I could have you arrested for what you did."

Tara's heart sank. "Michael wanted me to look after the children if anything happened."

"Oh, really. I suppose you have that in writing?"

"Of course not, Moyna. There was no time. The ship was sinking and … on fire. The children were hastily put in a life raft with me when theirs had trouble being lowered, and Michael… looked at me… " Tara could see his expression so clearly. It was burned in her memory. "I could only describe it as … beseechingly…."

"Are you telling me he never actually *asked* you to take the children?"

"He didn't speak the words, but he didn't have to…"

Moyna looked smug. "Then you assumed that is what he meant. He could just as easily have been *beseeching* you to get the children to me."

Tara had no reply. She was certain Michael did not want the children to go to Moyna any more than Maureen did, but she could not say so without causing offence.

"The children should be with family," Moyna said. "I am taking them back to Ireland with me."

Tara almost choked on a sob. She leapt to her feet and fled the room in tears.

Elsa sat down opposite Moyna, whom she had decided was a woman completely lacking in compassion. "My daughter did what she thought was best for the children, Mrs. Conway. She had no way of contacting you…"

"She made no effort, did she? The authorities found me to tell me my brother-in-law had died."

"Your sister had told her you have a big family of your own."

"My three eldest girls are making their own way in the world these days." She didn't say that they had gotten out as soon as they could, going into service for wages, instead of slaving for her for nothing. "Although I still have the four youngest at home…" Two of which were boys, and her husband had insisted they find work to bring in extra money, leaving Moyna and the two girls to look after the farm. "I love children, and my sister's two deserve to be brought up with kin."

At that moment several boisterous boys came leaping down the stairs, followed by two more who slid down the banister. Elsa noticed the noise they were making seemed to irritate Moyna, a hint that what she had said about loving children was not quite the truth. Jack closely followed the boys, who ran out of the front door ahead of him, chasing

Shellie. As he passed the sitting room, Jack glanced in, and instantly recognized the back of Moyna. He stopped in his tracks, his features ashen.

"Aunty Moyna…"

Moyna Conway turned. "Jack…"

"What are you doing here?" Jack asked in a less than friendly tone. It crossed his mind that Tara had sent for her, but he could hardly believe she'd do that.

"That's no way to greet your Aunt, Jack," Moyna said with a wooden smile pasted on her face. "I've come to take you back to Ireland. You and your sister are going to live with me."

Jack appeared devastated. "I don't want to go back to Ireland."

The fake smile evaporated like the first drops of rain in the desert. "You are too young to know what's best for you, Jack," Moyna claimed. It was obvious to those watching that she was restraining herself. Sweat was beading above her unruly brows and her lips were twitching as if she wanted to let fly with a few choice phrases. "Your parents would have wanted you to live with family."

"The children are happy here, Mrs. Conway," Victoria insisted.

Moyna took a deep breath, again a hint that she was holding back. "I'm sure you have cared for them as best your can, Mrs. Milburn, but they'll soon settle with us." The fact that her entire house was smaller than the sitting room she was sitting in made Moyna feel envious and resentful.

"My daughter loves those children, Mrs. Conway," Elsa said. "She'll be broken hearted if you take them. I'm begging you not to do it."

Victoria was thinking the house would not be the same without Jack and Hannah.

"I sent a telegram to the relatives of a Mrs. Tara Flynn…And you didn't even bother to reply…"

"There's a simple explanation for that. We did not receive it," Victoria said.

"Well, I received a reply from a Reverend Jim Malally, who told me the children were not happy here, Mrs. Killain, so who am I to believe?"

Victoria frowned in confusion. "I do not know of a Reverend Jim Malally, Mrs. Conway, and I know everyone in the area." Victoria suddenly had an inkling of what might have happened. Tadd had intercepted the telegram and replied to Moyna. Anger made her shake. She suspected such a malicious action was Tadd's revenge.

"Please have someone gather the children's belongings, Mrs. Milburn. I'm taking them, now."

Tara reappeared. "You can't take them, Moyna. I won't let you. Maureen didn't want you to have them. She told me you were unkind to your own children." She placed her arms around Jack's shoulders protectively and felt him trembling.

Jack could tell Tara was distraught at the thought of losing him and Hannah. Any doubts he had that she had contacted his Aunt were gone.

"How dare you say such a thing," Moyna shouted, no longer able to control her temper.

"I won't go with you," Jack cried. "And I won't let you take my sister to be your slave."

Moyna gasped in shock, her face turning carmine with rage. Victoria and Tara both noted her clenched fists, and knew Jack and Hannah would have a terrible life with her.

At that moment, Lottie came into the room carrying a tea tray, a look of concern on her face.

"You have no choice, Jack," Moyna said. "I have the law on my side. This woman," she gestured rudely to Tara, "had no right to take you from Port Adelaide."

"I asked Tara to take me and Hannah, so we wouldn't be separated. Tara has been good to us, and we love her. She's going to be our new momma."

Tara glanced at Jack, her eyes filling with tears. She wanted to be their mother with all her heart. She had never been more certain of anything.

Moyna's eyes became bulbous. "Your momma! That woman will never be your momma. I'm your legal guardian. These people are just after the compensation being offered by the shipping line."

"You know that's not true, Jack," Tara whispered. "I had no idea the shipping line were offering any compensation to the survivors."

Jack turned to his aunt. "I don't care about money, Aunty Moyna. I like it here, and so does Hannah. We want to stay with Tara, and her aunt. They're our new family. If you try to take us, I'll run away with Hannah and come back here."

"You'll do no such thing. Bring Hannah to me, at once."

Jack turned and fled outside.

Moyna leapt to her feet as quickly as her bulk allowed. The result was an ungraceful, snorting, struggle. "Come here, at once, Jack, or so help me…"

Jack ignored her.

Tara left the room and went upstairs to find Hannah, vowing that if she had to, she'd go bush with the children rather than let Moyna take them.

"Please don't take Jack and Hannah?" Victoria said. "Tara loves them so much." "They're my sisters children, and I'm raising them."

Elsa stood up in disgust and left the room to find Tara and comfort her.

"Victoria," Lottie interrupted. "May I have a word with Mrs. Conway?"

For a moment Victoria looked confused, but she nodded, fighting tears. She left the room looking every day of her age.

Lottie watched her friend go, her heart breaking for her. She knew Tara and Victoria were good people. They did not warrant the pain Moyna Conway was putting them through. Injustice always angered Lottie. She'd seen so much of it. She'd also been the victim of people like Moyna many, many times. Something drastic had to be done.

"Mrs. Conway, now that it's just the two of us, let's get down to the real reason you are here." Lottie had met all types, and she was sure she had Moyna Conway pegged.

Moyna was seated again. It was obvious her legs were giving her grief. They were so swollen; her ankles and knees were no longer visible. "Whatever do you mean?" she said, thumping her fist on the sofa beside her.

"Your theatrics do not impress me, Mrs. Conway, so save your energy. How much do you want, to go away, and leave my friends and the children in peace?"

Moyna gasped indignantly. "How could you suggest…."

Lottie interrupted. "How much, Mrs. Conway? You must have an idea what the shipping line is paying in compensation, so I'm sure you have a figure in your head."

Moyna studied Lottie as if trying to ascertain whether she was serious or not. She tipped her head back and her beady eyes squinted like a rat's, her nose and hairy upper lip twitching in anticipation.

"If he doesn't run away, Jack is going to make your life miserable for the next ten years. Why not let Tara deal with him?"

Moyna suspected this was true, but she'd lock him in a shed indefinitely if she had to, as long as she could use his compensation money. But she needed Hannah to work for her. Lottie watched the workings of her cunning mind. She was sure there was no love for the children, whom Moyna saw only as a meal ticket, and free labour.

Moyna scowled. The compensation was sure to be very good…

Lottie could see she wasn't about to relinquish her hold on the children without a little more incentive.

"You know, Mrs. Conway, people have been known to just disappear out here in the outback… never to be seen again."

Moyna's eyes narrowed. "What do you mean?"

"I was just thinking how lucky you were to find us out here, but of course you had Rex's help, which I doubt you can count on for your return trip. That puts you at the mercy of the elements. There are thousands and thousands of miles of open country out here, and so few people, and more deadly species of spider and snake than you'll find anywhere else in the world. I've seen ants an inch long. They could completely devour a woman your size in less than an hour, leaving nothing but a few bones. Call me bizarre, but I find that sort of thing so... fascinating. Did you know some of the aborigines are cannibals? If you were to become... lost... there aren't enough people out here to search..."

"What about the police?" Moyna said.

"The nearest police are in Marree, and they won't go too far from any form of civilization. Not that I blame them." Lottie suddenly gasped in fright, as three fearsome aboriginal's peered through the living room window. Their faces and bodies were painted in ochre, and they had a menacing expression. One carried a spear, which he pointed at the women.

Moyna turned to see what had frightened Lottie, and shrieked in terror.

Lottie studied the faces, and thought there was something familiar... Suddenly, it was all she could do to keep a straight face. Then, as unexpectedly as they had appeared, the faces vanished.

"Where have they gone?" Moyna asked, her bulbous eyes almost popping out her head.

"I don't know... perhaps our stockmen scared them off. I'm sure we are safe, for now. Victoria always keeps a loaded gun at hand."

Moyna continued to look out of the window, where in the distance, swirls of dust could be seen rising in the sky. Her mind was running rampant with unimaginable horrors, and she was suddenly very homesick for Ireland. "How much are you offering me?" she asked, her tone taking on a tinge of desperateness. "Keep in mind that I had to borrow the money to come all the way from Ireland, and the trip was very expensive." For the first time she noticed the expensive rings and gold chains Lottie was wearing. They looked to be worth a fortune. "I'm very fond of those children...."

Lottie noted that although she claimed to be fond of Jack and Hannah, that fondness didn't stretch to concern.

"I will give you a cheque for a hundred pounds right now, on one condition. You must sign the children over to Tara, legally. You can then go home with what we both know you came for."

Lottie called Ethan on the radio. He was up at his cabin, tending the camels. "Ethan, I'd like a favour, and I'm willing to pay generously."

Ethan was curious. "You know that is not necessary, Lottie. What is it?"

"Has Saladin left for Marree yet?"

"No, but he'll be gone in less than an hour. Why, Lottie? What's going on?"

"I'd like him to take someone with him." Lottie went on to explain the situation, asking for Ethan's vow of silence on the matter.

"I'm sure that can be arranged?" Ethan said. "I'll have Saladin saddle up *Horace* if you like." Ethan was half joking. *Horace* was as predictable as rain in the outback.

Lottie gasped. "Have you still got *Hurricane Horace*, Ethan? I thought you would have shot him years ago."

"You know I haven't the heart, Lottie. He's Hannibal's sibling. Old Bill MacDonald had him for a few months, but I brought him back two days ago."

"Whatever did Bill want with him? Nobody in their right mind would want to ride him."

"Horace hates dingoes. He was attacked as a youngster and has never gotten over it. Bill used him as a kind of watchdog for his calves, while he was away drafting and branding sheep. Unfortunately, he developed a liking for chasing the cattle dogs and almost killed two of them. He is better behaved with people these days, as long as he doesn't see a dingo, but I wouldn't use him to transport any fragile cargo..."

Lottie grinned wickedly. "He'd be perfect, Ethan."

"I'll have Saladin call there shortly. Have his passenger ready."

"Thank you, Ethan. As a special favour to me, could you ask Saladin to take the longest possible route to Marree?"

"Ah, the scenic route, alongside the Oodnadatta Track. That takes in Dead Man's Leap, Poison Sister's Lookout, the Hanging Tree and the Sulfur Pools, but shouldn't your unwelcome guest be going to Wombat Creek to get the train?"

"Yes, but I'd like her to see a bit of our fine country before she returns home." Lottie wanted to be certain Moyna Conway never returned to Tambora. "I hear she didn't hit it off with Rex, so I know he would be especially grateful."

CHAPTER THIRTY-SIX

"No matter what Moyna Conway says, I refuse to let her take Jack and Hannah." Tara paced Hannah's room. The little girl was playing beside the bed with Mary, amidst a pile of smooth stones they had collected. They were locked in their own fantasy world, innocently oblivious to the drama unfolding around them.

"I don't know what you can do, Tara?" Elsa said. "She does have the law on her side. I'm just praying she doesn't follow through with her threat to have you arrested."

Tara heard the tremor of fear in her mother's voice, and it angered her that Moyna's action was also affecting her. She'd also noticed that her Aunt was upset.

"They'll have to catch me first, and they won't do that if I take the children and go walkabout with the Aboriginals."

"Tara, what kind of life would you have on the run, with no roof over your head?"

"Not ideal, granted, but the children and I did spend a couple of days in the bush, and it wasn't so bad. It's not like I'm not used to camping out."

Tara was dreading such a life, but she did want to give her mother some reassurance they'd be all right.

Elsa knew Tara was thinking with her heart and not with her head. "At least as a gipsy you had the shelter of a caravan. Spending two days in the bush is virtually no indication of how difficult such a life would be indefinitely. From what Victoria has told me, there is no water out there and plenty of snakes and I can't bear to think what else, not to mention this intolerable heat. It would be a terrible life for you and the children. Jack may find it an adventure at first, but think of dear little Hannah."

Tara looked at Hannah's soft blonde curls and cherub face and knew her mother was right, but the thought of losing the children was unbearable. "Anything, mother, including living in the bush, would be better than being separated from Jack and Hannah."

At the balcony doors, Elsa looked out at the vast, inhospitable country surrounding them, which was shimmering in a heat haze. She couldn't imagine spending one day out there herself, but the thought of Tara and the children disappearing into that void terrified her.

As Elsa stood at the balcony doors, Saladin came into view aboard a camel. Her first thoughts were that he had come to take Moyna Conway and the children back to Wombat Creek, and she panicked, but then she noticed he had only one other camel with him. When they stopped in the grounds below, the spare camel, an enormous wild-eyed beast, growled and hissed so aggressively, it caught Tara's attention, as she hastily threw odd articles of clothing into a suitcase.

"Is Ethan here?" She stopped what she was doing in mid action. "No, it's the robed one."

"Saladin?"

Tara went out onto the balcony and looked down. "Oh, my Lord. He's here to take the children away." Her hand covered her mouth, as tears filled her eyes, and she turned to flee.

"I don't think so, Tara," Elsa said calmly. "They won't all fit on one camel, will they?"

Tara stopped. "No, they won't!" She came back out onto the balcony and watched as Moyna Conway appeared and awkwardly climbed aboard the growling beast. Along with plenty of reassurance, Lottie gave her a broad brimmed hat, and introduced her to Saladin, who barely acknowledged her as he tied her small case onto the camel. As if sensing she was there, the Afghan looked up at Tara with that cold, unemotional expression of his, and then something unusual happened. His lips moved in the barest of a smile, softening the expression in his dark eyes. Then he turned away. It happened so quickly that Tara could almost believe she had imagined it.

"Hold on tight," Lottie said, as the enormous, shedding camel got to its feet, but Moyna shrieked, and nearly tumbled off, the hat flying away. Lottie retrieved it, and Moyna and Saladin set off.

"She's leaving, mother," Tara said. "I can't believe it. She's actually going… without the children. What could have made her change her mind?"

Moyna looked a frightful sight. Her derriere was wider than the camel's and her swollen legs jutted out like oversized oars from a rowboat. Even as they moved away, Tara and her mother could hear her complaining bitterly.

"I have no idea, Tara. Let's go downstairs and find out."

When Tara and Elsa got to the bottom of the stairs, Victoria was standing in the open doorway. Lottie had just turned from waving Moyna off.

"I saw Moyna Conway leaving," Tara said to her aunt.

"And she won't be back," Lottie said, as she came through the door.

Tara visibly sagged, and tears of relief sprang to her eyes. "What made her change her mind? She was adamant she was taking the children."

Tara was looking at Victoria for answers, but her aunt was looking at Lottie.

"How did you convince her not to take the children?" Victoria asked Lottie, clearly baffled.

Lottie caught the hint of suspicion in her voice and went through to the sitting room, and the other women followed.

"Did *you* change her mind, Lottie?" Tara asked.

"I can't take all the credit," she said smiling, "but I'm so relieved she's gone.' Lottie laughed. "She's going to have a Hell of a trip with Saladin. She's riding *Hurricane Horace* all the way to Marree."

"Oh, my Lord! I didn't recognize him." Victoria laughed.

Tara looked at her mother and aunt in bewilderment.

"Unless he's changed, which I very much doubt," Victoria said. "*Horace* is the nastiest, most unpredictable brute to ever hold the title of domestic camel. Heaven help Moyna!"

"Ethan assures me he's better behaved around humans these days," Lottie said. "But dingoes still send him into a frenzy. It's a long story, but he was attacked by a dingo as a youngster. If he should see one on their travels, Moyna Conway will have an experience she will never forget."

"What are the odds they'll come across a dingo between here and Marree," Tara asked.

"Pretty darn good," Victoria said.

The women laughed until tears ran down their faces.

When Tara finally pulled herself together, she asked Lottie to explain how she convinced Moyna to leave without the children. "Until I know *why* she changed her mind, I'll always fear she'll return."

Lottie noticed Victoria was watching her closely. "To be honest, Tara, I'm ashamed to say I tried to frighten her by hinting she may get lost out here… and never be found again."

"Well, that could happen, and it certainly crossed my mind," Victoria said.

Lottie grimaced. "I also told her that some of the aborigines are …cannibals."

Victoria gasped. "Lottie!"

"I wouldn't have thought that would frighten Moyna Conway," Elsa said. "She didn't seem the nervous or panicky type to me."

"Quite right, Elsa," Lottie said, "But as fate would have it, I'd no sooner told her about the aborigines, when we looked up to find three fearsome fellows looking through the window at us."

"What!" Victoria said. "You must have been imagining things, Lottie. There are no fearsome aborigines around here, let alone cannibals."

"I know." Lottie laughed. "It was Nugget, Bluey and Charlie. You should have seen them. They were in full ceremonial war paint. Nugget was even carrying a real spear. They almost gave me a heart attack, until I realized who they were. After that it was hard to keep a straight face."

"What on earth were they doing?" Victoria asked.

"I have absolutely no idea, but their timing was brilliant. They terrified Moyna."

At that moment, Nerida came into the living room, giggling.

"Let me guess," Victoria said. "You've just seen Nugget, Bluey and Charlie."

Nerida continued to chuckle. "They look so …funny, Missus."

"I'll go and see what they were up to."

When Victoria returned a few minutes later, she was also laughing. "It seems Jack told Nugget and the boys about Moyna, and they thought she was a government official come to take him and Hannah. They didn't know what to do, so they got into their war paint and thought they'd frighten her." Victoria laughed again. "It's a good thing she didn't see Charlie's feet. He still had his boots on." Victoria raised her brows. "He's never been able to go barefoot. You'd never think a man so large would have skin like a baby's on his feet, but he has."

They all laughed.

"I can't believe they did that, Aunt," Tara said.

"They're very fond of the children, Tara. They pretend to be tough stockmen, but underneath that gruff exterior, they're softies. I've seen Bluey cry when he's had to destroy a calf."

Tara had never felt more loved by so many people, but her thoughts went back to Moyna. "What if Moyna returns with the law?"

"She won't, Tara," Lottie said.

"How can we be certain?"

"Because while she was in that frame of mind, I got her to put it in writing that she would not stand in your way when you legally adopted the children." She handed Tara a piece of paper that clearly stated that Moyna was relinquishing her rights as the children's legal guardian.

"Oh, Lottie. You are wonderful." Tara threw her arms around Lottie's neck.

"You put that paper in a safe place," Lottie said, embarrassed.

"I will." Tara gazed at the paper as if she could hardly believe it was real. "I should frame it."

"Where are the girls, Victoria?" Lottie asked. "It's time we headed back to town, if I can get Rex to come out and get us."

"They're upstairs with Sorrel."

"You can't go yet," Tara said. "This," she waved the paper, "is something to celebrate."

"Tara's right, Lottie," Victoria said. "Besides, I doubt Rex will come back today or even tomorrow."

"I must go and tell Jack and Nugget and the boys the good news," Tara said. "Jack will be so relieved."

"Lottie, you are a good woman," Victoria said, when Tara and Elsa had left the room.

"Nonsense." Lottie blushed, which made Victoria even more suspicious.

"I didn't do anything extraordinary, Victoria, so lets say no more about it." She turned away to avoid scrutiny.

"I believe you did, Lottie, and I can't thank you enough."

Despite her obvious discomfort, the lines on Lottie's hard face softened, taking years off her age. "I'm just so grateful to see Tara happy. She deserves to have the children. They would have had a terrible life with that woman."

"There's never been a truer word said." Victoria suspected Lottie had paid Moyna Conway off, but she knew her well enough to know she wouldn't like anything made of her generosity or selflessness.

"I don't understand how Moyna knew the children were here, Victoria, and who is the Reverend Jim Malally? I've never heard of him."

"To both questions, I believe the answer is Tadd Sweeney."

Lottie gasped. "Then it was the telegram from Moyna that I saw Tadd reading around the side of the hotel."

"I believe so. He's got a lot to answer for, and I'm going to see that he does. I've let that man get away with far too much, but sending for Moyna was purely malicious, and those innocent children would've paid an awful price. I can't prove he sent Moyna a telegram, but I can have him charged for forging my signature on bank records, and raping Nerida."

Lottie looked shocked.

"He's done some terrible things, Lottie. I'm ashamed to say that he did them right under my nose. I always thought of myself as sharp-witted…but somewhere along the line, I must have lost my insight. Becoming dependent on Tadd was the worst thing I could've done." Victoria looked vulnerable for the first time in weeks.

"You trusted him, Victoria," Lottie said, placing her arm around her shoulders. "We all have to place our trust with someone at some time in our lives. Occasionally that trust is violated."

Victoria knew Lottie was speaking from experience. "It doesn't make it any easier, does it?"

Lottie shook her head.

The two women heard whoops of delight coming from outside and knew Tara had given Jack and the men the good news.

After the children had eaten an early dinner, they followed Sorrel up to the reception room where she was going to teach them mime. Sanja had made a special cake for Jack and Hannah, to commemorate their new lives as Tara's children. Tara was touched by his kindness and wanted to thank him. She also had something else on her mind that she wanted to talk to him about.

"Sanja."

Not having heard Tara enter his kitchen, the cook turned in surprise.

"I want to thank you for the cake," Tara said. "The children really enjoyed it, and it was very thoughtful of you."

The cook half smiled. "Jack and Hannah good children, Missy."

"Yes, they are. I'm very lucky."

The cook regarded her keenly. "The children very lucky too, Missy."

Tara smiled, her eyes becoming bright with moisture. "Thank you, Sanja."

"The vegetables are growing well, Missy. Some day soon I will be able to make an Irish stew."

"Really?" Tara realized she had all but forgotten about the vegetable garden while helping the men. "Have you been looking after the garden, Sanja?"

"Can't let all that hard work go to waste, Missy."

Tara smiled. "And it was very hard work, Sanja."

The cook nodded, and turned back to continue cutting up meat, as if dismissing her. "Sanja, I want to ask a favour of you."

The cook turned, and Tara could see he was wary. She almost changed her mind. "As my Aunt told you… tonight is a special celebration dinner."

Sanja folded his arms.

"I'd… well, Sanja, everyone on the station has been so kind to me and the children, including you, and it's so hot, so I was thinking…"

"You want me set up a table outside, Missy?"

Tara was hesitant. She couldn't gauge his mood. "Yes, Sanja. I'd also like you to set a place for yourself if you'll join in the celebration."

Sanja's eyes narrowed and Tara suspected he had guessed what she really wanted. "Me, Missy?"

"Yes, as I said, it won't feel like a real celebration, unless everyone is there. All the adults, that is. The children will be asleep, I hope." She tried to smile, but Sanja was regarding her so intently, it was difficult.

"All right, Missy. It your night," Sanja said, and turned his back.

Tara was unsure whether he completely understood. "Do we have enough… place settings?" she asked nervously.

Sanja turned back slowly. "Yes, Missy." He noted the apprehension in her eyes. "Fourteen!"

Tara had already done a mental head count. She sighed with relief. "Thank you, Sanja. It looks as if this night will be perfect."

Sanja shrugged. "Out of my kitchen, Missy. I've got a dinner to prepare."

Smiling, Tara turned to go. "Yes, Sanja." She would have liked to ask what they were having, but as it didn't smell like curry, she thought she had better not press her luck.

At eight o'clock, with the sunset making a spectacular backdrop for the station, the guests gathered for dinner under the stars at the back of the house. Tara was wearing a pale green gown that her mother had bought her. The colour complimented her honey-coloured skin and copper hair. She was delighted to see that Ethan had made a special effort with his appearance. He was wearing a white shirt and dark, hip-hugging moleskin trousers. His hair was still damp, and neatly combed, and he was clean-shaven. He looked handsome, Tara thought, quite unlike her first impression of him, the wild frontier man. The other women complimented him, which seemed to make him self-conscious, but Tara didn't say a word. She smiled at him, a smile he returned with a warm gleam in his dark eyes.

When he pulled out a chair for her at the table, he whispered, "Congratulations. You'll make a wonderful mother."

"Thank you," she replied, turning to look up into his dark eyes.

"I'm glad to see you men changed for dinner," Victoria said, looking at Nugget and the boys, who were wearing clean shirts and trousers. "I think you missed a bit of war paint when you washed, Bluey," she said, pointing to the bottom of his left ear, but he only laughed.

The dinner was absolutely delicious. It was lamb cooked in a light pastry and served with Dhal. Tara began a round of applause when Sanja served dessert, a Semolina pudding with raisins. The cook beamed with pleasure.

"The pie was magnificent, Sanja," she said. "The best I've ever had." At that moment, her words of praise were absolutely sincere. The balmy night, the wonderful company, and her abundant happiness had all combined to make the night and the meal, perfect.

Her pleasure in everything was heightened a thousand times over.

"I wonder what Moyna is having for dinner?" Lottie said, pushing her empty pudding bowl away, and sighing in repletion.

Victoria laughed. "What do you think, Ethan? Snake, goanna, termites?"

Ethan grinned wickedly. "Saladin is partial to kangaroo rat."

"If she makes it back to Marree, I doubt she'll ever want to hear the word 'Australia' again," Lottie said.

"It'll be an adventure to tell her grandchildren," Belle said with her usual optimism.

"She'll probably wake up screaming in a cold sweat for the next six months," Maddy added, and they all laughed.

"On a serious note," Ethan said, "I'd like to propose a toast to Tara and the children." He smiled at Tara warmly. "May you have long and happy lives together."

They all raised their glasses. "Here, here."

"Thank you," Tara said. "I'm so glad we are able to share this night together." She glanced around the table, but her gaze lingered a moment longer on Ethan.

When the desert bowls had been cleared, Tara got to her feet. "While we're all together I'd like to take this opportunity to say something." She thought for a moment, wondering how she was going to express what was in her heart.

"When I first came out here to Tambora, I wasn't sure I wanted to stay." She paused. "Actually, that's not quite the truth, I was sure I didn't want to stay. I hated the dust, the flies, the mosquitoes, and most of all, the heat." She glanced at her aunt, expecting to see surprise, even disappointment, but instead, Victoria was looking back at her with complete understanding.

"I wouldn't have even made it to Tambora without Ethan. When I got off the train in Wombat Creek, after an awful week in Marree, I was bitterly disappointed with the town, and collapsed in the dust, sobbing in self-pity. Ethan literally picked me up and gave me a browbeating to bring me to my senses. Although I needed it, I resented it and said some pretty terrible things. It's long overdue, but …I apologize."

Ethan smiled. "You're forgiven," he said.

"After that, I dropped myself on Lottie's doorstep, and she offered her friendship without even knowing who or what I was. It's that unconditional friendship that has enabled me to keep two children who mean more to me than the world, and I'll never forget it." Tara saluted Lottie with her glass, and Lottie did the same.

"I'd taken Jack and Hannah, when I had no idea how I was going to support them or put a roof over their heads. I didn't even have any skills as a mother. I was blindly following instincts that said it was right, but I had more doubts and questions than answers. I was frightened, terrified actually. Sorrel got me through the first doubts with her poise and wisdom, and you, Aunt Victoria, opened your heart and home without hesitation. We'd always been close as I was growing up, but I was apprehensive that things may have changed. I should have known better. Through the difficult days and weeks that followed, you were all so kind. Nerida took the children under her wing, particularly Hannah, and Nugget, Bluey, Charlie and young Karl, offered their friendship and their hospitality without reservation. You men may not have thought you were doing anything special, but you'll never know how much your acceptance meant to me. I was even pretty cocky with Sanja, but it seems he's forgiven me if this wonderful meal is anything to go by."

The cook smiled. "You all right, Missy."

"When my mother came out here, I was cold towards her, for which I'm ashamed." Elsa lowered her head, knowing she had deserved her daughter's reservations.

"I'm in awe of what you've done to help save the station and our relationship, mother. I've never felt closer to you than I do at this moment. I hope you stay for Christmas and every other Christmas to come."

Elsa dabbed her eyes with a handkerchief. "I'll stay for as long as you need me."

"I'll always need you. Always."

It was being needed that felt so wonderful for Elsa. For the first time in her life, she felt she was doing something worthwhile. For that reason, she had turned down an offer from Riordan to go back to Ireland with him.

"What's of the greatest surprise to me," Tara said, "is how much I've come to love this country. I didn't realize what Tambora meant to me until I thought we were going to lose it. Once more, you all rallied around. You men could have deserted us." She looked at Nugget and the boys. "But you didn't. And Nerida and Sanja, you stayed on without wages. Lottie and the girls even went on strike for us, which I'm sure will go down in local history."

"Do you think we'll be part of the folklore?" Belle asked mockingly. The women laughed.

"Seriously, to all of you, your devotion to this station, to my Aunt, and now to me and the children, leaves me... speechless."

"You'd never know it," Victoria said, and everyone laughed.

Tara smiled. "It seems I've said enough, but I just want to add one thing more." She looked around the table, at each face watching her. They were a mixed bunch, socially and characteristically, and it was under the most unusual and unique circumstances that they had all come together in one place, for the one cause, and for each other. "I'll always think of all of you, as much a part of my family as Jack and Hannah."

There was silence for a few moments, and Tara smiled at the faces filled with awe around her. "But that doesn't mean you can take liberties. Let's toast to many more evenings like this... One big, happy family."

"Here, here."

Victoria got to her feet. "I'm not going to make a speech, but I do have something to add, something I'm sure all of you will agree with. Tara, we may have lost Tambora without your courage to challenge Tadd. I'd become dependant on him and it was a bad thing. My sight was fading, but my insight had gone, too. Yes, everyone pitched in, but you started the ball rolling. I've said it before, and I'll say it again, the day you came here was a blessing... for all of us, which reminds me. I've had word that our wool left Port

Adelaide today for India."

The table erupted in excitement.

When things quieted down, Lottie said, "Tara's got your grit, Victoria, and her mother's spirit."

"She's also got Victoria's stubbornness and caustic tongue," Ethan added. "You lot have only seen her sweet side, but believe me…"

"That's enough out of you, Ethan Hunter," Tara said smiling.

A kangaroo and her joey hopped into the clearing near the tables. Two emus followed. Attracted by the brightness of the cutlery in the lamplight, the emus came right up to the table to see what was on it.

"When you are having a party, the word soon spreads," Victoria said, shooing the emus away.

"Trust the Vine sister's to turn up," Lottie said, and they all looked at the nosey emus and laughed.

Throughout the evening, Maddy had been watching Tara and Ethan closely, observing the glances that had passed between them. She'd maneuvered herself into a seat beside Ethan, but Tara was opposite him. Earlier Ethan had asked where Riordan was, and had been told he'd gone back to Ireland. Maddy had noticed how pleased he looked, and the warm glow in his eyes whenever he looked at Tara. She thought bitterly of the years she had longed for him to look at her like that. She'd also noticed that Tara kept glancing in his direction. At times, it was as if they were the only two people at the table, which made her burn with jealousy.

After dinner, Nugget and the boys returned to the bunkhouse. They were always up with the sun, so they usually retired early. The rest of the guests wandered into the sitting room, where Victoria opened another bottle, a tawny port from the Barossa Valley. Tara slipped out onto the veranda to be alone for a few minutes. She gazed up at the stars thinking it had been one of the most unbelievable days of her life.

"A penny for your thoughts?"

Tara turned to find Maddy beside her. "I was just thinking what an amazing day it's been."

"I know what you mean."

Tara thought she caught a hint of something secretive in Maddy's tone, and she glanced at her quizzically.

"Oh, I can't keep it a secret a moment longer," Maddy said. "I hope you don't mind me confiding in you…"

"Of course not."

"Ethan and I are planning a future together."

Tara was stunned. "I… I had no idea," she stammered.

"We've been close for some time. I think all this talk about families, and children, spurred him into action." Maddy glanced sideways at Tara. Even in the darkness she could see she was devastated.

"What … What are your plans, if you don't mind… me asking?" She could hardly believe it was true, unless she heard the details.

"After we're married, we'll build a home… not something grand like this, of course, but something a little better than his cabin. I'd like to travel with him before we start a family."

Tara made no comment. She felt numb. She hadn't realized just how much she cared for Ethan until Maddy had given her this news.

"I'm happy for you, Maddy! If you'll excuse me, I'd like to go for a walk and let… everything sink in." Tara stumbled off into the darkness of the grounds.

Maddy watched Tara disappear amongst the shadows of the ghost gums. She felt a small stab of regret, but nothing that compared with her jealousy.

"Maddy!" Ethan said. "I thought …I saw Tara come out here…"

"No." She took his arm possessively, hoping Tara was watching. "Are you disappointed?" she asked provocatively, tilting her face up to his.

"No. Of course not."

Despite his claim to the contrary, Maddy caught the disillusionment in his voice, and it broke her heart. She was sure Ethan was falling in love with Tara, and was almost certain that Tara was in love with him.

"I think Tara has a lot to think about," Maddy said, watching Ethan closely.

"Yes, I imagine she has."

"Her mother told me earlier that she is planning a future with Riordan Magee, in Ireland. You were aware that he asked her to marry him, weren't you?"

Ethan felt a crushing pain in his chest. "Yes… but I thought…"

"He is a very handsome man, and he does own a gallery, so I imagine she'll have a wonderful life."

Ethan made no comment, but he felt sick at heart.

"She did tell me that after living the life of a gipsy, she wanted a settled life, with a real home of her own. She said she wants a husband that would sleep beside her every night."

Maddy noted the look of despair in Ethan's dark eyes, and a violent rush of jealousy swept over her.

Rex came to collect Lottie, Belle and Maddy early the next morning. Clearly, he wasn't pleased about having to return so soon, especially with the possibility of having that bullock of a woman pounce on him.

"What's this fantastic news you lured me out here with?" he asked Lottie, as he glanced around warily. He didn't need to be lured. He could never say no to Lottie.

"Saladin has taken Mrs. Conway on a wild camel ride to Marree," Lottie announced.

Rex dropped her bags in the dust. "Are you serious?"

"They left yesterday, and she's riding *Hurricane Horace*."

Rex roared with laughter. "That's the best Christmas present I could ever get, Lottie." He picked her up and twirled her around.

"Put me down, before you do me and yourself harm," Lottie declared indignantly.

Rex placed her on her feet. "And mind how you drive back to town."

As they climbed into the Packard, the four of them squeezing in the front, Rex insisted on hearing all the details.

Tara, Elsa, Sorrel and Victoria waved them off, with the children cheering from the upper balcony.

"What's wrong, Tara?" Elsa asked, as they ascended the stairs. "You don't seem yourself this morning."

"I'm fine, mother. Just a little tired…"

Elsa wasn't convinced. She could see dark circles around Tara's eyes.

Tara kept to herself for most of the day. She didn't feel like talking, although her mother tried. In the afternoon Victoria came up to her room to see her. She noted the clothes dropped on the floor, and the bed unmade.

"What's wrong, Tara? You should be on top of the world."

"Nothing, Aunt. As I told mother, I'm just tired."

Victoria studied her. "Are you missing Riordan?"

"No."

Victoria wasn't surprised, but she had wanted to be sure. She'd been watching Tara and Ethan. "Do you remember me telling you Ethan keeps his feelings to himself?"

Tara nodded.

"In all the time I've known him, I've never heard him talk about a woman, or how he felt about one. I've never even noticed him really look at a woman, until... last night."

"You mean... Maddy?"

"Maddy? Heaven's no. I mean you, Tara. The love shining in that man's eyes was as bright as today's sun light."

"You can't be serious, Aunt. Maddy told me last night that she and Ethan are planning a life together."

"Only in her dreams, Tara."

"Surely she wouldn't lie about something so serious, Aunt."

"I'm sure she would, if it suited her purpose. That romance has been one sided since it began. Naturally, she's jealous because Ethan had eyes for only one woman last night, you. It was almost as if no one else was at the table, including Maddy."

Tara's spirits soared.

Victoria smiled. "Dinner will be ready shortly. You can't leave me, Sorrel and your mother to contend with all those children by ourselves, so I expect to see you in the dining room." She smiled. "Do you realize it's Christmas in less than a two weeks? I must talk to Ethan about shopping for Christmas presents for the children. I want this to be a Christmas they'll always remember."

Suddenly bursting with energy, Tara opened her wardrobe door to hang up her green evening gown, which she'd carelessly discarded the night before when she threw herself onto her bed and cried in despair. As she hung the dress on the railing, her gaze caught sight of something red at the bottom of the wardrobe. She picked it up, recognizing the material of her beautiful evening gown. As she held it in her hands, pieces slipped through her fingers. It had been ruthlessly shredded.

"Momma. Momma," Jack said, as he came running into the room. "Have you seen Harry...?"

Tara turned in a daze, and looked at Jack without really seeing him. She was still holding the thin threads of her once beautiful gown.

Jack looked from the gown to Tara, in confusion. He wondered for a moment if she thought he had destroyed whatever she was holding, but then a sense of security washed over him, casting aside any doubts.

"Jack, did you... see anyone come into my room last night?"

"No, momma. I did see Maddy by the door, but she said she had made a mistake trying to find her own room."

"Maddy!" Suddenly everything fell into place so clearly. It wasn't Saladin who had slashed the buggy tyres, or Jack. It was Maddy!"

Tara looked at the remnants of her once beautiful gown, and wondered at the hatred that would make someone so destructive. Could jealousy be such a wicked emotion? She suddenly began to wonder about what Maddy had told her about Ethan. Even though she was sure he couldn't look at her the way he did, or kiss her the way he did, if he was in love with Maddy, last night she had been too blinded by pain to think clearly.

Downstairs in the radio room, Tara called Ethan at his cabin, but there was no answer. She then radioed Lottie's home. If Ethan was there, she'd leave it be, but if he wasn't, she'd try to find him.

"Lottie, it's me, Tara."

"Tara."

"You made it home in one piece, then?"

"Yes. Rex was so happy about Moyna Conway, he drove like an old woman."
"Lottie... is Ethan there?"

"No, dear. He called in, but he's gone."

Tara didn't know what to think. Ethan had been there...

"Lottie, could you tell me ... is he... romantically involved with... Maddy?"

"Whatever gave you that idea?"

Tara exhaled the breath she had been holding. "I have to find him, Lottie. Do you know where he is?" Tara was sure Lottie would know if Ethan and Maddy were more than acquaintants. That she didn't meant almost certainly that Maddy had been lying.

"No, I don't. He does go to the lake to think, and he did seem in a pensive mood..."
"Lake Eyre?"

"Yes, he has a special place there..."

"Thank you, Lottie. Over and out."

Tara marched into the dining room in her riding attire, announcing that she was going to Lake Eyre. Everyone was just about to begin their meal.

"Lake Eyre?" Victoria said. "Whatever for?"

"I can't explain, Aunt. I have to go…"

"Wait, Tara," Victoria said. "You do realize it's going to be dark soon and Lake Eyre covers thousands of miles?"

Tara looked surprised, as if that hadn't occurred to her. "I have to find Ethan, and Lottie told me he may be there. Apparently, he goes there to think…"

Victoria had noticed he looked strained when he left the night before. "Then take Nugget with you. I'll not have you getting lost."

Tara nodded. "You'll see me when you see me, so don't worry." Tara kissed Victoria, her mother, and Jack and Hannah.

"I think I'll get my Christmas wish," Jack said grinning broadly, which made the women look at each other in amazement.

"I know where to find Ethan," Nugget said, as they neared the Lake. They had ridden hard to get there before sunset, but there was barely enough light left to see the shapes and outlines of the landscape. As they neared the lake, they could hear music drifting on the breeze.

"The Kokata clan are having a corroboree." Nugget said, pointing to the south, where several hundred yards away they see the glow of several fires and shapes moving to the music. The haunting notes of the didjeridoo echoed over the vast salt flats of the lake, giving it a spiritual feeling. Tara felt as if she was stepping into a scene from millions of years past. The spirituality of the area was almost tangible.

At the edge of the salt flats, Tara and Nugget dismounted and began to walk towards the sand hills. Tara stepped onto the crusty surface of the lake, and gazed over the salt flats, trying to imagine the same area covered by water. It would be a spectacle. She smiled with irony when she remembered she had wanted to learn to swim in the lake. Nugget pointed out an area that was like quick sand, and told her to be careful.

As they neared the sand hills, they could see the glow of a campfire. Nugget stopped. "Over there is Ethan's special place," he said.

Tara felt suddenly nervous. "How can we be sure it's him?"

Nugget was certain it was Ethan, but he humoured Tara. He knew she was nervous.

"You go, Missus. I stay here. If you don't come back…" He grinned.

"All right, Nugget." Leading her horse, Tara walked towards the glow of the campfire, and the man she knew she loved.

Tara's horse snorted, alerting Ethan that someone was approaching. He stood up as she came into view.

"Tara! What are you doing here?"

"I..." Tara was suddenly lost for words. "I found my red gown slashed to ribbons this afternoon," she said.

"What?"

Tara's throat went dry and she suddenly felt very uncertain of herself. "I believe Maddy did it. I also think it was Maddy who slashed the buggy tyres."

Ethan knew Maddy was a very jealous woman, but he hadn't imagined she could be malicious.

Tara could see he didn't know what to think. "Last night, Maddy told me... you and she... were planning a life together."

Ethan looked confused. "She told me you were going to Ireland to marry Riordan."

Tara shook her head. "I could never love Riordan. My heart is lost to another..."

Ethan couldn't mistake the love in her eyes. His heart began to thud wildly.

"I never expected to find someone like you... out here," he said. "I never expected to feel... so drawn... attracted. Attracted isn't the right word... what Is feel for you is so powerful, I can hardly think straight."

"Oh, Ethan." Tara's heart overflowed with happiness.

Ethan didn't trust himself to say another word. He took Tara in his arms and kissed her until she was breathless.

Tara felt a rush of emotion so strong she thought she might faint. As his lips devoured hers, they sank to the ground beside his campfire. The magic of Lake Eyre enveloped the lovers as the haunting sounds of the didjeridoo and the words of the aboriginal's age-old songs swept over them.

The sun rising over the lake was the most spectacular sight Tara had ever seen. As each minute passed, the salt flats changed colour. From silver to pink and then blue, until finally it shimmered like a white layer of frost.

Tara lay against the silky mat of hair on Ethan's chest. "I've never been so utterly contented," she said. "As corny as it sounds, I feel as if I've come home. I finally feel like I belong."

Ethan's arms tightened around her half-naked body. "You do realize you have to marry me now, don't you?"

Tara smiled. "I can't imagine a more wonderful fate."

"Do you mind having a husband who is not at home every night?" He couldn't imagine wanting to be anywhere else but beside Tara, but knew it was not always possible in a land so vast.

Tara had no intention of letting him get away from her for a while. "I won't mind as long as you don't object to living on Tambora."

Ethan smiled. "That's a fair compromise." He liked the idea of Tara not being alone with the children while he was away.

"There's something I should have mentioned earlier, much earlier in fact…"

Tara turned to face him. "What is it, Ethan?"

"I don't know how to tell you this," he said, looking concerned.

"Ethan, you are frightening me. What is it? Tell me before I die of curiosity."

"This particular area is an aboriginal sacred sight."

Tara looked puzzled. "Have we desecrated it?"

He grinned. "I wouldn't call what we did all night…desecrating it."

Tara felt herself blush when she thought of their passionate lovemaking.

"It's a fertility sight. Men and women come here to make love, to conceive a child. The area has special powers."

Tara shook her head, thinking of the years that she had been unable to conceive.

"What nonsense, Ethan. How can an area help a couple conceive?"

"I'm telling you, it's true. It has never failed once, not in thousands of years."

Tara looked around her. She heard the wind whistling softly across the salt flats and through the grasses in the sand hills. It was an eerie sound. With a man like Ethan, who had captured her heart and soul, and in the right place, a place that did seem magical, then perhaps…

She smiled, never more happy and contented. A child, if she had conceived, would be an extra blessing, but she was perfectly happy with her son and daughter.

"I do love you, Ethan Hunter," she said, kissing the corner of his mouth.

"And I love you, Tara Flynn, with all my heart and soul."

THE END

Printed in Great Britain
by Amazon

60753507R00268